OCCITANIA

ASSIF CENTRAL

•Aurillac

Truyère

Lot

Conques

Allier

Loire

•Valence

Rhône

Rodez

Tarn

•Millau

IGEOIS

Agout

es

Hérault

MONTAGNE NOIRE

•Cabaret

Minerve

Minervois

•Saint Pons

Orb

•Servian

•Béziers

Aude

ssonne

•Narbonne

•Fontfroide

Villerouge-
Termenès

Termes

CORBIÈRES

Peyrepertuse

•Quéribus

•Perpignan

ROUSSILLON

to Barcelona

Montpellier

St. Gilles

Gard

Nîmes•

Avignon

Durance

Beaucaire

PROVENCE

•Arles

to Marseilles

Rhône

MEDITERRANEAN SEA

ATLANTIC
OCEAN

BRITTANY

NORMANDY

ILE DE
FRANCE

HOLY

ROMAN

EMPIRE

AQUITAINE

NAVARRA

Area of Detail

LEON

PORTUGAL

CASTILE

LANGUEDOC

ARAGON

PROVENCE

CORSICA

DOMINIONS OF THE ALMOHADES

SARDINIA

MEDITERRANEAN SEA

The Fire and the Light

Brigid's Fire Press

A NOVEL of the CATHARS and the LOST TEACHINGS of CHRIST

GLEN CRANEY

Published by Brigid's Fire Press, Los Angeles, CA (www.brigidsfirepress.com)

Contact information for all distributors is available at www.brigidsfirepress.com. For ordering or special discounts for bulk purchases, please contact Greenleaf Book Group LLC at: 4425 South Mo Pac Expwy, Suite 600, Austin TX 78735, (512) 891-6100

Art by Greg Spalenka–Spalenka.com; Design by Jeff Burne
Montsegur Painting by Ivan Lapper (Enhanced by Greg Spalenka)
Map by Jeffrey Ward (Enhanced by Greg Spalenka)

Illustrations from the Royal Fez Moroccan Tarot reproduced by permission of U.S. Games Systems, Inc., Stamford, CT 06902 USA. Copyright ©1975 by U.S. Games Systems, Inc. Further reproductions prohibited.

Inside title page illustration: *Quest for the Holy Grail*, tapestry from design by Sir Edward Burne-Jones, woven by Morris & Co., Birmingham City Museums & Art Gallery, by permission of Bridgeman/Art Resource, New York.

Library of Congress Catalogue Number: 2008903998

Publisher's Cataloging-in-Publication Data (prepared by Cassidy Cataloguing Services)

Craney, Glen

    The fire and the light : a novel of the Cathars and the lost teachings of Christ / Glen Craney. -- 1st ed. -- Los Angeles, CA : Brigid's Fire Press, c2008.
    p. ; cm.

    ISBN: 978-0-981-6484-7-7
    Includes bibliographical references.

    1. Esclarmonde de Foix, 1155-1240--Fiction. 2. Women priests--Fiction. 3. Albigenses--France--Fiction. 4. France--Church history--987-1515--Fiction. 5. Christianity--Origin--Fiction. 6. Inquisition--France, Southern--Fiction. I. Title.

PS3603.R3859 F57 2008
813.6--dc22 0809

Printed in the United States of America on acid-free paper.

11 10 09 08   10 9 8 7 6 5 4 3 2 1

First Edition

For
Mom and Dad

In the creation of the world, light from a central source is confronted by a return of its own vibrations. It is as though light were faced with its own echo. This confrontation produces flame. Fire appears out of light as it does in this world when the rays of the sun are concentrated through a burning glass.

- Arthur Guirdham, *The Great Heresy*

Foreword

One night I awoke from a vivid dream of a robed priestess who walked amid the ruins of a mountain castle. The word "crusade" was chanted in my ear while the letters *Mallorca* flashed below the scene. Around this spectral woman's feet sprouted dozens of crosses that shifted between possessing two and three horizontal beams. They seemed to mark the location of forgotten graves. I was struck by their resemblance to the logo used by the American Lung Association in its modern crusade against tuberculosis.

The priestess, bathed in a lucent radiance, beckoned me toward her with outstretched arms and pleaded, "Peace, child, let the Light."

Heeding Yeats's admonition that in dreams begin responsibilities, I hurried to the library the next morning. The medieval papacy, I discovered, had claimed possession of the triple cross for reasons that remain shrouded in mystery. According to the esoteric classic *Meditations on the Tarot,* one who wields this cross is empowered to regulate spiritual respiration between the angelic and earthly realms.

The double cross—also known as the Cross of Lorraine—was carried by the Knights Templar on their first journey to the Holy Land. Only decades later did those crusading monks replace it with their splayed cross pattée. Hermeticists would adopt the double cross as a symbol to denote their primal law: As above, so below. During World War II, the French Resistance embraced it as a rallying insignia in its struggle against the Nazi occupation. Today, the cross can be seen painted on walls in southwestern France as a call for the return of independence to the region once known as Occitania.

Several weeks into my research, I met Dr. Norma Lorre Goodrich, the late scholar of myth and ancient religions. In her book *The Holy Grail,* she identified the triple cross as a medieval watermark called the Catharist Cross. I wondered if the Vatican had confiscated this cross after exterminating the medieval Cathars, a sect of pacifist healers. The alternating number of traverse beams on the crosses in my dream suggested a connection between these doomed heretics and the recurring struggle for freedom in France. Although raised a Roman Catholic, I had never been told of the war of genocide sanctioned by the Church during the Albigensian Crusade. Yet as my investigation into these mystics deepened, I could not shake the conviction that the mysterious woman who appeared to me that night brought a warning for our own time, plagued as it is by religious intolerance and terror.

Months later, I was climbing the heights of Montsegur in the Ariege region of France. That desolate mount and its haunting castle ruins looked strikingly similar to the landscape in my vision. This discovery would prove to be only the first of many déjà vu experiences that I would have in Cathar country.

This novel, based on historical characters and events, is the result of my years-long quest to unveil the identity and message of the Priestess of Light who chose me to tell her story.

Potissimus Personae

Alice de Montmorency, *wife of Simon Montfort.*

Arnaud Almaric, *Cistercian General and the Abbot of Citeaux.*

Bernard d'Alion, *Occitan vassal of Raymond of Perella.*

Blanche de Castile, *Queen Mother of Louis, King of France.*

Cecille de Foix, *mother of Esclarmonde of Foix.*

Corba de Lanta, *daughter of the Marquessa of Lanta.*

Dominic Guzman, a *preaching monk from Castile.*

Esclarmonde de Foix, *sister of the Count of Foix.*

Esclarmonde Chandelle, *daughter of Corba and Raymond of Perella.*

Esclarmonde Loupe, *daughter of Phillipa and Roger of Foix.*

Folques de Marseille, *an Occitan troubadour.*

Giraude de Lavaur, a *Cathar perfecta.*

Guilbert de Castres, a *Cathar bishop.*

Guilhelm Montanhagol, a *Knight Templar.*

Innocent III, *Lothario Conti, an Italian pontiff.*

Jourdaine L'Isle, a *Gascon knight.*

Marquessa de Lanta, *godmother of Esclarmonde of Foix.*

Otto L'Isle, *son of Esclarmonde of Foix and Jourdaine L'Isle.*

Peter d'Aragon, *King of Aragon.*

Pierre-Roger de Mirepoix, *an Occitan knight.*

Phillipa d'Albi, a *Cathar perfecta.*

Raymond de Perella, *vassal of the Count of Foix.*

Raymond VI, *Count of Toulouse, the suzerain of Toulousia.*

Raymond VII, *son of Raymond VI.*

Roger de Foix, *Count of Foix and Esclarmonde's older brother.*

Roger Trevencal, *Viscount of Carcassonne and Beziers.*

Simon de Montfort, *a Norman knight.*

William Arnaud, *a Dominican inquisitor.*

Part One

The Courts of Love

1194-1206 AD

*Real changes in human sentiment are very rare—
there are perhaps three or four on record—but I
believe that they occur, and that this is one of them.*
                    - C.S. Lewis, The Allegory of Love

Blessed is he who stands at the beginning.
That one will know the end . . .
- The Gospel of Thomas

1

County of Foix, Occitania

April 1194

To be in love is to reach for Heaven through my lady.

Lounging deshabille on her bed, Esclarmonde de Foix whispered those scandalous words again. The troubadour's flirtations in the sitting niche had been harmless enough, but his singing of such verses to her in the square, only steps from the church, placed both their souls in jeopardy. The parish priest usually paid scant attention to wandering singers, dismissing them as a notch above half-wits and barking dogs. Yet Folques de Marseille was no common minstrel. If reports of his latest chanson reached Toulouse, the bishop might construe it as a declaration that she, not the Almighty, would lead the bard to eternal salvation. Still, to be courted by the most celebrated—

"Again you're not listening to me!" screeched Corba de Lanta.

Flipped pages fanned a rude breeze under Esclarmonde's nose. She snatched the codex from her irksome friend and thumbed through its myriad prescriptions for love compiled by Andreas Capellanus, a lecherous old cleric who clearly knew nothing about women. She recited the next maxim to be memorized from the *De Arte Honeste Amandi:* "Thou shalt not indulge in gossip of love affairs." She flung it to the floor in exasperation. "What amusement is left us? We might nigh well enter a nunnery and take vows of silence!"

Horrified, Corba ran to rescue the precious tome, the only one of its kind in Foix, copied on linen palimpsest and stitched between leathered boards. "If you keep complaining, we'll never learn them all in time!" She forced the book back into Esclarmonde's hands and returned to the maddening task of adjusting a barrette in her unruly red hair. After several attempts, she gave up in tears. "We're to be judged in two hours! How can you be so calm?"

"You fret enough for both of us." Esclarmonde soothed Corba by fixing her friend's mussed bangs. In truth, Esclarmonde was more anxious than her feigned nonchalance revealed. After turning twelve, she and Corba had been required to focus their scattered attentions on a year-long study of Romance and its dizzying maze of protocols. Now their long-awaited day—the most important in the life of an Occitan lady—had finally arrived. Foix's fabled court of love would convene that afternoon to determine if they had attained the refinement necessary for admission. Corba's mother, the Marquessa de Lanta, would preside, and their training had been in accord with the matriarch's first commandment: If a gentleman is expected to expose his heart on the ramparts of Eros, he is entitled to the assurance that the combat will be waged under the Code of Courtesy and its duly promulgated precedents.

Esclarmonde could not fathom why an emotion so natural as love required education and litigation to flourish. Unlike Corba, she drew courtiers with ease, having inherited her father's fiery Catalan temperament and her mother's luscious sable hair, dark Levantine features, and lithesome grace. So striking were her luminous agate eyes that a spice merchant from Outremer once christened them the Jewels of Kaaba, marveling how they reflected the sun like the polished celestial cube said to mark the center of creation for the infidels.

The Marquessa always nullified such protests to the study with a warning that love becomes more complicated as one grows older. Its dispassionate analysis, the grande dame insisted, was as essential as theology and rhetoric: Knights carried their blades, troubadours their verses, and ladies their maxims. None should travel the world unarmed.

Esclarmonde emerged from the wardrobe wearing her favorite kirtle, an emerald damask woven with gold thread and lined with slashes at the hem. She cinched its waist with an opal-studded belt to reveal her budding figure.

Corba was aghast. "Your brother will never allow *that*!"

Esclarmonde struck a seductive pose. "It's the new fashion. The Saracen courtesans girdle their seraglio raiments to draw their master's eye."

"How would you know?"

"I heard it in a song."

"From that Marseilles troubadour again? He follows you like a stray cat!"

Esclarmonde twirled to test the silk's sway. Although she'd relish Corba's reaction, she dared not divulge Folques's latest tribute. "Mayhaps I heard it from a knight in Mirepoix who croaks like a frog."

"Lord Perella? You saw him? Tell me!" Only then did Corba register the slander of the man she loved from afar. "And he does *not* croak!"

Esclarmonde cocked her head in affected rumination. "So many men seek my attention. Impossible to keep them straight." Suddenly, she bounced with excitement. "I do remember!" When Corba came rushing up, Esclarmonde pushed the page in question under her friend's nose. "Rule Forty-eight. A lady shall not engage in gossip of love affairs." She danced off with a lording smirk.

Corba reddened in anger. "I can't wait until Mother interrogates you!"

"Folques will love me even if I fail the examination."

Corba sighed as she curled up in a ball on the bed. "No one has ever sung to me." Ruddy in complexion, freckled, and a bit awkward, she was always being eclipsed by Esclarmonde's radiance. Her hips and calves tended toward plumpness and her lips, the shade of plums, were in constant flux, pursing and smacking in betrayal of every feeling. Her intellect could be charitably described as deliberate, mirroring the languid pace of her movements and mannerisms. By her own admission, she was no match for Esclarmonde's ripostes.

Despite such perceived faults, Esclarmonde secretly envied Corba's innocence and pureness of heart; her own lacerating wit and mordant tongue often erected unintended barriers to genuine affection. Regretting her cruel quip, she smothered Corba with a hug. "Raymond offers more in virtue and steadfastness than any lady could—" Her nose wrinkled from a whiff of cassia.

Before the girls could alter their diversion, Corba's mother invaded the room a step behind the vanguard of her Genoese perfume. "Continue to dally and you will both end up emptying chamber pots for the Benedictines at Fabas!" The Marquessa examined Esclarmonde's choice of attire with her usual endearing scowl. "Have I not told you that connoisseurs of fine wine distrust a fancied bottle? Now quickly, prepare yourselves!"

"Tardiness is an arrow in Cupid's quiver," reminded Esclarmonde. "Those were your very words when—"

The regal doyenne of the chateau was already off to attend to the hundreds of details that had established her reputation as the wisest arbiter of Courtesy in Occitania. She might have become a queen had the right eyes met hers in one of the many courts she had attended as a maiden. Instead, she fell in love with a Scots knight on his way to the Holy Land. He had stayed long enough to wed and give her Corba, then had revived his sacred mission, never to be heard from again. The Marquessa's broad shoulders and flaxen hair came from her Iberian forbears who had inhabited the Pyrenees long before the Romans arrived. Her innate air of authority gave credence to the legend that those mercurial, fiercely independent Fuxeens—the name given to the ancient natives of Foix—were once ruled by women. She had raised Esclarmonde and her brother, sixteen-year-old Roger, after their mother died in childbirth. Ten years later, Esclarmonde's father, Count Bernard-Roger, had been killed in a hunting mishap.

The loss of both parents at such a young age filled Esclarmonde with an insatiable desire to learn more of her family's glorious past. The Marquessa was one of the few who could remember when the troubadours had first arrived in Foix. She said that the goddess Venus, desiring a more potent argot for the casting of her spells, invented their Occitan tongue—called Provencal by foreigners—from an alchemy of Latin, Catalan, and Arabic. Set to flight by the dulcet dialect, so many poets began expounding on love's conundrums that people became hopelessly confused. Having been the subject of many a competing verse herself, the Marquessa had decreed the creation of an orderly system to resolve disputes of the heart without resort to violence. After all, as she was wont to prophesy, this was the dawning of the thirteenth century, a new age when ladies were to be heralded as the true guardians of haute wisdom and culture.

The two girls hurried down the tower stairwell and made their way along the battlements. The attendees were already queuing up at the garlanded entrance to the great hall. Esclarmonde lingered at the crenelations to take in the color-splashed tapestry and listen to the musicians tune their rebecs. The first blooms of the pink oleander had opened with fragrant fanfare along the conflux of the Ariege and Arget rivers, which wedged the lower town like a pair of St. Blaise's candles at the throat. Their currents raged from the spring melting of the snowcaps. On the lush banks, the high-booted orpailleurs sifted their trough chutes in search of gold dust.

Esclarmonde's father had often held her aloft on these vine-trellised walls, telling of Visigoth battles fought in the bracken-choked elbows of the surrounding peaks. She could twirl in any direction and face lands strikingly different in people and custom. From the west, across Aragon and Catalonia, had marched Hannibal and his man-crushing African elephants. North, beyond Aquitaine, sat

Paris and its dour Franks, as foreign to her as Greeks. The Languedoc's verdant vineyards and arid limestone plateaus were spread out toward the northeast. On clear days, she conjured up hazy images of Saracen sails entering Perpignan on the Mediterranean. Her home stood at a crossroads of many worlds, a launching point for knights and holy men on their way to gain glory and God. Eyes closed, she leaned over the parapet and exclaimed, "Isn't it breathtaking?"

"Indeed, I may expire from such rarefied beauty."

She turned with a start—her hand had been taken captive by the Marseille troubadour. Corba had rushed on into the hall without her.

Esclarmonde's neck tingled from Folques's mint-tinctured breath. Everything about the bard was as sharp as a serpent's strike. His penetrating copper eyes hovered like fangs and a pointed beard punctuated his words with manic flourishes. Lacquered black locks danced above his two thin lines of brows, enhanced with a mummer's pencil. He was forever in agitated motion, leaving the impression that he had been gifted with more brilliance than his slight body could contain. As if his poet's effusive nature were not outlandish enough, he had designed the coral reds and jonquil yellows of his garish tabard to test the limits of the local sumptuary laws. He descended to a knee and, lifting his gaudy gaze like a saint's to Heaven, said with a wistful sigh, "Sweet look of love encouraged."

Esclarmonde's mind went blank until—*say nothing*—she remembered one of the maxims. *Silence is the kindling of passion.*

Folques resisted her half-hearted attempt to pull away. "My lady continues to leave me without means of navigation. Pray advise, am I off course?"

She cast her gaze down—a tactic said to be potent in stoking a gentleman's interest—and took the opportunity to admire his maroon buskins stitched with the finest Cordwain leather. Her discreet inquiries had confirmed the rumors: Folques had left his father's shipping business at the age of twenty and was paid handsomely for his poesy by barons from Italy to Ireland. Although not of high pedigree, he counted both England's King Richard and Count Raymond de Toulouse as drinking friends. There were also whispers of an abandoned wife and child, but she dismissed these as slanders propagated by jealous rivals. A natural cynosure of the fair sex, he traveled with a host of musicians and doggerel scratchers, who roamed from court to court with him seeking some explanation for their existence. Drawn like pigeons to a crust, his fawning entourage rushed up in the hope of hearing some new inspiration from his lips.

Surrounded, Esclarmonde played coy. "Sir, your words are so leavened with erudition, I fear they transcend my modest understanding."

Folques curled a seductive grin. "After this day, my shy fledgling, you'll not be allowed to hide behind that shell of innocence." He circled her and sang:

Good lady, if it please you, suffer that I love you
Since it is I who suffer therefrom, and thus
would I be unharmed by pain,
but rather we would share it equally.
Yet if you wish me to turn elsewhere,
take away that beauty, sweet laugh, and
charming look which drive me mad,
and only then shall I depart.

Dozens of moist eyes turned on Esclarmonde pining for an expression of requited love. Singed by the heated scrutiny, she managed an awkward half-curtsy. Being chosen for adoration in the troubadour's chansons was indeed exhilarating. Her name was even being mentioned in the royal courts. And Folques *was* persistent, having ensconced himself in Foix for a month to woo her. But she had never been in love. Was this what it was supposed to feel like? She proceeded to do what she always did when flustered—she fled the scene.

Abandoned, Folques bounded to his feet and recovered his swagger. He reassured the vexed crowd by producing a scarf kept hidden in his sleeve for just such exigencies. "The lady has left me a token of her heart!"

Esclarmonde slipped furtively into the great hall through the servants' postern. Hundreds of nobles stood admiring the architectural renovations with their heads upturned and mouths gaped like goslings. The Marquessa had transformed the once-stolid chamber into a temple of lucent conviviality by replacing the sinking rafters with stone arches and studding the melon dome with golden flecks to mimic a starry night. The new bas-reliefs and lozenged wainscotting drew murmurs of a Moorish influence. Fresh rushes had been strewn and cloves were roasting in the warming kettle to chase the winter's mustiness. Yet the matron's proudest alteration was also the most miniscule: In the niche above the dais sat a stunning triptych of the Adoration of the Magi, painted in tempera by an Italian monk named Master Esiguo. The artist had portrayed the Holy Family with such shocking realism that the Cardinal of Padua was threatening to launch an investigation. The Marquessa relished the brewing scandal as only adding to the work's virtue and value.

While the attendees pressed up to see the icon, Esclarmonde covered her head and eddied against the flow in the hope that her tardiness would go undetected, but the flash of her gown's sheen gave her away. Her brother captured her arm and pulled her into an alcove.

"Do nothing to disgrace us this day," ordered Count Roger de Foix.

She fought off his rough hold. "I'm old enough to manage my affairs!"

Roger's face was shadowed in the grisaille monochrome that mirrored the morose state of his soul. He bored in upon her with his smoldering gray eyes so bloodshot that his veins seemed on the verge of overflowing. "Keep away from those scheming minstrels. The Bishops of Toulouse and Narbonne will be in attendance. I warn you. Give them no reason to find you licentious."

"I am *not* licentious!"

Roger's unchecked inspection alighted on her revealed waist. "Then dress yourself accordingly. And speak only when addressed. There are those here whose alliance would do much to ensure our survival."

"I'll not be dangled as bed fodder for some greased pig!"

"The churchmen will seize upon any excuse to annex our lands."

"If Father were here he would—"

"Your provocations will not return him from the grave!" said Roger. "No matter how much you would benefit from the back of his hand!"

Esclarmonde escaped Roger's clutches and huffed off. She had suffered too many times the Marquessa's apologia for her brother's brooding temper. Nicknamed "Wolf" because of his predilection for prowling about in search of affronts, he had been forced to take charge of their remote province while still a callow boy. The burden had filled him with a simmering, melancholic rage, and when taunted about his immaturity and stunted height, he was quick to remind anyone at the point of his dagger that the Lionhearted had dispatched ten thousand infidels before turning twenty. She was about to round back and lecture him on her own rights as a viscountess when the Marquessa caught her eye.

Corba enforced her mother's silent command and pulled Esclarmonde to the seat beside her. Corba frantically scanned the hall for the knight to whom she had secretly vowed her heart. "Lord Perella is not here."

"I'll never give myself to a man!" vowed Esclarmonde. "They are brutes!"

"I must announce your decision at once," said Corba.

"You'll do no such thing!"

Corba clamped on Esclarmonde's hand. "My prayers are answered!"

Raymond de Perella, the vassal who maintained Roger's chateau at Mirepoix, stood at the entry. Bearded and auburn-haired, he was stout and bowlegged from a life in the saddle—an eligible seigneur, Esclarmonde conceded, if not particularly comely. Only eighteen, he had already grown the bountiful girth of a man twice his age, the fruit of an almost-religious devotion to never missing a feast. Jocular and sanguine, he regaled all he met with rippling jests and slapped backs as he made his way to the next round of salutations.

Esclarmonde's attention swiveled to a tall, lean-boned knight accompanying Raymond. The stranger possessed a mutinous jaw and a narrow Nordic face that was fair and devoid of beard. His chatoyant eyes, permuting from azure to gray with the light, swept the hall as if assaying the order of battle. A thin scar—the remnant of a blade wound, she suspected—marred his right cheekbone. The imperious manner in which he carried himself brought to her mind the ruthless discipline of a caliph's shakiriya bodyguard. When he removed his riding mantle, the nobles hushed and backed away as if visited by the Devil himself. Underneath he wore a white habit emblazoned with a splayed red cross.

What is a Knight Templar doing here?

Esclarmonde had heard stories about the secretive order of celibate monks recruited by St. Bernard to protect pilgrims in Palestine. The Templars had grown so mythic as a fighting force that they were widely regarded as a species of exotic beast, half lion and half lamb. They answered only to the Holy Father, an accommodation that made them suspect with both clergy and royalty.

Raymond spied the girls from across the hall and wedged a path through the crowd. "My fond demoiselles, I'd not miss your initiation into the mysteries."

Freckles flaming from blush, Corba fluttered her fan awkwardly. "I pray, sir, you'll not be too harsh in your judgment."

"I will always appear harsh next to *your* beauty, Lady Corba."

Esclarmonde rolled her eyes at their palaver. She studied the Templar, who lingered two steps behind Raymond, equally disgusted by the cooing. He discovered her locking stare on him and blinked in a moment of disrupted concentration. She smiled in conquest; her beauty had discomfited a warrior who spent years disciplining his mind to focus only on God and the flash of scimitars.

Raymond detected their silent exchange. "My ladies, may I introduce Guilhelm de Montanhagol, most recently of Caesarea."

Esclarmonde extended her hand. "You are a first for us, sir. We have never enjoyed the attendance of one of God's chosen warriors at these proceedings."

Not one to stand on ceremony, the Templar did not reciprocate the warm welcome. "I am here on a charge more pressing than this frivolity."

Esclarmonde retracted her hand as if it had been bitten. "Frivolity? What could be more important than defending Love from its detractors?"

"Well struck!" chortled Raymond. "On your guard, Montanhagol. The Viscountess has bested many a knight errant in a joust of wits."

Unimpressed, the Templar maintained his defiant stance. "I have been summoned to this god-forsaken wilderness to apprehend heretics hiding in those mountains."

Esclarmonde cocked her head in a parry, loosing a strand of hair. When the Templar tired of their sparring and moved to depart, she stopped him in mid-step. "Why not save yourself the effort and arrest everyone in this hall?"

"Esclarmonde!" scolded Corba.

"Seeking God's grace through the intercession of a lady is heresy in the eyes of the Church," said Esclarmonde. "Is that not so, sir?"

The Templar turned on her with a glare of withering scorn. "I never discuss blasphemous matters, particularly with credulous fillettes who have never stepped beyond the boundaries of their own shadow."

Esclarmonde's chin recoiled. *Tactless knave! How dare he?*

The Templar lorded over her his spoils—her flabbergasted silence.

Raymond broke up their standoff. "We must take our leave and allow you ladies to prepare for your shining hour." He kissed Corba's hand and whispered, "You shall pass the test with banners flying."

When the men were out of earshot, Corba spun on Esclarmonde and berated her through set teeth, "Must you antagonize every man that has the misfortune of walking within bow shot of your mouth?"

"Do you think he despises me?" asked Esclarmonde.

"Of course not. Raymond knows your flighty moods."

"I don't mean Raymond."

A moment passed before Corba realized Esclarmonde was referring to the Templar. Flushing, Corba nearly shouted, "Why not just seduce a priest?"

The girls were burned by surrounding stares. Esclarmonde acted as if she had not heard Corba's outburst. When suspicions were finally allayed, she said sotto voce, "He wasn't honoring his celibate's vow when he looked at me."

This time, Corba channeled her outrage into a quivering whisper. "You are insufferable! A blind beggar could stumble over your feet and you'd be convinced he'd just swooned. This very morning you professed devotion to—"

A bell rang the session to order. On the dais, the Marquessa called the docket. "Our first case is brought by Pierre Vernal. State your dilemma, sir."

A rakish poet bedizened in a side-pointed *au courant* cap and crimson silks came to the fore with a mincing step. "May it please the court, I and another gentleman vie for the affections of the same lady. She first deigned a held glance upon me. Not until the day after did she touch the hand of my rival."

Esclarmonde paid no attention to the pompous cad. Instead, she monitored the infuriating Templar who stood with folded arms at the rear doors, shuffling impatiently as if planning his escape.

The Marquessa detected her distraction. "May I introduce one of this season's initiates? My goddaughter, Esclarmonde de Foix."

Corba kicked under her gown at Esclarmonde's ankle.

"Stop your fidgeting or I will—" Esclarmonde discovered all eyes riveted on her. Lashed by Corba's irritating smile, she stood slowly.

"My dear, you have studied the Code," reminded the Marquessa. "What is your proposed ruling? The glance or the touch?"

Esclarmonde saw that the Templar had delayed his departure to witness her comeuppance. She blistered him with a pinching sneer. *Apparently you've not taken a vow against snickering. I'll wipe that off your face soon enough.* She straightened her posture as she had been taught and replied, "The glance is the more profound gesture and must therefore be given precedence."

The Marquessa betrayed no hint of her opinion. "Your deduction, please."

Esclarmonde aimed her answer at the Templar. "For some, the caress is forbidden. For others, it is easily avoided. But Love will not be denied the eyes."

"Continue," said the Marquessa.

"One alone can steal a touch. Two must conspire in the shared glance."

Impressed by her cleverness, the audience gave shouts of *bon trabalh*—all but the Templar, whose wry smile was transmuted into a frown of disappointment on finding that Esclarmonde had turned disaster into victory. Yet she was afforded no time to enjoy the triumph—her attentions had alerted Folques's honed intuition of what passes between a gentleman and a lady. Before she could disarm the bard's suspicions with a reassuring glance, he shot to his silk-hosed feet and stood between her and the monk.

"Madame Justice," said Folques. "I would pose an interrogatory."

"Good sir," said Marquessa, "It is to *you* that inquiries about Romance should be addressed. Many believe you have crafted the art to its highest form."

Folques paused to bask in the admiring nods. "Lady Esclarmonde displays wisdom equal to her beauty. I would be remiss if I did not seek her counsel. May I ask her: Is it possible for one to be married and still be in love?"

Esclarmonde's mind raced. What could he intend by such a strange question? After a hesitation, she replied, "Not to the same person."

Folques held the confident look of a fisherman reeling in a catch. "No? But what if one is wedded to God? Shall he be allowed a lover outside his sacred betrothal?" He punctuated the question with a spearing glance at the Templar.

Esclarmonde had expected a more difficult query. "But of course."

The assembly murmured its surprise. Folques came to a jangled halt, eyeing Esclarmonde with one lid raised and then the other. He had not expected *that* answer. "I am certain, my lady, that you do not mean—"

"God Himself wishes it," insisted Esclarmonde.

Folques was thrown on both heels. "Of course you're not suggesting that you have firsthand knowledge of the Almighty's intentions."

"Did He not tell the Israelites that 'I am a jealous God. I shall have no other gods before me?'"

"So I am told," said Folques, his voice tentative. "Though I hasten to advise that neither of us are studied in theology."

"Rule Five," explained Esclarmonde. "Love exists not in the absence of jealousy. If God loves us, He must be jealous. By divine law, then, we must have other lovers. For God is all-knowing and would not be jealous without cause." She waited for the applause, but a dangerous silence rebounded on her. Too late, the Marquessa's stricken look informed her of the grave error: She had forgotten her godmother's admonition against revealing her covert instruction in Latin. Lay reading of the Vulgate, particularly by women, was viewed by the clerics as evidence of possible demonic seduction. Roused from their lethargy, the Bishops of Toulouse and Narbonne conferred in susurrant exchanges and ordered their scribes to retrieve their pouches. Folques paced with an inward gaze that suggested he was weighing a gambit of great import. He stole an sobered glance at her, one so out of character yet mirroring her own throbbing angst. Had he been trying to dissuade her from the very line of questioning that he had initiated? Why had she not decoded his warning sooner?

After a pensive circumnavigation, Folques turned to the Marquessa and said, "I wish to make a legal proclamation of love."

The matriarch lurched forward. "Sir?"

"To Lady Esclarmonde."

The proclamation—Courtesy's equivalent to a thrown gauntlet—set off a clamor of excitement; a singer's immortality could be set by such bold tactic.

The Marquessa gripped her armrests in barely suppressed vexation. "I trust you understand the full import of this request?"

Folques preened with confidence, but the worry crinkles and labored breathing divulged his recognition of the proposal's gravity. Yet if he did not divert the clerics, and quickly, Esclarmonde might be called to answer for heretical utterances. Worse even, his own reckless verses could be drawn into the inquiry. "If the lady accepts, I shall forever forego singing to other ladies."

"And she in turn would be required to decline the advances of other gentlemen," cautioned the Marquessa.

Esclarmonde sat in a fog. She had never learned the defense for such a motion. Yet this much she did remember: The Rules required a lady to present an answer forthwith, for to delay or seek counsel was tantamount to an insult. If she refused, no troubadour would ever again attempt her heart for fear of suffering the same indignity. If she accepted, her name would be immortalized. Yet she would be tied to Folques in a kind of monogamy, banned from accepting the verses and flirtations of others. His proffer was more binding than a betrothal; a married lady could still be courted in matters of a chaste heart. She had always dreamt of such a moment. Why was she paralyzed with indecision? She scanned the chamber—the Templar held her in his inscrutable gaze.

He is your champion.

She searched for the source of that discarnate command. From a high pedestal, a statue of the Blessed Virgin looked down on her with serene ebony eyes. Waves of light and shadow flickered across the icon's glossy face, imbuing it with changing expressions. She heard another voice—was it her own?—announce:

"I wish to invoke the Beloved's Prerogative."

Never in this august assembly had such reckless words been uttered. The air was so volatile that a single spark threatened to ignite a conflagration of protest. The Beloved's Prerogative was an arcane procedural tactic that permitted a lady to challenge the worthiness of a professed lover.

Esclarmonde knew at once that she had panicked. The desperate legal maneuver would only delay the inevitable. There were several talented wordsmiths in attendance, but none had come close to besting Folques in competition. As the troubadour searched for some hint of her intention, she prayed he would divine her disinclination and retract his motion.

Like a wilted lilac in sudden bloom, Folques reclaimed mastery of his insouciant air and met her challenge with a speculative smile. "I am grateful for the opportunity to prove my good faith."

The Marquessa had no choice but to allow the motion to proceed. "The lady must appoint an advocate to test the affiant. Each gentleman shall address a verse drawn on the spot. Judgment shall be by acclamation. Should the advocate prevail, the lady shall remain unfettered, with no mark against her honor."

Esclarmonde glared at the contemptuous crusader-monk who had caused this catastrophic cascade of events. If she had to forfeit her freedom to be courted, at least she could require him to share the humiliation. "I choose the Templar."

The astounded audience turned toward her unlikely selection.

For the first time, the Marquessa saw the Templar standing behind the others. Dubious of the choice, she asked, "Sir, will you accept the charge?"

The crusader shot a quick glance over his shoulder, making certain that a path to the door was cleared. "I am a contender for faith alone."

"In this domain, a man of arms serves both God and Courtesy."

Folques dismissed the proffered opponent with scowl of hauteur. "My lady, I implore you to choose an advocate from my profession. The monk is illiterate. It is beneath my station to contend with one so poorly armed in the agon of verse."

Before Esclarmonde could rescind the cruel appointment, the Templar marched up and removed his gloves defiantly, making no attempt to hide his contempt for the syrupy Marseille popinjay. "Am I permitted the use of Latin?"

"You will be at a disadvantage," warned the Marquessa. "The language of scholars is bereft of sentiment. But the Code permits it." When the Templar did not waver from his request, the matriarch reluctantly relinquished the dais—but not before scathing Esclarmonde with a chastising glare.

Shaken by the confrontation that she had spawned, Esclarmonde reluctantly took the high seat facing the assembly. Below her, Folques warmed his voice while stealing glances at the suspicious bishops. The Templar had more reason than any to be nervous, given his lack of experience in such a venue, but he stood stoically, a fixed planet in a tempest of agitated anticipation. He stared down the swishing troubadour who orbited him like a dazzling comet.

The sun had eased into early evening, benighting the hall in a trail of occult shadows. When the audience came to order, Folques beckoned his retinue of lute and harp players, then bent to one knee and sang:

> *Since Love so wishes to honor me*
> *As to let me bear you in my heart,*
> *I beg of you to keep it from the flames,*
> *Since I fear for you much more than for myself.*
> *And since, Lady, my heart has you within,*
> *If it is harmed, you, inside, will be harmed as well . . .*

Esclarmonde shuddered from the effects of the troubadour's mellifluous voice. If he moved the audience with such force, the Templar stood no chance. She was roiled by confused emotions, riven as to which man she would have prevail.

> *Do with my body what you will, but keep*
> *My heart as if it were your dwelling place.*
> *Since each day you're more lovely and charming,*
> *I curse the eyes with which I gaze on you,*
> *For their subtle contemplation can never be*
> *To my advantage but only cause me pain.*
> *Yet in the end I know I'll be more helped*
> *Than wounded, my lady, for I should think*
> *That you'd get little joy from killing me,*
> *Since the pain would be yours as well.*
> *Lady, I cannot fully tell you of my loyal heart,*
> *Out of fear of seeming foolish, but I hope*
> *Your wisdom will perceive the words unspoken.*

Folques lowered his chin to his chest in a dramatic coda. He had conjured up a magnificent performance, excelling all of the renowned troubadours who had preceded him in this hallowed court. Triumphant, he arose like an unfurling swan and swept his hand to offer the position.

The Templar removed his sword from its side harness with a chilling sang-froid and placed it on the dais. Tousled shocks of lichen-blond hair unfurled to his shoulders as he lowered his mesh coif. The musicians moved to his side, but he motioned them away. He looked up at the Virgin and, eyes shuttered, whispered a prayer, "Lady of Heaven, use me as thine instrument." After nearly a minute of meditation, he looked directly at Esclarmonde and chanted:

> *I am of low birth, untrained in the art of verse,*
> *Nor have I studied the ways of women.*
> *But I have dedicated my life to the Virgin,*
> *Who resides at the right hand of the Lord*
> *And has never failed to protect me in battle.*
>
> *I can offer you, my Lady, little else but the promise that,*
> *Should you ever be in need of a defender,*
> *You may call upon the services of one*
> *Who has fought a path to the rock where*
> *The Holy Mother knelt before her dying Son.*

Not even a cough broke the punishing silence. The audience seemed to be waiting for something more, another stanza perhaps—until a sharp crack of embers startled them from their stupor, drawing gasps and muffled sniffles. Someone dropped a goblet; its rattling clank echoed across the flagstones.

Esclarmonde cast her gaze down.

The Templar retreated a step, convinced that he had offended her.

Folques kept his back to the audience with his head bowed in the artifice of humility. He could not deny himself a congratulatory smile. Just as he had predicted, the monk's unskilled maundering had insulted all in attendance. Sure-footed, he prepared to come forward to accept the judgment—

The assembly shot to their feet in frenzied applause.

Folques milked the triumphant moment. Nodding at the popular confirmation, he rehearsed a few words for a victory speech. A second round of applause grew louder. The audience had no doubt witnessed Esclarmonde's confirmation. He allowed the adulation to continue a few beats more—timing was the art superlative of his profession, after all—and then he turned with an akimbo pose to acknowledge the accolades.

The assembly's collective gaze was trained beyond him.

They are cheering the monk.

Staggered by the incomprehensible sentiment, Folques silently begged Esclarmonde to countermand the popular verdict.

Only then was Esclarmonde assessed with the true cost of the dalliances in which she had so cavalierly engaged during the past weeks. The Marquessa had been prescient in her admonitions; there was indeed a vital purpose for these Rules of Love. Esclarmonde now understood, too late, that the capricious glance or wanton touch could prove more lethal than the sharpest weapon. If a woman held the power to lift a man to Heaven, she could also cast him into Hell. She had not been in love with the troubadour. She had only craved only his attentions and the fame that had accompanied them. Ashamed, she turned her eyes from Folques in rejection.

Voice cracking, Folques allowed, "My lady is freed of the offer."

With that concession, the troubadour managed an unsteady bow and walked from the hall through a gauntlet of judging glares. He paused only once—to memorize the face of the Templar who had eclipsed his reputation.

I seem like a stranger to them because I come from another race.
- Jesus Christ, Odes of Solomon

II

The Tarascon Forest

May 1194

The first day of spring hunting was always a cause for celebration, but this year's outing promised to be particularly delightful. The weather had turned temperate and the mountain air was redolent with the heady fragrances of lavender and marjoram. Warmed by the midday sun, the girls unclasped their riding cloaks and spread a blanket atop their favorite point of vantage, a mushroom-shaped stone in an herbage clearing that held a panoramic view of the Pyrenees.

Corba meticulously arranged the delicacies that she had packed for their picnic: Toast with almond sauce, currant dumplings, and hippocras sweetened with cinnamon. She had also baked a special cake of eggshells, sea salt, and barley. St. Mark's Eve was the traditional date for divining the future, a window into time when ladies could learn the true heart of their lovers. If Raymond came to her side this afternoon and upturned the pastry, she would have confirmation that he was to be her destined husband. After arranging the settings to her satisfaction, she asked, "Will you take jam or honey?"

Esclarmonde had not heard the question, preoccupied as she was with watching her brother's lathered hounds flush a buck from the brush. She silently willed the frightened animal into a thicket of pines that bordered the river gorge. If the buck reached the chalk escarpments, it might stand a fair chance of prolonging the chase.

"Esclarmonde!" demanded Corba. "Jam or honey?"

Esclarmonde edged up to her hands and knees, tensing with anticipation. The spooked buck zigzagged and disappeared down the cliffs, causing Roger to bite off a litany of curses. She laughed at her brother's ineptitude. The embankment was too steep for the horses to take on directly and the men would have to circle to the end of the gorge and wind their way down into the riverbed. When at last the hunters disappeared over the slope, she leapt to her feet and dragged Corba down the rock, scattering the basket and food.

"Have you taken leave of your senses?" cried Corba.

Esclarmonde led Corba on a breathless run across the brow of the hill and down a path overgrown with bramble. It had taken all of her talent for deception to convince Roger to allow them to accompany the hunt. He had relented only after concluding that they would be less likely to get into trouble under his watch. Little did he know that she secretly promoted these excursions to escape his smothering supervision. If the buck made it to the river, she would have at most an hour of freedom. She was not about to allow Corba's plodding to cause her to miss the adventure that she had so cleverly contrived. After several false turns, she followed the circling jackdaws and retracted the familiar tangle of briars that covered the entrance to Lombrives cave.

Corba's eyes bulged in protest. "No!"

"I'll go alone."

Corba feared the wild beasts in these woods even more than the creatures that inhabited Lombrives's vast antediluvian world of chasms and grottes. She kicked the ground in anger at being taken hostage by trickery. "Only as far as the first chamber."

Esclarmonde found the sack of flints and tinder that she had buried after their last excursion. After several striking attempts, she lit the torch.

"What is it you expect to find in there?" asked Corba.

Esclarmonde waved the flame at her. "The Devil's tail."

"Stop it!"

Esclarmonde placated her balky friend with a calculated hug. "It's the only diversion we enjoy. Please?"

"Your silk bliaut," demanded Corba. "At next month's court."

"You cannot possibly fit into—" When Corba launched upon a determined retreat, Esclarmonde relented grudgingly. "One night!"

With the bargain struck, she coaxed Corba a few steps deeper into the dark recesses, far enough to dispense with the bribes. After several minutes of groping along the narrow walls, they came to an almond-shaped rotunda that was large enough to hold St. Volusien's Church. The chamber's slimy floor was pocked with depressions that held pools of dripping water. Several galleries branched out from its perimeter. In the center of the chamber stood a giant stalagmite with its core carved out to form a perching seat.

Esclarmonde climbed atop the stalagmite and sat on its niche. Four years ago, her father had brought her here for the first time to visit the abode of the woman who gave a name to these mountains. "This was Pyrene's throne. Formed from her frozen tears. She died of grief when Hercules cast her aside."

"Lesson finished," said Corba. "Now let's get out of here."

In a musing mood, Esclarmonde nestled deeper into the arch. She pulled out the penknife kept in her belt purse and began carving words into the stalagmite's crystallized facing. "Do you think I'll ever see him again?"

"You'll end up worse than Pyrene if you keep talking about that monk," scolded Corba. "Must you always want what you can't have?"

"Templars can leave the Order."

"In a coffin! Beside, he wouldn't make a decent husband. All he knows is fighting. And have you forgotten that he dismissed you as a trifling filly?"

In the days since their encounter at the court two weeks ago, Esclarmonde had fantasized about surrendering to the Templar's embrace. "He may be reticent in showing affection, but he knows how to reach a woman's heart. That is more than—"

"Be quiet!" Corba searched the cavern. "Someone could hear you!"

"Yes, the entire kingdom of cave knights and damsels are listening to my every word." Esclarmonde stood atop the imaginary dais to address her subjects. "Hear ye one and all, I pronounce my love for the Templar Montanhagol. I shall turn him into a troubadour and—" Something dissonant in the corner of the chamber crossed her line of vision: A ladder reached to an upper ledge.

Corba read her mind. "I forbid you!"

Esclarmonde couldn't recall seeing the crude construction of poles on her last visit. Armed with the torch, she leapt down and began scaling the rungs. Corba had no choice but to follow. Halfway up, she slipped and groped for Esclarmonde's foot, nearly dragging her down. Esclarmonde firmed her hold and pulled Corba to the ledge. She waved the flame for more light.

A herd of mammoths, reindeer, and hyenas rushed at the girls.

Esclarmonde stifled a shriek. After regaining her breath, she inched closer and found that the walls were covered with paintings in charcoal and red ochre. Smudged by centuries of smoke, the drawings depicted animals being expelled from what looked like a giant birth canal. She came nearer and stepped on something brittle and serrated.

Human skulls and bones.

The girls were too frightened to make a sound. The ossified remains of ten bodies were embedded into the limestone floor. Their bones radiated out like the spokes of a wheel and their heads met at the hub. A slab set upon two large stones held a skull whose jaws were stretched open in a final torment. On the wall was carved a cross with one vertical line and three horizontal bars, each longer than the one above it. Nearby, a stone lamp sizzled with grease fat.

"I want to get out of here," cried Corba. "Now!"

Cat-like eyes rimmed in red pierced the darkness. Hobbling into the dim light came a frail old man with flowing white hair and temples webbed with fine purple lines like those of a drained cadaver. His lean face possessed a sharp patrician nose, tremulous gray lips, and sallow skin that hinted at the eastern regions of the world. He wore a frayed black robe tied at the waist with a link belt of alternating silver circles and squares. Armed with a root staff for support, he could have passed for a resurrected Merlin.

Hands reached out from behind the girls and covered their mouths.

The old man raised a finger to his lips to beg their silence. From the shadows emerged a dozen men and women, emaciated and clad in ratty black robes. Their bare feet were bloodied and ulcerated, and their haggard faces, pinched with rheumy eyes and jutting cheekbones, were so pale from lack of sun that they resembled the chalked masks worn in theatricals to evoke the underworld. A smattering of coughs grew into a chorus of diseased hacking. For a fleeting moment, Esclarmonde thought she saw a flash of golden light around their heads similar to the halos she had seen painted on icons.

The old man lowered himself to his knees and ran his palsied hand across the calcified bones. "The Romans walled up the entrances to starve them."

"My brother is the Count of Foix!" Esclarmonde affected as much false bravado as she could muster. "If you harm us, you'll be sorry!"

The man remained transfixed on the bones. "The Druids knew the secrets."

"What secrets?" Esclarmonde demanded.

Eyes welling, the man shook his head in heavy sadness. "This is the fate of those who seek to preserve the sacred mysteries." He looked up and studied

Esclarmonde from head to foot, but also seemed to look past her, boring into another realm of her being. He suddenly brightened and held his hands over her head in a form of benediction. "Behold the Light of the World."

The old man's accomplices dropped to their knees in homage.

Esclarmonde exchanged an amazed glance with Corba. How did this man know her name and its meaning?

"You shall help lead our people to the Kingdom," he said.

Esclarmonde's body tingled with a pulsing heat. Dizzied, she lost her balance and nearly stumbled from a deep sense of terror. She could not tell how or why, but she knew that something had shifted in the instant that it had taken the old man to make that pronouncement. Corba gazed quizzically at her as if she too had sensed the transformation.

"I am Guilbert de Castres. Bishop of the Cathars."

Corba screamed and crawled for the ladder. "Heretics! They'll eat us alive!"

Esclarmonde captured Corba's arm to keep her close. The priests had warned them never to come in contact with these agents of Satan who preyed about in the mountains. Cathars—so named because they claimed to purify themselves with occult rituals that offered necromantic catharsis—came down at night and trolled the villages for weaklings to consume in their demonic orgies. Young girls were particularly susceptible to their snares.

"Don't be afraid." Castres offered his upturned palms in a sign of peace. "We harm none of God's creatures."

Among these huddling wretches was a waif with bloodless skin and straight black hair, shorn haphazardly. Timid as a field mouse, she lurked behind the others and maintained a keen watch on Esclarmonde with patina-filmed eyes glazed from malnourishment. Castres smiled paternally and motioned her forward. She was gauze-like in her ethereal presence; an angel would have had more substance. She was clearly cherished by her fellow refugees, who watched her every move with evident pride. She kissed Esclarmonde on the cheek in a gesture that seemed a form of ritual, then hurried back to her comrades.

"Phillipa studies to become one of our priestesses," said Castres.

"A nun?" asked Esclarmonde.

"We call our female initiates 'perfectas,'" said Castres. "Pure Ladies. They conduct our rites with the same authority possessed by men."

Esclarmonde found it suspicious that these heretics allowed females to lead their worship. No doubt it was one of their tricks of temptation. In more of a challenge than a question, she asked, "You ordain women?"

"As did the Master Jesus," said Castres.

"The Bible doesn't say that," said Esclarmonde.

"You have studied the Roman version, not the true story."

How did he know of her secret studies? Aided by the Marquessa's complicity, she had read the gospels many times, but she had told no one except Corba. "My missal was copied from the abbot's tome at Montserrat," said Esclarmonde, bristling at the dismissal of its value. "My godmother paid good coin for it."

Castres pulled an ancient scroll from his knapsack and his followers gathered round him to shield it from the sparks. The frayed parchment was covered by a script of angry-looking letters whose terminals were flourished like the tips of scimitars. "The Gospel of the Righteous Teacher," said the Cathar bishop. "Written by the eldest brother of the Master."

Esclarmonde scoffed at that claim. "Our Lord had no brothers."

Castres sighed wearily. "The Master's Nasorean followers smuggled this gospel from Jerusalem before the impostor Saul could destroy it. What you have been taught, my child, is the false rendering of the Antichrist."

"Why haven't you taken it to the Holy Father?" Esclarmonde asked.

Castres pressed his hands together in a gesture meant to forgive her naïve suggestion. "There are many things you will come to understand. This is the only remaining evidence of what truly happened in those blessed days. If the Whore of Rome gains possession of it—"

Lights flickered below the ledge, followed by voices echoing up from the rotunda. The Cathars scattered into the dark corners. Castres hid the scroll under his robe and whispered, "If I am taken, this gospel must be saved."

This heretic monk was very strange, thought Esclarmonde, but he seemed prepared to give his life for what he believed. Had God revealed the nimbus to her as a sign of his holiness? After debating the risk, she confided, "My father once told me of another entrance."

"We are at your mercy," said Castres.

As the voices came closer, Corba pulled Esclarmonde aside. "If we get caught with them, the priest will send us to Toulouse!"

"We can't leave them here to die," said Esclarmonde.

"What do you intend to—"

Esclarmonde crawled to the end of the ledge. The ladder moved from the weight of a climber. She pushed it off. A moan came from below, punctuated by a curse. Having gained a few seconds at most, she hurried back to the Cathars and felt a tug. She feared she had ripped her skirt, but there was not enough light to inspect the damage. She led the heretics deeper into a fissure and soon came to a fork with branching tunnels. "The Devil always takes the left-hand path?" she asked. Reassured by Castres's nod, she chose the tunnel on the right. "They'll expect unbelievers to take the sinistral way."

Corba and the Cathars followed in single file on hands and knees. After several minutes, the passage narrowed, forcing Esclarmonde to abandon the torch and crawl on her belly. The tunnel became so impenetrable that she could not see her hands. Was this the same route her father had taken years ago? She turned onto her back and slid headfirst, sensing what it must feel like to be buried alive. The smell of sulfur and bat guano stung her nostrils.

Panic swept over her—she was stuck.

Castres brushed her foot. "Breathe slowly, my child. Turn within."

His touch inexplicably calmed her. She exhaled slowly, and the walls gave way just enough to unlock her foot. She kicked forward, and after several more lengths, the walls flared. Her arms were freed sufficiently to allow her to turn onto her stomach. Moist air attacked her face. She heard gurgling. Silver rippling reflected in the blackness below her. Cave crickets buzzed her ears and the blackness stirred with scorpions. They had reached an underground stream.

"We have to jump," she whispered. "Tell the others."

Distraught over the fate of his scroll, Castres ran his hand across the wall and found a crevice. He hid the parchment and covered it with rocks.

Esclarmonde offered up a silent prayer and dived blindly into the stream. Her foot came down hard on the bottom—a bolt of pain shot through her ankle. She almost blacked out until a splash near her head revived her. Cries were followed by the thuds of bodies hitting the black water. Arms grabbed at her neck and dragged her down. She surfaced with Corba clinging to her shoulders. Together they struggled to keep their heads above water as the stream hurled them through the darkness.

*P*hillipa patiently awaited her turn to jump. Hearing no voices behind her, she assumed that she was the last in line. When the Cathar man in front leapt into the water, she prepared to push off and—

A rope snared her foot and dragged her back through the tunnel. Two soldiers wrestled her to submission and wrangled her down into the rotunda. They threw her next to another captured Cathar named Sacchioni. A knight wearing a white mantle with a red cross limped out from the shadows and angrily kicked the fallen ladder.

"Montanhagol?" Raymond de Perella held up a torch to inspect his compatriot's bloodied shin. "Are you injured?"

"I'll roast the devil's whoreson who shoved that ladder!" Guilhelm grasped Phillipa's chin and pulled her face into the light. "How many were with you?"

Phillipa trembled with fear, but she remained mute.

"They never talk," said Raymond. "Come. We'll deliver them to Toulouse and be done with this damnable business."

While the two prisoners were herded toward the cave's entrance, Guilhelm climbed the ladder again to make certain that no other heretics were cowering on the upper level. Finding none, he prepared to descend when he saw a piece of green cloth hanging from a jagged rock. He retrieved the swath and sniffed it. The scent was oddly familiar. Perplexed, he looked down at Phillipa as she was led away and saw that she had been watching him intently. When she averted her eyes with a look of knowing guilt, he became suspicious.

Raymond discovered him lingering behind. "What have you found?"

Guilhelm hid the cloth in his fist. "Nothing." He waited until Raymond had turned back and then displayed his discovery to Phillipa. He shook his head in a warning that she should never speak of their mutual secret.

Esclarmonde came to consciousness coughing up water and shaking with nausea from the pain in her swollen ankle. The Cathars carried her to a grassy clearing near a stream that emerged from the mouth of the underground cavern. She recognized the landscape—they had been deposited nearly half a league from the entrance to Lombrives.

Corba lifted Esclarmonde's head. "Are you hurt?"

"I fear my foot is broken."

Castres gently cradled Esclarmonde's ankle in his ancient hands while speaking prayers over it in a foreign-sounding tongue. The other Cathars placed their hands over her heart and joined him in the incantations. Soon she felt a balm of heat course through her foot. She searched the faces hovering over her and discovered one missing. "The girl?"

Castres shook his head, fighting back tears. "Our dear Phillipa did not receive the last rites. She will be forced to incarnate again into this world. Three others from my flock have also been lost."

Hunting horns blared in the distance.

"You must get away!" warned Esclarmonde. "I'll come back in the morning with food and clothing."

"You will not!" insisted Corba.

"They'll starve out here."

"You've done enough, child," agreed Castres. "If the Roman churchmen discover that you've helped us, your family will be in danger."

Esclarmonde pushed to her elbows and struggled to her feet. She took a tentative step—the pain had eased. Stunned, she embraced Castres in gratitude for the healing miracle. "Where will you go?"

"If the God of Light so wills, our paths will one day cross again." Castres looked up at the skyline to memorize the location. "What is this place called?"

"Niaux cave," said Esclarmonde.

Castres delayed as if wishing to tell her something more, but he had no time. He hurried with his flock to the protection of the trees only moments before the Foix men galloped over the horizon.

Roger caught sight of the girls and spurred to a charge, shouting, "By God, I'll have you both thrashed!" He reined up his sweating steed and stared incredulously at their drenched clothing. "Where in Hell's name have you been?"

"We went swimming," said Esclarmonde, shivering.

Roger stared at her as if questioning her sanity. "Swimming? We've been searching two hours for you!"

Esclarmonde knew from hard experience that the best tactic in such a predicament was to throw her brother on the defensive. "I am the viscountess of this domain."

Roger screwed his face into a knot; he did not need to be reminded yet again that, under Occitan law, this forest had descended to Esclarmonde through the tradition of matrilineal descent. "What does that have to do with—"

Esclarmonde ripped a bundled cloak from Roger's saddle and draped it over her shoulders. "I shall inspect my holdings in any manner I choose. Now stop sitting there like a boorish philistine. Provide us your horses."

Roger was still trying to understand how the two girls had swum so far from the clearing. He dismounted in a cloud of confusion and assisted her onto the saddle. Another knight offered his stallion to Corba.

In a weak protest, Roger warned, "Don't overtax the—"

Esclarmonde lashed the lathered horse toward Foix. When she had gained a safe distance from the men, she turned to Corba with a shaken glance. Both knew that this day had seen the last of their girlhood idylls.

Read this little book, then, not as one seeking to take up the life of a lover, but that, invigorated by the theory and trained to excite the minds of women to love, you may, by refraining from so doing, win an eternal recompense and thereby deserve a greater reward from God.

- Andreas Capellanus, De Arte Honeste Amandi

Foix

May 1194

As Vespers came to a close, the sleepy villagers filed out through the rear doors of St. Volusien's Lady Chapel. Esclarmonde arose slowly from the front kneeler, extending her prayers so that she would be the last of the congregants to depart. The distant splash of holy water confirmed that the priest had retreated into the sacristy. She lingered a few steps behind the others and eased the doors shut in front of her. Alone in the dark chapel, she retraced her steps and felt her way along the wall until she found one of the Stations of the Cross: Christ was being nailed to the beams. The altar, she calculated, was only a few paces away.

After her contretemps in the Court of Love, the Bishop of Toulouse had confiscated her *missale plenum*. Fortunately, he did not inquire as to how she had come into possession of the rare compilation of gospels and epistles. During his service to the Cross, her father had become an admirer of Eleanor of Aquitaine, the erudite wife of King Louis. Detecting the same precocious talent for letters in his daughter, the elder Count of Foix had secretly employed a Catalan Latinist from Montserrat to catechize Esclarmonde in the trivium of Latin grammar, rhetoric, and dialectic. After the Count's death, the Marquessa had continued the private tutelage, but with suspicions recently aroused, she deemed it prudent to terminate the monk's services with an annual benefice conditioned on his promise never to divulge the arrangement.

Esclarmonde, however, would not be so easily thwarted. She remembered that the parish priest often left his breviary on the altar for dawn service rather than lock it in the vestibule library. Although it was rare for the village clerics to sing their Office in public, Father Jean was so proud of his voice that he would open the chapel on Sunday evenings and permit the parishioners to sit in and admire his chant.

Bone-weary from the chase that afternoon, she was nevertheless determined to find evidence of the heretic bishop's assertion that Jesus had possessed an older brother. Why had she not been told of this brother's existence? And how could the Blessed Mother have been a virgin? She crawled down the side aisle to avoid being seen should the priest return. A few coals still flickered in the hand-warming dish. She lit the candle that she had hidden under her cloak and followed the eyes of the pedestaled Madonna toward the altar.

The breviary was still on the lintel—with its clasp unlocked.

She held the candle above the tome and turned to the first gospel. The historiated calligraphy was in a strange hand, most likely from a northern abbey. It had never occurred to her that two versions of Holy Writ could appear so different. She pored over the Latin, slowly gaining speed, but she found nothing about Our Lord having a brother. If St. Matthew made no such reference, certainly none of the other saints would have done so. The words of Scripture were divinely inspired. God was neither forgetful nor inconsistent.

The Cathar hermit was exposed as a falsifier. Disillusioned, she prepared to leave when a dollop of hot wax dripped onto her hand. She stifled a scream— her elbow knocked the breviary from its perch. She snuffed the candle and hid behind the altar. When the priest did not return, she thanked the Madonna for the protection and relit the candle. The tome had landed face down. She turned it aright and was confronted by a passage from St. Mark:

> *He went away from there and came to his own country; and His disciples followed him. And on the Sabbath He began to teach in the synagogue; and many who heard Him were astonished, saying, "Where did this man get all this? What is the wisdom given to him? What mighty works are wrought by his hands! Is not this the carpenter, the son of Mary and brother of James and Joseph and Judas and Simon, and are not his sisters here with him?"*

Four brothers, and sisters, too? She read on:

And they took offense at Him. And Jesus said to them, "A prophet is not without honor, except in his own country, and among his own kin, and in his own house."

How could Christ's own family not believe in Him? And why had St. Mark recorded such an important incident when the other saints had not? She could not remember seeing these passages in her own copy of Scripture. The scribe at Montserrat may have considered them too blasphemous to record. Her thoughts turned to the many arguments that she had waged with Roger. The same blood in siblings, she knew, could run hot and cold. But Our Lord had worked miracles in His own family's presence. Why had they not accepted His teachings? She reread the passage to make certain the Devil was not playing tricks. Perhaps *this* passage was the amendment of a renegade scribe. If this James did in fact disown Jesus, why would he have felt the need to write his own gospel? And why was it not included in the New Testament? Whom could she consult about this? The Marquessa had no expertise in theology. The local priest might report such an inquiry to Toulouse. She had to find the old Cathar mystic again. She turned to leave and saw a shadowy figure standing at the far end of the aisle. With trepidation, she raised the candle for more light.

"Father?" she asked.

Through the murk of incense, Folques took an unsteady step toward her. His unshaven face was the sickly color of cider pomace and his black eyes swam with pain. In a hoarse voice, he rasped, "It was not my intent to frighten you."

Recovering from the fright, Esclarmonde cursed her carelessness in failing to bolt the rear doors. "Is it your practice, sir, to remain in the shadows of a closed church while eavesdropping on a lady's private supplications?"

"You are not the only one who seeks spiritual comfort," said Folques. "And from my vantage, you were doing more reading than praying."

"I thought you had departed Foix weeks ago."

"I came here this night to petition a miracle. The novena was still warm on my lips when you appeared before me like an angel."

"A miracle? For what purpose?"

He captured her hand. "I beg you hear me out. I am trained in locution, but I know not how to commence. Sleep has abandoned me since I failed you."

She glanced nervously at the sacristy door. "Please, lower your voice."

"I ask only to be given another chance. The court at Puivert convenes next month. I shall raise you to the heavens with song so bold that all shall forget my abject fall from grace."

She drew him toward the rear of the chapel to prevent the priest from overhearing. "We must not be found here."

"I care not who hears me! I'll scream it to the world!"

She gathered a shallowing breath for resolve. "Sir, I owe you an apology. I accepted your attentions without regard to the consequences. I cannot continue to give you hearing."

Folques descended to his knees. "I live only for you! A sign of your affection is all—"

"Please, no . . . I have no feelings for you."

The troubadour's face turned slate with harsh accusation. "You are not betrothed! What has caused this sudden change of heart?" He tightened his grip on her wrist. "That Templar has beguiled you!"

"You do me grave injustice!"

"I saw your heated glances at him!"

"I will not be interrogated!"

Folques arose in a pique and circled her. "There are rumors of a sordid history with that ogling celibate."

She tried to escape, but he blocked her path.

"Are you not curious why the monk no longer fights the infidel?"

"Enough!" she screamed, forgetting the proximity of the sacristy.

Folques stepped back, repulsed by her raw fury. He stood aside and left her an opening toward the doors, then smiled grimly when she refused to leave without hearing the rest of his report. "Montanhagol was assigned to guard the King of Jerusalem. During his watch, assassins infiltrated the royal confines and cut out the monarch's heart. As punishment, the Lionhearted ordered the Templar's beard be sheared. The Grand Master banished from Palestine."

In truth, she had found the Templar's breach of custom passing strange, for it was common knowledge that the monk warriors were required to wear beards, even in the stifling heat of the desert. This information would have been of great value to her that day at the court.

"That treacherous monk will guard your heart with the same dereliction."

She slapped him. "Base indictment from a man who has never raised a sword in the defense of person or principle!"

Folques clenched his fist but held back from striking. Instead, he took satisfaction at having elicited some emotion from the woman he loved. He captured her shoulders and pulled her closer, lusting to taste her lips.

She looked up at the Blessed Mother to remind him that he stood in a house of God. "I pray one day you'll find a use for your talent in a cause more noble than slandering those who exceed you in chivalry."

Heaving with anger and arousal, Folques drove her against the wall and tongued her ear in a taunt. "You'll never have him," he whispered hotly. "You may be the most beautiful woman in all the Languedoc, but you stand no chance of winning that Templar from God. Mark me, one day you'll know the agony I now endure."

She fought off his clutches and rushed crying from the chapel.

Folques staggered to his knees and slumped in self-loathing. He gaze up at the icon of the Virgin and begged, "Why am I afflicted with this fever?"

The Blessed Mother's eyes remained cold. She too had abandoned him. Resigned to his wretchedness, he arose and turned to leave when he saw the breviary on the altar. He examined the page that had so intrigued Esclarmonde:

A prophet is not without honor, except in his own country . . .

That passage had not been meant for her! No, the Almighty had left it for *him*! What was a troubadour if not a prophet? He had been rejected by his fellow Occitans just as the biblical visionaries had been shunned by the Israelites. The divine message was clear: He must renounce his profligate ways to regain his good name. But what profession would have a ruined man with no skill but the clever crafting of words? He looked up at another icon above the altar: Jehovah, the God of Judgment, was calling to him.

"My life for an answer!" he cried. "Why does this disease burn in me?"

He pressed a coin between the Scripture's bindings as an offering for the oracle, then he opened to the page chosen by the Almighty. Before him appeared a verse from the Song of Songs:

Set me as a seal upon your heart,
As a ring upon your arm;
For love is strong as death,
Jealousy is cruel as the grave,
Its flashes are flashes of fire,
A flame of the Eternal.

He was shattered by this revelation. His best years, he realized, had been wasted in frivolous versifying. With the sneer of a jilted lover, he cursed the Virgin, "Inconstant woman! I sang your praise! And you turned against me! I am forever finished with you!" He looked to the towering Jehovah for sustenance. "To you, Father, I now devote my life. In Your name, I will cleanse this pernicious land of the Serpent's harlotry."

Many set out from the very spot
where the object of their quest is to be found.
- Jalaoddin Rumi

IV

Foix

May 1194

The Marquessa angrily ripped the blanket from Esclarmonde's bed and exposed her legs to the frigid morning air. "Your brother returned last night in a frightful rage!"

Corba peeked out from behind her mother's gown. "He vowed to have you married off by Michaelmas!"

Esclarmonde abandoned her feigned sleep. "He cannot do that!"

The Marquessa latched the door to avoid waking Roger, who was slumbering from a hangover in the solar. "Corba told me of this business in the cave."

Esclarmonde took a swipe at Corba, but missed. "Traitor!"

Corba remained at a safe distance. "Where did you go last night?"

"To Vespers."

"You never attend the chant," said Corba, suspicious.

"You both will be severely disciplined!" Finding Esclarmonde tearing up, the Marquessa regretted her strident tone and stroked her goddaughter's hair in a plea for forgiveness. "My love, you do not understand the gravity of this encounter. There are things from which you have been sheltered."

"It would not be the first time! You and Roger tell me nothing of what goes on here!"

The Marquessa retreated to the window and studied the signal tower atop Roquefixade, several leagues away. She remained there in tortured contemplation for several minutes, occupying herself by stirring the brazier embers. At last, she drew a constricted breath and revealed, "I have kept something from you for much too long . . . Your mother did not die during your birth."

"What do you mean?" asked Esclarmonde.

"After Roger was born, Cecille was told she could never again bear children. The news cast her into a despond. She so desperately wanted a daughter."

"Why don't I remember her?"

"Child, allow me to finish," pleaded the Marquessa. "One morning, she and I were climbing Montsegur. That tor was her favorite place. On its summit, an itinerant holy man appeared from behind the rocks and offered to cure her of the barrenness. Only your father and I knew of her condition."

"This hermit," said Esclarmonde. "What did he look like?"

"He wore a black robe," said the Marquessa. "And his eyes burned hot like coals. I will never forget the chills I felt looking into them."

"Did you run?" asked Corba.

"I tried, but Cecille insisted on speaking to him. The monk placed one hand on her womb and the other toward the sky as if calling down God's grace. He promised that she would give birth to an angel who would fly to Heaven from that mount." The Marquessa brushed lint from Esclarmonde's nightgown in a play for time to gather courage. "A year later, you arrived, my love. Cecille insisted on returning to Montsegur to thank the monk for the miracle."

"Did she find him?" asked Esclarmonde.

"I was too afraid to go with her." The Marquessa turned aside with her smoky eyes hooded in shame. "I never saw her again."

Esclarmonde stole an interrogating glance at Corba. Fortunately, Corba seemed not to have made the possible connection between the old Cathar in Lombrives and the hermit who had healed her mother years ago.

The Marquessa sought comfort from the wall crucifix. "Your father was convinced that Cecille had been seduced into the heretic fold. He scoured the mountains, but she had vanished. After that, he exiled the cloggers from the villages. There were rumors . . ." She debated the wisdom of finishing her confession.

"Tell me!"

The Marquessa spoke rapidly to release a heavy burden from her soul. "Two years after Cecille disappeared, a tinker reported seeing a woman among the prisoners at Carcassonne who bore a striking resemblance to your mother."

"Does Roger know of this?"

"Your father made him promise never to tell you. The Count feared you would try to find her. You must forego all contact with these heretics."

"But if they healed her, why not—"

"Speak no further of this!" ordered the Marquessa. "The clerics in Toulouse already suspect us of giving sanctuary to the false believers. Your brother has tried to remove the suspicion by allowing our county to be searched."

Esclarmonde now understood why Roger harbored such deep resentment toward her. He no doubt blamed her birth for their mother's disappearance and the troubles it had spawned.

The Marquessa loosened the calyx of her necking and drew forth a small medallion that hung on a chain. "The hermit gave this to Cecille. I found it on the mount years later. She would have wanted you to have it."

Esclarmonde inspected the talisman. She was struck by its resemblance to the pax tablets worn by priests and kissed by worshippers when offered the blessing of peace. Engraved on one side were two robed figures in an embrace, accompanied by markings of an esoteric alphabet. The reverse side held a triple cross—the same symbol she had seen etched over the skeletons in the cave.

"Stay in your room and make no more trouble for your brother," warned the Marquessa. "This is no time to test his patience."

The slumbering guard at the chateau's gate was awakened by the pounding of hooves. Alerted, he jumped to attention. "My liege, I was not told you would be practicing today."

Accoutred in his jerkin and tilting helmet, Count Roger cantered his jaunty Arabian from the stables and dug his heels into the mare's flanks. He barely afforded the guard time to crank up the portcullis.

Two leagues beyond the walls, the Count reined up on seeing another knight on the horizon. Wisps of low fog impeded his view. He identified himself as suzerain of the domain by brandishing his shield with the Foix heraldry, a golden wolf clawing at a thunderbolt. When the distant knight circled, Roger lifted his shield a second time for good measure. The rider spurred to a rowelled gallop, rising and sinking across the valley. Roger nodded with satisfaction at finding the man hurrying forth to offer homage. Yet when the stranger neared, he did not abate his pace but angled low in the saddle and aimed his lance. Roger tried to swerve aside, but his Arabian was trained to dig in against such onslaughts. A few paces from the collision, he ripped off his helmet.

Esclarmonde—disguised in her brother's armor—sat on the Arabian.

The charging stallion skidded to a joint-locked halt and vaulted its rider airborne. The knight landed with a thud on his sacrum and lay sprawled on the ground for several seconds until a groan came from his helmet. Thrashing and picking sod from his ocularum, he resembled a silver beetle upturned.

Esclarmonde cantered over to him. "Are you bereft of all good sense, sir? Or do you always bear down on travelers like a brigand?"

Her accusation so flummoxed the knight that he lost his balance and fell again. He finally lurched to his knees and threw off his helmet. "Am I bereft?"

The Templar.

Esclarmonde patted her mare to calm its skittishness and gain time to dissemble her own blush of surprise. Delighted by this unexpected meeting, she opted to keep him on the defensive. "You needn't raise your voice to me. I'm not one of your pew mates rendered hard of hearing by too much chanting." From her high vantage, he appeared less gallant than he had in the court. She stifled a laugh while watching him roll from side to side in a frenzied effort to stand. "You truly give new meaning to the appellation 'Poor Knight of Christ.'"

The Templar leveraged up and angrily dusted his breeches. "Why in God's name did you raise your shield?" He only then recognized the absurdity of the question. "Why are you even carrying a shield?"

She affected hurt by daubing her eyes. "Can you not see that I am shaken by this barbaric assault?"

"If you insist on parading across the countryside, you'd best learn the rules of encounter. Why are you in battle gear?"

"That is none of your concern."

The Templar shook his head in exasperation. "First you dispute with churchmen. Now you ride about like Lancelot seeking the Grail. What could possibly be next? A one-woman crusade?"

It occurred to Esclarmonde that by now Roger would have discovered her theft of his livery. Having the Templar at her side when she was apprehended might prove beneficial. Not even her brother would suspect her of searching for the heretics if she were accompanied by the monk. She cast her hand to her forehead. "I am so weakened from the shock, I must petition your escort."

The Templar was blindsided by her audacity. "The rules of my order do not allow me to travel alone with a woman."

"So much for that promise of protection at the court! I do wonder what your brothers-in-arms will say when they learn that you were unhorsed by a lady?"

The Templar bolted upright. "You wouldn't."

She circled him as if addressing an audience in the round. "Saladin's princesses will no doubt sing of it to give their men courage. What shall we call it? 'The Quest of Esclarmonde?' No, perhaps 'The Unseating of Montanhagol.'"

The Templar could not deny a grudging smile at this infuriating creature. "I trust you are not intent on Jerusalem."

She swung a leg over the saddle to dismount and accept his apology, but she forgot the weight of the hauberk and tumbled to the grass. Immobilized on her back, she found the Templar standing astride her with a punishing smirk. She presented her hand to him for assistance. "Are you going to just stand there like an imbecile?"

The Templar milked this agreeable turn of fortune. "Perhaps the minstrels will instead sing of the Amazon from Foix who was buried in her brother's breastplate." She doubled her efforts without success, but he refused his assistance until she answered him. "Where are we going?"

"I will tell you then!"

He pulled her halfway off the ground and withheld his full leverage until she complied with the demand.

"To Montsegur."

Informed of her intent to visit the notorious heretic lair, he released her hand and crossed his arms, sending her plummeting to the grass again.

She cursed like a washerwoman as she wiggled out from under the hauberk like a butterfly shedding a cocoon. Gaining her feet, she bent over and shook the dry leaves from her hair. She turned to find the Templar gazing at her derrière, revealed by the tight cut of her riding breeches. In all likelihood, he had never seen a woman without the modesty of robes. She decided to take advantage of his sheltered existence. "What use would you be to me anyway? You're obviously too blind to tell a knight from a lady." She stole a sideways glance to confirm that her verbal cut had landed, then raised herself to the saddle, ensuring that he had clear view of her ascent. Before he could protest, she kicked the Arabian into a loping run.

Minutes later, the Templar charged past her and eased into a plodding gait, two lengths ahead. *Does he think me an invalid?* She had no intention of being led on a slow procession like some wizened nun on a pilgrimage. Yet each time she tried to sidle up to him, his stallion thwarted the attempt. "Has your horse also taken a vow of chastity?"

The Templar ignored her taunt and rode on.

The Templar's contemplative silence allowed her to ponder a vexing question: Why had he first refused to accompany her, only to acquiesce so quickly? She would solve that riddle in due course. The more pressing task at hand was to educate him on the consequences of ignoring a lady, even for the call of God. She spurred to a gallop and gained ten lengths on him before he was wrenched from his meditation. She lashed her mare down into the blue-green valley toward the crest of a massif formed by the first eruptions of the Pyrenees. She looked back and, for the first time, saw him laughing.

Not even the descriptions of the holy places in the Bible could have prepared her for the dissonant sight. The towering crag of Montsegur was an alien eruption amid rolling sheep fields and sporadic oak groves. The mount looked as if the gray head of a giant dragon had long ago broken through the earth and turned to stone. The summit of the pog was not sharp like the surrounding Pyrenean caps but rounded off like a thimble, and the pitch on three of its sides was so severe that no vegetation could survive there. The east approach alone looked passable; its steepness was alleviated by a green finger of land that swept halfway up the limestone face. A winding shepherd's path split the crag and disappeared on its ascent into tufts of shrubby trees. Had Noah known of this place, he might well have chosen it over Mount Tabor as the site best suited to build his ark.

The Templar finally caught up. He was about to chastise her for extending the horses when he caught his first glimpse of the mount. "Impregnable."

Esclarmonde was astonished at how a man could view the world so differently. It had never occurred to her that such a place should hold a fortification. "We should get started if we're going to make the top before sundown."

The Templar blinked hard. "You don't intend to scale it?"

"I do indeed."

"I would attempt the walls of Acre first," he protested.

She dismounted and tethered her horse to a tree. "Come. Whilst we climb, you can tell me about your many deeds of valor in Palestine."

The Templar sat in the saddle muttering Arabic-laced curses. Finally, he removed his mantle and slung the scabbard over his brocaded shoulders, framed even more prominently by his slender waist and lean legs. Bared for the first time, his muscular arms appeared pale next to Esclarmonde's copper complexion. In times past, his fellow brothers had refused to expose their skin, even under the deadliest desert sun. Only after scores had died from heat prostration did St. Michael appear to the Grand Master of the Order in a dream and order the rule be rescinded.

Esclarmonde followed him up the switchback and wondered anew why he was submitting so meekly. Perhaps he had been taught to obey without questioning. All men would do well to spend time in such training. When the climb became more arduous, she extended her hand for assistance. "Guilhelm." She had never addressed him by his first name. He hesitated and cast his eyes down, but accepted her reach. His fingers trembled slightly as he pulled her up the precipice. Having won this hard-fought prize, she was not about to relinquish it. "I've not thanked you for coming to my aid at the court."

He huffed with derision. "Someone needed to silence that inane warbler."

"It was not I who inspired you?" she asked flirtatiously.

"My lady—"

"Will you not call me Esclarmonde? Combatants should be on less formal terms, no?"

He increased the pace of their climb, uncomfortable with the intimate direction of the conversation. "We've twice locked shields in the short time I've known you. And I always seem to get the worst of it."

So, he has been thinking of me. She risked his withdrawal by closing the space between them. "Do you know that you are a poet?" She sensed his flinch at her forwardness. "Your words are simple and direct, but they find the heart. Promise me you'll pursue your gift."

"The prophets and saints have written all the words required."

She saw that he was a taciturn, self-contained man who could not linger long without performing some useful task. But he continued to hold her hand, and that gesture was more telling than a thousand musings of love. As they angled their way through the brush, her thoughts turned to her mother and how she would have made this same punishing climb alone on the day of her disappearance. It was a possibility long on odds, but if she could find the old Cathar healer atop this crag, she might learn more about her disappearance.

After a half-hour of labored climbing, Guilhelm lifted her to the flat promontory that crowned the mount. A tangled garden of limestone rocks surrounded them. They stood so elevated that the horses looked like ants in the valley four thousand feet below. The sun's rays painted the jagged scarp with changing hues of pinks and purples and at eye level to the west, twenty leagues away, the cordillera of the Pyrenees pierced the gray clouds. On the far side of the summit, the ruins of an old chateau lay imprisoned in an eerie stillness.

Exhilarated by the rarefied air, Esclarmonde twirled in the breeze. Soon she became so light-headed that she felt she might fly. Was it any wonder that her mother so loved this place? Without warning, her euphoria gave way to an unbearable ache of sadness. She stopped to catch her breath, fearful that her heart might explode from the rush of ineffable emotions. Perhaps God's beauty here was too intense for mortals. She found Guilhelm resting on an ancient dolmen hewn by the Druids of old. "Could Heaven be more beautiful than this?"

He studied the charred remains of a fire, no more than a week old.

"Guilhelm," she repeated. "Is this not Heaven?"

"One man's heaven is another man's hell," he said dismissively, refusing to acknowledge her whimsy.

"What, pray tell, does *that* mean?"

Only then did he vouchsafe a direct glance—the same smug look that had so infuriated her at the court of love, the one suggesting that he knew more than she did about life. "In Syria, the caliphs ply boys with hashish until they fall into a stupor," he said. "The fools are then taken to mountain palaces in the clouds and awakened amid harems and gardens. After a week, they are drugged again and returned to the desert. The old men tell the foolish whelps that Allah granted them a vision of Paradise and would reward them with its perpetual repose if they died in battle . . . There *are* many heavens and hells."

The strange story unnerved Esclarmonde. Beneath the Templar's rock-hard faith and imperturbability lurked a dangerous cynicism, she feared. She wondered if Folques had not been entirely wrong about him. Perhaps he *had* been altered for the worse by his contact with the infidels. She was about to question him further when she felt a swirling heat on the spot where her mother's medallion rested under her blouse. A horrid vision flashed across her mind—for a fleeting moment, the summit appeared engulfed in flames. She turned, certain that she had felt her mother's presence behind her. Frightened, she hurried back to the boulder and edged next to him.

Guilhelm was baffled by her swift flights of mood. Uncertain how to comfort her, he awkwardly wrapped an arm around her waist. She nestled into the crease of his shoulder to seal their intimacy. Safe again in his embrace, she loosed her hair in the wind and sank into his chest. She felt the beating of his heart quicken. *He has never held a woman.* The thought that she was his first thrilled her. Eyes closed, she slowly, almost imperceptibly, inched closer. When she could no longer endure the denial, she pressed her mouth to his lips and was swept away by an annihilating rush of passion.

He returned the kiss, then released a soft cry of pleasure—or was it anguish? He pulled away suddenly, his head hung in shame. He abandoned her on the boulder and walked off to find solitude near the precipice.

She was jolted by his abrupt retreat. "It was my doing. Let God punish me if He must. But I cannot believe He would condemn such feelings!"

"You are naive about this world and the next."

She recoiled as if slapped. What had she done to deserve such reproof? She had only followed her heart's lead as the troubadours prescribed. "I may not have traveled to far lands like you, but I am not some ignorant naif!"

Guilhelm stood at the cliff and watched the tumbling brume merge and part over the mountains. After an extended moment of private debate, he reached into his tunic and pulled out a shred of green cloth. With a chary eye on her, he revealed, "I know why you came here."

Esclarmonde examined the swath. A moment passed before she realized it was from the skirt she had worn in Lombrives cave. She retraced the events of that day in an effort to make sense of how he could have found it. "*You* were with the soldiers?"

"I was ordered—"

"You led me here to find the others!"

"Hear me out, woman."

She charged at him with such a fury that he nearly lost his footing. "I dealt a fall to one of your murdering kind. I wish it had been you!"

His jaw dropped. "You pushed that ladder? I still suffer the bruise!"

She slammed a foot into his shin. "There's one to match it!" She ran crying for the shepherd's path that descended to the base of the crag.

Guilhelm limped after her. "Stay away from those heretics! Two of them were taken to Toulouse for interrogation."

She spun back. "The girl is alive?"

"Not for long if—"

She scooped up a handful of rocks and hurled them at him as fast as she could fire and reload. "Folques was right! You *are* a coward!"

"That lying knave? What did he—"

"I never want to see you again!" she screamed.

Guilhelm took the brunt of the assault against his back. When it was safe to turn, he peered over his arm. She had disappeared down the scarp.

The Pharisees and the Scribes have taken
the keys to knowledge and have hidden them.
- The Gospel of Thomas

V

Rome

February 1198

The golden travertine of the Lateran's scalloped piazza shimmered under the brutal midday sun, broiling the thousands of monks, pilgrims, and citizens who had stood for three hours waiting for Lothario de Segni to appear for his papal coronation. The fever season with its bloodsucking mosquitoes and shrieking cicadas had arrived on Candlemas, four months early. The oracle hags who trolled the ruined Baths of Constantine warned that the arrival of the preternatural summer was an evil omen for the new pontiff who would take the name Innocent III.

Pressed into the crowded ranks of his fellow Cistercian monks, Folques sopped sweat from his tonsured scalp. "What could be the delay?"

Arnaud Almaric, the bald, diminutive Abbot de Citeaux, sucked on a ball of spit to ease the dryness in his mouth. "Lothario is no doubt meditating on the fate of his predecessors. On the day of his procession, Gelasius was anointed with boiling pitch and driven from the city tied to the back of an ass."

"Jesus weeps!"

The Abbot was amused by his novice's naive innocence. "You must count him blessed, my son. At least he survived. On his first day, John III was sent to his heavenly reward with hammer blows."

Folques was so unnerved by this litany of mayhem that he stumbled from faintness. The monk behind him retaliated with a sharp elbow. Folques waved air to his nose and begged forgiveness for his spiritual weakness. This sweltering tribulation was slight compared to the torments endured by the first Christians here. Four years had passed since he knocked on the doors of Thoronet Abbey in Provence, but he had only recently adjusted to St. Bernard's regimen of two hours sleep each night, the weekly pittance of fish, and the tortuous rash raised by the burrell cloth. Despite these mortifications, he remained plagued by one persistent failing: Evil thoughts of the woman whose name he had vowed not to speak since the night of his conversion in Foix.

His talent for the plainsong had caught the eye of the Abbot during an inspection visit to Thoronet. As General of the Cistercian Order, Almaric took pride in grooming promising proteges, having himself climbed the ecclesiastic hierarchy at a young age, in no small part because his father had provided distinguished service to King Louis. Yet Almaric looked and acted nothing like the holy men he governed. Some even whispered behind his back that God would never have given such repulsive countenance and preening ambition to a man meant for the religious life. His long face and beakish nose were framed by cheeks striated with slashes of mauve capillaries; these features, combined with his queer habit of blowing balls of air into his jowls, brought to mind a gilled sea reptile. His carbon eyes were ringed with ash-pallored circles and his folds of adipose hung so slack on his bent frame that he seemed perpetually on the verge of collapse. A deformed right leg, shriveled since birth, had thwarted his dream of becoming a knight. Detecting in Folques a similar disappointment so early in life, he had brought his new charge to Rome to undergo the cure that had lightened his own dark night of the soul—Vatican politics.

Folques was fortified by the knowledge that he would soon be blessed with a gift that no troubadour could ever hope to attain: a papal audience. But he would first be required to undergo the most strenuous test yet of his fledgling faith. The pontiff-elect's procession through Rome to receive the keys in St. Peter's basilica was an ancient tradition adopted to permit the masses to observe their new spiritual father up close. In recent years the ritual had deteriorated into a harrowing gauntlet under fire. He took measure of the route the procession would take down the haze-choked Via Major. The old Aurelian walls now enclosed vast, weed-infested barrens so overrun by wolves that bounties were offered for the predators' ears. Hundreds of churches stood abandoned and the city's thirty thousand inhabitants, many rife with heresy, had migrated to the core like worms in a rotten apple. On this day, they were in an ugly mood. To emulate Christ's poverty, Lothario had announced that his traditional gift to the populace would consist of a mere pauper's dole.

The rest of Christendom was in no better condition. Henry VI had died four months earlier, leaving his son Frederick to run roughshod over northern Italy. Feuding among the Christian barons in Outremer had allowed the Moslems to regain Jerusalem. In the East, the schismatic Byzantines wallowed in decadence while the Turks watched for an opportunity to cross the Hellespont. Even in the peaceful regions, heretics flourished from the Balkans to France. To confront these menaces, Lothario would have in his arsenal only the threats of excommunication and eternal damnation.

A roar across the piazza flushed thousands of pigeons.

At last, an acolyte armed with a towering crucifix led the pontiff-elect from the Lateran stables. Clad in a plain white chasuble, Lothario lashed his stippled palfrey into a canter and fixed his fierce gaze on the unruly flock. In a miracle of transformation, the tears of Christ melted his scowl. Splotched since childhood from bouts of malaria, he appeared much younger than his thirty-seven years. His protruding upper lip curled into an arc of determination as he rode toward the Tiber. Three columns of monks came up behind him and broke into a low chant of "Kyrie, Kyrie Eleison" to drown out the jeers.

Almaric bit off a new curse with each agonizing limp as he was herded into the maelstrom. When the mob became more vociferous, he retracted his robe to reveal the dagger at his belt, reassuring Folques that they would not be relying on God's grace alone to survive the ordeal.

An hour into the punishing march, the pavement narrowed below the Coliseum and forced Lothario within earshot of every imaginable slander. The arches of that hallowed necropolis of martyrdom were desecrated with mangonels and gangs of thugs. Spurred on by the hostile faces, the monks tightened their formation like a besieged phalanx.

"Show us your trained bird!" screamed one of the cretins.

Almaric laughed grimly. The city was rampant with jokes about the dove that Lothario claimed had flown into his lap to signal his election during the conclave. "Even fools can stumble onto the truth."

"But the cardinals confirmed the Holy Spirit's sign," protested Folques.

Almaric shoved an elderly monk to speed his pace. "They also believe Lothario gained his wealth from honest trade, not stolen Vatican funds."

The procession passed under the looming shadow of a half-constructed turret that bore the Conti escutcheon. The tower was on the verge of becoming the tallest structure in a city ruled by height. Folques had been in Rome only a week, but during his requisite circuit of the sacred relics—including the skull of John the Baptist, the sinews of St. Anne, and the foot of Mary Magdalene— he had witnessed numerous skirmishes between the two most powerful Italian clans, the Orsini and the Conti. If the Conti were allowed to complete their fortress, Lothario would control both the city and the papacy, a monopoly that had never been permitted. Yet Folques could not believe that the Almighty would allow St. Peter's city to be so defiled by such crass enmities. "The Holy Father endures the taunts with humility. He must be a spiritual man."

Almaric snorted. "He is haunted by premonitions, if that is what passes for spiritual gifts these days. He claims to have had visions of marrying his mother and seeing the basilica collapse in a ball of fire."

Folques swallowed the lump in his throat. He himself would soon be standing under those dry-rotted timbers. Like every pilgrim, he knew the story of how St. Peter's had once come crashing down in divine retribution for Rome's faithlessness. "But Lothario prepared Celestine's body for interment while the other cardinals rushed to the Septozium to choose a successor. Surely no man who lusts for the throne would embrace such subservience."

"Unless he nurtures a morbid fascination for corpses."

Horrified, Folques stopped abruptly. The column crushed upon him from the rear, spurring imprecations and kicks.

Almaric captured Folques's arm to keep him abreast. "You must study the writings of those with whom you are forced to deal. I attended the university with Lothario in Paris. He spent three years writing an exhaustive treatise on the corruption of the flesh." Finding Folques shaken by these revelations, the Abbot reassured him, "Popes come and go like the leaves of the seasons, but the Church remains steadfast as the tree. Our Italian with the actor's tears may not be a saint, but he possesses the one quality we now require."

"And that would be?"

"The mettle to wield Christ's mace against the heretics."

The procession ground to a halt on the Palantine Hill near the Forum of Nero. The Draconarii guards, the city's militia whose allegiance was always in doubt, fought back the rabble. Dozens of ragged men broke through the cordon and ran at Lothario, screaming, "The Conti stole from us!"

Lothario's palfrey spooked and reared. Several monks rushed up to shield the pontiff from the rocks and debris. The Conti henchmen infiltrated the onlookers and attacked the Orsini partisans. Lothario signaled for his deacons to open their sacks and throw coins to the street. "Silver and gold are not mine!" he cried, repeating the time-honored profession of poverty.

The momentary diversion allowed the Draconarii to flog Lothario's palfrey free from the mêlée. Certain that the smattering of ducats would only enrage these firebrands, Almaric hurried Folques through the scuffle. Arm in arm, the two Cistercians led the frightened monks in a hobbled run for the protection of Castel de Angelo, the turreted papal fortress on the Tiber.

Exhausted from the morning's riots, Folques fell prostrate at the foot of the Scala Santa, the Lateran's hallowed staircase. He followed Almaric and the seven bishops of France on hands and knees up the twenty-eight steps walked by Christ to the Praetorium of Pilate. After fifteen minutes of this excruciating penance, the heaving clerics reached the vast portico of the Triclinium and found Innocent waiting for them on a high-backed chair that had been carved whole from a block of red porphyry. At his side was his brother and clan enforcer, Ricardo, armed with a jeweled dagger, ostentatious evidence of the Conti wealth. The pontiff listlessly offered his garnet ring to be kissed.

The corpulent Bishop of Narbonne raced forward to be first. Breathless and beet-faced, he flapped his mouth like a beggar's clap-dish. "All Occitania prays in gratitude for your election, Holiness."

Innocent arose and retracted his hand in disgust, nearly slicing the truckling cleric's nose with his beveled ring. "That is difficult to believe, Bishop. Prayer, I am told, has become a lost practice in your land. The churches are unattended and the coffers empty. Yet the shepherds appear well fed."

The bishops plimmed in umbrage, their faces scarlet as Rahab's thread.

Innocent glowered through the latticed window at the riffraff still milling below the palace. The panes rattled from thrown rocks. He whipped his sleeves to his elbows in frustration. "I cannot travel my own city without being accosted by demagogues and mendicants babbling prophesies of doom!" He strode angrily to a sheepskin map of Christendom that was draped across an illuminator's desk. "What is the state of the Languedoc?"

"The Occitan strain of heresy has proven quite virulent," said Almaric. "Carcassonne, Beziers, Toulouse. All are overrun by these Albigensee spreaders of lies who are called Pure Ones by the deceived masses."

"Cities under the supervision of those before me," reminded Innocent.

Almaric suppressed a smile at the expense of the cowering bishops and directed the pontiff's attention to the western borders of Occitania. "The Manichean disease is particularly rampant here, in Foix. The inhabitants translate the Scriptures in their vernacular and openly encourage personal revelation. They hold mortals to be the equal of our Lord in works and miracles."

"They deny the sanctity of St. Peter's succession?" asked the pontiff.

"The miscreants refer to your Eminence as—" Almaric lowered his head to mark distance from the blasphemy—"the Whore of Babylon."

Innocent's cleft upper lip twitched with indignation. He gazed across the vast chamber, drawing strength from the artistic depictions of saints in the throes of various agonies. "Do they expect me to rule from an anchorite's cell?"

"They expect you not to rule at all," blurted the Bishop of Toulouse.

Innocent stood motionless, his salmon-pink face sealed in an expression of sour incredulity. The Curia's physician tried to daub beads from his forehead, but the pontiff repulsed the ministration and pounded a table with his fist. "Sons of Satan! God damn their blackened souls!"

The bishops squirmed with mouths twitching, stunned to hear such a distempered curse by the Vicar of Christ, in holy confines of the Lateran no less.

Almaric allowed the bishops to bridle a moment more before breaking their discomfited silence. "The Occitan heretics are indeed demon-possessed. They abjure taking up arms, even to defend Christ's kingdom. They also avoid eating meat for fear that the animals may be their kin."

The bishops tried to negate that revelation with nervous titters, hopeful that the absurdity of the heretics' beliefs might soften the pontiff's ire.

Innocent glared them into a chastened submission. "Is it true that these people abstain from sexual union?"

"Not for reasons of purity," said Almaric. "They deem it a tragedy when a soul is born. Their provocateurs walk from town to town mimicking the Apostles and passing off black magic as the working of the Holy Spirit."

Innocent's interest was piqued. "What form of magic?"

"They claim to heal by touch as did Our Lord," said Almaric. "It is clearly communion with Hell's succubi. The men seduce illiterate women into their ministries and masquerade them about like pagan priestesses."

Innocent strode before the craven bishops and examined their wan faces closely. "You have been given the powers of excommunication, exile, and forfeiture of life. Why have you not eradicated these thistles from your fields?"

"The secular rulers must impose the penalties," reminded the Bishop of Narbonne, his voice suddenly falsetto. "When we demand enforcement, the

Count of Toulouse tarries and offers excuses. His vassal, the Count of Foix, is no better. It is rumored . . ." The revelation caught in his throat. The only sound heard was the chirp of crickets in the damp silence of the lower gardens.

"Do not try my patience!" shouted the pontiff.

The bishops hemmed and hawed, unable to gather the verve to finish the report. Almaric underscored their cravenness by revealing, "The Counts of Toulouse and Foix are believed to be enamored with the Cathar beliefs."

"I once heard the Count of Foix's sister engage in scurrilous exegesis of Holy Writ," confirmed the Bishop of Narbonne, eager to segregate himself from his colleagues, whose dioceses were more proximate to the offending domains.

"That woman is a wanton whore!" cried Folques.

The clerics turned on Folques, shocked that a deacon would dare speak in the pontiff's presence without permission. Almaric moved quickly to blunt Innocent's ire. "My scrivener is unschooled in the protocol."

Innocent circled Folques. "A Gregorian gamut. Sing one for me."

The bishops were perplexed by the odd request. With a stern look of reprimand, Almaric nodded for Folques to perform the requested task. Folques cleared his throat and filled the chamber with a series of dulcet plainsong notes.

Innocent closed his eyes and swayed with the rhythmic chant. When Folques had finished, the pontiff sighed as if roused from an ecstatic state. "Remarkable tone. I am constantly tormented by discordant sounds. My ears are extremely sensitive. You have given them a blessed respite, my son. For that, I should think we might hear what you have to offer on the state of God's realm."

Folques glanced contritely at Almaric before acceding to the invitation. "Holiness, I once lived among these false Christians. They flout all conventions of chastity and speak the crude langue d'oc, which says yes to every lust. Instead of attending mass, the men spout poetry like Moors and the women parade about in dress more promiscuous than the silks worn by the daughters of Belial. The songs of their troubadours are veiled hymns to the dualist heresy."

"A conspiracy?" asked Innocent. "Among the errant bards?"

"The singers swear allegiance to a secret brotherhood called the Church of Love. Their code equates the passion for a woman to one's love for God."

"How do you know this?" asked Innocent.

"Until redeemed by Our Lord," said Folques, "I was one of them."

"What course of action would you propose I take?" asked Innocent.

"St. Michael raised his blade against Satan," said Folques. "If the Occitan barons refuse to cleanse their land, should we not act in their stead?"

The bishops repulsed that outlandish proposition with a corporate gasp. Delivering souls to the secular estate for the pyres was warranted under Church law, but to suggest that the Church itself take up violence was as uncanonical as the errors being rectified. St. Augustine had centuries ago established that a just war could be waged only by rulers of kingdoms, not men of God.

The Bishop of Toulouse was determined to quash Folques's temerity by exposing his ignorance of ecclesiastic law. "You would have *us* shed blood?"

"The Knights of the Temple are allowed to take monastic vows while fighting the infidels in Palestine," said Folques. "Why not sanction an order of God's warriors to put down the unbelievers in our own domains?"

"The infidels meet sword with sword," reminded the Bishop of Narbonne. "The heretics threaten us with lies, not weapons."

While the bishops browbeat Folques with biblical citations, Innocent stood at the sill and studied the mobs festering in the piazza below. When the clerics fell silent to await his indication, he gave a paternal pat on Folques's shoulder. "Our Lord banished Satan with the Word alone, my son. I do indeed require an army. On that you have spoken wisely. But my ranks must be filled with preachers, not soldiers. Regrettably, I possess neither. Instead of steadfast servants of Christ, what stands before me is an ostentation of preening peacocks."

Stung by the calumny, the bishops stirred with affront.

Almaric seized the opening to expand his authority at their expense. "Holiness, may I propose your legion of preachers be recruited from the enemy's own territory? My monks know these Occitan recreants firsthand. They grew up in the same villages and understand their devious ways."

The bishops burned Almaric with searing glares, having long suspected him of scheming to insert his Cistercians into their pulpits to siphon off donations.

The Bishop of Toulouse sputtered, "We have conducted sermons—"

"With dolorous effect!" reminded Innocent.

"I meant only—"

Innocent silenced the Toulouse bishop with the point of his horny forefinger. Lips compressed white in dudgeon, the pontiff retreated to a painting of St. Sebastian being slowly impaled by arrows. After indulging at length in the saint's pained rapture, he turned to Almaric and ordered, "Abbot, draft a missionary campaign for the Languedoc. I wish it led by your Cistercians." He came to Folques and pressed the former troubadour's hands into his own. "Find me more silver-throated champions of Christ like this one. What prodigal soul would not return to the Church after hearing such a voice?"

Ears lit scarlet, the Gallic bishops bowed stiffly and hurried from the chamber before the choleric-tempered pontiff could issue more punishing directives. Relishing his victory, Almaric moved with Folques toward the doors.

"Abbot, will you remain a moment?" asked Innocent. "Accompany me. You may bring your songbird."

The pontiff escorted the two Cistercians from the Triclinium and down a corridor of dark galleries until they reached an iron-studded door. A functionary standing guard allowed them entry into a long, windowless room that was filled with shelves of ancient scrolls, codices, and manuscripts.

"The archives," said Innocent. "Some are Ebionite, Docetist, and Marcionite tracts confiscated from Alexandria and Ephesus, a few from Jerusalem. I remembered your love of books during our school days in Paris. I thought you might enjoy seeing some of the scurrilous works that have been collected over the years." He dismissed the custodian and locked the door behind him. After a hesitation, he asked the Abbot with a studied nonchalance, "In your encounters with these Occitan heretics, did any speak of a gospel not written by the saints?"

"They rant on about all manner of fables and forgeries," said Almaric.

Innocent debated if his next line of inquiry was worth the risk. Finally, he asked, "One authored by an older brother of our Lord?"

Almaric's brows narrowed in confusion. "The Blessed Mother was a perpetual virgin unstained by original sin. How could—"

"A blasphemy, of course," said Innocent, waving off the question. "The Jews and Greeks concoct such lies to propagate their mischief. It would not surprise me if a few scrips by Simon Magus and the Gnostics had escaped our nets."

"Some of the captured Manicheans claimed knowledge of a tradition older than St. Paul," said Almaric. "I dismissed it as ravings of the weak-minded."

"But no writings?" asked Innocent.

"They spread their disease by word of mouth to avoid a trail of evidence," assured Almaric. "Should such forgeries be uncovered, I will burn them."

"No!" said Innocent, too abruptly, then retreating to an air of indifference. "In the unlikely event you encounter such a manuscript, simply bring it to me." Finding the two Cistercians bewildered by his directive, he moved to allay their suspicions. "We must study Satan's sorcery if we are to prevail over him."

As Almaric bowed to take his leave, he saw the pontiff's admiring gaze linger upon Folques.

The Whole on high hath part in
our dancing. Who so danceth not,
knoweth not what cometh to pass.
- The Acts of John

VI

The Languedoc

March 1198

The journey north on the mud-slogged road to Toulousia was proving as taxing as Roger had warned it would be. But Esclarmonde would not hear of missing the christening of the infant Raymond VII, the future count of Toulouse, an eagerly awaited ceremony that promised to be one of the most memorable in Occitan history. Richard the Lionhearted, recently ransomed from an Austrian prison, would stand as godfather for the child of his sister, Johanna, thus bringing together the kings of England, France, and Aragon for the first time in a decade. Those three irascible monarchs shared but one trait—a hatred for the other two.

As an escort led the Foix contingent from Carcassonne, Esclarmonde studied her brother in the vanguard and wondered why he had surrendered so quickly to her demand that she and Corba attend the baptism. Could he be up to some intrigue? More likely he didn't trust her to remain in Foix unsupervised.

Raymond de Perella doubled back and captured Corba's bridle to ease her gelding into its pace. "Another day's ride, my dear, and you shall have a rest."

Corba stole back the reins in a tease. "We're not fragile dolls!"

"Yes, Raymond," chided Esclarmonde. "Do you mistake us for Northern ladies who insist on being carried about in palanquins?"

Raymond arched with laughter. "I truly pity those Parisian damsels. They are soon to find themselves eclipsed in beauty and endurance." Before returning to the van, he and Corba shared a glance pregnant with a secret.

When out of his earshot, Corba found Esclarmonde locked on her with an insistent glare. Finally, she broke under the silent inquisition. "There's something I've been meaning to tell you. But you must promise to keep it between us."

Hurt by the implication that she was a gossip, Esclarmonde placed her hand over her heart and vowed, "By all I hold dear."

After a hesitation, Corba whispered, "Raymond has proposed."

Esclarmonde screamed with delight, throwing the column into disarray. She dismounted and pulled Corba from the saddle to smother her with a hug. "We must prepare the banns and announcements!"

The men rushed up on hearing the shouts. Finding the women frolicking, Roger was about to chastise them when Esclarmonde left him speechless.

"Raymond and Corba are engaged!"

"Esclarmonde!" cried Corba in horror. "I just asked you not to—"

Roger grasped Raymond's hand in congratulations. "Nary a word to me?"

Corba could only shrug at Raymond's look of utter dismay.

"Bring the goblets and the best wine from the pack!" Esclarmonde led the foursome to seats on a limestone curb that overlooked the lush vineyards of the Argot valley. When all had gathered, she offered up a toast: "To Love, and to this Paradise in which we are blessed by God to live."

Raymond clanked his goblet against hers. "Esclarmonde, it is a state of bliss that I dare say you will soon enjoy yourself."

Esclarmonde saw Corba furtively tug at Raymond's sleeve in a signal to avoid that subject. Her instincts told her something was amiss, for Roger had acknowledged the prediction with a troubling smirk. Yet she dared not challenge him before they arrived in Toulouse. There was a restraint in Corba's expression of joy. Perhaps they were all sensitive to the fact that, at eighteen, she herself had passed the age when ladies were considered desirable for marriage. She had entertained no suitors since her public humiliation of Folques, and Roger incessantly threatened to take matters into his own hands. When he confronted her with the growing necessity of an arrangement, she would lash back by reminding him that he himself had yet to take a wife and produce an heir. A sudden wave of sadness swept over her. Who would have thought that Corba would be the first to marry? She knew it to be divine retribution for the many times she had lorded about her own throng of admirers.

Corba took Esclarmonde's hand and walked her away from the men. "You are thinking of him again."

"I cannot help it." During these past five years, she had tried to wean her thoughts from Guilhelm, but his face still came to her, flashing that laugh on the day she had raced past his steed for Montsegur. She had only herself to blame; he was a man who needed be told only once to avoid a lady's presence. Perhaps it was just as well. The notion of a betrothal to a Templar was as senseless as a desire to flatten the mountains.

"I can ask Raymond if he has heard news."

"It's best I not know."

"Raymond said Guilhelm was ordered to search for the heretics."

"You told Raymond of our quarrel?" snapped Esclarmonde.

"He is to be my husband. And who are you to talk of indiscretions?"

"I suppose he'll hand me over to the tribunal like he did that heretic girl!"

"What in God's name has come over you?" demanded Corba.

Esclarmonde turned away, repelled by her own outburst. "Guilhelm has this hold on me. I cannot shake it."

Corba stroked her hand. "You will find someone else. I am certain—"

Esclarmonde flinched from a report that sounded like the crack of lightning. A shimmering orb of gold suddenly appeared over Corba's shoulder, radiating with a centrifugal illumination unlike any she had seen, paradoxically both distant and within reach. She was struck with the inexplicable conviction that the vision was not formed by her corporeal eyes. She blinked repeatedly to chase the phantasm away, but its swirling grew more brilliant as it spun toward her. "Do you not see it?"

Corba turned. "See what?"

Esclarmonde collapsed in a spasm. Pulsations coursed down her spine and she heard words only dimly, as if submerged in water. The alarmed faces of Corba and the men hovered over her, blurred as if looking through a gauze. A balm of calming ecstasy suddenly dissolved her fear—she sank into what felt like a hidden chamber of her own flesh, enveloped by an emotion stronger than any she had ever experienced, painful as it was rapturous. The golden ball of light split into two serpents, one black and one white. They hissed and intertwined in a desperate struggle to swallow each other. The black serpent subdued its opponent but then choked on its conquest. A white dove flew from the mouth of the dead serpent and transformed into the orb that had given birth to the vision.

This is the Star followed by the Magi.

She was hearing the Voice that had spoken to her in the court of love. *Follow this Light, even unto the mouth of the Serpent.*

sclarmonde came to consciousness strapped to a stretcher. Her head pounded and her limbs ached horribly. An elderly woman with dark skin knelt over her, accompanied by a heavyset knight with bushy side whiskers. The woman pressed a wet compress to Esclarmonde's heated forehead. "I am Giraude, the chatelaine of Lavaur. This is my brother, Aimery. We have no physic here, so I tend to the ill . . . Can you hear me?"

Still disoriented, Esclarmonde nodded her head.

"She suffered a seizure," said Roger.

Giraude drew water from a well located in the center of the small village and brought the ladle to Esclarmonde's lips.

"There was a sun, but it was not like the real sun," said Esclarmonde. "And two snakes became entangled in a fight."

"It must have been the wine," said Corba.

"Perhaps sunstroke," said Aimery.

Giraude frowned knowingly on hearing Esclarmonde's mention of the serpents. The chatelaine monitored the reaction of the others, but to her relief, they remained perplexed. She ordered the men to carry Esclarmonde into her small chateau. When the others had departed, Giraude bolted the latch. She poured several pinches of crushed herbs into a cup, then stirred up a thick concoction and brought the tonic to Esclarmonde's tongue. "A posset of vernain and sorrel. It will aid the blood humour." She waited until Esclarmonde regained strength, then asked, "This scintillation of light you saw . . . Did it speak to you?"

Esclarmonde nearly spilled the drink. "How did you know?"

"You are the daughter of Count Bernard-Roger of Foix?"

"Yes, but—"

"I knew your mother."

Esclarmonde tried to arise, but she fell back from dizziness. "Do you know what happened to her?"

Giraude battened the oiled linen coverings over the windows to prevent anyone outside from overhearing. "Your mother and my sister, Blanche of Laurac, were ordained perfectas in this room."

"You're a Cathar?"

Giraude examined the necklace at Esclarmonde's breast and found its talisman. She pulled a stone from the wall and produced a small pyx chest, which when opened revealed an identical medallion. "They are called merels. We wear them to identify those of our faith. The twin riders represent the Rule of Two. Perfectas are attached to travel and live together in pairs. Your mother and my sister were such companions."

"Then if I find—"

"My sister was burned at Carcassonne."

Esclarmonde sank with despond. If her mother and this woman's sister were inseparable, they would have suffered the same end.

"You have been led to me for a purpose," said Giraude. "What I am about to impart to you must be kept in confidence until the day when another will be brought to you for initiation into the gnosis."

"How will I know?"

"You will know, as I know now." Giraude bathed Esclarmonde's fevered cheeks with the cool cloth. "You have heard of the Magdalene?"

"Mary, the repentant whore?"

Giraude muttered a curse under her breath. "That lie is what the priests wish you to believe. The Magdalene was trained in the temple arts. It was she who initiated Our Lord into the mysteries of the Light. After His death, she and the Master's brother, the one called James the Just, attempted to preserve the teachings by forming an order of believers known as the Nasoreans. But Saul of Tarsus, the Teacher of Darkness, conspired to alter the arcana and spread falsehoods to the uninformed."

Esclarmonde had discarded to distant memory her discovery on the night that Folques had accosted her in St. Volusien's chapel. Now the details of that quest came flooding back to her. "Yes, I've heard of this brother."

"He was exiled from Jerusalem with the Magdalene."

"Why?"

"He knew the Master Jesus too well."

"But he is mentioned in the Gospels."

"The usurpers could not deny James's existence," said Giraude. "Too many in Jerusalem remembered him. So they committed a more devious act. They diminished his importance."

"What happened to the Magdalene?"

"That well outside was blessed by her hand. She and her brother Lazarus—"

"The one raised from the dead?"

"He was in a meditative trance, called back by the Master from his ascent to the Light realms. When the Tarsian imposter purged the Nasoreans, Lazarus fled Jerusalem with his sister and together they found refuge at Marseille. The Magdalene preached the true teachings of the Master throughout Provence. She spent her final years in a cave not far from here."

"Tell me of these teachings."

"They are given only when the aspirant is ready."

"How did you come by them?"

"Before converting to the Christian faith of my father, my mother was raised in a Persian mystery sect called Qadiriyyah. Her people quested for the same sacred emanations that came to you today. The Magdalene studied the mysteries of this Light with the priests in Egypt. She returned to Galilee and Judea to show her Nasorean disciples how to find its salvation."

"These Arab mystics. Are they connected to your Cathar faith?"

"They are streams that flow from the same river," said Giraude. "Do not be led astray by names. The true ones of the hidden Church of Love are to be found in all faiths. You must look beyond the outer trappings to sift the essence of the teachings." She retreated to a closet and returned wearing a white robe gathered at the waist with a red silk sash. She closed her eyes and began turning, slowly at first, then faster. Soon she was whirling with such abandon that she seemed propelled by an invisible force. Esclarmonde thought she saw the faint outline of a halo around Giraude's head. Had she fallen into the hands of a madwoman?

"This is the door to the Peace that passeth understanding," said Giraude as she whirled. "When the Sun at Midnight comes to you again, you must not fear it. Dance and merge with it. The Nasoreans called it the Jesus Dance. The Lords of Darkness have long schemed to suppress its power."

"Why?"

"Because it releases us from the chains of our senses."

Esclarmonde arose from the bed and tried to imitate Giraude's spinning. Within minutes, her normal thoughts were obliterated by a tingling that ignited at the center of her breastbone. "What is this warmth I feel?"

"It cannot be named," said Giraude. "Nor sold by a church. The seductions of the flesh impede its gifts."

"How then am I to describe it?"

"By stories and song, and by the example of your life," said Giraude. "Did you truly think that the troubadours were only simple-headed minstrels? They spread the secret words that open the heart and channel the Light . . . Now, tell me of this man you love."

Esclarmonde lost her balance, astonished by the woman's clairvoyance.

"The heart has its own eyes," said Giraude with a knowing smile.

"He is a Templar."

Giraude nodded. "Why am I not surprised?"

"He's nothing like me."

"I doubt that. Two souls with a common destiny are drawn together on the same ray. Your monk has not revealed to you all he knows."

"But he hunts down the adherents of your faith."

"He hunts no mortal prey. The Temple set its headquarters in the bowels of the Jerusalem Temple for good reason. The monks discovered that the secrets of the gnosis were guarded there long ago. If your Templar has the inner sight, he will know that you have been transfigured when next you meet."

Esclarmonde averted her eyes in shame. "I fear there will not be a next time . . . I ordered him never to speak to me again."

Giraude bolstered Esclarmonde's flagging spirits with an embrace. "This is your first lesson of the Light. Listen well. Once, a maiden came to her Beloved's door and knocked. 'Who is there?' asked a voice from within. The maiden answered, 'It is I.' But the voice replied, 'There is not enough room here for you and me.' The distraught maiden retreated to the desert. After spending a year in solitary prayer, she returned to the door and knocked again. 'Who is there?' the voice asked again. This time, the maiden replied, 'It is thyself.' And the door was opened."

Esclarmonde felt a surge of joy at the thought that Guilhelm could be her twin soul. But she quickly dismissed the possibility of their being together as man and wife. "He is vowed to God."

"There are two grades of women in this world," said Giraude. "There are the many who, by force of past actions, must reincarnate and give physical birth. And then there are the few who are placed on this earth to procreate in another way."

"What other way is there?"

"The way of the Magdalene, who gave birth to the Light. The Vessel that follows this path must sacrifice its womb to the Higher Wisdom."

"I'm trying to listen with my heart, but I still don't understand."

"Understanding will come," said Giraude. "Just know for now that, on this day, the seed of a new life has quickened within you."

Drowsy, Esclarmonde retreated to the bed. As she slipped into a deep sleep, she heard Giraude offer another admonition. "One thing more you must never forget. Every birth requires a sacrifice. It is the Way of the Light."

Jesus said: "If some say to you,
'Where have you come from?'
Say to them,
'We have come from the Light.'"
- The Gospel of Thomas

VII

Pamiers

<hr />

March 1198

Almaric abstained from all secular pastimes such as falconry and boar spearing, deeming such popular obsessions uncouth for a man of God. But that did not mean he denied himself the thrill of the chase. Come each spring, when the hawking mews were thrown open and the gamekeepers exercised their lymers with loping runs across the greening parks, he would order his black Frisian saddled and his favorite riding habit—expertly tailored with darts and hidden slits to inspire reverence while allowing freedom of movement—brought out from storage.

This morning, the orange Ariege sun was a socket of welcoming warmth, breaking fast above the cornflower-blue lavognes, the small pools that trailed across limestone causses of this alluvial plain like the tears of the Blessed Mother on Calvary. A thousand strands of crystal snow water tinkled down the pleats and rucks of the foothills, rushing from melting caps to placid lakes. The village markets were abuzz with the clanking of hawked wares and the hum of salacious gossip, and from the street stalls came the irresistible aromas of fresh-baked sourdough, roasted asparagus, and spitted turnips—all time-proven baits for the elusive prey that the Abbot stalked this time every year.

Heretic-hunting season had arrived.

This year he had chosen for his base of operations a sleepy burgh situated on a crossroads a few leagues north of Foix. The Occitan town of Pamiers was unremarkable save for one fact: It had long been a notorious haven for the Cathar heresiarch Guilbert de Castres. Because of the degenerate proclivity of its inhabitants, an old keep here called the Clocher des Cordiers—the Tower of Ropes—had been converted into a dank dungeon to incarcerate petty poachers, cutpurses, and heretics who did not warrant the expense of a trial.

Armed with the weapons of his sport—a crucifix, a vial of holy water, and a knapsack stocked with foodstuffs—the Abbot led the reluctant Folques down the Clocher's occulted stairwell, which corkscrewed into a dripping cavern once used to cure cheese. Escorting the two Cistercians was the establishment's one-eyed gaoler, whose houndish nose and drooping ears had taken on the features of the vicious Pyrenean mastiffs he bred to sniff out escaping prisoners.

Folques braced his hand against the moss-slimed stones. Assaulted by the stench of rancid flesh, he flashed a torch. A few steps more and he came upon dozens of decomposing bodies that hung from manacles.

The gaoler jingled a half-moon of rusted keys to chase off the cockroaches and rats. "Ye needn't worry. They're all shackled." He emitted a monosyllabic sound that approached a laugh, then added, "Unless they've bitten through their limbs." He kicked one of the prisoners in the hope of drawing a response, but the only sign of life was the scrum of maggots that squirmed under the wretch's stripped skin. He cursed the dead man for the loss of income. "Devil damn you!"

"Utter another word of profanity in my presence," warned Almaric, "and you will join them."

The gaoler spat a black jet of root mash into the cadaver's face, the only act of protest he dared raise against these haughty Cistercians. Mumbling a litany of his lifelong afflictions, he led the monks deeper into the foetid pit until he saw something move in the far corner. A closer inspection revealed a sunken-eyed ghost of a girl chained at the feet. She blanched into the shadows and hovered next to an emaciated man locked in wrist irons. Clad in filthy rags, the two prisoners blinked painfully from the light. The wall above them was covered with suspicious pagan etchings. The girl shook her head at her cell mate in a warning not to speak.

The gaoler pulled the wasted urchin to her feet to demonstrate that her blackened ankles, rubbed raw by the manacles, would not prevent her from walking out. "Brought in from Foix. Three, four years ago."

"Their crimes?" asked Folques.

"This li'l quail's a witch. How else how could she survive?"

Almaric retreated a step. Although protected by the crucifix at his breast, he did not take lightly the power of Satan to channel his sorcery through the female form. After examining the two prisoners, he chose to begin his interrogation with the whimpering man. "Your name?"

The girl rattled her chains in a plea for her comrade to remain silent.

The man was too frightened to obey. "Sacchioni."

Almaric offered him a cut of salted jerky as an inducement. "We are men of God, my son. You need not be afraid . . . Who brought you here?"

Sacchioni chomped down the sliver of meat and retched it up.

"If you confess your sins, we can remove you from this suffering," said Almaric. "Otherwise, you face an agonizing death."

Sacchioni rocked nervously on his haunches and tried to avoid the wild-eyed girl's admonishing glare. He had the queer habit of closing his lids when speaking to the monks. At last, he blurted, "Ten soldiers. Their leader was short. Another one wore a red cross."

Almaric offered a wineskin to slake the man's thirst. "Tell me more about the soldier who wore the cross."

"A strange rood, it was," mumbled Sacchioni, wine dribbling down his neck. "Like four petals of a flower. And he had a scar—"

"What did you say?" demanded Folques.

Sacchioni's eyes darted maniacally, fearful that he had declaimed something punishable. "On his face. He had a scar under his eye."

Montanhagol.

Folques had never forgotten that marred cheek. The Templar must have been ordered to Occitania to search for heretics as penance for his dereliction of duty in the Holy Land. Such an assignment would have been too demeaning for members of his Order in good standing. The Abbot nodded him toward the girl, indicating that she would be his first test in the saving of wayward souls. Folques knelt beside her and held his crucifix before her face. "The blessings of the saints cannot be invoked without your name." When she persisted in staring blankly beyond him, he flushed with anger. If he could not break this half-starved pigeon, how would he ever subdue the wily Cathar leaders? Imitating the Abbot's example, he tempted her with a scrap of bread, but she would not weaken. He turned and brought the crumb inches from Sacchioni's lips.

"Phillipa!" shouted Sacchioni, snapping up his reward.

The girl dropped her head in defeat.

Folques pressed his thumb into the floor grime and marked her flailing forehead with the sign of the Cross. "Phillipa, accept Jesus Christ, who died for your sins." He began to feel ill. Was she bewitching him? He grasped his crucifix to thwart the demonic spirits and asked the question designed to ferret out suspected heretics. "Do you accept the one God indivisible?"

She muttered incoherent prayers and looked away.

"Answer me, I implore you. For the sake of your soul."

Almaric could no longer endure this pitiful exercise of ineptitude. He pulled Folques to his feet and pushed him aside. "You have much to learn about dealing with these cloggers."

"But the Holy Father said—"

"Innocent will discover soon enough the futility of persuasion." Almaric ordered the gaoler, "Leave us."

"That's twenty francs for the two!" Cowed by the Abbot's baneful glare, the gaoler threw the shackle keys at his feet and skulked away.

Almaric traced his finger along the collar of Phillipa's tunic, pausing to caress the pale chevron of flesh below her throat. He played with the drawstring on her tunic and slowly untied its knot. She fought wildly and scourged him with the chains, but her struggle only aroused him more. An odd expression, half pain and half rapture, shadowed the Abbot's face as he unlocked her ankles. She sprang for the gate but stumbled and fell from weakness. He limped after her and came astride her waist, then leaned down and pressed his chest against her frangible body. "If you're not a heretic, prove it." He tore open her tunic and groped her breasts. She clawed at him with her long nails, drawing a swash of blood across his stubbled jawline. Heaving from the exertion, he restrained her wrists and shouted with saliva dripping from his mouth, "The witch is revealed to be abhorrent of normal relations!"

Folques stood frozen in disbelief.

"Record it!" ordered the panting Almaric, his face crimson with heat.

Folques fumbled for parchment in his pouch.

"You Romans don't take wives!" screamed Phillipa.

"Satan speaks!" Almaric slapped her against the stones and came atop her again. This time, she did not struggle. He looked down in horror at his white robe—it was splattered with blood. "The Sabine opened her veins on me!"

Sacchioni crouched in the corner. "Am I to be released?"

Reclaiming his pious composure, Almaric arose from the half-conscious girl and smoothed his stained robes. He shook his sleeves to his wrists and wiped his bald head with the meticulous care of a priest about to exit the sacristy to say mass. "Released you shall be, my son . . . to the heat of God's wrath."

"Not the fires!" Sacchioni crawled screaming in an attempt to catch the departing Cistercians. "There were others! Lasses of privilege."

Phillipa roused from her stupor. "You took the Last Touch!"

"One of them helped us escape!"

Folques turned at the cell entrance and rushed back to the Cathar man. "These maids. How do you know they were highborn?"

"They wore finery and spoke the court Oc."

"No!" pleaded Phillipa.

"Father Castres called one of them—"

Phillipa sprang at him. "Don't sin! You'll be born again!"

"—the Light of the World."

Almaric was perplexed by Folques's stunned reaction. "That means something to you?"

Folques hesitated. "He speaks of the Count of Foix's sister."

Almaric broke a fiendish grin. "I've sought the arrest of this Castres for years. He appears and vanishes like a spectre."

Folques raised the whimpering Sacchioni to his feet. "The man who wore the red cross. Did he conspire with the noble maids?"

"I saw him pick up a shred of the dark-haired one's dress and hide it."

Almaric mulled the revelation, then shook his head to dismiss its value as evidence. "A tribunal would never believe the ravings of this wretch over the sworn attestations of a viscountess and a Templar. These two are no use to us."

"Then we must see to it that they condemn themselves," said Folques.

"How do you propose to accomplish that?"

Folques led his superior out of earshot of the two heretics. "You are to officiate the baptism of the infant Raymond?"

"A week hence. In Toulouse. "

Folques turned sloe-eyed with the hatching of a scheme. "I once saw a monger drop a filleted mackerel into a vat of fish. The other mackerel flopped in a frenzy, but the carp and monkfish remained unperturbed."

"So?"

"The mackerel sensed that one of their own had been gutted."

Taking his meaning, Almaric affectionately slapped Folques's cheek in pride. He pulled a handful of coins from his pouch and threw them at the gaoler lurking just beyond the gate. "Deliver these two to Toulouse."

There is no tyranny on earth like the tyranny of priests.
- Averroes

VIII

Toulouse

March 1198

The interrogatories that resounded through St. Sernin's ancient basilica were chanted by a voice that rang distantly familiar. Standing three rows from the baptismal font, Esclarmonde was denied a closer look at the hooded deacon who declared the ordo at the Abbot's side. Yet she could not shake the presentiment that his exorcisms were being directed at her.

"Do you renounce Satan?" the deacon bellowed.

Count Raymond de Toulouse answered for his infant son. "I renounce."

Esclarmonde monitored the tempestuous baron as one might a volcano about to explode. Draped in a robe of maroon and gold, Count Raymond maintained a telling distance from his rival, Richard the Lionhearted, whose green eyes still held a hint of his infamous temper despite the ravages of hard crusading. With bulgy face grooved like a walnut, the Count was no less dissipated than his English brother-in-law, if for less gallant reasons; few ladies or goblets had ever passed his debauching reach. It was commonly said that the Languedoc vineyards would grow purple oranges before these two old enemies met in peace. But Richard had grown weary of war against Toulouse and, in a stroke of diplomatic cunning, had bonded a treaty by marrying his widowed sister to Raymond. The two leaders had thus outfoxed their mutual nemesis, King Philip of France, who in a pout had reneged on his commitment to attend the ceremony.

Esclarmonde repulsed Corba's attempt to take the temperature of her forehead. "Stop treating me as if I'm deathly ill."

"Tell me if you feel the least bit faint again," whispered Corba.

Esclarmonde regretted her choice of attire, a cerulean gown creweled in pearls. Surrounded by the somberly-garbed Northerners, she stood out like a blue-white flame in a cluster of smoldering coals. Above her hung the basilica's famous frieze of Herod's soldiers murdering the Innocents, a fitting tableau for this humiliation the Toulousians were forced to endure. A few feet away stood the bronze plate that marked the spot where Saturnius, the city's patron saint, had challenged Druid priests in a test of Christ's power. He had paid for his faith by being dragged to his death tied to a raging bull. She wondered if, looking down now from Heaven, Saturnius rued his martyrdom on finding that these arrogant Cistercians had merely exchanged robes with those pagan necromancers.

The deacon's chant rose in ferocity in its demand for renunciation of Satan's pomps. Almaric kept the babe submerged in the piscina. When the Count delayed the concession, the deacon's voice shook the nave anew. "Do you renounce Satan's armies and the dualist heretics who infest this land?"

Count Raymond reached his fill of such insolence. He retracted the deacon's cowl and was stunned to find himself face to face with the old troubadour friend he had not seen in four years. Esclarmonde held fast to Corba. Folques, beardless and tonsured, stood unflinching in his exposure. His vengeful eyes were trained on her as if he had practiced this moment a thousand times.

"Twittering quisling!" shouted Count Raymond at Folques. "*You* of all people dare alter the liturgy in my church?"

Almaric came to Folques's defense. "This basilica, and your good standing in it, belong to the Holy Father."

The Count repulsed his wife's attempt to calm him. "I allowed the baptism to take place here rather than in St. Gilles, where my forefathers received the sacrament. But I'll not stand by to hear my family slandered by this fluted cad!"

"The ceremony will be suspended." Almaric spoke loud enough for the thousands gathered outside to hear. "I shall report your decision to Rome. Should your heir succumb, he will languish in Limbo."

Grumbles of indignation and alarm rippled through the congregation. All present understood the gravity of that threat. The Cathars who resided in Toulousia did not believe in infant baptism, but taught that Jesus had never transmitted the Light before a person could understand the import of the decision. For them, the birth sacrament was a fabrication designed to herd people into the Church before the Pope's sovereignty could be questioned. Though Esclarmonde would never admit it openly, she sympathized with their objections. Yet if Count Raymond refused to allow the baptism to proceed, such defiance would be seen in Rome as a public espousal of the heresy. Nothing was more feared than a papal interdiction and its resultant horrors of unburied corpses, bastards born out of wedlock, and loss of lucrative pilgrimage trade.

Seeing his tenuous alliance on the brink of collapse, Richard of England drew Count Raymond aside. "They are only words. Be done with it."

"That conniving Italian sends legates to usurp my authority!" seethed the Toulouse baron. "Arrest this one! Execute that one!"

Johanna captured her husband's arm. "Raymond, please."

"Leave this to me, woman!" shouted Count Raymond.

Richard bristled. "Speak harshly to my sister again and—"

"Gentlemen!" interjected King Peter of Aragon. "Whoever holds temporal care of this church, it remains God's sanctuary. You both have performed great service to Christ. Do not stain that memory." He admonished Almaric, "Abbot, the call for renunciation would best be offered by you, not your deacon."

Almaric knew the Aragon monarch to be on close terms with the Holy Father. Eager to avoid a damning report, he reluctantly agreed to amend the ordo. "Do you renounce Satan and his armies, be they spiritual or mortal?"

Count Raymond swallowed the bitter compromise. "I do renounce."

Almaric immersed the infant for the final time. "I christen thee Raymond VII of Toulouse, servant of the Holy Roman Church." The pronouncement was met by a low pattering of unenthusiastic amens. Before Raymond could retrieve his wailing heir, the Abbot carried the infant to the portico and held it aloft so the multitudes outside could witness their liege's capitulation.

Count Raymond rescued the child and delivered it to a nursemaid. "Your duty here is finished. You may return to your abbey."

"I would be remiss if I did not attend the afternoon's celebration," said Almaric. "I have brought a gift from the Holy Father."

The Count was in no position to banish these snout-poking monks whose influence was growing more troublesome by the month. He angrily waved off the confrontation and descended the steps to greet his adoring subjects.

When the Foix contingent passed under the narthex, Almaric stepped in front of Roger. "I plan to visit your county soon, baron."

"You needn't waste a journey to our humble domain," said Roger.

"The Church follows God's example by taking interest in all its children, be they great or small." Almaric turned with an expectant smile upon Esclarmonde. "I believe, madam, you know my deacon."

She refused to meet eyes with her former courtier. "I am heartened, sir, to see that you have found your true calling."

"I was admonished once to make better use of my talents," said Folques.

The Abbot monitored their reunion like an alchemist combining volatile vapors. "I am told you have an unusual familiarity with Scriptures."

Esclarmonde's stomach tightened. *He is testing me.* She forced a pale smile, having become more adept at crafting facial expressions to erect barricades to her thoughts. "I am certain the spiritual protector of the Languedoc has more pressing concerns than the trivial reading habits of ladies. Now, I must apologize for monopolizing your excellency's good graces."

Almaric blinked hard at the backhanded escape. "I trust we will enjoy your company at the banquet?"

"I shall be in attendance," she said, flatly.

Almaric shared a knowing glance with Folques. "We look forward to it."

That afternoon, the guests mingled and dined around the two rows of linen-covered trestles that had been set in the verdant valley below the sangria-hued walls of the Chateau Narbonnais. A flourish of trumpets from the tower's kitchen unleashed yet another cadre of scullions carrying platters laden with the fourth course of the sumptuous feast: Muscalades of minnows, porpoise, and peas; baked herring; roasted eel; and cockatrice with heads of chickens sewn atop the bodies of suckling pigs.

Corba moaned with gustatory rapture as she garnished another slice of Alexandrine gingerbread with kirsch-flavored blancmange. She forced the delicacy on Esclarmonde. "Heaven in a spread! You must try this!"

Esclarmonde declined the offer and continued searching the crowd, fearful that any moment she might again encounter Folques. "I have no appetite."

"What can he do to you? He's a monk now."

"He has never forgiven me."

"You worry needlessly. The churchmen would not allow a novitiate into their ministry if he had not repented of his sins."

Raymond de Perella returned from his glad-handing rounds and presented his flask to a mounted wine steward for refilling. "Esclarmonde, you would quite enjoy your brother's predicament. He has been held prisoner to the Aragon delegation for the past hour while King Peter drones on about his plans to drive the Moors from Seville."

Corba studied the culinary choices before settling on a leg of duck for her fiancé. "Eat well, darling. Soon you will be forced to endure my cooking."

"You're fattening me for the kill!" Raymond laid siege on the drumstick. "I fear our wedding feast shall pale in comparison to this."

"Nonsense," teased Corba. "Esclarmonde will be in charge of the festivities. She'll refuse to be outdone."

Esclarmonde put up a façade of interest, listening with half an ear to their banter while nervously scanning each passing face. "Yes, with your purse, Raymond, I'll have no trouble eclipsing this slight repast."

Raymond nearly choked on her threat. Before he could recover, a blond lad styled in a lavish turquoise shirt bounded up and bowed to their group. With chest puffed out and twinkling eyes as cobalt blue as the hills of Lorraine, the boy applied a rather mature kiss to the back of Esclarmonde's hand. "So, it is true," said the young newcomer. "I've oft heard about the unmatched beauty of the demoiselles from Foix."

Esclarmonde stifled a chuckle. "Who might you be, sir?"

"Roger Trevencal. One day to be the Viscount of Carcassonne and Beziers. They call me the Gallant Trevencal."

Esclarmonde magnanimously accepted his effusive offer of courtesy. "You're so young to have received such a lofty sobriquet."

"I'm eighteen." Detecting her incredulity, he amended, "Fifteen."

"Shall we settle on twelve?" Esclarmonde had not felt such lightness of heart in years. The Trevencals were a renowned family related to Raymond de Toulouse that held Occitan domains small but influential in diplomacy. The House of Trevencal also held a distant lineage to her mother, Cecille. The boy reminded her of Guilhelm, not in his speech, which was much more effusive, but in his confident air. "You must have many lady admirers."

"I've waited for the one who would do me high honor."

"Have you not yet found her?" she asked.

"Only today." Trevencal lowered to one knee. "Will you, Lady Esclarmonde, accept my offer of marriage?"

Corba and Raymond could no longer suppress their good-natured laughter.

Deeply touched by the gesture, Esclarmonde untied a scarf from her wrist and handed it to the boy. "If I were younger, I would deem it an honor. But I

fear you would soon tire of me. When I'm old and shriveled, you'll still be fluttering the hearts of maidens and I would be consumed by jealousy. But, please,
accept this as a token of my heartfelt gratitude."

The treasured gift was rudely snatched from the boy's grasp.

"Seems the Trevencals lust for wenches as well as fiefs." Hovering over the
boy stood a barrel-chested man with uneven eyes the color of dirty ice and skin
pitted like Portuguese cork. He was accompanied by two knights accoutred in
the blacks and grays of the North.

"Be gone with you, whelp!" growled another of the intruders. Shorter than
his comrade, he was cursed with a bull neck that leaned to the left, suffusing
his frame with a sinister tendency that personified his malformed soul. He
clamped on the boy's chin. "Come back when you have whiskers."

Trevencal fought to reclaim the scarf. "If my father were here—"

"Your father is a dolt-witted coward." The taller Northerner spoke loudly
in the crude Anglo-Norman patois of langue d'oeil, bleating hard consonants
and whistling heavy breaths through his mucous-clogged nose.

The struggling boy turned crimson. "He is bedridden, else he'd clap your
ears!" He wrangled loose but was sent sprawling by a straight-arm.

Esclarmonde intervened before Raymond could call out the interlopers.
"Who are you, sir, to treat this young man so basely?"

The tallest Northerner plunged his hand into a bowl of pudding and licked
his fingers like a common beggar. "Jourdaine L'Isle. This is Simon de Montfort
and his brother, Guy, from the Ile de France. No doubt you've heard of us."

Esclarmonde brought Trevencal to her side for protection. "We rarely
receive dispatches from the backwaters."

With chest hair crawling from his neckline, Simon de Montfort resembled
a squinting bear as he blinked with a rapid tic from nearsightedness in an
effort to assay her features. "Where we come from, women aren't allowed to
speak with such impudence. But then we're not cuckolded like you Ocs."

Raymond took a threatening step. "I warn you, sir!"

Jourdaine leered at Esclarmonde's bosom. "You're not yet married?"

"What concern is that of yours?" asked Esclarmonde.

"Your brother would be well-advised to find you a husband before your
ripeness turns to rot. One who can teach you proper Christian humility."

Trevencal filched the dagger from Raymond's belt and charged at the miscreant. Jourdaine shifted sideways and drove a hip into the boy, causing him to
fall somersaulting from his own wild momentum. "You Ocs are all alike." He

kicked the dazed Trevencal in the kidneys and departed with his malicious confederates. "All crow and no cock."

Esclarmonde helped Trevencal to his feet. "Are you injured?"

Trevencal retrieved the prized scarf and tucked it away for safekeeping.

"Why do they harass you?" she asked.

Trevencal glared a promise of reprisal at the gauche Northerners as they disappeared into the throngs. "They covet my father's lands. Jourdaine is a second-born from Gascony. He has no demesnes of any worth. The two de Montforts are Norman scum who hold claims to lands in England. The cross-eyed one is twice-spawned from Satan's seed. They make their way on tournament winnings and stolen estates. You must warn your brother. I've heard it said they have designs on Foix."

Before Esclarmonde could make sense of this unsettling news, a fanfare called the guests to the dais.

On the rostrum, Almaric stood to address the assembly. "The Holy Father cannot rest knowing that Christians still languish in Saracen prisons. On this day, he calls on all warriors to return Jerusalem to its rightful protectors."

The petition was met with a stony silence. Most Toulousians could name at least one kinsman who had failed to return from the Holy Land. The zeal once held for such enterprises had long since dissipated, replaced by disgust at the onerous Saladin tithes levied to finance them.

Almaric nodded, having expected the contumacious reaction. "To honor this display of steadfast faith, I have arranged a gift."

"You've spouted that promise repeatedly," said Count Raymond. "On with it, so we may return to more important matters."

The gates of the Narbonnais tower were thrown open. Constables in the employ of the Cistercians dragged out two barefoot prisoners whose heads were hooded. Brandishing a staffed crucifix, Folques led the wretches toward a clearing where men-at-arms dug postholes and piled faggots around two stakes.

"What is the meaning of this?" demanded Count Raymond.

"What better way to affirm your son's entry into the Army of Christ than to rectify two fallen souls this day?" asked Almaric.

"You push me too far, Cistercian!"

"You wish me to release them?"

Count Raymond realized that he had been drawn into a trap. Refusing to enforce the judgment in such a public forum could bring harsh consequences from Rome. He had no choice but to wave the soldiers to the task.

Folques removed the hood from the head of the first heretic.

Esclarmonde was too far removed from the clearing to gain a clear view of the delirious man. She edged closer and caught her breath in a flash of terror. "Is that not—" Corba's hand covered her mouth, stifling the question.

The soldiers lit the faggots. Folques stepped back from the lurid flames as Sacchioni's skin blistered in a blackened mass of snapping veins. Finally, too slow in coming, it was over. Green from his first burning, Folques staggered to the second stake and lifted the hood from the remaining prisoner. Phillipa saw Sacchioni's charred body and dropped her eyes in despair.

Esclarmonde shoved Corba aside and rushed past the barricade.

Folques intercepted her. "This is not your court of manners!"

Esclarmonde escaped his grasp and ran to the royal dais. "I beg of you, my lord! Don't let them burn this girl!"

"The heresy spreads like a plague here," said Almaric, enjoying the fruits of his ploy. "Even ladies of exalted pedigree are not immune to its seductions."

"She is too young to have offended God," insisted Esclarmonde.

"That is for the Church to adjudge," said Almaric.

Count Raymond could not look at Esclarmonde. "My hands are tied."

"Mine are not!" Trevencal broke through the pressing crowds and leapt to the platform. "Are we to be ordered about by foreign monks who have never drawn a verse or bent a knee to a lady?"

"Hold your tongue, pup," warned Almaric. "Ere you find it cut out."

"And who'll do the cutting?" Trevencal pleaded with Count Raymond, his uncle. "Would your father have permitted these monks to blacken the day of your own christening?"

Almaric was determined to finish the execution before the Toulouse baron wavered. "The order has been given."

"I demand a trial by combat!" shouted Trevencal.

"This is an ecclesiastic proceeding," said Almaric.

"Are we not governed by Roman code?" asked Trevencal. "Have I not the right to champion the accused by a test of arms?"

A roar of acclamation drew a tight smile from Count Raymond. "It seems, Abbot, the stripling has bested you on a point of law."

"The Church has outlawed such barbaric spectacles," said Almaric.

"As Cistercian General, you have the authority to grant exemptions," reminded the Count. "Sanction the tournament, or I shall allow my subjects to decide the maid's fate. Then you can condemn the entire city."

Finding his stratagem unraveling, Almaric grudgingly acquiesced to the affair. "Who shall defend the Church? Indulgences shall be granted."

Jourdaine L'Isle climbed to the dais and shoved Trevencal aside. "This tadpole needs to be taught a lesson in obedience." Simon de Montfort and his brother Guy joined the Gascon on the platform to serve as advocates ecclesia.

Esclarmonde rushed to Trevencal. "You don't have to do this!"

"I'd not wish to live after witnessing such a day," said Trevencal.

Roger drew Esclarmonde aside. "Do you know that girl at the stake?"

Esclarmonde hesitated. "She was with those . . . in the cave."

"Then she is a heretic as they charge," said Roger.

"She saved my life."

"How do you know that?"

"She could have offered me up to save herself." Esclarmonde directed his attention toward the smoldering faggots. "If someone had stood up for our mother . . ." She realized too late what she had unwittingly revealed.

Roger was stunned. "Who told you?"

A few steps away, Jourdaine watched their animated discussion with a smirk. "There's a pretty sight! An Oc bitch shaming the Wolf to howl. For certain, it is their old man's litter."

The proximity of listeners prevented Roger from interrogating Esclarmonde further on how she had come to learn of their mother's fate. Although outsized by a hand's span, he came up fast on the Gascon spoiling for a fight. "You should try an opponent your own size!"

"Loose tongues seem to run in this litter," said Simon de Montfort.

Raymond of Perella tried to dissuade Roger from being drawn into the scuffle. "Save their spitting for the field."

Seething, Roger climbed the steps to the dais. "We stand with Trevencal for the maiden."

Count Raymond gave his hearty imprimatur to the contest before Almaric could retract the ratification. "I call a Pas D'Armes on the morrow! Best of three runs to determine the fate of the accused!"

The crowds shouted wagers and the yeomen rushed to build the railings.

When Esclarmonde was distracted by the jostling, Corba hurried Trevencal behind a tent. "Do you know the town of Mirepoix?"

"A half day's ride," said Trevencal.

Corba slipped a note into his hand. "Deliver this with all speed."

Think ye with what grief and sorrow the twain did asunder part.
- Wolfram Von Eschenbach, Parsifal

IX

Toulouse

The Next Morning

Surrounded by the fluttering pomps and gaudy trappings of pageantry, Raymond de Toulouse arose from his viewing chair on the tournament grandstand and announced, "Any lady who takes issue of Courtesy may strike the helm of the offender."

Esclarmonde glowered at Jourdaine's conical headgear as if covering it with a curse. The Gascon's boorish behavior on the previous day had been sufficient cause for disqualification under the code of *chevaliers sans reproache*. She forced him to await her decision while she fingered a denier, then whispered to him, "I would see you immortalized this day."

Jourdaine was impressed that she had so quickly—

She tossed the coin to a minstrel. "To commission a verse. One telling how a courageous boy avenged a petty baron's insult." She stepped back and left the Gascon's helmet untouched, preferring to see him shamed on the field.

Jourdaine lost his grin.

The two teams retired to their respective positions. Those who had not merited seats fought for position along the railings. Thousands of commoners had filled the surrounding hills to witness the rare *à outrance* joust that offered the possibility of injury and even death.

At the south end of the lists, Roger assisted young Trevencal onto the saddle to face Simon de Montfort for the first encounter. "You've made runs?"

"Of course . . . against quintains."

Roger quickly dissembled his misgivings lest the boy be needlessly discouraged. "Keep your lance traverse. You'll not have time to maneuver it."

Trevencal was hotfoot to charge. "I'm going to run him through!"

"You need only unhorse him." Roger sliced away the fancy embroidery on the lad's gambeson. "The lance will catch. You want the blow glance off."

Trevencal bridled his rouncy toward the stake in the tilting corridor and found Phillipa shivering in the wind, covered only by a scrim tunic. He placed his riding cloak around her shoulders. "Your healers, my lady, have done much to ease the suffering of my dying father. I would ask the Consolamentum of you."

Phillipa was astonished that one of noble birth would so publicly request her faith's most solemn sacrament, given to the uninitiated only when death could be imminent. "You know you must forever abstain from sins of the flesh?" When he nodded, she said, "I must touch you to transmit the blessing." She spoke a Cathar prayer as he placed his hand to her cheek, "Have no pity on the body of corruption, but have pity on the spirit imprisoned. Go always with the Light."

"We will meet again," he promised. "In this world or the next."

The crowds rustled with a scaling hum of anticipation as Trevencal returned to his starting position. Count Raymond gave the hand signal. The herald blew his long-necked horn and scurried behind the barriers. The field erupted in two converging clouds of sawdust. Esclarmonde held tight to Corba, unable to watch. Halfway to the meeting of lances, de Montfort leaned to reduce his exposure, but Trevencal remained upright with his weapon bouncing wildly.

"Tilt!" screamed Roger.

Trevencal's shield exploded at impact—he catapulted from the saddle and landed with a sickening thud. The Northerners hooted and threw dung at him.

De Montfort circled his destrier around the stunned boy, splattering him with mud. "My regards to the imbecile who sired you."

Esclarmonde intercepted the stretcher-bearers. She ripped away Trevencal's bloodied hauberk and found a shoulder wound. The physic daubed the puncture with a styptic balm, then assured her, "He'll live for more foolishness."

Corba rushed to Raymond, who had already mounted. "Don't do this!"

Raymond set his helmet. "Darling, would you fetch me a leg of lamb from the tables? I'm always ravenous after a joust."

Buoyed by his brother's easy victory, Guy de Montfort pranced and reared his charger to its hinds in a taunt. Trevencal had barely been carried off the field when the herald scampered into the lists and sounded the second run. Raymond managed an agile start; even and level, his smaller horse stayed the course without veering toward the rails. Their collision was announced by a sharp crack followed by chilling equine whines. When the sawdust cleared, Raymond sat slumped in the saddle as his steed angled aimlessly across the field. Guy de Montfort, sprawled in the ooze, angrily threw off his helmet.

Esclarmonde and Corba hurried to Raymond, who tottered precariously near the rails, dazed by the hit. "I am fine," he said. "A little tossed is all."

On the dais, Count Raymond settled back into his high-backed chair and turned to the Lionhearted. "So, it comes down to the Wolf."

"A hundred francs says the heretic burns," said Richard.

"Bold wager by a man who just emptied his treasury for ransom."

"I once passed through Foix," said Richard. "There's not a stretch in that sparrow's nest flat enough to practice a run."

Folques overheard their exchange and narrowed his eyes in rebuke. "The Church abhors the laying of odds on matters of God's judgment."

"Yes, Raymond," said Richard dryly, having never forgiven their once-mutual friend for abandoning the singing profession. "We must follow the example of our humble holy man here and wager on proper subjects. Such as which of the many asses he's kissed will one day fart on St. Peter's throne."

"You slander me, sir!" said Folques.

Richard curled a sardonic smile. "Another hundred says the Abbot wrangles a bishop's mitre for his yapping lapdog before year's end." When Almaric stood to confront the calumny, Richard met the challenge by arising to hover over the two Cistercians. "You feckless monks exhort the battle, but when the blood flows, you're always found behind your altars."

Almaric and Folques could only stew in their enforced silence.

At the south end, Roger blinded his flighty Arabian with leather flaps. Sun flashes came from the far chute. Jourdaine had hung his charger's neck with a taffeta trapper spangled in tiny bells, a contraption designed to create a ringing hysteria in the ears of the opponent's horse. When Roger turned to mount, the Gascon surreptitiously slipped an illegal extension onto his lance.

Esclarmonde offered Roger a sip from the wineskin to fortify him. "Be on your guard. That Gascon will resort to any means to obtain what he wants."

"Then he must be a man of strong faith to so earnestly wish the death of that heretic girl," said Roger. "Accompany me to her."

At the stake, Roger studied Phillipa, too long for propriety. He tried to discern from her countenance what it was about her faith that had caused his mother to forfeit family and life. His cold glare of judgment evanesced into a flustered look of dislocation. He seemed to have fallen under the same spell that had seized Esclarmonde in Lombrives. For once, he displayed none of his usual gruffness. "My sister tells me you are worth risking a kingdom to save."

"I am forever in your debt, my lord," said Phillipa.

Roger found it difficult to break from Phillipa's mesmeric eyes. Finally, hearing the crowd clamoring with impatience, he slapped the Arabian to awaken its mettle, then bowed to her and rode to his starting slot.

Jourdaine raised his triangular shield to indicate his readiness. The herald sounded the final blast. Roger charged fast, taking steady aim at Jourdaine's left breast. Just before impact, the Gascon yanked his shield across his pommel. Roger tried to adjust, but his shifting confused the Arabian and caused it to lose speed. He was driven violently into the cantle—the lance slid from his hands. His destrier careened and fell against his ankle, then bolted up in a panic and dragged him through the dreck. A stunned silence was broken by Esclarmonde's shriek. Writhing in pain, Roger finally extricated his arms from the harness and flung off his helmet. Phillipa hung her head and waited for the flames.

"God wills it!" shouted Almaric, exultant.

Count Raymond removed a handful of coins from his purse and dropped them into Richard's lap. With a sigh of remorse, he prepared to signal for the firebrands to be thrown to the faggots when a rumble of surprise creased the assembly. A helmeted knight blazoned with a red cross on his mantle cantered methodically down the hillside. Reaching the viewing pavilion, the stranger pulled a rock from his saddlebag and threw it at the Lionhearted's feet.

Richard shot up from his chair. "Knave!"

"I've come to collect a debt."

"Reveal your face!" When the knight complied, the English king cursed under his breath. "Montanhagol . . . I counted myself rid of you."

"You promised a gold piece for every stone taken from the walls of Acre." Guilhelm stole a sharp but fleeting glance at Esclarmonde, as if directing his next admonishment at her as well. "You also owe me my good name."

"What I owe you is the edge of my sword!" said Richard.

"Let us in on this little mystery," said Count Raymond. "Who is this Templar who invades my tilting ground as if he owns it?"

"A coward who once refused to obey my orders," said Richard.

"Orders to commit butchery," corrected Guilhelm.

Richard paced the dais in agitation. "It was necessary!"

Guilhelm rode down the length of the grandstand. "Three thousand Saracen prisoners were beheaded in a single day by order of that man! Men, women, and children! He is called the Lionhearted only by those who never fought at his side! Some required ten strokes to die! All murdered to slake his rage at losing an engine! When I protested such treatment as contrary to Christian justice, he exiled me with a false report that I had betrayed the King of Jerusalem!"

Esclarmonde flushed with shame. Had she wrongly condemned him?

Richard flung a coin in mock payment, but Guilhelm threw it back. "There is interest due."

"Damn you!" shouted Richard. "What is it you want?"

"The maid's life."

Folques shoved his way to the fore. "This apostate Templar conspired to protect the heretics! The burned sinner confessed it!"

Guilhelm rode closer to the stands and only then recognized his old nemesis. "So, the Pope now employs your prattle."

Jourdaine confronted Guilhelm. "I and my men won the joust."

"Then I challenge you."

"Your vows forbid profane combat," reminded Folques.

"Salic law allows suspension of the ban if justice requires," said Guilhelm.

Esclarmonde watched with held breath as Folques and Almaric confided privately. She yearned to go to Guilhelm and beg his forgiveness, but he refused to even acknowledge her. Had he forgotten her? Before she could gather the courage to approach him, the Cistercians broke off their whispered discussion.

"The ordeal shall be allowed on one condition," said Almaric. "If the Gascon prevails, the Templar must again take up the Cross for the Holy Land."

The crowds pressed closer to hear Guilhelm's answer to the demand, which was tantamount to a death sentence. Templars were always positioned in the vanguard of battles and the order's hierarchy refused to pay ransom for prisoners. A taut muscle twitched in Guilhelm's neck; he had vowed never to return to that sandpit of Hell. Finally, he nodded his grudging assent.

"And my recompense if I win?" said Jourdaine.

"Name it," said Guilhelm.

"The hand of the Viscountess de Foix in marriage. With a dowry of five hundred francs and the land of Montsegur."

A rumble of astonishment met the Gascon's brazen proposal. Guilhelm delayed his response, desperate to find some way of circumventing this unforeseen dilemma. "The lady alone can accept such a condition."

Esclarmonde stood paralyzed by indecision. She could not let Phillipa die, but the thought of marrying the Gascon caused her stomach to curdle. She looked at Guilhelm and for the first time found consternation in his eyes. He *had* come because of her. *A birth always requires a sacrifice. That is the way of the Light.* Where had she heard those words before?

Roger took her aside. "You needn't agree to this."

At her request, three men had risked life and limb to save the Cathar girl. How could she refuse when she had asked so much of others? She had no choice but to trust that God would deliver Guilhelm's victory. She turned from Guilhelm's locking gaze lest she lose resolve. "I accept the terms."

Jourdaine insisted, "I must also hear it from the Wolf."

Roger could manage only a bitter nod.

"Broadswords!" announced Raymond of Toulouse. "First blood!"

The two combatants placed their helmets on the dais. While Esclarmonde whispered a prayer over Guilhelm's gear, the Gascon came aside her and gibed, "No acid-tongued quips this time?" Fighting tears, she walked away.

Jourdaine chased her with a punishing smirk, then retrieved his helmet and took his position in the center of the lists, twirling his broadsword deftly over his head to demonstrate its lightness in his massive hands. Simon de Montfort placed a cube of sugar into his comrade's mouth to prevent parching.

The herald blew the signal horn. Drooling sweet saliva, Jourdaine lunged and drove his round shield into the Templar's left shoulder. Guilhelm was plunged to a knee by the force of the impact. The pain in his elbow rang like a tuning fork. Their first clash of blades spawned a crackle of sparks.

On the dais, the Lionhearted dropped another sack of coins into Raymond of Toulouse's lap. "The Gascon."

Count Raymond laughed scornfully. "You may pay for this feast yet."

"Do you know what day it is?" asked Richard.

"Did that Syrian desert fry your brain?"

"Templars fast on Friday. Your man fights on water rations."

Count Raymond tried to retrieve his wager, but Richard's hand was too quick. Grinning, he threw the pouch to an attendant to hold in escrow.

In the lists, Jourdaine threw his shield across his body as a counterweight. He heaved his sword but narrowly missed his mark. Guilhelm remained behind his shield and waited for an opening. Jourdaine swung again but caught the edge of Guilhelm's shield. He extracted his blade with a grunted curse. "You fight like a damned Turkish eunuch!"

"You wouldn't know a Turk if another one bedded your mother!"

Guilhelm reproached himself for having breached the Temple's first rule of engagement: Never return the taunts of an opponent. Such distractions only drained one's concentration. Denied the warning of the Gascon's eyes, he riveted his watch on Jourdaine's friezed hauberk; the blade always followed the hand, and the hand the trunk. He swung low at the Gascon's exposed legs but his blow was blunted. The Gascon hammered at his helmet and caused him to stumble with blurred vision. He tasted the salt of his streaming sweat.

Esclarmonde clutched Corba's arm. "The Gascon pushes him at will!"

"Jourdaine outweighs him by four stone," said Roger, confined to a pallet. "The Templar had best finish him soon, or he'll be worn down."

Jourdaine grew annoyed with Guilhelm's defensive tactics. He dove into the clutches and flailed again and again. Guilhelm maintained the disciplined tactics of the Temple, standing rooted to the soil. Drilled on slot work, he repulsed every lunge and pounded at the crease between Jourdaine's collarbone and shield. The struggle deteriorated into a series of staggering assaults with both men panting like ravenous animals. Weak from the fasting, Guilhelm feared that he might soon black out. He had no choice but to resort to snaps. He lashed his hilt like the handle of a whip and sent the blade behind the Gascon's head. The torque threatened to fracture his wrist. Jourdaine's reach was too long—he wedged his tip inside Guilhelm's shield.

"He's jamming you!" shouted Roger. "Wheel out of it!"

Guilhelm was driven back with his right side exposed. He tried to pull the shield to his side, but Jourdaine locked it with a knee, then pivoted and whipped his sword around his torso. Guilhelm raised his right arm to block the smite, too late. Blearing fatigue slowed his reaction—the hot sting of metal sliced into his thigh. He fell and his nose smashed against the nasal guard. Wetness oozed from his mouth. Distant screams echoed in his head.

"Blood!" shouted the herald.

Esclarmonde's cries brought Guilhelm back to consciousness. The physic applied a tourniquet to a nasty gash on his thigh. She pressed her palm to his sweltering forehead, at a loss how to ease his suffering.

"Is that proper conduct for a betrothed lady?" Jourdaine hovered over her. "I expect your presence at L'Isle in six months."

"I ask only that the ceremony take place in Foix," she said, eyes cast down.

"You'll live in Gascony," said Jourdaine. "You'll wed in Gascony."

Folques rushed to light the faggots, but Jourdaine intercepted him and commandeered the torch. He forced Phillipa to wait for death, then slashed her bindings. "The lass is a wedding gift. To my future bride."

ells inside the Templar commanderie in Toulouse summoned the holy brothers for midday contemplation. Three hooded monks made their way along the cloister shadows and fell in with those already ambulating in prayer. After their third circumnavigation of the garth, the monks slipped unnoticed through the door of a cell near the infirmary.

Inside, Guilhelm lay half-delirious. "I told you! Let me die!"

"I have brought you good medicine." Raymond de Perella lowered his cowl and led Esclarmonde and Phillipa to the cot. The women knelt and retracted the Templar's linen braies to inspect his wound. The crude stitching had turned black with abscess during the three days since the combat.

Phillipa regarded Esclarmonde with a doubtful look. "If he is to survive, the flesh must be cut away, but . . ."

"But what?"

"He's so weak . . . he may die from the loss of blood."

Esclarmonde placed a wooden spoon between Guilhelm's teeth. "I'll not let him rot to death."

"There will be pain," Phillipa told Guilhelm. "I will try to be swift."

Guilhelm restrained her hand. "I don't deserve your help. In the cave . . ."

"You were only abiding the dictates of your faith."

Phillipa commenced the surgical procedure taught to her by Bishop Castres. She smothered Guilhelm's nose with a sponge soaked in mandrake. When his eyes fluttered, she took the knife that Raymond had heated over the fire and carved a chevron around the wound. She dug out the diseased flesh, careful not to slice the artery. Esclarmonde flinched with each cut and gripped Guilhelm's forearm as if the suffering were her own. After cauterizing the incision, Phillipa sutured it with a thread of spiderwebs and applied a poultice of wort. As she placed her hands over her work in prayer, Guilhelm eased the clench in his fists as the pain subsided. He was unable to fathom how she had finished so quickly.

"You must hurry!" Raymond stood watch at the door. "If they discover us, he'll have worse problems than a split thigh."

Esclarmonde held back, desperate for a moment more. Raymond reluctantly agreed to her request and slipped out the door with Phillipa.

Esclarmonde tried to squeeze the good humors back into Guilhelm's hand. "I feared I would never see you again."

"Was that not what you wished?"

"You have little understanding of women!"

"On that I can attest. Your friend sent for me. You are the worse for it."

"How can you say that? You saved a precious life."

His voice trailed off. "And lost a love."

Esclarmonde was not certain if she had heard correctly. "You speak of love, Guilhelm?"

He stared up into her hopeful eyes. "I will burn in Hell for it but . . . I have loved you since the day we first met."

"Then take me with you when you leave here!"

He enlivened at the thought, then sank defeated into the cot. "We are both constrained by vows. The Temple would hunt me down and the Gascon would bring a legal writ against your brother. The dowry lands and the girl's life would be forfeited."

"But we would be together!"

"In broken faith."

Esclarmonde did not want to believe him, but she knew he was right. She held him in her arms and pressed her cheek to his. Finally, she forced herself to pull away. At the door, she turned back, unable to depart without asking, "Guilhelm, have you ever had . . . visions?"

He struggled to his elbow, studying her with a look of grave apprehension. "I have seen things untold in our religion, but—"

"What things?"

"You must shun such inquiries."

"I have been cast into a world I do not understand!"

He regarded the door. "Tell no one of this."

"I feel as if I am going mad!"

"Heed me!" he insisted. "To speak of these things is too dangerous."

Raymond cracked the door. "We must go."

She clung to Guilhelm. "Promise you will return to me."

"I will die in Palestine."

Tears coursed down her cheeks. "Promise me! Or I'll not find the strength to face what awaits me!"

Shaken by her desperation, Guilhelm sealed one oath with a kiss and broke another.

...Hidden things of the mysteries of Light and the ways of Darkness.
- The Book of Secrets, Dead Sea Scrolls

X

Foix

September 1198

With the dreaded hour of their departure for Gascony fast approaching, Esclarmonde emptied her closets while the Marquessa packed the trunks, cursing and sighing at every folded bundle. It would be the first year in memory that the matriarch did not preside over her court. The calamity in Toulouse had thrown her into such a gloom that she could find no reason to celebrate the ideals of Courtesy that were passing away with the century. They hurried to finish their tasks before an autumn snowstorm blocked the passes, for they knew that Roger would be in no mood to tarry at dawn.

"Please don't attempt this journey," said Esclarmonde.

The Marquessa stripped the ornaments from the walls with a surging vehemence. "Perhaps I can yet reverse this misfortune!"

"The Lord L'Isle is not a man to be swayed by threats or entreaties."

"Had I accompanied you to the baptism, I might have shamed Count Raymond into standing up to those Cistercian thieves! Puivert and Perpignan have also cancelled their courts rather than risk accusations of heresy."

"Folques is much behind it, I fear." Esclarmonde immediately regretted that indictment. She had been careful not to mention the former troubadour's name for fear of sending her godmother into another fit of apoplexy.

"If I meet that crowing rooster again, he'll prefer the presence of Satan!" The Marquessa watched Esclarmonde halfheartedly pick through the array of bright dresses she had worn in the courts. None seemed appropriate. Observing her dilemma, the Marquessa went to her chamber and returned with an emerald satin dress embroidered with a fleur-de-lis brocade and gold meshwork. "Your mother's wedding gown. Your father imported it from Cyprus for her."

Esclarmonde held the dress to her shoulders and tried to imagine her mother walking down St. Volusien's in its sweeping lines. She fought back emotion as she returned the gown and chose an austere black dress in its stead.

The Marquessa smothered her with a tearful embrace. "I've instilled you with hopes much too lofty. All of this talk of chivalry and romance was a blind path to disappointment."

"Corba has found happiness."

"She is a simple girl. You have always longed for the unreachable. Your mother had the same dangerous yearning."

Esclarmonde retreated to the window and watched the snow drifting high against the walls. The last ships en route to the Holy Land had launched from Marseille a month ago. Guilhelm was likely on one if he had not already succumbed to the gangrene. Still, she was grateful for the six months she had been granted to prepare for the marriage. All she had once taken for granted was now burned into her memory: The sunset walks along the rustling Ariege, the riding excursions to Montsegur, the smell of baked bread in the market ovens. What she missed most was Corba's companionship. They had planned their weddings together in this room, but perverse Fate had denied them both their dreams. Corba and Raymond married soon after returning from Toulouse, foregoing a fete for a modest ceremony. Corba had visited Foix only once since. Radiant and joyously in love, she had transformed Raymond's austere chateau in Mirepoix into a home of felicitous warmth.

The Marquessa broached a subject too long delayed. "Child, on your wedding night—"

"Do not speak of this now!"

"The man will expect the marital duties to be consummated."

"I cannot!"

"It will go worse for you if you do not submit. Men become savage when denied. You will learn to distance yourself from the act."

"I will endure it only until Guilhelm comes for me."

"You must give up that fantasy. It will only prolong your sorrow."

"He promised to return."

"Return to what? You have foolishly sworn him to a doomed errand."

"You cannot take this hope from me!"

The Marquessa captured her shoulders to enforce the admonition. "Never mention that Templar's name again. We must take up our crosses. Look forward to children. They will be a comfort."

Esclarmonde pulled away. "You talk to me of children? By that man?"

The Marquessa grasped the bedpost for support. "Corba is gone. Now you. How will I manage to—"

At the door, Phillipa appeared with a steaming pot of jasmine tea. Embarrassed at having intruded on their conversation, she hastened away.

Esclarmonde rushed to stop her. "Please! Don't leave!"

The Almighty, it seemed, never took with one hand without giving from the other. This wispy spirit was the only glimmer of light in the chateau now. After the tournament, Roger had insisted that the Cathar girl come to Foix and live as part of their family. Phillipa at first declined his offer, fearful that the Cistercians would learn of her whereabouts. Hospitality to a heretic, even one legally released, would only bring more trouble. But Roger would not take no for an answer. The Marquessa had found it difficult to accept the girl whose faith had brought such sorrow to her family, but Phillipa's selfless ways soon won her over. Under her tutelage, the docile creature who once spoke hardly a word had miraculously bloomed into a winsome lady.

Phillipa poured two servings. "I can finish the preparations in here. I've already packed what little I need."

Esclarmonde nearly dropped her cup. "Go with us? I'll not hear of it!"

Phillipa tightened the trunk straps. "The Gascon lord would not jeopardize his bargain by arresting me. Besides, you must have a maid of honor."

Deeply moved, Esclarmonde tried to think of a way to repay the kindness. With a glint of mischief, she sized up Phillipa's lithe figure and brought forth a gown of burnt rose from the wardrobe. "Do you like it?"

Phillipa admired its luxurious sheen. "It's beautiful."

"It no longer fits me. We'll wrap you in disguise."

Phillipa removed her tunic and stepped into the gown. While she shuffled across the floor for Esclarmonde's inspection, the Marquessa slipped out of the room unnoticed to give the two of them a few moments alone.

Esclarmonde so wished that Bishop Castres could see his little priestess in training now. Her thoughts often turned to the enigmatic Cathar leader and his unsettling prophecies in Lombrives. She did not want to leave Foix until she had gained some understanding of the man who had shaken her life to its core. "Have you heard any news of your bishop?"

Phillipa's smile vanished. She hurriedly removed the gown, thrust back into the world of denial. The expensive dress was a temptation dangled by the Lords of Darkness so despised by her faith. While she was lodged and well-fed, the Bishop and her fellow Cathars endured harsh deprivations in the caves and forests, constrained even from enjoying the warmth of a fire for fear of being captured. She placed the gown on the bed and stepped away as if its very touch was fraught with sin. "I was wondering when you would ask about him."

"I didn't mean to upset you."

"No, it's good you wish to know more about him."

Esclarmonde helped Phillipa into her bare tunic and retrieved the sewing basket to repair a tear in its sleeve. "How did you find him?"

"He found me," said Phillipa. "I was ten years old. Turned out into the streets of Albi after my mother died. He took me to one of his safe houses."

"He spoke with a strange accent."

"His people were called Bogomils," said Phillipa. "They migrated to Bulgaria from Jerusalem."

"That's halfway across the world. What brought him here?"

"He came to spread the true teachings of the Master."

"Why didn't he come to your aid in Toulouse? He must have heard that your burning was to take place."

"He did come."

Esclarmonde was so astonished that she nearly pricked Phillipa with the needle. She could remember no one that day who remotely resembled the bishop.

"When one of our people is led to the stake, the Father is always in the crowd offering prayers and comfort. He takes on disguises to avoid the Cistercians."

"If he was hidden, how did you know he was there?"

"We have a sign," said Phillipa tersely.

Esclarmonde recalled the nimbus she had seen around Castres's head in the cave. She wondered if the Cathars identified their fellow believers by second sight. Phillipa was doing her best to put up a stoic front, but Esclarmonde sensed that her new friend was deeply distressed by the Bishop's absence. "He was in tears that day at Lombrives when he thought you had perished."

Phillipa smiled sadly. "He was the kindest man I've ever known."

"Why does he not come to us now?"

"He always chooses the right moment to appear."

"I don't understand. How could he just stand by and watch you die?"

"Our faith is difficult for many to accept. We do not seek death, but neither do we fear it. We won't cling to life if it means compromising our beliefs."

"Why must you give up all that is pleasurable?"

"The Master said His Kingdom was not of this world. Your Church insists that our way is perverse, but we only follow the Master's example."

Esclarmonde marveled at how two faiths could interpret the teachings of Jesus so differently. The more she learned about these Cathars, the more she questioned what she had been taught by the priests. She looked down at the trunk that held the linen nightgown she would wear on her wedding night. Her stomach knotted with revulsion. There were so many questions that she could not ask the Marquessa. "Have you known a man . . . intimately?"

Phillipa's face darkened. "You've heard the slanders."

"I was told your people do not believe in such relations."

Phillipa flashed with uncharacteristic anger. "If that were true, the Pope would not need to burn us! He could just wait until we all died out!"

Esclarmonde suddenly recognized the absurdity of the claim. How could there be Cathar families if they did not procreate? They both enjoyed a rueful laugh, chasing the momentary tension.

"The Romans twists our beliefs," said Phillipa. "We're no different than your monks. If a woman or man wishes to become a perfecta—"

"A nun?"

"A priestess. In our faith, women are treated as equal to men in the eyes of God. Some accept a life of celibacy to meditate and perform good works, but it is never forced on them. Those who wish to remain believers are free to marry and bear children. They are called credentes. We seek to avoid the wheel of rebirth. To return to the Light, we must escape the bonds of this existence."

"Our Lord established His Church to rule in tandem with kings and queens. He must have meant us to make the best of life here."

"He did not establish a church."

"The Scriptures say that St. Peter was chosen as the foundation rock."

"I can only tell you what Father Castres taught me," said Phillipa. "The Romans alter the Master's words to fit their purpose. There were no churches in the time of Christ. He was a Jewish rabbi. If he *had* created a place of worship, He would have called it a synagogue. But He had no interest in erecting houses of worship. His disciples expected the world to vanish within weeks."

"Are you saying that Jesus failed in His mission?"

Phillipa nervously regarded the door. "Why would He have created a church after promising those with Him that they would witness the End of Days? The Romans had to explain away this contradiction, so they falsely added the claim that He named Peter as His successor."

"Why then did Jesus come to die for us on the Cross?"

"He did not die for us," said Phillipa. "We do not glorify that rood of torture. What loving father would send his only son to suffer so horribly? The Master came to show us how to return to the Light *before* physical death."

"Return how?'

"By meditation and healing and discourse with the angels. Only the Magdalene and His brother James understood these mysteries."

"But the disciples saw Him resurrected in the flesh."

"They saw only what their minds could perceive," said Phillipa. "The Master returned to them in His Body of Light to demonstrate his teachings."

This explanation transported Esclarmonde back to that day in Lavaur when the mystical orb had thrust her into a paralyzing ecstasy. Perhaps the Apostles had confronted the same ineffable radiance. If so, she could certainly empathize with their confusion. "Phillipa . . . I think I've seen this Light."

Phillipa showed no surprise. "Father Castres said you are one of us. Perhaps one day you will become a perfecta."

"But I'm to be married."

"Many hear the calling after their families are raised."

For the first time, Esclarmonde began to understand how a life of a perfecta could attract a woman; no worries about men and their demands, to be left in peace to pray and seek God.

Seeing Esclarmonde's eyes hood with fatigue, Phillipa locked the packed trunks and teased, "Last one up in the morning must wake your brother."

P hillipa walked down the hall and tiptoed passed the sleeping guards. The kicking of the horses in the stable gave the only evidence of life in the shuttered castle. She came to the solar and discovered the door ajar. She cracked it open a bit more and found Roger standing at the hearth with his back turned. She inquired softly, "My lord?"

Roger whirled and let fly with a goblet. "Leave me be, woman! I'll suffer no lectures this night!"

The goblet sailed past Phillipa's head and bounced off the door frame. She allowed him a moment to recover his bearings, then replied with a hint of gentle reproof, "I am sorry for disturbing you."

Only then did Roger realize that she was not the Marquessa hounding him again. "Wait . . . I thought—"

"Is there anything you require before I retire?"

He stared at her, too long for discretion. "Do you have an army?" She melted him with that same tender smile. "No, you'd slay the enemy with that Greek fire you shoot from those eyes."

Phillipa blushed from the strange compliment as she busied herself with cleaning up the mess that he had created. While sorting the papers on his desk, she saw the parchment that contained the terms of Esclarmonde's dowry.

He detected her interest. "You know of Montsegur?"

"My people cherish it as a holy place."

He hissed with contempt. "The rock has been nothing but a curse to me. I'll be glad to be rid of it. It will be the Gascon's problem now."

"Will he build upon it?"

"The crest is too misshapen for a chateau. He'll use it as stakes for a gamble and some other malcontent will stumble into its possession."

"A treasure is often hidden in the most useless location."

"Then the gold of Midas must be stashed inside that pog." And yet, he was forced to admit that if this girl could be so wondrously transformed in the few months he had known her, perhaps even that misshapen thrust of limestone might one day prove of value. He staggered from the wine and lack of sleep.

Phillipa assisted him to the bed and removed his boots. She examined his ankle scar to ensure it was healing, then drew the covers over him and turned to leave. At the door, she hesitated. "My lord, I have meant to ask you . . ."

"Will you not call me Roger?"

"Roger, then . . . Why did you come to my assistance in Toulouse? You have made it clear how much you despise my faith."

He looked away. "You reminded me of my mother. I chose not to abandon you, as she abandoned me."

"I am certain she did not mean to leave you."

Without warning, his mood turned black again. "Isn't that what you Cathars do? Leave your families and go find God on some cloudy perch away from us flesh-eating mortals?"

She calmed him by tucking the covers to his neck. "Have I left you?"

Eyes closed, he muttered, "You will."

I came out of Light and the gods.
Here in exile am I from them kept apart.
- The Soul's Fate, a Manichean hymn

XI

Gascony

September 1198

*H*ad the Almighty wished to hasten the remorse of sinners with a glimpse of Purgatory, He might with equal effect have led them down the lone street of L'Isle. Michaelmas was the traditional day for celebrating the harvest, but the squalid village appeared so abeyant that the calendar could have been mistaken for Good Friday. Gascony was the only province in France still held by the Plantagenets of England, a vestige of Eleanor of Aquitane's marriage to Henry II. The region bordered Toulousia, yet the Basques who lived here were foreigners in both tradition and attitude. King Phillip and his court in Paris found them such perfidious people that they coined the phrase *promesse de Gascon* to denote an empty vow. Even pilgrims walking to Compostela were warned to take a circuitous route to avoid the gangs of robbers and cutthroats that lurked in these marcher wilds.

Punished by icy spits from the early-season storm, Roger led the Foix women on horse toward the church, a converted warehouse crowned by a rusted iron cross that rattled in the wind. Perched high on a hill overlooking this ramshackle cluster of waddle-and-daub cabins stood Jourdaine's austere tower of ruddy limestone. A desultory finger of green-wood smoke coughed up from its sooted vent. The church door, nailed with the banns of marriage, creaked open. Jourdaine ambled out with Simon de Montfort, both armed.

Jourdaine snarled, "You've kept us waiting."

The Marquessa dismounted with Roger's assistance and attacked the snow-blanketed steps to inspect the Gascon's pocked face up close.

"Cease bewitching me with that evil eye, woman, or I'll have you banished."

"I'll not leave this festering sty soon enough!" said the Marquessa. "So you are the cretin who hatched this scheme."

"The contract was freely accepted."

She drove a finger into his chest. "There was a time—"

"Spare us your kitchen tales." Jourdaine shunted her aside and came to Esclarmonde, half-expecting to see her fair features altered in some perverse attempt at revenge. "Are you well?"

"My health was not part of the arrangement."

"The passage of time has not tamed her tongue," said de Montfort.

The Marquessa glowered the Norman to silence. "I had the misfortune of meeting your caitiff father, the Count of Evreaux. You share his lack of couth."

The villagers began cautiously emerging from their huts to steal a glimpse of the foreign woman who was about to wed their liege. Roger attempted to escort the ladies into the church to shelter them from the cold stares and raw gusts, but Jourdaine blocked his path and insisted that the legal dispensation be conducted outside for all to witness. With an impotent huff, Roger produced the marital contract for inspection.

Jourdaine quickly read the document. "This is not what we agreed. I'll not allow Montsegur to revert at my death."

Stunned, Esclarmonde caught Roger and Phillipa sharing a knowing glance. She had not been told of this late addition to the terms. Her brother so despised the mount where their mother had disappeared that she could not fathom what motivated him to negotiate the possibility of its repossession.

"Occitan law requires the land be returned to the bride's family should no heir be produced," said Roger. "If you wish to contest the matter, we'll submit it to the justiciar in Toulouse and delay the wedding pending the litigation."

Jourdaine weighed the challenge, then scratched his signature to the agreement. He quirked his mouth at Esclarmonde and threw open the doors. "I have another wedding gift for you."

Folques, in full clerical regalia, stood under the architrave.

The Marquessa had to be restrained from charging at the former troubadour. "This scapegrace will not sanction the vows!"

"The Bishop of Bordeaux has ordered me here to perform the ceremony."

"You are sent by that bastard of Satan, the Abbot of Citeaux!"

"I'll not abide blasphemy in God's sanctuary!" warned Folques.

"You blaspheme with your presence!" She slapped his face. "I once showered you with all the courtesy our modest principality could offer!"

Eyes watering, Folques captured her wrist and sought her removal, but Jourdaine merely snorted with amusement. Denied his retribution, Folques shoved the Marquessa from his path and led the congregation down the aisle.

The cloud of incense and dust inside the church was so thick that Esclarmonde was forced to cover her mouth to stifle a cough. The moldering vault, devoid of pews, was dimly lit by two facing wall slits that produced a tormented whistling. The floor of pounded clay held an altar of rough-hewn rock furnished with one unlit candle.

Only when Folques reached the ambulatory did he notice the hooded figure following Esclarmonde. He recognized her as the heretic girl who had escaped the stake in Toulouse. "She will not be permitted in holy confines."

"She is my sister's maid of honor," said Roger.

Phillipa moved quickly to diffuse the confrontation. "I will wait outside." She hugged Esclarmonde and whispered, "Send me your thoughts. I will send you mine. You will never be alone." With difficulty, she broke from the embrace and rushed from the church.

Before Esclarmonde could recover from the enforced abandonment, Jourdaine intertwined his fingers with hers and formed the handfasting symbol of infinity. She struggled to pull away, but he subdued her. He had not given her time to remove her cloak—a small blessing, she now counted it, for the added layer provided a welcome boundary to his noxious proximity.

At Jourdaine's insistent nod, Folques dispensed with the preliminaries and commenced the vows. "I charge you both, as you will answer on the Day of Judgment when secrets of all hearts shall be disclosed. If either knows any impediment why you may not be joined in matrimony, confess it now."

Jourdaine's grip tightened in a warning for Esclarmonde to remain mute. She begged a miraculous intervention from the chipped icon that stood over the sacristy, but the Blessed Virgin's plaintive eyes remained downcast.

"There is no love in this binding!" protested the Marquessa.

"Your rules of romance hold no weight here," said Folques.

"They were weighty enough when you fished for amors. Now you cast about for any means to drain the rancor from your malignant heart." The Marquessa told Jourdaine, "This faux monk burns for the woman you barter to marry."

The Gascon was too preoccupied with the curve of Esclarmonde's bosom to hear the Marquessa's indictment.

"He intends to ruin her if he cannot—"

"Desist, woman!" shouted Folques.

The Marquessa would not be silenced. "I curse every reprobate involved in the crafting of this unholy attachment!"

"Finish it!" ordered Jourdaine.

Folques pronounced the rest of the recital in a faltering stutter. "Jourdaine L'Isle, will you have . . . have this woman to be thy wedded wife to live . . . together after God's ordinance?"

"I will."

"Esclarmonde de Foix, will you have this man to be thy wedded husband, to obey and serve him, keeping only him in your heart"—Folques choked up—"for as long as you shall live?"

She kept her gaze inward. "I take him . . . as my husband."

Folques saw through her temporizing. "You must give oath to all demands."

"I'll not mock God by falsely swearing my heart," said Esclarmonde. "The Lord of L'Isle knows he will never have it."

Jourdaine dismissed that prophecy with a cold laugh and jerked an impatient nod for Folques to speed the ceremony.

Folques was embroiled in his own war of wills with Esclarmonde. "I will not confer the sacrament unless—"

Jourdaine shouted, "She is not marrying *you*, monk!"

"I am the Church's representative here."

"Her prostration will suffice," said Jourdaine.

Aghast, Marquessa pulled Esclarmonde to her side. "I forbid it!"

"Then the heretic will be returned to Toulouse this hour," said Jourdaine.

Esclarmonde descended to her knees and lowered her head to Jourdaine's muddied boots to perform the ritual of obeisance. She would fain accept the disgrace if it meant not having to swear against her love for Guilhelm. Unable to endure the humiliation further, the Marquessa lifted her from the floor.

Folques clumsily placed the lace betrothal cloth on Esclarmonde's head while she burned him with a glare meant to haunt the rest of his days. He tried in vain to avoid her vengeful eyes. "Who gives this woman?"

Roger stepped forward. "I stand for her father, a knight of the Cross who will seek justice from Heaven should any harm come to her."

The fierce reputation of Esclarmonde's father was so storied that the mere invocation of his ghost would give most mortals pause. Jourdaine, however, was not a man to dwell upon the spiritual consequences of his acts; with a hiss of contempt, he slid a crude band on Esclarmonde's finger and held her hand aloft. When he released it, the band fell to the stones. Eyes as round as coins, he questioned if the Marquessa had invoked the omen by witchery. He retrieved the ring and searched Esclarmonde's hand until deciding on her index finger.

Esclarmonde offered up a silent prayer of gratitude for this small sign of divine protest. When Folques crowned the couple's clasp with his gloved hand to form the symbol of the Trinity, she turned away, repelled by the simultaneous touch of the two men she most despised.

"In the name of the Father, the Son, and the Holy Ghost, I pronounce thee man and wife," said Folques. "What God has joined, let no man put asunder."

After an awkward pause, Jourdaine turned to kiss Esclarmonde, but she shrank from his attempt. He chose not to press the rebuff and led her out with a hand clamped to her elbow to force the pace. When they reached the portico, he dismissed Roger and the other Foix women. "You may take your leave."

The Marquessa searched for an excuse to delay their parting. "The bed must be blessed. We will serve as witnesses."

"De Montfort will perform the task," said Jourdaine.

With an embittered wave of resignation, Roger descended the steps to retrieve the horses. The Marquessa hung back; she had kept her family together through many tragedies, but now she was near collapsing with despair.

Esclarmonde pulled her godmother to a shaking embrace. "Do not burden Corba with the details," she whispered. "I have darkened enough of her joyous time." She kissed the Marquessa goodbye and tried not to look back.

Jourdaine ordered her, "Be undressed when I return."

Esclarmonde had never encountered a room so woefully maintained. Shadowed by an indifferent fire in a charred hearth, the wedding bed consisted of an uncanopied mattress stuffed with straw and was covered with a quilt stained the color of fermented cider. She thought of bolting the door, but she knew the futile act would only enrage him. Finding no means of escaping her predicament, she removed her mother's Cathar medallion from her neck and slid it under the matting. She retrieved a phial from her baggage and gulped the infusion of cloves and cabbage juice that Phillipa had prepared as a contraceptive. She fought to keep the bitter liquid down.

The door opened—she closed her fist to hide the phial.

Jourdaine stripped off his shirt and breeches. "Are you deaf? I told you to get out of that dress. They'll be here soon."

She had rehearsed this horrid moment a hundred times, but she could not force herself to disrobe. "I am overwhelmed with fatigue."

"By God, I'll get it done myself!"

She ran for the window. He caught her and threw her onto the bed.

"Unhand me!"

He hammered her against the headboard. "I'll not tell you again!" He pulled her hair back and forced his tongue down her throat. Choking from tears, she slowly unfastened her bliaut. He became impatient and cut the strings with his dagger, then saw that her chemise was splattered with blood. Horrified, he inspected his blade and found it clean. "What sorcery is this?"

Esclarmonde traced the trail of blood down her arm—the phial shards had embedded into her palm.

"Oc bitch!" He slammed a fist into her stomach. "You think you can deprive me of an heir?" He rifled through her baggage and slung her belongings across the floor. "What other pagan charms did you bring?"

"It's only a medicinal!"

He shook her shoulders violently. "You take me for a fool? Expel it!" He punched her in the plexus again. "Give it up, damn you!"

"I see you've commenced the marital education without us."

De Montfort stood grinning at the door with Folques. Esclarmonde scrambled under the quilt to hide her nakedness and spied the merel hanging over the edge of the mattress. When Jourdaine turned, she covertly slid it back under the matting. She held her breath as he crawled back into the bed and rolled over the talisman.

"She's just had her first lesson," said Jourdaine, his hirsute chest heaving. "She may need a few more." Seeing Folques mesmerized by Esclarmonde's bared shoulders, he threw a boot to stir the monk from his unholy rapture. "Bleat your hosannas, Cistercian, then it's back to your hair shirt."

Folques was sent reeling by the heel against his forehead. He recovered to his clerical duty with hands shaking as he sprinkled the betrothed with holy water. "I bless this bed in the name of the prophets. May Christian progeny result from it."

"Progeny *will* result from it," promised Jourdaine.

Folques circled the bed with an uncertain gait, unable to take his eyes from Esclarmonde in her revealing chemise. He, not the Gascon, had been destined to be in her arms this night. For years he had tried to chase the lustful fanta-sies. She was to blame for this deviation from God's will. Now evil thoughts of adultery would be added to his shameful list of required expiations. "It is the prescription of the Church, woman, that you submit to your husband. You are forbidden to take pleasure from the consummation."

She escaped Jourdaine's hold and rushed at Folques. "That will be the only wish of yours I'll ever gladly fulfill!"

Jourdaine wrangled her back to the bed. "Rattling cow! You're not in that stinking mountain crib anymore. You'll not speak unless ordered!"

"You bless this, Folques?" She forced him to examine the mottling bruises under her eyes. "You bless this bed of blood?"

Jourdaine's hand sent another wave of prickly numbness across her face.

Folques made a start to go to her aid, but de Montfort held him back and teased his old tilting mate with a lascivious wink. "Does she deny you your just reward, Jourdaine?"

"She and that runt of a brother thought they could deceive me of an heir," said Jourdaine. "I'll have a son if I have to beat it out of her."

Distraught by the rough handling of Esclarmonde, Folques resolved to remind Jourdaine of the Church's prescription against violence, even against recalcitrant wives. But before he could summon the words, de Montfort thumped the back of his tonsured head to speed his departure.

At the door, de Montfort turned to impart a last indignity. "I leave on the morrow for the Holy Land, Madam L'Isle. No doubt I'll encounter your Templar acquaintance. Shall I convey a message for you?"

Esclarmonde could not bear the thought that this might be her last chance to communicate with Guilhelm. As Jourdaine's hands caressed her throat with a promise of retaliation, she remembered Phillipa's warning about the Demiurge and his Lords of Darkness. She had given little credence to the Cathar belief in such evil archons, but now she knew with certainty that they were all too real.

She was surrounded by them.

For the time will come when you will say:
"Blessed is the womb that has not conceived
and the breasts that have not produced milk."

-The Gospel of Thomas

XII

Gascony

October 1201

*A*fter three years of holding daily vigils at the window, Esclarmonde had given up hope of receiving news from Foix. To ease her boredom and loneliness, she would often escape to the church in L'Isle and brighten its walls with whitewash. The reward for this service was her discovery that the Benedictine friar who visited the village every third Sunday left a missal unlocked in the sacristy, confident that none in this isolated outpost could read Latin. Always confirming that she was alone, she would pore over the Scriptures, rewriting the verses in Occitan and adding her own exegetical commentary on scraps of linen. She argued with herself about the parables and allowed her imagination to run wild with their possible meanings. When finished, she was careful to burn the evidence of her study.

On this frigid evening, suffering from one of her lowest moments, she hurried to the church and knelt before the Blessed Virgin. With the missal opened, she again begged to know why she had been cast to this Hell on earth. Receiving no answer, she was about to leave in dejection when the church shook with a thunderous crash. Her head exploded with the same swirling orb of Light that had incapacitated her in Lavaur. When she regained her sight, she felt compelled to focus upon the whiteness that surrounded the missal's script. Her intuition of this command could only be described as the invisible giving form to the visible.

The Light of the body is thine eye. If therefore thine eye be single, the whole body shall be full of Light.

Tears of joy trickled down her cheeks. She had not been abandoned after all. The Voice from her youth had returned. She had always read the references to this Light as a metaphor for purity and goodness, but now she knew it to be a real force, one that acted directly upon the body. She looked down again at the Gospel of St. Matthew and there, coruscating on the page, were the very words she had just heard. She narrowed her concentration on the white borders only.

John.

This shift of attention from foreground to background of the letters had the inexplicable effect of admitting her into another realm of understanding. But what did the Voice mean by "John"? St. John the Baptist? The Gospel of St. John? She turned to John, her favorite of the gospels. Feeling vertiginous, she took the sensation as a sign to reread the passage she had just looked upon:

The words that I speak unto you I speak not of Myself, but the Father that dwelleth in me, He doeth the works.

Could this be the same Voice that had spoken to Jesus? Dare she let herself believe such a thing? She had performed no miracles or healings. Perhaps Satan was whispering these thoughts into her head.

Verily, verily, I say unto you. He that believeth in me, the works that I do shall he do also. And greater works than these shall he do, because I go unto my Father.

Her questions were being answered by Our Lord's own words! If she could hear the same Voice that had guided Him, how could any person, great or small, be required to give up such a gift as the Church demanded? She searched for the passage cited by the monks to demonstrate the righteousness of Rome's worldly rule. She found the verse in St. Matthew:

Thou art Peter, and upon this rock I build my church, and the gates of Hell shall not prevail against it.

Flaming tongues consumed the passage as the whiteness bordering the words fought against the blackness of the ink. She rubbed her eyes in amazement: A new verse took form from the substance of the disappearing words:

Jesus said, "Let one who seeks not stop seeking until one finds. When one finds, one will be disturbed. When one is disturbed, one will be amazed, and will reign over all."

Reign over all? If the Church was the supreme arbiter of God's will, how could a mere mortal reign over all? She searched the passages in all four gospels, but she could find no evidence of that claim.

The true revelation, said the Voice. *The Gospel of Thomas.*

St. Thomas wrote a gospel? Why was it not included the New Testament? The Voice of the Light seemed to be advocating not a blind obedience to the Pope and his doctrines, but a personal search for God.

The line of script transformed anew:

The Father will love you, and make you my equal.

Had Jesus come into this world to reveal that all of us were His equal in potential? Was the Voice saying that we are gods? Or that Jesus was *not* God?

James the brother.

The older brother, again. If a gospel written by St. Thomas was rejected by the Church, then James, the brother of Christ, might also have authored a suppressed tract as the Cathar bishop had claimed. But why were these gospels not recognized in the canon? She waited, but this time the Voice did not answer.

The rumbling of hooves shook the walls. She hid the missal under the floorboard and hurried from the church to find Simon de Montfort riding through the gate. In a crass demonstration of brute strength, he grasped the iron loop that hung from the arch keystone and braked his horse. Accompanying him on a palfrey was a wimpled lady with hard cyan eyes and a severe, mole-ridden face.

Jourdaine ran out from the chateau to greet the unexpected arrival of his old comrade. "If you break my gate, you whoreson's father, you'll pay!" He inspected de Montfort's new female consort. "What booty is this? A Greek princess from the emperor's harem?"

"My new bride," said Simon in an uncharacteristic tone of rectitude. "May I present Lady Alice de Montmorency."

The lady waited with an air of hauteur until de Montfort came to assist her from the saddle, then she repulsed his tardy hand and dismounted of her own accord. She harrumphed at finding Esclarmonde still watching from the church steps. "I am accustomed to being greeted by both castellan and chatelaine."

Jourdaine jerked his head to summon Esclarmonde. "My wife was raised in Foix. They learn manners there from the cloggers and Saracens."

"I'll abide no heretical talk in my presence," warned the lady.

"The Lord of L'Isle is a stickler on that discipline, my love," assured de Montfort. "You can be certain he's weaned her of such baneful influences."

"She's become as meek as a lamb," confirmed Jourdaine with a grin.

Without waiting for an invitation, Alice marched nose retroussé into the chateau and coldly inspected the poorly lit walls that were hung with only a few frayed bargellos, a testament to Jourdaine's niggardliness. She shook her head in abhorrence and threw her gloves at Esclarmonde's feet. "See to my baggage."

Before Esclarmonde could recover from the woman's astounding rudeness, Simon came sniffing up on her. "You remember me, I dare say."

She resolved to endure the debasement if it meant coaxing news about Guilhelm. She led them to the table and brought out a platter of cold duckling. Simon dug in with abandon. His wife refused to touch the serving.

Jourdaine allowed Simon another ravenous bite before demanding, "Well, out with it! What news from the crusade?"

Simon nearly choked from laughter. "Crusade? Is that what they're calling that death march here? I left that rot-gut rabble before it set sail." He remained oblivious to his wife's glare of disgust at his reversion to camp manners.

Jourdaine quaffed the last of the cheap cellar wine in his goblet, so thick that the dregs collected on his gaped teeth. "I've never known you to abandon an enterprise before the plunder is gained."

"The Franks are being played for fools," said Simon. "The Venetians have taken them hostage on the galleys." He gazed longingly at his new bride. "I returned to Paris and found my true love in the Capetian court."

Jourdaine chortled at his old friend's unwonted display of affection. "A pity. I hear the Doge has designs on Constantinople. There's enough gold in St. Sophia's basilica to buy us both a kingdom."

"Greece is no place for a civilized man," warned Lady Montmorency.

Simon saw that Esclarmonde was hanging on every word. He broke a waggish grin and asked Jourdaine, "You remember that rogue Templar?"

"I trust he dutifully fulfilled that vow we saddled on him?"

"I encountered the lout at Corfu. He was—"

"I wish to pray before retiring," interjected Lady Montmorency.

"Take her to the church," Jourdaine ordered Esclarmonde with a wave of his knife. "Simon and I will plan our next tournament."

Esclarmonde tarried, desperate to learn if Guilhelm was alive.

"My jousting days are over," said Simon.

Jourdaine could not believe his ears. "What say you?"

"My beloved has convinced me that God holds greater use for my talents than breaking lances for hire. I've been graced with a newfound faith."

Lady Montmorency challenged Jourdaine's hoot with a glare of threat. "Take heed of your own soul, sir, and leave my husband's to my care."

Jourdaine's mirth gave way to hot anger. "I knew your husband and his soul long before you leeched upon them, madam!"

The lady retaliated by shoving Simon's plate from his reach. "Apparently not long enough, or you would know that he will never take up the sword against fellow Christians, even if they be filthy Greeks."

Esclarmonde admired the lady's mettle, however poisonous her tongue might be. She had never witnessed anyone leave Jourdaine speechless. Yet she was amazed at how little the woman knew about the reprobate she had married.

"I am intent on Palestine," revealed Simon sheepishly.

Jourdaine greeted the revelation of that ambition with a dismissive huff. "You'll pay your own freight. No Venetian will ever ship you over there."

For once, Lady Montmorency agreed with Jourdaine. "Why must you cross the sea when there are infidels here in our own lands to exterminate?"

Jourdaine pounded the boards in mock excitement. "A crusade in Occitania! What say you? Gain our indulgences without suffering the heat of a desert!"

Simon turned serious as he leaned across the table. "You jest, but the Cistercians say Innocent plans to rid the South of these wretched cloggers."

Esclarmonde tried to conceal her listening by removing the cutlery. She had been kept deprived of all news regarding the developments in Occitania. This was the first she had heard of the new directive from Rome. If Phillipa's people were in danger, she had to find a way to send a message to Foix.

"Innocent would never use force in a Christian kingdom," said Jourdaine.

"He'll learn soon enough that these damnable heretics won't be converted from the pulpit," said Simon. "Let him send his monks into the Languedoc churches. When the Ocs toss them out on their asses, we'll swoop—"

"I wish to leave this outpost at first light!" The lady had suffered enough of their vulgar conversation. "Simon, will you join me for evensong in the chapel?"

Arising, Simon caught Esclarmonde watching him intently at the door. "Jourdaine, I believe your wife wishes me to finish my news about that Templar."

Jourdaine erupted from his chair and struck Esclarmonde across the face. Stifling painful coughs, she opened the door for the de Montforts to exit.

"Wait!" Simon turned. "I nearly forgot." He motioned for his lady's handbag and pulled a letter from it. "The nuns at Grandselve asked me to deliver this."

Annoyed, Jourdaine tore open the wax-sealed letter. "What do those hags want now? I gave them their annual donation." He read its contents and nodded with grim satisfaction. "They've bestowed a Mass on my behalf."

"For what purpose?" asked Simon.

"They wish to pray over me . . . that I be granted an heir."

"They're angling for an endowment," insisted Simon.

"Signed by the Abbess herself." Jourdaine sneered at Esclarmonde. "It's heartening to know that at least one woman wishes me so rewarded."

Shamed by their judging glares, Esclarmonde rushed to remove the serving platter. She had submitted to Jourdaine's advances, but he continued to accuse her of plotting to avoid becoming with child. She acceded to his inane regime to improve the chances of conception: Crossing her legs, avoiding sudden movements after coitus that might jar the seed, gorging on chestnuts and leeks, reciting the Nicene Creed ten times before bed. He constantly monitored her for generative signs such as shivers or the grinding of teeth and was now insisting that she place garlic cloves in her womb to fertilize it. Her spirit had long given up the resistance to his demands, but her body had not.

Jourdaine tucked away the letter with a troubling grin. "The Abbess has also offered to examine you for demonic marks."

Esclarmonde dropped the tray and sent the tableware crashing in shards. "I'll not have sterile nuns pawing my person like some altar relic!"

"Impertinent cow! They're no more sterile than you!"

"Then take one of them as your wife!"

Jourdaine slapped her to the floor. From her knees, Esclarmonde looked up to find Lady Montmorency tapping her foot in irritation at the delay.

T wo hundred veiled nuns and widowed conversi filed into the choir stalls of Grandselve, a dour Cistercian compound that sat like a giant dovecote amid the sweeping vineyards north of Toulouse. The abbey's most notable feature was its sprawling double houses of monks and nuns separated by a high curtain wall that prevented the holy orders from leering at each other with lascivious intent. The buttressed church with its thick corner turrets and machicolated arches looked more like a fortress than a place to inspire worship. Instead of being gifted with a clerestory, the thick perimeter of its lugubrious single nave was rimmed by slatted allures that allowed access to its narrow embrasures, so constructed to permit the firing of arrows from within.

The Abbess, distinguishable from the other nuns only by her red mantle, led Jourdaine and Esclarmonde down the aisle to the front pew. Esclarmonde's bruised face remained covered, as was required of women in the presence of the Eucharist. A ringing bell on the far side of the screen signaled the Introit.

The Abbess whispered, "The inspection will be conducted now."

"I must witness the perusal," said Jourdaine.

"It would not be wise," warned the Abbess. "If there is necromancy at work, the demons could attach to your own soul. Remain here and say the Pater Noster five hundred times without error to seal the spiritual protection. Should your mind wander, you must start the recitation anew."

Jourdaine forced Esclarmonde to her feet. "Don't be long. She's not to be left out of your sight."

Esclarmonde put up a struggle, but the Abbess managed to drag her to the rear of the church and down a winding stairwell into the crypt. In a small warming room, three veiled nuns waited to conduct the examination. "You have twenty minutes." The Abbess departed and locked the door behind her.

Esclarmonde clawed away the reaching hands and was stopped short by sounds of weeping. The Marquessa threw off her habit and rushed to hug her goddaughter. Corba and Phillipa dropped their disguises and joined in the embrace. They caught Esclarmonde before she fell from the shock.

"Child, what has this man done to you?" asked the Marquessa.

Esclarmonde heaved with sobs. "It is bearable."

"We must report this to Roger!" insisted Corba.

"No!" begged Esclarmonde. "I have caused him enough trouble."

"You have brought him his greatest joy," said the Marquessa.

"He is that relieved to have me gone?"

The Marquessa placed Esclarmonde's hand on Phillipa's distended stomach. Esclarmonde felt a kick and looked at the women in confusion.

"Roger and I were married," revealed Phillipa with a puckish grin. "We've tried to send news, but Jourdaine intercepts our couriers."

Stunned, Esclarmonde turned to her godmother for confirmation. "Under our noses, she was winning his heart! And not a peep!"

"She has nearly tamed him," said the Marquessa with pride.

"But what about your religion?" asked Esclarmonde.

"Roger allows me to pray to the God of my choice," said Phillipa. "And I have agreed to refrain from advising him on politics."

Thrilled, Esclarmonde hugged Phillipa. "I'm to be an aunt!"

"That's not quite true." With a twinkling eye, Corba opened a door to an anteroom. A wet nurse walked out and placed a swaddled infant into Esclarmonde's arms. Corba watched with mischievous glee as Esclarmonde tried to make sense of this new arrival. Finally, Corba revealed, "You *are* an aunt. Or at least the honorific aunt of your godmother's granddaughter."

"She has your chin!" exclaimed Esclarmonde.

"I pray she takes after her grandmother in looks," said Corba. "Neither Raymond nor I have much to offer in that regard."

"Nonsense," said Esclarmonde. "What is her name?"

"On that matter," said Corba, "we require your arbitration."

"We both wish to name our child after you," said Phillipa. "If mine is a girl."

"Your brother's heir is entitled to the name," said Corba. "But watch." When she spoke Esclarmonde's name, the infant flailed its tiny hands in excitement.

Phillipa agreed, "You must decide."

Esclarmonde was brought to tears. Yet she could not bear the thought of disappointing one of them. "You cannot force such a choice on me."

The Abbess cracked open the door. "The priest is dispensing the Eucharist."

Bereft of any other means of making the decision, Esclarmonde rested one hand on Phillipa's womb and the other on the head of Corba's child. She spoke her name aloud. Phillipa's baby kicked and Corba's baby pumped her hands. She knew intuitively that Phillipa carried a girl. Mulling the dilemma, she kissed Phillipa's womb and announced her judgment. "I name this child Esclarmonde Loupe, the 'She-Wolf,' for she kicks and fights like her father."

Too moved to speak, Phillipa hugged Esclarmonde in gratitude.

Esclarmonde took Corba's infant into her arms again. When the candle's heat came near its pink cheeks, the babe playfully waved its arms and legs. She knew it to be a divine sign. "This precious girl I name Esclarmonde Chandelle—'Little Candle'—for her beautiful face reflects the light."

"It is an inspiration," said the Marquessa.

Esclarmonde held tiny Chandelle to her bosom and thought about what it would feel like to suckle her own child. She looked into its blue eyes with the hope of eliciting a smile—she shuddered with a foreboding.

Corba sensed her alarm. "What's wrong?"

Esclarmonde moved the candle back and forth, but the infant did not react to the flame. She gave the candle to Phillipa and motioned for her to walk several steps away. The child's eyes continued to look off into the darkness.

"You're frightening me!" cried Corba.

The babe's head jerked toward her mother's cry. While Phillipa held the candle, Esclarmonde walked two steps away and called out, "Chandelle!"

The infant turned toward her voice. Esclarmonde gestured for the candle to be brought nearer the child's face. Its eyes remained trained toward the direction of her call. The flame reflected oddly in its glassy corneas.

"My God!" cried Corba. "She's blind!"

Esclarmonde rescued the infant before Corba collapsed in despair. She blessed the child with a prayer of welcome to the world, and felt a strong connection. She knew in her heart that this soul was special.

The Abbess reentered the room. "We must return now."

Esclarmonde reluctantly placed Chandelle back into Corba's shaking arms. "She will bring much joy into our lives, Corba. I promise you."

"I cannot curse God," said Corba, stifling her weeping. "I've been given a loving husband and child. It is you who needs our prayers."

The tearful women embraced Esclarmonde one last time.

The Abbess hurried Esclarmonde to the staircase, but Phillipa stopped the nun and pulled her aside to ask something out of earshot of the others. The Abbess hesitated, then nodded her reluctant assent to the whispered request.

As the Mass neared its final benediction, the veiled Abbess walked down the aisle alone and came to the pew where Jourdaine was half-asleep. She whispered to his ear, "There are marks."

"The witch!" said Jourdaine, rousing with a start. "I knew it!"

"Inflicted by the hands of a demon for certain," said the Abbess. "Touch her again in violence and your seed will be forever cursed."

Jourdaine lurched up, bollixed by the charge. Had that bitch of a wife told those nuns of the beatings? He itched to strike out at the insolent Abbess, but he was thwarted by the many witnesses around him. "The Bible prescribes discipline. I'll suffer no woman to tell me otherwise."

"Do you read the Bible?" asked the Abbess.

"Of course not. It's forbidden for laymen."

"Then how do you know what it permits?"

"Damn you! Reveal your face!"

Before he could rip away her veil, the Abbess removed her red mantle and threw it to the floor. She retreated into the sea of nuns that was pouring out from the stalls into the nave. Jourdaine shoved open a path to give chase, but the Abbess had disappeared into the anonymity of black habits.

Esclarmonde stood waiting at the rear doors for Jourdaine. As the veiled nuns flooded past, one captured her hand and squeezed it. Esclarmonde knew that blessed touch. She tried to reciprocate the gesture, but Phillipa—disguised in the Abbess's habit—had escaped into the cloister courtyard.

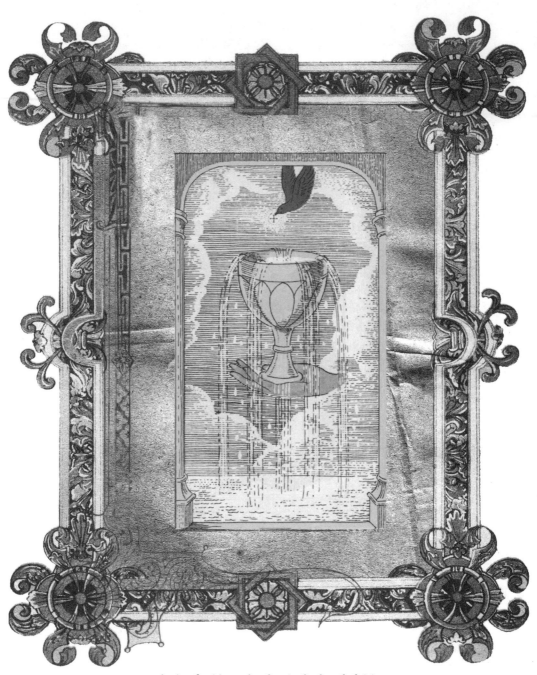

And the Brotherhood holdeth hidden
the Grail from all strangers' eyes . . .
- Parsifal

XIII

Constantinople

April 1204

uilhelm could hear the Greek drungaries across the Golden Horn shouting orders for their arbalests to be loaded. Repulsed in their first attempt to capture the Byzantine city, he and thirty thousand seasick crusaders had stood for two days festering in a muck of brine and manure on the decks of their assault galleys. They watched with suspicion as the Venetian sailors measured the winds in preparation to raise anchors. If the dangerous currents shifted, their armada would be carried into the swirling Straits of St. George, where the galleys would be easy prey for Turkish pirates.

Enrico Dandolo, the blind Doge of Venice, was rowed across the bows to exhort the assault that he had spent thirty years planning. Cardinal Peter of Capua sat at his side pronouncing the assurances of victory, "See how the Almighty parts the winds! Just as He splayed the sea for the Israelites!"

From deep within the crowded ranks, Guilhelm shouted, "And did the Israelites sack and murder their own people?"

The Cardinal searched the decks for the source of that blasphemous utterance. "Who dares question God's mission?"

Guilhelm removed his helmet and pushed to the fore. "A Christian! As are the men on those battlements!"

"The schismatics purge their altars with vinegar after our services and lower baskets of crumbs to us as if we are lepers!" countered the Cardinal.

Guilhelm spat his disgust into the putrid Bosphorus water. He had long suspected the Pope of intriguing to bring Byzantium to heel. This motley force of Germans, Franks, and Angevins had been beguiled into delaying its advance on the Holy Land to attack the most fortified city in the Christian world. A second crusader army had already sacked the nearby city of Zara and stood waiting near the Castle of Bohemond, assigned the task of taking the inland walls from the north. He surveyed the temper of the men around him. Most were petty knights, debtors, and sinners on pilgrimage, all led by a few land-hungry barons. Yet surely even these dregs would have qualms about such an unprovoked aggression. He tried to shake them from their moral lethargy. "The Doge and his circus trainers have led us by the nose for their own designs!"

The shriveled Methuselah who wore the ostentatious Lion of St. Mark signaled for his drummers to drown out Guilhelm's protest. Having long nurtured a vendetta against the Byzantines, the Doge was not prepared to see it scuttled at this final hour. As a young diplomat in this city, he had lost his sight to a royal eunuch whose expertise was the manipulation of a reflecting glass to burn the corneas of unsuspecting victims. He now made tactical decisions based on his faded memory of the city's defenses—a fact that Guilhelm feared the Greek spies had discovered. With his high-pitched screech of a voice, the old Venetian harangued the crusaders for their cowardice. "You Franks ask us to risk our ships and plead penury when you are aboard! You promised to take those walls if I forgave your debts!"

"We are the blind ones!" shouted Guilhelm. "If we weren't burdened with Venetian usury, we'd be in Jerusalem by now!"

The Doge resorted to a time-proven tactic to abort the brewing insurrection. "There are vast storehouses of gold within that city! You shall all be wealthy beyond your dreams! God's reward awaits you!"

His promise elicited the expected response. The crusaders donned their armor and rattled their blades in a clatter of greed. Filled with a loathing for this spectacle of bloodlust, Guilhelm prepared to disembark, preferring starvation on the plains of Chalcedon to such an abomination. But the Doge's guards blocked his path off the galley.

Advised that the malcontent was a Templar, the Doge curled a devious smile. "If your conscience prevents you from fighting apostates, monk, we will gladly relieve you of your weapons to help you avoid the temptation of sin."

Guilhelm had no choice but to return to his station. These thieving Venetians might force him to remain with this army, but they could not require him to kill fellow believers once the battle was commenced.

Satisfied that the mutiny had been strangled, the Cardinal of Padua raised his hands and shouted the traditional martial benediction, "God wills it!"

Thousands of sails unfurled at once. Oars sliced into the sea and lifted the quilled galleys in a great surge forward, stretching as far as the eye could see. Halfway across the Horn, Guilhelm heard a low whistling and saw the torches atop Constantinople's ramparts disappear from view. He lifted his shield seconds before a hail of catapulted missiles rattled the decks. Impaled men and horses dropped to the boards with a horrific groan. The stiffening winds had cleared the skies, affording the Byzantine gunners an open vista. Puffs of smoke crackled amid tongues of low lightning. The sea rocked as if struck by an earthquake.

"Greek fire!" shouted the coxswain.

Streams of ignited sulfur and linseed oil arced from the Byzantine walls. The crusaders were given enough warning to take cover, but the slaves shackled below the decks were flayed horribly. The Venetian gunners retaliated by pumping jets of boiling naphtha from the mouths of the brass lions perched atop their bow beaks. The beachhead came into sight and the galleys tightened their formations. The severest test was now at hand: Five of the largest ships had been tethered together to carry an assault tower with gangplanks. The ramps of the first galleys ashore dropped into the frothing waves and disgorged a tangled exodus of horses, knights, and siege guns.

Guilhelm cursed his fortune. Directly above him stood the Petrion tower manned by the Waring Guards from Daneland. These moustached mercenaries—descendants of the Vikings who had swept across the British Isles—were armed with their infamous battle-axes. He had drawn the task of confronting the most hardened of the city's defenders, who were sworn to fight to the death for Murtzuphulus, the notorious usurper of the Byzantine crown. The long-bearded Archbishop of Constantinople stood at their side brandishing the venerated Palladium, a miracle-working icon that had repulsed every assault on these walls during the last eight hundred years.

Guilhelm could only stand by and watch from his galley as the Warings split the skulls of the first Franks up the ladders. He girded his breastplate and prepared to take his turn in the second assault when a hand grasped his arm.

"You are not alone, brother." The knight at his side angled his shield to display within its concave interior the beausant insignia of the Temple. He lifted his visor, revealing the weathered face of an elderly man with with sharp, intelligent eyes. "I am Baroche. Preceptor of the Lombard commanderie."

"I was told the Temple had forsworn this siege," said Guilhelm.

"This enterprise is a ruse by the Doge to get his hands on the Emperor's treasures." A missile whistled past their ears and crushed several Franks to their rear. Baroche leaned closer for a whisper. "The Greeks possess relics of incalculable worth. I have been sent by the Grand Master to recover them. Will you assist me?"

Guilhelm angled his shoulder to prevent the other knights from overhearing. "If I am to risk my life, I must know more."

After a hesitation, Baroche allowed, "The relics are from Jerusalem."

Guilhelm's curiosity was whetted. "The true Cross?"

Baroche snorted with contempt at the suggestion that he would undertake such a dangerous quest for a slither of useless wormwood. "A manuscript. And with it a remembrance of Our Lord far more precious than you can imagine." He tugged at Guilhelm's Templar mantle. "Discard this. The Greeks will take aim for it first."

Their galley rammed the shoals—the sally ramp exploded into the sea. Guilhelm was swept out into a whirlpool of thrashing men and frightened horses. He kicked to find the bottom but his armor drove him deeper into the churning undertow. He went black as he lost the last of the air in his lungs. The din of battle transformed into a peaceful quiet.

There are worse ways to die.

He was pulled upward. Salt stung his eyes as they broke the surface. Baroche was dragging him to the shore. Spitting sea wash, Guilhelm crawled to his horse amid the churn of drowning men. On the beachhead, the sappers dug furiously at the base of the wall. Those crusaders who had managed to crawl to land now confronted a new terror—boiling pitch.

The two Templars mounted their skittish horses and rode the length of the narrow beachhead in search of a breach. Guilhelm turned back toward the Horn and saw the galleys retreating for the far piers of Galata. "The Venetians are abandoning us!" His warning spread like fire down the ranks. The panicked Franks discarded their armor and swam for the galleys.

A crazed Carthusian monk loosed a bloodcurdling hosanna. Refusing to see Christ's will denied, he dived headfirst into a small hole that had been bored into the tower's gate. The Franks were so astonished by the monk's reckless act that they rushed back to pull his dangling legs from the hole. His torso reemerged—with his head hacked off. Filled with a collective madness at the gruesome martyrdom, the crusaders converged on the gate and hammered wildly until the beams caved in.

Guilhelm and Baroche drove their horses behind the knights as they swarmed through the gape. Inside the walls they found no defenders. Murtzuphulus and the Warings had retreated into the central city to use the vast network of streets as a firebreak. The citizens strolling along tree-lined parks reacted to the appearance of the Franks as if a pack of wild dromedaries had escaped from their city's famous zoo. The bloodthirsty crusaders poured down the broad avenues and exacted revenge on the effeminate-looking Greeks, who were easily identified by their painted eyes and perfumed curls.

Guilhelm and Baroche broke free of the scrum and galloped toward the chariot Hippodrome, where the smoke of pillage swirled around the towering Egyptian obelisks. They came upon a mob of crusaders dragging nuns from the Church of the Holy Apostles with the intent to rape them. Guilhelm reined back to go to the aid of the holy women, but Baroche intercepted him.

"Leave them to the Lord's mercy," ordered the Templar commander.

When they reached the Aqueduct of Valens, Baroche halted to gain his bearings of the city's famous seven hills. Reoriented, he led Guilhelm north past the thousands of kneeling Greeks who begged for their lives by traversing their forearms in the sign of the Cross. The main crusader army cut a bloody swath toward the Hagia Sophia to ransack its priceless icons and ornaments, but the Templars reversed course and climbed the Petrion Hill. There they were stopped short by a fire raging through the wooden bazaars. Caught in the maze of smoke-filled wynds, Baroche searched frantically for an escape route.

Guilhelm's helmet clogged with soot. Nearly overcome, he lashed his balking steed deeper into the flames. He stumbled out on the far side of the holocaust and dropped gasping from his saddle. Baroche had not followed him. Guilhelm hurled himself back into the inferno and found the Templar commander ghastly burned. He dragged Baroche from the flames, too late.

Convulsing in death, Baroche muttered, "Blachernae."

Guilhelm signed the brother to his salvation. He looked toward the looming citadel that sat in the far northwest corner of the city. The isolated fortress stood at the opposite end from the Boucoleon Palace and the Hagia Sophia.

Why Blachernae?

lachernae Palace, the fortified summer residence of the Emperor, appeared abandoned. Only the gurgle of a distant fountain broke the eerie silence in this magnificent edifice of red brick and granite, designed as an escape into a world indifferent to the travails of mortals. Guilhelm passed through the gold-gilt gates and walked from opulent apartment to apartment, all interconnected by labyrinthine galleries lavished with crystal chandeliers, arras-hung walls, tesserae ceilings, and marbled mosaics. A bowl of ripe pomegranates sat on a table. He tasted one to savor its sweet juices.

A distant patter of footsteps reverberated down the polished floors.

He quickly skulked behind a fluted colonnade with a hand on his sword. The echoing steps, light and swift, became louder. Had the Warings returned to defend the palace? No, the feet sounded too feminine and softly sandaled. Royal eunuchs, most likely. Even with their loss of manhood, eunuchs could be dastardly creatures, for they were trained to foil assassins with the use of their hands alone. He might take a couple of them down, but if they shot upon him like wasps, his armor would be his coffin. His only hope lay in their deeply inculcated fear of Franks. The emperors had warned them that the foreigners from the West would debauch them in heinous ways. With a fortifying breath, he raised his sword quietly and leapt into the hall.

Crouched and at the ready, he rounded his eyes wide as platters and contorted his face in the most fearsome mask of devilry that he could summon. He blinked in astonishment. Were those pomegranates laced with a narcotic poison to foil intruders? Or was he losing his mind before giving up his spirit?

Before him stood a menagerie of bizarre animals, as surprised to see him as he was to confront them. The motley herd was led by a pony striped in black and white. At its side was a miniature elephant with a horn protruding from the center of its forehead like a unicorn. Hovering above all of these cross-bred beasts of Satan stood a frightful creature with a neck as long as a jousting lance and legs so slender and fragile that they seemed incapable of holding up the torso. Another quadruped possessed the head of a deer atop the body of a giant rabbit; the most unsettling of its aspects was the succubi twin of itself that it carried in a pouch hanging under its stomach. Below the undergird of these monstrosities paraded a gaggle of queer birds with fanning feathers that held dozens of unblinking blue eyes.

His reverie at the Emperor's escaped collection of exotic animals was interrupted by a woman's scream from a far chamber. The spooked creatures erupted and scurried past him in a stampede. He recovered from the near-trampling and followed the screams to a chapel. He rammed open its burnished doors.

A crusader had his hand clasped over the mouth of a comely blonde lady and was preparing to ravish her. The lusting Frank pinned his frightened captive against the altar and sliced away the tressings of her bodice.

Guilhelm calculated that he could not rescue the woman without risking her throat being cut. "Perhaps you should take her to another chamber."

Desperate for his intervention, the lady sank in despair.

The Frank laughed demonically and dug another lascivious bite into the lady's pale neck. "What difference where I have her?"

"The Virgin looks down upon you," said Guilhelm.

The Frank glanced up at an icon of the Blessed Mother on the balustrade. With a curse of annoyance, he dragged his conquest down the aisle and into an antechamber. Having escaped the Virgin's judging glare, he renewed his assault on the lady by shredding her blouse to expose her alabaster shoulders. He found Guilhelm still watching him. "Why don't you go find your own?"

Guilhelm's vows forbade the taking of a life within an arm's reach of a holy sanctum. He had to lure the man a few steps closer. "I passed the Emperor's bedchamber down the hall. Think of the story you could tell."

The Frank traced the point of his blade across the lady's breast, drawing a slender line of blood. "When I'm done with her, I'm going to cut off your balls and hang them from your ears. Think of the story *you'll* tell."

"Have you forgotten you're a Christian?" Guilhelm slid his sword across the marbled floor and raised his hands in a gesture of pacific intent to coax the knight nearer. "Are you all cock and no blade?"

The Frank threw the lady aside and charged at him. "Damn your wagging tongue! I'll have your name before I carve you up!"

When the crusader crossed the chapel's threshold, Guilhelm whipped the dagger from under his hauberk and skewered the man in the gut. Eyes bulging, the Frank buckled to his knees. Guilhelm twisted the blade as he whispered into the crusader's ear, "Since you asked so graciously, the name is Montanhagol the Templar. Where you now go, they will know it well. I've dispatched many a deserving resident to its heated lodging."

A bubble of blood gurgled up from the corner of the dying man's mouth. He looked up in disbelief at Guilhelm's unmarked tunic as if protesting that some law of required identity had been breached.

Released, the lady covered her nakedness with her torn blouse and studied Guilhelm intently. "So, there is a rose among the Latin thorns."

Guilhelm was surprised to hear a Greek woman speak fluent French.

"I am Mary Margaret of Hungary."

Stunned, Guilhelm bent a knee to give courtesy to the wife of the Emperor. "My lady, why have you been left here unattended?"

"The Warings have sold their loyalty to the usurper. They blinded my husband and strangled my son."

"I must escort you to safety at once."

"I would only be hunted down and married off again." She waited as if expecting something more from him. "You said you were a Templar. Do you not have an indication for me?"

"An indication?" he asked, perplexed.

The Empress placed a finger to her attacker's jugular to make certain he was dead. Reassured, she circled Guilhelm and tried to make sense of his apparent lack of knowledge about her mission. "I have been in clandestine communication with your superiors. A meeting was to take place in this chapel. A sign was agreed upon. Are you not the one sent?"

"I was ordered here by a brother who met his Maker this day."

The Empress lowered her head in prayer for Baroche's soul. "Did he reveal to you his purpose in coming to Constantinople?"

"Only that he sought to save possessions of great value."

The Empress debated whether she could trust him. The Venetians were notorious for subterfuge. The Doge may have assassinated her Templar contact and sent an imposter in his stead. Yet she had no choice. The Franks would soon be swarming the citadel in the thousands. She led Guilhelm into the chapel and barred its doors, then drew a key from her bodice and retracted a curtain that hung behind the altar. From its recesses she brought forth a glass-encased reliquary that was half the size of a shield. The ancient container rested on a slender stone cask annealed and blackened by age.

Guilhelm was dropped to his knees by an ineffable force. Under the reliquary's pane was a fragile cloth that held the image of a bearded man. The sepia lines of its features seemed burned into the linen and its eyes were closed in repose after suffering some unspeakable torture. Guilhelm felt compelled to shield his gaze. "What is this countenance that bears down on me?"

"The Mandylion Shroud. It rests on the Keramion, the cup that held Our Lord's blood."

Guilhelm had heard stories in Jerusalem about the precious syndoine that had been wrapped around Our Lord after His death and resurrection. "I was told the holy cloth was kept in Santa Sophia for all to see."

"Your fellow Latins are wrangling over that forgery as we speak."

"I'm not worthy to be in its presence."

"You are, or you would not have been led here." She delivered the relics into his possession. "Take them. Before Rome's agents discover them here."

"Take them where?"

The Empress stared into his eyes as if reading his soul. "You are a Templar sworn to celibacy. And yet there is a woman in your heart."

Guilhelm felt more exposed than if he had been stripped naked. "How do you know this?"

"You must return to her at once. The lady requires your aid. She will take my place as guardian of these precious remembrances of Our Lord's Light."

Alarums sounded outside the palace followed by the familiar smell of pillaging smoke. The Franks had arrived and were searching for loot.

The Empress rushed Guilhelm through a side portal and down a hidden staircase. "There is little time."

"But your safety—"

"Is in God's hands. As my life's purpose is now in yours." She led him to a faux door that opened to a descending tunnel. "The cisterns lead to the port of Eleutherius." She removed a signet ring from her finger and handed it to him. "Display this to the harbor commander. He will provide you safe passage."

Two steps down into the passageway, Guilhelm turned back. "The brother also spoke of a manuscript."

"The scroll was taken from here years ago. If you are meant to find it, the Mandylion and the Cup will lead you to it. Together, the relics and the scroll unlock a hidden truth that must be preserved at all cost." She placed her palm to his forehead in a blessing. "May God go with you."

. . . Lord, sometimes you urge us on toward
the Kingdom of Heaven, but at other times you turn us away.
Sometimes you encourage us, draw us toward faith,
and promise life, but at other times you throw us out . . .
- The Secret Book of James

XIV

Gascony

January 1205

Jourdaine arose naked from the bed and stood staring at the spent embers in the hearth. After several minutes of debate, he said without turning, "I will have an annulment. The petition will be sponsored by the Bishop of Bordeaux and sent to Rome with your affidavit of acceptance."

Was he testing her? Esclarmonde chose to feign dismay, fearful that any display of hope might cause him to retract his decision. "On what grounds?"

"Grounds? Has your head turned as useless as your womb?"

"I have acceded to your desires."

"With all of the fervency of a tenant paying arrears. You avoid taking pleasure in the act to deny me a son."

She had long since become accustomed to his penchant for latching upon new superstitions to explain her failings, but this latest claim was so preposterous that in the heat of outrage she unwittingly abandoned her plan to lure him into carrying out the threat. "You cannot believe *that* inanity!"

"The physicians say that the Almighty gave women rapacious lust so they would strive to be filled with the perfection of man."

"Leeches and coffin robbers! What do they know about women?"

"Bruys of Toulouse once opened the entrails of a childless hag. Her canal had become shriveled because of her incessant frowning."

Esclarmonde leapt from the bed to confront him. "Perhaps if that blood-letter had split his own gut, he too would fail to peal with laughter. Your priests tell us it is a sin to take pleasure. Now your doctors tell us it is an impediment. What are we to do but ignore—" She caught herself, too late.

The flame's inconstant light glinted in Jourdaine's malefic eyes. "Limp rag! I'll soon be rid of that wagging tongue!"

She braced for the blow, even wished for it. One last beating would be a small price to seal his impetuous demand to end their marriage. But this time he held back his fist. *Why does he not strike?* She thrust out her chin to taunt him. "Take your leave from me, then! You've cost me the best years of my life!" When he merely grinned, she realized that she had just forfeited what small advantage she had held in the negotiation. Even Jourdaine was clever enough to know that most women, no matter how wretched their lot, would cling to a marriage rather than face the ignominy of being turned out on the charge of a fruitless womb. He was prepared to offer her concessions, but she had revealed her willingness to agree to the annulment too soon.

"Sign Montsegur to me," he said, "and you will be free to go."

"That land was my dowry! By law I am entitled to retain it!"

"Consider it recompense for the misery you've caused me."

"You will not steal that mount!"

He drove her into the wall. "Scheming wench! You accuse *me* of thievery?" He pinned her to the floor and forced the quill into her hand.

Crushed under his weight, her mind flooded with visions of home. She could live with Phillipa and the Marquessa, never again to be a victim to his violence. All that was required was this one stroke. She tried to focus her eyes on the terms of dissolution—and flung the quill across the room. Enraged, he drove a fist into her stomach. Something inside her broke apart. The blows came so fast that she was certain this would be the end. "I'll deny it's mine!"

He forced her to scratch out a line. "Don't you see that de Montfort has witnessed your signing?" He play-acted as if his old comrade was testifying. "What say you, Simon? Did she not rush to pack her bags?" Satisfied with her signature's look of authenticity, he fell back into the bed and guttered the candle. "Fetch me some wine from the cellar. We'll toast our parting."

Esclarmonde spat blood as she crawled away in the darkness. She was fearful of what he would do to her if she passed out. She groped for the hinges—the door creaked open of its own accord. She tried to look up to find the source of the movement, but she was overcome by the sickening blackness.

A trencher clanked on the table next to the bed.

"You move quickly enough with a little encouragement." Jourdaine took a hearty swig. His eyes widened from a hellish stench. He spewed the contents of the trencher and stumbled across the room to light a taper.

The chamber pot was overturned.

"Poisoning shrew!" He kicked at the darkness with offal drooling down his chin and found her sprawled near the door. He was about to finish her with a stomp to the head when an apparition appeared above the hearth:

The Face of Our Lord Jesus Christ looked down upon him.

The Holy Countenance, shimmering in shades of blue and red, approached him with eyes closed in harsh judgment. Jourdaine fell back upon his haunches, but the avenging ghost continued to stalk him. "Call it off!" Jourdaine pressed his hands together in desperate supplication—until a sharpness nicked his throat. "St. Michael spare me! I've fought the infidel!" The tip of a sword came under his Adam's apple. In the dim light, he saw a red cross—followed by a second face more menacing than the first. He lunged at his old nemesis, but the blade aborted his attack. He was lifted and driven toward the spectre that had been levitating—the necromantic face was encased in glass. He spat at Guilhelm. "I was told you lay under a heap of Greek stones."

"It was a near enough thing," said Guilhelm. "But God grants all who take the Cross one boon before leaving this world. He has fulfilled half of mine this night. My next meeting with de Montfort will make it complete." He stifled Jourdaine's attempt to call his guard with a sharp turn of the blade. "He's out searching for your horses."

Jourdaine's neck was strained to its limit. "Take her and be gone!"

"I see you've been practicing your martial skills since last we met." Guilhelm offered his raised jaw as a target. "Have at me."

The sword thwarted Jourdaine's advance. "Fight me fairly!"

"Fairly? Like you fought her?"

Jourdaine's throat was streaked with blood. "You're gutting me!"

"Would it help if I put on her nightgown? A more familiar target, perhaps?"

The blade came perilously close to Jourdaine's jugular. He had no choice but to shred the annulment petition and write new terms.

Guilhelm dictated to him, "I, Jourdaine L'Isle, do hereby grant—"

"She grants the dissolution to me!"

"You've acquired quite a familiarity with the law."

"The dowry forfeits upon the proof of the wife's sterility!"

Guilhelm lowered the weapon to the crease at Jourdaine's ungirded loins. "And does the law also grant the same right to a wife whose husband is sterile?"

Jourdaine's hands were now freed, but he dared not risk a move.

"Did de Montfort in his many tales of adventure relate to you the manner in which Greek palace boys are rendered eunuchs? The secret is dispatching the appendage slowly. If the cutting is too quick, one bleeds to a slow death."

Jourdaine needed no convincing that the Templar would carry out the mutilation. He finished scribbling the terms of the new contract: *I hereby attest that during the course of my marriage, I inflicted bodily harm upon my wife. Having caused no progeny to issue, I relinquish all rights to the dowry of Montsegur.*

Guilhelm examined the document and returned it to be signed. The Gascon reluctantly inched the quill toward the signature line and—

"Guilhelm?"

Esclarmonde staggered toward him from the shadows. Guilhelm was forced to drop his weapon to prevent her from falling. Catching her, he was straightened by a blow to his shoulders. He fell with her clinging to his neck.

Jourdaine drove a punishing heel into Guilhelm's ribs. "I should've run you through the first time I laid eyes on your scrawny bones!"

"No!" Esclarmonde lurched to her knees. "You'll kill him!"

"That's a plan! Yours will come!"

The moon's light through the embrasure revealed Guilhelm's abandoned sword several feet away. While Jourdaine rained blows on the Templar, Esclarmonde crawled for the weapon. She raised the blade with all of her waning strength and aimed its quivering point at Jourdaine's back. "Get off him!"

Jourdaine ignored her—until his spine was pricked.

She struggled to keep the heavy blade aloft. "So help me God, I'll do it!"

"Don't your grass-eating heretic friends forbid murder?" Jourdaine turned and backed her against the wall. "You've prayed every night for this chance. But I don't think you have it in you!"

She gripped the hilt so tightly that her knuckles turned white. If she could not dredge the courage to impale him, he'd wrest the weapon away.

"You've finally found a use for that fallow pit." He pressed the hilt knob into her stomach. "What are you waiting for?" He laughed at her reluctance to drive home the weapon. "I'm going to count to three. Then I'm going to take it from you and dispatch your monk's head from his neck."

She had no doubt he would carry out the threat. No court in Gascony would convict him for killing an intruder.

"One."

It would mean the hangman's noose for her, even with the marks on her face. The tribunal would ask why the Templar had been in her bedchamber. Adultery, the judges would find. Even if she only maimed Jourdaine, he would still obtain his divorce and she would forfeit Montsegur.

"Two."

She was barren, already half-dead. To have it all over would be a blessing. If Guilhelm had to die, she would go with him. She released her grip on the sword to surrender it and—

"Three!"

Jourdaine lurched for her with eyes distended. His quivering mouth gaped inches from her face—but it had not uttered that final count. A trickle of blood bubbled over his teeth and trailed down her chemise. She shrieked as the knob continued to press against her, pulsing with his death spasms. He grasped at the handle and fell face-first, driving the hilt to its limit.

Guilhelm stood on the spot vacated by the Gascon.

The Templar collapsed. Esclarmonde dragged him to the bed and lay next to him convulsing in shock and clutching his face. She stared at Jourdaine's blood channeling down the floor's mortise joints. "What have we done?"

"It was my deed alone," muttered Guilhelm.

"I brought this on you!" she protested.

Guilhelm winced as he lifted to his elbows. "You must leave before the body is discovered." He tore off a portion of the parchment that Jourdaine had left on the table and scribbled a message. "Take my horse to Saverdun and deliver this to the preceptor there. He'll arrange to have you taken to Foix."

"It was self-defense!"

"No one will believe that," he insisted.

Several moments passed in fragile silence before Esclarmonde comprehended that he did not intend to go with her. Despondent, she cursed Jourdaine's corpse. Even in death, he had conspired to keep her from the man she loved. When Guilhelm tried to pull up from the bed, she eased his head back to the pillow. She tore a strip from the sheet and wrapped his shoulder to stanch his wound. "We have a few hours before daylight. The washwoman who comes in the mornings has orders not to intrude. Grant me this night. If we are doomed to count our time together in hours, let us make the most of it."

Guilhelm was too weak to deny her request. She stroked the crosshatched lines of his sunburnt forehead and wondered if she had altered as much in appearance. He had grown a beard, streaked with gray and closely cropped, and his once-taut muscles now sagged a bit with age. Alarmed to find him so thin, she slipped from the room and returned with a plate of cold victuals.

He studied her closely while she fed him. "What happened to the brash maid I left behind?"

She turned aside to avoid his inspection. "I tried to banish you from my thoughts."

"And I you . . . in my hopes, if not my thoughts."

"You doubted my love?"

"De Montfort said you were content with the Gascon. I'd have understood if you made the best of your lot."

"You believed *that* pernicious man?"

"I assumed even he would not utter a falsehood on holy crusade."

"But you came back."

"I do not make promises lightly."

She sighed in bitter resignation. A trail of misbegotten vows had led them to yet another crossroads. She resolved never again to undertake an oath. What use were such commitments if they brought only sorrow? She wondered what judgment Jourdaine was now confronting. If there *were* two gods, as Phillipa and the Cathars insisted, to which divinity was he now answering for his depravity? Would his malformed soul be reborn into this world? She sank with despair at the thought that their paths might merge again in another lifetime.

"If Hell has a toll gate, he'll stand in a long line," said Guilhelm. "I saw thousands of his kind commit every atrocity imaginable."

"Against the infidels?" she asked.

"Nay, fellow Christians. A man who becomes a cannibal first eats the flesh of a stranger. But soon he turns on his own children."

"What are you suggesting?"

"I fear this madness in the East may soon be unleashed on our own land." He found her staring at the relics that he had brought back from Blachernae. Set on the mantel above the flickering hearth, the Mandylion shroud seemed enlivened by the shadows that swept over it. "The emperor's widow in Byzantium told me to bring them to you."

"To me? Why?"

"She said the woman in my heart would protect them."

Esclarmonde closely examined the unsettling facial features that had been burned into the aged cloth. The Holy Countenance appeared to be an inversion that exhibited darkness where light would normally be found. There was an unsettling depth to its pile, as if the creases formed in its creation had been preserved. What had caused this unnatural transformation? She was certain no illuminator could have fashioned such a lifelike icon; the deep nap of the linen had been darkened, but there was no evidence of dye or pigment. The shroud seemed to represent a reversal of all that was tangible and real. "Do you ever question what we've been told by the Church?"

Guilhelm shrugged. "I've heard all manner of claims. I once encountered an old Jew in Aragon who spent nights rearranging the letters of the Scriptures."

"To what purpose?"

"He told me that every person, every physical object even, had its converse in the spiritual realm. If you could find its ephemeral antipode, you would hold the secret of its essence."

Esclarmonde recalled that day in the church when the Light had visited her. "Are not the white borders of a written letter the contra of the letter itself?"

The example she posed took Guilhelm by surprise. "One night in Rhodes, I was awakened by a vision of blazing letters. The white surrounding the word transformed into a heavenly cathedral that seemed built of crystal."

"What were the letters?"

"AMOR."

She laughed in sudden discovery. "The cathedral must have represented the Church of Love!"

Guilhelm was astonished by her insight. "Like you, I was compelled by some inclination to rearrange the letters. But I could make no sense of it."

She performed the mental operation by reversing the letters: ROMA. "If your Jewish sage spoke true, then the Church of Love must be the opposite of the Church of Rome. But what then is the Church of Love?" Before she could solve that mystery, she was doubled over by a sharp pain in her stomach. The nausea that she had suffered during the past weeks had returned.

Guilhelm braced her forehead and soothed her with a sip of wine. "You must rest to gain strength for the ride in the morning."

She sank into his arms. "Where will you go?"

"The Temple's gendarmes will expect me to flee west across the mountains. I'll make for Aquitaine and the north."

Esclarmonde retrieved her mother's Cathar medallion from under the mattress and placed its cord around Guilhelm's neck for a keepsake of her. As he fell asleep in her arms, she begged the sun to delay its rebirth.

Watch and pray that you may
not be born in the flesh, but that you may
leave the bitter bondage of this life.
- The Secret Sayings of the Savior

XV

Foix

August 1205

he wizened midwife stopped at the threshold of the lying-in room to search for evil shadows. Satisfied with the thoroughness of the lime wash, she traced a pentagram on the floor stones. "The moon is waning. A baneful hour, it is. She'd best give up the litter before midnight."

"I did not bring you here to cast horoscopes," scolded the Marquessa.

"A hen crowed this morn below my window."

"You heard no such thing!"

The midwife traced her finger along the window battens to find cracks that might allow the insipid demons to enter and foul the birthing. "A hen turned rooster is an evil omen."

"Cease your inane prattle before she hears you. It's her first."

The midwife nudged the door to the hall and found Roger waiting alone, evidence for the village gossip that the father may not have been Esclarmonde's husband. "The succubi flock in droves to a bastard. My fee is doubled."

"You delivered my daughter for a third of that!"

"A fatherless babe fights the world. Twice the trouble, twice the pay."

Extorted by the ever-present sword of death that hung over a birthing room, the Marquessa had no choice but to wave the wily crone to the task.

The midwife commenced her preparations by spreading straw around the birthing stool and sprinkling it with wax, snakeskins, and herbs. In the center of this menagerie she set a miniature carving of St. Margaret, the patron saint of laboring women. She opened the cupboards, tightened the oiled linen curtains, and tossed pinecones into the hearth to sweat away any lingering spirits. The chamber soon became a stinking, oppressive oven. She clapped her hands to chase the flies and clucked, "In with the heifer."

Phillipa led Esclarmonde to the stool at the foot of the bed. Loupe and Chandelle, both four years old, followed them a few steps behind. Esclarmonde's stomach was distended and her turgid eyes were rimmed pink with pain.

The midwife wrapped Esclarmonde in the frayed birthing girdle that had been kept for generations in St. Volusien's sacristy. She dropped a pebble and ordered her to pick it up in a test. "How close are the grippings?"

"I've lost count!" gasped Esclarmonde. "My God, I ache!"

"Her water is pallid," warned the Marquessa.

The midwife measured the womb's descent and shook her head woefully. "The belly rides high. The child should have lowered by now."

"I'm suffocating!" cried Esclarmonde.

Phillipa pressed a wet compress to Esclarmonde's blistering forehead. "Won't you allow her to rest?"

The midwife thrust three magical stones into Esclarmonde's palms and pulled her up from the stool. "She must stay on her feet. To the stairs. Avoid moving her in circles."

Esclarmonde was marched up and down the tower staircase until she became so enervated that she could not stand without assistance. When that torment produced no results, she was placed over a heated cauldron to steam the birth opening. Throughout this torturous ordeal, she cursed Jourdaine for having found a way to continue his violence on her from the grave. Soon after leaving Gascony, her moon flux had stopped. She arrived days later in Foix racked by morning sickness. In the intervening seven months, she had grown increasingly despondent over the lack of news about Guilhelm and the prospect of giving birth to a child sired by the man she had detested.

When dawn arrived with no progress, the midwife resorted to more drastic measures. She allowed Esclarmonde to lay on the bed and required her to swallow scraps of cloth inscribed with the names of saints. Esclarmonde struggled to force the imitation hosts down her throat while the midwife chanted charms to speed the magic:

This be my remedy for hateful slow birth,
this be my remedy for heavy difficult birth,
this be my remedy for hateful imperfect birth.
Up I go, step over ye,
with living child, not a dead one,
with full-born one, not a—

The door flew open. Folques, draped in his red sacramental stole, invaded the room. "What pagan abomination of the Eucharist is this?"

Outraged by the trespass, the Marquessa covered Esclarmonde with a sheet for modesty. "You have no warrant here!"

"The Almighty has warrant against infanticide!"

"You believe I'd harm my own child?" cried Esclarmonde.

"You absconded before testifying at the murder inquest."

Esclarmonde gasped, breathless from the piercing pangs in her lower back. "Give proof of my complicity!"

"The crime has already been solved," said Folques. "The heinous deed was committed by the Templar Montanhagol."

Bathed in sweat, Esclarmonde bolted up from the bed. "That's a lie! You banished him to the Holy Land!"

Folques produced a confession signed in the Templar's hand. Esclarmonde tried to focus her fractured thoughts. Guilhelm must have planted the evidence to exonerate her after she had fallen asleep that night in Gascony.

Folques enjoyed her discomfited reaction. "He will be apprehended in due time. And your assistance in the crime will be demonstrated."

"Call my brother!"

Folques thwarted Phillipa's attempt to leave the room. "The Count has been served with the decree ordering the child's baptism."

Esclarmonde was about to protest the illegality of that injunction when she was seized by another spasm. The midwife placed a sponge soaked in henbane under her nostrils, which were already inflamed by the pepper applied to induce sneezing. Her vital signs were so weak that the midwife dared not raise her to the birthing stool.

Unnerved by the shrieks and curses, Folques retreated a step, having been warned by his Cistercian brothers that a birthing chamber was particularly susceptible to attaching fiends. "Has she been bled?"

"I'm not running a plague charnel!" snapped the midwife.

Folques circled the bed with his crucifix hoisted for protection. "Heaven requires a predetermined number of souls be saved on Judgment Day. If she denies the child the salvation of the Church, she must be cut open."

Esclarmonde lurched and convulsed. The midwife tried to assuage her throes with the palliative sponge, but Folques captured her hand.

"Desist from the medicinals!" commanded Folques. "Scripture forbids relief from the sorrows wrought by Eve's sin!"

"The child is trying to come by the feet first!" said the midwife.

"What does that mean?" asked Folques.

The midwife spat a black wad of root chew at the monk's sandals to curse the stupidity of men. "In most cases, a body follows!" While being sermonized on the travails required of woman, she escaped under the sheet to examine the womb. The fetus was unnaturally reversed and the cervix would not dilate. The harder Esclarmonde struggled to push it out, the more the infant resisted.

"Unleash it!" said Folques. "Holy Church commands it!"

Rattled by his threats, the midwife worked desperately to shift the breach. "I can't deliver the babe without risking injury to the lady!"

Folques fumbled for the chalice in his traveling bag. He hurriedly performed the miracle of transformation and held the Body of Christ to Esclarmonde's exerting face. "Surrender it! Or I'll force the Eucharist down your throat!"

Esclarmonde turned purple from the exertions. "You darkened me with one of your damnable sacraments! You'll not curse me with another!"

"It comes!" shouted the midwife. "Heat the canal with screams!"

The women elbowed Folques aside and wailed over the bed to raise the vibrations. Esclarmonde feared the infant was going to leave her dead. A roll of linen was forced into her mouth to protect her tongue. A piercing cry shook the room—the women suddenly ceased their shrieking.

"A boy!" announced the midwife.

Folques rushed up to pronounce the sacrament over the newborn and was stopped short by a horrific discovery. Denied a view by the arched sheet over her knees, Esclarmonde could not understand why the pain had not subsided. Why was the midwife still splitting her if the child was freed?

"Lord Christ protect us." Ashen-faced, the midwife brought out a second fetus—a blue-faced girl whose neck was wrapped by the birth cord. "The lad has strangled his sister."

Esclarmonde heard those words only vaguely. As if trapped in a distant dream, she could make no sense of the commotion swirling around her.

Phillipa took the infant girl from the midwife and frantically dug mucus from its clogged mouth. The tiny body hung limp. She swigged a mouthful of wine and sprayed the liquid into its throat, but the babe's caked eyes remained closed. She placed a feather under its nose and prayed for movement, to no avail. With a crazed look, she forced the stillborn girl on Folques. "Will you baptize her? Where is your god for her?"

Folques recoiled from the mucous-slathered clump. "Take it away!"

Phillipa kissed the stillborn's head and prayed for her return to the Light.

The midwife mumbled lamentations while measuring off four finger lengths on the birth cord. She doubled the ligature and powered it with crushed chervil, then lifted the bloodied Armor of Fortune to inspect the blackened caul for signs. When the surviving boy wailed in a demand not to be ignored, she looked down and saw a blue vein striating his temple—the infamous Artery of Death. She glanced ominously at Esclarmonde and muttered, "This one will kick at you for the rest of your days."

Folques crossed his breast as an antidote against the malignancy. "The fouled birth is the result of illicit coitus!"

"Enough!" cried Phillipa.

Folques pointed an accusing finger at Esclarmonde. "The surviving child was sired by your dead husband, a fervent Christian! There is no mystery about the fornicator whose seed produced the dead one!"

Little Loupe latched onto Folques's leg like a rabid pup. With the gnawing child in tow, Folques limped around the bed filling his scepter with holy water. Before he could dispense the baptismal sacrament, Phillipa rescued the newborn boy from the midwife and ran from the room.

Two weeks later, Almaric and Folques rode into Foix accompanied by a carriage and twenty armed men. The soldiers set up an inquest dais in front of the church. Almaric mounted the boards and announced to the gathered villagers, "The viscountess of this domain is to be interrogated."

Roger emerged from the castle to confront the clerics. "Since when does the Cistercian General concern himself with the birth of a child?"

"The smallest seed can spawn a field of thistles," said Almaric.

Roger assessed the mood of the townsfolk, but few appeared willing to support him in defying the monks. The Abbot's gendarmes commandeered the women from the chateau. Punished by the hot sun, Esclarmonde feared she might pass out while she rocked her infant boy to sooth his choleric crying. The soldiers led her to a stool that had been placed below the dais. Folques entered the church and removed the small casket that held her stillborn daughter. He set it beyond the borders of consecrated ground.

Roger tried to put a halt to this base treatment of the child's remains, but the soldiers forced him back. "My sister is not well. At least allow her to be questioned in the cool of the chapel."

"She remains unchurched," said Folques.

"I shall endure it," said Esclarmonde.

Almaric took his seated station under the shade of the church lintel to satisfy the ecclesiastical requirement that judgment be rendered within sanctified confines. "Do you know why you have been summoned?"

Esclarmonde stood unsteadily to meet the indictment. "I presume it is because of my lack of good manners in failing to die during childbirth."

"You are accused of withholding the sacrament of baptism." Almaric turned to Folques. "I will hear from the defender of the soul."

"Defender?" yelped the Marquessa. "I'd rather the Devil plead the case."

Folques circled behind Esclarmonde to avoid the spell of her eyes. "The Devil is much invoked in these parts."

Esclarmonde tried to turn and face him, but the effort proved too painful. Near fainting, she fell back onto the stool and found Folques staring at her bodice, which had become wetted by her lactating breasts.

Folques asked, "Have you ever uttered incantations?"

"You mean prayers?"

"I mean scriptural words falsely manipulated."

She shuddered with alarm. Had the Cistercians somehow learned of her surreptitious study in Jourdaine's chapel? No, that was impossible. She had been alone at all times and had told no one. "If that were a crime, *you* would have hanged by now. Every person here once heard you spew your poesy and seduce maids with words falsely manipulated."

"You play with me, woman!"

The Marquessa shouted, "When it comes to mediating God's mercy, you merit only playing with!"

"You may soon alter that opinion . . . I call Margery de Santi."

The villagers watched in confusion as a foreign-looking woman was led from the carriage and brought before the dais.

Folques asked the new witness, "Do you know this lady?"

The woman shot a vengeful sneer at Esclarmonde. "She was the wife of my dead lord, God rest his soul. I served as their laundress in Gascony."

"Did you witness her activities when Lord L'Isle was away?" asked Folques.

"She bade me to leave her alone in the church on certain days. But I watched her from the sacristy window. I knew she was up to no good."

"And what did you see?"

"She stole a book from the priest's quarters and copied words from it. She wrote them on scraps and whispered them over and over."

"And what did she do with those charms?"

The woman glowered at Esclarmonde with wicked satisfaction. "She threw them into the fire."

Perspiration beaded on Esclarmonde's brow, but she dared not swab it for fear that the act would be seen as a sign of guilt. "I can explain—"

"The playing has only just begun," said Folques. "I next call Mary Peraud."

The guards prodded up the Foix midwife. She cowered in terror under the stern inspection of the Cistercians.

"You delivered the dead infant?" asked Folques.

"And the living one!"

"Was it an unnatural labor?"

The midwife hesitated. "It was queered from the start."

"Could the infant girl have been saved?"

"Only if I cut the lady open."

"Was that remedy not proposed to the mother?"

"Yes, but—"

"And she refused? Placing her life before the salvation of the child?"

The midwife turned toward her fellow villagers to plead the case that she had done nothing wrong. "The viscountess was sufferin' terrible."

Folques reclaimed her attention by pounding his fist on the dais. "Did you mock the Eucharist and draw pentagrams in the birth room?" He nodded ominously in a warning that she had best answer with caution for her own soul.

"I was taught the way by my grandmother."

"Was the boy infant offered the mother's breast?"

"He was."

"And did he take it?"

The midwife glanced helplessly at Esclarmonde. "He refuses her milk."

"A damning portent!" shouted Folques. "The innocent babe recoils from the tainted nourishment of a murderess!"

Almaric forced Esclarmonde to suffer the full impact of that mark of culpability. "What say you to this evidence?"

Starved for sleep, Esclarmonde tried to respond, but her mind was slowed. She had suffered recurring bouts of memory loss during the past weeks. The ravages of the difficult labor and the many blows from Jourdaine's hand had taken a cumulative toll, dulling her senses and slowing her reactions. She closed her eyes in an effort to marshal her thoughts. "The God I love would not consign innocents to a pit of isolation and abandonment."

"All mortals must be baptized by water before they are allowed entry into Heaven," said Almaric. "All are stained by the sin of Adam and Eve, even children. God's laws allow no exceptions!"

"Where in the Scriptures is that stated?"

"Holy Writ is beyond the understanding of the laity," said Almaric. "The Holy Father clarifies and mediates God's Word."

"And bends it to his designs," said Esclarmonde. "This monk who questions me was once a laymen. He took no schooling in theology. How is it that he suddenly gained such insight into God's opinions?"

"Blasphemy!" Almaric turned to his notary. "Record it!"

"Christ never condemned unbaptized children," said Esclarmonde. "Where is it written that He baptized *any* children?"

Almaric glared the murmuring crowd to silence. He had expected insubordination from these primitives, infected as they were by the vilest of beliefs. The heretics taught that only those who fully understood and accepted the teachings of Christ should receive the Holy Spirit. He had been warned that Esclarmonde would attempt to turn the inquest into a debate on scriptural justification. Yet he could not back down now in such a public forum. "Father Augustine affirmed that such infants are relegated to Limbus. There they share the common misery of the damned and are denied the beatific vision."

"Did Jesus not say that he who is baptized and believes shall be saved?" she asked. "Infants have not developed the faculty for belief."

Cornered, Almaric moved to end the proceedings before she could stir the crowd further. "Summarize the evidence!"

Folques was forced to shout over the protests. "This woman conspired by magical means to remain barren! Her conjuring with the Devil cause her to become seeded with the perverse state of duality!"

"Rome was founded by twins!" cried Phillipa. "Does all evil then come from that city?"

Folques spun on Phillipa with an accusing finger. "This woman, a known heretic, conspired with the accused to prevent the baptism!"

Phillipa saw Esclarmonde stumble and falter. She broke through the cordon of guards to brace her and prevent the child from being dropped.

Almaric stood and took a halting step on his deformed leg. "It is the finding of this tribunal that the accused— "

"She must be allowed rebuttal witnesses!" demanded Roger.

Almaric turned his fearsome glare on Loupe, who stood at her father's side. "Has *this* child been baptized?"

Esclarmonde silently begged Roger to say no more lest he place Loupe in danger. At Phillipa's insistence, their daughter had not received the Catholic sacrament. For once, Roger acceded to his sister's better judgment.

Almaric held no illusion about his chances for proving a charge of heresy against Esclarmonde at a full tribunal in Toulouse. But he wielded another cudgel of punishment, one that would admirably serve his purpose this day. "The unbaptised stillborn is denied burial in sacred ground. The son of the deceased Jourdaine of L'Isle will be taken into this church and christened in the true Apostolic Faith. He shall then be remanded as an oblate to the wardship of the Order of St. Bernard."

Esclarmonde rushed the dais. "You'll not take my child!"

Folques forced her back. "The baptism will proceed! Or your brother's child will also be taken into custody!"

Mad with despair, Esclarmonde fell to her knees shrieking and crying. "I've not named him!"

Folques stole the wailing infant from Phillipa's fighting grasp. "His surname has been chosen by the Abbot. He will be called Otto L'Isle, after his paternal grandfather."

Esclarmonde clawed to break past the guards. "The son must also take the name of the mother's lineage! It is the law of our people!"

"He will take the Christian name of his father." Folques lorded his revenge over her as he cradled the infant to ease its crying. There was justice in God's wisdom. This child should have been *his* firstborn. He would raise it as if it were his own.

Esclarmonde reached Montsegur several hours after midnight. Despite the debilitation of her illness, she climbed the crag with her swaddled dead daughter strapped to her back, forced to stop every few steps to gather strength. She finally reached the approach to the summit and found the small dolmen where she and Guilhelm had first kissed. The moon's crescent seemed to dip in grief as if to confirm the destined spot. She knelt there and dug a hole with a knife. Coughing back tears, she placed the tiny body into the shallow grave. "The Church does not permit me to give you a name. Forgive me." She heaved with sobs as she covered the grave with dirt and stones.

A few steps away, the cliffs fell off sharply. She looked down at the welcoming darkness. What blessed relief it would be to walk away from this world. The night would make it easier. She would be eternally damned, for all suicides were denied Heaven. But at least her baby girl would not be alone. She came to the edge and tried to push off. *Do it, coward!* Eyes closed, she released her hold on the boulder and—

Two hands pulled her back.

"Preparation for death takes a lifetime." A hoary old man dropped the hood of his black robe, revealing a flowing white beard.

She fought against his restraint. "Let me die!"

He held her in his embrace until she calmed. "To seek release from this world is the mark of wisdom. But only if accomplished in the manner that allows one to avoid returning to the flesh."

"Who are you?"

He smiled sadly. "You don't remember me?"

The old man's face suddenly came back to her memory—he was the Cathar bishop she had encountered years ago in Lombrives. "My God . . . How did you know I was coming here?"

Guilbert de Castres led her from the precipice. "There is much suffering in this cracked world. You incarnated into this life to show others the way back to the Light."

"My life is in ruins. How could I show a way to anyone?"

"Our people are prisoners trapped in a dark cave," said Castres. "Like you, they are disheartened and blinded. Do you offer them a torch and leave them to their blindness? Or do you show them how to strike the flints?"

Esclarmonde sifted her fevered mind for an answer to the riddle. "The torch would soon go out. They would only be lost again in the darkness."

"The Church of Rome begrudges us a few sparks and commands us to be satisfied with the dimness of our existence. The true god, the God of Light, would have us break the bondage to these priests who monopolize the spiritual sun."

"What kind of God denies an innocent child entry to Heaven?"

"The God of Darkness," he said. "The God of Rome."

"How do you know the God of Rome isn't the beneficent one?"

"The Master said the Almighty created us in His image. Would a loving father send his son to a brutal death to rectify his own misbegotten creation?"

"My babe is doomed to Limbus!"

Castres pressed his palm into the fresh dirt. "No, this precious one has been called home. Be thankful she did not suffer long."

"She was sent here to die? Without even taking a breath?"

"If not for her sacrifice, would you have come to this crisis in your faith?"

Esclarmonde flushed with hope. If the heretic bishop spoke true, her daughter had not been consigned to perpetual darkness after all. Perhaps the babe's suffering had not been in vain. As she looked back on her own life, she saw that everything taught by the priests of the Roman Church had caused her only pain and despair.

"Our sole means of escape from the cycles of incarnation is the gnosis that rids us of ignorance," said Castres. "Rome insists that blind belief alone will offer us salvation. The Pope spawns sacraments for every occasion and demands remuneration to build his towers of Babylon. But his dogmas and creeds are designed to keep us enslaved."

"These mysteries you teach . . . Can they give me back my life?"

"They will bury your old life, not revive it. Our way leads to the ineffable joy sought by the Magi since the beginning of time. But its ascent is difficult and fraught with dangers."

Esclarmonde looked toward the rocks, thousands of feet below. Had it not been for this holy man's intercession, she would be dead. Here, on this pog, her mother had chosen the same path now being offered to her. "My life was meant to end here, on this night. That's the only thing I know with certainty."

"Then end it."

"But you said—"

"Die and be born again in the Light."

"How do I do that?"

"The first step is always the most difficult. You must cast aside the chains of desire and attachment."

Esclarmonde hesitated. "There is a man I love."

Castres took her hand and led her down the pog. "A greater love exists. I will help you find it."

The Lord. . . allowed us to communicate those divine
mysteries, and of that holy Light, to those who are able to receive them.
He did not certainly disclose to the many what did not belong to the many.

- Clement of Alexandria, Stromata

XVI

Foix

April 1206

Esclarmonde was led blindfolded down a long, descending corridor of uneven steps. After being administered a bitter concoction of belladonna and wolfsbane, she was lowered onto a dank surface that smelled of mold and incense. The swish of robes receded and she heard a heavy slab being slid over her head. Minutes passed, then an hour. Yet she could not be certain of the time; the absence of sound and sight combined with the narcotic effect of the brew skewed her senses.

Her breath shallowed and quickened. She had spent the past year meditating and fasting in preparation for this night. Thousands of Cathar credentes, or believers, lived in the Languedoc, but only a few had undergone such rigorous training to attain the highest station of their faith. Shivering from the cold, she tried to turn onto her stomach, but the sarcophagus was too narrow. *We are exiled from our true home, left helpless to find our way back, trapped in the rotting coffin of our physical sheath.* To avoid panicking, she concentrated on a point between her eyes and repeated another tenet of Bishop Castres's teachings: *Seeing involves not seeing something else.* Her skin ignited with heat and a disorienting flash was followed by what appeared to be an image of her body hovering above her. The Bishop had instructed her that all mortals were wrapped in a Robe of Light, an invisible spark of the soul from the divine Sun that was often mistaken for an angel by the uninitiated.

I am not my body. I can see without my eyes.

She willed her Light Body higher until only a slender cord connected it to her heart. She was suddenly propelled through a swirling vortex of opalescent colors. Before her stood two gold-gilt doors with corners embellished by images of a lion, an eagle, a bull, and a bearded man. The portal opened to a grotto that had been carved into shimmering crystal. A knight with his back to her knelt before an alabaster altar and prayed to the Mandylion shroud.

The Holy Image on the cloth came alive.

She was being drawn back into time. She was shown how the frightened Apostles had huddled together in Jerusalem after the crucifixion. In this room of their hiding, Jesus appeared to them in His vitalized Robe of Light. He was blazoned with such blinding illumination that they were required to turn away. The Magdalene placed a linen sydoine over the Master's emanating face and body to singe His features into the cloth. He removed the imprinted shroud and offered it to His disciples as a remembrance, and then He vanished.

In a cascade of successive visions, Esclarmonde witnessed how the future of Christianity was set upon an erroneous and disastrous course in the crucial hours after the Master's return to the Light. Disheartened by His second disappearance, the disciples argued over what they had just witnessed. His brother James and the Magdalene knew that Jesus had come to demonstrate the illusion of the physical body, but Peter and the others insisted that Jesus had been resurrected in the same flesh that had hung on the cross.

When these visions finally receded, the knight on the kneeler turned toward her. Her heart leapt with joy—she rushed into Guilhelm's embrace burning with desire. She was lost in a kiss a hundred times more powerful than their first on Montsegur. She opened her eyes to stare into his loving gaze.

Folques—not Guilhelm—was kissing her.

The Cistercian held her so forcefully that she feared her soul would be stolen through her breath. She knew with a frightening certitude that if she did not escape his clutches, she would suffer a fate worse than bodily death. She began praying the Cathar Pater Noster. "Our Father, who art the Light . . ."

Folques captured her face with his tightening hands. "Who art in Heaven!"

She refused to speak the Roman version of the prayer that had transmogrified Christ's original words. "Hallowed be Thy *hidden* name!"

"Not hidden!" demanded Folques. "It is Jehovah!"

"To Thy Kingdom lead our return!"

"His Kingdom shall come *here*! On Earth! As it is in Heaven!"

"Of Thy nature grant us to learn—"

His hands tightened around her throat. "You must *believe*!"

She fought against his grip. "Give us this day our suprastantial bread and forgive us our trespasses! As we forgive those who trespass against us!"

A searing Light descended and forced Folques to release his hold in order to shield his face. Repelled by the power of the authentic Cathar Prayer, his simulacrum began to dissolve. He raised a host of leavened bread to her in a last desperate plea. "Eat the body of Christ!"

An explosion percussed Esclarmonde backwards.

She was transported to a circular classroom circumscribed by fluted capitals. Castres and three elders, draped in white robes, sat above her. She had never seen the Bishop in any attire but black. She then remembered having been taught that in the Realm of Light, the true nature of a corporeal object is the reverse of what our outer eyes perceive.

"You are in the Temple of the Brotherhood," said Castres.

She heaved from the pounding in her chest, still recovering from Folques's spiritual attack. *How did I get here?*

"By willing it with your heart."

Castres was answering her thoughts before she spoke them. He descended the steps and crowned her with a golden band that held a carved serpent's head and a tail. A buzzing sensation began to build inside her skull. He lifted his staff and cast it to the floor. The rod came alive and slithered toward her feet.

"Why was the Serpent condemned?" he asked.

A jolt of heat shot up the meridian of her core. "Because it tempted Adam and Eve to eat the fruit."

Castres and the elders evaluated the timbre of her responses with equal interest as their content. "What did the serpent have to gain by such a temptation?" Finding her at a loss, Castres answered his own question, "Perhaps the serpent's offer of knowledge was not a temptation, but a selfless sacrifice."

Esclarmonde felt as if she was extracted from normal consciousness—another voice now spoke through her. "The world was flawed at creation. The God of Light wished to send his goodness forth, but the Demiurge imprisoned its sparks in grossness of this world." This was the voice she had heard during every crisis of her life: the voice of her own Robe of Light.

"You have learned to trust your higher self. Ask now, and receive."

"How do I attain enlightenment?"

"The gnosis unfolds like a flower with constant nurturing, and not before its time. Rome would have you believe that a paradise awaits after one lifetime, to be gained by blind obeisance to its laws . . . Did you not experience a sense of recognition when we first met in the cave of Lombrives?"

Yes, she had always been drawn to that mysterious place.

"You and I lived in caves when the Master preached in the Judean desert," said Castres. "We were called Essenes."

"Why was I required to return to the world?" she asked.

"The lost sparks from the central Light reincarnate together, as do the souls of the Dark legions. The two armies have stalked each other since the beginning of the aeons. In Judaea, we failed because we were divided. Some of us chose to fight the Roman oppressors in a wasteful slaughter. We swore off the sword and took refuge in the hills above the Dead Sea to meditate on the Light. We were called perfects."

"As we are now," she said.

"The discipline does not change. We healed the sick and refused to eat the flesh of animals. We kept no personal possessions. Our ways were persecuted, as they always are. Many of us chose suicide rather than submit to the defilements of the Demiurge."

"Were our teachings lost?"

"Manuscripts can be burned and wise men martyred, but the memory of souls will never be destroyed." Seeing her slumped with despond over the prospect of an endless cycle of earthly struggles, Castres reassured her, "The sacred gnosis is only awakened when the Spear has pierced the heart and the Cup has been filled with new blood."

"You mean this knowledge is already within me?"

"'Look not for it over there, or over here,' said the Master. When the serpent rises, the old skin is shed and the new is reborn."

"How am I to know what is real and what is not?"

"The recorded past is the first illusion perpetrated of the Demiurge," he said. "Point your finger at my nose. Is your finger now my nose?"

"Of course not."

"If a road sign says 'I am the Way,' do we worship the sign? Or do we continue on our journey toward our destination?"

"Even a fool would know the answer to that," she said.

"Why then does Rome falsely claim that Jesus is the Godhead?"

She was stunned by the unadorned power of this example. "Why is this not revealed to all?"

"Few have the courage to cast off the blindfold of ignorance, as you have done this night," said Castres. "It is easier to believe than to seek and know. Did the Master not warn us against throwing pearls to swine? Did He not say His parables were only for those who had ears to hear? Did He not promise that we would perform His miracles and more?"

"But what about those who haven't the faculties to learn this?"

"This broken world is not just. The newborn cannot read. Does faith alone allow the babe to learn the alphabet? We are all cast as exiles into a foreign land, unable to speak the language that would free us. Yet the Way is marked for those who seek return to the Light. You must never forget your mission here. You have come back to illuminate the way home for those who will follow."

Before Esclarmonde could ask another question, she was thrust back into her physical body. Her head pounded and her heart ached from a fathomless sadness. She heard the sarcophagus slab being drawn back. Still blindfolded, she was led up the staircase and left standing in the bitter cold. Several minutes passed until she could no longer endure the silence. She pulled off the blindfold to discover the identity of her escorts.

She was alone atop Montsegur.

Not since the courts of love had there been such excitement in Occitania. After undergoing her covert initiation, Esclarmonde announced that she would take the vow of a perfecta. So many dignitaries and countrymen insisted on attending the unprecedented event that Bishop Castres was required to dispense with the tradition of holding the ordination in a modest house. Instead, he made arrangements for her ascension in the chateau of Fanjeaux, a renowned meeting place of troubadours that was situated equidistant from Toulouse, Foix, and Carcassonne. The ancient city sat on a high spur of rock that held the ruins of a Temple to Jupiter and overlooked the Lauragais plains and Montaigne Noir forest.

On the morning of the ceremony, the philandering sun withdrew behind legions of cadaverous clouds that rolled ominously across the pocked plateaux and descended on the spires and rooftops, encompassing the burgh in an oppressive gloom. In an anteroom of the great hall, Esclarmonde prepared for her life-altering step by fasting and praying alone. As the early hours passed, a gradual darkening settled in like a solar eclipse. Since undertaking the regimen of a novitiate, she had become more sensitive to the spiritual signs abounding around her. Shaken, she could not determine if this preternatural occlusion of day was an approval of her worldly denial or an omen of warning.

Roger entered the room to make one last attempt to dissuade her. "The barons have looked the other way when the perfects arrived in their cities. But no noblewoman of your stature has ever openly embraced this Cathar faith."

"No one is requiring you to follow my example."

"This undertaking will cause severe repercussions in Rome. A sister who is a heretic is the sister *of* a heretic.

"You married a heretic."

"My wife does not flaunt her faith before the entire aristocracy of the Languedoc. We will all pay dearly for this conceit of yours."

Hearing her husband's raised voice, Phillipa hurried into the room with Loupe. She tried to calm Roger. "My love, how much more harm can the monks do to us? You must permit her to follow her calling."

Exasperated, Roger made a move to leave, but Esclarmonde called him back. "My vows require that I relinquish all of my possessions."

"Empty your closets into the streets for all I care," he said. "No doubt you'll take great pride in throwing away all that our father sacrificed to give us."

"The perfects have no place to take refuge. I wish to give them Montsegur."

"The Cistercians will deem that a blatant act of defiance!" said Roger.

"The mount is holy," said Esclarmonde. "God gave it to us to protect."

When the belfry chimed to announce the ceremony, Roger stormed out in a huff. Phillipa hugged Esclarmonde and offered up Loupe for a kiss.

The congregation fell silent as Castres escorted Esclarmonde into the hall. The walls shimmered from the light of a hundred streaming candles. Attired in a plain linen tunic, she came to the kneeler on the dais and looked down on the hundreds of Occitan nobles whose fiery reds and satin blues contrasted sharply with the somber garb of the robed Cathars.

Castres commenced the ritual by washing his hands in the ablution bowl. "Where two or three are gathered together in my name, there I am. On this day, Esclarmonde de Foix accepts the life of a perfecta." He raised his hands over her head. "Do you give yourself to God and the Gospel?"

"I do."

"And do you promise that you will eat neither meat nor eggs, nor cheese, and that you shall live on the vegetable of wood and the fish of water, that you will not lie, that you will not swear oaths, that you will not kill, even should your own life be forfeited, that you will not abandon your body to any form of luxury, and that you will never abandon your faith for fear of water, fire, or any other manner of death?"

"I so promise."

Castres held aloft the Gospel of John, whose description of the Light was committed to memory by every member of their faith. "This is the true baptism of the Holy Spirit, given by the hands of Our Lord and his Apostles."

Esclarmonde recited the next verse. "Love not the world, neither the things that are in the world. If any man loves the world, the love of the Father is not in him. For all that is in the world, the lust of the flesh and the lust of the eyes and the pride of life, is not of the Father but is of the world. And the world passeth away and the lust thereof, but he that doeth the will of God abideth forever."

As she spoke, a pall descended over the assembly. The revelry and gaiety of the love courts had long since vanished. Gone were the flirting eyes, the merry dances, the hopes and dreams of a young girl. All the Languedoc now seemed a vast shriveled vineyard that had been worked for too many years.

The damp-eyed nobles joined her in the recitation. "While ye have Light, believe in the Light, that ye may be the children of Light. I am come as a Light unto the world, that whosoever believeth in me should not abide—"

A courier muddied from a forced ride hurried down the aisle and whispered a message to Roger. After a stunned hesitation, Roger stood and announced to the assembly, "On this day, Folques de Marseille has been installed as the Bishop of Toulouse."

A cry of disbelief swept the assembly.

The Marquessa gathered her granddaughter into her arms. "Ah, child, what unhinged world are we leaving you?"

Castres calmed the distraught congregation. When silence was restored, he nodded for Esclarmonde to proceed with her final rite, the public confession.

Esclarmonde was still unsettled by the perverse symmetry of the news. Folques had cynically chosen to make his ascension on the same day as hers. She stood slowly from the kneeler and confessed for all to hear, "I have held pride and vanity in my heart. I ask forgiveness of the Bishop of Toulouse for the injuries I inflicted on his reputation. I pray he will not hold others responsible for my actions."

Roger shouted, "That traitor will never be forgiven!"

Esclarmonde gazed down at Roger with compassion. "I have crossed wills with my brother and have brought him much strife. I fear my decision this day will cause him more. I ask his forgiveness and understanding."

Roger was softened by her unexpected gesture.

She scanned the hall and searched for one more face. Denied in that forlorn hope, she resolved to accept the most difficult of the conditions for her conversion. "I have kept a man in my heart. He has been nearer to me than God Himself. I know not whether he still lives, but I ask his forgiveness for leading him astray from his sacred vows. In what I am about to do, I will break a solemn promise that I once made to him."

Castres draped Esclarmonde's shoulders with a black robe and tied her waist three times with the costi, a belt made from white linen threads. Phillipa presented her with a copy of the New Testament that she had secretly labored on each night for two years, copying the words in Occitan and illustrating the margins. Phillipa and Castres placed the small tome on Esclarmonde's head and supported her at the elbows to transmit the Touch of Love.

A white dove flew through the window and fluttered across the ceiling beams. Startled, Esclarmonde opened her eyes at its flapping. The dove circled and escaped toward a distant hill where a lute player commenced a plangent melody. Several chords into the song, an unseen troubadour accompanied the musician with these words:

> Fear not, my Lady, that thy Love did cruel havoc play,
> What wind shakes not the rooted flower to seed a new spring's lay?
> Look close upon those wetted cheeks so near to thee this day,
> And know if granted second chance, not one would wish away.

Esclarmonde's heart leapt at the familiar voice. Could it truly be him? Had he received the news of her conversion and come back to claim her? Why did he wait until this last hour?

> As for this mismatched troubadour, who carries blade not tune,
> His Love is not the mannered type that dies without the swoon.
> He begs, before his soul God calls, she grant one final boon,
> That from the holy peak again they'll gaze Diana's moon.

No longer able to deny herself the temptation, she turned and searched the horizon for the singer of the monody. There was no one on the knoll. Had it only been her imagination? Here was the last chance to change her mind before the ritual kiss sealed her fate. Cruel world. She found Castres staring at her intently, awaiting her decision. Had the Bishop contrived this vision as a final test? She lowered her eyes and prayed for the strength to release Guilhelm from her heart, then she nodded her readiness for the final acclamation.

"This day," pronounced Castres, "you are reborn of the Spirit."

The knights and ladies in the audience turned to one another and exchanged the Cathar Kiss of Peace. They filed up in a single line to offer Esclarmonde the ritual greeting of the Melioramentum and genuflected three times before asking of her the traditional blessing:

"Help me, Perfecta, to make a good death."

Part Two

The Vineyards of Death

1206-1231 AD

To know is more than to believe.

— Clement of Alexandria

It is not I alone whom the Holy Spirit visits.
I have a large family on earth, and at certain times, on
certain days, and at certain places, the Spirit gives Light.
- A Cathar prisoner's confession

XVII

Montsegur

October 1206

alfway up the sinuous climb, Esclarmonde begged a moment's rest
to catch her breath. Finding Loupe staring at her with the silent
verdict that she had become old, Esclarmonde smiled ruefully and
accepted her niece's judgment as unassailable.

Chandelle, holding fast to Loupe's hand, was drawn toward a small clearing near the path. Her blind eyes suddenly filled with tears from some inward
terror. "It feels hot over there. Like fire."

Esclarmonde brought the sensitive child into her embrace. "Whatever it is,
love, it's only in your mind and cannot harm you."

The company of these two girls, both now five years old, had done much
to ease the grief that she had suffered after Guilhelm's disappearance and the
loss of her son to the Cistercians. Corba had sent Chandelle to Foix for a week's
visit, and though the girls were starkly different in both features and temperament, they immediately became inseparable. The blonde, wispy Chandelle wore
a perpetual smile as if unaware that another expression was possible. There was
the clairvoyant wisdom of the ancient sibyl in her silky voice; she often cobbled
together the most astonishing juxtapositions of descriptions and observations.
She was not been embittered by her blindness, but reveled in the gifts offered

by her other senses, laughing in ecstatic pleasure at the unexpected trilling of a lark or the whiff of a sage bloom.

The taller, dark-complexioned Loupe was a few months younger than Chandelle but more precocious in strength and willfulness. Her distrustful eyes resembled hard black currants and her narrow face shadowed so swiftly with rankled emotion that those around her remained perpetually on guard for the inevitable tantrums. Fiercely protective, she would gambol through the village with her new companion playing knightly escort with a wooden sword and thwacking the knee of any malingerer who dared look askance at them. She had inherited her aunt's questioning nature and her father's saturnine, pugnacious temperament, a mixture that Esclarmonde feared would one day prove volatile.

Despite such antipodal personalities, the girls did share one trait: a craving to hear more about Esclarmonde's childhood adventures. Spurred by their pleas, Esclarmonde had decided it was time they visited the holy mountain.

Loupe interrupted her nibbling on a carrot to ask, "Did you once love a troubadour, Aunt Essy?"

Chandelle nudged Loupe, whispering, "Momma said never mention that."

Esclarmonde found a seat on a boulder and ran her fingers across the pocked surface heated by the midday sun. She recognized the clearing as the spot where she and Guilhelm had first held hands. She nestled closer to the girls, then answered Loupe's question, "I did . . . but now I love God."

"Can't you love a boy and God at the same time?" asked Chandelle.

"God's the biggest boy," explained Loupe. "He'd beat the others up."

Esclarmonde conceded with a bittersweet sigh, "Sometimes what we want is not what God wishes for us."

"So God wanted Chandelle to be blind?" demanded Loupe.

Esclarmonde never failed to be taken aback by the alacrity with which Loupe's vehemence could surface without warning. Yet she herself would have asked the same perforating question in her youth. "I think there are two gods, a good one and a bad one. The good God never wanted Chandelle to be blind. But when our souls became lost, the bad god captured us and put us into bodies."

"Like the Devil," insisted Loupe.

Esclarmonde stroked Loupe's curly black hair while searching how best to explain something quite complicated. "The pope in Rome says that the original sin of our first ancestors caused Chandelle to be born blind. But you must never let anyone tell you what to believe if it doesn't feel right. The good God talks to all people, and He will talk to you if you ask."

Chandelle sensed that the answer had left Loupe unsatisfied. "It's okay."

Loupe exploded to her feet. "The good God should never have let the bad God do it!" She grabbed Chandelle's hand and raced up the path in a rage.

"Come back!" ordered Esclarmonde. "You mustn't run!" The girls disappeared into the scrub brush. In her haste to catch them, she stumbled on a burrow hole and wrenched her knee. She tried to stand but the sharp pain sent her crumpling back to the ground. "Loupe! Where are you?"

Loupe came hurrying back, her face contorted in fear. "Chandy's fallen!"

Esclarmonde crawled in anguish toward the crevice. A wide section of the path had caved in. Through the fissure she saw Chandelle, bloodied and thrashing near a parlous ledge several feet below. A few garrigue roots were all that kept the lip of the rocks from avalanching. "Chandelle, don't move!"

Disoriented, Chandelle groped the ground. "Where am I?"

Esclarmonde searched for a way down, but the rift was too narrow. Loupe could not ride alone to Foix. If she herself tried to go, she would need Loupe's support to make it down the pog. Chandelle would be left helpless. She went blank with panic. Loupe bolted from her grasp and squeezed past two boulders, lowering herself down along the edge of the cliff.

"No!" cried Esclarmonde.

Loupe wiggled through the narrow cleft and slid from rock to rock. Her hand dislodged a clod. Slabs of shale crumbled off and narrowly missed Chandelle. Loupe lost her balance but broke her fall by grasping a branch. If the larger boulders cut loose, both she and Chandelle would be crushed.

Despite the pain of her injury, Esclarmonde knelt on the precarious scarp and pressed her hands together in desperate supplication. This mount had taken her mother and daughter. She could not bear the thought of it also devouring these two girls.

Build it here.

She searched for the source of that command. On the summit, the sun's rays fell on the ruins of the ancient chateau. The outline of the rubble seemed to have transformed into an image of a ship, docked and ready for a deluge.

My Ark of Light.

She did not understand the enigmatic utterance, but she promised to find a way to obey it if only the girls were saved. In that instant, clouds sailed overhead and swept shadows across the cliff, causing her to look down.

Loupe was leading Chandelle to the safety of an overhanging cleft. "I'm sorry, Chandy," Loupe repeated. "I'll never leave you again."

Although her knee was still swollen, Esclarmonde insisted on returning to Montsegur a fortnight later. A few nights earlier, she had been visited with a fleeting dream of the ark that she had been commanded to build. Assisted by Castres and Raymond de Perella, she managed the onerous climb with difficulty and led the two men past the Visigoth ashlars scattered across the summit. She had delayed revealing the reason for their journey for fear they would dismiss her plan outright before she could defend it.

Castres lost patience with her coyness. "Now, child, what is this undertaking of such great secrecy you would have us consider?"

She spoke rapidly to lessen the impact. "I wish to build a temple here."

Castres dropped his eyes in sharp disappointment, but Esclarmonde had steeled herself for the censorious reaction. He had been always been adamant in expressing his distaste for embellished edifices, deeming them seductions of the Demiurge to keep mortals chained to the material world. She persisted, "Our people have nowhere to seek refuge and lift their spirits. Those of the Roman faith are permitted to make pilgrimages to Compostela and Jerusalem."

"We have the mountains and the forests," reminded Castres.

"I once stood in the nave of St. Denis," she said. "The light filtered through its rose window is said to deeply transform all who experience it."

"Thousands could have been fed with the monies wasted on that vanity."

"You teach that we can transfigure our bodies," she said. "Think of the blessings possible if we could speed the work with a configuration of stone."

Her contagious passion for the project gave Castres pause. "What sort of temple do you have in mind? We don't possess the coffers of the Vatican."

"The night of my entombment . . ."

Castres frowned at her cavalier mention of the ritual. Sensing the Bishop's unease, Raymond retreated to a far corner, aware that certain matters could only be discussed by initiates. When alone with Esclarmonde, Castres whispered, "You were buried to experience the true nature of death and rebirth."

"Buried in stone," she reminded him. "Why not create that transforming experience on a grander scale for all who come here?"

"The gnosis could be stolen and misused."

"The wisdom can be concealed from those not worthy of it."

"Concealed how?"

"With the vibrations of sacred form." When that possibility was not immediately rejected, Esclarmonde called up their escort before the Bishop could change his mind. "Raymond, I'd have you rebuild this chateau."

Raymond waited for Castres to countermand the impractical request, certain that the wise cleric would never sanction such a folly. But Castres merely shrugged to indicate that he had already lost that battle. Incredulous, Raymond prosecuted his protest alone. "I have no means for such an undertaking."

"I will raise the funds," said Esclarmonde. "And you'll have no shortage of volunteers. It will be a special place."

Raymond shook his head as he scanned the rocky spine. "This terrain is too severe and uneven to support towers and battlements."

She smiled with the memory of Guilhelm offering a similar tactical assessment. "It won't be a defensive fortress. More like a cathedral. I intend to commission masons from Toulouse, men branched from the Druidic schools who will be in sympathy with our faith."

"The quarry contracts would have to be drawn up immediately if we're to commence the work by spring," said Raymond.

"We won't wait for the thaw," she said. "I've already sent orders to Lavalanet for scaffolding timber. I want to celebrate the spring equinox inside its walls."

That winter, hundreds of perfects and laymen from the far reaches of Occitania converged on Montsegur to help build Esclarmonde's temple. The snow-shrouded pog resembled a giant anthill as one line of black-robed volunteers hauled up material on sleds while a second line descended to repeat the task. On the summit, the women stoked bonfires to boil soup in giant cauldrons and provide beacons visible from ten leagues away. The troubadours competed with the screech of mortise chisels and carpenter planes and took turns singing chansons to inspire the workers.

Two months into the preparations, Esclarmonde decided that the auspicious moment had arrived for the laying of the plat. Accompanied by Phillipa, Corba, and the girls, she walked across the crag and unrolled a ball of cord knotted in the sacred proportions while a musician played a lute at her side. "Listen," she instructed. "The harmony is sweeter in certain places."

Corba shot a look of exasperation at Phillipa, questioning if their mutual friend had gone soft in the head.

Esclarmonde gathered up Chandelle into her arms. "You can tell the difference, can't you, Little Candle?"

The blind child nodded and swayed with the music.

Watching this strange ritual with unchecked contempt was the project's master mason, a bald Provencal named Berengar, who had a round, sunburnt face and thick hands gnarled from fifty years of working stone. He dismissed her intuitions as womanly nonsense, having argued for the enclosed cruciform plan used in cathedrals. But Esclarmonde would approve no design that incorporated the Roman cross. Instead, she had opted for a more ancient method of determining the temple's appropriate shape. She was convinced that telluric lines of a healing force, heated by underground streams, coursed through the pog's limestone shafts. On certain days, the effect was as if mercurial serpents slithered up the tail of the rock toward the highest point.

When Esclarmonde had finished her dowsing, the perfects and laborers stood atop the stones to examine what she had traced: A five-sided structure whose corners, when connected, would form an elongated pentagram. A rectangular chapel would crown its northern end.

Castres was astonished by the result. He had never confided to Esclarmonde that their faith treasured the power of the pentagram, whose points embodied the soul of Light entrapped within the four corners of the world's foundation stone. The ancient graves of his Bogomil ancestors in Bulgaria were engraved with the esoteric symbol to represent the inner heart of the divine spark. He blessed her layout with his arms raised in benediction. "It is divinely inspired."

That night, after the masons and perfects retired to their lodgings, Castres led Esclarmonde to a flat area within the staked enclosure. "Your geomancy was more accurate than you know." With a spade, he dug into the hardpan and exposed a hewn capstone that opened to an underground grotte.

Esclarmonde realized that they were standing on the spot where she had been abandoned on the night of her secret initiation.

Castres replaced the capstone and concealed it with pounded dirt. "We bury our perfects in a necropolis below to hide the bodies from the Romans. I've been thinking about what you said about our need to preserve the mysteries. I haven't many more years to live. I must find a way to ensure that the location of this grotte is not lost."

Esclarmonde studied the perimeter of the scarp and tried to imagine how the temple would look when completed. The moon, attended by the constellation of Sirius, crowned the St. Barthelemy massif to the west. This pog was a natural observatory of the heavens. Struck by an epiphany, she led Castres to the cabins along the north ridge and pounded on the master mason's door.

A grumpy voice inside bellowed, "The guild requires no work at night!"

She had learned during their many arguments that the gruff mason could not resist a challenge in Pythagorean geometry. Winking at Castres, she said in mock resignation, "I told you we were wasting our time. Only the Paris masons know how to determine the cardinal points without a compass."

The door flew open. Berengar, in his nightshirt, confronted them. "Overpaid chisel hacks! I can do that with one eye closed! You calculate the high and low reaches of the sun on the shortest and longest days of the year. Divide the angle to find east and west, then draw right angles for north and south."

Esclarmonde primed the mason's conceit. "Can you also predict the precise angle of the sun between two points?"

"Of course! Angles! The world is angles!"

"Then it is possible to construct archere slits on opposing walls to focus the sun into a ray that would travel the length of the temple during the solstices?"

The mason warmed to her conundrum. "It has been done."

"And at some point on the ground, the solstice rays would cross?"

"The dawn would have to be unimpeded by clouds," said the mason. "And the same person would have to be present on both solstice days to discover the spot where the lines intersect."

Esclarmonde smiled at Castres in conspiracy. "I wonder who would choose to climb this mount every solstice?"

"Only an initiate," said Castres, finishing her thought.

The mason's eyes widened. "Sun worship? I'll not abet idolatry!"

"Rest your fears, brother," said Castres. "The fiery orb merely represents the outer manifestation of the Kingdom of Light. By mapping the heavens, we will locate the secrets of the constellations within our hearts."

"Even if what you say is true, the monks will accuse me of devilry."

"The purpose of the design will never be disclosed," promised Castres.

Esclarmonde marked an "X" in the middle of her drawing to indicate the concealed entry to the necropolis. "The alignment of the slits must be so precise that the solstice rays will cross here, at a location we will reveal only to you."

Berengar's look of astonishment confirmed his growing realization that Esclarmonde was much more clever than he had first believed.

At dawn on Easter morning, the day chosen for the temple's dedication, Esclarmonde lay awake in her hut below the crag. Too excited to sleep, she climbed from her pallet and found Chandelle sitting up and listening to the chirping of the blue jays. She placed a finger to the child's lips in a warning not to awaken her mother. "Shall we go bathe?" Hand in hand, they walked to the gurgling Lasset creek. The lit tapers on the summit flared above the beeches. Castres and the perfects had spent the night atop the pog, fasting and preparing for the ceremony. She left Chandelle on the bank and waded into the cold stream. The sun was just breaking over the horizon, but the morning was still dark enough that she felt safe in removing her robe and allowing it to cleanse. Minutes into the bath, her solitude was interrupted by a tornado of leaves on the hoar-frosted ground.

"Remove yourself from my sight, despicable Eve!"

She sank to her neck and retrieved her robe. In the water's reflection, she saw a tonsured monk, barefoot and clad in a ragged black habit with a hood that dropped to his waist. He had long eyelashes and a sallow forehead stained with a quarter-moon birthmark. He leapt from his lean-to, scattering a ratty knapsack filled with notebooks, and began flogging his back with birch twigs.

How odd, she thought; perfects always traveled in pairs. "Who are you?"

The monk kept his welted back turned. "Away, Satan! Tempt me not with voluptuous flesh! I call upon the legions of St. Michael to chase you!"

"Remove yourself! I am equally entitled to enjoy God's creation."

"Aunt Essy?" cried Chandelle, frightened by the man's voice.

"It is only a perfect who has lost his way," said Esclarmonde.

Hearing the Cathar denomination for a cleric, the pigeon-legged monk girded for spiritual warfare by signing his breast three times with the Roman cross. "Give up the black tunic of sin, woman!"

"Your garb is the same color as mine."

The monk looked down in horror at his habiliment, severely vexed why God would allow such similarity to abide. "Allow me at least to save the child. I've installed a new convent in Fanjeaux. Only this week I returned to Christ two wayward souls whose simple minds were overwhelmed by your false doctrines."

"If their minds were so simple," she asked, "how is it they came to understand the superiority of yours?"

The monk's face filled with a vein-raised fury. "Faith, woman! Faith! God makes amends for His lesser creatures who, like you, have not the faculties to comprehend the logic of His cosmic plan."

"Do you have a name? Or does your pious humility preclude such vanity?"

"I am Dominic Guzman. Prior of the cloister in Osma."

She was puzzled how a monk from Espagna could have strayed so far from home. "You are the lost one. Castile is on the other side of the mountains."

"I know where I stand, both in this world and the next. I've come here to seek out the heresiarch Guilbert de Castres."

"What is it you want from him?"

"Capitulation unto God's righteous judgment! My superior, Bishop Diego de Osma, proposes a challenge. Four clergy of our True Faith shall hold a disputation with your sorcerers in Pamiers on the fourth Sunday of next month."

"And who is to judge this disputation?"

"Arnaud de Crampagna, if it be any of your womanly concern. The man is a Waldensian, a fallen soul. Yet so assured is our victory that even a stray dog will choose God's path over the briars of heretical iniquity."

Esclarmonde backstroked to the far bank. "I will convey your request, but I cannot promise to do justice to its condescending tone."

Oblivious to her sarcasm, Dominic lugged his meager belongings over his shoulder. "It is your misfortune, sister, that you'll not witness the glorious refutation. Many eyes and ears shall be opened." He looked up and for the first time saw the torches atop Montsegur's temple. "What is that shining tower?"

"A lighthouse. Built to guide those like you who are cast adrift."

As Dominic disappeared into the forest, he twisted his face in confusion, unable to comprehend the need for such a beacon with no sea nearby.

The temple's dedication was delayed by Esclarmonde's report of the Castilian's challenge. The Cathar hierophants hurriedly convened in their new adytum to decide if they should agree to the proposed disputation. Among them were Pons Jourdaine de Verfeil, Benoit de Termes, Arnaud Othon de Cabaret, and Lady Giraude de Lavaur, the perfecta who had nursed Esclarmonde to health. The Marquessa, Corba, and the girls remained in the bailey with those who had not been initiated into the higher mysteries.

"This monk Guzman is called the Spanish Mangonel for good reason," warned Bernard Marti, the filius major, second in rank for the Cathars behind Bishop Castres. "He hurls curses like shots from engines. The challenge is a snare set by the Cistercians!"

"If entrapment is indeed their intent," said Castres, "then their bait is the hope that we'll lose the resolve to risk our faith against their theologians."

"I have met this Waldensian they've chosen to arbitrate," said Giraude. "He loves the jangle of coins and cannot be trusted."

"Transcripts of the disputation will be circulated across Christendom," said Castres. "We'd reach thousands who might never hear us otherwise."

"Ours is a faith of the heart, not the mind," reminded Giraude. "We have never excelled in the hairsplitting arguments of the Romans."

"If one soul might be saved," asked Castres, "is it not worth the risk?"

As the eldest of the initiates, Giraude was afforded great respect in her counsel. She contemplated the dilemma for an extended moment before cautioning the Bishop, "Guzman hails from a family steeped in the military orders of Santiago. He will attack us like a caballero against the walls of Toledo."

Castres was given pause by her concern. He turned to Esclarmonde and asked, "Child, you looked into his eyes. Do you think him honorable?"

"He sleeps on the bare earth and ignites the leaves with his smoldering faith," said Esclarmonde. "He is also full of himself and schooled in the artifice of rhetoric. But I don't believe him to be deceitful."

"Then we shall accept the challenge," said Castres.

Marti came to the Bishop's side to show his support for the decision. "Who else shall accompany us?"

"I will take only one," said Castres.

"We will be overwhelmed!" said Marti. "At least allow Pons or Arnaud to join us."

Castres braced his longtime subordinate with a hand to the perfect's shoulder. "Take no offense, Bernard . . . but I intend to have Esclarmonde with me."

The initiates met that announcement with a stunned silence. Marti had always accompanied the Bishop on the preaching tours. Humble as he was, he could not dissemble his wounded pride. "She is untried," said Marti. "And the Catholics will not suffer a woman to debate theology in their presence."

"She is more versed in Scripture than any man here," said Castres. "If the Romans refuse to accept her participation, the rot of their spurious religion will be exposed."

With a manner of grave concern, Giraude took the Bishop aside for a private conference. "This confrontation may well determine our fate, Guilbert. No one denies that she has a quick wit and an impressive knowledge of the gospels. But she has never been subjected to the ruthless tactics that the Cistercians will bring against us. You must choose wisely."

Castres pressed Giraude's hands in great affection, but he remained firm in his decision. He then announced to all, "Now, we must not allow our day's celebration to be delayed further. Esclarmonde, you said you have something to present to us on this momentous occasion?"

From behind the altar, Esclarmonde brought forth a draped frame and removed its covering. The Easter sun broke through the embrasure and bathed the Mandylion sydoine with a brilliance so intense that the chamber dazzled.

The perfects descended to stunned genuflections. Castres approached the relic with tears of joy. "I saw this precious cloth as a boy in Constantinople. It is the remembrance of the Master's Robe of Light." He turned to Esclarmonde in amazement. "How did you come into its possession?"

"The Templar brought it back from the East."

With palsied hands, Castres reached into his knapsack and unrolled the Nasorean gospel that he had carried with him since coming to Occitania. "Could there be a more profound sign of the righteousness of our mission?" He read aloud from a passage in the gospel:

And then, on Easter morning, the disciple Thomas approached Jesus and placed his hand upon the shining Robe of Light. 'Master,' said Thomas, 'You have risen from the dead.'

'Do you not yet understand?' lamented Jesus. 'Those who say that they will die first and rise are in error. Be not deceived. They must receive the resurrection while they live.'

Deeply moved by the benefice, the perfects exchanged the Cathar Kiss of Peace as they walked in emotive silence to the outer sanctum. Lining the path from the chapel were hundreds of credentes and lay Occitans who knelt and petitioned the blessing of the Touch from the holy ones.

When Giraude reached the horseshoe-shaped western gate, she turned back for one last look at the magnificent edifice that Esclarmonde had inspired. "Permit me a moment. I'll not have the strength to make this ascent again. "

The venerated lady began shuffling her feet, turning slowly and swaying with her eyes closed. She was performing the sacred whirling, the dance that she had demonstrated for Esclarmonde years ago in Lavaur. It was the same ritual that the Magdalene had performed in the Jerusalem Temple, the same ecstatic movement that the first Christians had called the Dance of Jesus.

The Marquessa intertwined arms with her old friend Giraude and joined in the dancing. Esclarmonde clasped hands with Corba, Phillipa, and the girls, and together they surrounded the two grande dames, whirling and fusing the Midnight Sun with the serpent of the mountains, as Pyrenean women had always done in bygone days when great stones were brought together.

Now seekers after knowledge must
know exactly how to make out true orthodoxy
for themselves by using natural examples; and especially such as we
draw from our very selves, for they are surer and are a true means of proof.
- St. Gregory the Sinaite, Discourse on the Transfiguration

XVIII

Pamiers

May 1207

"This is a leper colony of the faithless!"

The audience crowded within the great hall of Apamea Castle turned toward the monk who had shouted that incendiary charge.

Jangling from a chain strapped to his loins, Dominic Guzman strode through the rear doors. Halfway to the dais, he fell to his knees in an ecstatic seizure. Those spectators who were perched on the rafters leaned down for a closer glimpse of the infamous Castilian whose neck crawled with the strands of a hair shirt. After nearly a minute of this inert prostration, the monk arose in a whirl of flailing arms, his exerting face pigmented in the shade of breath-deprived aubergine. "Mutilate my limbs! Display my hacked arms before my eyes! I beg to share the agony of Christ!"

Dominic's entrance had the scattering effect of a hound sticking its nose into a chicken coop. Yet the animus of the Occitans at this fulmination paled in comparison to that ignited by the arrival of his fellow Catholic disputants. Crowned with a miter, Folques walked down the aisle basking in the indignation. Accompanying him were Bishop Diego de Osma, an ancient Spaniard with a haggard face, and Peter de Castelnau, a sneering firebrand sent by Rome to monitor the proceedings. A column of Cistercian monks trailed the delegation with the disciplined step of a conquering legion.

Roger de Foix erupted from his seat to confront Folques. "I told you never to set foot in this county again."

"As I predicted," said Folques. "The cloggers have no stomach to stand against us." He taunted Roger to reach for his sword, welcoming any pretext to impose harsh measures on the recalcitrant Southern nobles.

Arnaud de Crampagna, the Waldensian mendicant chosen to judge the debate, separated them. "This is a day for the clash of theologies, not arms."

"If it were my decision, we wouldn't waste breath arguing with fools," said Folques. "Be advised, Wolf. The Holy Father has ordered King Philip to cleanse the festering heretic squalor on his borders."

"That provocation will be met in kind!" warned Roger.

Dominic silenced their squabbling. "I am here to save souls!"

Folques shunted Roger aside and resumed his advance toward the dais. He paused at the front row expecting to find Esclarmonde seated with Phillipa. "I see your consort in sin chose not to attend. No doubt she foresaw the outcome."

Phillipa refused him the satisfaction of a glance. "Perhaps she detests the company of kidnappers."

Folques ignored the insult and stepped grandly onto the rostrum. With a sweep of his white-gloved hand, he pointed to the two empty chairs set opposite the Catholic position. "Can they find only two heretics in all Occitania willing to submit to our scrutiny?"

The Catholics laughed and hooted—until Castres emerged from the side door with Esclarmonde at his side.

Folques had removed his mitre and was about to lower to his chair when he froze in mid-descent. "You expect us to contend . . . with *her*?"

"If a minstrel can be transformed into a bishop," asked Castres, "are not all things possible?"

Dominic circled Esclarmonde, his chains chiming with each step. Suddenly, her face came back to him from their encounter below Montsegur. He turned away from her with sour disdain as if by a feat of concentration he could remove her from God's creation. "Had Christ meant for the weak of mind to preach the Word, He would have been born a woman."

"And if He wished both men and women to preach?" asked Esclarmonde. "Would he have entered the world with a beard *and* a bosom?"

The crowd roared with laughter. Castres chastened her with an admonitory eye for the quip. She had been instructed to limit her participation to whispering scriptural references, but she could not allow such inanities to go unchallenged.

"Our Lord took no females as apostles," insisted Dominic.

"Mayhaps the writers of *your* gospels chose not to reveal them," she said.

Dominic raised his fluttering eyes to the heavens as if channeling the saints. "St. Paul wrote in Timothy 2:12: 'I permit no woman to teach or have authority over men. She is to keep silent.'"

She countered, "He also wrote in Galatians 3:28: 'There is neither male nor female, for you are all one in Christ Jesus.' Apparently he could not make up his mind. One wonders why we women are always accused of inconstancy."

"Go back to your spinning, widow!" shouted Castelnau.

The Occitan nobles shot to their feet, incensed by the papal legate's contumely. Bernard de Grenac, a knight from the Count of Toulouse's court, leapt to the dais and drove Castelnau against the wall. "Speak basely to this lady again and I'll show you a religion forged of steel!"

Castelnau fought him off. "Your liege stinks of the heresy!"

Esclarmonde had fully expected the Catholics to foment violence. Her Cathars had the most to lose if the disputation were suspended; the Romans would cite such an altercation as evidence that its arguments for orthodoxy could not be countered. She stepped between the two men before blows could be landed and shouted above the din of threats, "Jesus Himself said that to achieve perfect consciousness, male and female must be perceived as one!" Her tactic had the desired effect—all turned on her in astonished silence.

"Nowhere in the gospels is such vile statement to be found!" said Dominic.

"That is because your gospels do not contain the full truth," she said. "There are other accounts of Christ's teachings. Suppressed accounts."

"Polemics fabricated by schismatics," dismissed Castelnau. "Judgment was rendered on the sins of the Greeks when Constantinople fell."

"And did your god also order the nuns of that Christian city to be raped and murdered by the Holy Father's crusaders?"

"The Church sheds no blood!" insisted Folques.

"No, you exhort the butchery with assurances of Heaven's attainment," she said. "But you shed no blood."

Dominic resorted to rapid-fire retorts in an attempt to overwhelm her. "You judge against rightful wars?"

"We judge against all wars." Her initial nervousness gave way to a rising confidence. All of the years she had spent in secret study of Scriptures now seemed in preparation for this moment. She knew she could stand with these men. "Did not Our Lord command Peter to sheath his sword in the Garden of Sorrows?"

Dominic played on the sentiments of those present who had taken up the Cross. "This woman would allow the infidel to trample the Holy Sepulcher!"

"And where was your god during that star-crossed quest?" she asked. "The Latin Kingdom has been reduced and Jerusalem is lost."

Folques was so eager to rebut her that he shoved Dominic aside. "If you have writings on these matters, produce them. We will test them against the ordeal of fire. If they leap from the flames unscathed, God's sign of their righteousness will be confirmed."

"Cast your own gospels first," said Esclarmonde. "If what you propose is a true test and they levitate unharmed, we'll match the demonstration."

"I'll stoke the flames!" shouted the Marquessa.

Thrown on the defensive, Dominic turned to the Waldensian and insisted, "The woman must be banned from debating God's word!"

The arbiter took careful measure of the tinderbox mood in the hall. After a hesitation, he ruled, "The lady seems capable enough. She may participate."

The assembly clamored its approval, galvanized by the prospect of a bedazzling agon between the famous monk and priestess.

Esclarmonde nodded in gratitude to the Waldensian. She wondered if Giraude had in fact misjudged him. He was the leader of a harassed sect from Lyons who, like her Cathars, sought to spread Holy Writ in the vernacular. She suspected that the Cistercians had chosen the mendicant as arbiter because he did not wish to split from the Church of Rome, only reform it. They no doubt based their choice on the old adage that rival heretics were like cats in a sack: They would claw each other to death before attacking the rat. Yet she began to hold out hope that the Cistercians had been too clever by half.

Folques stood in front of Castres to prevent Esclarmonde from coming to his aid. "Admit that you deny the stain of original sin."

"Nowhere in your own canon is the responsibility— "

Dominic cut off the Cathar bishop's attempt to respond. "In Genesis! Adam was seduced by Eve!"

Castres's inchoate thought splintered into lost fragments. He struggled to regain his faltering focus, having never confronted the sharp-elbowed style polemics in which disputants teamed to hurl ripostes. He stammered in an effort to counter the Castilian who spit his points like a hissing snake.

Esclarmonde led her bishop to his seat and answered for him. "The Old Testament is the chronicle of the Demiurge. We do not recognize the legitimacy of the work or the archon that authored it."

Dominic blinked rapidly as if flipping scriptural pages across his mind's eye. "The dualist rears her dragon's head! A god who is not unique is not god."

Esclarmonde had trained for the disputation by walking alone in the woods and projecting her voice to the birds, mimicking the dramaturgical elocution of the troubadours who drew their verses from deep within the viscera. She now put that practice to the test. "A god who is all-powerful cannot abide suffering and still be good."

Dominic had never heard a woman speak with such authority on theological matters. "A righteous God is Yahweh!"

"And jealous god, by His own admission," she said. "Is He not also all-powerful and all-knowing?"

"He is! And He sees your evil ways this day!"

Folques edged up on his chair to warn the Castilian against traveling down that slippery slope. "What Brother Dominic means—"

Esclarmonde pressed the point home before Dominic could be saved. "So, if God is both all-knowing and jealous, there must be other gods. Otherwise, He would have no reason to be jealous, for he could not be jealous of an inferior being. There *is* another god. The God of Light. The God who opposes Yahweh of the Pharisees."

Folques glared at Dominic with disgust. The reckless Castilian had fallen for the same trap that snared him years ago in the Foix court of love. He had replayed that fateful exchange a thousand times. Had he kept silent that day, he and Esclarmonde might still be lovers. Now the Lord had given him a second chance. He walked across the dais to demand that the feeble Castres answer his question. "If there *are* two gods, as this woman claims, what proof is there that *yours* is not the God of Darkness masquerading as the beneficent deity?"

Castres looked to Esclarmonde for assistance. She leaned to whisper a suggested answer, but Folques quashed her attempt, insisting, "You must speak directly to the assembly! Those are the rules!"

Caressing her bishop's hand, Esclarmonde spoke this time in such a subdued voice that the Catholics were required to tilt closer. "I was suggesting to him that we might benefit from examining how Yahweh treated His people. But I must confess that I am as perplexed by your wishes as I am of your Church's commandments. First, you order me to remain silent. Now you instruct me to speak louder so that all might hear."

The Marquessa screeched with delight.

Red-faced, Folques could only manage a weak nod for her to continue.

The hot intensity of Esclarmonde's coal-black eyes threatened to set the chamber ablaze. "Yahweh ordered a bear to maul the children of Bethel, but the God of Light said we should all be as children. Yahweh commanded the massacre of all Canaanites in Jericho, but the God of Light tells us to love our enemies. Yahweh created Adam and Eve, then withheld all essential knowledge while cruelly imbuing them with an insatiable hunger for it. He exiled them, persecuted their descendants, burdened them with laws of prohibition, threatened them with annihilation, and carried out the threat by wiping out humanity with a flood." She raised her voice to drive the dagger to its hilt. "And when the children of Noah returned, Yahweh started over by hurling fires and catastrophes on them again!"

A lute player twanged a fortissimo chord to punctuate her winning point.

Dominic jangled to his feet, his preening arrogance unraveling like a rolling ball of twine. "The Jews deserved to be punished! They worshipped idols and murdered Our Lord!"

Esclarmonde exposed the shrillness of Dominic's diatribe by modulating her own tone. "There was one Jew who did not worship idols. By Yahweh's admission, Job was a righteous man. And yet Yahweh inflicted suffering on him merely to enjoy a wager with Satan. What father tortures his own son to atone for the sins of his family? Do we throw the son into prison for the debts of the father? You would have us worship a god who does precisely that."

The audience bolted to its feet with raucous applause.

Face scorched, Dominic pressed the hair shirt against his chest, as if by distressing his flesh he could gainsay the power of her refutations. "The venerable Augustine clearly demonstrated how a woman caused—"

"The Bishop of Hippo was himself a dualist at heart." Esclarmonde would not allow the monk to gain wind for his billowy sails. "He transformed his self-loathing into such hatred for my sex that one wonders how he ever looked upon a statue of the Virgin. You cannot have it both ways, Brother Guzman. Either your god is all powerful and responsible for evil, or He is in constant battle with an equally potent god of darkness."

Intrigued, Bishop Diego grasped Dominic's arm for assistance to arise. He was a Catholic version of Castres; both were tired old men whose faith was of the heart, not the head; both had been worn down by the wrangling of youthful minds. His trips on horseback to Denmark to find a wife for the Castilian Infanta had worsened his fragile health, but the Holy Father refused his pleas for retirement. To enforce his obedience on this mission against the heretics,

Innocent had saddled him with the legate Castelnau, whose invective was so incendiary that he had already received several assassination threats.

"My lady, I see a different world than do you," said Diego, softly. "The harmony of the birds flying to the south in winter, the sun breaking the horizon on a crisp fall morning. Is there not a Oneness in all of this?"

Esclarmonde mirrored the aged cleric's gentleness. "Have you not also seen starving wolves tear at their own pups for sustenance? Is not nature itself imbued with both good and evil?"

"But Christ died to change all of that."

"Then He died in vain. For evil still pervades the world."

Dominic prowled the dais, tortured by their civil exchange. Unable to endure it further, he pointed a waspish finger at Esclarmonde in accusation. "Enough of this sophistry! You trample the crucifix!"

Castres came to her defense. "Does the condemned man worship the garrote? The Demiurge seduces us with the illusion that the body is real."

"Our Lord is nothing but a spectre to you cloggers!" charged Folques.

"The Master came to show us the way back home," said Castres.

"To Heaven!" corrected Dominic.

"Not to Heaven," said Esclarmonde. "Christ taught that we should not look for the Kingdom here or over there. He said the Kingdom is attainable in this life without physical death."

"A blasphemy against the Resurrection of the flesh!" shouted Castelnau.

Esclarmonde refused to be cowed. "When your flocks discover that the Kingdom of Light can be gained without the Church—"

Folques tried to shout her down. "If you hide heretical writings with such false claims, they will be your undoing!"

"Why should people not be allowed to read what they wish?" she asked.

Folques held up a Bible to demand its obeisance. "Laymen untrained in theology are incapable of understanding the Word."

"So *your* god made *our* nature inferior?" she asked.

Dominic double-teamed her. "He made us exactly the way He wished!"

"Why then did He have to save us from ourselves?"

Exasperated, Dominic flogged the air with his floppy sleeves. "What salvation would you claim for us, woman?"

Esclarmonde suppressed a prescient smile. She had coaxed the acidic monk into violating the first rule of disputation: Never ask an opponent a question whose answer you do not know. "The salvation of gnosis. The soul must be elevated by meditation, fasting, and prayer, not by blind belief. The Lord came to show us the way to the Light, not to enforce the dogma of men. He refuted the priests of His day, who condemned Him, as you now condemn us."

Diego wanted to hear more about this Cathar gnosis. "How does one know when such elusive enlightenment has been attained?"

Esclarmonde took quick advantage of the dissension in the Catholic delegation. "The way to the Light cannot be described. It is like a man who becomes drunk with wine and then becomes sober. He is aware that he knows *more* when he is sober, and he knows *when* he is sober. Yet no one can convince him while he is drunk that he is befuddled. When people cease experiencing God, they are left only to believe in Him."

Dominic cried, "You would turn every man into a church unto himself!"

"By their fruits ye shall know them," she reminded the Castilian, quoting Christ. "Examine the lives of those who spread God's teachings. Do they sit on thrones of gold and porphyry? Or do they walk among the people sharing all they own, as did the Master?"

Dominic fell to his knees as if possessed by the Holy Ghost. "Our Lord never rejected anyone, be they master or slave!"

Esclarmonde was prepared for this tactic of divine inspiration. In a low but firm voice, like a mother chastening a child from a tantrum, she admonished, "Even St. Paul preached that only the few could understand the true teachings."

"The woman is an elitist!" cried Folques.

"You call *me* an elitist? You who dismiss my sex as incapable of understanding Holy Writ? You who deny the laity the right to read the Bible? The freedom of the Garden of Eden is turned on its head into an accusation of guilt, appeased only by your lust for emoluments."

"The Church must be financed!" said Folques.

Esclarmonde was so charged with exhilaration that she could hear the blood pulsing in her ears. Folques had stumbled into her second trap: Divide and conquer. "And must poor Christians finance your silks and sapphires? When did Christ ever dress as finely as you?"

Folques retracted his jeweled fingers into his miniver-cuffed sleeves. "You expect us to walk in rags? The City of God is entitled to tithes."

"And to a lucrative trade in relics," she said dryly.

Folques appealed to the assembly, "Who here has not been blessed by grace from gazing upon the bones of a saint?"

"And who here has not seen enough pieces of the True Cross to build a bridge across the Ariege?" she countered.

The Catholic disputants stewed in bridled agitation, unable to dredge up a controverting point. The spate of snickering in the hall during the caesura flooded their ears like screams. Dominic carried on the disquisition with himself, expostulating on Aristotle's assertion that the female was a deformity of nature, citing the encyclopedist Vincent de Beauvais's insistence that woman is the confusion of man, an insatiable beast, a daily ruin. But the audience was no longer listening to him. All eyes had turned toward the Waldensian judge, who shifted anxiously while awaiting a response from the Catholic side.

Folques moved to change the trajectory of the debate. "You deny the transformation of the Eucharist!"

"An invention of your priests who wish to control our path to God," said Esclarmonde. "The God of Light calls us with the shedding of the physical. He has no need to wallow in our mouths and intestines."

"Your own hermits lay on hands on the infirm in a demonic transmission of spells," accused Dominic.

"Our healing is given freely," said Esclarmonde. "Any member of our faith may transmit the Light. Nor do we ask remuneration for the service, as do you in your selling of God's grace."

Folques paced the dais in spiraling frustration. "Do you deny swearing off sexual relations in order to strangle God's creation?"

"Do you deny that you have done the same?" she asked. "Or was the vow of chastity not included in your ordination, as seems to be the case with the Abbot of Citeaux, who slakes his wanton desires on innocent virgins?"

The Catholic delegation shouted protests against the slander. Folques stole a sharp glance at Phillipa, fearful she might confirm Almaric's lapse from propriety in Lochers dungeon. "The Abbot of Citeaux is an honorable cleric!"

"As am I," said Esclarmonde. "Yet you afford me no respect. I have taken my faith's vow of celibacy, as have you. We believe the Light can be reached sooner by avoiding the physical act. And I have done my duty as a woman."

"We know well enough how you performed your wifely obligations," said Folques. "A husband lies murdered and a daughter languishes in Limbus."

Stung by that calculated aspersion, Esclarmonde struggled to maintain her composure. "You accuse us of an unnatural hatred for the body. Yet this Castilian mortifies his flesh in every imaginable perversion."

"An offering!" protested Dominic.

"If God so loves the flesh, why would He wish you to scourge it?" she asked. "We do not tempt the flesh. But neither do we hack at it in abominable pride."

The Catholics fractured into heated whispers. Unnerved, Folques turned to the judge and ordered, "We submit the decision."

The audience lurched up from their seats to protest the attempt to abort the disputation. "Answer the Perfecta's question! It is not finished!"

The Waldensian looked nervously to Castelnau for guidance. The papal legate dipped his chin in a prearranged signal for the proceedings to be concluded. With trepidation, the arbiter arose unsteadily to issue his judgment. "I find the arguments of Rome have prevailed by—"

"No!" The outraged Occitans pressed forward and shouted to drown his verdict. "Treachery and artifice!"

Fearing for his safety, the Waldensian dropped to his knees in front of Dominic. "I ask to be returned into the True Church."

Dominic placed his hands on the judge's head. "This day you are saved."

"Sold to the Devil!" screamed the Marquessa.

Dominic turned toward the riotous assembly with open arms. "Come to me, all of you! Do not pass up this last chance for redemption."

Two Waldensians disguised in Cathar robes rushed up from the audience and prostrated themselves before the Castilian monk.

Dominic screamed their penance over the scoffs of ridicule. "On every Sunday for three months, you shall walk with your bared backs flogged. And for the rest of your lives, you shall wear the yellow cross of heresy on your breast." He waited for more apostates to come forward. When not one Cathar accepted his offer, he shook his fist at them and shouted, "You are not Christians!"

Esclarmonde stood her ground. "St. Bernard said he found nothing contrary to Scriptures in the manner of our living."

Pale with rage, Dominic aimed the tip of his staffed crucifix at her. "We have used words of sweetness to no avail! Now shall be called forth the rod and the sword! God's fiery wrath shall be brought down on this faithless land!" While he harangued the Occitans on the certainty of Hell's approach, his fellow Catholics scurried for the doors.

Grenac, the hot-headed knight from Toulouse, manhandled Castelnau and pinned him against a column. "You profess to know all there is about salvation. You'd best prepare for it."

The legate burned the knight's face into his memory. "Advise the Count of Toulouse that he'll soon hear from Rome."

In the bedlam, Esclarmonde was left forgotten on the dais. She saw Folques standing a few steps away, monitoring the enfilade of threats and imprecations with riveted interest. The courage she had managed to muster for the disputation was trivial compared to that she now required. She approached him with trepidation and whispered, "Sir, may I have a word with you in private?"

Folques drew an inward breath of surprise. Assured that the other members of his delegation had hurried off, he retreated with her into an alcove.

"I beg of you," she said. "Grant me some news of my son."

Concealed behind a chamfered column, Folques weighed her plea, assaying if some advantage might be gained from it. If he were to return the most notorious Occitan heretic to the Church's fold, he would be lauded as the great hope of the Languedoc, eclipsing even Dominic as a fisher of lost souls. He had no illusions about which side had won the disputation. His old troubadour competitors would spread word across the Continent that Esclarmonde had matched the greatest minds of the Church. Did the Almighty give him custody of her son to bring this moment of reconciliation to fruition? Yes, the boy was the bridge back to her heart. In time, she would come to recognize God's original plan for them to be together, an Abelard and Heloise in reversed fortune. He revealed to her, "He is being instructed in catechism at Grandselve."

"Does he ask of me?"

"He has been told the truth. That his mother abandoned him for her heretic faith." Seeing her eyes dampen, Folques placed a hand on her arm in an attempt at intimacy. He lowered his forehead to hers and, with a sigh in remembrance of more joyous times, whispered with measured solicitude, "Publicly repent of your apostasy, my lady, and I shall see that he is returned to you this night."

Esclarmonde's throat constricted as if coiled by an adder. Would men never cease tempting her faith? Jourdaine had offered her freedom in exchange for Montsegur. Now Folques was dangling her own son as bait to gain her betrayal. She shuddered with revulsion at his touch, as calculating as it had been during their first encounter in Foix. She had committed a fatal error by asking him this boon, exposing her most vulnerable weakness. She feared that one day she would pay dearly for it.

She removed his hand and walked away.

Jesus said: Woe to the Pharisees,
for they are like a dog sleeping in the food
trough of cows; the dog neither eats nor lets the cows eat.
- The Gospel of Thomas

XIX

St. Gilles

June 1209

Disguised in mendicant's rags, Guilhelm dragged his scarred feet through the brackish muck of the Camargue wetlands and fell in with the hundreds of dry-shod travelers who were walking the levee road into St. Gilles, the patron city of cured cripples and the ancient home of the counts of Toulouse. During his four-year hegira, Guilhelm had eluded the Cistercians by traveling at night through the forests of Aquitaine and Brittany, then moving south in the hope of finding transport to the British Isles. On this sweltering morning, he was forced to abandon the protection of the delta's tall reeds to refill his water skin at the city's common well. He slipped past the gate gendarmes and merged into the anonymity of the dusty pilgrims being herded down the corbel-shaded warrens.

A street hawker pulled him aside and offered a drink from his ladle. When Guilhelm's thirst had been slaked, the pedlar shoved a strand of obsidian beads into his hands in the hope of making a transaction. "Brother, you must have the latest in miracles. A holy man from Castile passed here with them only last month."

"A holy man in this godforsaken land," grumbled Guilhelm. "*That* would be the miracle."

"Dominic was his name. The Blessed Virgin drew rosebuds from his lips to form the beads. He calls them 'rosaries.' I am certain he will be declared a saint. These are the only ones left that were touched by his hand. Because of your evident piety and mortification, good brother, I will give you a deal."

Guilhelm fingered the cord, which resembled the Arab worry beads he had seen carried by the Caliph's soldiers in Palestine. "What brings these hordes into the city on such a hot day?"

The hawker flipped up the brim of his floppy hat in astonishment. "God bless you, Lazarus! Have you just risen from the dead? Our liege is to be scourged in front of the church for murdering Peter Castelnau."

"Murdered? When?"

"A week after the disputation at Pamiers."

Guilhelm tossed the rosary back to the huckster. The man was obviously a spinner of lies. Raymond de Toulouse might be an adulterer and a wastrel—he had been married five times, and two of his former wives still languished in nunneries; as a boy, he had even bedded his father's mistress—but he didn't have the balls to kill a papal legate in cold blood.

Repulsed in his bartering, the hawker suspected Guilhelm's sympathies lay with the heretics. Under the cover of his sleeve, he furtively displayed a miniature dove carved from mahogany, the symbol of peace so treasured by the Cathars. "Some say the Bishop of Toulouse had a hand in the deed."

The bustling crowds suddenly parted to make way for a column of monks chanting Te Deums. At the head of this procession walked a cleric dressed in the regalia of high rank. He led the half-naked Count of Toulouse by a rope tied to his neck and periodically thrashed the corpulent baron's bloodied back with a stave of birch twigs. The punishment drew groans and cries for mercy from the horrified onlookers.

Guilhelm elbowed closer to gain a better vantage of Raymond's tormentor. Cursing his discovery, he pulled his hood over his head and tried to slink back into a side alley.

"You!" ordered Folques. "The beggar!"

A covey of deacons captured Guilhelm and shoved him back into the street.

Folques forced the birches into Guilhelm's hands. "The penitent will be abused by the lowest of his subjects."

Count Raymond was bent low with exhaustion from the humiliating ordeal. He turned and looked up into the recesses of the mendicant's hood. His sweat-stung eyes widened in recognition. To avoid suspicion, he offered his back to Guilhelm for another blow, then whispered, "Stroke hard."

His identity still undetected, Guilhelm brought the birches down as gently as he dared. The throngs shouted promises of retaliation, but he preferred the anger of the crowd to the risk of being unmasked by Folques. Satisfied with the arrangement, Folques renewed the procession's advance toward the church. Guilhelm tightened the noose in mock abuse and drove the Count to his knees. He exhorted the baron through fixed lips, "Stand firm against these treacherous priests! The people will rally to you!"

The Count labored and heaved, breathing loudly through his teeth. "The Abbot of Citeaux marches from Lyons with a host of thousands!"

"Why has Trevencal not mustered his forces with you?"

The Count hung his head in shame. "My nephew and I are estranged."

"You can still turn them back."

"It's too late for me. You must warn the Wolf. These Cistercians will not be appeased until they have his sister in chains."

Guilhelm brought the birches down, this time with real force. He was about to punish the feckless baron again when he saw his twelve-year-old son, Raymond VII, walking behind the procession and sharing every wince. He sensed in the resolute lad all the mettle that was lacking in the old man. He forced the Count to look at his heir. "If you persist in this groveling, that boy will not inherit a kingdom!"

Folques halted the punitive cortege at the Abbey Church, a popular pilgrimage sanctuary whose doors had been nailed with a papal declaration of a crusade against the Cathars. He climbed to the portico and read aloud Rome's condemnation of the Occitan heretics:

Damned are they when they are asleep and awake.
Damned are they everywhere and at all times.
Damned are they at day and at night.
Damned are they when they eat and when they drink.
Damned are they when they are silent and when they speak.
Damned are they from their heads to the soles of their feet,
That their eyes may become blind,
That their ears may become deaf,
That their mouths will be dumb,
Damned are all parts of their bodies.
Damned are they when they stand, lie down, or sit,
That they may be buried with the dogs and the donkeys,
And that the violent wolves may tear their bodies apart.

Three archbishops and nineteen bishops—nearly the entire ecclesiastic hierarchy of France—emerged from the nave armed with the reliquary that bore the consecrated femur of the city's namesake. A prelate shouted the malefaction issued by the Pope: "Raymond de Toulouse, pestilent man, tremble! Thou art like the crows living on carrion. Impious, cruel, and barbarous tyrant, thou art declared anathema for the murder of Peter de Castelnau."

The Count gazed up with blood-filled eyes at the lintels that held the world's only sculpted depiction of the Lord's Passion: The Four Evangelists floated undisturbed above a gory Apocalypse in which lions devoured saints and Satan's legions fought archangels in the final battle for the world. He found the scene a fitting allegory for his own blackened fate.

"What proof?" screamed one of his subjects.

Folques tightened the rope against the Count's throat. "The legate's body was exhumed and found redolent of a sanctified fragrance!"

"Drenched in myrrh and honey!" shouted another Occitan in the crowd. "I was there when they gutted him! He stank like that Norman whorehouse he was born in!"

Unnerved by the rising foment, Folques yanked the noose to speed the Count's acceptance of the prearranged punishment.

"I take responsibility," muttered Raymond, half audible.

"In the words agreed," required Folques.

The Count finally relented, "I am duly suspect of guilt."

"And your accomplice, Bernard Grenac?"

"He has taken flight."

"The felon who wielded the dagger will soon be apprehended," said Folques. "Pronounce the sentence of death on him."

Another lash spurred Raymond's cry, "It shall be done!"

"And you shall relinquish all rights to the bishoprics and monasteries."

That demand stoked the mob's rage. Such a catastrophe would cost the citizens of Toulousia precious earnings from the local ecclesiastic estates and force them to pay more tithes to the rapacious Cistercians.

"Answer, or you shall remain excommunicate," insisted Folques.

With a huff of anguish, the Count gave up the final concession. "Be gone with them all!"

The fractious crowds surged forward. "Go back to your abbeys!"

Pummeled by a fusillade of rocks, Folques and his vespiary of monks retreated into the church, dragging the Count with them. They tried to bolt the doors, but the rabble broke through before the beam could be jammed. Guilhelm was swept into the narthex with the surge.

Folques cowered behind the Count on the chancel platform. "Command them to desist! Or the army will be ordered to attack this city first."

Count Raymond weighed his bitter dilemma: Lose the respect of his people or forfeit St. Gilles. He stole a guilty glance at Guilhelm, then erupted to his feet. "I join the Holy Father's crusade!"

His subjects fell silent, unable to comprehend their liege's betrayal.

Folques pulled the shifty baron behind the altar to demand an explanation. "What treachery is this?"

Raymond raised his head to be heard. "Rome has promised protection for those who take the Cross! Toulousia must be spared!"

The Occitans suddenly saw the cunning in Raymond's turn of allegiance. Roaring their approval, they stormed the altar to congratulate their liege on outwitting the officious Cistercians. Guilhelm withered the conniving baron with a glare of accusation. Both knew that once the Pope's army was unleashed in the Languedoc, it would not return north satisfied with a few conversions. Deprived of Raymond's cities to sack, Almaric and Folques would divert their hordes against the lands of Trevencal and Foix. Desperate to get a warning to Esclarmonde and her brother, Guilhelm searched for some means of slipping out. Across the nave stood the church's renowned spiral staircase, the Screw, which funneled up to the belfry tower. He sank into his cowl and navigated against the crush to reach it.

"The wretch escapes!" shouted a man in the crowd. Guilhelm dashed up the steps, but the mob pulled him down and set to thrashing him. "Dog! See if you lay hands on our liege again!"

Folques watched with indifference as the beggar was passed through a gauntlet of fists and kicks—until the captive's hood was ripped off. He lurched to the fore and shouted, "Bring that man to me!"

The gendarmes dragged Guilhelm to the altar.

Folques circled his old nemesis and grinned at his good fortune. "The Lord's nets are cast, and we know not what they bring. This Templar is a fugitive from justice. Convicted in absentia for the murder of a Christian knight in blood revenge for a tournament loss." He turned on Raymond with a punishing smirk. "As I recall, baron, the combat was held in honor of your son's baptism."

Raymond nervously assessed the mob's reaction to that revelation. "I've never before laid eyes on this vagabond."

Folques motioned to a deacon for his diocesan pouch and produced the indictment that he always carried with him. "The wife of the dead knight, an adulteress and heretic, conspired in the deed. The finding against her was duly recorded in Toulouse."

Guilhelm rushed at Folques, but the guards subdued him. "The Viscountess of Foix had no hand in it!"

"The heretic woman will receive her justice in due time." With a smile of anticipation, Folques turned to hoist Count Raymond on the petard of his own cleverness. "Great crusader that you've just become, baron, the Almighty has presented you with an opportunity to demonstrate your newfound faith. Proceed with the felon's execution."

"You have no authority to order his death," insisted the Count.

"The Holy Father has granted me plenary powers to issue all necessary decrees. This man is a condemned consort of the heretic conspirators."

With his own murder indictment hanging over his head, Raymond had no choice but to begrudge his consent. The constabularies dragged Guilhelm from the church and prodded him toward a beam that had been erected in the square. They hoisted him on a timbrel and tied his hands behind his back.

Seeing the relic vendor in the crowd, Guilhelm swallowed his pride and begged Folques, "Allow me to die with the beads of the Virgin."

Folques savored this pitiful display of groveling. He motioned the hawker forward to grant the Templar's last request.

Guilhelm whispered to the vendor while the rosary was wrapped around his neck, "The medallion under my shirt. When they cut me down, deliver it to Foix. Tell the viscountess there what you have heard. She must seek safety at once." He choked with emotion. "Tell her also . . . that I love her."

"Last words, Montanhagol?" taunted Folques, out of earshot. "Allow us all to hear your minstrel's lament. You have always been so facile with them. A doggerel, perhaps, about the wind kicking at your heels?"

"This purchased bishop is the Devil's confessor!" shouted Guilhelm.

Folques glared at the Toulouse baron to give the order. Averting a shamed glance, Count Raymond raised his hand to send the Templar to his death.

Guilhelm closed his eyes and prayed to the Blessed Mother, his protector. She had extricated him from the clutches of the Saracen mamluks at Acre and had nursed him back to health when he had been given up for dead in the frying Egyptian desert. He could not accept that She had walked him through so many valleys of death only to deliver him to Judgment under the pernicious leer of this seducer-turned-cleric. He looked down at the money beads strung around his neck and cursed that damned Castilian Guzman for falsely claiming the Virgin's special fondness. The cart lurched and rocked ominously. The rope dug like a saw into his jaw. He drew a final breath. The cart inched forward—and came back to rest.

Damn him! Have done with it!

The gendarmes cut the rope from the beam.

He fell tumbling to the floorboards. The back of his head rebounded, surging blood into his nose. The hissing strands of hemp snapped and coiled around his shoulders. When he recovered his bearings, he slowly realized that his neck had not snapped. He looked up and found Folques standing astride him with an arched smirk.

"You have earned a more appropriate punishment," said Folques.

I bring evil from the north and great destruction; the Lion has
gone up from his thicket; a destroyer of nations has set out.
- The Book of Jeremiah

XX

Beziers

July 1209

ooled by a pleasant summer zephyr, Esclarmonde sat on a bench atop the observation terrace of Foix castle and tutored Loupe and Chandelle on their Latin grammar assignments. The two girls reminded her of a yoked pair of mismatched carriage rakkers. One was high-strung, quick-gated, and easily distracted; the other tranquil, even-tempered, and inwardly focused. Each had learned to compensate for the other's contrary tendencies.

Loupe kept one eye on the board and the other on the persistent flurry of birds that circled the tower, an activity that interested her a great deal more than the Latin. After several unsuccessful attempts to decipher a sentence, she tossed her writing board aside in frustration. "This is boring!"

Chandelle was startled by the loud report. Assured that it was only one of Loupe's tantrums, the blind child returned to her task of pressing the stylus with precision into the wax and running her fingers across the surface to make certain that the letters were formed correctly. She fastidiously blew away the shavings, collecting them in her free hand to rework them into the board.

"You mustn't neglect the punctuation," reminded Esclarmonde.

Shamed at being outdone, Loupe grudgingly retrieved her board. "Papa says Oc is the only language anyone needs to know."

Esclarmonde was wise to Loupe's strategy of pitting her against Roger. "I'll remind him of that next time he asks me to translate a letter."

"He also said that knights don't marry ladies who are too smart for their own good," said Loupe.

"He married your mother. And she's smarter than him by the length of a church aisle. He doesn't seem to mind, does he?"

"Maybe he doesn't know," chirped Chandelle.

The three shared a chuckle to celebrate their secret: As the women of the chateau, they wielded an ulterior power over the lone man in residence. Phillipa and Corba had coaxed Esclarmonde into helping with the girls' education, an assignment that provided a welcome respite from the demands of her new notoriety. Montsegur was being besieged weekly with appeals for her to preach in lands as far away as Italy, but Castres rejected them all, citing the dangers of travel. His real reason, she suspected, was that he could not bear the thought of losing her companionship and assistance. The disputation at Pamiers two months earlier had taken a heavy toll on him in both body and spirit.

"Latin is the language of lovers." Chandelle carefully enunciated each word as she pressed the letters into the wax.

"Is not!" said Loupe. "Troubadours sing in Oc."

A natural diplomat, Chandelle chose not to embarrass Loupe with a correction. Instead, she would ask a question whose answer she already knew. "Did the Romans have troubadours, Aunt Essy?"

Esclarmonde stroked Chandelle's hair in approval of her subtle method for handling Loupe. "Yes, they did. Ovid was a Roman bard who knew all the secrets for pleasing ladies. But he wrote in Latin, so Loupe probably doesn't want to hear about him."

Loupe wrestled with the dilemma. "Just this once."

Esclarmonde caressed Chandelle's arm to confirm that their conspiracy had succeeded. As the girls nuzzled closer to her, Esclarmonde opened a small book and began by reading its title, "De Arte Honeste Amandi."

"What does that mean?" asked Loupe.

Esclarmonde required a moment; hearing those words again brought up a torrent of memories. Here was the book written by Andreas Capellanus on Ovid's maxims, the same tome that she and Corba had studied for their initiation into the court of love. Recovering her voice, she explained, "It means 'The Art of Honest Loving.' As I recall, there are three sections of prescriptions. The first advises men on how to win a lady. The second instructs how to keep her happy. And the third suggests strategies for a lady to win the heart of a man."

"Is there a section that tells how to keep boys away?" asked Loupe.

Esclarmonde noticed that Chandelle had become oddly silent. "Chandy, where should we start?"

"No knight will ever wish to court me," said the blind girl. "I needn't learn these rules, I think."

Esclarmonde smiled dolently, her eyes serous with tears. She was determined to instill the blessed child with the requisite *amour-proper*. "You possess a great advantage, my love. When the gentlemen discover that you care only for their gallantry and goodness of soul, they will flock to you in droves. Now, listen closely while Loupe reads us the first rule."

With that promise, Chandelle's melancholy sailed with the clouds.

Loupe stumbled on the Latin translation. "Let it be your concern to know the handmaid of the lady who is to be won. She will faculate—"

"Fa-cil-i-tate," corrected Esclarmonde.

"Facilitate your approaches," continued Loupe. "Make sure she is the one nearest to the deliberations of the lady and is an entirely trustworthy confidante in your secret games."

"What does *that* mean?" asked Chandelle.

Esclarmonde was about to explain the time-honored tactic when she saw Loupe distracted by a freckle-faced boy who was hiding behind the stairhead. Loupe flexed like a cat about to pounce on a bug—until Esclarmonde tapped her arm to regain her attention. Denied her raid, Loupe was forced to settle for sticking out her tongue at Bernard Saint-Martin, the son of Roger's castellan at Laurac. She held an ominous glare on the twelve-year-old lad while she answered Chandelle's question. "It means that if a boy likes me, he'll get friendly with you so you'll tell me how nice he is."

"Would a boy really do that, Aunt Essy?" asked Chandelle.

"It has been known to happen." Esclarmonde monitored the developing drama with a latent smile. "Let's read on."

"'The pleasure that comes in safety is less prized,'" read Loupe. "'Invent a fear, even if you are safer than Thais.'"

"Who is Thais?" asked Chandelle.

"She was Alexander the Great's lover," said Esclarmonde. "When Thais became tired of men, she walled herself inside a cell."

"Maybe Loupe should try that with Bernard," quipped Chandelle.

Loupe sprang to her feet. "You promised not to tell!"

His lurking exposed, Bernard scampered down the stairs and nearly careened into Phillipa, who had been listening to the lesson from afar.

Esclarmonde winked at Phillipa. "Has a young knight been calling on you, Loupe?"

"He keeps singing annoying songs to me."

"Oh, well. I'm afraid you may have to suffer many a shrill note before finding the one sweet melody."

"I don't think this Ovid knew what he was talking about," said Loupe.

"Let's keep reading and find out."

Loupe continued, "'Love is a species of war. Night and winter and long roads and terrible sorrows and every hardship are native to this gentle camp.'"

"Being in love doesn't sound like much fun," said Chandelle.

Esclarmonde had not heard that last observation, lost as she was in her thoughts about Guilhelm. How strange. The two of them had indeed been like warriors. Why had their few moments together always been heightened by conflict? She had heard nothing from him since that night in L'Isle. Folques would have spared no effort in bringing him to trial for Jourdaine's death. If Guilhelm had survived, he would have found a way to get a message to her by now. Still, she could not bring herself to accept that he—

Chandelle, ever intuitive, kissed Esclarmonde to chase her dark thoughts.

Phillipa seized the moment to interrupt their lesson. "Girls, go put on your best dresses. We have visitors."

Esclarmonde interrogated Phillipa with a questioning look, but she was given not even a hint about the arrivals. Intrigued, she rushed down the steps into the great hall and gasped with delight. She was embraced by Lady Giraude and her brother, Aimery, her benefactors from Lavaur whom she had not seen since the dedication of the temple. The Marquessa and Castres hurried in from a side door and hugged their unexpected guests in a gushing reunion.

Giraude lavished Esclarmonde with kisses. "How I wish I'd been at Pamiers! You are all the people talk about now."

"You are all my sister can talk about, that is for certes," Aimery genuflected three times in courtesy. "She lords it over every man in Lavaur as evidence of the superiority of the female mind. I have become somewhat of a pariah."

Esclarmonde blushed at the report of her fame. "It was Father Castres who carried the day."

"False modesty is the wife of willful pride," said Castres. "And let us not forget that we lost the decision."

"I warned you about that Janus-faced Waldensian," said Giraude. "His judgment has been the object of much mockery." Turning solemn, she took Esclarmonde by the arm for insistence. "The Bishop has something to tell you."

Esclarmonde's expectant look drove Castres to a difficult admission. "It is time, child."

Giraude gave the Bishop no chance to reconsider the decision that she had extracted only after much persuasion. "The Cistercians have launched another preaching campaign," she said. "They harass our perfects in the villages. We have no universities. We need you there."

Nothing terrified Esclarmonde more than the thought of leaving Foix again. Her escape from Gascony had been nothing less than a miraculous reprieve, one that had cost her Guilhelm. Yet she knew her Cathar vows required her to travel to those in need of ministry. "I've never preached."

"You more than held your own against Folques and the Castilian," reminded Giraude. "The people are clamoring to hear you. It will be a grand tour. Marseille, Nimes, Perpignan. But first, Beziers. In the county of our young friend Trevencal."

"What would I say?"

"You'll speak from your heart," said Giraude.

"Allow Phillipa to go with me, at least."

"She must tend to our houses in Carcassonne," said Castres. "I will accompany you to Beziers. We will leave in the morning."

Esclarmonde silently begged Phillipa for support in her attempt to avoid their call to service, but she saw that her friend was resolved to do her duty.

The girls came running into the chamber. Phillipa gathered Loupe into her arms. "I have wonderful news, love. Corba is going to take care of you for a few weeks. You'll get to stay with Chandy even longer."

"You're going away?" asked Loupe.

"Aunt Essy and I must go help others."

"I don't want you to go!" screamed Loupe. "Aunt Essy, tell her not to go!"

Esclarmonde smothered Loupe with kisses, dousing the looming conflagration of the child's explosive temper with the loving wetness of her lips. "You must be brave. When your mother and I return, we'll throw a birthday fete for you. And you mustn't marry Bernard until I get back."

"I'll never marry Bernard!"

Esclarmonde found Chandelle's head dipped in sadness. She picked up the blind child and gave her a hug. "Love, say a prayer for me each night."

Chandelle's drained face held a look of terror. In a voice repressed of emotion, she said, "You shouldn't go. But I will pray for you."

Esclarmonde was unnerved by the child's strange warning.

Phillipa squeezed Esclarmonde's hand in reassurance. "We'll be back before the leaves fall. Have I ever failed to keep a promise?"

The citizens of Beziers came rushing down from their terraced houses above the Orb, a trout-teeming river that slithered through checkered squares of vineyards and sloping fields awash in sunflowers and lavender. The local Cathars lined the Pont Vieux to ask for Esclarmonde's transmission of the Light. Their Catholic neighbors had also turned out to see the heretic woman who was emptying their churches.

Esclarmonde crossed the stone span and was inspired by the breathtaking view of St. Nazaire. The cathedral's famous towers, built with pale limestone that had been scavenged from Roman ruins, sat atop an acropolis that once had served as a Gallic fortress. The cobbled road that she and Castres had walked from Foix ran only three leagues inland from the Mediterranean, and the trade winds from the nearby chain of lagoons and dunes mixed their sea salt with the kitchen aromas of mushroom fricassees and crayfish stews to form a wondrous olfactory welcome. She could well understand why the twenty thousand inhabitants here claimed that the Greek gods had fashioned their city as a winter retreat when Mount Olympus became too cold.

She climbed the cathedral's steps and stood under the dazzling rays that streamed from its rose window, a marvel of lead and alchemy excelled in magnificence only by the stained glass of Chartres. The local Cathar perfects carried up their sick and crippled family members to gain her blessing. Among the infirm lay a man marred by leprosy, too ashamed of his sinful condition to meet her eyes. She placed her palm against his festered forehead and prayed, "The God of Light has not forgotten you."

In the crowd stood the stooped, white-haired priest who had taken care of the cathedral for thirty years. He raised his folded hands to her in hospitality. The magnanimous gesture instilled her with the courage to walk among the petitioners and listen to their heartbreaking stories of suffering. "Your pain is not a judgment cast down by the God of Light," she assured them. "He seeks to cleanse you of your sickness, as did the Master Jesus. The radiance that flows through me is from the same spiritual Sun that Our Lord drew upon to offer His healing powers. All of you, man or woman, may transmit this touch of Light to your brothers and sisters. The work of God does not require the sanction of the Church or the Pope."

An old woman with desiccated legs struggled to her elbows. "The priests tell us to accept our suffering as punishment for our sins."

"Your priests mean well, but they are misguided," said Esclarmonde. "They preach only what their bishops mandate. Did Our Lord abandon the lame when the Pharisees declared them unclean?"

"No!" shouted several voices.

"He called the sick to Him and drove out the impurities from their bodies. The Church of Rome forfeited the gift of healing because it has rejected the Master's true teachings. The Pope orders you to accept your plight and give thanks to God for the opportunity to share in Christ's agony on the Cross. I tell you that Jesus wished no one to endure torment. Suffering was not the Father's plan for his Son. Nor is it the Father's plan for us."

The elderly priest shuffled to the fore of his parishioners. "How then would you have us overcome our failings of the flesh?"

"Disease is a deception perpetrated by the Demiurge," she said. "The world of matter is an illusion. We must refuse its seductions. Only then can the Light transform the flesh and permit the spirit to escape the cycles of imprisonment."

The old priest pondered her explanation. "That is not unlike what I preach of God's grace."

"My faith does not teach that salvation can be purchased with indulgences and extortions," she said.

"The Lord interceded for others," reminded the priest.

"Not in exchange for tithes or compensation. He sought to show us how to fish the spiritual waters for our own sustenance. We wish to teach people to live in His example, to meditate and fast, to do no violence even if attacked. And we allow all to follow their own conscience."

The elderly priest climbed the steps with difficulty and offered his faltering hand to Esclarmonde in goodwill. "I have little learning. I know not if what you say about the Scriptures is true, but I believe you to be a good woman. You are welcome in my— " A low rumbling shook the hillside.

Roger Trevencal and the city's Catholic bishop, Reynaud de Montpeyroux, led an entourage of knights across the bridge. Both Catholics and Cathars shouted huzzahs at the sight of their youthful viscount who had been away for months. Trevencal had taken a wife, but his boyish charm still drew the unabashed admiration of the ladies. Favoring the shoulder wound suffered from de Montfort's lance in Toulouse, he dismounted and genuflected to Esclarmonde, a courtesy that drew a scowl from the Catholic bishop. Trevencal ignored the cleric's disapproval and pressed a kiss to her hand. "My lady, accept my apologies for not having been present at your arrival."

Esclarmonde broke a glowing smile as she lifted her former champion to his feet. "You've become a man."

Trevencal stood taller to merit the observation. "Not soon enough, I fear, to have prevented a gross injustice." They shared a moment of silence while recalling that tragic day when she had been forced to betroth Jourdaine. "Lady Phillipa is well, I trust?"

"She travels to Carcassonne." Esclarmonde saw that Trevencal's eyes had gloomed over with the mention of his capital city. "And you, my lord? Do I detect a chink in that armor of high spirits?"

Trevencal surveyed the city's ramparts with a sullen look of gravity. "I've just come from an acrimonious parlay with the Abbot of Citeaux. He and the Bishop of Toulouse lead an army of twenty thousand against us from Nimes. My uncle has deserted to their ranks." Met with cries of alarm, Trevencal put up a brave front. "These walls are strong! You shall be defended!"

The Catholic bishop produced a document to contradict that hope. "I come bearing a generous offer from the Abbot. Deliver up the heretics in your midst and you will be spared." He glared menacingly at Esclarmonde. "Your name, woman, is on this roll."

The citizens of Beziers argued over whether they should accept the offer. One of the burghers called for silence and asked Trevencal, "My lord, would you have us betray our own neighbors?"

"I'd not condemn some of my subjects to save the others," said Trevencal. "Whatever name you give to the god of your faith, remember that you are all Occitans, lovers of freedom!"

"We'll follow you into the bowels of Hell!" cried another man.

"Hell will be the preferred venue if you reject this condition," warned the Catholic bishop. "Be advised that routiers accompany this army."

A collective gasp sucked the air. Routiers were roving bands of prison rejects, thieves, and beggars who lusted for rape and plunder. The Northern barons found the wretches useful as human fodder, sousing them with cheap wine and whipping them into a frenzy before throwing them against the walls of a besieged city to waste the defenders' missiles. That these depraved creatures laughed in death's face was no surprise; eternal damnation could be no worse than their squalid existence. They were so loathed that Rome had forbidden Christian monarchs from recruiting their services. Now Innocent III and his henchmen found their employment to be advantageous.

Trevencal maintained a steadied front. "Stand fast! I implore you! Don't allow these monks from foreign soil to destroy our tolerance of creed!"

The frightened populace looked to their pastor for guidance.

The local priest bowed his head in deference to his superior. "I disagree with those who profess the existence of two gods. But this woman and her flock have never harmed us. I believe Christ's mercy begs their protection."

The Bishop glowered at the priest with a promise of retribution. "Have you forgotten what happened to Constantinople?"

Trevencal stole the condemnation list from the Bishop's grasp and threw the parchment to his subjects, who shredded it in a frenzy of patriotism. The Viscount ordered up the Bishop's horse to indicate that his presence was no longer welcome. "You have your answer."

"May God have mercy on your souls!" snarled de Montpeyroux.

When the cleric had been hounded off across the bridge, Trevencal turned to Esclarmonde and advised, "Gather your perfects. I will provide as many mounts as I can spare for those who cannot walk."

Esclarmonde was riven by indecision. Had she not just preached the need to refuse the seductions and illusions of the material world? If she fled to safety while others stayed in harm's way, she would be exposed as a hypocrite. "I can't abandon these people."

Trevencal drew her aside. "You are here because I asked you to come and preach. I won't allow you to remain in danger."

"Your Catholic subjects have agreed to risk their lives to save my followers." Pressing his hand for reassurance, she turned and walked among her Cathars. "If any of you wish to go to Carcassonne, no judgment will be held against you." When none of the Cathars stepped forward to accept Trevencal's offer of escort, she brought the tottering Castres to the Viscount's side. "Father, I have followed your guidance for many years. Now you must follow mine. Go to Phillipa. She must be warned to turn back for Foix."

Castres hung his head in surrender to her order.

Trevencal climbed to the highest step and shouted, "I leave to prepare the defenses of Carcassonne! You will be in the trusted hands of my seneschal! Provisions are stockpiled and the moats will be strengthened!"

Esclarmonde saw a blind rabbi huddled with his terrified congregation beyond the border of the cathedral grounds. The Jews had retrieved their precious scrolls from the city's synagogue and were clutching them to their chests. She feared they would fall victim to a pogrom, as had their grandfathers when the crusader armies passed through the Languedoc in past times to embark from Marseille. She pleaded with Trevencal, "Take the Jews away from here."

A younger rabbi translated her intercession into Hebrew for his blind elder. The aged rabbi bowed to her in heartfelt gratitude.

Abiding her request, Trevencal detached a small contingent to escort the Jews on their exodus west. Assured that his orders for the preparations had been understood, he mounted and took a last look at his adoring subjects. "Citizens of Beziers! You are my Thermopylae! God be with you!"

Thousands ran after the Viscount and dampened his dust with their tears.

For two days and nights, the Occitans deepened the ditches around Beziers with picks and shovels. The seneschal of the garrison, Bernard de Servian, led raiding parties into the countryside to burn the crops and salt the wells while Esclarmonde helped organize a hospital in St. Nazaire to ease the suffering of the refugees who were straggling in by the hundreds from neighboring towns.

On the morning before the feast of St. Magdalene's Day, a piercing cry came from the ramparts: "They are on us!"

So many citizens rushed to the allures that Esclarmonde feared the scaffolding would collapse. When she reached the crenelations, her heart sank. The far banks of the Orb were filled with a horde more vast than the Roman legions that she had read about in the Annals of Tacitus. The Northern army paraded across the valley with banners from Auvergne, Burgundy, Limousin, even Germany. A golden rampant lion on a red field—Simon de Montfort's herald—led up the Cistercians and their towering crucifixes. Behind the main army came the routiers, roistering down the hills like savages and diving naked into the water with no regard for modesty. She pleaded with Servian to avoid a violent confrontation. "Perhaps if I speak to the Abbot."

"That would be taken as a sign of weakness," warned Servian. "Let them batter their heads against these stones. They'll soon tire of their folly."

During the night, the Occitan garrison monitored the crusader campfires for suspicious movements. Informed by his scouts that the French sappers were testing the foundations, Servian ordered vats of boiling pitch be poured over the ramparts, a tactic that drew screams from the darkness below.

By dawn, the besieged Occitans had worked themselves into such a frenetic expectation of attack that their nerves could no longer hold. A mob of three thousand— mostly barefoot peasants armed with clubs and pitchforks— converged on the gate and demanded to be let out to fight the invaders.

Esclarmonde tried to stop them. "Heed the orders! I beg you!"

"Our knights cower behind these walls like Saracens!" cried one manic-eyed farmer. "Those filthy Northerners laid waste to my village at Bedarius!"

The mob unleashed an inhuman bray as it pushed past her. The Occitans hemorrhaged through the gate and hurdled down the embankment toward the bridge. Halfway across the river, they halted to shout goading curses at the Franks who were sleeping on the far banks.

The routiers roused and regarded the Occitan rabble with hectoring amusement. A giant Northerner with a face like pounded dough strode onto the bridge and shook his beefy fist. "Who wants it first?"

The Occitans swarmed the foolhardy Goliath and lifted him aloft like ants stealing a crust of bread. With a collective heave, they threw him to the treacherous rapids. Enraged, his fellow mercenaries erupted from their bed sacks and attacked the bridge en masse with cudgels and tree limbs. The first light of dawn was greeted by an unworldly screech as the two hordes collided. Those wretches in the van of both gangs were propelled into the river by the crush.

Awakened by the alarums, Almaric and Folques came running up in their nightshirts. They found the Count de Nevers watching the skirmish while spitting the night's dryness from his mouth with vinegar wine. The other barons stumbled cursing from their tents. They relieved their bladders and bowels with a concatenation of hissing arcs of urine and detonating farts.

"Shouldn't you disperse them?" asked Almaric.

"My knights won't go near that scum," said Nevers, gargling loudly. "Let the devils exhaust themselves. It'll save us the trouble of having to hang a few for general mischief." When he and his fellow barons prepared to retire in search of breakfast, they found Simon de Montfort strapping on his armor.

"What are you doing?" asked Folques.

Simon squinted repeatedly in an attempt to monitor the progress of the fight. "Opportunity gestates in this melee."

Nevers and the other barons laughed at the nearsighted Norman. "You can't even see your own hand in broad daylight. There on the bridge, de Montfort! The Lionhearted rides to meet you! Your day of fame awaits!"

Simon strode with grim determination toward his horse. "With your superb eyesight, Nevers, you can watch me gain glory from afar, as is your custom."

Before Nevers could counter that slander, de Montfort saddled and took his position on the crest of the hill that overlooked the bridge. One by one, the crusaders reconsidered their bluster and began following his lead. Soon the horizon was lined with knights mounted and at the ready. Simon drew his sword as the Beziers peasants began getting the worst of the scuffle. When the Occitans broke into a retreat, the Norman baron spurred to the charge. His advance on the river was so swift that the yeoman bringing up the siege engines abandoned their stations to avoid being left behind for the looting.

On the ramparts, Servian rang the tocsins for his garrison spread throughout the city to converge on the gate. "Don't allow the damn fools back in!"

His knights were too slow in ramming the planks into the gate slots. The bloodied Occitan horde debouched through the portal and eddied back into the city, swallowing all who came within its panicked undertow. Montfort galloped across the bridge at the head of his Northern knights and cut an indiscriminate swath through the laggards. The routiers running alongside him overwhelmed Servian's garrison at the gate and poured into the burgh like the demon-possessed swine sent by Christ over the Galilean cliffs. De Montfort and the crusaders were so stunned by their ease of entry that they were forced to fight a second battle with their own thugs for control of the narrow streets.

On the tower, Esclarmonde stood immobilized. The Northerners were dragging half-naked women from the houses and throwing infants from the windows. The cathedral priest knelt down before the onslaught with his crucifix raised to remind them of Christ's pacifism. A routier armed with an ax sliced the priest's scalp and the icon with one stroke.

Entrapped by the mash of his own men, de Montfort reared his charger to kick open a path. He looked up to the walls in discovery and rubbed the soot from his blurred eyes to confirm that they were not deceiving him. "Ten gold pieces to the man who brings me that black-shrouded minx!"

Dozens of routiers clambered up the hoarding like monkeys. Esclarmonde could not comprehend what was happening. The hellish phantasmagoria was playing out in slowed time—her body seemed to float above the screams and blood-spurting churn of heads and limbs. An Occitan knight shook her back to her senses and dragged her across the allures. They had nearly reached the next tower when her protector straightened from an arrow in his back. With his last breath, he ordered her, "To the cathedral!"

A frantic pealing of bells called the survivors toward the protection of the city's two churches. Esclarmonde leapt from the allures and was swept into the whirlpool of mayhem. She saw the spires of St. Nazaire above the smoke and ran for its doors, but so many Occitans had pushed their way inside that corpses were being thrown from its towers. A perfect reached a hand out to pull her to safety. She neared his grasp—and was dragged back.

"I am a nun!"

A routier with half an ear ripped at her robe. "I fulken know who you are! A little romp and then ten shillings from—" His head snapped back violently. A crusader in black armor circled his horse around her attacker. Eyes glutinous as oysters, the routier bared his canine incisors and lunged for the reins. "Getch yer own!"

Denied a full arc for his sword, the crusader pommeled the routier's scalp with the knob of his hilt. Tusks of blood drooled down the corners of the wretch's mouth as he hung on and dragged the knight's horse down with him. The knight cried out in anguish—his leg was pinned under the steed's flanks.

Freed, Esclarmonde staggered on hands and knees toward the cathedral. The crusaders charged past her and funneled through the splintered door planks, hacking away as if cutting through bramble. Curdling screams echoed from the nave. Rivulets of blood oozed down the steps. The church reeked from an effluvium of urine, vomit, and evacuated bowels. The local Catholics made the sign of the cross and recited the Apostles' Creed, to no avail. Some climbed the pillars only to tire and fall like spitted salmon on waiting spears. Those who escaped into the murk of the crypt were smothered in heaped piles. The Cathars in their black robes were easily spotted; their limbs were sliced off one by one to prolong their suffering. Old men, women, children, invalids—none were spared by the French knights who high-stepped through the muck bashing skulls and cutting gold fillings from teeth.

Esclarmonde crawled across the corpses on the outer portico. Her hair was yanked back to expose her windpipe for the knife.

I commit my soul.

A viscous wetness splashed across her face. She opened her eyes in horror—she had been splattered by the routier's brains. She stumbled to her feet and was concussed by an onrushing horse. The crusader who had skulled the routier was hoisting her to his saddle. The last sounds she heard before passing out were the screams of Occitans jumping to their deaths from the cathedral's tower.

A detachment of mounted crusaders led Almaric and Folques through the carnage-strewn city toward the Church of St. Mary Magdalene, where the last of the Occitan survivors had barricaded themselves. The Northern barons and their exhausted men sat near a battering ram at the front doors of the looming brick edifice that was winged with flying buttresses and protected by thick walls constructed like those of a fortress.

"Why haven't you taken it?" asked Folques.

"The beams are too stout," said de Montfort.

Nevers sat peeling an apple with his dagger. "We can wait and starve them out. There's plenty of gold still to be found in the city."

Almaric studied the thick oak planks that framed the church's bell tower. "Will the roof take a flame?"

The barons turned on the Abbot in disbelief. There were ten thousand people crammed inside the church, most loyal Catholics.

"I don't intend to spend the summer laying sieges to these heretic nests," said Almaric. "An example needs to be made."

"There is precious treasure within those confines," said de Montfort with a percipient grin. "You may wish to recover it first."

"I have enough chalices," said the Abbot.

"I'm talking about a vessel more valuable than gold . . . I saw the Count of Foix's sister running down that street."

Nevers laughed and tossed his apple core at de Montfort's boots to dismiss the absurd claim. "What would she be doing this far east? Besides, you couldn't tell a fox from a chicken if both were hung on your nose."

Folques broke the two scrapping knights apart. Shaken by the possibility that Esclarmonde was trapped inside the church, he suggested, "Perhaps we should take the viscountess alive to make a spectacle of her capture."

Almaric chastised his protege with a peremptory glare, suspecting him of harboring a more personal motive. "The woman can burn now or burn later." He glowered with intimidation. "I am certain the Bishop of Toulouse agrees."

Folques gave up a reluctant half-nod.

"What about our own believers?" asked Nevers. "There are more of them in there than the cloggers."

Almaric meditated on the jeweled crucifix at his breast. After nearly a minute of prayer, he made the sign of the Cross on the church doors as if dispensing the sacrament of penance. With his face shuttered in cold indifference, he turned to the barons and ordered, "Kill them all."

The crusaders traded startled glances, uncertain if they had heard the Abbot correctly. De Montfort reminded him, "There are innocent—"

"God will know his own," said Almaric.

De Montfort shrugged at the inscrutability of the Almighty's ways and ordered his men to jam the doors with wooden wedges. His archers swabbed their arrows with oiled rags and shot the flaming missiles to the roof timbers. Within minutes, black smoke churned from the embrasures in the cathedral's walls and screams could be heard above the crackling firestorm inside. The doors rumbled from the violent pounding of bodies and fists.

Folques could not bear the agony that Esclarmonde was now enduring in the inferno. In a reflex of pathos, he risked the Abbot's censure by rushing to the barred portal, but the scorching flames leapt at him like Hell's salamanders and drove him back. The buttresses crumbled and the rose window exploded. Shards of glass rained down on him as he crawled for cover. With a groaning heave, the church's brick walls imploded in a billowing cloud of black smoke and debris. He reached the nearest awning seconds before streams of hot cinders shot onto the thatched roofs of the surrounding buildings.

De Montfort and the barons cursed the unforeseen catastrophe and whipped the routiers to the task of forming bucket brigades to douse the shingles before the flames could spread. But the mercenaries were so embittered at being denied a share of the booty that they began fanning the embers with their rags, laughing and dancing like demented fools as the afternoon winds stoked the conflagration.

That night, after the burned city had cooled, Almaric and Folques were carried in a baroche around the smoldering battlements to inspect the results of the holocaust. Satisfied with their work, the Abbot ordered a report be sent to Rome expressing gratitude that fifteen thousand Occitan souls had been sent to the Almighty's righteous judgment.

If in the darkness of ignorance you don't
recognize a person's true nature, look to see
whom he has chosen for a leader.
- Rumi

XXI

Carcassonne

August 1209

Esclarmonde came to consciousness pinned over the saddle of the helmeted knight who had abducted her in Beziers. Disoriented, she could not lift her head to see where she had been taken. The ground was covered in thick cotton grass and her eyes stung from a sea-blown wind that was peppered with the stench of burnt flesh. She listened for sounds of fighting but heard only the peaceful chirping of kestrels.

The crusader had brought her into the wilds to have his way with her.

She fought frantically to break loose from his hold. He did not react to her jostling but kept his elbows pressed against her back. Had he expired from a wound and stiffened in rigor mortis? She jabbed a knee against his leg and finally elicited a sign of life. His chin dipped and recoiled, then came back to rest on his chest. The kidnapper was asleep! She waited until his groggy agitation eased again into slumber, then stole the reins and pulled the aimless horse to a stop. She shoved him from the saddle and galloped off.

Several lengths into her escape, a whistle halted the Arabian.

She kicked and cursed, but the horse would not move. Two more whistles turned it into a determined canter back toward its master, who was on one knee taking stock of the abrasions to his leg. Before she could dismount and run, the knight captured her. He subdued her thrashing arms.

"Unhand me!" she shouted. "Damn you to Hell!"

"I thought the famous Perfecta of Montsegur didn't believe in Hell."

Confounded by that reminder, she yanked off the knight's helmet. A ghostly spectre stood before her, so gaunt in body and spirit that she feared the strain of the day's horrors had cracked her mind. There was a hint of familiarity in his features, but they were more of the visage she might have imagined of him in old age. His limbs were so emaciated that she could see the blue blood pulsing in their strained veins. His ashen-rimmed eyes were hollow from hunger and his copper face was indelibly scored with deep sun lines. She raised a hand to his stubbled jaw to confirm its reality.

"I'm only half dead," he assured.

Overjoyed, she fell into Guilhelm's arms. Only when she had recovered from the shock of his miraculous arrival did the troubling circumstances that had brought it about suddenly dawn on her. The pendulum of her emotions swung from relief to hot anger. She shoved him away and attacked his chest with her fists. "You joined those murderers?"

Guilhelm restrained her until she had spent her fury. Too weak to move, he rested his forehead against hers, as if her touch alone could nourish him back to health. In a voice husky with fatigue, he explained, "Folques forced me to accompany the crusade to witness your capture."

He buckled from faintness before she could question him on how he had fallen into the clutches of the Cistercians. She eased him to the ground and dipped her hem into a pool of rainwater to wipe the caked blood from his face. She only then saw that he was not wearing his Templar mantle. "Your cross?"

"I am done with that Order and its lies."

"You must never go against your promises to God."

He unfastened his breastplate and flung it aside. "What promises has God kept to me?" He seized her shoulders roughly and turned her toward the black plumes curdling over Beziers. "Haven't you seen enough killing this day to know there is no God?" He hesitated to gather the words that he had rehearsed a thousand times. "Sail with me to Ireland. They say the monks there let you live by your own conscience."

She had prayed for years to hear that request. But now she·turned away, avoiding his expectant eyes. "I'm not the same woman you once knew."

"You care more for those heretics than me?"

"Phillipa and Corba have daughters who carry on my name." Her voice cracked from shame. "After you left . . . a girl did not survive. Folques keeps her twin brother in a monastery."

Several moments passed before Guilhelm deciphered what she could not bring herself to reveal explicitly. He fixed on her with a incredulous stare and tried to recreate the chain of events that had culminated in such an abomination. "If the Gascon sired the boy, then you are better off rid of him."

"You don't understand what it is to lose a child!"

"I'll give you more sons and daughters."

"I took an oath—"

"To damnation with your oath!" he said. "That is where mine resides. Did you not beg me to take you away that night in Gascony?"

"And you refused!" She had never before admitted the depth of resentment she nurtured against him for choosing duty over love during those fateful hours in Toulouse and Gascony. Now he was reproaching her for the same act of allegiance. Would she never be freed of the hypocrisy of men? "You said our vows were more important than—"

He stole her breath with a forceful kiss.

She surrendered in savage abandon, giving vent to years of rage, all the nights under Jourdaine when she had willed her skin to numbness during his many invasions. She would finally have recompense against the flesh! She rolled him onto his back and came sitting astride him. She ripped away his sweat-soaked shirt and pressed her face into his chest, luxuriating in the matte of coarse hair that branched from his taut abdomen. His calloused hands found her waist and traveled up her sides with such force that she feared her ribs might crack. *Why am I shaking?* He cupped her breasts and with a pant of desire pulled her down. No, it was *his* hands that were quivering. *He has never lain with a woman.* She found his lips again and felt him rise with arousal. St. Augustine's famous prayer came to her:

Make me chaste, Oh God. But not yet.

She surfaced to gain a breath, but she could not find air. An unbearable weight pressed against her chest, as if the aethers were congealing to collapse her lungs. *I am strangling.* She tried to warn him but could not force a sound from her mouth. Guilhelm looked up at her in confusion, as if questioning whether she was enthralled in some arcane feminine rapture that traveled the border between pain and ecstasy.

What is happening to me?

A flitting vision of a sarcophagus flashed across her memory's eye. She shuddered in recall. On the night of her initiation, she had suffered the same panic of suffocation, crafted by the elders to test her recognition of the world's illusion. She was being sent a warning—the Demiurge was tempting her.

She finally recovered and pulled away, overcome with guilt for having desired Guilhelm so wantonly. She loved this man, that she could not deny even before God, and all she had ever dreamed was to be his wife. Yet she could not abandon Bishop Castres and those who had sacrificed so much for her. Guilhelm had saved her life, but they had saved her soul. She covered herself and turned aside to reconcile her conflicting thoughts. After several moments of agonized debate, she spoke in a hushed tone to blunt the impact of what she was about to ask. "Will you take me to Carcassonne?"

Guilhelm, still recovering from her abrupt retreat, could make no sense of what he had just heard. Had the horrors of the day fractured her sanity? Or were all women this inconstant in the throes of passion? Why would she wish to put them both in harm's way again? He began to question if the heretics had instilled her with a death wish fueled by some nihilistic obsession for tempting fate's wrath. She knew that Folques carried a warrant for her arrest. Did she *want* to be captured? Perhaps she still held a perverse attraction for the former troubadour. The hope of taking her away from Occitania was all that had sustained him during these five long years. Crestfallen, he interrogated her with a brittle glare. When she would not waver from her request, he cursed this depraved world whose workings made less and less sense to him. He watched the scudding clouds rush west over the willow-lined Orb river and imagined them as sails of the Catalan carrack that could take him far away from this war. He could not shake the premonition that this would be his last chance to escape the madness descending upon the Languedoc.

Taking his protracted silence as a refusal, Esclarmonde mounted the Arabian and headed alone for Carcassonne, refusing to look back lest she weaken. A whistle halted the Arabian again.

The orange tiles of Carcassonne's conical towers glistened under the last spikes of daylight. Esclarmonde sat behind Guilhelm on the saddle as they angled across the distant ridge that rose above the marshy banks of the Aude river, which approached from the west and flirted with the pink-hued walls before turning north. Lauded by the troubadours as the Paris of the South, Carcassonne had been built in the shape of a distended oval on a rocky eminence that overlooked the main trade route from the Mediterranean to Toulouse. Although blessed by a rich diversity of culture, the Occitan city differed from its northern rival in one critical aspect—it had no equivalent of the Seine flowing through its center. Here Caesar's legions had confronted the same predicament that would hamper subsequent defenders: The highest ground in this corrugated verdure was several hundred paces from the river.

Guilhelm tacked through rows of staked vines to gain a clearer view of the parched ribbon of flatland that sloped down from the walls. He cursed under his breath—the van of the Cistercian army had arrived and was throwing up palisades between the river and the city. "Trevencal is finished."

Esclarmonde was perplexed by Guilhelm's dire assessment. Although the Northerners had marched west with stunning speed, Trevencal was afforded several days to strengthen the already-imposing castellated defenses. The city's thick walls, twice the height of Beziers's ramparts, were protected from the north and south by the Bourg and Castellare, suburbs of mud shanties surrounded by ditches and barbicans. The Chateau Comtal, Trevencal's impressive palace, sat in the northwest corner of the ville like a hard kernel in a chestnut. "The city appears heavily fortified."

Guilhelm pointed toward the lone bridge now under the control of the crusaders. "Trevencal could be sitting behind the walls of Jerusalem and they would do him no good. Do you see the placement of that aqueduct?"

"It runs parallel to the Pont du Gard."

"Why do you think the Romans built it there?"

She was growing annoyed with his pedantic tone. "Tell me."

"There are no wells on that rock. The Cistercians have cut Trevencal off from his only source of fresh water."

Esclarmonde reflexively slid her swollen tongue across her dry mouth. On their forced ride from Beziers, she had tasted only a few drops from Guilhelm's depleted flask, for the cisterns in the abandoned villages they had passed en route had been salted. She scanned the teethed bastions and searched for the black robes of her perfects. She prayed Castres had intercepted Phillipa in time, but she had to make certain. "I must get inside."

Guilhelm knew better than to renew his remonstrance against such a fool-hardy attempt. Dismounting, he stroked the Arabian's nostrils to allay its nickering and wrapped its hooves with sackings to muffle its clop. His aggrieved silence made all too clear his opinion that such a crossing would not be for the faint of heart. When the gloaming finally gave way to night, he mounted again and this time positioned her in front. They advanced on the bridge at a rising canter and took aim at the unsuspecting guards lounging along its entry. She tried to monitor their approach, but Guilhelm pressed her face into the mane to shield her from missiles. His arms tensed around her with such tenacity that she found it difficult to breathe. *So this is what he feels during battle.* A few paces from the bridge, he spurred to a jolting gallop.

"Breakthrough!" shouted a sentry.

The crusaders scrambled for their bows. The night air whistled with fletches and the water was stippled with pings. Halfway across, Esclarmonde escaped Guilhelm's restraint long enough to look back. The crusaders were giving chase and gaining ground. Guilhelm whipped their struggling horse past the far entry and rushed up an earthen ramp that ran parallel to Carcassonne's walls.

"Fire!"

She braced for the impact. To her relief, she discovered that the command had been shouted by an Occitan sergeant directing the defense on the walls. She heard shafts glancing off Guilhelm's cuirass and the whinnies of stumbling horses. The herse spikes of the portcullis lifted. A band of knights sallied out and held off the crusaders long enough for Guilhelm to reach the archway.

Inside the city, Esclarmonde lifted her eyes in the dismal light to a ghastly scene: Trevencal and Castres stood surrounded by thousands of panicked Occitans whose lips were cracked and bleeding from thirst. The wretches fought for what little space could be found amid bony cattle swarmed by armies of black flies. Several rushed for Guilhelm's empty flask and begged for water.

Castres was splotched and pasted in sweat from a fever that was spreading rapidly through the populace. "Child, why did you come here?"

Esclarmonde searched the panicked faces. "Where is Phillipa?"

"God be praised!" cried Castres. "She was not here when I arrived. She must have been warned to turn back."

Trevencal assisted Esclarmonde from the saddle. "My lady, what is the news from Beziers? We have been cut off from all communication."

Esclarmonde could not summon the courage to tell him in the presence of so many Occitans whose relatives had been murdered in the conflagration.

Breaking the apprehensive silence, Guilhelm answered for her, too harshly for compassion's need. "The city is razed. Your subjects are massacred."

Trevencal could barely form the next question. "*All* of them?"

"To the child."

A great wailing surged and cascaded down the streets as the report was passed through the pressing crowds. Trembling with rage, Trevencal motioned for his armor. The knights in his garrison girded their livery in preparation to ride out and meet the crusaders.

"You're outnumbered," warned Guilhelm. "Wait them out."

"I have forty thousand people inside these walls," said Trevencal. "There is water in the cisterns for two days, at most. I have to get to the river."

Amid the tumult of preparations, Esclarmonde caught sight of the limestone bust of Dame Carcas that hung over the main gate. As a girl, she had listened to her father tell how the city's maternal namesake saved these walls from Charlemagne by feeding the last of the grain to a calf and releasing it into the enemy lines. When the Franks had cut open the calf, they were so discouraged to find meal pouring from its gut that they lifted the siege and went home. Perhaps, thought Esclarmonde, a variation of the heroine's strategy might work again. She beseeched Trevencal, "Hold off your attack until I signal you."

The perplexed Viscount waited for an explanation for the queer request, but Esclarmonde was already leading the women and children to the cisterns. They filled their pots with what little water could be siphoned from the stagnant pools and carried them up to the allures. She ordered the torches lit so that the Franks could better see them on the walls. Dipping a ladle, she poured water down her face and threw the remainder of her gord to the rocks below. The other women followed her example, laughing and jesting as if they had not a care in the world. The men stripped their shirts and bathed, regaled by musicians who strummed their instruments as if playing for a festival. Out of sight of the Northerners, the children stood below the allures and caught the precious water droppings with skins.

At the river, the crusaders and routiers watched in disbelief as the Occitans cavorted on the walls. Seeing the Northerners abandon their weapons and draw closer to confirm the city's seemingly bountiful supply of water, Esclarmonde nodded for Trevencal and Guilhelm to unleash their attack. Four hundred knights came galloping in silence under the long shadows through the Narbonne Gate on the opposite side of the city. She fought the temptation to monitor their advance, fearful of giving away their advantage of surprise.

Minutes later, Trevencal's cavalry swept around the corner with a curdling whoop and ambushed the unarmed crusaders in the Castellare suburb. A jubilant cry shook the ramparts as the Northerners retreated in disarray toward the bridge. The Occitan knights dismounted at the banks of the river and began filling as many water skins as they could carry.

The celebration on the walls suddenly gave way to screams of warning—Simon de Montfort was leading a squadron back across the bridge.

Trevencal and his knights had no time to finish filling their skins. They scrambled back to their water-gorged horses to meet the assault. Guilhelm took aim at de Montfort's nasal, but his blow failed to faze the Norman. De Montfort heaved his blade and forced Guilhelm to slew against his crupper to avoid the cut. The smote caught the nape of Guilhelm's stallion and sent it crumpling to its forelegs. Guilhelm catapulted and rolled to his knees with the wind knocked out of his lungs. He looked up to find both forces retreating. He was abandoned with wounded men and horses writhing around him.

Trevencal turned back to rescue Guilhelm. De Montfort lashed up in a race to reach the Templar first. Inflamed by the memory of his boyhood humiliation, Trevencal charged and sent his old tormentor airborne with a scything slash. Grounded violently, de Montfort slowly regained his senses, only to be prodded and forced to crawl like a dog to avoid being trampled. Guilhelm crawled to his feet and climbed to the saddle behind Trevencal.

"My dead father sends his regards!" shouted Trevencal.

Staggered on hands and knees, de Montfort spied his sword, several paces away and out of reach. His nearsighted eyes darted wildly as he waited for the death clout. Finding Trevencal holding back, de Montfort taunted him with a gallows grin. "Sniveling calf! You don't have it in you!"

Trevencal raised his blade—and sheathed it. He deemed it unchivalrous to kill an unarmed man, no matter how much knavery he had committed. "Take a message to those mongrels of Satan. Tell them I will see their bones bleached whiter than their habits for what they did to Beziers!"

Stunned by the reprieve, de Montfort limped to his horse and lashed for the safety of the bridge. The Occitans abused him with curses and stones as he passed under Carcassonne's walls. He had nearly reached the river when his eye caught a silhouette on the ramparts framed by the full moon. He reined back and squinted in disbelief at the occulted face looking down upon him.

Had she returned from the dead?

De Montfort screamed at Esclarmonde, "This night belongs to you, witch! We'll see about the morrow!"

he few skins of water that Trevencal's bold foray gained did little to ease the suffering inside the city. The next morning, the populace was roused from its misery by distant chants of the *Veni Sancte*

Spiritus, the hymn that Innocent III had authored as the crusading anthem for the Languedoc war. In the field below the eastern wall, Almaric and Folques rode forth with a deputation of white-robed canons waving staffed crucifixes. The two clerics exhorted a phalanx of crusaders forward for an assault.

"They intend to try for the Bourg!" warned Trevencal.

Guilhelm, hobbled by the leg injury suffered in the previous day's fight, had to be assisted to the hoardings. Every man and woman capable of standing took stations on either side of the catapults that fringed the teethed walls. Those with no weapons loaded their tunics with rocks. Some panicked and let loose too soon. Their stones fell harmlessly into the ditches, far short.

"Hold your fire!" shouted Guilhelm. He shielded his eyes from the blinding light. The Northern barons had cleverly chosen to place the sun at their backs. Squinting, he saw Almaric and Folques ride through the crusader lines accompanied by ten catapults and battering rams whose frames were covered with animal skins. "The Cistercians are up to some artifice," warned Guilhelm. "Those cowards would never expose themselves in battle."

Almaric halted his engines just beyond the range of Trevencal's catapults. "Citizens of Carcassonne! Surrender the heretic woman and her followers, and you will be spared!" His offer was answered with a fusillade of stones.

"As you spared Beziers?" challenged Trevencal. "These walls have never been breached! Have at it!"

Almaric signaled for the hides covering the engines to be removed.

Esclarmonde shrieked in horror.

Phillipa, bloodied and half-conscious, was tied to the lead battering ram. On each side of her stood twenty captured Cathars strapped to the guns. Phillipa slowly raised her head and slumped in despair on finding that Esclarmonde had come into the besieged city looking for her.

Almaric ordered the engines and their human shields forward.

"If they reach the berm," warned Trevencal, "these walls will suffer gravely."

Esclarmonde tried to escape from the allures and run to the gate, but Guilhelm restrained her. He braced her shoulders and fixed on her with an insistent stare. "Nothing can be done," he said. "You must commend her to God."

De Montfort's men cranked the catapult latches and loaded the slings. Another twenty paces and their fire would be deadly. Trevencal held his archers at bay and looked to Esclarmonde for a decision. She was too numbed with grief to train her mind. Castres was on his knees at her side, praying incoherently, undone by Phillipa's plight.

Guilhelm led Esclarmonde behind a tower to prevent the Cistercians from witnessing her loss of resolve. He pressed his cheek to hers and whispered, "Do you not believe she goes to a better place?"

Sobbing, she sank into his chest. "I cannot bear to lose her!"

"Esclarmonde!" shouted Phillipa.

She looked down into the vale, A golden aura surrounded Phillipa's head. It was the same nimbus that she had observed during their first meeting in the Lombrives cave. Was it a sign from the Light?

A single tear fell like quicksilver to Phillipa's battered cheek. She closed her eyes in acceptance and prayed the Cathar Pater Noster. When finished, she looked up at Esclarmonde and cried, "Tell Roger and Loupe I love them!"

Esclarmonde collapsed. She knew Phillipa meant the request as a plea to sacrifice her life to save the city. Esclarmonde pressed a kiss to her shaking palm and raised it in a farewell, then turned away, the only act of assent she could manage. Guilhelm ordered the archers to take aim. When their bows were drawn taut, Esclarmonde begged them to hold off. She took Guilhelm aside and whispered to him. The Northern crusaders watched in bewilderment as Guilhelm commanded a bow and nocked an arrow. Esclarmonde touched the shaft to transmit the last rites of the Consolamentum. Phillipa nodded in relief to see that Guilhelm would attempt the shot. She arched her chest to offer him a better target.

Esclarmonde could not release her hand. Guilhelm pulled away from her reach, and fired. Phillipa kept her eyes fixed on Esclarmonde as the bodkin point sped toward her. She sank into the ropes—the shaft impaled her heart. A rain of missiles from the walls released the other hostages to the Light.

Their stratagem foiled, the Cistercians reared their spooked horses and retreated to a safe distance beyond the Occitan range of fire. Folques sat paralyzed with disbelief as he watched Esclarmonde pray over her martyred followers. He muttered to himself, "These people go willingly to their deaths for her. We will never command such allegiance."

Almaric snorted with disgust at the heretics' insipid disregard for life. He signaled for the full assault. Unleashed, the routiers dove into the moat and clawed up the banks to gain a foothold under the walls. Sheets of arrows whistled down as they attempted to throw planks across the moat.

"Loose the catapults!" shouted Trevencal.

De Montfort angled to avoid the bombardment and scrambled across the backs of wounded routiers. Scaling ladders rattled against the ramparts.

Trevencal's defenders sent the first wave of Franks crashing to their deaths. Repulsed, de Montfort turned to reform the ranks for another attempt when he discovered the other barons had deserted him. Pelted by stones, he discarded his armor to gain speed and beat a zagged retreat on foot toward the bridge, which was gorged with panicked men and horses.

The Occitans tried to loose a cheer, but their throats were too raw from thirst to make a sound.

During the days of misery that followed, the sun bore down upon Carcassonne like the tip of a red-hot branding iron. Trevencal begged Esclarmonde to keep her tongue wetted so that she could continue to preach, but she refused the additional ration of water. She did what little she could to nurse Castres, who was grief-broken and manic with fever, as were most of the besieged Occitans.

On Sunday morning, the church bells interrupted the city's languorous silence to announce an unexpected arrival at the gate. Esclarmonde came running from the hospital and found King Peter of Aragon riding his magnificent sorrel bay up the Rue Grande d'Aude. Christ entering Jerusalem on Palm Sunday could not have received a more glorious welcome. The Occitans roused from their wretchedness and threw themselves before the monarch in a frenzy of relief, certain that their benefactor had crossed the Pyrenees to save them.

Trevencal broke through the throngs. "My liege, you are a blessed sight!"

"I fear less so than you wish." With an upturned nose, Peter scanned the multitudes of walking skeletons and spotted among them a frail woman in black robes. Several moments passed before he recognized Esclarmonde in her haggard condition. "It deeply saddens me to find you here, my lady."

"Have you brought us water and medicinals, my lord?" asked Esclarmonde. "Our people die by the hundreds from the flux."

The King glared in pique at Trevencal for having caused this trouble with Rome by placing the welfare of a few heretics above the demands of statecraft. "I have crossed the mountains with two hundred knights at great expense."

"I will attack the bridge while you hit them from the rear," said Trevencal. "There is no time to waste. The strength of my men wanes by the hour."

"You are in no condition to fight. Your only hope is to negotiate terms."

The King's inconceivable counsel of surrender spiraled Trevencal into a fit of coughing. "With those madmen? Did you not hear what they did to Beziers? They used our own people as cover for their engines!"

Peter turned toward the hushed citizens in the hope of convincing them to give up their doomed defense. "The Abbot of Citeaux will allow the Viscount and eleven of his knights to leave unarmed."

"And the rest of us?" asked Esclarmonde.

Peter would not look at her directly. "Forfeited to the barons to dispense with as they see fit."

Trevencal had to be restrained from rushing the monarch. "You bring me such an offer from that murderous knave?"

Peter vented his frustration at Trevencal's ingratitude by yanking his mount's bit. "Save yourself. There will come another day for fighting."

Regretting his outburst, Trevencal sought the King's hand in contrition. "Good liege, would you abandon your kingdom, as you now ask me to do?"

The King repulsed the gesture and brought a kerchief to his nose to chase the gagging stench. He deemed the question too absurd to merit a response. No Christian monarch of his intelligence and stature would ever allow himself to be brought down so low by a rabble of Franks and Normans. "What answer do you wish me to convey?"

Trevencal swallowed painfully to ease the grate in his throat cords. After a hesitation, he straightened in defiance. "You may tell those Cistercian thieves they'll see donkeys fly before they enter this city."

The King waited for a public remonstrance to that reckless bravado. To his astonishment, the citizens lodged no protest to their leader's obstinacy, but walked back into their corners of suffering, determined to renew their resistance. He shook his head in disbelief. "You Occitans are a stubborn breed. My troubadours shall sing of your courage, ill-advised as it surely is." Before departing, he warned Esclarmonde, "Whatever happens here, my lady, you must not allow yourself to fall into the hands of those Cistercians."

After two weeks of the siege, the carrion crows were so satiated by the abundance of putrid flesh that they no longer flew over the city. The Northerners left the bodies of Phillipa and the Cathar martyrs tied to the engines, where they were gnawed at by wild dogs and used for target practice by the routiers. Trevencal banned all but his garrison from climbing to the walls for fear that the sight would drive his subjects mad.

When her flagging strength permitted, Esclarmonde canvassed the waste-fouled streets and brought the worst of the afflicted to the lazar house. Each day that passed under the cloudless sun seemed like a month in duration. She learned to her horror that a city dies much like a human body, rotting slowly from the extremities first, then shutting down in its central organs.

In the relative cool of the early mornings, the cremation gangs would ring their bells to collect the corpses of those who had expired during the night. Trevencal refused to give the Northerners the satisfaction of watching the bodies thrown over the walls. Instead, he ordered cremation pyres kept fueled without cessation. The noxious smoke exacerbated the unbearable heat and poisoned air. Most of the dead were found huddled below the eastern wall overlooking the city's cemetery. Denied burials, the Occitans would crawl there to be near their ancestors. Some wrapped themselves in shrouds and sewed the seams to their necks to save their families the trouble. Those who survived the nights made their way to St. Nazaire the next morning to lick condensation from the cathedral's marble pillars. Others drank their own urine or the blood of rotting cattle, only to find their agony increased. Yet throughout this ordeal, not one Catholic called for Esclarmonde and her Cathars to be surrendered.

Trevencal, however, was beginning to crack under the strain. On this morning, he rode forth from his palace in full armor, his sunken face sealed in an expression of manic fixedness. The people gasped at how altered in appearance their youthful liege had become. Patches of his once-thick blond hair had fallen from his scalp and his lips were the morbid shade of dark plums. He tried to hide the pallor of disease by daubing his face with rouge, but the effect made him look as if he had been embalmed with a thin layer of wax.

Esclarmonde hurried to intercept him. "My lord, where are you going?"

Trevencal's febrile gaze remained trained on the gate. Christ on His way to Cavalry could not have looked more tortured yet accepting of the bitter cup being offered. Finally, he looked down at her with pain-soddened eyes and rasped, "I must negotiate with the Abbot."

Guilhelm captured the reins and tried to dissuade Trevencal from leaving the protection of the city. "The Northern barons are only pledged for one more week. Wait them out. They will abandon the Cistercians."

"Another week and I will command a charnel house," said Trevencal. "My uncle is with them. I will plead my cause with him. He is one of us."

"The Count of Toulouse cares not a whit about your kingdom," reminded Guilhelm. "Unless it falls into his hands."

"His father was a man of honor," said Trevencal.

Helpless, the Viscount's officers turned to Esclarmonde, the only one among them of sufficient stature to dissuade him from this folly. She was so depleted by illness that she could only grasp Trevencal's hand in a silent plea.

Trevencal forced a sluggish smile to allay her fears. "You would do the same for your flock." He wrapped his shoulders in his ceremonial sash and ordered his horse watered to prevent it from expiring before he crossed the river. The Cistercians, he knew, would closely examine him for an indication of the city's condition.

Guilhelm ordered his own mount be brought up from the stables.

"You don't mean to go with him?" said Esclarmonde.

"I'll not stand by and watch him thrown to those wolves alone."

The guards fought back the throng of citizens who begged to accompany their liege as guardians. After bidding Trevencal to remain just beyond the portal, Guilhelm left the city and advanced toward the crusader lines waving a white gonfalon from his lance. He reached the Northern headquarters and waited for de Montfort and the Cistercians to emerge from their tents.

"Trevencal wishes a parlay," said Guilhelm.

De Montfort gripped the handle of his sword, itching to strike. "I'll have a parlay of a different sort with you, Templar."

Almaric studied the distant mounted figure at the gate. "The baron is willing to discuss terms with us in person?"

"Upon your vow of safe conduct," said Guilhelm.

The Abbot mulled the proposition. "Agreed."

"I must hear it from this Norman swine as well."

The Abbot nodded a command for de Montfort to submit. The Norman bit his lip, but finally he acquiesced. "My blade rests for an hour."

Guilhelm crossed back over the river and made a detour to the siege engines. He took advantage of the brief truce to cut the ropes holding the rotting Cathar corpses. He wrapped Phillipa's remains in one of the skins and delivered them to the Occitan soldiers manning the gate.

Trevencal maintained a keen watch on the Cistercians, who stood waiting across the river. "Did they give their word?"

"For what it's worth," said Guilhelm.

Trevencal cantered back toward the Port d'Aude and whispered something in confidence to Esclarmonde. Guilhelm monitored their exchange, but he could divine no hint of its purpose, except that she seemed discomfited by what she had been told. She tried to call Trevencal back, but he was off on an unsteady gallop for the bridge, blessed by the waving scarves of his subjects.

Guilhelm caught up and together they threaded the gauntlet of routiers and crusaders, who needed only a twitch of a threat for an excuse to draw their weapons. Escorted into the Cistercian pavilion, Trevencal walked up to Count Raymond of Toulouse and stared nose to nose at his uncle. Several seconds passed before the paunchy Raymond realized that the wraith standing before him was his nephew. The Toulouse baron stole a guilt-laced glance at Guilhelm, whose life he had cowardly condemned in St. Gilles. Unable to bear Trevencal's insolent inspection, Raymond broke off their war of wills and shoved him aside. "Have you fallen dumb?"

"I am trying to discern how we could share the same blood."

"Impudent ass!" shouted Raymond.

Trevencal had to be restrained. "You think you can nest with these snakes and not get bitten?"

Almaric sniggered at the spectacle of family dissension. Finally, he had his fill of the hurled threats and curses. "Have you something of importance to say? Or did you ask for this meeting to trade insults?"

Trevencal swayed from weakness. He braced his palms against the table behind him, careful not to let the Northerners detect his need for support. "I wish an audience with the Holy Father."

Folques laughed at him with scorn. "What makes you think the Holy Father grants hearings to heretical barons?"

"I will go to Rome to offer my defense."

"It is a bit late for that," said the Abbot. "I have been delegated the authority for exorcizing this land. The siege will not be raised until all of the cloggers under your protection are handed over."

"We know all too well how you distinguish heretics from believers," said Trevencal. "You let the flames decide."

The Abbot circled Trevencal with a calculating step. "I've heard it said that you were educated by Bertrand de Saissac, a notorious heretic. Reprobates who protect Christ's enemies must accept the consequences of their malfeasance."

"The only enemies of Christ in this land conspire in this tent."

Almaric offered Trevencal a goblet of water to test his resolve. "Your people suffer needlessly because of your allegiance to these heretics. Why should your sinful pride cause good Catholics to endure eternal damnation?"

Trevencal accepted the goblet and gazed at his reflection in the cool water. He blinked with shock, apprised for the first time of the ravages that the siege had taken on him. He raised the goblet to his lips—and poured the water at the feet of the Cistercians. He threw the cup aside and strode with a faltering gait toward the portal flap. "I am prepared to wait out the summer."

A step from the exit, the two Occitans were grappled to the ground by de Montfort and his officers.

"*We* are not," said Almaric, smirking.

Guilhelm fought in vain to reach the treacherous monks. "Lying dogs!"

Folques slammed a foot into Guilhelm's ribs. "Contracts with Satan's advocates are not binding. The Holy Father wishes new overlords installed in Occitania. Barons who will prosecute the heretics with zeal. And you, Templar, have your own list of crimes to answer."

The prisoners were dragged from the pavilion and paraded in tethers across the bridge. A moan of despair swept across Carcassonne's ramparts.

Almaric shouted at the Occitans who had crowded atop the walls, "Within the hour, every man, woman, and child in this recalcitrant city will walk out wearing only shirt and breeches. Defy Holy Mother Church in this command and your liege will suffer grievously."

Trevencal tried to scream for his subjects to disobey the Abbot's demand, but de Montfort and the crusaders knocked him senseless.

When the allotted hour had passed, the gates of Carcassonne were swung open. Thousands of half-naked Occitans staggered forth from the city and filed past a waiting gauntlet of crusaders and routiers. The Northerners howled with laughter as they beat the wretches forward with clubs. Some of the Occitans broke through the cordon and risked decapitation to slake their thirst at the river.

Almaric and Folques sat shading under a canopy while surveying this passing train of misery to ferret out the Cathars among the inhabitants. When the last of the disgorged Occitans had been searched and interrogated, no heretics were discovered among them. Incensed, Almaric ordered de Montfort to scour the city's nooks and cellars to drive Esclarmonde and her craven followers from their hiding.

At day's end, de Montfort and his men returned with the report that not even a rat could be found inside the walls. Seething at the inexplicable deception, the Cistercians rushed to the prison cart where they had ordered

Trevencal and Guilhelm clamped in chains. Trevencal peered out with a grim smile from the cramped confines of the small dovecote that had been converted into a pronged cage.

Folques slapped the Viscount's face. "Where have the heretic woman and her brood absconded?"

Guilhelm turned on Trevencal with a look of confusion, unable to fathom how Esclarmonde could have escaped.

Trevencal spat blood at Folques. "You tonsured devils insist that she's a witch. Mayhaps she cast a spell on you and flew away."

One who gazes into
the vision of the Chariot first descends
and then ascends . . . He has rays from His hand,
and His hidden face is there. What is His Hidden Face?
This is the Light that was stored away and hidden . . .
— The Bahir, Kabbalah

XXII

Foix

November 1209

Esclarmonde whispered a prayer of relief on seeing Foix's towers pierce the clouds like the pillars of Hercules. She arose from her crouch in the tussocks of heathland broom and motioned up Castres and eight perfects from their hiding behind the high rocks. Two agonizing months had passed since their escape from Carcassonne. Before his disastrous meeting with the Cistercians, Trevencal had told her of a tunnel that ran from St. Nazaire's ossuary crypt to a faux grave in the cemetery outside the walls. She and her five hundred Cathars had hidden in that underground passageway until the Northern army decamped. To avoid capture, she had divided the perfects and perfectas into bands of ten with orders to make their way separately to Montsegur. She led her own clan of bedraggled refugees on a detour to Foix, surviving on mushrooms and berries while traveling at night through the wilds of the Pierre-Lys Gorge.

With the safety of her brother's chateau now only a river's breadth away, she tried to find the courage required to tell Roger and Loupe of Phillipa's death. She prepared to make the run across the dangerous open ground when she heard moans from a nearby grove. Alarmed, she signaled for Castres and the others to drop into the tall grass.

A ragged man, more demonic than human in aspect, staggered out from the coppice with his scabrous, blood-clotted face missing an eye. He snorted with excruciating breaths as he snapped a rope tied to his wrist. Piles of dried leaves stirred. Fifty tethered men emerged from dugout holes—all with both eyes gouged out and noses sliced off.

Esclarmonde fought the urge to retch. "Who did this to you?"

"A Northern excrement named de Montfort." The one-eyed leader swiveled his head in a pitiful attempt to gain depth of vision. "You wear the black robe."

"I am the Count of Foix's sister."

The men fell to their knees and reached for her hand in the hope of a miracle. Castres and the perfects came running and spread out among the men to administer the healings.

"De Montfort mangled us in Bram while the Cistercians watched," said the leader of the men. "Saissac. Alzonne. Montreal. All have fallen."

"Why did they leave you alone with one eye?" she asked.

"The Norman forced us to draw lots. When I won, he ordered me to lead them here to tell your brother that he's coming to give him the same treatment."

Roger came bounding down from the chateau to meet Esclarmonde as she climbed the hill. "We'd all but given you up for lost."

She tried to turn him back. "Don't let the girls come out!"

"They've stood waiting at the window for weeks!" Roger shook off her restraint and found the other perfects lurking below the brow, attempting to avoid his detection. He came closer and saw the men with faces covered by swathes torn from their cuffs. He ripped off the ragged bandanas to reveal their identities. Slack-mouthed, he turned on Esclarmonde, questioning if she had undertaken some perverse heretic ritual against the flesh. Before she could explain, he discovered that Phillipa was not among the returned Cathars. "Where is my wife?"

Esclarmonde drew him aside. "Roger . . ."

Roger repulsed her attempt to take his hand. "Damn you! Answer me!"

"Phillipa . . . is dead."

Roger stood rooted to the ground, incapable of comprehending what he had just heard. Shaking from the dawning impact of the revelation, he manhandled the Bishop, who meekly accepted his wrath.

Esclarmonde shielded Castres. "The Cistercians have declared war."

Roger shoved her aside and circled aimlessly, bereft of a target. "I warned you this damned religion of yours would—"

"Aunt Essy! Aunt Essy!"

Loupe and Chandelle came scampering down ahead of Corba and the Marquessa. The two girls latched onto Esclarmonde's robe and leapt with joy at finding her returned. Wet-cheeked, Esclarmonde tried to turn Loupe away.

Loupe found her father on his knees with his face twisted. "What's the matter, Papa?" She saw the disfigured soldiers and shrieked. "Where's Mama?"

Esclarmonde took Loupe into her arms. "My love, be brave." She spoke rapidly for fear of losing her voice. "Your mother . . . has gone to God."

Loupe turned purple. "Mama is . . . I told you not to let her go!"

"There was nothing I could—"

"You killed her!"

Roger yanked Loupe from Esclarmonde's grasp. "How did it happen?"

"The Cistercians tied her to the siege guns. Trevencal had no choice."

"Trevencal fired the shot?"

Roger's fearsome glare drove her answer. "Guilhelm."

"The Templar . . . killed my wife?"

Esclarmonde stole a helpless glance at the Marquessa and Corba, but they were too enmeshed in grief to offer a buffer to his vehemence. "Blame me if you must. I asked him to release her from—"

Roger ran toward the stables, swearing against God and quavering with such spuming rage that he seemed on the verge of choking. The small garrison and the villagers, drawn by the screams and wails, began congregating in the bailey. Roger pulled a sword from its brackets and climbed the railings of the foaling stall. He hacked away at his favorite steed, the magnificent Arabian that Phillipa had so loved. He seemed possessed of a primeval urge to expiate his wife's death by sacrificing the one creature that had remained loyal to him in this depraved world ruled by betrayal. The blade sliced into the animal's neck and splattered blood across the stable. The bawling Arabian knifed to its forelegs.

Loupe tried to go to her father, but Esclarmonde held tight to her, fearful that Roger would flail away at anything that came within his range.

After several more blows, Roger fell to his knees, exhausted and slathered with entrails. In a deadened voice, he ordered his men, "Issue the summons."

"You can't mean to go after them!" cried Esclarmonde.

Roger staggered to his feet and drove her against the wall. "I've had enough of your damned religion and its turn of the cheek!"

"If not for *my* religion, you'd never have met Phillipa! I beg of you! Leave it in God's hands."

Roger threw her from his path with such force that she fell. "It *has* been in God's hands! Now it will be in mine! Take these troublemakers to that den of Hell and stay forever from my sight!"

Esclarmonde crawled after him. "Banish me if you wish, but leave Loupe in my care. You cannot raise her if you mean to fight."

Roger drove a boring finger into Castres's forehead. "You stole my mother *and* my wife. If I ever find you in my daughter's presence, I'll gut you!"

"Where are you taking her?" cried Esclarmonde.

"To learn how murderous monks are dealt with."

"She's only a child!"

"I grew up before my time," said Roger. "She'll do the same."

On her knees, Esclarmonde pleaded for her niece to stay. "Loupe, come with me to Montsegur."

Loupe burned her with a glare of hatred, then ran off to join her father.

That winter, a heavy snow buried Montsegur under a pall of despair. Each day brought more refugees from the Northern army's swath of terror. De Montfort and the Catholic barons ravaged the Aude Valley opposed only by Roger's small force of Occitan raiders. For the first time since her ordination, Esclarmonde could not find the strength to minister to her people. Beset by a paralyzing melancholy, she sequestered herself in a small hut on the north face of the mount and gave orders that she not be disturbed. With Raymond off soldiering, Corba and Chandelle came to stay with her at the temple. Each day they left food on her sill, but she would not touch it.

This morning, streams of harsh sunlight invaded the hut. Lying on a straw pallet, Esclarmonde shielded her eyes and found Chandelle standing at the opened door. "Leave me be, child."

From the shadows, an elderly man with a wispy gray beard came into the glim holding Chandelle's hand. Phylacteries hung from his head and his waist was wrapped in a blue sash. His foggy eyes remained fixed with a distant stare.

"Please talk to this man," begged Chandelle.

"I cannot give spiritual sustenance today," said Esclarmonde.

The stranger took another unsure step and swiveled his head from side to side. "I have come to give, not to ask."

"I'm sorry?"

"You don't remember?"

"You must forgive me," said Esclarmonde. "I've not been well."

"You saved my life in Beziers. I am known as Isaac the Blind."

The features of the rabbi Esclarmonde had sent to safety with Trevencal slowly came to her memory. "Yes, of course. But why have you come to Montsegur?"

"This war between you Christians has cast my people upon another diaspora. We were told of a haven in these mountains."

Esclarmonde tried to arise, but her vertigo thwarted the effort. "I would do more to ease your plight, but . . . we have little to offer."

"Aunt Essy, he can help you feel better." Familiar with the room, Chandelle led the blind rabbi to the pallet. He knelt with difficulty and pressed his palms to Esclarmonde's forehead as if reading her soul by touch.

Esclarmonde felt a warmth around her temples. "Are you a healer?"

The rabbi maintained his silent concentration. After several minutes of this spiritual inspection, he removed his hands from her head and settled into a seated position. He asked Chandelle, "You are certain we are alone?"

"The others are in the temple," said Chandelle.

Reassured, the rabbi edged closer to the pallet. With lowered voice, he said, "That day in Beziers, you spoke of a Light."

"Forgive me," said Esclarmonde. "That is a teaching I can discuss only with the initiates of my faith."

The old Jew was undeterred. "Our secret tradition for imparting these mysteries is called Kabbalah."

That strange Hebrew word filled Esclarmonde with a rush of energy.

"It means 'to receive,'" he explained. "The secret of drawing down the divine Light was delivered to Moses by the Egyptian priests. He taught it to the prophets, who transmitted it by word of mouth to the Essenes. They in turn taught it to your Master Jesus ben Joseph. All who attain the keys to this arcana confront the same persecution that you and I now endure."

"You are attacked by those of your own faith?"

"Charlatans who claim no enlightenment is possible beyond the written Word dismiss me as a demented magician. One who approaches the Throne of the Unspeakable is never accepted by the jackals who scheme to hoard its spiritual power."

Esclarmonde had never considered the possibility that the Jews, sons and daughters of the Old Testament, might quest for the same divine radiance. Did searchers for the Light reincarnate into all faiths? If so, it followed that the angels of Darkness would also infiltrate every religion. Something about this rabbi's quiet confidence led her to believe she could confide in him. Despite her fervent petitions for guidance, her Voice had offered no guidance since the day she had been directed to build Montsegur. Perhaps this mystic Jew could tell her why she had been abandoned. "I've lost that which once sustained me."

"You are being emptied. Old wine must be discarded to give way to the new."

"Darkness drags me further into the abyss with each passing day."

"You require the Chariot."

"Chariot?"

"In our tongue, it is called the 'Mer Ka Bah.' Ezekiel warned long ago that the higher spheres cannot be reached without it."

As a girl, Esclarmonde had been haunted by that prophet's visions in the Book of Revelation. "Ezekiel was the one who saw the Ark of the Covenant."

The rabbi rocked on his haunches in a ritualistic movement that seemed designed to connect him to the higher realms. "The seals are not broken unless one has studied these mysteries in past lives. Is it not written in your gospels that the Rabbi Jesus asked his disciples whom the people thought he was?"

"It is."

"And did His disciples not say that some held Him to be the Baptist, and others Elijah, and still others Jeremiah? Why would they answer this way if they did not believe in the return of the soul?"

Esclarmonde was amazed. If this rabbi spoke true, then Castres had been correct in his claim that the Church fathers neglected to excise from the gospels certain telling fragments about transmigration. She watched as the rabbi began drawing several shapes in the dirt—triangles, circles, and crosses.

"The first elders of your faith embraced the truth of reincarnation," he said. "But when the wife of the pagan emperor Constantine learned that she would suffer rebirth to pay for her promiscuity, she demanded her husband outlaw the doctrine. Your bishops from the West conspired to gain the emperor's conversion by condemning transmigration as heresy."

Chandelle snuggled closer to the Jew, giving the first hint that she had been listening intently. "Did Jesus study your Kabbalah?"

Isaac placed the stick in Chandelle's fingers and helped her sketch the sacred images. Together they created a cross with one vertical bar and three horizontal bars—the same symbol that Esclarmonde had seen as a girl in Lombrives. The rabbi embellished his drawing by connecting the lines and adding circles. His finished schematic looked like an intricate tree that bore fruit. Inside the circles he formed Hebraic letters that carried powerful vibrations.

"Your Rabbi Jesus knew that Ezekiel's vision was a veiled description of the Chariot," said Isaac. "The throne of glittering ice was the final approach to the Light's center. Ezekiel witnessed these during his ascension on the paths."

Esclarmonde rubbed her temples in an effort to awaken her dormant mind, dulled by the stupor of her illness.

Sensing her frustration, the rabbi pointed to his breastbone. "The teaching must be taken here, in the heart. The high priest of the Temple wore the jeweled breastplate to facilitate the heart's connection to the upper regions."

Esclarmonde did not fully understand this mystery of the spiritual Chariot. Yet it seemed to her to be steeped in a profound truth.

The rabbi persisted despite her frown of confusion. "To gaze upon the Ancient of Ancients with our outer eyes invites disaster."

She noticed for the first time that his eyes did not look like those of other blind people, including Chandelle's, but were glazed white and striated like marbles, as if the pupils had been seared by heat. "Is that what happened to your—"

"The petty travails of my life are of no importance!" Vexed by her allusion to his own impairment, Isaac fell silent, lost in painful memories.

Chandelle broke the tension. "I see angels every day."

Isaac surrendered his melancholy and blessed the blind child with a toothless grin. "You and I have an advantage, little one."

"I feel as if I am the blind one here," said Esclarmonde in contrition.

"I have the only antidote for spiritual blindness," said Isaac. "Now, where was I? Ah, yes. Some of the angels lusted for the unmediated illumination. They ripped away the veils before they were prepared to received its mediated force. The Light broke the vessels that held it in check. It was like a great river bursting its dams. These ambitious angels were swept away, and when they awoke, they were trapped in the flesh, prisoners of the Demiurge."

Esclarmonde realized that the rabbi's explanation of the world's calamity was similar to that taught by Castres. Yet one tradition was Christian and the other Jewish. "Are we then condemned to remain lost forever?"

Isaac directed her attention to his drawing: Nine circles in three rows were connected by lines, resembling an ascending scale. "This is the only escape."

"It looks like Jacob's Ladder," she said.

The Jew smiled at her perspicacity. "Jacob climbed the same path ascended by your Master Jesus. These spheres are called Sephiroths. Each represents a spiritual level created by the Ain Soph—the Unspeakable Name—to repair the catastrophe and ration the downward flow of the spilled Light. When you meditate, you must concentrate on riding the Chariot up these planes."

"Do these spheres and paths truly exist?" she asked.

"Can you see the air you breathe?"

"No, but—"

"Yet you never doubt the air. Did your Master not promise many mansions in the Kingdom? These paths take you to the gates of true salvation."

Esclarmonde traced her finger up the Tree of Life until she came to the highest station. "What will I encounter on this ascent?"

"The Lords of Light post an archangel at each portal. If you are found worthy, you will be allowed to pass to the next station. What appears depends on the seeker's needs and merit. There are three primary routes. The left is the Pillar of Severity, chosen by martyrs and ascetics. The right path, the Pillar of Mercy, is traveled by those who ease the suffering of others."

"The two outer paths appear symmetrical. Do they depend on each other?"

He nodded to confirm her astuteness. "Those who suffer are equal in number to those who ease suffering. Likewise, both male and female are present in the Unspeakable. Only when this truth is accepted will the Middle Path open."

"But Rome insists that God is male."

The rabbi bobbed his head as if attempting to liberate a trapped answer. "The Wife of the Almighty is Sophia, the feminine Wisdom. Together they sit on the dazzling Throne. Fools and usurpers describe divinity by the reflection of their own cross-eyed gaze. Where there is grasping for spiritual power, there will be disharmony. Where there is disharmony, there will be ignorance. And where there is ignorance, there will be injustice."

Inspired, Esclarmonde fought the dragging ballast of her lassitude and curled into a seated meditation position. She required all of her wan strength just to remain upright, but she had been given the gift of renewed hope, and for that she was deeply beholden. "Thank you for saving me."

"I save no one," said Isaac. "Your salvation depends solely on your will and courage." Before departing, he turned back with a warning. "There will come a time on this ascent when you have to make a choice: Leave your body forever, or return to help others find the Light."

For five days and nights, Esclarmonde meditated furiously. Yet all she encountered were the tortured thoughts of her own cracking mind. Weak from hunger, she finally collapsed to the floor, convinced that both Isaac and Castres were deluded about the existence of this higher realm. If the God of Light did exist, He had long ago abandoned her. She had lost a niece, a brother, a lover, and a son. All in the bidding of a deity who—

A violet flash illumined the room. The glowing presence took on the form of a resplendent figure with long dark hair and a countenance of avian intensity. The man—or was it a woman?—wielded a flaming sword and a scale of measures. A serpent curled around the legs of this illuminated figure.

"Who are you?" she asked with trepidation, backing away.

"Mikael."

"Where am I?"

"At the crossing to the Splendor, the first gate . . . You have a question."

She remembered the rabbi's admonition: Meet all with courage and the truth in one's heart. "Why does your God allow my people to suffer?"

"Who made them *your* people?"

"They come to me for answers," she said. "I cannot ask them to die for a faith that I myself do not understand."

"There is a war."

"I know there is a war!" she shouted. "I have seen it too close!"

"I speak of a war that has been waged since the beginning. Yours is but a skirmish in the greater struggle."

"Why do you not defeat these legions of Evil?"

"You must first prevail," said Mikael. "We depend on you."

"You ask the impossible! The Northern armies overwhelm us."

"You possess a weapon they lack."

"Weapon? We abjure all violence!"

Mikael offered her the shimmering blade, whose tip sparked with a phosphorescent effulgence. "The Sword of Love."

The weightless blade resonated from an ineffable force. She tried to return it, but the archangel refused the attempt. Before she could ask him what she was suppose to do with the weapon, he receded into the Light.

Another vortex spawned—Phillipa emerged from its emanating center.

Overjoyed, Esclarmonde rushed to embrace her departed friend.

"The radiance is too dangerous," warned Phillipa, backing away. "You must put my death behind you. Do not lose heart."

Esclarmonde wept uncontrollably. "Roger is consumed by vengeance."

"He must go through his own trials," said Phillipa.

"Loupe follows him."

Phillipa's face darkened. "His bitterness must not take root in her heart."

Mikael reappeared, signaling to Phillipa that it was time to depart.

"I have to know what has happened to Guilhelm!" cried Esclarmonde.

Phillipa disintegrated into the brilliant Light.

At the portal, Mikael turned back to Esclarmonde and warned, "All now depends on you."

The doors of Fanjeaux Abbey slammed open. A startled archdeacon dropped his chalice and backed away from the altar. His fellow monks retreated to the ambits of the nave. Ten Occitan knights marched down the aisle. Loupe walked at her father's side grasping his hand.

"Where is the Bishop of Toulouse?" demanded Roger.

The archdeacon gauged the distance to the sacristy door. "With Simon de Montfort on the road to Carcassonne."

The one-eyed Occitan retracted the archdeacon's cowl. "This one was in Bram when the Norman cut us."

Roger clamped the archdeacon's chin and lifted him off his feet. "And the Castilian Guzman? Where is he skulking??" When the red-faced archdeacon glared his canons to silence, Roger dragged him down the steps of the chancel to confront Loupe. "Your Abbot murdered this child's mother."

"You cannot hold us responsible!" cried the archdeacon.

"Isn't that what your God does?" demanded Roger. "Hold each of us responsible for the sins of Adam?"

"He does, but—"

"And did your God send His only son to die for the sins of others?"

The archdeacon whimpered, "He did."

"Then, by God's own law and example, you must be held answerable for the sins of your Abbot, no?"

The archdeacon cowered on his knees. "Spare me! I beg of you!"

Roger brought Loupe a step closer. "She will decide."

Loupe glared at the frightened monk. "Did you see my mother die?"

"War has its victims, child."

"Has she gone to Heaven?"

The monk withheld an answer until spurred on by Roger's blade. "Your mother was a heretic. She fell into Satan's clutches, but you can yet be saved."

Loupe escaped crying into her father's arms, distraught to learn that her mother had been damned to Hell.

Roger dragged the monk to a Bible. "Find the passage about the eye."

The archdeacon trembled as he frantically thumbed through the tome. He stopped at a page and slowly lowered the red ribbon to mark the place.

"Read it," ordered Roger.

The monk's face drained whiter with each word. "'If any harm follows, then you shall give . . . life for life, eye for eye, tooth for tooth, hand for hand, foot for foot, burn for burn, wound for wound, stripe for stripe.'"

Roger shoved the archdeacon's nose into the crease. "Tell this child if your God requires an eye for an eye." When the monk surrendered a reluctant half nod, Roger asked, "Then I would be a heretic if I did not obey it, no?"

"The Lord Jesus allows mercy!" sputtered the monk.

"Be assured that I will be more merciful than you Cistercians." Roger spread out a parchment and forced a dipped quill into the monk's hand. "Confess that the Scriptures are in error. Confess that God never required an eye for an eye, and you will live."

"I would suffer the fires of Hell!"

"Your faith seems to have cast you in a dilemma," said Roger. "The Pope says the God of the Old Testament was righteous. The heretics say that He was a tyrant. I wonder which version you will choose."

The monk slung the quill to the floor and made a dash for the sacristy. The Occitans wrestled him down and splayed his limbs. "This is Rome's justice!" Roger drove his sword into the monk's right eye. The monk howled and crawled down the nave gushing blood. The Occitans dragged him back to the altar and quartered him. Roger gutted the monk's remaining eye.

Loupe stood over the writhing monk and watched him bleed to death.

The Savior said: "Blessed Thomas, the visible Light
shines upon you not to keep you here, but to make you leave."
- The Gospel of Thomas

XXIII

Carcassonne

November 1209

De Montfort slammed the papal communiqué to the table. "I cannot win this war with masses alone!"

Almaric hacked from the chill that had settled into his lungs as he hovered over the scalloped hearth of his new headquarters in Trevencal's former palace. "Prayers from His Holiness are worth more than gold."

De Montfort glowered at Folques, expecting support in his protest. "Are you going to stand mute while Rome pisses away your bishopric?"

Folques dared not challenge the Abbot, even though he shared Simon's frustration with the Holy See's sporadic financial patronage of the war. When the forty-day pledges expired, the Northern barons had returned home with their spoils. Simon threatened to do the same until Almaric offered Beziers and Carcassonne as inducement for taking command of the army. Simon drove a hard bargain, extracting a commitment from the Cistercians that they would champion his claim for suzerainty over all of Toulousia when the Occitan fiefs were reapportioned by the Vatican.

Yet the Lion of the Languedoc—the epithet bestowed on de Montfort by his enemies—now found himself embroiled in a grinding war of attrition with no end in sight. The rebels had retreated to their lairs atop the Pyrenees and most of his own troops had been siphoned off to defend the many chateaux in Trevencal's domain. In a hostile territory scavenged bare of food and fodder, he could count on only a hundred knights to answer a day's muster. Adding to his woe was news from England that the earldom of Leicester, devolved to him after his mother's death, had been confiscated by King John for unpaid debts.

"Ours is not the only army in need of reinforcements," reminded Almaric. "The Holy Father has called for another mission to the Holy Land."

Simon upended a velvet chaise. "Damn that man's malevolent timing! No knight will join me when he can win Heaven in Jerusalem!"

"You must hold out for the Lenten season," said Almaric. "In the spring, I will return to Paris and preach the indulgences."

Simon paced in spiraling agitation, rubbed raw by the patronizing military counsel of these clerics. "How am I to defend this shit hole until then? Peter broods beyond the mountains like a dog deprived of his favorite bone."

"The King of Aragon is loyal to Rome," assured the Abbot.

"And the Wolf? He harasses me without cease."

Folques finally found the nerve to speak up. "The Count of Foix's rectification will come soon enough on the open field."

Simon's rancor came to a sudden boil. He throttled Folques's neck and drove his nose into the window slit. "You arrant imbecile! That whoreson and his phantoms know better than to attack me on the plains! While I sit here rotting inside this tower, he plans his resistance from those pigeon roosts!" He sent Folques floundering to the floor with a flick of his wrist.

"The Wolf is a mere irritant," said Almaric. "Nothing more."

"The two of you have made him of consequence with that half-baked scheme to use his wife as arrow matting. Foix has become infested with every miscreant who escapes our fires."

"His sister professes to be a pacifist. She will keep him in check."

"His sister? From what I hear, he won't even speak to her! Even though you've managed to make her a subject of song in every court from Castile to Rome!" Simon searched the chamber for some accessory that had not suffered his abuse. "I'll never command the allegiance of these Ocs as long as they hold Trevencal and that Foix bitch in their hearts!"

"Then you must rid their hearts of such attachments."

The intrusion of that new voice at the door was accompanied by a chilling gust of wind. Alice Montmorency de Montfort stood at the threshold, slapping a cropper against her gloved hand.

All strain sailed from Simon's face as he rushed to the wife whose companionship he had been denied for nearly a year. If there was anything that stirred his juices more than a well-preached sermon or a battle rife with booty, it was this mole-studded woman whose thin auburn hair was bound as severely as her lips were pursed. "My love! You've come at my blackest hour."

Alice repulsed Simon's embrace. She circled the Cistercians with her face so thickly glazed in white powder that she might have passed for an apparition of the biblical Lilith. "So, these are the buglers who send the hounds to the hunt."

The Abbot bowed with his hand extended, exuding a cloying charm as was his method upon meeting a new acquaintance who offered the promise of some advantage. "Madam, I've not had the pleasure."

She fingered the sarcenet silk of his scapular. "By the impressive thread count of your garb, Abbot, I'd venture there is precious little pleasure you've not had." She rifled through the correspondence on his writing desk. "Why have more troops not been provided to my husband?"

"It is a complicated matter of Vatican policy and—"

"I'll not be condescended to by priests relegated to the marches!"

Rather than taking umbrage, Almaric was fascinated by this Amazon who imitated Eleanor of Aquitane's example by traveling on campaigns and participating in the war strategies. "The Holy Father cracks the whip, but the sting must come from the pulpits. The bishops in the Languedoc are too craven to confront the nobles and the Northern clergy have little interest in our cause."

"Where are the Counts of Champagne and Nevers?"

"With Beziers and Carcassonne cashiered, the barons saw no reason to continue fighting," said Folques. "There is also some sentiment, clearly uninformed, that Trevencal was illegally removed from his rulership."

Finding Simon slouched in despond, Alice braced his shoulders with her vulturine hands. "I have brought you four hundred German knights, paid up until Easter." She shot a sneering glance at the Cistercians. "It seems a woman has more influence than the Pope in raising troops."

Simon was alarmed by her blasphemy. He knew that Almaric often weaved such offhanded statements into his correspondence to Rome.

Unfazed by her husband's cautioning glance, Alice pressed her interrogation. "Am I to understand that the petty seigneur of this city sits in chains while the Ocs hold out hope that he will return to save them?"

"We dare not release Trevencal," said Folques. "He is so beloved, he could raise an army of thousands within a week."

"I am not talking about releasing him!" she shouted.

The guards came running, drawn by her shrillness. The Abbot waved them back to their posts, then poured the lady a libation of sweet Alsatian wine.

Retreating into an icy tranquility, Alice accepted the Abbot's offer with a thin smile of intrigue. "Trevencal is a heretic, no?"

"He refuses to confess," reminded Folques.

"Were the heretics at Beziers formally adjudicated?"

Almaric's brows pinched. "No, but—"

"Does God favor some sinners over others?"

Almaric suddenly deciphered what Alice was suggesting. "Burning a few peasants is one thing. But to execute a viscount . . ."

Alice buttoned the fur-lined cloak around the Abbot's neck in feminine concern for his health; the gesture also carried a more veiled implication. "You must take better care of yourself. The flux, I am told, is rampant on these frontiers. The disease knows no distinction of station."

Simon was becoming disconcerted by the obliqueness of their conversation. The haughtiness of learned monks always made him defensive about his dearth of intellect, particularly when they acted as if he were not in the room.

"You forget Trevencal's wife and son," reminded Folques.

"Given the alternative of starvation," assured Alice, "his family will abdicate their rights in exchange for a generous annuity."

Only then did Simon grasp the deviousness of his wife's proposal. "Even if I'm rid of Trevencal, how will I subdue the Languedoc with so few troops?"

Alice condescendingly pinched her husband's jowls. "*Mon ami*, why do you bang your head against these Southern nobles when you can exterminate the instigators who inflame their passions?"

"If I corner the heretics in one village, they scatter to the mountains like rats and infest some other outpost. The whole pack now hovers in the clouds."

"Every rat has a nest, and every nest a queen mother." In a breathtaking alteration of mood, Alice turned on the monks with eyes slanted in sharp reproof. "Why has the Count of Foix's sister not been apprehended?"

"She continues to slip our nets," said Folques.

"That broken colt I encountered in L'Isle?"

"The Ocs are bewitched by her," said Simon.

"She has ensorcelled the three of *you*, it seems! Each time you fail to apprehend her, she only grows in legend!"

"Foix Castle looms upon a massive rock," reminded Folques.

"Then smoke out her brainless brother. He has a temper. Make him lose it." Alice retreated to the window, impervious to the harsh wind. "A pyre of charred corpses will prove more valuable to us than a battalion."

The Abbot raised his goblet to toast her guile. "If only all women were as devoted to seeing Our Lord's Kingdom come on earth as it is in Heaven."

For three months, Guilhelm and Trevencal had been forced to remain standing on their toes, hung by their arms from pinions in the dungeon below the Comtal palace. Their existence had become the interminable agony of making the choice between allowing the irons to cut their wrists or suffering the cramps caused by stretching to relieve the pressure. Fed just enough slop to stay alive, they had been given no information regarding the progress of the war. Guilhelm suspected that the Occitans were still holding out. If the war was lost, Trevencal would have been traded for ransom.

Trevencal roused from his misery with inflamed eyes too heavy to keep open. "What day is it?"

Guilhelm counted the scratches on the web-clotted wall that he had made with his toenail. "The fourth Sunday of November."

Trevencal wheezed, "I'll not see another Christmas."

"You must keep your spirits raised."

Trevencal retreated into an uncustomary silence. After several difficult exhalations, he asked, "Tell me, Montanhagol . . . Why did you join the Temple?"

"God wanted me to experience Hell before my Judgment Day."

"No, in truth. Was it to see the Holy City?"

Guilhelm hoped Trevencal would take his sarcasm as a hint to desist from wasting strength in speech. He himself had been taught to endure long periods without communication, but Trevencal was an outward-directed soul who craved discourse. Guilhelm grudgingly revealed, "I joined the monks to eat."

"Not from faith?"

"I cared nary a whit about killing Mohammedans. My widowed mother survived by turning whore. When she tired of scrounging scraps, she left me on the preceptory steps. One of the brothers made the mistake of cracking the door. Four years later, I was dodging Saracen missiles below Jerusalem."

"Does Our Lord's tomb still glow from His transfigured Light?"

"I never saw it."

Trevencal straightened with astonishment. "You fought your way across the desert and did not set eyes upon the Holy Sepulcher?"

"My Master had no interest in tombs. His passion was for other quarry."

"Diggings?"

"I've said enough."

Denied, Trevencal sank into the chains with despair etched into his face. His breathing was becoming more labored, a transformation that Guilhelm had witnessed in Muslim prisoners hours before they surrendered their spirits. If he did not give the baron a reason to fight on, Guilhelm feared he would soon expire. Besides, what allegiance did he owe the Temple? Trevencal was more a brother to him than any of those monks with whom he had been forced to share meals and cells. He scanned the far reaches of the dungeon to make certain no one was listening. "We stabled our horses under the base of Solomon's Temple."

"You committed sacrilege in the holy sanctuary?"

"The stabling was only a ruse. At night, we were ordered to burrow into its foundations with picks and axes. We drowned out the clang of the tools with chants. We were assigned shifts every other night so that none of us knew of the prior day's discoveries."

"You were searching for Our Lord's chalice from the Last Supper."

Guilhelm shook his head at the gullibility of fools. "That tale was put out to keep the barons and friars off our tracks."

"What *did* you seek?"

Guilhelm hesitated, fearful of what Trevencal might reveal if racked. But the longing in his dimming eyes demanded an answer. "The Ark."

Trevencal strained against his chains. "The Ark of the Covenant? You found the miraculous tabernacle of the Israelites?"

"I found nothing. You asked what we sought. What others unearthed I cannot say. All I know is, during the infidel assault, half of my brethren were ordered to continue digging rather than man the walls. When Balian surrendered the city to the Arabs, my Master was so desperate to finish the excavation that he had to be dragged from the tunnels for his own safety."

"Then the Ark must still be there."

"If it ever existed." Guilhelm glanced guardedly beyond the grille. "We did find something else. Something none of us could have wished."

"The True Cross?"

"The true *story* of the Cross . . . if racked infidels are to be trusted."

"What do you mean?"

"Some of the prisoners claimed to have seen scrolls buried in jars by members of a Arab sect that called themselves Nasoreans."

"Our Lord was a Nasorean."

"Not for the reason the Church would have you believe," said Guilhelm. "He was not from Nazareth."

"From whom were these writings being hidden?"

Guilhelm met that question with a scornful laugh. "The Romans. Followers of St. Paul. Rival Jewish sects. God only knows."

Trevencal stretched his manacles to their limit to draw closer. "What did these scrolls reveal?"

Guilhelm shook his head in admonition for him to lower his voice. "The jars we found under the Temple had been emptied. But the captives swore they had once contained evidence proving that Christ never intended to die on a cross for our sins. He was executed to be silenced."

"Silenced of what?"

Guilhelm shrugged, having asked that question a thousand times.

Trevencal shook his shackles in protest. "Another infidel blasphemy! You don't give credit to it?"

"I too dismissed it as a deceit, until I encountered your Cathars in the mountains. Esclarmonde told me she once saw such a scroll . . ." He stopped short of finishing the thought. "I no longer know what to believe. Perhaps it's best not to believe in anything."

"You don't share your lady's faith?"

"Faith is like bottled magic," said Guilhelm. "Discover the first flask empty, and all desire to open another is lost."

"Then you undergo these trials for the viscountess, not God."

"Her embrace is the closest I've ever come to approaching the Almighty's grace. Yet she and I are both required to break sacred oaths to attain it." He saw that Trevencal had become deeply troubled by these revelations. "And you? Why do you defend the cloggers?"

"I have tried to live as a good Christian. I fail to understand the arguments of theologians. For me, it has always been a feeling of brotherhood. The perfects ask nothing for their ministry. They imitate the Apostles and keep only the possessions they carry on their backs. They have shown great kindness to my family. Did Our Lord not say that we shall know His disciples by their fruits?"

"So it is written."

"Unconditioned love and goodness are shown to all by the *bon hommes*," said Trevencal. "Their roots must reach to some deep—"

The cell door creaked open—Guilhelm hissed a signal for silence.

Torches cast a blinding light on their pallid faces. De Montfort and Folques, accompanied by two guards, stood before them.

De Montfort kicked Trevencal's shin. "Look at me!"

The guards unlocked Trevencal's chains. He tried to arise and meet their haughty grins, but he collapsed to the floor, too weak to stand. Folques laughed at his pitiful effort and forced a parchment to his eyes.

Restrained by the guards, Trevencal read the terms of the document that required the forfeiture of his kingdom to de Montfort. He spat on the space left for his signature. "Not if dipped in your blood."

The guards dragged Trevencal to the wall and pinned his arms behind his head. They wrapped a buckskin strap around his throat with a knotted cord and twisted it with a rod. "Your hand *will* do its work," warned Folques. When Trevencal clenched his fist to prevent the quill from being forced into his hand, Folques ordered the executioner, "Leave no marks."

The guard rotated the garrote rod another turn. Eyes bulging, Trevencal motioned for Folques to come closer to his quivering lips. Folques smiled as he leaned in to hear the Viscount's concession.

Trevencal bit into Folques's ear.

Folques escaped with blood trickling down his neck. Enraged, he clasped Trevencal's chin and ordered another turn of the garrote. "The bards will sing that you passed tragically from the flux. We will lament that all was done to save you. Your body will lie in state in St. Nazaire with not a scratch upon it. Tears of pity will be shed for your poor widow and son."

Trevencal's legs buckled. A lesser man would have offered up Guilhelm's revelations about the Jerusalem Temple to save his life, but Trevencal remained mute, staring out in silence as death welled up in his straining eyes.

Guilhelm fought to escape. "Murderous bastards!"

While the garroter prosecuted his grisly work, de Montfort kicked Guilhelm in the ribs. "What about this one?"

"Throw him with the others," said Folques. "He's earned a slower demise."

As he was dragged away, Guilhelm remembered what a Syrian mystic had once told him: At the moment of passing, one must chase all doubt if the soul is to avoid becoming lost on its journey to Paradise. He turned back to his dying cell mate and screamed, "Trevencal!"

Trevencal opened his eyes as the garrote stole his last breath.

"I believe!"

That lie released a chivalrous soul to the Light.

uilhelm regained consciousness in a larger gallery of the Comtal dungeon. Aching from the previous day's beating, he was surrounded by dozens of prisoners, most of whom had long since passed the threshold of sanity. His throat was so swollen that he could barely swallow saliva. He moaned for water.

A long-nailed hand poured a few drops into his seared mouth. He gurgled the offering, lubricating his inflamed cords. A crone with wild white hair and bare gums came over him. Her skin was striated with the purplish splotches that foreshadowed death. He felt a stirring under his shirt. She was examining the Cathar merel. He pulled it from her grasp. "I'll rip off that thieving hand!"

The woman recoiled into the darkness. "Forgive me. I once owned such a talisman. I thought you might know of its origins."

He pulled her hoary face into the vague light and tried to reconstruct her features as they might have appeared in youth. "What is your name?"

The woman glanced worriedly at the grille door. "Cecille."

That name meant nothing to him. He cursed the trouble she was causing and rolled over to find respite from his misery in sleep.

"An old hermit once gave such a merel to me in Foix."

He sprang to his knees with such alacrity that the other prisoners regarded him with suspicion. He waited until they had returned to their lethargy, then asked her in a whisper, "Do you know the count of that domain?"

The woman was uncertain if he could be trusted. "I am his wife."

Guilhelm waved her off as deranged. He had dispatched Phillipa with his own hands. The Wolf would not have taken another wife in such a short time, particularly an old hag like—

"I've not seen him in thirty years."

He assayed her face again—she had the same elegant Catalan chin and piercing black eyes. "You are the mother of Esclarmonde de Foix?"

She glared at him with suspicion. "You know my daughter?"

He hesitated. "I . . . love her."

She studied him with damp, shrouded eyes. "Tell me of her."

"She was told you were burned as a heretic." When the crone began sobbing, he tried to comfort her. "She is renowned throughout Christendom. The troubadours sing of her as the Lady of Montsegur."

"Montsegur? What does she have to do with that rock?"

"She built a temple on its pinnacle."

"A temple? Why?"

"She teaches the faith of the Cathars within its walls. The Pope and his assassins prosecute a war against her."

Cecille unleashed a weak shriek of despair and began clutching at her thinned hair in self-recrimination. ""Does my husband not defend her?"

"He died in a hunting mishap. Your son is hard-pressed by a ruthless Norman named de Montfort." In a disorienting flash, Guilhelm saw in the crone's wasting frame an image of Esclarmonde as she might look in old age. "I must get a message to Foix at once. Your son will come for you."

"No!" Cecille dug her nails into his arm to protest such an attempt. "You can never reveal that I am here. Promise me! My children would place themselves in harm's way to obtain my release."

Guilhelm knew she was right. Besides, in her wasted condition, she would not survive much longer. He reluctantly nodded his agreement to her demand.

Cecille eased into her corner with a distant, reminiscing look. "It is a misfortune that you did not meet my daughter before she took the vow."

Guilhelm snorted at the irony in that observation. "I did. She was an initiate in the Marquessa de Lanta's court."

The crone smiled, drawn back to her youth. "The Marquessa was my maid of honor. I met my husband in that hall during one of our many courts. I can still hear him singing our wedding ballad." She looked deeply into Guilhelm's eyes as if weighing his soul. "Does Esclarmonde share your love?"

He was not accustomed to sharing such intimacies, particularly with a woman he had only just met. "She has said as much."

"Why did the two of you not become betrothed?"

"At the time, I was bound by a Templar oath."

"Have you abandoned the Order?"

"No one is allowed to leave the Temple, at least not alive. When I returned from the Holy Land, your daughter was . . ." He thought it best to spare her the news of Esclarmonde's marriage to Jourdaine. Instead, he mercifully conflated the history of her life. "She had taken the vow of perfecta."

Cecille grasped his hand. "The two of you are joined at the heart. One day you will come together again."

"Our natures are as different as night and day. I fail to understand your faith. Your people die without offering resistance."

"As a Templar, you have fought against evil, no?"

"It has been my profession, it seems."

"Did good come of it? Or did only more suffering arise?"

He pondered the question. Which would have been preferable: Allowing Esclarmonde to remain bound to Jourdaine, or releasing her to confront the Cistercian menace? A shuddering thought came to him: What if true Evil was the very violence that he had always employed to confront it? Could the Demiurge so hated by the Cathars have constructed a world in which acts of resistance spun one deeper into its stranglehold? He remembered having once come upon a Muslim ghazi warrior who had stumbled into one of the many quicksand pits in the Egyptian desert. The infidel's horse had become completely submerged and he was up to his chin in the quagmire. The ghazi knew that he was doomed to suffocate, for the more he struggled against his fate, the deeper he sank. He could only sit and accept the horrid death that Allah had decreed to him. If these Cathars spoke true, then the world was like that sandpit. The more one fought against its depravity, the stronger became its choking grip. Finding Cecille still waiting for a reply, he conceded, "It does seem that perdition has stalked me on every road I have taken."

"The Lords of Darkness tighten their chains by seducing us to strike back in violence," she said. "If we purchase into their lust for vengeance, we will only be forced to incarnate to learn the lesson again."

"I will always draw the sword and—"

The approach of torches elicited howls from the half-dead inmates.

Guilhelm removed the medallion and offered it to its first owner, but Cecille shoved it back into his hands and crawled into the shadows.

De Montfort strode through the dungeon with two guards. "Get up, Templar. You're going out for some fresh air."

Guilhelm signed his breast in preparation to meet his death. The guards unlocked the shackles on his ankles and dragged him toward the door.

De Montfort stumbled over Cecille. He drove a heel into her side in retaliation for tripping him. When Guilhelm moved to go to her aid, the Norman became intrigued. He pulled the woman to her feet and studied her scabbed face.

The crone broke away from de Montfort's nearsighted inspection and charged at Guilhelm with flailing hands. "He tried to have his way with me!"

De Montfort studied the woman for a dangerous moment, then laughed and threw her aside. "I doubt that, sweet one. Comely as you are, this monk is trained to mount goats and sodomites."

Cecille slithered back into the darkness. From the shadows, she turned and risked one last glance at the man who loved the daughter she never knew.

Then there was so great a killing that I believe
it will be talked of until the end of the world.
- Guillaume de Tudela, *La Chanson de la Croisade Albigeois*

XXIV

Lavaur

April 1211

The infidel catapults that Guilhelm had confronted in Palestine were primitive imitations of David's sling compared to de Montfort's new trebuchet. Cut whole from giant Argonne oaks, its beams had to be transported to the Languedoc on forty sleds. Folques and Almaric, adorned in their purple Lenten mantles, consecrated the wooden colossus with holy water while Dominic tapped his staff against its foundations to banish demons.

"What think you of my newest recruit, Templar?" asked Simon. "I've christened it 'Malevoisine.' I'm told that's Oc for 'Bad Neighbor.' I dare say it will wear out its welcome here soon enough."

Shackled to the engine's front girders, Guilhelm measured the distance to Lavaur's redstone walls. He was reassured by the depth of the briar-thicketed gorge that separated the village from the crusader army. The German engineer in de Montfort's employ might build cathedrals that defied the limits of space, but he held no credentials in weaponry. "If you emptied your purse for this contrivance, you've been robbed."

Simon answered with a dismissive snort. "We'll find out soon enough. One thing is for certe. You'll have the best view."

Guy and Amaury de Montfort, Simon's brother and eldest son, had arrived from the Holy Land earlier that month and had wasted no time in demonstrating cruelty to be a familial trait, convincing Simon to keep Guilhelm alive merely to increase his misery. Yet despite their many punitive campaigns, the de Montforts had failed to subjugate the Languedoc. The massacres at Minerve and Termes had only caused the Southern nobles to fight more fiercely, the Cathars to accept martyrdom more willingly, and the Occitan peasants to believe with more certainty that an evil god ruled from Rome.

Confronted with these setbacks, Almaric persuaded Simon that capturing the perfecta Giraude and her four hundred Cathars in Lavaur would provide the *coup de grace* against the heretic hierarchy on Montsegur. But the Abbot was becoming alarmed at how quickly his donations were being spent. He opened Simon's coffer and found only a few coins. "How was the engine financed?"

Simon gave a jerk of his head toward a near hill where a swarthy burgher held court in a well-appointed pavilion.

Almaric and Folques shared dismayed glances. Simon was resorting to usurious loans. The Abbot asked him, "You summoned me from Paris to bless a trebuchet that has yet to be purchased?"

"If Rome insists on withholding funds, I have no choice but to find other sources," said Simon. "The man has credit with the Jew bankers in Seville. If he is satisfied with the engine's capabilities, he will provide the backing."

"What advantage is in it for him?" asked Folques.

"The town's gold and jewels."

The Abbot whipped his sleeves to his elbows in protest. "Property confiscated from the heretics belongs to the Church!"

Simon slammed the coffer's lid, nearly smashing the Abbot's hand. "If his offer offends your haute sensibilities, I can return to Carcassonne."

Guilhelm strained against his chains to overhear their confrontation. The Cistercian war would be set back a year if the Lavaur siege was abandoned. Simon alone now held the allegiance of these troops, who fought for forfeited estates, not indulgences. To Guilhelm's disappointment, Almaric grudgingly agreed to postpone his decision until after the engine's demonstration.

Simon collared the elfish German engineer. "If I don't see stones flying from that wall on the first shot, I'm going to sell your hide for reimbursement."

Duly motivated, the engineer herded the clerics from the trebuchet like a stable master preparing to liberate a wild bull. When the trebuchet was brought to life, Guilhelm knew at once that he had underestimated the German. The Bad Neighbor was evidence that the Arabs did not hold the patent for ingenuity. Braced by thick buttresses, the engine featured a large counterweight box that when loaded with stones pulled a sling along a railed trough. The German brought down a sledgehammer on the latch, jolting Guilhelm violently. The sling raced down its track and jerked its load high into the sky.

"The path's too steep!" warned Simon.

The engineer watched the missile like a falconer judging the trajectory of his bird. Just before impact, Lavaur's defenders leapt from the walls to avoid being hit. The stone smashed a ragged hole in the corner tower. Guilhelm dropped his chin to his chest. He knew that the village stood no chance.

"How quickly can you reload and fire it?" asked Simon, grinning.

The German accepted the question as an apology. "On the half-hour, provided I am kept supplied with a sufficient arsenal."

"And to breach the main tower and wall?"

"A month, if we have clear weather."

Simon's good cheer evaporated. "I don't have a month."

"I cannot alter the natural laws of God."

While Simon and the engineer argued, Folques walked to the edge of the gorge and watched as Lady Giraude's brother, Aimery, and his Occitan knights scurried to replace the stones in the breach. At such a languid pace of firing, the defenders could repair the walls as rapidly as the trebuchet could bring them down. Perhaps a different kind of missile would have more effect. He dragged up twenty Cathar prisoners and chose one man and one woman. He turned to Guilhelm with a sinister smile. "Do you see the irony of it, Templar? Because of their depravity, these two sinners have abstained their entire lives from touching the opposite sex. Now they will go to their deaths arm in arm."

The German engineer suddenly fathomed what Folques was proposing. "I'll not allow my engine to be profaned!"

Simon turned toward the burgher, who signaled his agreement. "It's no longer your engine," Simon said. "Fire it, or take the cloggers' place."

The engineer spat with disgust and reluctantly waved his yeomen to the task. The two Cathars chosen for martyrdom offered no resistance as they were thrown into the sling. When the engineer refused to wield the hammer, Simon pushed him aside and unleashed the latch. The bound Cathars were launched on a high parabola and deposited into the gorge with a sickening thud. The defenders on the walls looked down in seething anger at the mangled bodies.

Simon shouted at the Occitans, "Each day you resist, two more will be sent over to join you!"

Simon made good on his promise. Six more heretics were dispatched into the rocks and Lavaur was punished with a quarry haul of stones. Yet Giraude and the Occitans refused to yield. On the fourth night of the siege, the weary crusaders suspended their bombardment until dawn and retired to their tents for wine and much-needed sleep.

Guilhelm was left chained to the trebuchet with the surviving Cathars, forced to endure the blood-sucking mosquitoes and lurking wolves. After several hours in the chill, he finally fell into a fitful slumber. Hours into the night, he was awakened by choking smoke. Groggy, he looked up to find Aimery and his knights filling the engine's rigging with pitch and setting its bowels afire. The raiders cut the Cathar prisoners free and delivered them to Lady Giraude, who herded them toward the gorge. She discovered Guilhelm chained to the far side of the trebuchet. "What about this one?"

"Leave him," whispered Aimery. "He's likely a deserter."

Giraude was distracted by a metallic flash reflected in the growing flames. She came closer and found the merel around Guilhelm's neck. "From whom did you steal this?" When he turned aside to deflect her inspection, she persisted, "Answer me! I knew a woman who wore it."

"I can best that," said Guilhelm with indifference. "I have known two."

Stunned, Giraude brought the torch closer to Guilhelm's battered face. "You are Esclarmonde's Templar. But how could you know . . . Cecille is alive?"

Guilhelm remained silent, refusing to break his vow made in Carcassonne to Esclarmonde's mother.

Aimery rushed back from the ravine. "Hurry!"

"You must save this man," insisted Giraude.

Aimery had no time to question her reason. The night winds were fanning the flames and the Northern sentries would be alerted within minutes. He yanked at the chain on Guilhelm's wrist but found it fastened firmly by a bolt. He brought his blade down on the links, but the weapon bounced off with no effect. He shook his head in defeat. "The shackles are too strong."

Shouts of discovery rang out from the crusader camp.

Guilhelm chased Aimery off with a kick. "Away! Both of you!"

Giraude knelt before Guilhelm and forced him to look into her searching eyes. "Is your love for Esclarmonde not worth a hand?"

Guilhelm was speechless. How did this woman know of his feelings for Esclarmonde? The flames, fueled by the dry brush, swirled closer, singing his face. A horrible death was only seconds away if the crusaders did not reach him first. He flexed his left hand, trying to imagine an existence without it. Yet he could not bear the thought of never seeing Esclarmonde again. He went blank with indecision—why did he lack Trevencal's courage? He threw his arm across the beam. Giraude held his face away and prayed the Cathar Pater Noster. The heat was so punishing that he sensed what it must feel like to burn alive.

"It is finished," said Giraude.

Guilhelm looked up at her in astonishment. He had felt nothing. Could the blade truly have done its work? He relaxed his arm and—

Aimery brought down his sword.

Giraude stifled Guilhelm's scream. Blood spurted across her cloak. A bolt of searing pain crawled up Guilhelm's spine as he rolled free and grasped his severed wrist. She tore a strip from her sleeve and ligatured his gushing artery while Aimery and his knights covered their retreat.

The chateau's wall reverberated from a thudding crash. Guilhelm awoke with a fire raging in his head and a cauterized stump staring back at him. His delirium slowly gave way to cold reality: The Occitans had failed to destroy the engine. Through the window, he saw from the damage to the village that de Montfort had intensified the fusillade in punishment for the raid. He studied the space where his left hand had once existed. He could still feel his fingers, but the stump remained motionless when he squeezed.

Giraude swabbed his beaded brow. "The fever has eased."

"I cannot hold a shield or grip reins . . . I am useless to you."

At the door, Aimery brought forward a blacksmith who carried a hollowed iron tube that had been cast with slits to resemble the curved fingers of a hand. Giraude slid the prosthetic over Guilhelm's stump, which she had treated with the Cathar red oil, a concoction of St. John's wort and olive oil that possessed miraculous healing properties. "We took some measurements while you were asleep." She threaded two leather thongs through holes in the tube, tied their ends over his elbow, and wrapped them tightly against his biceps.

Guilhelm waved the arm. The prosthetic was heavy, but he was confident of building the strength required to wield it. "I wish I had a miracle for you."

Giraude dismissed her brother and the blacksmith from the room. When alone with Guilhelm, she revealed, "We have sent messengers to Foix for help. None have made it past de Montfort's lines."

Guilhelm tried to envision how he might ride with one good hand. It would be suicidal, but he was determined to attempt it. "Bring me your best horse."

Giraude bolted the door to prevent entry. "My brother must not hear what I am about to tell you . . . I will not survive this siege."

Guilhelm tried to rise from the cot in protest. "My lady . . ."

She gently bade him rest while he still had the time. "I am prepared to leave this world. You, however, still have much to live for. Should you reach Foix, you must take caution."

"Why?"

"The Count nurses a blood revenge against you. He has exiled Esclarmonde to Montsegur. You must find a way to convince them to heal their animosities. They will need each other in the times ahead."

"Let me try to take you from here."

Giraude packed a few dried beans in a knapsack for his sustenance. "I would only slow you . . . Deliver a message to Esclarmonde for me. In our faith, I cannot return to the Light until I seek pardon from all whom I have wronged. I selfishly insisted that she and Phillipa leave their homes to preach. She must hold me coldly in her heart for what I have cost her."

"The heart I know does not descend to such degree."

"There is also another from whom I must beg forgiveness."

"Who, my lady?"

"You."

"Surely you have never injured me!"

"More gravely, I fear, than you can imagine." After a hesitation, she revealed, "When Esclarmonde was first brought to me for instruction, she spoke of her love for a Templar. I convinced her that she was destined for a higher purpose."

That admission stung Guilhelm more sharply than the pain in his arm. Had it not been for this Cathar woman, he might now be married to Esclarmonde and far away from this war. Yet he could harbor no malice toward her. She had only followed the dictates of her religion, as he had done when he turned Phillipa over to the Cistercians. "She made the choice of her own will."

"Will you take the Consolamentum before you leave?"

"I don't adhere to the beliefs of your faith."

"But you wear the merel?"

"It carries Esclarmonde's touch."

She removed the Cathar talisman from her neck and handed it to him. "Place this in Montsegur's chapel. In remembrance of me."

By the eighth day of the siege, the walls had been reduced to rubble and there had been no sign of a relief force from Foix. Resigned to their fate, Aimery and his starving garrison, depleted to forty men, manned what remained of the defenses near the gape while Giraude gathered her perfects into the church to exchange their final Touch of the Light.

An hour after dawn, the Bad Neighbor fell silent. A serried phalanx of three thousand crusaders swarmed over the gorge and converged on the walls. Aimery fought bravely, but the Northerners tightened their pincers and drove the defenders into a scrum so packed that they could not raise their swords. Exhausted, Aimery and his Occitans dropped their weapons.

Simon cudgeled Aimery to his knees and ordered the Occitans bound. "Where is your heretic sister?" Receiving no answer, Simon rammed his blade through the throat of a prisoner. He wiped the blood on the hair of the next Occitan knight in line. "I can make it slower."

"In the church," sputtered the man.

Before the sanctuary could be stormed, Giraude unlocked its doors and came out with her fellow Cathars. The Cistercians chanted Te Deums as the soldiers dragged the perfects into the square. Dominic pressed his crucifix against Giraude's forehead to imprint it with the image of the cross. "Woman, accept the mercy of the Lord Jesus Christ. These wayward souls will follow your example."

"I have accepted *my* God," she said.

"You must accept Him under the authority of the Holy Father in Rome and the Apostolic Church!" insisted Dominic.

She maintained a defiant glare. "I will obey your demand when you tell me where it is written that the Apostles ransacked towns and committed murder."

Dominic turned white with fury. "Here Satan makes his habitat!"

"I know who you are," she said. "My only regret is that I was not present in Pamiers when the Perfecta of Foix bested your arguments."

Indignant, Dominic appealed to Folques. "I prevailed that day!"

"Not one of our people converted under your threats," reminded Giraude.

"Swear against the existence of two gods!" demanded Dominic. "Repeat the Nicene Creed! I believe in One God, Father Almighty, maker of heaven and earth, of all that is seen and unseen!"

"Did He create that hurling abomination of destruction?" she asked.

"He did! To pound you for your sins!"

"I will worship no god who sanctions violence against fellow Christians," she said. "My brothers and sisters are free to do as they desire."

None came forward to take up Dominic's offer. Impatient with the standoff, Simon dragged Aimery up a staircase and forced him to stand on a plank that had been set under a beam. He looped a rope around Aimery's neck and yanked it tight. Simon's kinsmen prepared the other Occitan knights for hanging. Giraude rushed up to transmit the Consolamentum, but she was thrown back.

Twirling his sword, Simon strode below the creaking plank. "Where is that conniving Templar? I have something of his." He pulled a wrapped bundle from his saddlebag and threw Guilhelm's severed hand at Giraude.

Aimery looked down at his sister to reassure her that a better life awaited them. "I will see you soon. I love you."

With a scorning laugh, Simon brought his sword down on Aimery's ankle, drawing a cry of agony. Weighed down by their armor, the noosed Occitans stood helpless as Aimery struggled to maintain balance on his good leg. Simon hacked off Aimery's remaining ankle. The boards split asunder and dropped the knights into the nooses. Giraude turned away, unable to watch them strangle. A great crash was followed by unearthly moans—the beam had collapsed under their weight. The Occitans writhed and kicked on the ground, some dying from broken necks, most still half-conscious.

Simon glanced toward the heavens, questioning if divine intervention had thwarted him. Reassured by Dominic that the Almighty approved of the executions, the Norman finished off Aimery by slitting his throat. Those Occitans still alive were dispatched in the same grisly manner. When the butchery was finished, Simon removed his bloodied gloves and threw them at Almaric's feet. "The cloggers are yours to deal with. I have a thirst to quench."

Almaric stepped back. "You know I am precluded from drawing blood."

"Yes, I am constantly reminded of your purity."

Almaric looked to Dominic, who had conveniently fallen to his knees in tranced prayer. The Abbot delegated the duty to Folques. Eager to lay waste to the town, Simon's men dragged the Cathars to a palisade that they had constructed outside the gate. The perfects walked willingly into the piles of brush and stacked the kindling around their own feet.

Giraude prepared to climb into the pyre, but Simon held her back. "I have other plans for you."

The crusaders barred the palisade's gate with poles. Simon offered the torch to Folques, but he could not bring himself to light the fire. Disgusted, Simon stole the torch back and flung it over the logs. "That Templar was right. You'll never be more than a juggler of words."

The faggots quickly took flame. Revived by the heat, Dominic erupted from his rapture and held his crucifix toward the billowing smoke to speed the wayward souls to their damnation. When the holocaust was finally finished, not one scream from the dying Cathars had been heard.

Giraude shook with grief as she knelt before the charred pyre. She turned upon Folques with a promise. "Our suffering lasts for minutes. Yours will consume an eternity."

Green from the stench of burnt flesh, Folques heaved his morning's meal.

Simon chortled at Folques's notoriously weak stomach and tossed him a handful of grass to wipe his robes. He dragged Giraude into the square and stood her in front of the well once blessed by Mary Magdalene, the same spring that had nourished Esclarmonde during her first initiation into the Light.

"I have had a divine revelation," said Simon. "The men of this land are mere puppets of their women. It is time we dealt with the true source of our troubles." He hammered Giraude to the ground. "That harlot in Foix needs to be sent a message. From this day forward, I will administer the same justice to you witches that I would to any traitor."

Bloodied, Giraude stood unsteadily and reclaimed her condemning gaze. "Yes, I am a witch. I *can* see the future. I see that you will die at the hands of an Occitan woman. I see that generations will forever ring their bells on the anniversary of your death."

Simon gave up a half-hearted laugh to disarm the strange oracle. "If it is a woman to be the death of me, I can make certain it won't be you." On his signal, the crusaders quartered Giraude across the well. Simon tossed a rock into the hole. Several seconds passed before a distant splash was heard. "Our God has shown us a shortcut to Hell." He placed a large stone on her stomach. "You will take it."

Giraude closed her eyes and prayed.

The crusaders dropped her into the darkness. A thud from the depths was followed by several weak moans, then silence.

"Fill it," ordered Simon.

Every soldier and monk in the crusader army was required to file by the well and drop a stone. By dusk, the sacred spring no longer offered up its healing waters. That night, many of the Northerners could not sleep, convinced that they heard the lamentations of the Magdalene echoing from deep within the earth. Several crusaders pleaded with Simon to restore the well, but he mocked their fears and ordered the village razed.

The Essenes despise danger and
conquer pain by sheer willpower; death, if it comes
with honor, they value more than life without end. Their
spirit was tested to the utmost by the war with the Romans,
who racked and twisted, burnt and broke them, subjecting
them to every torture yet invented to make them blaspheme
the lawgiver or eat some forbidden fruit.

- Josephus Flavius, The Jewish Wars

XXV

Foix

June 1211

There is another way to die.

That was the promise Bishop Castres made to his flock before leaving Montsegur to minister to those of the faith on the other side of the mountains in Catalonia. Placed in charge of the temple during his absence, Esclarmonde had intensified her quest to find the way back to the Light through that spiritus incognita once blazed by the Essenes and Nasoreans.

Yet after two years of meditating on the kabbalistic Tree of Life, she had come no closer to reaching the elusive Middle Way to the Throne. With de Montfort's army closing in, she was joined in this desperate mission by the hundreds of perfects and perfectas who had taken refuge with her on the pog's vertiginous terraces. What these navigators of the higher realms sought was not the uninitiated passing by physical death, which would only return them to the world to repeat their sufferings, but the mystical release that came by degrees, the same radiant transfiguration of the body that the Master had tried to teach before His mission was cut short by the crucifixion.

Esclarmonde's frustration with her slow spiritual progress was heightened by her discovery that the inner planes did not seem to adhere to the same cause-and-effect laws governing the world of the senses. Each morning, she would gather with her students for a light breakfast and discuss their nocturnal dreams, sifting through the dredge of meaningless harlequinades and chimera for jewels of insight. She became so fixated on the narratives of these visions that she often found it difficult to discern what was real and what had merely been created by her imagination. Months into this discipline, she came to suspect that what she saw during waking hours was no more substantial than the objects in her dreams. At times she would take up a fistful of dirt and stare at it for hours while trying to winnow its essence from the form. Everything in this realm of earth and water and air seemed to be the props of a clever illusion created by the Demiurge.

In fact, the deeper she delved into the arcana of the Light, the more the outer and inner worlds appeared to operate like a series of mirrors. As a child, she once encountered a street jongleur in Toulouse who, by angling two concave plates of polished silver, had conjured so many multiplied images of her face that she seemed to recede into eternity. When she questioned him about his trickery, he revealed himself much wiser than his frivolous profession might warrant. The jongleur had taken her aside and to explain that when the sun falls on an object, some of its light is reflected, some is absorbed, and some is stolen. For a smooth surface to serve as a mirror, it must reflect the sun's benefice while retaining as little as possible. The grace of God's Light, he told her, worked in much the same manner: A soul must be without blemish to reflect the Almighty's saving effluence upon those in greater need. He then whispered to her the secret key that she had never forgotten:

As above, so below.

Years later, she discovered that many of the joculators and mummers who performed with the troubadours were alchemists in disguise. They adopted such debased trades as cover to travel from city to city and work with fellow practitioners. In recent weeks, the image of that jongleur's multiplying contrivance had reappeared in her meditations. She was struck by an intuition: Enlightenment unfolds much like the sun's rays against the mirror of this world, with each reflection absorbing just enough Light to form its own image, then offering back the rest to the Source. Perhaps the stations of the Tree were like mirrors facing mirrors that reduced each multiplied reflection until the false outer shell disappears. Castres once said that when one stands in the Light but does not offer its blessings to others, a shadow is formed in the spiritual world.

Yet when she examined her own reflection in water, she saw that the image differed from its source in one important respect: It formed a perfect opposite in polarity. This epiphany led her to posit a second law of the Chariot: Everything has its opposite, in this world and beyond. These contraries were drawn together by an invisible force, like iron shavings to a lodestone. She had been warned that the demons who tempt the aspirant are chosen by the Demiurge for their ability to expose the searcher's weaknesses. For this reason, the initiate is obliged to thoroughly examine the dark aspects of her own soul.

On this evening, a summer rain pummeled her wattle hut, settling in with a dripping humidity. The thatched roof was so leaky that she feared it might collapse. She cored the drainage rut with a spade, then chewed a few fava beans to chase the hunger pangs and spread her threadbare mat in preparation to again attempt the Gate of Yesod.

This station, the second on the kabbalist's Tree, was the most dangerous. It was in Yesod—the Hebrew word for Foundation—where the archons were said to work their most elaborate delusions by devising a bestiary of soul-sucking demons that masqueraded as angels and beneficent beings. If she could not reach this lower mansion, she had no hope of making it up all twenty-two paths. In previous sessions, she had meticulously followed the rabbi's prescriptions, taking the most oblique approach, watching, ever watching, for the moment of opportunity. But her patience and strength were ebbing fast.

She sat with eyes closed and tried not to think about the starving cat that was mewling somewhere on the eastern ridge. On the summit above her, a loose shutter rattled against the chapel's embrasure. Whom had she placed in charge of the sanctuary this night? Ah yes, the new perfect from Barcelona, a Gorgonish little man with skeins of ratty hair and pimpled skin like that of a plucked chicken. No, she must not think of him in such harsh terms. She would speak to him discreetly about his body odor. A converted Jew, he apparently labored under the misapprehension that the admonition about cleanliness being next to godliness was a falsehood propagated by the Pope.

She would have given the perfect no further thought had she not overheard him gossiping about a group of young adepts who had formed a mystery school in Gerona. According to his account—which she suspected might be apocryphal—these upstart students had broken away from Rabbi Isaac's tutelage after discovering another route up the Tree, one that took less time and effort. They called their mysteries the Way of Zohar—the Hebrew term for Splendor—and their revolutionary technique, the Flash of Lightning. The insurrectionists claimed to have bypassed most of the outer paths by leapfrogging up the nine major trajects in a zigzagging bolt; hence, its tantalizing sobriquet. She traced a schematic of the Tree of Life in the wet clay and studied how this Flash of Lightning overlaid the paths:

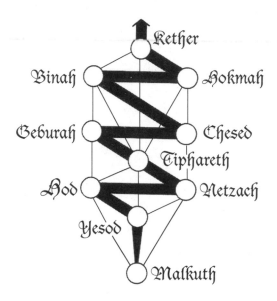

The shortcut was intriguing, but she chased the temptation. She smoothed the ripples of her mind by picturing the surface of a limpid lake on a summer day. Her respiration slowed—inhale, hold, exhale, hold—until each breath became almost imperceptible. Her chin sank to her chest as she allowed all intrusive images to sail past. She watched for the gate of Malkuth, the first entry where she had encountered the archangel Mikael. Slowly the swirling colors of that station emerged; the familiar russet hue became tinged with the flaming aura of citrin. Malkuth was like the outer portcullis of a walled city. All who entered the spiritual realms, novices and initiates alike, were required to pass through this gate before reaching their ultimate destinations.

She waited and waited, fighting the seduction of sleep and the growing numbness in her legs. How much time had passed? An hour? Agitated, she eased her breathing again and restarted the process. The swirling colors began receding. Where was the infernal gate?

Damn this delay!

How long would she be required to endure this crushing ennui? And why was Malkuth closed when she had already attained it months ago? Had she forgotten some incantation for unlocking its entry? Perhaps Castres and Blind Isaac had grown so forgetful in their senescence that they neglected to impart all the essential steps for the ascent. She could well understand why the rebel kabbalists had taken matters into their own hands.

Had she not been admonished that boldness was essential for this work? Perhaps the delay was a test. She could bypass Malkuth and Yesod by climbing directly to Hod, the first sphere on the Pillar of Severity. From there she could ride the Flash of Lightning all the way to the Crown. Hod was the station of mental acuity and artistic expression where the vibrations of sacred words were honed. She had always been blessed with a faculty for language; that station should open to her like petals of a blooming flower. After all, those Jewish adepts had accomplished their breakthrough with less meditation experience than she possessed. During her initiation, she had stood shivering in the wind on this pog until she had enough verve to remove her blindfold. How foolish she had felt that night, waiting to do what in retrospect had been quite obvious.

She would attempt it.

She drew a deep breath and again summoned the image of the Tree. She launched her spirit up the left rung and bypassed the first two vessels. Within minutes, she felt exultant, freed of all constraints. Waves of deepening blackness rushed at her—she was being hurled through a tunnel that appeared carved into pure agate. Without warning, she was braked to a jouncing halt. Before her hovered a brilliant silver orb circled by ribbons of red, yellow, and green; a bloodless moon studded its center. There was something both beautiful and devastating about the radiance of this pulsation. She could not take her inner eyes from it. A swirling heat ignited at the base of her spine and began coursing through her limbs. Her skin crawled as if bitten by thousands of fire ants and a liquid fire lapped up into her core in spasms. She was heaving and breathing so fast that her lungs felt on the verge of bursting.

What is happening to me?

She tried to pray the Pater Noster, but her throat tightened and her head began jerking back and forward so violently that she feared her neck would snap. Her insides felt as if they were being bubbled up and expelled from her mouth. She had breached the floodgates of the Light too soon. Her body was an athanor boiling her soul in the bellows of spiritual calcination. She feared that her throbbing heart could not take much more.

I will die and be forced to start over.

In that instant, the spears of incaldesence gave way to gentle whooshes that wound through her like the undulations of a rising serpent. The ineffable force reached the top of her head and detonated in a fountain of dazzling diamonds. Her face aglow, she heard a faint thrum of angelic music; and then the strangest of thoughts came to her:

This is the radiance of Moses and the Burning Bush.

The floating moon transformed into a golden sun. She could only approach describing the experience as being released from a tomb into the brilliance of a cloudless day. She felt light enough to float away. Her fear was swallowed up by a consuming ecstasy a thousand times more pleasurable than any she had ever experienced. She begged to remain there forever. No sooner had she offered up that plea than Guilhelm's face appeared within the sun's nimbus. She thought nothing could increase her rapture—until she shivered anew from spikes of intensified pleasure. Her loins burned with an obliterating lust. She melted into Guilhelm's arms and found his lips to share her joy with him.

The Demiurge.

Conniving bastard! He had chosen the one disguise that might turn her from the path. She thrashed against the demon's snare and fought desperately to escape. "Away from me! I know who you are!"

The simulacrum would not be banished. "You don't recognize me?"

How cleverly the Evil One contrived Guilhelm's voice. She raised her fist to strike but the hellion pinned her with its supernatural strength. She struggled loose and slapped something iron-hard—*that* was proof enough that this was no mortal she was wrestling. The fiend tried to frighten her into submission with a demonstration of its grotesque powers.

"Would Satan tempt you with a vision like this?"

Disoriented, she touched a scarred stump. The serried flesh felt as real as her own skin. The spectre dragged her from the floor and forced her pale face into the sunlight at the opened door. The harsh rays jolted her back into the physical realm—but the tempter did not vanish. She stumbled from faintness and nearly fell before being caught.

Guilhelm slapped the blood back into her cheeks. "Get up!"

Haltingly, she recovered her equilibrium. She caressed the furrowed lines of his face and her heart danced—it truly was Guilhelm standing before her. Having heard nothing from him since Trevencal's murder, she had assumed the worst. She stared at the horrid wound. "What happened to you?"

Guilhelm returned the iron prosthetic to its place with practiced speed and wrapped its bindings around his biceps. "De Montfort besieges Lavaur. He'll come south if the village falls. We must leave for Foix at once."

She paced the floor staggering, her mind still ajar from the abrupt intrusion. "You'd have me abandon this temple to de Montfort's destruction?"

"This rock is not what he wants to crack. He wants you. Your brother's towers offer the only protection."

She reclaimed her meditation position. "Take the others."

Guilhelm stared at her in utter incredulity, his eyes as sharp as talons. "Damn you, woman! Have you lost all will to live?"

When she would not answer, he threw her over his shoulder with his good hand. He was astonished at how diminished she had become in her asceticism. The clews of her spine protruded like the beads of Dominic's rosary. He wrangled her from the hut and into the bailey where the other perfects stood waiting, having gathered their belongings on his orders. The Cathars watched in stunned silence as their pacifist priestess was carried down the crag screaming like a banshee and pounding at Guilhelm's back.

Esclarmonde hurried across the rope bridge that spanned the Ariege and was stopped short. Foix looked like a deserted, plague-ravaged town. The main rue was a river of mud clogged with a flotsam of dangling shudders, abandoned buildings patrolled by wild dogs, and mews full of rotting fowl carcasses, all crowned by a vapor of flies so thick that a black oscillating cloud seemed to have descended. The lavender distillery and tanner's house had been dismembered. At the far end of the square, the ochre-hued frame of St. Volusien's church stood gutted, its slate tiles caved in on the altar and its lacquered pews hacked for firewood. Warned that de Montfort was on the march, the Fuxeens had retreated south carrying all that they could pry loose from their walls. They had emptied their excrement buckets into the streets to serve up a foul reception for the murderous Norman.

Esclarmonde looked to Guilhelm for commiseration, but he had long since become inured to such scenes of desolation. Although they had exchanged only a few words on their run from Montsegur, she learned enough to know that he had seen more horror in the past months than he cared to reveal. At Lavaur, he had made it past de Montfort's guards during the night by strapping a dead Occitan knight upright on a horse and slithering behind it on foot. Halfway down the chasm, he had slapped the phantom rider into a gallop to draw the Northerners off on a chase. Freed to cross the gorge, he had hurried south to deliver disheartening news. De Montfort was concentrating his forces in the western foothills to make an example of the poorly defended villages.

If the Lion captured Foix, Montsegur would be cut off and isolated from the other Cathar chateaux in the region.

Esclarmonde high-stepped her way through the detritus and met her brother, wild-eyed and reeking of wine, stumbling sottish down the path from the chateau. Roger studied her with an uncertain gaze, at first not recognizing her in such macerated condition. He repulsed her attempt at an embrace and swung his fist into Guilhelm's jaw. "That's for murdering my wife!" When the Templar offered no defense, Roger turned his fury back on Esclarmonde. "I told you never to set foot in this castle again."

Guilhelm stepped in front of Roger. "I forced her to come."

"You don't decide who enjoys my protection."

"You think you're the only one who's been wronged by this war?" demanded Guilhelm.

"Why should I suffer for her sins?"

"De Montfort besieges Lavaur," said Esclarmonde. "Will you at least go to Giraude's aid?"

Roger turned aside to deflect the impact of what he was forced to reveal. "We reached the village two days ago. The walls had been breached and the ground salted. Every man and woman inside . . ." He could not bring himself to finish the report.

Guilhelm kicked at the ground, angered to find that he was too late.

Before Esclarmonde could recover from the news that Giraude had been lost, the girls came running from the tower. Corba and the Marquessa hurried after them. Chandelle rushed into Esclarmonde's arms, but Loupe held back. Sobbing, Esclarmonde pressed Chandelle to her breast. "I've missed you so!"

The blind girl tugged at Esclarmonde's robe and refused to be released. "Will you stay with us, Aunt Essy?"

Roger could not bear to see Chandelle disappointed. With a huff of disgust, he walked back toward the chateau and ordered his men, "Lodge them in the north tower where I don't have to look at them."

Esclarmonde called to Loupe. "Love, do you have a hug for me?"

Loupe ran off to join her father, shattering Esclarmonde's heart like glass.

The next morning, Esclarmonde was awakened by an explosion that rocked the foundations. She donned her robe and climbed to the allures in time to see a stone hurtling toward the walls. She ducked below the merlon, certain that the chateau would be hit. But Guilhelm, who had become proficient at judging the trajectory of missiles, watched without a flinch as the stone fell short of the scarp. De Montfort and his army had arrived during the night. His engineers were laboring to increase the Bad Neighbor's range by wedging beams under its front sleds for leverage.

"The angle is too steep," said Guilhelm.

"Are we safe?" she asked.

Guilhelm rubbed his bruised jaw as he glowered at Roger, who was directing the defenses on the far rampart. "We would be had your hotheaded brother stocked sufficient water and victuals. But he thought it more important to vent his rage by running chevauchees on monasteries."

De Montfort forded the river with Folques and rode toward the walls waving a flag of parlay. The Lion cursed under his breath on finding that the Cathars had been evacuated from Montsegur. He sneered a promise of revenge at Esclarmonde, then offered, "Wolf, there is no need for us to ram heads. Surrender the keep. You and your men may leave with your mounts."

"Your generosity overwhelms me," said Roger. "To walk away with my horse and lose only my wife and my home is indeed a windfall."

Folques could not hide his relief at finding Esclarmonde alive. His countenance, however, turned black when he saw Guilhelm at her side. He shouted to Roger, "That devil-seeded Templar is to blame for your wife's death! Hand him over and I will see to it he receives due justice."

"And where do you propose my horse and I go?" asked Roger.

"Rome would look favorably on a pilgrimage to Jerusalem," said Folques.

"Where is that cripple of Satan?" asked Roger.

"The Abbot has returned to Paris. He has assigned me spiritual governance of the Languedoc in his absence. We can resolve this without resorting to arms."

Below the allures, the Occitan soldiers silently loaded a sling with horse dung. Roger kept Simon and Folques preoccupied by observing, "You are bold to come out from your tents on such an inclement day."

De Montfort squinted at the clear sky in confusion. "You must be mad from thirst, Wolf! There's not a cloud in—" A large globule of damp compost flew over the walls and splattered the two Northerners.

Roger slacked his jaw in mock surprise. "The weather in these parts alters as swiftly as your honor."

Folques angrily wiped the steaming refuse from his face. He unrolled a parchment containing a papal decree and read it aloud:

By the Statute of Pamiers, ratified by the Holy Roman Church, all fiefs that do not surrender to the forces of the Holy Father shall be distributed to those barons who have taken the Cross. It is hereby ordered that Occitan barons shall not pass across the frontier borders of Foix without permission and shall employ only Frankish knights in their service. Widows and female heirs of all Occitan chateaux are prohibited from marrying any man who is not a citizen of a domain in the good graces of his Holiness. All heirs shall inherit land and holdings according to the customs and usage in Paris and that part of France surrounding it.

Esclarmonde's face bleached. She tried to nullify the sting of this news by acting as if it was already common knowledge. In truth, such draconian terms had never been imposed on a Christian kingdom. The Pope, she realized, was now resolved to exterminate her faith and the entire Occitan aristocracy. Before her brother could answer, she shouted in his stead, "We will never agree to become a colony of Paris or a priory of Rome!"

"I encountered a woman in Lavaur who spoke of knowing you," said de Montfort. "That is, before she descended to Hell."

"You've gained quite a reputation for murdering innocent women," she said. "No doubt the Pope is preparing your sainthood."

Simon's teeth made the sound of flint striking tinder as he surveyed the imposing towers. He debated adding a concession to the negotiation. "I'm a reasonable man, Wolf. Why risk your kingdom for a godless cause? Hand over your sister and I'll leave your domain untouched. She's been nothing but a thorn in your side."

Roger mulled the proposal, too long for Esclarmonde's comfort. Finally, to her relief, he answered, "Bring me the offer with the Holy Father's seal and I'll consider it."

Simon protested, "That would take months."

"I have months to spare."

Simon wrapped the papal edict on a lance shaft and hurled it over the walls. "I'll melt this rock like grease over a flame!"

July brought the hottest temperatures in Foix's memory. Three weeks into the siege, the blue-green pastures and chartreuse lemon groves below the chateau turned brown—not the natural desaturation of the dry season, but the tawny dunning that presaged death deep in the roots. The surrounding vales were a bonescape of calcareous downs, ribbed black as if flayed on a grille. Even the jackdaws were dropping dead from the sky, roasted in flight. Yet the Almighty in His infinite wisdom decreed such *damnum fatale* insufficient. A rare tramontane had turned inland to blister the drouthy vapors. So hard did these infamous tempests blow that some Occitan districts promulgated laws absolving murders committed during them due to the madness they engendered. De Montfort bolstered the effect of the climatory disasters by laying waste to the vineyards and firing bales of vines below the walls to stoke the heat and further foul the air.

Esclarmonde wiped the smoky haze from her eyes as she watched Simon and Folques lounge under their open pavilion. "It is not like them to wait like this. How long can we hold out?"

Guilhelm studied the gray-tipped mountains, whose white caps had long since melted. The cistern levels had been drained so low that the water ration was already cut in half. "Without rain, two weeks."

Esclarmonde saw that the disastrous endgame of Carcassonne was being played out again. This time, she would not stand by and watch her own family suffer thirst and starvation. "Take me to Folques this night."

Guilhelm stared at her as if questioning whether the months of solitary meditation had unhinged her mind. "Have you forgotten what happened to Trevencal?"

"Perhaps I can convince him to raise the siege."

"That crowing rooster won't be reasoned with. Especially by you."

"I don't intend to reason with him." She descended the tower steps and left Guilhelm shaking his head. She knew that brooding silence. He would pout, but he would eventually do as she had asked.

Hours later, deep into the night, Guilhelm appeared at her door provisioned with a scaling rope. Esclarmonde disguised herself in a soldier's cloak and followed him under the shadows along the walls. When Guilhelm offered to take the watch at the postern gate, an exhausted sentry eagerly accepted the exchange. Guilhelm motioned Esclarmonde from her hiding and together they slithered out and swam across the shrunken river, careful to avoid the light of the waxing moon. She waited below the crest of the bank while he crawled into the camp and knocked a guard senseless with a blow to the neck. He motioned her up. They stole from tent to tent until they found the Cistercian insignia.

Guilhelm pierced the flap and found Folques sleeping alone. He lowered a dagger to the throat of his old nemesis. Startled, Folques awoke and tried to call for help, but a sharp prick from the blade caused him to reconsider.

Esclarmonde heard Guilhelm's hiss and entered. She stared at Folques for several moments, then ordered Guilhelm, "Leave us."

Guilhelm stood dumbstruck. Her tenacious glare finally drove him to comply, but not before he gave the dagger another half-turn under Folques's chin. "I'll return to those walls with the lady or your worthless manhood." He tried to divine Esclarmonde's purpose for this risk, but she would not even look at him. He warned her before departing, "New guards will be posted on the hour."

Alone with Folques, Esclarmonde tied the tent's bindings, then came closer into the candlelight's glim. She slowly unhooked her soaked cloak and dropped it to expose her shoulders. Folques cowered into his cot, unable to fathom what she intended. He was possessed by her ravishing form revealed through the sheer wet blouse. Though still slender from the spartan heretic diet, she had regained much of the weight she had lost in the siege at Carcassonne. She approached him with a heavy-lidded look of seduction. "Take me."

"What . . . what are you doing?"

"Have your way with me."

"You know I am sworn to celibacy!"

"You are sworn only to the bile in your heart." She loosened the crease of her chemise to reveal her bosom. "You started this war because I denied you this night. Stop the killing and I am yours to do with what you wish."

Folques's cheeks flamed with rising heat. He was mesmerized by her nakedness, unable to marshal a coherent thought.

She pulled the strings of her under-blouse and dropped it to her waist, revealing the fullness of her breasts. No man but Jourdaine had ever seen her so uncovered. "Is this not what you want?"

He made a halfhearted attempt to shield his eyes. "Your love is all I've ever wanted!"

She brought his quavering hand to her breast. "You can have what Guilhelm will never have. Take this as recompense for the injury I have caused you."

Folques winced with agonized passion. It had taken years of mortification to tame his urges. Now the temptations had returned, more forceful than ever. "I would stop it all if I could! It is beyond me now!" He slid to his knees, sobbing. "I beg you! Help me! I am constantly plagued by visions of the burnings!"

She lifted his chin and brought his fevered gaze to her provocative eyes. "If you save my people—*our* people— you can still gain God's forgiveness."

He stroked her wrist, as he had done years ago in that tower across the river. "Let's return to how we once were. I'll sing you songs and you'll blush."

"I have seen too much to ever blush again."

He arose and cradled her face, desperate to taste her lips. "You haunt every hour of my existence!"

She surrendered without resistance, remaining rigid, drawing the strength she required from the memory that she had survived worse in Jourdaine's bed. Eyes closed, she retreated into the refuge of meditation. For months she had practiced the art of disconnecting from the flesh. This was only dust upon dust, she told herself.

He surfaced from the cold kiss and pushed her away. "Your heretic body means nothing to you! You're trying to deceive me!" When she dropped the chemise to her feet to tempt him, he knelt before the crucifix and fixed his eyes upon the mortified Christ. "You think your faith is stronger than mine?"

Standing exposed, she prayed for him to weaken. He tore away his night-shirt and began whipping his back with the knotted cord of his rope belt, crying out and sobbing with each welt. Resigned to failure, she gathered her robe around her shoulders and retreated toward the flap.

He crawled after her. "What does that Templar offer that I cannot?"

Without turning, she said, "The courage to let me go."

G uilhelm slipped back into the chateau with Esclarmonde and quietly called the guards to him, making certain that the tocsins were not sounded. Roused by the commotion, the perfects crawled from their sleeping niches along the walls. Roger rushed to the armory convinced that they were under attack, too distracted to question why the Templar and his sister were soaking wet. Guilhelm halted the Wolf's frenzied preparations with a finger to his lips to demand silence. The Occitans watched in confusion as Guilhelm filled a ceramic bowl with water and placed it on the rampart. Seconds later, the water in the vessel reverberated slightly.

Guilhelm whispered, "De Montfort is sapping the south tower."

"How do you know?" asked Roger.

"I saw the mining shed in their camp."

Roger blinked hard. "When were you in their camp?"

Guilhelm allowed him no time to press that inquiry. "If they've been digging for a month, the tunnel will be near the walls."

Roger ordered up his armor. "We must counterattack at once."

"Their defenses are too heavily manned," said Guilhelm.

"I won't wait until they collapse the foundations."

Guilhelm searched the bailey and saw three bony cows suckling half-starved calves in the livestock pen. "How much grain is left in the bins?"

"Enough for three weeks if we are judicious," said Roger.

"Feed it to the calves. When they founder, cut their throats and store the carcasses in the cellar."

Roger could make no sense of the bizarre order. "I have three hundred people to sustain here. And you want me to gorge the beasts?"

Guilhelm climbed to the parapets and scanned the brambled cleft in the camp where he had spotted the mine. This limestone promontory was riven with underground channels. If de Montfort's sappers hit one, the Northerners could be digging under the tower within hours. He traced a line in his mind's eye from the shaft's entrance to the base of the chateau. He hurried back down to the bailey, walked off ten steps from the wall, and impaled his sword to indicate the spot where the counter-mine should be commenced.

During the next five days and nights, the Occitans burrowed their narrow shaft while the Cathars prayed aloud to muffle the clang of the excavation. Even in the dead of night, the heat was so stifling that the miners had to pace themselves to avoid prostration. When they reached a depth judged to be ten feet below the crusader tunnel, Guilhelm ordered the sides of the hole braced with planks that had been scavenged from the stable stalls. Accuracy was critical; if their shaft was dug too near the crusader mine, the soft veins in the limestone would collapse and the ramparts would cave. The diggers meticulously angled their tunnel horizontally to pass just under the foundations, leaving barely enough space for one man to creep on his stomach through it to the elbow.

Three hours before dawn, Guilhelm reconnoitered their progress. He reemerged from the shaft downcast. "De Montfort will reach the wall before morning."

"What can we do?" asked Esclarmonde.

"We have no cloth long enough for a fuse."

"You wish our prayers?"

"I need your robes."

Esclarmonde was thrown on her heels. She and her Cathars placed little value on material possessions, but their black habiliments were their most sacred possessions, blessed at their ordinations. "Our vows forbid us from making accoutrements for the prosecution of violence."

Guilhelm's patience with her inane faith had run its course. "You were willing enough to give up your virtue! Now you refuse to relinquish your rags?"

Esclarmonde was stunned—how had he divined her proposal to Folques?

Guilhelm spun her to face Loupe and Chandelle. "If you want to throw away your life, so be it. But you've no right to abandon these girls to de Montfort's cruelty. This tower will come down before the day is finished."

"I'll not order my flock to forfeit their souls!"

Guilhelm tightened his insistent grip on her shoulders. "Would you see destroyed the very hall where your mother met your father? Had she not fallen in with these damnable . . ." Too late, he realized what he had just disclosed.

Esclarmonde turned on the Marquessa with wide-eyed suspicion. How had Guilhelm obtained such intimate details of her mother's life? She herself had never revealed the place where her parents had met nor the fact that Cecille had disappeared on Montsegur.

"I told no one," insisted the Marquessa.

Roger slammed Guilhelm against the wall. "You said my mother was taken. What do you know about her?"

Guilhelm had no time to parry questions; he was forced to break his commitment to Cecille. "I found her in de Montfort's dungeon. She required from me a promise never to tell you."

"My mother," cried Esclarmonde, "is alive?"

Guilhelm's lowered eyes betrayed the horrid truth: In Cecille's wasted condition, she had likely expired soon after their encounter.

The blood drained from Esclarmonde's sunken cheeks. She circled in a tempestuous daze of grief and rage, at a loss over how Guilhelm could have kept the discovery from her. Had she been told in time, something might have been done. The Cistercians stole her son. Now they had condemned her mother to a miserable death. Each time she relinquished someone dear to her, the demand for sacrifice was doubled. She knifed to her knees in obliterating despair. There was only so much denial she could bear. No, she would *not* deliver up her home! To Hell with God and His betrayals! If necessary, she would come back in the next life to this detestable existence and kill those murderous bastards across the river with her own hands! Eyes brimming with hot tears, she rent her robe and threw the stripped rags at Guilhelm. The Cathars followed her example by tearing their outer garb into ribbons and binding them end to end.

One of the miners peered out from the tunnel. "We hit rock. There's a crevice, but it's too narrow for us to pass through."

"How far from the wall?" asked Guilhelm.

"Not far enough."

Seeing the men drop their heads in defeat, Loupe escaped from her father's grasp and ran to the tunnel.

"No!" screamed Esclarmonde.

Loupe disappeared into the hole.

Guilhelm restrained Roger from going after her. "You'll risk knocking out the props."

After several seconds, Loupe clambered back up the rope in the shaft. "I can do it."

"I forbid it!" shouted Esclarmonde.

Roger searched Loupe's determined eyes and nodded with pride. "She's the daughter of the Wolf. Braver than any man here."

The miners dragged out the bloated carcasses and lowered them into the shaft. Guilhelm soaked a kerchief in water and wrapped it around Loupe's face to protect her from the stench and dust. He mixed a pulverized concoction of sulfur, ground hooves, and hemp, then poured the powder into a knapsack hung around the neck of one of the carcasses. "At all cost, you must avoid rupturing the guts. Do you understand?"

Loupe nodded, swallowing her fear.

"When you reach the crevice, climb in first. Then pull the carcasses through behind you and tie the bindings to this bag." As she descended, Guilhelm called her back and patted her head. "Your mother would be proud of you."

For the first time, Loupe did not burn him with her usual glare of hatred for having killed Phillipa. "I know it wasn't your fault." She signaled to her father that she was ready to be lowered into the blackness.

Esclarmonde paced around the hole, unable to watch. She rushed up on seeing the uncoiling of the makeshift fuse come to a halt. "Has she made it?"

Guilhelm pressed his ear to the orifice. "Loupe?"

The child's faint voice echoed back, "I'm stuck."

Guilhelm's heart raced. With a blood-drained look of apprehension, he searched the bailey for any means of saving the girl. A gripping madness swept the chateau. Esclarmonde and the women fell to their knees crying and beating their breasts with their fists. The Marquessa stomped the ground as if convinced that the earth had betrayed her. The perfects huddled in silent prayer, bowing and rising with gathering intensity as if the propulsion of their bending bodies would speed their pleas to the Light. The livestock and bloodhounds, exorcised by the hellish wailing, erupted in a caterwaul so dinning that the stale air felt sucked from the cramped confines.

Roger tried to enter the hole, but Guilhelm forced him back. "You'll block what air she has left."

Chandelle stepped forward. "I'll go."

"My God, no!" shrieked Esclarmonde.

"The darkness doesn't scare me," said Chandelle.

Corba pleaded with Roger to spare her daughter from the suicidal attempt. Esclarmonde rushed past Guilhelm and tried to capture the blind girl. "She's only a child! What does she know?"

"You would throw away your life for an indifferent god," said Guilhelm. "She's willing to risk hers for a friend. I'd say she knows more than you."

Withered by that indictment, Esclarmonde pulled Chandelle aside. "You don't have to match Loupe in courage."

Chandelle groped for the hole. "She saved me on the mountain."

Guilhelm tied the rope snugly around Chandelle's waist. "When you get to the bottom, feel for the fuse and follow it."

The blind girl was lowered into the shaft. Nearly a minute passed, but no sound from her could be heard.

A thunderous report shook the night sky—the chateau rumbled.

Guilhelm rushed to the allures in time to see the Bad Neighbor's cogwheel being cranked for another launch. The Northerners had renewed their bombardment at the worst possible moment. Dirt trickled and then cratered into the mine hole. Roger scooped furiously to hold the edges while his men retracted the rope. Another missile rocked the scarp and caused the tunnel to crumble faster.

The girls emerged arm-in-arm and slathered with loam. Esclarmonde ran to them with a cry of relief. The girls were grasping the rope so tightly that their hands had to be peeled off. The men drove slats into the partially collapsed tunnel and pulled up buckets of dirt until the bottom was reached.

Guilhelm lowered himself head first into the hole. He came back up and hugged the two girls. "The sides have held. The fuse is still in place." He poured the remaining oil down the shaft to drench the fuse. The women and children retreated to the tower while Roger and his knights strapped on their armor in preparation for an assault. If the mine backfired and the walls collapsed, the defenses would be overrun by the Northerners.

Guilhelm lit the fuse. The strips of cloth took the flame and the fire snaked into the hole. He hurried up the rampart steps to monitor the ground over the crusader mine. When several minutes passed with no detonation, he shook his head in exhausted failure. The fuse spark should have reached the carcasses by now. He prepared to descend the steps and—

An explosion catapulted him from the allures.

He recovered his senses and clambered again to the wall slats. Below him, the embankment had imploded into a sinkhole thirty paces from the chateau's foundations. A second detonation nearer the river lit up the night sky again.

Panicked shouts rang out from the crusader camp.

He raised his fist in triumph. His crude imitation of Greek fire had not failed after all. The sulfurous gases inside the bloated calf bellies had ignited to form natural bellows that blew out the props holding up the crusaders' mine. Those Franks not crushed in the sinkhole were crawling out of the mine, seared with burns and gagging from the noxious fumes.

At dawn the next day, a heavy rain began to fall, the first in a month. Hundreds of crossbills and finches eructed from their thirst-induced somnolence in the chalky trees and serenaded the chateau with a deafening whir of excitement.

The weary Occitans peered over the walls, half-expecting to discover that the Northerners had unleashed a plague of disease-carrying birds. To their amazement, they found the crusader camp abandoned. The pavilions had been left pinioned to the ground, still covered with the debris from the previous night's explosions. Roger threw open the gates and led his cheering men in a splashing race across the trickling river to search for foodstuffs and provisions.

Weak from hunger, Esclarmonde panted her way with difficulty to the ramparts. She was forced to pause at the top to chase an attack of dizziness. When she recovered, she looked into the valley and was confirmed in her hope. "God has granted us a miracle."

Guilhelm gently braced a hand against her back to steady her, ensuring for her peace of mind that the other Cathars did not witness the gesture of intimacy. He assisted the Marquessa and the two girls to the allures to allow them to see the fruits of their bravery. "These lasses, not God, gave you the miracle. But the Lion will return."

That prediction dashed Esclarmonde's hope for an end to their travails. "Then we have accomplished nothing."

"We've gained time," said Guilhelm. "That is victory enough for this day. The Lion will limp back to Carcassonne for the winter to lick his wounds."

Esclarmonde could find little to celebrate in the temporary respite. She muttered to herself in despair, "This war will never end."

Guilhelm was not one to sweeten bitter medicine to ease its consumption. "If your brother does not find an ally, it will end sooner than you wish."

"Is there no one who can turn back that bloodthirsty man?"

The Marquessa overheard Guilhelm's dark prognostication. With her pensive gaze set on the distant crests, she challenged him with a prediction. "There is one who can . . . the Hammer of the Moors."

Guilhelm shook his head to dismiss such foolishness. "The King of Aragon will not cross those mountains again. Not to risk his kingdom to save a few heretics."

"I know him better than you do," insisted the Marquessa. "He is of my generation. He can be brought to our side."

"Peter is a loyal Catholic," scoffed Guilhelm. "Besides, he has his hands full fighting the infidels on his own borders. What could possibly entice him to bring his army to Occitania?"

The Marquessa glanced speculatively at Esclarmonde as if sharing a mysterious knowledge that only women could comprehend. "In his youth, the King was possessed by two passions," said the matriarch. "He could never keep a dry eye on hearing a well-phrased verse."

"And the second?" asked Guilhelm.

The Marquessa's gray eyes smoldered with a plan. "A certain chatelaine of great beauty who lived in Cabaret."

Just as in a candle flame, the obscure light
at the bottom adheres close to the wick, without which it cannot
be. When fully kindled, it becomes a throne for the white light
above it, and when these two come into their full glow, the white
light becomes a throne for a Light not wholly discernible.
- The Zohar, Kabbalah

XXVI

Aragon

October 1212

sclarmonde climbed atop a high scarp worn smooth by centuries of pilgrims who had fallen to their knees in prayer after surviving the Pyrenees on their way to Santiago de Compostela. Thrilled to find España's fertile plains spread before her, she dropped her hood and basked in an arid breeze redolent with the bloom of autumn oranges. Guilhelm did not stop to share her exultation but continued his descent into the Aragon foothills, cautiously guiding her black meren jennet through the tufts of blue thistles. He had said little during their strenuous two-week trek through the Ariege gorge and across the high ranges, where they had found shelter in the primitive refugios that bordered Andorra's chain of crystal lakes.

Esclarmonde allowed her imagination to evoke the many celebrated personages who had trudged this ancient route: Julius Caesar rushing his legions to the Ebro river to subdue Pompey; Hannibal and his African elephants slipping through the pass to reach the back door of Italy; Roland and Oliver trading chansons de gestes on their campaigns against the Moors. According to legend, so many pagans and Christians after them had trampled though this defile that the dust raised by their feet had formed the Milky Way. Young couples in particular were drawn to the pilgrimage; a bounty of children was promised to those who reached the end of Creation on the Galician shores and gathered the scallop shells held sacred by the goddess Venus.

She studied Guilhelm and wondered if he too saw the irony in their circumstance. Both were sworn to celibacy. Yet here they were, treading together a path that promoted fertility. At times she wondered if God became so despondent over the world's misery that He contrived such mismatched adventures for His distraction. Since his contretemps during the Foix siege, Guilhelm had not spoken of her attempted tryst with Folques. His silence was more unbearable than open recrimination, for she could not determine if he had forgiven her or was so heart-injured that he had locked the pain within. She dared not broach the matter now, when they were so near their destination. It had taken all of her talents for persuasion just to win his escort. She caught up with him and tried to coax a conversation. "Guilhelm, do you think you've lived before?"

He turned on her with a look that hovered between astonishment and harsh dismissal. "Has the elevation made you light-headed?"

"Don't tell me you've not thought about it. Who were you? Caesar? No, you brood more like Brutus."

"Was he the one that bedded that Egyptian harlot?"

The quip stung Esclarmonde like the asp that killed Cleopatra. She knew the allusion was meant to suggest that she was loose with her virtue. "She was only trying to save her kingdom from the domination of insipid men."

"And did she succeed?" he asked, knowing the answer.

Esclarmonde was stopped speechless. What an infuriating man he could be at times! How was she expected to argue with such a cynic who held fast to no creed? The Cistercians could be cornered into their blind wynds of flawed logic, but Guilhelm never took a rooted stance, contending in philosophy with the same shifting tactics that he adopted in combat. She tried to outflank him with another approach. "Do you believe that God is just?"

He studied her like a chess player trying to predict an opponent's next move. "What does the great polemicist of Pamiers believe?"

"You dodge and weave like a Paris juggler on ice. Humor me this once."

"Is God just?" He ruminated for a moment. "Efficient, perhaps."

She licked her lips in anticipation, having exposed his board queen to her strength—a discussion of theology. "Can God be both just *and* inefficient? If the world does not work in accordance with divine law, is not unmerited suffering the inevitable result?"

"What is your point?"

"Cleopatra sacrificed her body to save her people. Yet the Egyptians did not claim her to be their risen god. The only difference I see between Cleopatra and the Roman version of Christ is that she was a woman and He was a man."

"What does *that* have to do with what we were just talking about?"

Nothing at all, she conceded to herself. But she was still smarting from his barb hinting at her compromised chastity. Now that her feint had thrown him off balance, she was in a better frame of mind to resume their game. "Would you send off a squire under your instruction to fire one practice arrow, then judge him for the rest of eternity on the merits of that single shot?"

"Of course not."

"Why then would God allow us only one chance at salvation?"

Guilhelm screwed his eyes into a mental clench. "You deem it a tragedy to be returned to this world. The Pope declares it an abomination to believe that a soul would transmigrate and take on flesh again. What if both of you are wrong? If we *are* returned here again and again, might it not be a blessing?"

Esclarmonde laughed from astoundment. "If one of us suffers from the thin air, it's certainly not me. Why would you want to relive—"

"Hear me out, woman! You ask my opinion, and before I manage half a thought, you dismiss it. You are as pig-headed as the Pope!"

She affected mock injury. "You'll pay for that slander."

He displayed the back of his good hand. "Slap it."

"I certainly will not!"

"Ah, I forgot about your pacifist vows. No loss. You wouldn't be quick enough anyway, being a woman and—"

She punished his wrist with a darting smack and followed it up with a lording smirk. "How's that for womanly quickness?"

Her alacrity did not elicit the expected response. Guilhelm gently took her hand in a gesture of conciliation. Moved by his plea for clemency, she arched her wrist to receive the courtesy, impressed by how far he had come since that first day in the court of love. Indeed, her companionship seemed to have had a rather salutary effect on his manners. She closed her eyes to savor the full effect of the kiss and—"Ouch!" She yelped from the sting of his retaliating slap. Her eyes flew open and examined with horror the red contusion that had been raised on her wrist. "Why in blood's name did you—"

"How did that feel?"

"How do you think it felt?" she snapped.

"Would you have empathy for the pain had you not received it in turn?"

"So, you champion an eye for an eye? What did that ever solve?"

He captured her hand again, this time calming her flinch and rubbing away the lingering discomfort. "Have you considered the possibility that both you and the Pope misinterpret the Old Testament? Perhaps the eye for an eye is not demanded in the same lifetime. Perhaps one must return to this world to experience the same injury to understand his error? You consider suffering unjust only because you don't remember inflicting it on others."

"That is absurd."

"You insist that God is efficient. What would be the most efficient way of teaching people to do unto others as you would have them do unto you?"

"Tell me, oh Master Abelard."

"If the Cistercians knew that they would suffer the pyre in the next incarnation, would they be so hell-bent on inflicting their mayhem? You and the Pope are not so different. He wants to ascend to Paradise and sit in Abraham's lap. You want to escape to some elusive realm you call the Light. Each of you hates this world in your own spiteful way. Perhaps the most just *and* efficient result would be for you and Innocent to exchange places in the next life."

She could not determine which had shaken her more: his assault on her hand—which seemed motivated by more than just education—or his searing condemnation of her faith. Was it any wonder that all three estates despised the arrogance of Templars? He may have abandoned the Order, but he had not forsworn its condescending method of discourse. Yet she had undergone sufficient introspection of her own soul to admit that she had goaded him into the challenge. He had reason to be cross with her; she had cost him years of misery and humiliation under de Montfort's heel. If she could not accept his criticism with good grace, then in truth she was no better than the Roman pontiff. Finding him stewing, perhaps even a bit regretful of his outburst, she resolved to change the subject. "When will we reach the King's palace?"

"Within the week, provided the Caliph's scouts don't find us first."

That was not the question to brighten his mood. He was still in a foul temper over her refusal to heed his counsel against making the journey. King Peter of Aragon had defeated the Moors three months earlier in a decisive battle at Las Navas de Tolosa, but these frontiers were still infested with infidel marauders who made their living selling Christian captives to the North African slave markets. She resorted to another tact to tease away his grumpiness. "Didn't you once suggest we run away together to a foreign land?"

"I proposed a locale far from Rome's reach. You have led us into the very cauldron of its devotion. If you think de Montfort and the Cistercians are fanatics, wait until you deal with these Spaniards."

"King Peter arranged the marriage of his sister to an excommunicate," she reminded him. "How devoted to Rome can he be?"

"He has also bonded his son's future marriage to de Montfort's daughter. He plays both sides."

Esclarmonde shook her head in exasperation. She had always found it nigh impossible to unravel the intricate bonds of vassalage that webbed the Languedoc. Nor could she understand how in statecraft, unlike in love, fealty could be multiplied and divided without apparent impairment. The Count of Toulouse was cousin to King Philip of France and brother-in-law to Peter of Aragon. The House of Foix thus owed allegiance to Toulouse and Aragon and possessed the right to seek redress and protection from both. Yet these two domains separated by the mountains were ancient enemies, a harsh reality that rendered all the more difficult her plan to yoke them as allies to save Occitania. The Cistercian war had dragged on for another year. De Montfort had intensified his savagery, massacring the populations in Mossaic and Mountabon and drawing her brother into a costly battle at Castelnaudry. If she failed to convince the Aragon monarch to take up their cause, it would be only months before Foix and Montsegur were also lost. Guilhelm lifted her to the saddle and led her palfrey down into sloping fields striped by rows of olive groves. Sensing that he had become more restless than usual, she risked another question. "Is there something besides brigands that worries you?"

"Alcaniz is governed by the Order of Calatrava," he said. "The Spanish caballeros despise Templars."

"Both are Christian orders. Do they not abide by the same ideals?"

"Years ago, the kings of Aragon and Castile placed their possessions under the Temple's protection," he said. "When the Moors sent reinforcements from Africa, my Master recalled our brothers to France rather than defend the castles. After that treachery, the Spanish kings formed their own military orders and vowed to never again trust the Temple."

"Will you be in danger?"

"Only if they discover my affiliation."

"Is there anyone in Peter's court who might recognize you?"

"To my knowledge, no."

"Then you fret needlessly," she assured him. "No one would ever suspect a Templar of escorting a heretic lady across the mountains."

The white-mantled Knights of Calatrava greeted Esclarmonde with glares of contempt as she entered their headquarters, the Encomedia of Alcaniz, an austere fastness that sat on a sunbaked hill overlooking the Guadalope river and the trade road from Barcelona to Toledo. The ancient palace's latticed stucco walls were studded with the black hammered armor of these caballeros so feared by the Saracens.

To her relief, King Peter did not share in the cold greeting. He broke a wide grin and rushed to her with open arms. "My lady, it gladdens my heart to see you in good health." He was surprised to find her accompanied by a man not attired in the black robes of her Cathar faith. "Do I know you, sir?"

"I was at Carcassonne," said Guilhelm vaguely, eager to avoid the subject.

Peter's face darkened at the mention of Trevencal's lost city. "You were fortunate to escape that infernal pit. The foolish lad would not heed my counsel."

"He refused to abandon his people," reminded Esclarmonde.

Peter brushed aside their disagreement on the murdered viscount's virtues as no longer worthy of his attention. "I have been in the field fighting the Almohads. What is the news from the Languedoc?"

"De Montfort prosecutes a reign of terror with a savagery never before witnessed in a Christian district," said Esclarmonde.

The King was distressed by that unexpected report. "My eldest son resides with the man. I was told by the monk Guzman that the Norman was merely cleaning up a few rebellious enclaves."

Pierre Vidal, the most senior troubadour in the Aragon court, limped forward and genuflected with difficulty to Esclarmonde. "The lady speaks true, my liege." Vidal's voice was still as mellifluous as she remembered it from her youth, but there was now an odd thickness in the way he pronounced his words. "Last year, I saw with my own eyes the Lion's depravities in Toulouse."

The King detected Esclarmonde's distraction. "Our good friend here suffered the worst calamity that could befall a member of his profession. A married lady fell in love with the cleverness of his tongue."

"That is no mark against a man of song," protested Esclarmonde.

"The lady's betrothed did not see it that way," said the King. "My physician reattached the appendage. He now warbles again like a spring robin."

"My gracious benefactor took pity on me," said Vidal.

Esclarmonde looked across the hall and recognized several former dignitaries of the singing guild. "My lord, it appears you've given refuge to every troubadour who once traveled my homeland." She offered her hand in greeting to an aged but still-handsome bard whose most prominent feature was a perpetual grin of mischief. She laughed in delight, thrilled to make the reacquaintance of the only Occitan singer so famous that he was referred to by the name of his Provence home. "You, Miraval, I shall never forget."

King Peter arched with a loud guffaw. "My lady, you are much too young to remember this old bag of pipes!"

The Calatravans, seeing how Esclarmonde's arrival had exalted their monarch into such high spirits, eased the severity of their martial stances. She could not remember the last time she had enjoyed the warmth of such a well-appointed court. When Miraval kissed her hand, she felt transported as if a maiden back to the love courts. She giggled girlishly and in a good-natured taunt reminded him, "My father oft spoke of his rival."

Miraval surrendered a bemused confession. "The Count of Foix and I were hot-blooded *jeune hommes*, held in thrall by the unrivaled beauty of your mother. You have her high cheeks and alluring eyes."

The King saw that Miraval's last observation had chased Esclarmonde's good cheer. "Is your mother not well?"

"She was last seen near death in de Montfort's dungeon." She blinked back tears. "There is a saying in our land, my lord. When your neighbor's walls are on fire, your own property shall soon burn."

Before the King could offer his condolences, a shout from the entrance interrupted their shared moment of grief. "Fire shall be the fate of any who traffics with this heretic woman!" Peter and his knights turned toward the doors and found the Bishop of Toulouse blustering into the hall with a claque of sour-faced canons from Dominic's parish in Castile.

Esclarmonde shot a consternated glance at Guilhelm. How had Folques learned of their decision to come to Aragon? Did the Cistercian spies deduce it from her absence? Worse even, could the Calatravans have sent copies of her correspondence with Peter to Citeaux?

Folques came bounding up before the King with the same slashing swagger of his troubadour days. Dispensing with the usual diplomatic preambles, he unrolled a parchment and read aloud:

> *To the Defender of the Faith in Spain, the King of Aragon, from his Holiness Innocent III: My prelates have reported that you harbor within your court persons suspected of sympathy with the Occitan heresy. You are ordered to restrict your attention to the reconquest of God's land in Hispania and give no hearing to those who seek to seduce you into the holy*

*war being waged in the Languedoc. Such is the command that your Serene
Highness is invited to obey, in every last detail. Failing which, we should
be obliged to threaten you with Divine Wrath, and to take steps against
you such as would result in your suffering grave and irreparable harm.*

The King was lifted from his chair by the affront. "The Holy Father threat-
ens *me*? The Church's champion who drove the infidel from Las Navas?"

Miraval circled Folques and pinched the rich ermine purfling of his almice.
"Well, if it isn't the prodigal son. The vow of poverty has not diminished your
exquisite taste in garb. What happened to you? You were once one of us."

Folques brushed off Miraval's pawing hand. "Our Lord saved me from the
seductions of frivolous verse. Besides, I bested all of you. There was nothing
left for me to accomplish."

"As I remember," said Miraval, "there was one you did not best."

Folques shot a narrow-eyed glance at Guilhelm in a warning that they
would both be served by not revealing their first encounter in Foix. "The lady
held a preference that day. I was denied a fair hearing."

"Indeed, I cannot fathom why the maiden would not have preferred you,"
said Peter dryly. "Considering the effervescent company you offer."

The hall rumbled with laughter, pricking Folques's bilious swell of hauteur.
He spun to ferret out the source of the whispered jests.

The King retreated to his chair and mulled the delicious possibilities presented by this rare confluence of characters. "When an accusation of foul play
is filed in my court, I must see to it that reparations are administered. I am
inclined, Bishop, to grant you a chance to redeem yourself."

"I fail to take your Excellency's meaning," said Folques in puzzlement.

"Tomorrow eve," said the King, "I intend to sponsor the greatest contest of
verse ever held in Aragon."

Folques retreated a step, having ciphered the monarch's intent. "My vows
do not permit participation in such base games."

"Your vows may bend when you hear the stakes," said the King. "The victor
shall be granted a valuable benefice. Should you prevail, you may advise His
Holiness that I will wash my hands of the Languedoc. That would carry you a
step up the Vatican staircase, no?"

Folques surveyed the chamber. Most of the bards in attendance were long
past their prime in the art of the chanson. After the Cistercian banishment
of the love courts in Occitania, these former stalwarts of the profession had
become soft and untested in the heat of competition. True, he himself had

not attempted a performed verse in fifteen years, but he had kept his voice tuned with the daily chanting. Notwithstanding the monastic discipline, he had never forgotten the secular songs. He bowed with calculated humility to accept the invitation. "For the greater glory of God."

The King watched with gleeful anticipation as the most emboldened of the troubadours threw their signets into an esquire's hat to indicate their entry into the contest. He stood to announce the roll. "We shall reconvene—"

"I would offer another competitor," interjected Esclarmonde. "That is, if it is not too late."

"By all means, my lady," said the King. "Who among these crafty veterans of the song would you have perform in your honor?"

Esclarmonde kept her eyes trained ahead lest she lose resolve. "My escort."

Guilhelm spun on her with a glare of disbelief. He had no choice but to accept, for to lodge a public objection would prove too dangerous.

Peter examined him more closely. "Your name again, sir?"

Guilhelm bit his lower lip in anger. "Montanhagol."

Intrigued, the troubadours converged around Guilhelm to assay his features. In a burst of discovery, Miraval announced, "It is the Templar of Foix!"

The Calatravans tightened their circle around Guilhelm in provocative threat. The King held his knights at bay, perplexed why the intruder did not wear the mantle of the order. "Is this true? A Knight of the Temple slinks into my chambers in deceptive garb?"

"I have served the Cross," said Guilhelm, barely containing his pique at Esclarmonde for the inconceivable indiscretion. "As have your worthy knights."

Miraval shook Guilhelm's hand in admiration. "And yet, your Excellency, this warrior's greatest victory came in an epic battle of song. I was present that day in Foix. His was the voice that sent the Devil's bishop to the cloister." Miraval pivoted to aim a finger at Folques. "Admit it, Cistercian!"

Folques stood stone-faced, refusing to acknowledge the claim.

Savoring this tantalizing agon, the King ordered up a draught of wine and made a toast, "I pray you are up to the task, Templar. I'd rather fall defenseless against the Moors than walk unarmed into a skirmish of song with these blue jays. A body on the battlefield can be buried. A bloodied reputation cannot." He quirked a smirk at Folques. "You could attest to that, eh, Bishop?"

Incensed by the laughter at his expense, Folques whipped his flowing sleeves to his elbows and marched from the chamber, cuffing Guilhelm's shoulder as he passed.

The evening tapers cast dancing shadows across the checkered inlays of Alcaniz's great hall. Of the thirty troubadours in attendance, only five had been confident enough to enter the fray. On the dais, Peter held court over an elite audience comprised of his knights, the Cistercian monks, and dozens of aspiring singers who had rushed here from afar to witness this rare display of poesy. No woman had ever seen the sun set within the monastery, but the King had decided to allow Esclarmonde to attend over the protest of the Calatravan commander, who deemed abhorrent any act that smacked of the Moorish belief that women were the equal of men in intelligence.

Monkish stares of disapproval singed Esclarmonde as she took a seat in the front row next to Guilhelm. She had tried in vain to convince him that she had not schemed his participation in advance. When Peter made the offer of the Languedoc to Folques, she could not stand by and allow her homeland to be so cavalierly bartered. She had rehearsed Guilhelm on all she could remember about the peculiar strategies and mannerisms of his competitors. Still peeved, he had refused to share with her the verses that he had chosen to sing.

One by one, the competitors walked down the aisle and drew the lots that would indicate their order of performance. Their careers, for some even their lives, depended on this night. Esclarmonde's heart went out to all of them. They had lost patrons in the Languedoc war and had been forced to retreat to Aragon, too proud to beg in the streets. Peter could not lodge them indefinitely, particularly with Rome growing suspicious of their affliction with the Occitan heresy. The victor would win both immortality and the protection of the last champion of song; the losers would be turned out into the crumbling world to fend for themselves.

The King commanded silence. "Who has drawn the first slot?"

Miraval arose and came before the monarch. "My lord, I have the first. But I beg to defer to the Adam who gave birth to our profession."

His fellow troubadours nodded with approval and turned in reverence toward Vidal, ancient of the ancients, the feisty but beloved Druid who had wandered the earth from Palestine to Ireland. He was shrunken by age and bent from the many disappointments of life, but his watery eyes—one blue and one hazel—still dazzled. He had been present at the dawn of Chivalry and was rumored to have learned the secrets of Merlin, a legend that had grown from his promise that words commissioned from his mouth always came true.

Two knights leveraged the tottering Vidal to his feet. He waved off their assistance and gazed sadly across the assembly, clairvoyantly aware that this would be his last performance. When a viol player strummed a melancholic chord, Vidal sang in a husky but powerful contratenor voice:

Sir, had I a goodly steed,
Soon would my enemies for mercy plead;
For even when they hear of men my name,
They fear me more than quail doth fear hawk's greed;
Nor prize their life a doit, so fierce of deed,
So stern they know me, and so great my fame.

When donned my glitt'ring, steel-lined coat of mail,
And girt my sword, his gift that cannot fail,
Whither I go, the earth doth shake with fear;
No foes I meet that do not fore me pale,
And yield me place; nought doth their pride avail,
So great their terror when my step they hear.

Esclarmonde marveled at how, within a few blinks, the dotaged gentleman had transformed his ravaged body into an instrument of divine resonance. Some believed that the bards of Eire had taught him the secret of shortening his throat cords and embouchuring his lips, allowing air to flow in such a way that he could move up and down the register of notes without breaking his voice:

Great joy have I to greet the season bright,
And joy to greet the blessed summer days,
And joy when birds do carol songs of praise,
And joy to mark the woods with flowerets delight,
And joy at all whereat to joy were meet,
And joy unending at the pleasance sweet
That yonder in my joy I think so gay,
There where in joy my soul and sense remain.

Tis Love that keeps me in such dear delight,
Tis Love's clear fire that keeps my breast ablaze,
Tis Love that can my sinking courage raise,
Even for Love am I in grievous plight;
With tender thoughts Love makes my heart to beat,
And o'er my every wish has rule complete—
Virtue I cherish since began his reign
And to do deeds of Love am ever fain.

Even the hardened Calatravans fought back coughs of emotion. Exhausted, Vidal managed a half-bow and shuffled back to his seat. Too moved for words,

Esclarmonde captured his frail hand to express her admiration. An old ache stirred in her heart; the verses had reminded her how much she treasured these Occitan songs that were now threatened with extinction.

Pierre Cardenal, the youngest of the contestants, was next to perform. Raffishly splashed in frayed silks of red and green, he stood quickly and stroked his beard to its point, as if by swirl of motion he could break Vidal's spell. Esclarmonde feared this singer's performance less than the others. He had always played the court jester, mocking and needling his opponents to throw them off their tilt, often resorting to motley attire and buffooneries such as acrobatics and coaxing his horse to beat a tambour with its hind legs. His ribald voice, while florid, was less formidable, requiring him to rely upon tricks such as warbling inflections and gaudy falsetto riffs through the octaves.

Cardenal took an exaggerated stance as if bracing for a stiff wind. He whirled toward Folques with a glare of accusation:

> *Vultures fierce and kites, I ween,*
> *Scent not rotting flesh so well*
> *As the priests and friars keen*
> *Scent the rich where'er they dwell;*
> *Soon the rich man's love they gain,*
> *Then if sickness, grief, or pain*
> *Fall on him, great gifts they win,*
> *Robbing thus his kith and kin.*

Esclarmonde was swept by rush of panic. Cardenal had dispensed with his usual frolicking virelays and rondelets, choosing instead a stinging sirviente to indict the most notorious traitor of his profession. She had underestimated him; the mark of a great troubadour was the ability to improvise on his feet. He was hurling *bon mots* like Cumaean curses, thrusting his eyes into their sockets to mimic the trances of Folques's notorious confederate, Dominic Guzman.

> *Priests and Frenchmen ever seek*
> *All ill to praise for love of gold;*
> *By usurers and traitors eke*
> *Is this world of ours controlled;*
> *Lies and fraud to men they've taught,*
> *And confusion 'mongst them brought;*
> *Order none can be discerned*
> *That this lesson has not learned.*
> *Know ye what on them will fall,*

Unto whom great good belong?
One will spoil them of their all,
Death, a robber fierce and strong,
Fells them, strips them, thrusts them down,
In four poor ells of linen brown,
To a dwelling dark and low,
Where great misery they'll know.
Man, great folly thou dost do,
God's commandment why transgress?

Well playd, Esclarmonde conceded. She fixed an uneasy eye on the King and saw that he had been thrust into a deep melancholy. Cardenal milked his pose for effect; then, with a sudden break of his held stance reminiscent of an unfrozen mime, he bowed and marched back to his seat.

She was afforded no time to estimate his ranking, for the elegant Miraval, the most renowned bard in Toulousia, had taken the singing position. He was cherished by none other than the Count of Toulouse, who referred to him in public as "Audiart," the pet name for a beloved friend. Miraval possessed an aura of dignity that seemed misplaced in one of such common birth. He was equally adept at the panegyric, the leer, the braggadocio, and the taunt; a savant of the measured metre, he could conjure dozens of rhyming patterns and marry them with an arsenal of syllabic lengths, assonances, and alliterations.

Miraval stood in contemplation, tortured by a private dilemma. Finally, he said, "My lord, I am unworthy to follow such luminaries. The great Vidal has sung of battles past. The brilliant Cardenal of clerics evil. I can offer only a modest dessert to their sumptuous courses. Good liege, your generosity has long sustained me. You must forgive an old singer for storing in his quiver no stinging words against infidels or indulgences. My wars have been fought on the ramparts of love." Cueing the musicians, he looked up to the statue of the Virgin Mary that stood on a pedestal, and sang in bewitching largo:

Lady, if Mercy help me not, I ween
That I to be thy slave am all too mean,
For thy great worth small hope to me has given
Aught to accomplish meet for dame so rare;
Yet this I would, and nowise will despair;
For I have heard, the brave, when backward driven,
Strive ever till the conquering blow they deal,
So strive I for they love by service leal.

> *Though to such excellence I come not near,*
> *Nor eke of one so noble am the peer,*
> *I sing my best, bear meekly Love's hard burden,*
> *Serve thee and love thee more than all beside,*
> *Shun ill, seek after good whate'er betide;*
> *Wherefore, methinks, fair dame should liefer guerdon*
> *With her dear self a valiant knight and true,*
> *Than the first lord that haughtily may woo.*

The master was on his game. He still possessed his signature mannerism of tapping his chest with his right index finger. When Esclarmonde had seen him perform in her youth, she had thought he was keeping time with the hand tic. But the Marquessa had confided Miraval's close-held secret: He plumbed his sternum to locate the faint buzzing sensation that gave his voice its peculiarly soulful aspect. This drone in his cavity was not unlike the vibration of a bagpipe; it made his breath feel as if it brushed against the rib cage, elongating the lungs before building pressure against the lips and escaping like a dove from a cage. To summon the desired effect of pouring spiritual fire on the listener, he had to moan, not sing, from the depths of his being. With each succeeding stanza, his voice rose an octave, and he thumped his chest with more force:

> *Against cruel Love I ever fight amain,*
> *As wars a vassal 'gainst his suzerain,*
> *That him with scanty justice would disinherit;*
> *Such vassal, seeing warlike enterprise*
> *Avails him not, perforce for mercy cries,*
> *So I, the better Love's sweet joys to merit,*
> *Seek pardon for what faults in him I find,*
> *And pray his pride may turn to pity kind.*

> *Her eyes so lovely yet so full of guile,*
> *At that which makes me weep and sigh do smile,*
> *That graceful form, that frank and noble bearing,*
> *Slay me with longing, yet the dear delight*
> *Of calling mine that lady fair and bright*
> *I ne'er may know, nathless as her true knight*
> *E'en unto life's last hour my faith I plight.*

Miraval finished with an unexpected staccato for dramatic effect.

A transfixed silence hung over the awed assembly. Recovering, the King loosed a heavy sigh and daubed his eyes. "Who dares follow such lightning bolts into the heavens?"

Folques nervously fingered the ivory chip that held his draw. He arose slowly, his baleful eyes bathed in the same intensity they had held on that fateful day long ago in Foix. He walked down the aisle and leaned to Esclarmonde's ear for a whisper. "How long I have dreamt of this chance for redemption." Receiving only a flicker of her lashes in reaction, he curled a wicked smile and pointed to the other troubadours in accusation, then sang:

> *The dogs across the peaks now cower,*
> *And howl upon the moon;*
> *Lamenting long the Oc whore's dower,*
> *That once did pay their swoon.*
> *From Mother Church their backs they turn,*
> *Her bed is much too hard;*
> *Yet Heaven's gate soon shall they learn,*
> *Doth not admit the bard.*
>
> *Good Peter, wielder of the mighty rod*
> *That did the Muslim bruise,*
> *Betray not the Church of God,*
> *Whose cause they pray you lose.*
> *If Rome be such the Devil's den,*
> *As these heretics so want to claim,*
> *Why has it grown in vast dominion,*
> *Lest blessed by God's Great Name?*
>
> *These damp-eyed mongers of verse and sigh*
> *Who sell with winks and nods,*
> *Fool none with talk of Woman high;*
> *She, the faith of their two gods.*
> *The witch of Foix, black-gowned,*
> *Doth spin across this keep*
> *Dark webs of false-made sounds*
> *While her wolves attack the sheep.*

Folques took his seat, savoring the shattering silence.

Guilhelm stood and stared at his old rival, aware that the calumny against Esclarmonde had been calculated to throw him off balance. He thrust his left arm into the Bishop's face and removed the iron prosthesis to reveal his cauterized stump. "Tell us, Cistercian! When has a lamb ever bitten a wolf like this?"

The battle-hardened Calatravans were not easily impressed by wounds, but they drew closer to inspect Guilhelm's mutilation.

Folques turned aside and refused to be interrogated. When Guilhelm took the performance circle and waved away the musicians, Folques erupted to his feet to protest the tactic that had cost him the decision in Foix. "The Templar must sing with music! It is required!"

"Words alone will work this spell," insisted Guilhelm.

"Proceed as you wish," ruled the King. "But no bard has ever prevailed in this chamber without the accompaniment of the lute or viol."

Guilhelm walked across the length of the hall, his eyes boring a challenge into each expectant face. He opted to forgo the trappings of rhyme and lyricism to tell a story that demanded unadorned prose. "Mine is a tale of three ladies from Occitania. Maidens who would have merited high courtesy from any knight here. The first, her name was Phillipa, a generous soul to all who crossed her path, be they Catholic or Cathar. Against the walls of Carcassonne came the Bishop of Toulouse and his mangy henchman de Montfort. These so-called Christians brought up their engines with Lady Phillipa tied to the beams. They used her chaste flesh as a shield for their cowardice."

A swell of indignation filled the hall.

The King demanded, "She was released before the assault!"

"Released to the mercy of Our Lord," said Guilhelm. "By my own arrow. The Cistercians were prepared to ram her against the walls."

Folques bolted to his feet. "I had nothing—"

"Silence!" Peter threatened Folques with a warning finger. "Your time has come and gone, Cistercian!" He gestured for Guilhelm to continue.

Guilhelm punctuated each revelation with a clank of his heel as he strode across the stone-flagged floor. "At Lavaur, a holy lady named Giraude defended her chateau against de Montfort's deadly sling. When the Lion and this purchased bishop captured her, they deemed the flames too quick a death. So they threw her into a well and stoned her slowly, rock by rock." Guilhelm was about to say something more, but then took his seat.

Deprived of a finish, the audience lurched up in protest.

The King edged forward in his chair. "You said there was a third lady."

Guilhelm crossed his arms in defiance. "I thought none wished me to go on without music."

"Finish!" begged several voices. "Finish!"

Acceding to the shouted pleas, Guilhelm took to the floor again and shot a glare of promised retribution at Folques. "There was indeed a third lady. One who suffers even more than the others, if that be conceivable. She suffers more because she still lives with the shame of knowing that, in a nobler time, her indignity would not have gone unpunished. At Cabaret, where many present this night once sang for a meal, the bloody-toothed Lion and his tonsured trainer drove the lady from her home to suffer in the freeze of winter.

"You knew of her plight," asked the King, "and did not go to her aid?"

"This warbling bishop clamped me in chains. But I asked of the lady, 'Is there no knight who will defend you?'" He took a fractional pause for effect.

A furrow of concern pinched the King's brow at the mention of Cabaret. "Well, out with it, Templar! What did the lady say?"

"She told me there was indeed a troubadour knight who had once professed his undying love. But he had long since forgotten his vow."

"A name!" cried the King. "Did you extract the knave's identity?"

Guilhelm nodded. "I too could not believe that a knight worthy of the honor would abandon a lady merely because of the passage of years."

"Damn you!" cried the incensed Peter. "Tarry longer with me on this, Templar, and I'll have you strung up from these rafters!"

Despite that threat, Guilhelm delayed a moment more to ratchet the tension. Finally, in lowered voice, he said, "The lady's champion is of great station and resides in a far land. But she is too proud to send for him."

The King bolted from his chair. "Do you know this negligent miscreant's whereabouts? Or must I search him out myself?"

"His face is known to many," said Guilhelm.

The King was livid with rage. "Expose the fiend! I swear by the Holy Blood of Christ that I will have him tracked down!"

Guilhelm lowered his gaze as if contemplating the monarch's demand. When the hall had hushed to hear the offender's name, he turned back toward the dais and revealed the secret of long ago that the Marquessa had supplied him. "It is you, Excellency."

The chamber sizzled with outrage from the effrontery. Bollixed by the incomprehensible slander, Peter staggered back into his chair. The Calatravans lunged at Guilhelm and manhandled him down the aisle. Folques grinned at the Templar's foolish miscalculation. The knights had nearly driven Guilhelm through the rear doors in banishment when—

"Wait!" ordered the King. "The lady's name?"

Guilhelm fought off the Calatravans' restraint. "Azalais."

The King's eyes extruded from their sockets and his mouth twitched as if he was seized by some malady. His knights rushed to his aid, but he pushed them aside. He charged off the dais and drove Folques against the wall. "Does the Templar speak true?"

Folques grasped the crucifix at his breast to remind the monarch that he remained under the protection of the Church.

"Answer me, damn you! Or I'll send you to Rome by the limb!"

"The woman gave sustenance to heretics," said Folques.

Pale and tremulous, the King turned with guilt-hooded eyes toward Guilhelm. In a quavering voice, he said, "State your petition."

"Name it, Templar," agreed Vidal. "You've earned the prize fairly."

The other troubadours nodded their agreement to the King's decision.

"The lady shall exercise my right," said Guilhelm.

Shamed by the exposure of his negligence, the King could not bring himself to look at Esclarmonde. "I am at your command, my lady."

Esclarmonde had not yet recovered from the dolorous effect of Guilhelm's story. He had not warned her in advance of his intent to employ such an unorthodox strategy. After debating how burdensome a benefice she could risk seeking from the King, she said, "I ask only that you open your kingdom to my people as a refuge from the Cistercian massacres."

Folques fought past the Calatravan guards to deliver a white-lipped warning. "Allow one heretic past your borders and you'll lie buried in profane ground for the rest of eternity!"

The King turned to his Calatravans for counsel. The knights raised their swords to indicate a willingness to follow him even under the threat of a papal damnation. Anguished by the dilemma, Peter mulled Esclarmonde's request. Finally, eyes reddened with emotion, he shook his head in reluctant refusal. "As a Christian monarch, I cannot sit idle and allow your people under interdiction to straggle across the mountains to my land."

Esclarmonde's shoulders sank in numbing defeat. She fought back tears and nodded her acceptance of his judgment, then wrapped her cloak over her shoulders in preparation to leave the hall. Folques chased her out with a lording glare. At last, he had cornered her outside the lair of Montsegur. Denied Peter's protection, he would see to it that she was served with an arrest warrant within the hour and returned to Toulouse to face the tribunal. At last, the backs of the heretics would be broken and—

"I will go to *them*!" Peter bolted to his feet with such propulsion that his chair was sent flying. "I will cross the mountains and avenge this outrage against our Occitan brothers and sisters!"

Folques's smugness melted into slack-jawed disbelief.

Cheered by their monarch's decision, the Calatravans drove the stunned Folques down the aisle with jeers and stabs. He fought off their harassment long enough to come face to face with Esclarmonde. With a voice crackling in bitterness, he vowed, "You'll not work your sorcery on me again. As God is my witness, the next time our eyes meet will be the last."

The Sons of Light and the Forces of Darkness
shall fight together to show the strength of God with the roar of a
great multitude and the shouts of gods and men; a day of disaster.
- The War Scroll, Dead Sea Scrolls

XXVII

Muret

September 1213

Simon spied a caulk-dusted rider trotting up the Saverdun road with a bloodied Aragonese knight dragged at the end of a rope. In a foul mood from having needlessly driven his weary cavalry across the barren causses, Simon spurred into a gallop to berate his tardy brother whom he had sent ahead to scout the Wolf's whereabouts. "Where in Hell's name have you been? You've left me blind for two days!"

"You've been blind since you fell ass-first from the womb." Guy dismounted and produced a letter from his hauberk. "Here's more reconnaissance than you'll wish to stomach. The Spaniard put up quite a fight for it."

Simon pressed his nose to the captured correspondence to aid his myopia. He read a few lines and broke an incipient smile. "Bring the lad to me."

Folques prodded up the Aragon king's firstborn, Jaimes, a sensitive seven-year-old who had been left in the custody of the Cistercians pending his marriage to Simon's daughter. Simon clasped the frightened boy's chin and tried to divine Peter's intention from the son's reaction to the news. "Your old man has crossed the Venasque Pass. Would you like to see him?" When Jaimes brightened at the prospect, Simon flung the boy onto his rump. "You'd best hope he's as eager to see you . . . alive."

"Raymond will march out from Toulouse to join forces with Peter," warned Folques. "And the Wolf will be drooling for a fight."

Simon crushed the letter in his fist. "Then we'll finally get to see their craven faces by the light of day. I've almost forgotten what they look like."

"We should return to Carcassonne at once," said Folques.

Simon nullified that advice with a contemptuous spit. "I'll not be holed up by these meddling Spaniards." He drew his dagger and pressed it against the prisoner's jugular. "How many knights does Peter bring?"

"A thousand," said the Aragon courier. "More in infantry."

Simon chortled with feigned indifference to reassure his apprehensive troops. He read the letter again, this time aloud, mocking Peter's famous lilt:

> *Dearest Azalais,*
>
> *I find myself bent low with grief by the report of your misfortune. I leave on the morrow to avenge the offense dealt to you by this contemptible Norman. If you can find it in your heart to forgive my tardy response, meet me within the fortnight at Muret, where I shall endeavor to shower upon you love enough and more to amend a lifetime of indignities.*
>
> *Your neglectful champion, Peter*

Simon twisted the whimpering boy's earlobe. "I fear, pup, that your mama's not the wench being courted."

The soldiers cackled and made swooning sounds, but Folques did not share in their mirth. "You know the woman. You threw her out at Cabaret."

Simon's eyes darted to and fro, a certain sign that a stratagem was forming between his ears. "The memory of a man's first lover always grows more false with time. Is that not true, Bishop? You were once schooled in the mysterious ways of seduction." When done needling Folques about his troubadour past, Simon ordered Guy, "Find me a red-headed Delilah with a comely face."

Folques and Guy traded dubious glances, questioning if Simon had become punch-drunk from too many days in the saddle. While they were distracted, the Aragon prisoner attempted to crawl away. Simon captured the man by the scalp and sliced his throat from ear to ear.

Peter's son burst into tears, terrified by the grisly execution. "My father will come for me!"

Simon grasped the boy's nape and forced his eyes inches from the pooling blood. "You must give up that hope, lad. My victory against that whoreson's bastard is not in doubt, for God is on my side. If you behave, I may let you sit on my lap while I fart on your pappy's throne."

uilhelm rushed into the Aragon royal pavilion breathless from his forced ride from the front lines below Muret. "The conscripts have breached the Sales gate."

Elated by the unexpected breakthrough, Roger de Foix and his Occitan knights converged on a map to plan their assault against the small crusader force that they had trapped inside the walled bastide, which was situated a few leagues south of Toulouse. Count Raymond's militia, ill-disciplined and green, had been set loose on its western bulwarks to sap the garrison's strength in preparation for the full attack on the morrow. The Southern barons knew they would have to move quickly to capitalize on this propitious turn.

King Peter remained reclined on his chaise, in no hurry to settle upon an order of battle. The flaps had been retracted to allow him to lounge in comfort while monitoring the siege in the vale below. Raymond of Toulouse paced impatiently, forced to endure yet another debate between the monarch and the troubadour Miraval on the superiority of Provencal poetry over Arab verse.

"All in harmony with God's plan," said Peter with a wine-induced yawn. "My congratulations to your amateur sappers, Raymond. I dare say my Turkish ballistae had a hand in it."

Guilhelm was alarmed by the King's lethargy. "De Montfort rides this hour to relieve the garrison. We must cut him off before he reaches the river."

Peter sank into his silk-cased pillows and waved his goblet at a scullion for more wine. "All in due time, Templar. At Las Navas, I stared down the Moors for two weeks to weaken their knees. I even managed to write three chansons during the—"

Count Raymond slapped the flask from the startled attendant's grasp. "Enough of your insufferable tales! My lands hang in the balance!"

The King arose to confront Raymond, the only baron present with sufficient stature to speak to him so boldly. "I have this Norman churl exactly where I want him. Now he has no choice but to meet me on the open field."

Guilhelm and the officers traded sullen glances, fearful that the adulations showered on Peter during his march through Occitania had gone to his head. Greeted as a conquering hero, he had accepted without blush the comparisons with Caesar and Alexander. Guilhelm sympathized with Count Raymond's frustration, but the baron's own vacillations were so notorious that he held no coin to spend on demands for quick action. "My lord, de Montfort follows no code of honor," warned Guilhelm. "He'll employ any ruse to gain an advantage. I implore you to strike him while his forces are still divided."

The King walked unsteadily, impaired by the evening's drawn-out imbibing. "How many men do we have?"

"A thousand knights in your camp," said Guilhelm "The Counts of Foix, Toulouse, and Commiges command five hundred each."

"And de Montfort?"

Guilhelm hesitated. "Eight hundred."

"Infantry?"

"The thirty men holding the city."

The King took another healthy draught and licked his lips, confident in the developing calculus of his case. "Our foot soldiers?"

"Forty thousand," conceded Guilhelm.

The King withered his officers for doubting his judgment. "Who here says I cannot defeat de Montfort on the plains with such odds?" Finding none willing to take up his challenge, he stumbled back to his chaise and launched a loud belch. "Order the Toulousians to stand off. When de Montfort enters the city, I'll have him snared like the spotted skunk he is."

Incredulous, Count Raymond attempted to raise another protest, but seeing Peter marinating in such a languid state, the baron could only sulk from the pavilion muttering imprecations.

Peter waved off Raymond's petulance and motioned up a courier who had been waiting in the wings. Hearing the whispered message, the monarch broke a wide grin and smoothed his robes. "Out! All of you! And make certain the flasks are filled." As the knights departed, Peter winked at Guilhelm. "Templar, I have you to thank for this night."

"My lord?"

"Lady Azalais calls on me."

Guilhelm considered such a visitation unseemly on the night before a battle. Yet after being chastised for questioning the King's strategy, he deemed it imprudent to say more. Making his way to his own quarters, he crossed paths with a hooded woman being led to the pavilion by two Calatravans. He was afforded only a fleeting glimpse of the lady from Cabaret. She was still beautiful with full lips painted red and skin as white as a swan's neck. He had not seen her since the banishment from her chateau. She seemed not only remarkably recovered from that calamity but younger than he remembered.

He turned to offer a greeting, but the Calatravans whisked her into the royal pavilion before he could speak to her.

Simon and Folques led their eight hundred crusaders across the Muret bridge under a full moon. The Toulousian militia, massed between the river and walls, held back from attacking in accord with Peter's orders. But the Lion's taunts became too much for them to endure. The Occitans charged across the span, too late to prevent the crusaders from gaining the gate. Exhilarated by the ease of his crossing, Simon sped through the bourg and made his way to the citadel where his beleaguered garrison greeted him with cries of joy. Hearing the roar, the pursuing Toulousians beat a disorganized retreat to their earthworks, convinced that the Lion was launching a counterattack.

Simon scaled the tower's stairwell and found Dominic Guzman holding a prayer vigil in the donjon's chapel. The Castilian monk loosed a hosannah and fell prostrate at Simon's boots. "The Lord hath answered my prayers!"

Simon's eyes dampened from their emotional reunion. He pulled Dominic from his knees and shot a glare of disgust at Folques. "At last I have with me a man of God who preaches the wrath of Hell instead of retreat."

"Strike them!" howled Dominic. "The archangels shall fly with you! Break the nefarious legions of Lucifer!"

The two old comrades climbed arm-in-arm to the ramparts and inspected the lay of the Aragon camp on the Perramon plateau to the north. Simon snorted with derision on finding that Peter had positioned his army several leagues from the Count of Toulouse's headquarters. "The Languedoc is not large enough for two fluttering peacocks."

Folques pointed to a more sobering discovery in the low valley between the Aragon camp and Muret's walls. "The Wolf protects the King's center."

Simon cocked his ear at the faint thrum of a troubadour's song in the Aragon camp. "They spend the night in revelry."

"They can afford to sit and chirp," said Folques. "They know we have only a day's supply of victuals left."

Simon closed his bloodshot eyes in deep contemplation. After nearly a minute of this entranced prayer, he roused with a maniacal look and ordered, "Muster the men in the square."

Folques feared that Simon had finally buckled under the strain. During the past months, the Norman had adopted nonsensical tactics, some even suicidal. "We've had no sleep for two nights! Allow me to negotiate terms."

Ignoring Folques's plea, Simon returned to his steed and rode across the ranks of his weary crusaders. "We attack from three directions!" he ordered. "A sacred aspect of the Holy Trinity will guide each squadron. I will remain in reserve with the Holy Ghost."

These veterans of the heretic war were accustomed to their commander's frequent conversations with the archangels. Yet they traded skeptical glances, dismayed to find him under the delusion that the Father, the Son, and the Holy Ghost would ride into battle with them. Every Christian knew that the Trinity had never been seen together, not even by the saints.

"Peter is protected by the Wolf," reminded Guy.

"The Wolf is a coward!" said Simon. "Our forebears conquered the Saxon and the Saracen! This day these song-sotted Ocs will join that roll!"

Guy warned his brother, "If Raymond sends his knights to our rear, our only escape route will be cut off."

Simon flogged his exhausted horse to keep it from collapsing to its forelegs. "We'll reach the Aragon camp before the Toulousians are even helmed."

Too weary to protest further, the crusaders slumped over their pommels and tried to catch a few moments of sleep before attempting the improbable sortie. To keep them awake, Dominic regaled them with stories of the biblical battles fought by the Israelites.

After an hour passed, a flash from the watch lantern announced the sun's approach. Simon stole a conspiring glance at Dominic, then ordered Folques, "Bishop, if you wish to send priests to parlay, do so now."

Folques released a sigh of utter relief, gratified that the few minutes of sleep had restored Simon to his senses. He drafted two barefoot friars and rushed them from the gate with instructions to seek favorable terms from King Peter by promising a new church built in his honor when Jerusalem was restored. While the friars hurried across the bridge as fast as their blistered feet would allow, Simon sat so lifeless in his saddle that some of his men feared he had expired. When sufficient time had passed for Folques's emissaries to reach the Wolf's sentinels, Dominic touched his crucifix against the forehead of Simon's ebony warhorse. The Lion resurrected and took the Eucharist to his tongue, savoring his first morsel of sustenance since the morning prior. Invigorated by the power of Our Lord's resurrected Body, he unsheathed his sword and motioned his crusaders into their three assigned columns.

Flummoxed by the sudden mobilization, Folques was nearly trampled by the horses of the marshalling crusaders. "What are you doing?"

Simon shared a shifty grin with Dominic to confirm that their ruse had purchased a few more minutes of rest while deceiving the Wolf into dropping his guard. "You must train your priests to walk faster."

Dominic's smoldering eyes ignited with the anticipation of God's approaching rectitude. He clambered to the walls testifying and exhorting the crusaders on with the fervency of an Old Testament prophet. "And Yahweh ordered the Israelites to rise up and smite the Moabites and fill the river with the blood of their pagan king!"

Simon snapped his horse into a fast lope toward the Sales Gate. His squadrons followed in a silence that was broken only by Dominic's hellfire and the clack of hooves echoing in the cold morning air.

Bedded down on the far banks of the river, the Toulousian militiamen were awaked by the earth shaking below their heads. They hurried to their weapons, certain that the Northerners were sallying forth along the slender path beyond the walls to attack their position. But Simon bypassed the bridge and kept close along the shadows, turning left at the angle to follow the banks of the Louge. His crusaders split off into their assigned squadrons and took aim at the marshy ford just beyond the Aragon camp.

"The King is attacked!" screamed the Toulousians.

Guilhelm was jolted from sleep by the same clarion blast that he had heard below Lavaur. He rushed from his tent and was met with a spectacle that would have churned the most battle-hardened of stomachs. In the valley below Muret, the burnished shields of de Montfort's knights flashed under the dawn sun like streaks of lightning. Roger and his Foix men, their horses unsaddled, stood conferring with the two friars sent by Folques. They had no time to don their armor.

Guilhelm ran into the royal quarters and found Peter surrounded by empty flasks and reeking of debauchery. He pulled the drowsy King from the bed. "You must rise at once, my lord!"

Racked by a hangover, the King bent over the bed and retched. "I feel as if I'm drugged!"

"Rally your men! De Montfort attacks!"

Peter stumbled out in his stained nightshirt and floundered to his knees. The Aragon knights stared aghast at their King's peccant condition. His attendants hurriedly wheeled up a wooden contraption that resembled a miniature gallows and cranked a lever to raise the heavy suit of royal armor gilt in turquoise above Peter's wobbling head. Before the breastplate could be lowered, the King spied one of his guards rushing to his horse without armor. "Good man! Where is your hauberk?"

"No time, my liege!"

"Take my breastplate! I'll have no knight less protected than me."

Given no say in the matter, the attendants fitted the reluctant knight with the royal armor and draped his head with the coif of gold-embroidered silk. Peter rummaged through the livery piles and found an unadorned breastplate and helmet. Satisfied with the exchange, he saw Guilhelm mustering the bataille of thirty Aragon knights placed under his command. "Templar! No assault until I give the order!"

A clattering report of splintered lances echoed up from the lower field. Guilhelm turned in time to see the two crusader squadrons drive into Foix's cavalry like the flanges of a pitchfork. Amid the horrid grind of metal, Roger and his ambushed knights fought bravely and shouted, "Remember Trevencal! Remember Beziers!"

Guilhelm quickly set his echelon in formation. "No sorties! We fight as one!" The Aragon knights turned on him as if expecting something more, perhaps a prayer or some rousing quote of Scriptures. But he had no use for such florid platitudes. Battle was discipline, pure and simple. What difference did it make if a man believed God wished him to prevail? He had killed too many Saracens who were convinced of the same preordained victory.

The onrushing crusaders did not stop to melee with the Foix survivors, but galloped up the ridge toward the Aragon left flank, which was still in chaos. A light rain began thrumming an achromatic tune on the gleaming iron bonnets and soddening the soft turf into a curdled paste of red clay and manure. The half-dressed squires scrambled to bring up their masters' mud-clodded horses. The King's Navarrese dart throwers fired their curled Turkish bows to give cover, but the crusaders had made up too much ground—the arrows fell harmlessly behind them.

On the right flank, Guilhelm saw that Peter had yet to form his bataille. He ordered his echelon to the center of the field to afford the monarch a few more precious seconds. The charging crusaders lowered their lances and leaned into the necks of their steaming warhorses for protection. He waited for the signal for the countercharge. In the distance, under Muret's walls, he saw Simon holding back a squadron of three hundred horsemen.

He intends to try the flank!

Armored at last, Peter took his position of honor on the left echelon. Guilhelm drew a breath of renewed confidence—all was now ready. With the high ground, his Aragonese knights still held the advantage if they moved quickly. Inexplicably, the royal banner remained unfurled.

Give the order, damn you!

To Guilhelm's dismay, King Peter sat inert, unwilling to meet de Montfort's dastardly attack, as if to do so would grant his deceitful ploy an imprimatur of correctness. If the monarch did not advance at once, he would suffer the same lesson learned by the Saracens in Palestine: Monfort's ponderous chargers on the run would overwhelm the smaller, stationary Aragon ponies. Guilhelm angrily slammed his helm into place and shouted, "Tighten the line!"

Fools and their damned chivalry!

He signaled for the frondejadors to let loose with their hand slings. The sky filled with rocks—the Northerners saw the launch in time and raised their shields. When that tactic failed to slow them, he ordered lances lowered in preparation to countercharge. His knights turned in astonishment, unable to accept that he would move without the King's command.

Guilhelm dug his spurs. "Advance!"

The Aragon destriers lurched to the impact. Guilhelm wrapped his reins around his left cast and held his lance with his right hand; if unhorsed, he would be dragged to his death, but he had no choice. His knights dropped their lances to eye level and took aim at the heads of the onrushing crusaders. The two armies were nearly in range to lock shields and—

The crusader squadrons splayed apart in a stunning maneuver.

Unnerved by the feint, Guilhelm's knights disintegrated into a vortex of tangled lances and spooked mounts.

"The King!" screamed a dozen Aragon voices to his rear.

Guilhelm reined back. The crusaders had outflanked his bataille and were reforming in a wedge to take aim at Peter's poorly organized phalanx on the left. The Aragon knights abandoned Guilhelm and rushed toward their royal banners, too late. The crusaders converged on Peter like wasps on a dollop of honey. Beset from all sides, the monarch fell from his white charger. The crusaders closed in on him and hacked down his outnumbered guards.

A Frank tore off Peter's helmet. "This is not the King!"

The royal Aragon guards were stunned—one of their dead comrades, not Peter, wore the monarchial armor. Rattled, they abated their fighting and gave way, uncertain who was friend and foe.

Peter came galloping over the ridge on a sleek black Arabian. Clad in a common hauberk, he shouted, "Here is your King! Follow me!"

The Aragon knights were now doubly paralyzed by confusion. Yet Peter fought so ferociously that the Northerners began to back away, educated as to why hundreds of Moors had fallen to his sword.

Abandoned in the mayhem, Guilhelm looked toward the Toulousian camp. Where was Count Raymond? His Occitan knights offered the only hope to turn the tide. A low rumble swept above the din of the battle—Simon had unleashed his reserve battalion and was angling athwart to encircle the dwindling Aragon line. Guilhelm spurred to the kill. He drove Simon from the saddle and lifted his broadsword with his good arm to deliver the coup stroke.

Simon captured Guilhelm's saddle riggings and wrangled his horse to the ground. "I'll have that other hand!"

Guilhelm had the presence of mind to relax his tensed muscles as he leapt airborne. He somersaulted to the churned muck and came to a jaw-rattling stop. He tried to crawl from harm's way, but his iron arm was entangled in the reins and the eye slit and airholes of his helmet were ajar, obscuring his vision. His parched mouth was so hard pressed against the caved metal that he feared he would suffocate. He heard the familiar laugh as the Norman raised his battle-ax.

"Where's my son?" shouted Peter, his round face latticed in blood as he ploughed a furrow of destruction to reach Simon.

Simon abandoned Guilhelm and charged at the monarch with a taunt. "Learning the catechism you failed to teach him!"

Peter heaved and retched as he ran. "I'll teach you penance!"

"Did you enjoy the lady?" asked Simon. "Did she find it in her heart to forgive you? That Toulouse whore cost me a fair coin!"

Peter stumbled to a halt, weak-kneed from shock. Only then did he comprehend that Simon had intercepted his letter and had given it to an Occitan prostitute armed with soporifics. Peter dropped his sword, undone by the code of chivalry that he had devoted his life to see prospered. The crusaders swarmed him from all sides, competing to mete out the final stroke. He slumped to his knees under the bludgeoning. A thrown lance pierced his mail shirt and impaled his lungs, drawing a guttural moan. He looked down in disbelief at his blood jellying in the links under his throat.

De Montfort dived into the fray. "Leave me the last blow!"

Guilhelm hacked free his tangled arm and yanked off his helmet. He corralled a balking mount and fought a path toward the Toulousian camp on the far hill. There he found Count Raymond pacing under his pavilion with head in hands while troubadours comforted him with chansons to lament the day. Roger de Foix, half-conscious from a leg wound, was surrounded by Raymond de Perella and the few Foix knights who had survived the onslaught. Tears streamed down Count Raymond's puffy cheeks as he kicked at the traitorous ground. "The fool has ruined me!"

"You can still turn them!" said Guilhelm. "Order your knights into battle!"

Count Raymond stared off into the distance, lost in a haze of misery and despair. He muttered to himself, "In one hour, our world has vanished."

After decimating Peter's army, de Montfort turned his squadrons back on the city and drove the Toulousian militia into the wedge formed by the walls and the river. Dominic and Folques stood on the ramparts waving their staffed crucifixes and hurling promises of damnation at the Occitans, who were forced to make the choice between death by drowning or the sword.

By dusk, four thousand Southern corpses floated down the blood-tinged Louge toward Toulouse.

Guilhelm rode all night to reach Foix. With his vision bleared from the loss of blood, he burst through the chapel doors and careened toward the women, who turned from their *prie-dieu* kneelers.

Esclarmonde knew at once that all had been lost. She assisted him onto a bench and tried to revive his strength with sweet tea. The Marquessa shepherded Loupe and Chandelle from the chapel to prevent them from overhearing the report of their fathers' fates.

Guilhelm rasped, "We must leave within the hour."

"My brother?"

"Wounded grievously. Peter is slain. De Montfort's advance guard will be here before the morn." He drew a painful, clotted breath. "Bring only what you must. The horses cannot be overburdened."

"I'll not hand over my home to that man!"

"Don't resist me on this!" he shouted, coughing up blood. "We'll head south to Perpignan and cross the mountains."

Esclarmonde was blinded by the news of the inconceivable defeat. She braced her forehead against the wall to reclaim her clarity, unable to bear the thought of another punishing trek across the mountains. The journey was difficult enough for stout men. To attempt it with the two girls and the Marquessa would be courting disaster. She took Guilhelm's swollen face into her hands and begged, "Take us to Montsegur."

Guilhelm's eyes flashed wrathful. "I have no men to defend that rock! The Count of Toulouse has absconded. His army is scattered to the winds."

"If I am to die," she said, "I would have it be in the temple."

Incensed by her stubbornness, Guilhelm rose up like a crazed Lazarus and seized her forearms. "It's over! Your religion is finished! They'll hunt you down. You've given all that you can to these people! Now save your family!"

"I've not given what Phillipa and Giraude gave."

He shoved his iron hand in front of her recoiling face. "I gave *this* to come back to you. I love you more than any miserable god loves you!"

She blanched from his blasphemy. "Guilhelm!"

"What has your god done for you except thrust suffering upon us?"

"He has given you to me," she said.

"But he has not given you to *me*! This god you worship does not exist! If he did, it would be de Montfort dead on that field instead of Peter!"

Esclarmonde caved to her knees, undone by his raw anger and torn with indecision. She had not heard from Castres for months and feared the worst. If the Bishop did not return, she alone would hold the fate of the Occitan Cathars in her hands. Panic would spread swiftly across the South with news of the Muret disaster. Her followers would be isolated and exposed, left undefended by the local barons. If she abandoned them, they would be driven into the mountains to starve or freeze. She was so weary of it all. To fall into Guilhelm's arms and let him take her where he wished would be blessed. But how could she live after such a betrayal? She had always championed the belief that women were equal to men in intelligence and courage. She alone was responsible for King Peter's sacrifice. If she fled Occitania now, she would be exposed as a craven hypocrite. With plaintive eyes, she turned back to him and implored, "The good in this world does not always prevail. Does that mean we should turn our backs on all that is good?"

Guilhelm's battle blood was still up. "Chivalry and its vanities were buried at Muret!"

"I love you more than life itself! I beg of you! Stay with me! I can't bear to lose you again!"

"You've never loved me."

She flushed. "Don't say that!"

"If there is a God, then He delights in the cruelty of requiring us to break promises. He must be as jealous as the Catholics insist." He stared into her frightened eyes for what seemed like an eternity, then broke their brittle silence. "You've made your decision. Now I must make mine."

"You cannot doubt my love!"

In that dreadful moment that hung between them, Guilhelm repulsed her grasping hand and lifted to his feet, wincing from his wounds. "You have every reason to live, but you welcome death. I want to live, but I no longer have a reason." He turned from her and limped toward the door.

Esclarmonde thought nothing could further darken the hour—until Loupe ran into the chapel and captured Guilhelm's hand. The child had escaped the Marquessa's watch and was listening behind the door. On the verge of tears, Loupe looked up at Guilhelm in empathy with his anger and begged, "Will you take me to my father?"

And there shall be others of those who
are outside our number who name themselves bishop and
also deacons, as if they have received their authority from
God. They bend themselves under the judgment of the
leaders. Those people are dry canals.

- The Apocalypse of Peter

XXVIII

Rome

November 1215

A halo of buzzing flies crowned Pope Innocent III as he bent to inspect his birthday gift: The corpse of a heretic who had succumbed under the interrogation weights of the *Peine Forte et Dure*. The victim's viscera, splayed flat across his skeleton like a flounder, had been packed in ice and transported from the Languedoc by Dominic Guzman and the Cistercians. Undaunted by the sulfuric stench, the pontiff peered with fascination into the skull's sockets. "Did worms partake of the sinful flesh?"

Folques covered his nose to calm his distempered stomach. "As you predicted, Holiness, we found only the black maggots of Satan."

"Last month, a Flemish knight released from captivity in the Holy Land was brought before me for judgment," said the pontiff. "The Saracens had ordered him to devour his children or suffer starvation."

"What did the man choose?" asked Folques.

Innocent shrugged. "He succumbed to original sin."

"A difficult case for prescribing penance," said Dominic.

"Not at all," said Innocent. "I forbade him from eating meat for the remainder of his life." Splotched from the fever that now struck him every third day with the regularity of a stigmata, he refused an offer of water in an act of mortification. A distant cackle of foreign voices reminded him of his current cross to bear: Four thousand clerics had descended on Rome to attend the Fourth Lateran Council, a conclave that promised to be the most momentous in Church history. The palace was so congested that three friars and a bishop had been trampled to death in the crush to hear his opening sermon.

Folques was alarmed by the deterioration in Innocent's health. A premature end to his pontificate would be disastrous; all that now stood in the way of the Languedoc's subjugation was the promised nuncio divesting the Occitans of their lands. In the two years since the victory at Muret, de Montfort had captured Foix and reinstalled Folques as defender of the faith in Toulouse. But that recalcitrant city remained embroiled in a bloody street battle between the Catholic mercenaries, the White Brotherhood, and the supporters of the Count of Toulouse, the Black Brotherhood. Esclarmonde and her Cathars on Montsegur had eluded capture and would continue to do so until the Southern barons who protected them were eviscerated of their titles.

Folques gently reminded the pontiff of his long-delayed pronouncement. "Holy Father, the heretic nobles will never lay down arms until you recognize de Montfort as their rightful ruler."

Innocent grimaced pettishly at being required to return to the burden-some affairs of the Council. "I am told the Norman seizes estates without compensating the Church its rightful share."

Folques's worst fear had come to pass. Arriving in Rome early, the Counts of Foix and Toulouse had bent the pontiff's ear with damning reports. Preoccupied with the siege in Toulouse, Simon had sent his dim-witted brother to defend the family's interests. This private audience was the last opportunity Folques would have to plead the Cistercian case before the plenary session opened. "You must not be deceived by these Occitans, Holiness. They will spout all manner of falsehoods to save their domains."

Innocent clutched his chest and gasped for air in the Lateran's stifling heat. "The Holy Sepulcher must be restored to the Church's protection before I confront my Savior. Philip sits idle in Paris waiting to pounce on Toulousia when de Montfort and the heretics have fought themselves to exhaustion. The French barons will never take up the Cross for Palestine while easier prey lurks on their borders. This war of yours is diverting tithes and recruits."

This war of yours?

Folques was stunned by Innocent's retrograding support for the heretic crusade. The pontiff now postured as if he had never preached its righteousness. He might be ill, but he had lost none of his cunning. To check the rapacious designs of the French monarchy, Innocent seemed prepared to relinquish all that his Cistercians had fought so hard to gain in Occitania. Folques glanced expectantly at his superior, but the Abbot, still nursing a grudge against Simon over being denied the countship of Narbonne, refused to raise an objection.

"I intend to place a new canon law before the Council on the morrow," said Innocent. "It will require every adult to take the Eucharist at Easter and give confession at least once a year."

Folques met that news with a lock-jawed look of consternation. Such impositions on his dwindling congregations would only stoke their hatred of Rome. "Holiness, my priests barely find the time to make their rounds for the masses, if they manage to enter the churches at all. How can I ask them to—"

"We will recruit more clergy." Innocent shared a knowing smile with Dominic. "Our brother from Castile has proposed the creation of a new order of preaching monks."

Only then did Almaric erupt from his pout, his neck spindling with ecclesiastic jewelry. Informed that the ambitious Dominic had been scheming behind their backs, he protested, "Eminence, my monks have made great strides—"

"You have plowed the field," interrupted Innocent with a peremptory hoist of his horny finger. "But now the tiller must give way to the harvester."

Dominic kept his head lowered in smug humility. "The mandatory confessions will assist us in ferreting out the heretics. The dualists despise the sacrament. Those who refuse it will be exposed as nonbelievers."

"There is no scriptural precedent for such a compulsion," said Folques.

Innocent rebuked Folques with a snap of his cassock sleeve, refusing to be lectured. Folques bowed in a plea for forgiveness, informed that he had overplayed his hand before the full Council had even convened. Innocent eased his petulant stance and accepted Folques's silent act of contrition. "Am I to understand that this woman in Foix still lives to spread her depravities?"

Dominic answered before Folques could soften the pontiff's ire. "The Occitans have raised the witch to sainthood. They go to the stake beseeching her spiritual intercession."

Innocent fixed his calculating gaze on an icon of the Blessed Mother, a gift from the Venetians gained in the plunder of Constantinople. Aureated in tarnished gold leaf, the Virgin's immense eyes, shell-shaped ears, and long nose had grown with Her holiness, surpassing the normal sense organs of mortals. "Perhaps we should send the most beloved of women to do battle with this Foix temptress. Even in these dens of sin, the people still love the Virgin, no?"

"Such fawning smacks of the pagan disease that gave root to this dualism," argued Almaric. "The Ocs set their Marian shrines on the same rocks and springs where the abominable whore-goddesses of Canaan once held court."

For once, Dominic sided with the Cistercians. "Excellency, you know my devotion to the Blessed Virgin. But if she is raised too near the throne of the Trinity, the falsifiers will trumpet their ordination of women."

Innocent waved off their objections. "I intend to instruct the Council to preach the virtues of the Holy Mother and promote pilgrimages in Her honor. The spiritual corrosion caused by the traveling poets who extol these Occitan courtesans must be suppressed. Deprived of their addictions, the balladmongers will soon take up the Virgin's cause to maintain their purses and—"

The pontiff's breath was stolen by a bird-like creature who leapt from the shadows. "I pray you give no credence to the visions of the Ludgard nun!" The intruder, a fur ball with bushy eyebrows and unwashed hair, fell to his knees. "She saw your Holiness condemned to Purgatory until the Last Judgment! But I am certain the Almighty would never allow such an injustice!"

Innocent fought off the interloper's pawing hands. "Who allowed this swineherd into my chambers?"

"I seek only to live like the Apostles!" cried the begrimed stranger.

Innocent angrily wiped the skirts of his soiled cassock with a kerchief. "The Apostles did not wallow in dung or preach to pigs!"

Dominic pulled the beggarish-looking man to his feet and wrapped an arm around his bony shoulders. "Holiness, this is Francis, from the village of Assisi. He has gained a reputation for great sanctity."

Innocent cast a narrow eye on the gaunt monk. "Did I not banish you from these confines a month ago?"

Francis kept the moon of his tonsured head aimed at the pontiff's sandals. "Father, you ordered me to convert the livestock to Christ before returning to your presence. Every night since, I have slept with the lowest of the beasts."

Innocent slumped in aggravation. "Has the grasp of a simple metaphor become a lost art?"

"I beg forgiveness if I misunderstood your command."

Dominic brought Francis closer so that the pontiff might discern his holiness. "Last week, I dreamt that another monk would join me in raising the crumbling dome of the Church. Together we held up Christ's edifice like two human pillars. I believe Francis to be the comrade in my vision."

Innocent was intrigued. "Speak quickly."

Francis pressed his fidgety hands together in supplication. "I wish to create an order of friars that will imitate Christ's poverty."

Innocent's chapped lips pursed with abhorrence. "That smacks of the detestable Joachim of Fiora and his barefoot rabble! God has ordained a hierarchy for his clergy."

"May only learned men spread the gospels?" asked Francis, meekly.

Innocent turned with a huff and marched down the hall. "If I allowed every shepherd to preach the Word, I'd have a thousand more heresies to quash."

Francis crawled after him. "A blessing! I beg of you, Holiness!"

Innocent turned and vouchsafed a halfhearted sign of the Cross over the foul-smelling monk, then washed his hands in the ablution lave. "I shall take your request under advisement. Until then, take care not to despoil my tapestries on your way out."

*L*oupe had never seen anything so opulent. The Lateran's basilica was embossed in hammered gold and washed in a resplendent blue light that filtered down from the stained glass of its high-arched windows. The ribbed roofing was so elevated and devoid of apparent support that it caused her to feel queasy. She held fast to her father's hand as he limped down the aisle, still hampered by his wounds suffered at Muret. Face set in truculent determination, Roger fought their way through the assembled ecclesia and its colorful array of cassocks, sashes, skullcaps, and simars. The ranks included the Patriarchs of Constantinople and Jerusalem, seventy-one archbishops, four hundred bishops, eight hundred abbots, and scores of ambassadors and diplomats, all craning their necks over the ropes to gawk at the notorious Languedoc heretics.

Loupe finally spotted a friendly face. She nodded a tense greeting to the elderly Raymond de Toulouse, who sat slump-shouldered in the front row next to his firstborn son, Raymond VII, who had eluded the Cistercian spies by arriving from his hiding in England on a merchant ship. The boy who walked behind his father during the scourging at St. Gilles was now a tall, handsome lad of eighteen with blonde shocks and broad shoulders set back in defiance. His bold demeanor stood in stark contrast to that of his decrepit father whose spirit had been crushed by the Muret debacle.

Since leaving Esclarmonde's care to go fight with the rebels, Loupe had undergone her own transformation. To her dismay, her athletic body with its slim hips and coltish legs had begun to blossom. She tried to mask her emerging womanhood, preferring loose flaxen tunics and riding breeches to the trappings of a lady's wardrobe. A tomboy at heart even at age thirteen, she could ride a horse and shoot an arrow as skillfully as any man in her father's troop. Dark-complected as a Moor, she abhorred rouge and wore her sable hair cut short and blunted. The whites of her carbon eyes were ringed with a pale rinse of red, a residue of torments and rage unnatural for one so young. Her unchecked gaze, fierce and predatory, repulsed the most intrepid of the flirtatious Italian young-bloods. None were left doubting that she was the daughter of the Wolf.

Her coming to Rome was fraught with risk, for if the Vatican's promise of safe-conduct to her father was abrogated, she would be left stranded in a hostile city. Yet she was determined to confront the men who had murdered her mother and stolen her home. Guilhelm remained in Aragon to avoid arrest, but she had prevailed on her father by arguing that to have her at his side might soften the pontiff's judgment. She took her seat and leaned forward to discover who the Cistercians had sent to prosecute the indictment against the Languedoc barons. Guy de Montfort met her stare with a yellow-stained sneer of intimidation. She retaliated by silently mouthing an Occitan word suggesting that, in the great spectrum of female chasteness, his mother sat opposite the Blessed Virgin.

An acolyte's bell silenced the assembly. The Lateran guards led Innocent into the chamber. Weighed down by his miter and embroidered vestments, the pontiff required support at his elbows and could manage only bated steps through the sea of clerics. He reached the ciborium-covered dais as the chants of the *Veni Creator Spiritus* finished. Loupe had expected a giant full of gas and thunder, but this bag of bones belied his fearsome reputation. How could *he* have caused so much suffering?

Lowered into his chair, Innocent swept the vast assembly with a leer of suspicion. Only days before, the Council had erupted in a riot during a debate over the German royal succession. This session promised to be no less tumultuous. His hands trembled from the fever's palsy as he sucked on a cut lemon to lubricate his swollen throat. He contorted his body in a drooping image of humility and spoke to the Occitans in French, "It pains me to learn that there are those in the Languedoc who still turn from our grace and—"

This pretension of meekness stuck in Roger's craw. He leapt to his feet and sheered off the pontiff's introit speech. "My land has been singled out unfairly!"

Startled by the interruption, Innocent dropped his lemon.

Folques stood to meet the challenge. "If anyone is to speak for these heretics, it must be the Count of Toulouse! He is overlord to this petty baron!"

Heated with ire, Roger pressed his demand to be heard. "I am no less in stature than are you to that gold-digging Abbot!"

The Council disintegrated into a cacophony of hoots and catcalls. Checked on that point, Folques tried to give way to Almaric, who by seniority should have taken to the floor to force Roger's hand. But the disgruntled Abbot was bent on letting their cause be lost out of sheer spite against the de Montforts.

Raymond de Toulouse, grossly obese and afflicted with gout, rose with difficulty from his chair. He refused to acknowledge the Cistercians and kept his hooded eyes fixed upon Innocent. When the assembly finally quieted to hear his defense, he said weakly, "We are both old men, Holy Father, worn out by the wrangling of ambitious underlings. I ask that the Count of Foix be permitted to speak on my behalf. He has shared my tribulations."

Innocent waved Roger up to the dais. Buoyed by the tactical victory, Roger walked the width of the chamber and stopped in front of the Cistercians. He pointed a finger at Folques and shouted with such vehemence that the latticed windows rattled. "This Bishop is responsible for a massacre of Christians the like of which has never been inflicted even by the infidels!"

"Lies of a heretic!" cried Folques.

"What proof is there that I am not a good Catholic?"

Guy de Montfort bolted to his feet and came nose to nose with Roger. "The blood of Muret on my sword is proof enough!"

"That blade is also stained with the entrails of the monarch who turned back the Moors," reminded Roger.

Aghast at the crass conduct of both parties, Innocent raised his palms to demand order. "You have failed to mention, baron, that the Count of Toulouse remains an excommunicate because of his egregious sins."

Roger comforted the elder Count Raymond with a hand to his shoulder. "My liege's complicity in the murder of your legate was never proven."

"He revealed his colors when he joined the heretics," said Folques.

"To defend his domain," reminded Roger.

Folques anxiously assayed the pontiff's reaction, knowing him to be obsessed with the law and its precedents. To sanction removal of these barons without clear evidence of heresy could foment unrest among the royal houses. "You wish proof? Is this Toulouse baron not your liege?"

"You know it well enough," said Roger.

"And thus is he responsible for the conduct of your domain?"

"I am answerable to him in vassalage. As I was to the King of Aragon before you gutted him."

"If I give proof that heretics have been protected within the Count's borders, will you concede his dereliction of spiritual duty?"

Roger suspected sophistry. "To my knowledge, he harbors no heretics."

"No?" Folques tarried for effect. "Was your wife not a Cathar?"

Apoplectic, Roger had to be restrained. "Had you not murdered her, she could answer for herself!"

Folques beseeched the Council with arms outstretched in protest. "I have never shed a drop of blood, let Christ be my witness!"

Roger rushed the platform like a snorting bull. "More than a hundred thousand souls, old and young, have been destroyed by this faux Bishop!"

The Council members gasped in disbelief, uninformed by the Cistercians, who had concealed the true number of casualties in the decade-long war.

Folques dissembled the slumped pose of a man assailed by slander. To divert the Council's attention, he resorted to his old troubadour flair for performance by striding down the length of the chamber, bobbing his head slightly as if entranced in a prayer of forgiveness for his accuser. Suddenly, drawn back from the rapture of unjust persecution, he turned on Roger with becalmed calculation. "Do you deny that your own sister is a heretic sorceress?"

Roger's indignation lost its edge. "I am not my sister's keeper."

"I can produce witnesses who will attest that she took refuge in your chateau at Foix during de Montfort's siege."

"When did hospitality to one's own family become a crime?"

Folques moved a step closer with each interrogatory. "The stronghold of Montsegur is part of your domain?"

"I have never set foot on that rock."

Folques swiveled sideways to confront Loupe. "And your daughter?"

"Leave her be!" demanded Roger.

Only then did Innocent notice that a young woman was present. His brows knitted into a frown on seeing Loupe's masculine attire, a trait deemed evidence of heretical perversity in a female. He motioned her forward, so close that she could see the broken capillaries in his flaccid cheeks. Their eyes locked and exchanged messages that words alone could never adequately convey. Her eyes said that if not for the guards stationed at the ends of the rostrum, she would pounce on him like the animal of her name and tear at his throat with her teeth. His eyes were those of Yahweh chastising Job, asking who was she to question him so defiantly, he who wielded God's power on earth. When she refused to back down, the pontiff broke off their battle of glares and ordered, "If she is of majority age, she shall answer the question."

Folques hovered over her. "You are the niece of Esclarmonde de Foix?"

"I am."

"Has that woman ever taken you to the place called Montsegur?"

Loupe glanced at her father, but he was powerless to intervene. "Yes."

"Is your aunt a priestess in the Cathar sect?"

"She is, but—"

"From the mouths of babes shall come the truth!" roared Folques.

"I have nothing to do with my sister's sins!" said Roger. "She was bequeathed the fief of Montsegur by my father. By law, I could not divest her of it. I swear by the crucified Christ that no pilgrim was ever mistreated in my county."

"The souls of those monks gutted at Fanjeaux would swear otherwise!"

"This Bishop is the Antichrist!" cried Roger.

Innocent gripped his armrests, unnerved by the hurling of charges. "Baron, you have set forth your right, but you have sorely diminished ours."

"He milks vengeance against my family!" said Roger. "When he was a paid singer of lewd songs, his advances were rebuked by the woman he condemns!"

The assembly surged forward shouting objections.

Innocent swooned from the clamor. His attendants rushed to his side with weak tea, but he brushed them away and closed his eyes in meditation. After a delay so lengthy that the deacons feared he had slipped into a coma, the pontiff lifted his lids and pronounced in a less-than-convincing voice, "I find no evidence that these Occitan barons are other than good Catholics."

Folques stood petrified in disbelief. The conniving Italian was attempting to rewrite the annals of his pontificate to remove all stain of controversy. Armed with this imprimatur, the Occitan barons would wage a clandestine war of attrition while proclaiming a disingenuous obedience to the Church. The de Montforts would be defanged and his Cistercians would be left to cower defenseless in their abbeys. He had to force Innocent to admit his role in front of the Council, or all was lost. Walking across the rows of canons and bishops, he spoke with dripping piety, "Holy Father, none will ever forget your stirring words to those who took the Cross in the Languedoc. 'Let them march as ones who had seen the Light bearing fire! Let them carry the Cross and the sword!' If you give back these lands to the heretics, good Christians will have died for naught, deceived in the sanctity of their cause."

Innocent's jaw tightened in anger at the public reminder of his complicity. He looked to Almaric for a countering argument, but his old classmate refused to come to his aid. Desperate for a moment's reprieve, the pontiff fixed upon one of the mosaics on the far wall, a depiction of St. Callistus trampling the schismatics under his foot. After contemplating the scene at length, he roused as if having been visited with a divine epiphany. "You must forgive the lapses of an aged mind. I have not been well, as you know. The Bishop of Toulouse has raised points that I had not fully considered. My ruling was incomplete."

Roger stood to protest a codicil to the judgment, but he was too late.

"Simon de Montfort shall keep all lands freed from the heretical plague except those inhabited by widows and orphans." The pontiff glanced at the elder Raymond with a faltering look of deflected culpability. "The Count de Toulouse has allowed this disease of the soul to flourish in his land. In punishment, he shall be disenfranchised and banished from the Languedoc for the remainder of his life."

A confused silence hovered in the stagnant Roman air. In the span of minutes, Occitania had been saved, only to be condemned. Folques eased into his chair and shot a lipless smile at the elder Count Raymond.

Stunned by the volte-face, Roger tried to salvage compensation for the younger Raymond. "The son has committed no crime! Why is he disinherited?"

Innocent studied the youthful Raymond, who had stood to hear his fate. "Do not despair, my boy. You walk in darkness now, but you must seek the sustenance of our Lord, and He will offer you light."

Young Raymond held a protective pose over his prostrate father. "So dark is the shadow cast by these Cistercian usurpers that there is no light left in my homeland! They have broken my father! But they have yet to deal with me!"

Incensed by that threat, the assembly's mood turned turbulent. Before the Pope could issue more punitive rulings, Roger rushed Loupe through the nave amid hissed promises of Hell's damnation. They fought their way through the doors and down the portico steps past the crush of beggars and pilgrims.

"May you yet find Christ," said a youthful voice.

Loupe spun toward the direction of those Occitan words, the first she had heard uttered by a stranger in Rome. She broke from her father's grasp and threaded back into the crowd to find their source.

The presumptuous blessing had been spoken by a Cistercian acolyte who looked about her own age and stared at her with the steely, deep-set eyes of a Caliph's assassin. He possessed a slightly stunted body and an elfish head, closely shaved except for an archipelago of hemp-colored tufts that ran above his ears. His truculent mouth was liver-lipped and his skin was so bloodless that it appeared to be marbled in variegated shades of gray.

"Traitor!" she said. "Keep your preaching to yourself!"

"You don't believe in praying for the salvation of others?" he asked.

The acolyte's self-possessed air of rectitude only inflamed Loupe's wrath. She shouted at him, "Your priests murdered my mother!"

"You are not the only one who has suffered such a loss."

"Was your mother taken away?" she demanded.

"Worse. She abandoned me for a pagan god."

Loupe noticed that the boy had a queer habit of angling his head to one side. Only when he was jostled by a passerby did she see the reason for his effort to maintain a profile to her inspection—his right temple was branched with a repugnant blue vein that throbbed with each beat of his heart. "Who are you?"

The acolyte shunted her behind a portico column. Assured that no one had seen them together, he revealed, "Your cousin."

"Otto?"

The son that Esclarmonde had lost to the Cistercians placed a finger to his lips for a whisper. "Bishop Folques brought me with him from Grandselve."

"You must leave that Devil's handservant and return home," she pleaded.

"Home to what? To a mother who murdered my father?"

"That is a falsehood fed to you by those monks. My aunt still loves you. The Bishop has kept her away from you all these years for his own evil designs."

"I don't believe you."

"Come with me to Foix and I'll prove it."

"I will take the novice vows next year," he said. "Folques is my stepfather. I no longer need a mother." Seeing Folques emerge on the top step, Otto escaped into the ranks of departing monks to avoid being seen with Loupe.

Loupe tried to go after him, but Roger elbowed his way back through the crowds and captured her arm. "I told you not to leave my side!" He detected her distraction. "What are you looking for?"

In her brief encounter with this cousin, Loupe felt an inexplicable closeness to him, had even understood his anger and feelings of betrayal. Yet she thought it best not to divulge their meeting, fearful that another confrontation could land her father in a Roman prison. She took his hand and ploughed past the leering Italians. As they hurried off, she glanced over her shoulder and saw Otto standing at Folques's side, still watching her.

The cardinal from Rome too, he comes
proclaiming that death and slaughter must lead the
way, that in and around Toulouse shall remain no living
man, neither noble lady, girl nor pregnant woman, no created
thing, no child at the breast, but all must die in fire and flames.

- Chanson de la Croisade Albigeois

XXIX

Toulouse

September, 1216

olques stood rooted at the embrasure and stared down in disbelief at the thousands of rioting Toulousians who had trapped him inside the Chateau Narbonnaise. The kinetic sky, gray and ominous as his vacillating fortune, was threatening to explode with a torrential rain. Only two weeks earlier, he and Simon had finally subdued this Occitan capital, the last of the heretical cities to hold out. Confident that the defeated remnants of the Black Brotherhood would not risk slinking out from their lairs in the mountains, they had dispatched most of their knights to bastides across the Languedoc to put down the few remaining pockets of resistance. Yet they had failed to plan for the one turn of fate that would revive the war.

Alice de Montfort circled her husband, who sat slouched and impassive, impotent to recall his scattered army. "That Italian snake abandoned us!" she railed. "Just as I knew he would!"

Folques reread the communiqué sent by his liaison in the Curia and tried to fathom how the most powerful man in the world could have been dealt with so basely in death. "The cardinals were in such haste to return to Rome, they didn't even bury him. Robbers ransacked the Holy Father's quarters and threw his naked body into a closet."

"I hope he strangled on his own lies!" shouted Alice. "God rot him in some rat-infested hole!"

Folques had long since become inured to the woman's vitriol. He offered up a prayer for the soul of Innocent, whose fever-swelled lungs had finally burst while he was convalescing in Perugia. "We must take heart. His successor is said to despise heresy with equal fervor."

"Honorius is a financier!" shouted Alice. "The Vatican purse strings will now be knotted twice as tight! Our only saving grace is that the fool is older than the Lateran timbers."

Folques burned the letter to prevent it from falling into the hands of the Black Brotherhood. Innocent's passing could not have come at a worse hour. Simon had only fifty knights to hold off the uprising and rumors were rampant in the streets that Count Raymond VII, who had succeeded his deceased father as Count of Toulouse, was on the march from Beaucaire with a large force. Dominic had fled north to raise his new order of friars and Almaric remained entrenched in Narbonne, refusing to answer their petitions for troops. More frequently as the years passed, Folques wondered if God was so entertained by this heretic war that when some hard-won advancement was gained, a catastrophe was decreed from Heaven to balance the scales.

"Did you hear me?" demanded Alice.

Folques was rudely jolted from his morose thoughts. "I would have to be deaf not to hear you, madam!"

"How do you intend to extract us from this disaster?"

"Me? Your husband is suzerain of this city!"

"And you are supposed to be the spiritual shepherd of that godless rabble," she reminded. "Threaten to renew their excommunication."

Folques bit off a half-laugh. "You think the prospect of Hell daunts them after what they have endured at your husband's hand?"

Simon suddenly roused from his slumped hibernation. "Go tell the Ocs that I wish to negotiate a truce."

Folques could not believe his ears, for Simon had never deigned to discuss terms with the Southerners. "They will take it as a sign of weakness."

Simon stomped his heels against the boards to loosen the thickening blood that threatened to clot in his arthritic legs. "There's not a rat in that infestation of black vermin that still does not fear me more than Satan. Promise them safe conduct and a full pardon."

Folques waited for Alice to countermand her husband's order, but for once the shrieking harridan remained silent. He had learned from hard experience that there was no reasoning with Simon once he had set upon a course of action. With trepidation, he donned his cassock and red sash in the hope that the clerical trappings might afford some small protection from the mob. He fingered his rosary nervously as he descended the tower stairwell and ordered the gates swung open. His unexpected appearance brought rushing toward him hundreds of armed Toulousians in their black bandanas and cloaks, adopted to mock the white habits of his Cistercians.

"Come get your last rites!" the mob shouted.

"Hear me out, my good flock!" Folques held open his shaking hands in pastoral supplication. "I come to you in Christ's peace."

"Any more of *your* peace and we'll all be dead!" The rebels cleared a path for their masked leader who had shouted that rebuttal.

"I would speak to you eye to eye," said Folques.

"These are *my* vestments. Discard those robes you've purchased with our blood, and I'll accommodate you."

Folques stole a worried glance at the tower. The de Montforts were watching him from behind the aperture. If he failed to gain the truce, Alice might order the door barred and leave him to the mob's mercy. He reclaimed silence and announced, "I bring an offer from your Count!"

"*Our* Count is on his way from St. Gilles," said the rebel leader.

"De Montfort is your liege! By investiture of King Philip!"

"Who is the King of France to us?"

"Return to your homes," pleaded Folques. "On the morrow, de Montfort will meet with your consuls to hear your grievances."

"How do we know that polecat won't fire our houses?"

Folques held up a Bible as a testament to his good faith. "You have my word as Christ's servant! All shall receive clemency!"

The Occitan leader removed his bandana to be heard by all. "Don't believe him! He shouted the damnations while the Lion slaughtered your kinsmen!"

Folques took a startled step back—he had been negotiating with the Count de Foix's daughter. If Loupe was left behind to lead the city's resistance, the Wolf and his ruthless band of guerilla partisans would not be far off. Determined to seize the advantage before her father could return, he shouted over her head, "Is the She-Wolf afraid to meet with de Montfort?"

Loupe was scorched by judging looks. She had heard more than a few grumbles when Roger placed her in temporary command while he led his main force into the Ariege valley to recruit more men and forage for supplies. She would never earn their respect if she waited for her father every time a decision had to be made. It sickened her to parlay with Folques, but she dared not show weakness in the face of his challenge. "All parties shall meet unarmed?"

"On God's word," said Folques.

T he next morning, Loupe led a delegation of twenty Toulouse burghers and noblemen into the expansive square of the Maison Communale. She and the Occitans took their seats on one side of the long trestle table that held the document bearing the terms of the truce.

Minutes later, Simon rode out from the Narbonnaise at the head of thirty unarmed knights. Raking the perimeter of the square with his blinking eyes, the Norman dismounted and spat in disgust as he commanded the seat across from Loupe. "Where is your feckless whoreson of a father?"

"Avenging my mother's murder."

"That heretic bitch that birthed you made two poor choices. The first was betraying God. The second was marrying Satan's bloodhound."

"God, it seems," said Loupe, "has now chosen to betray you."

Simon dug his grips into the edge of the table, unaccustomed to being spoken to in such a churlish manner, by an Occitan woman no less. "Tell me, does your aunt still bed that Templar coward?"

Loupe had not expected to find the Lion such an old man. He still snarled and clawed, but twelve years of war had taken a toll. His leathery skin was marred by scars and his jittery hands were twisted and knotted.

Unnerved by her judging glare, Simon turned aside and lobbed a verbal shot at the city's elders. "I'm not surprised you send a spayed rabbit to do your bidding. You eunuchs have done a poor enough job of it."

"I've given you several sleepless nights," said Loupe, reclaiming his attention. "Do you wish a few more?" While Simon glared at her in rankled agitation, she searched the ranks of the crusaders and was flicked by a twinge of foreboding. "Where is the Bishop? He must sanction the pardons."

Simon's tight-lipped sneer metamorphosed into a fanged grin. "You'll have your pardons . . . for thirty thousand marks." When Loupe stood to protest the treachery, Simon affected astonishment. "Did Folques fail to mention that condition? His mind must be turning to mush from drinking too much of that piss you Ocs supply him for altar wine."

"That's more than our entire treasury," sputtered a burgher.

"You might just make it if you melt down all of your silver."

Loupe shoved her chair from the table in hot anger. She turned to leave but was stopped in mid-step. Three hundred crusaders, some armed with crossbows, appeared on the tiled rooftops. Simon had used the night's truce to funnel in additional men from Carcassonne. More Northerners emerged from the warrens and tightened a cordon around the ambushed delegation.

Simon climbed atop the trestle table. "The other nobles in this putrid hole will be stripped and banished within the hour. The rest of you dregs will stay and raze these walls. Refuse, and your witless leaders will be hanged!"

During the ice-sheeted weeks that followed, Simon drafted every able man, woman, and child into his corvée gangs and forced them under threat of death to tear down their beloved rose-hued walls and towering belfries, which had survived since the days of Julius Caesar. With each falling sun, the Occitans grew more resigned to the bitter realization that young Count Raymond was not coming to save them.

On the morning that marked the third week of their imprisonment in the dungeon below the Narbonnaise, Loupe and her fellow consuls heard a key turning in the lock, followed by footsteps. She knew from the jangling of a sword that it was not the bailiff bringing their daily gruel. The burghers fell to their knees, certain that Simon had finished his demolition of the city and was coming to take them to the gallows. She hid behind the grille. The door creaked open and a knight armed with a torch emerged from the stairwell. She pounced on his back and dug her fingernails into the crease of his neck.

The man thrashed and spun to buck her. "Get off, you leech!"

"Carry me to de Montfort!"

"I'll drown the both of us in the Garonne first!"

Confused by his curse, Loupe loosened her clench.

The intruder hurled off his helmet to get a better look at his ferocious attacker. Tall and brocaded in the shoulders, he had thick waves of auburn hair and a bright, well-favored face; his hazel eyes held a spark of mischief as his impertinent mouth curled a broad smirk. "You don't remember me?"

Loupe's eyes rounded with recognition. She launched a punishing kick into the shin of Bernard Saint-Martin, the freckle-faced boy who had been her persistent admirer years ago in Foix. "*You* joined the Lion?"

When Bernard leaned down to rub his leg, Loupe slithered past him and escaped up the stairs. Outside she was greeted by her father and Count

Raymond. The Toulousians lifted her to their shoulders to celebrate the city's deliverance. Roger leapt from his saddle and hugged her. "We drew the Lion off toward Mossaic. We have his hag trapped in the donjon."

Atop the tower, Alice paced the battlements while searching the horizon.

Loupe shouted, "You'll soon be enjoying my accommodations below!" She warned Count Raymond, "De Montfort will be no more than three days away. The ramparts are in ruins."

Raymond weighed the risk of being caught inside the city if he stayed. He climbed onto a pile of stones to be heard by all. "Citizens of Toulouse! These walls must be raised before the Lion returns! Can you do it?"

With a thunderous acclaim, thousands ran to the surrounding fields and began carrying the scattered stones back to the foundations. Inspired by the rhythmic beat of gongs, the Toulousians labored throughout the night under the light of massive bonfires while the soldiers siphoned the Garonne into moats and Raymond's engineers raised cranes and scaffolds. The women and children carried buckets of mortar to the masons, damning Alice with imprecations each time they passed her tower to empty their loads.

Simon halted his cavalry on the ridge overlooking Toulouse and stared incredulously at the resurrected walls. He scampered back and forth along the river like a trapped fox, squinting with rising distress from each closer inspection. His crazed wife and her harried guard of ten knights still held the Narbonnaise, but they were being pounded mercilessly by the Occitan trebuchets. Although the donjon sat just beyond the restored walls, the Wolf had positioned his bowmen to prevent entry.

"Release my wife, Wolf!"

On the parapet, Roger taunted him, "Your mane looks a bit scruffy, you old mouser! We'll allow you to exchange places with your hissing kitty."

Simon's face contorted in purpled rancor as he led his troop farther down along the river. Finding a ford, he doubled back to the undefended suburb of Saint Cyprien, a section below the city proper that faced the weakest point of the reconstructed ramparts. Two parallel bridges built of ashlar stone—the only entries into the city—crossed the dangerous headwaters. He bit off a litany of curses. The Occitans had anticipated his maneuver by posting detachments on the gate towers situated in the middle of both bridge crossings, a hundred yards apart. Raymond de Perella commanded the Pont Vieux and Bernard Saint-Martin protected the Pont Neuf. Simon had no choice but to build a second city on the far side of the river. The fate of Occitania would be decided in the desperate fight for these two narrow bridges.

T wo months into the standoff, Loupe was awakened by a raging thunderstorm. She rushed from her bivouac in the Maison Commune and found that the Garonne had flooded during the night. Sections of both bridges had been washed away near a slogged no-man's island called Montfort's Purgatory because the dead of both armies were thrown there. Troubadours sang that the white lilies in this macabre charnel represented the Toulousian martyrs and the red lilies the Hell-burnt souls of the crusaders. All that remained of the Pont Neuf was its far abutment. Raymond de Perella and his men had ferried across to the surviving tower to aid Bernard and his garrison. Both Occitan detachments were now trapped together—and Simon, spying an opportunity, was launching an attack.

Roger braced a shoulder into the driving rain. "I can't get more men to it!"

Loupe found a bundle of rope. Drafting her best crossbowman, she ran with him to the river's edge. "Bind the rigging to your missile."

The dubious bowman did as ordered, but his missile fell short and caromed into the river. As de Montfort's crusaders poured onto the bridge, Loupe reeled in the rope and forced it on the archer for another try.

"Even if I thread the lancet, there's nothing to hold the binding in place."

"Aim for their backs!" ordered Loupe.

The bowman shook his head as he took aim and fired again. This time, the missile miraculously threaded the tower slit and impaled one of the Northerners who had fought his way into the breach. The crusader bent over the ledge with the arrow passed clean through his breastbone. Bernard extricated the rope from the dead crusader's entrails and hurriedly tied it to an iron ring.

Loupe knotted her end of the rope to four yoked mules. "Three at a time!"

"It won't hold one!" warned Roger.

Loupe leapt onto the rope and began rappelling across the raging currents. One false grip would send her to the freezing waters. Shamed by her example, several of the Occitans followed her onto the traverse. The mules dug in against the sliding mud. Halfway across, she heard a groan. The soldier behind her clutched at an arrow in his gut and fell to his death. Near exhaustion, she attacked the last few lengths with her hands bleeding from the rope's burn.

Bernard pulled her into the tower moments before de Montfort sent a second wave of attackers across the ruins. A large stone fired from a Toulousian trebuchet crashed into the far reaches of the bridge and sent dozens of charging crusaders plummeting to the water. One by one, the Occitan reinforcements scrambled across on the rope. Those Northerners who had navigated the remnants of the bridge discovered that their path of retreat was destroyed. Outnumbered, they flung off their armor and dived into the river to avoid being cut down.

A clamor of victory arose on Toulouse's walls.

Bernard hugged Loupe. "You saved my life, little She-Wolf." He dropped to one knee. "Marry me! Or I'll keep you hostage in this tower!" Before she could repulse his embrace, he stole her breath with a kiss.

A troubadour on the ramparts celebrated Bernard's bold advance by breaking out in song. Bernard surfaced from his conquest and shouted to Roger on the river's banks, "Wolf, I wish the hand of your daughter in marriage!"

Roger waved him off with a grin. "She's more than you can handle!"

Embarrassed by her stirred feelings, Loupe backed away and dived for the rope before Bernard could embrace her again. "You never could catch me!" she teased as she rappelled off. "And you never will!"

Nine more months of siege passed in bloody stalemate. With the onset of winter, Folques had decided to travel north to preach the crusade for funds and recruits. Simon had all but given up on the Bishop's return when, on this hot June morning, he saw his old comrade appear over the shimmering horizon with two thousand troops. He rushed from his tent to confirm the reality of the blessed sight. "Did you think I'd last forever?"

"I have brought you the hero of Bouvines," said Folques.

Mathieu de Montmorency, the foppish brother of Simon's wife, rode jauntily into the camp at the head of the reinforcements. Sniffing his perfumed kerchief to chase the stench, he regarded de Montfort's ragged army with a pinched nose as if encountering a demoralized band of squatters in a squalid ghetto. "This is what has become of the great victor of Muret?"

The Lion of old would have been at the insolent man's throat. But Simon merely dropped his hands to his knees in fatigue.

"Are you not well?" asked Folques.

"I am drained beyond all measure," whined Simon. "Those damnable Ocs nip at me like mad geese."

"Shopkeepers have brought you to this sorry state?" chortled Mathieu.

"You haven't fought them half your life!" snapped Simon.

"Nor do I intend to," said Mathieu. "I'm pledged for forty days. I spent half that time reaching this dung pit. I suggest you order an assault on the morrow."

Simon had heard his fill of such reports from Paris condemning his failure to take Toulouse. Anxious to reveal the true reason for his delay, he led Folques and Mathieu to a deep ravine on the far side of a forested ridge. Out of sight of the Occitans, his engineers were hard at work constructing an assault tower that rose more than five stories in height. The magnificent creation possessed retractable boarding planks and large wooden wheels that would roll it flush to the city's ramparts. Tanned hides covered its thick timbers for protection against Greek fire and its roofed penthouse was large enough to hold fifty archers who would fire deadly enfilades from a steep angle.

Simon kissed one of its newly notched beams. "God's glorious reward to me. It will lead me to my consummate victory."

"Let the Ocs have a look," said Mathieu. "They'll surrender at once."

"Not until the opportune moment!" insisted Simon. "I'm going to take the bastards by surprise!"

The next morning, Simon awoke at dawn to hear Folques say mass. The younger men in the army cracked jokes behind Simon's back about his rabid devotion, for he was constantly bragging that he had not missed the daily Eucharist since taking the Cross twelve years ago. Despite their frequent quarrels, these two old veterans of the heretic wars had come to cherish these early mornings together. In recent months, their conversations often turned to the subject of God's redemption, for both were increasingly hagridden by the doubts of advancing age.

"I had another dream," said Simon. "I cannot shake its hold."

"Have I not warned you that the night is Satan's porthole?" said Folques. "Give no heed to such visions. They were Innocent's undoing."

"This one has plagued me for years," said Simon.

"Expose it to the light of day and it will wither."

"It commences with a lion stalking a maiden. Instead of running away, the maiden approaches the beast. I always awaken in a cold sweat."

"That fairy tale frightens you?"

"Last night, for the first time, the dream ended differently. The lion allowed the maiden to grasp its jaws."

"Sleep is plagued by the bestiaries of the absurd," assured Folques. "Give no more thought to it."

Simon trembled from the recollection. "Hear me out! The lion could not overcome the strength of the woman's hands. It was as if she possessed some hidden power . . . What do you make of this?"

Folques was alarmed by the deepening fissures in Simon's fragile mind. The old warrior seemed even less stable and coherent than when they had last been together. "We must pray on it."

Tears flooded Simon's cataract-glazed eyes. "What year is it?"

"1218. The 25th of June. Why do you wish to—"

"Hear my confession." Simon stumbled to his knees before Folques could demur. "Blessed Father, I stand on the threshold of bringing this evil land under Your righteous hammer. You lit the fires at Beziers. You granted me the victory at Muret. My life is growing short."

"Simon, you must not talk like—"

"I beg just one more miracle." Simon fought in vain to prevent his clasped hands from shaking. "Merciful God, help me to breach those insolent walls that—"

A soldier rushed into the tent. "The Ocs are attacking the assault tower!"

"The tower?" sputtered Simon. "How could they reach the tower?"

"Lord Mathieu ordered it rolled to the walls last night."

Simon crawled screaming from the tent on hands and knees. "The damned fool! My tower! He's taken my tower!"

Below the ramparts of Toulouse, a fiery tempest swirled around the base of the wheeled citadel. The Wolf and his raiders had sortied from the city before dawn to ambush Simon's brother-in-law, who had moved the contraption closer so that he and his Parisian drinking companions could lounge on its roof and taunt the Occitans. The crusader encampment exploded with shouts and harried mustering. Guy de Montfort led a contingent of half-attired crusaders toward the burning tower in a desperate effort to save it. A bolt whistled across the sky and sliced through Guy's leg. He dropped to the ground in agony.

Simon did not stop to assist his brother, but stole his sword and limped in a jagged run toward the conflagration. "Save my tower!" He was stopped abruptly by something that crossed his line of vision. He looked up to see Loupe and four Occitan women loading a catapult on the ramparts. "Damn your blackened soul, Esclarmonde de Foix! I'll melt this mountain of Satan yet!"

Loupe realized that the half-senile Norman was under the delusion that he stood below Montsegur. She was determined to disabuse the old Lion of the notion that she in any way resembled the aunt she so despised. While the other women heaved and levered the catapult into position, she loaded a stone into the sling and whispered, "For you, mother." She cut the latch and unleashed the catapult's arm. The stone sailed smoothly into the cloudless sky.

Simon stood laughing like a madman at the absurd spectacle of the Occitan women trying to hit him.

Folques hurried to reach his old friend. Suddenly, he remembered the dying vow of the Cathar witch in Lavaur. "Simon! Take cover!"

Simon turned toward Folques's shout the stone smashed into his left temple. A flash of disbelief crossed his blackened face. Rivulets of blood streamed down his forehead and his right eye dangled from its socket. Staggered, he looked down at his chest with his remaining eye and ran his hand through the brains that had splattered his hauberk. He crumpled to his knees. His head, a mash of blood and bone, fell face first to the ground.

Both armies ceased fighting as if God Himself had decreed sound and motion stricken from Creation. The Occitans approached warily and looked down at the most feared man in the Languedoc.

"Simon!" cried Guy, writhing from his wound. "Simon, get up!"

Folques reeled back, pallid and lost. The crusaders around him broke into a panicked retreat. The Occitans were so astounded by Simon's refusal to rise that they could not organize a chase. Suspecting a trap, Roger stood astride the body and cautiously flipped it over with his sword.

The Lion stared up with one eye—in death.

On the walls, the cheering Toulousians carried Loupe to the field in a triumphant procession. Above them, on the allures, a troubadour blew his horn for silence. The Occitans halted their jubilation and bowed heads in remembrance of the thousands of countrymen who had lost their lives to the wicked man who lay before them. The troubadour sang a paean until his lungs nearly burst:

> *De Montfort es mort*
> *Viva Tolosa*
> *Ciotat gloriosa*
> *Et poderosa!*
> *Tornan lo paratge et L'onor!*
> *De Montfort es mort!*

The bells of Saint-Sernin tolled joyfully. Soon, the belfries of neighboring towns chimed in. By nightfall, every church in the Languedoc pealed with the announcement of a miracle.

Lady Giraude's prophecy had come to pass.

If the saint drinks a poison, it becomes an antidote.
But if the disciple drinks it, his mind is darkened.

— Rumi

XXX

Thoronet Abbey

November 1231

"Father, I have witnessed a glorious miracle."

Hunched over a kneeler, Folques interrupted his hymn singing and squinted into the obscured, dust-speckled light. "How many times must I tell you? No breakfast! I cannot keep it down!"

A slender monk entered the sparse dorter cell and drew a breath of shock at the wasted visage before him. "It is me . . . Otto."

That name rattled distantly in Folques's senescent ears. He then vaguely remembered having sent Esclarmonde's son to Rome several years ago to study at the Abbey of Casamari and gain valuable introductions. Otto assisted him to his cot in this Cistercian enclave where he had first sought refuge from heartbreak thirty-seven years ago. The swish of a black robe in the shadows near the threshold crossed his line of sight. He dismissed it as another of the many diabolic apparitions that now attacked him with greater frequency. "Otto, my boy, I am a walking martyr. Pray you die before growing old. My liturgics are all I have to ease my suffering."

Otto soaked a compress in tepid water and daubed Folques's heated forehead. "I have joyous news, father. Dominic Guzman is to be declared a saint."

Folques's sleepy eyes flared. "No more saints! There aren't enough days in the year!" He was distracted again by a distant cough. "Is that Dominic at the door? Bring him to me at once. I must hear of his work in Fanjeaux."

Alarmed by his stepfather's mental deterioration, Otto stole a quick glance of embarrassment at the unidentified companion who remained beyond the door's light. "Father, you remember . . . Dominic has been dead for ten years."

Folques's knees buckled from the revelation. "No! Simon would never allow Dominic to be captured!"

"De Montfort lies buried in a crypt in Carcassonne," said Otto. "The war is over. Count Raymond signed the Treaty of Meaux and agreed to marry his daughter to the King's brother."

Folques gasped for breath as he fell onto his pallet. "Raymond surrender? The mountains would fall into the sea first!"

Otto offered a cup of weak tea to aid Folques's faltering memory. "You and I stood on the steps of Notre Dame and watched the baron flogged."

Folques rubbed his mottled temples in frustration. During the past months, the Devil had twisted his thoughts so wickedly that at times he could not distinguish between the real and the imaginary. In his defense, he had witnessed the two recalcitrant counts of Toulouse scourged so many times that the punishments seemed to have merged into one perpetual rite of expiation. He looked up at Otto with eyes glazed in confusion. "What does it all mean?"

"Occitania will pass to the crown," said Otto. "The heretics are finally to be dispossessed of their lands."

Folques found himself weeping, not from joy, but from the cruel passage of time. In his lucid moments, he was haunted by the losses that had befallen him in the years following Simon's death. A few months after the Black Brotherhood broke the Toulouse siege, he was forced to abandon the city that had never accepted him as its bishop. He retired in ignominy to this abbey of his ordination where the younger monks regarded him as a curious relic.

It seemed only yesterday that he had led Simon's funerary procession across the burnt causses with the widow Alice and her three young sons. The Ocs threw so many rocks from the hills that day that the coffin nearly disintegrated. The Lion was soon joined in death by nearly all of the luminous stars that orbited his violent life. Almaric succumbed a bitter man in his embattled Narbonne tower. Honorius followed Innocent to a nondescript grave, passing the Keys of St. Peter to Dominic's fellow Spaniard, Cardinal d'Ostia, now Gregory IX, a firebrand whose hatred of heresy exceeded even that of his predecessors. Two kings of France had come and gone, leaving nine-year-old

Louis IX in the overbearing regency of his mother, Blanche de Castile. The ambitious Blanche now schemed to drag away the carcass of the Languedoc prey that he and de Montfort had spent decades subduing.

Yet he took some small solace in the knowledge that most of his old enemies had fared no better. The elder Raymond de Toulouse had died an excommunicate; his cursed head was still displayed under glass to pilgrims on their way to Compostela. That other thorn in his side, the Count de Foix, was permitted, for reasons known only to the Almighty, a natural death in some isolated mountain keep. The Dominicans had seized Foix and extracted a postmortem punishment on the Wolf by scattering his unshriven bones in a thistle field below his towers. The heresiarch Castres had not been heard from in years and had likely found his due entrance to Hell in some black Pyrenean cave.

"Did you hear me?" asked Otto. "Dominic is to be a saint."

"Dominic was no more a saint than any of us!" Folques tried to rise from the cot. "He stood at the pyres with me and fanned the flames!"

Otto nervously regarded the door. "Father, you must not say such things. Dominic converted thousands to the forgiveness of Christ."

"His only conversion was Innocent's ear!"

"If only you had been at the inquest," said Otto. "Thousands of believers pressed upon Dominic's tomb. If the legates had found a malodorous emanation, the pilgrims would have rioted."

Folques stood with a faltering effort and shuffled to the chamber pot in the corner. Steadying himself with one hand against the wall, he urinated and fouled the air. "He always stank of that hair shirt when I was with him."

"The most heavenly fragrance came from his opened sarcophagus," insisted Otto. "We fell to our knees weeping with joy."

Folques kicked over the pot as he stumbled back to his cot. "Remind me to douse my ass with oils before I croak! Better yet, I'll graze on honeysuckles and fart my way to sainthood."

"Father!"

Folques angrily waved off the scolding. After several moments of retreat into his tortured thoughts, he beckoned Otto closer to ease his effort to speak. "Your mother . . . Has Montsegur been taken?"

Otto angled his shoulder sideways to prevent his unidentified companion at the door from overhearing his whispered answer. "The heretics still infest the mountain, but—"

"Then the war is *not* over!" Folques thrashed away Otto's solicitous hands and glared at the irksome swishing that persisted near the door. "Bring me my crucifix, boy! You've let the demons slip in!"

A tall monk stepped forward from the shadows. Bald and gaunt, he possessed an austere forehead and the lean, sallow face of a greyhound. His flaccid hand gestures and mechanical, self-assured comportment dripped with the same smarmy unctuousness practiced by the sycophants who inhabited the inner circles of the Vatican. He kept his supercilious, heavy-lidded eyes fixed on Folques while he questioned Otto, "What was it the old fool asked about your mother?"

"What business is it of yours?" demanded Folques.

"I am William Arnaud," he said in a peremptory tone.

"That name means nothing to me."

"Then you are even more doddery than I suspected."

Folques looked to Otto for an explanation of this interloper's presence. "Why do you bring a jackal into my cell to insult me?"

Otto tried to find the courage to reveal what he had withheld too long. "Father, I wish to join the Black Preachers. I've come home to ask your blessing."

Folques did not want to trust his failing ears. He turned one eye on Otto, then the other coldly on the stranger who had beguiled his stepson. "The Rule of St. Bernard is no longer good enough for you?"

Arnaud placed a firm paternal hand on his new recruit's shoulder. "Brother Otto wants to cleanse the heretics from his motherland."

"We Cistercians fight the heretics!" reminded Folques.

"*Fought* the heretics," corrected Arnaud. "My Dominicans have been assigned the task of finishing what you could not. You and your brethren have been freed to pursue your calling in the cheese cellars and milking stalls."

Folques jerked upright. "Upstart! How many walls have you breached? How many disputations waged?"

Arnaud held a gloating half-smile. "There will be no more disputations."

Unsettled by the confrontation, Otto tried to calm Folques. "Brother Arnaud has been sent by Rome to lead the new Dominican mission. He has agreed to teach me how to convert our Occitan countrymen and renew Christ upon their hearts. My father would have given his—"

"Your father? I would never—" Folques suddenly realized from Otto's guilt-tinged reaction that he had been speaking of Jourdaine. The boy had always referred to *him* as father. Those sodomites in Rome had filled the boy's ears with promises of glory in the service of the saints, stoking him with fables that

Jourdaine had been a holy crusader and taken up to Heaven in martyrdom. Yes, that was how the preening eunuchs gathered their nets, twisting history and burning evidence. He had lost Otto to the machinations of the Curia schemers.

Could it truly have been thirty-three years ago? Every sensation came back to him from that sweltering day in Rome when he too had been seduced by the allure of spiritual power; climbing the Santa Scala, navigating the mazed archives, overhearing whispered intimations about the next appointment. He could still smell the sweet claret on Innocent's warm breath. Now the most precious person left to him in this world had stumbled onto the same path that led to this purgatory before death. These barking dogs of Christ—as the Dominicans were being derisively called by the villagers—had the audacity to claim that they were now the new legions of St. Michael riding forth to save the Church, just as his Cistercians had—

Otto jostled Folques back to the present. "Brother Arnaud has developed novel methods for bringing our strayed brothers and sisters back to the Church."

Folques shot a contemptuous ball of sputum toward the chamber pot, missing badly. The lad had already been indoctrinated into the high-sounding argot of heretic-hunting. *Strayed brothers and sisters, my wrinkled ass!* The boy would learn soon enough that dogs and cats stray. These Occitans who walk into the fires willingly would not be herded back into the fold by whistles and cowbells. "I'd pay pretty coin to see these novel methods."

"Perhaps one day your wish will be granted," said Arnaud. "In the interim, I have learned only this morning that a dying woman in the town here has requested her bishop for the last rites."

"She has asked for me?" asked Folques with a swell of pride.

"Who else could she mean?" said Arnaud.

Offered the rare opportunity to minister to a soul outside the abbey, Folques hurried to don his sandals and the white cloak that he always kept hanging on the wall peg. Arnaud watched with a smirk as Folques fumbled pitifully around the cell, unable to find his garb. Finally, the inquisitor provided a spare Dominican robe that he had brought for the occasion. Without giving a thought to its color, Folques gathered the robe over his shoulders and armed himself with candles and his dispenser of holy water. "I have never failed to timely convey the sacrament of death. It is truly a solemn undertaking. The lady no doubt remembers my high status and wishes my intercession."

"Yes, no doubt," said Arnaud with a sinister glint.

The morning was raw; the slate clouds scudding over the scrubland carried the promise of sleet. Careful not to step in the offal rut, Folques relied on his staff as he hobbled down the lone rue of Thoronet. He was taxed to keep up with Otto and Arnaud as they led him briskly into a cobblestoned warren darkened by the tilt of thatched-roof houses. He remembered similar winter days during the campaigns of old when Simon, refusing to take bivouac, would drive the army through storms so punishing that even the wolves refused to leave their dens. He prayed not to be late in administering the unction. Perhaps if he performed admirably the Abbot would offer him more assignments. Unaccustomed to the rush of the cold air to his lungs, he began to feel light-headed. He could not recall the last time he had ventured beyond the abbey walls. The gusts were strong but the sting against his face was bracing. He must get out more often, he reminded himself. It was good for the soul.

Arnaud reached a cul-de-sac and knocked on the door of a squat daub-and-wattle hut. "We have brought the Bishop as you asked."

A dirty-faced boy with eyes ringed like dark saucers cracked the door. Confirming that the three cowl-draped monks were clad in black robes, he opened it a bit more. "She suffers terrible. Can't swallow the soup."

"Fear not, lad," assured Arnaud. "We shall ease her pain."

The boy scanned the inscrutable faces. Finally, he allowed the clerics to enter. The humble room was thick with the stench of decay and poorly lit by a struggling fire. Otto began to cross his breast for protection, but Arnaud restrained his hand. The old woman lay in the corner on a ratty straw mattress surrounded by candles. She mumbled words that sounded like an Occitan version of the Pater Noster. Above her on the wall were etched pentagrams and other signs of witchery. Eyes shrouded with cataracts, she managed to turn her head just enough to make out the outlines of their black robes. The arrival of the holy men seemed to give her great comfort. She eased back into her matting and wheezed consumptive breaths. "I feel the darkness coming."

"Have you followed God's teachings?" asked Arnaud.

"I've tried my best to abide the faith," she said.

"You wish the Bishop to give you the last rites?"

"I've waited all my life for his blessing."

Cued to his moment, Folques lowered to his knees and fumbled through his knapsack. Finally, he pulled out an ampulla, spilling half the holy water. To aid his sight, he hovered over the woman's face and tried to place her features.

"Don't you remember?" the woman asked, disappointed. "Of course you wouldn't. We met years ago . . . on the sacred mount."

Folques's brow creased with confusion. He gave no more thought to the woman's ramblings and reached his palsied hand to her forehead. "Do you believe in Jesus Christ, the only begotten Son of God?"

"I do."

"And do you believe in the one true Apostolic Church of Rome, in one God, Father Almighty, Creator of Heaven and Earth?"

Something about his voice troubled her. "Bishop Castres?"

That name stung Folques's ear like a serrated arrow. Flustered, he looked up at Arnaud for an explanation.

Arnaud nudged him aside and grasped the woman's hand. "Tell us in your own words what you believe. God will be satisfied with that."

"I believe in the God of Light, just like the Bishop here taught," she said. "I believe that I will go to the Light and be with my daughter, blessed be her soul. She was burned at Toulouse."

"Your daughter was burned?" repeated Arnaud, savoring the moment.

The woman's face blackened from the memory. "By Folques the Butcher."

Folques sputtered and struggled to arise from his knees, but the inquisitor's hand pressed against his shoulder to keep him down. He tried to focus his befuddled mind. "What . . . what deceit is this?"

The woman's glassy orbs widened in agitation. "You don't sound nothing like the Bishop."

Arnaud firmed his hold on her hand in threat. "We have brought you a true bishop of God . . . Bishop Folques of Toulouse."

Several moments passed before the woman could make sense of the inquisitor's horrid revelation. She lurched up and pulled Folques's face to her failing gaze, then unleashed a terrifying wail. In that moment, she was drained of what little faith she had managed to hoard during her wretched life. She turned to the boy with a stricken look. Gurgling sounds came from her mouth as if she had just swallowed her tongue. "Child, what have you done?"

The frightened lad ran for the door, but Arnaud sent him tumbling to the corner. "Grandma, you told me to ask for the black bishop."

"At night, child!" cried the woman. "At night!"

Folques floundered on his hands and knees, drooling and bewildered. Otto was nonplussed by the discovery that he too had been kept uninformed of the inquisitor's true intentions.

Arnaud reassured his shaken charge. "Your first lesson, my son. We must ensnare these heretics using their own deceit as bait."

"The Touch!" begged the crone. "Don't let me die without the Light!"

Drawn by the screams, the sheriff of the village came running and threw open the door. "What goes on here?"

"A plague rampages through your burgh," said Arnaud.

The sheriff took a step back and examined the room. "A plague?"

"This woman is infected with heresy," said Arnaud. "By authority of Holy Mother Church, I order you to take her to the field of execution and cleanse her soul in the flames of Christ."

The sheriff stared at the inquisitor in disbelief. "The Devil I will! Agnes Broielel is a good woman."

"Any person who harbors a heretic is subject to examination," reminded Arnaud. "Now, you spoke of the Devil?"

The sheriff saw Folques prostrate on the floor and narrowed his gaze in sudden recognition. "You were the Bishop of Toulouse."

Folques enlivened at hearing his name. "Yes, my son?"

"I'm a devout churchgoer," said the sheriff. "The parish priest will attest to that. I don't know this woman's beliefs and I don't ask. She's only hours from death anyway."

Arnaud allowed Folques no time to form a defense. "If it is mercy you seek, constable, you are petitioning the wrong man. Difficult as it is to believe, this broken-down old mule once consigned thousands of souls to God's judgment."

The sheriff punished Folques with a glower of condemnation. "Aye, I saw plenty of his bloody work firsthand. I was conscripted into de Montfort's army. Where were you, Bishop, when this woman required tending? Off ransacking cities and stripping furs from corpses. Her only crime was turning to those who succored her with the Almighty's mercy."

Folques could only hang his head in shame.

"A fine speech," said Arnaud. "Now, what will it be? Carry out my orders, or appear at an inquest to answer for your own orthodoxy?"

Weighing the threat, the sheriff reluctantly surrendered to the inquisitor's demand. He tried to lift the dying woman to her feet, but she collapsed to the floor, unable to stand.

"Carry her in the bed," ordered Arnaud.

The inquisitor marched down the street pronouncing condemnations in Latin while Otto and the sheriff hauled the woman on her cot. Folques straggled several steps behind, stumbling and dazed, the strands of his ragged tonsure whipped up to resemble horns by the wind. Too frightened to come out of their homes, the townsfolk shuttered their windows and peered through the cracks. Arnaud led the execution entourage to a small clearing that was deemed an appropriate distance from the church and its sanctified graveyard.

When the sheriff could not drag the delirious crone from the bed, Arnaud ordered him, "Burn her where she lies."

The sheriff searched the square for anyone who would come forth and support him in a challenge to this injustice. But the village, dependent as it was on the abbey for sustenance, had turned so somnambulant that it might have been mistaken for abandoned. If he pressed the matter before a tribunal, it would be his word against these monks. He held no illusion of what the result would be. Given no choice, he whispered prayers for forgiveness as he tied the woman's frail wrists to the bedposts and surrounded her with brush.

Arnaud brandished a crucifix over the babbling woman. "By the authority of Holy Mother Church, I commend your unrepentant soul to the glorious judgment of God." The sheriff lit the torch and offered it to Arnaud, but the inquisitor declined it. "I am not permitted to shed blood."

With a huff of disgust, the sheriff threw the torch on the makeshift pyre and turned away, unwilling to watch. The mattress of hay quickly exploded. The woman screamed in agony as the flames enveloped her. Heaving and gasping, she disappeared under a billow of black smoke. Otto restrained the boy from going to her aid. Minutes later, the smoke finally cleared. The woman's charred arms were still tied to the smoldering bedposts.

Arnaud captured the distraught Folques by the elbow and walked him closer to inspect the blackened corpse. "Bishop, is it not like the fire called down by Elijah to confuse the priests of Baal? No doubt you were visited with such comparisons during your crusading days."

Folques caved to his knees, too overcome to form a response. The old queasiness that had attacked him below the flames at Lavaur and Minerve now swelled up in his throat again. He retched and soiled his robe, then looked down in horror—aghast not at the vomit, but at the black shade of the Dominican cloth he wore. He looked up at Otto and questioned in vain how such an abomination could have manifested.

Arnaud wrapped an arm around Otto's shoulder and led his young recruit away. "Come, my son. We must not be late for matins."

olques remained confined to his pallet, taking no food, his mind mean-dering in and out of saneness. During the two days since the old wom-an's burning, he had been constantly frightened by shadows flickering across the walls. At this hour, just before dawn, another nigrous presence came hovering over him to darken his face. He flailed and contorted and cried out, "Help me, for Jesu' sakes! The demons are on me again!"

Otto's voice cracked with grief. "Father, the hospitalier says you must take the last rites at once." He motioned five Cistercian monks into the room and bade them sing the hymns that Folques had composed during these last years in the abbey. "The brothers will comfort you with the chants. Pray fervently and I will return soon from the sacristy with the Eucharist."

Folques's terrors eased as he sank into the rhythms of the antiphonal plain-song. He took revenge in the assurance that he would be transported and buried at Grandselve, in the abbey overlooking the city that so despised him. There he would perpetually haunt the ungrateful Toulousians from the grave. He mouthed the chant, fearful of descending too deeply into sleep and not returning.

After several minutes, a woman's lulling voice overtook the song and melded it from Latin into Occitan. The strings of a lone viol strummed in the background. Folques tried to rise to find the source of this disturbing trans-formation, but he was prisoner to a deep paralysis. The words, oddly familiar, were not the ones he had written for the hymns:

> Love, have mercy! Let me not die so often,
> for you could easily kill me outright,
> but instead you hold me on the brink of life
> and death, thus increasing my martyrdom;
> but though half-dead, I am still your servant,
> and this service I prefer a thousand times
> to any other facile recompense.

The profane spewings punished him like hammer blows. He cried out, "Cease these damnable verses!"

> For you know, Love, that it would be a sin
> to kill me, since I have not rebelled against you;
> but too much service often does great harm
> and—or so I have heard—makes friendship flee.
> I have served you and still do not turn away,
> but since you know I await some recompense,
> I have now lost you and the service, too.

Unable to raise his head, he panicked, strafed by memories of the screams and the clawing nails of the heretics who had been buried alive at Minerve. "Otto! Remove this nun from my presence! Am I to be tortured in my final hours?"

But you, my Lady, who have the power,
persuade Love and yourself, whom I so desire,
not for me, but merely out of pity
and because my sighs thus plead with you.
For when my eyes laugh, my heart cries,
and through fear of seeming troublesome
I fool myself and bear the grievous loss.

He began weeping uncontrollably. The salt in his tears burned his chapped lips like acid. "Enough! I beg of you!"

The woman's singing gave way to a silence that was even more frightening. And then a voice asked, "Do you not remember them?"

"Ramblings of a love-sopped fool!" cried Folques.

"You wrote them . . . They are your chansons."

He gasped, "That cannot be!"

"You once sang them to me."

He gave an inward-sucking gasp. Could it truly be her? Why could he not turn his head? His field of vision was narrowing—had he passed across the veil? *She has come to escort me into Purgatory, or worse. No, the Almighty would not allow that! I served the Church faithfully.* Wispy shadows converged on the ceiling and metamorphosed into the most beautiful maiden he had ever laid eyes upon. Why was he being tempted?

Esclarmonde's fey face, not quite in focus, came closer and stared down on him from above. "There is still time."

"Let me die in peace!" he begged. "I want to meet my Savior!"

"Ask the God of Light for forgiveness," she implored.

A cascade of tormenting scenes swirled around Esclarmonde: Thousands burning in Beziers; the cloggers freezing in the snow at Minerve; Lady Giraude stoned in the well at Lavaur; de Montfort gouging out the eyes of the heretic knights at Bram. His heart raced from terror—he suddenly remembered the curse he had cast on her in the Aragon court years ago.

The next meeting of our eyes will be the last.

He cried, "No!"

"You must understand the purity of Love before you go," said Esclarmonde. "You were sent into this world to fulfill this task."

"I loved only you!"

"True love requires giving up this world for the beloved. And giving up the beloved for this world."

"Heretic lies!"

"Did Our Lord not teach that we are not of this world? Surrender what has been most precious to you, Folques, and you will be saved."

"I cannot . . . give you up!"

"I forgive you. Offer up your hatred to the crucible of the Light. This precious opportunity comes but once in a lifetime."

He felt as if he were drowning in a sea of crystal. The crushing radiance was a thousand times brighter than the lurid flames that he had stared into at Lavaur. "I did it all for you!"

Her celestial image began to recede.

"Esclarmonde! Don't leave me!"

The water of holy absolution splashed against his lips. Reviving, he looked up with red-streaked eyes. Otto was staring down at him in disapproval.

"Father, you must not speak that woman's name when you are so near to God's blessed reward."

Folques's heart sank. She had only been a figment of his fractured mind. And yet her presence felt so real. He remembered having taken the torture-induced confessions of several Cathar prisoners who claimed the ability to transport their spirits across time and space to comfort fellow believers in the final throes of the fires. Sweating profusely, he grasped Otto's wrist and begged, "Hear my confession."

"I will call the Abbot—"

"No! Only you! It must be written down."

Otto motioned the other monks from the room. Alone with Folques, he pulled up a chair near the bed and draped a penitential stole around his neck. He brought a quill and parchment to the table, then placed the Eucharist host to his stepfather's chapped lips. "You must not try to swallow it. Allow it to melt on your tongue."

Folques gagged and spit out the wafer, frantic to speak while he still possessed the faculties. "I have sinned grievously in my life."

"We all falter."

"I loved your mother! More than God Himself!"

Otto held back the quill. "I'll not write such blasphemous utterances!"

Folques convulsed with sobs. "I took you away from her. I wanted some part of her to hold forever." He locked on Otto's eyes with a look of fierce intensity. "Renounce the madness of this war! Go to her!"

"Never!"

"I beg of you! I gave you a life built on hollow stones. Make it right with her! For your sake and mine!"

"She abandoned me!"

His breath began to falter. "You had a sister."

Otto blinked hard in denial. "You're not in your right mind!"

"I am more clear than I have ever been in my misbegotten life." Folques arched with spasms as he fought for the breath to finish. "Your mother protects a mystery of Our Lord on that mountain . . . The Vatican has long sought to wrest it from her . . . You must not let those Dominicans find—" His neck arched in a paroxysm of coughing.

Otto placed a drop of water on his stepfather's blistered tongue to spur the revelation. "What does she possess?"

"Write it!" Folques's voice began slurring, his breath dying with each word. "Esclarmonde of Foix is declared free of heresy . . . By order of the Bishop of Toulouse." With the dictation completed, Otto placed Folques's trembling hand on the quill and helped him scribble his signature. Folques dropped the instrument to the floor. "Seal it with the impress of my episcopal ring . . . deliver it to her . . . tell her I ask forgiveness with—"

"Father! The mystery! Tell me!"

Folques gave a heaving sigh and fell back into the pallet. His gaze remained fixed on the icon of the Blessed Virgin on the wall.

Otto pressed his stepfather's lids closed in death and signed his soul to Heaven. Troubled, he walked to the hearth and studied the written confession, trying to decipher the heretic secret that Folques had desperately tried to reveal. Finding no hint of it, he dispatched the parchment to the flames.

Part Three

The Mount of Salvation

1242 – 1244 AD

Know that between the Faithful is an ancient union.
The Faithful are numerous, but the Faith is one.

- Rumi

Become Passers By.
- The Gospel of Thomas

XXXI

Montsegur

May 1242

Esclarmonde awoke with an aching rigor in her rheumy knees. Her sleeping Cathar priestesses sat huddled along the chapel walls with their heads sunk into their robes to retain the warmth of their breaths. The dawn sun pierced the mullioned window and inched across the floor, beckoning her outside. This temple was alive, she knew, and she had long ago learned to heed its callings. She arose with a wince of effort and clapped her hands softly. "Who feels like a walk?"

Chandelle roused and brightened at the prospect. "Wonderful idea! I've not yet seen the morning glories this spring." The women laughed at the blind perfecta's self-deprecating jest as they stretched with yawns and stored away their sleeping shawls. Chandelle brushed her hand across the Marquessa's mottled cheek. "Grandma, we will return soon."

The ninety-year-old matriarch lay on the same pallet that she had been carried on for ten years. She nodded weakly in disappointment, informed that her prayer to be taken by death in sleep had again been denied.

Chandelle always annulled these supplications by predicting that her grandmother would outlive them all. Having recently celebrated her forty-first birthday, Chandelle remained youthful-looking and cheerful despite the hardships of living on the mount. Some ascribed her optimistic disposition to being spared eyewitness to the war's depredations. In truth, she suffered more than the others, being prisoner to a powerful imagination that recreated the horrors from the descriptions of the refugees. Unable to share in many of the communal tasks, she tried to compensate for her infirmity by patiently listening to the tribulations of the other perfectas and lifting their spirits with prayers and encouragement.

Time had not been so kind to Esclarmonde. At sixty-one, her white hair contrasted starkly with her black robe and though she still possessed the statuesque posture, her lean figure and sun-weathered face betrayed the emaciating effects of the severe Cathar diet, which consisted of legume soup, an occasional whitefish, and what vegetables, nuts, and berries could be found. No longer able to manage the long walks without assistance, she took Chandelle's arm and together they led the women through the temple's eastern gate. The summit buzzed with activity as the perfects toiled at their looms and forges while the small garrison under Raymond de Perella's command carried up stones to build a new tower and barbican on the eastern spine.

Was that the faint glim of Foix's towers on the azure horizon? Esclarmonde wondered how the chateau was being maintained. If the Dominicans imitated their deceased founder in prideful austerity, the rooms had no doubt been stripped of all tapestries and furniture. In the pleated meads below, Roger's unshriven bones lay scattered, picked clean by the carrion crows. She turned aside to chase the memory of that indignity. After Folques's death, she had held out hope that the persecutions would end, but she had learned to her despair that the Demiurge kept fresh troops in reserve: De Montfort and the Cistercians had been replaced by the King of France and Dominic Guzman's Black Friars.

Before passing to the Light two years ago, Bishop Castres had assigned formal leadership of the surviving Cathars to her and Bernard Marti. Four hundred of them still lived in the cluster of huts on the terraces and in the vale below. Those who fled to the forests risked capture on feast days by returning to receive her blessing and what grain could be spared. The temple had avoided the fate of Lavaur and Minerve only because the Catholic engineers could not conceive a method for hauling their trebuchets up the crag.

Halfway down the path, the women hushed their conversations. Before them stood a jutting scarp crowned by a small pyramid of rocks. Esclarmonde stooped with difficulty and placed another stone on the grave of her daughter. Over the years, she had granted herself the indulgence of tending a small pleasaunce here; the sprigs of mint and absinthe gave off a welcoming bouquet and the orange lilies added brightness. She peered over the cliff where she had nearly taken her life. The serrated descent still looked threatening. Would her family have been better off if she had jumped that night?

Sensing the dark turn of Esclarmonde's thoughts, Chandelle nudged her on. Nearby sat a small dolmen nestled in tufts of thyme and lavender. The briars had been kept trimmed on the spot where she and Guilhelm had first kissed. On the far side, the roots of a stripling gripped the fissure where Loupe had rescued Chandelle. There, on the ledge below, lay the stones broken off by Chandelle's fall. Lord God, this was a via dolorosa of memories.

Esclarmonde stopped to regain her breath—her throat tightened with a frisson of foreboding. She knew intuitively that this would be her last descent down the pog. The Light had granted her this hoar-frosted morning to walk the path one more time. In a flash of gnosis, everything became clear: The pitch of her life, like this switchback, had not been straight, but spiraling. Often it seemed she had made no spiritual progress, but as she looked back, she realized that she had been climbing steadily all along. If she failed to merge with the Light in what little time was left to her, she would try to find this wondrous place in the next incarnation. She burned into her soul's memory every aspect of the landscape: The snowcaps crowning the St. Barthelemy massif; the dark holm groves hanging over the Ariege like weeping mothers; the lacerated profile of the pog's western approach—she stumbled from the accretion of remembrances.

Corba steadied her. "You mustn't let your mind wander!"

Esclarmonde smiled ruefully. "Time demands recompense for past slights. Do you remember how I'd tease you about being scatterbrained?"

"You'd have me so flustered I couldn't remember my name."

Chandelle playfully pinched Esclarmonde's arm. "Tell me. What were the two of you like as maidens?"

"My memory doesn't go back that far!"

"Mine does," chided Corba. "Your godmother is saintly only because she must do penance for her past intrigues with the poets."

Esclarmonde playfully slapped her wrist. "Corba!"

Corba leaned to her daughter with a smile of intrigue. "She'd always blackmail me into sitting near her intended conquest. I was required to casually mention that another troubadour had secretly offered his love to her."

Chandelle bristled with mock outrage. "Scandalous!"

"We were only practicing the lessons taught us by your grandmother." Esclarmonde's stride became lighter with the recall of their flirtatious idylls. "True jealousy always increases love's ardor."

"The maxims!" exclaimed Corba. "How many can you still recite?"

Esclarmonde demonstrated that the quick wit so lauded in the courts of old had not waned. "No one can love unless driven on by the prospect of love."

Corba took up the challenge. "At the sudden sight of the beloved, the lover's heart quakes."

Chandelle listened with delight as her mother and godmother transformed into coquettish conspirators. Their voices grew more girlish with each remembered rule of Andreas Capellanus's treatise on the art of honest loving.

"A love divulged rarely lasts," said Corba.

"No one can possess two loves at once."

Corba was stumped. "No one . . . should be deprived . . ."

Esclarmonde gave Corba no time to finish, just as she had been wont to do when they had studied for the exam as court initiates. "No one should be deprived of his love without very good reason." Drawing the same look of exasperation, she needled Corba with an elbow and came up with another rule. "Love is always growing or diminishing."

Chandelle interrupted their contest. "Can *that* one be true?"

Esclarmonde held fast to Chandelle's arm—the maxim about love diminishing had struck her heart with an unexpected force.

Corba felt Esclarmonde's forehead. "Are you not well?"

Esclarmonde shook off a wave of sadness. "I'm fine."

"They were silly games," dismissed Corba.

"No, I owe her an answer," said Esclarmonde. "We once pestered your mother with such questions."

Corba sighed with regret. "Those days are long gone."

Esclarmonde led them to the flat-surfaced boulder to sit. The younger perfectas tarried to hear more about her legendary life, but Corba, always protective of these rare moments of privacy, waved them on down the pog. Esclarmonde lifted her face to the sun's warmth while debating how best to respond to Chandelle's question. "It does seem that love requires undivided attention. At least, that has been my experience."

Chandelle straightened in surprise. "So, the God of Light is also jealous, just like the Demiurge?"

"Could you share the man you loved with another—" Esclarmonde thought it prudent to abort that example, solicitous as she was to the feelings of this goddaughter who had never experienced the embrace of passion. It was a subject that both of them had been careful to avoid.

Yet this time Chandelle would have none of Esclarmonde's attempt to evade the subject. "I'd be worried that my feelings would exceed his."

Esclarmonde shook her head in marvel at the many times this scriptural passage about God's jealousy had come to bear on her life. "Can we ask more of God than we could offer of ourselves?"

"You just said otherwise," reminded Chandelle. "The rules hold that true jealousy increases love's ardor. If God *is* jealous, would He not desire us to come to Him even more?"

Esclarmonde gave up a laugh of surrender, grateful that the Catholic disputants at Pamiers had not possessed such perspicacity. "It would seem so."

"What was Guilhelm like?" Chandelle ignored her mother's admonishing squeeze on her arm. She was determined to hear more about the man whose life had been kept a mystery. "I was only a child when he left."

Esclarmonde could not recall the last time she heard Guilhelm's name spoken, and yet her breath still quickened. This reaction severely vexed her, for she knew it to be a seduction instilled into the flesh by the Demiurge. "He suffered from a wound so deep that I was never able to plumb it. I believe his faith was severely tested early in life. Most draw closer to God as they grow older, but he wrestled his doubts more fiercely than Jacob fought the angel . . . We were so different." She raised her eyes to the sun to dry a tear.

Chandelle snuggled closer. "Has your love for him diminished?"

So many incidents of Esclarmonde's life had faded from her memory, and some she had buried intentionally, but not the image of Guilhelm's imperious face during their first encounter. No, that fateful moment in the love court had been forever inscribed upon her mind's eye. Lord Jesus, his gaze was hotter than that blood-red cross on his tunic. *Love of woman for her own sake is heresy in the eyes of the Church. Is that not true, sir?* How prophetic those words to him had been. Why hadn't she allowed him to just walk away? Was it truly her voice that had appointed him as her defender? Finding Chandelle still awaiting an answer, she dared not compound the sin of thinking about Guilhelm so intimately by offering up a lie. "No, it has not diminished."

"Then it has grown," insisted Chandelle. "The Rule says that Love must either diminish or grow. The emotion cannot remain unaltered."

Esclarmonde raised her palms in defeat. "You were always a shrewd learner. I would have been no match for you in the courts."

"You've not heard from him?" asked Chandelle.

"Not since we left Foix. What has it been, Corba?"

"Twenty-five years."

Chandelle fell silent, and Esclarmonde knew what she was thinking: How could she have grown in her love for Guilhelm and yet be capable of turning him away, as she had done after Muret? Playing for time, Esclarmonde arose from the boulder and renewed their stroll. Finally, she said, "Certain maxims are said to take precedence over others. For example, there is the rule that says one cannot love another unless driven on by the prospect of love."

Chandelle stopped abruptly. "Love is eternal. Surely it does not depend on requited affection? And how can you be sure Guilhelm doesn't still love you?"

Esclarmonde angled to hide the inculpatory surge of color in her cheeks. "Even if he is alive, he would have long since forgotten me. It was for the best that we parted. I brought him only affliction and pain."

Chandelle pawed at the dirt with her sandal, the most outward display of anger her gentle soul could muster. "If the God of Light demands abstention from passion, then He is no better than the Demiurge."

The three women turned a bend and nearly collided with Loupe, who was climbing the path at an impatient pace. Behind her came Raymond de Perella, Bernard Saint-Martin, and a contingent of soldiers laden with caches of swords and bows. The men genuflected to Esclarmonde—all but a short, barrel-chested stranger whose sunburnt face was framed by a unkempt red beard. His undisciplined green eyes were so closely set that their unruly brows were joined as one, a feature said to accompany an unbalanced temperament.

Esclarmonde felt an immediate dislike for the new arrival whose contemptuous sneer confirmed that the opinion was reciprocated. She complained to Loupe, "You're turning my temple into an arsenal. Have I not told you—"

"All Occitania is an arsenal," said the stranger, interrupting sharply.

Raymond moved quickly to defuse the confrontation. "This is Pierre-Roger of Mirepoix. He fought with your brother at Muret."

"You promised no more soldiers would be stationed here."

"I haven't enough men to hold the crag," said Raymond. "Pierre-Roger has agreed to provide reinforcements in exchange for a share of the command."

"Extortion, not altruism, is what he offers," said Esclarmonde.

Loupe abruptly reversed her resumed climb. "The French army is thirty leagues away and the Dominicans are in Lavelanet!"

"Young Raymond in Toulouse will protect us," said Esclarmonde.

"The Count no longer young," said Loupe. "And if you took interest in our welfare, you'd know that he is cuckolded by that detestable hag in Paris."

Esclarmonde questioned how two members of the same bloodline could be so different. Yet she had encountered other such examples: Eleanor de Aquitane, a kind soul who had patronized many a troubadour, was the grandmother of the current queen mother, Blanche de Castile, an intolerant harridan. This war against her faith had turned fathers against sons and mothers against daughters. The debts of past lives, it seemed, always held sway over shared lineage. Perhaps the Demiurge arranged such conflicting familial combinations for his cruel amusement. "Blanche's position must be difficult, surrounded as she is by ambitious men who seek to impose their dominion." Esclarmonde glanced with challenge at Pierre-Roger to drive home her point. "Let us pray she succeeds in convincing her son to embrace peace."

Loupe slung down her load of weapons in exasperation. "That scheming Spanish bitch wants to destroy us! And you defend her?"

Bernard tried to mollify Loupe, but she shunted him aside. Her nerves had been rubbed raw from being forced to live in such close proximity to the perfects whose pacifism she despised. Nor had she forgiven Esclarmonde for her father's death, which she blamed on her aunt's refusal to take her Cathars from Foix.

Esclarmonde softened her tone in conciliation. "This war has been waged for forty years. All it has gained us is more suffering." Rebuffed by Loupe's icy glare, she saw no purpose in trying to reason with her further. She whipped her sleeve to her elbow and resumed her walk.

"Mother!" demanded Loupe. "Where are you going?"

Esclarmonde flushed with anger. Her flock addressed her with the maternal title out of respect, but Loupe applied the honorific as an irritant, enunciating it with galling spite as a reminder of her advancing age and her role in taking Loupe's own mother from this world. This sharp-tongued niece knew where the deepest wounds lay and how to salt them. Without turning, Esclarmonde answered testily, "We are taking a walk along the stream."

"Don't stray from the sight of the guards," ordered Loupe.

Esclarmonde could no longer abide such impertinence. "I climbed this mount long before you were born! I don't need your permission to go anywhere on it! The Catholics would leave us alone if you did not use this place as a bolt hole for your raids!"

Raymond stepped between them. "If we don't station a garrison—"

"I never asked for armed protection!" Esclarmonde came within inches of Loupe's pinched face. "We are prepared to depart this life when God decides."

"We are not!" said Loupe. " I've had my fill of your self-righteous sanctity!"

"Loupe!" chastened Chandelle. "Show some respect."

Loupe rounded on her old friend with a shout so vehement that the blind perfecta nearly fell. "And you've become lost in her madness! While our countrymen die to free you of invaders, you sit babbling nonsense with her!"

"No one requires you to adopt our faith," said Chandelle.

"I cannot escape it! My mother and this aunt made certain of that!"

Drawn by the shouts, the other perfectas rushed up the path.

"Take them to the river," ordered Esclarmonde. When Corba hesitated, fearful of leaving her alone with Loupe, Esclarmonde insisted, "Please do as I ask!" Corba had learned from hard experience that it was no use attempting to placate Esclarmonde when she had her hackles up, so she hurried with Chandelle and the other women down the pog. When the perfectas and soldiers were out of earshot, Esclarmonde turned on Loupe with a fury. "I'll not hear you speak basely of your mother!"

"I'm not one of your nuns who falls at your feet in obeisance!"

Esclarmonde picked up one of the dropped arrows and forced Loupe to stare at its tip. "Phillipa gave her life to save us. You make a great display of defending this land. But you fight only to vent your bitterness."

"What do you know of love? You drove away the only man who—"

"Enough!"

"Loving that sun idol of yours is easy for you," persisted Loupe. "You make him whatever you want him to be. He conveniently speaks to you in that ghost voice that no one else hears. Everyone is told to accept your rantings without question. Guilhelm was a man. But a mortal man has his own needs. And Hell should pay if his ever got in the way of yours."

Esclarmonde pressed her fists into the creases of her elbows, fearful of what she might do with them. "I made a choice. And I hurt the one I loved because of it. But it was a choice made from conviction, not fear."

"You think I'm afraid?"

"Any animal can kill," said Esclarmonde. "To place your freedom at risk is true bravery."

"I fight for your freedom!"

"You fight to avoid what really frightens you."

"Nothing frightens me!"

With a sharp angling of her head, Esclarmonde directed Loupe's attention toward the battlements where Bernard Saint-Martin stood guard. "He does."

Loupe turned aside. "I have no time for that foolishness."

"Has he renewed his request to marry you?"

"That's none of your concern," said Loupe.

"First you assail me for avoiding the demands of this world. Now you wish me to do exactly that. I promised your mother I would look after you."

"God save us from your promises."

"Bernard is a good man. He has loved you since you were young. That is a gift you must not lightly dismiss."

"You swore off marriage. Why shouldn't I?"

"There will come a time when he won't ask again. Don't repeat the mistake that . . . You are as obdurate and wilful as your father."

"My father fought for what he believed."

"And he lies unburied for it."

"Because of a war you caused!" reminded Loupe. "Don't you understand? They've all died because of *you!*"

For a fleeting moment, Esclarmonde saw Roger's face in Loupe's knotted features, blaming her again for every mishap of their existence. She rushed at Loupe but caught herself, distressed by her own boiling rage. She took a protective step back and demanded, "I want these soldiers off my mountain!"

*E*sclarmonde was too exhausted from the quarrel to finish her walk to the stream. Pallid and fighting for breath, she returned to the temple alone and retired to her hut without a word to anyone. She collapsed to her pallet and fell into a fitful sleep. Soon she was enveloped by a recurring nightmare. In the vision, she emerged from her cell and found herself abandoned inside the chateau with the gates bolted shut. Left with no means of escape, she ran to the crown of the walls and prepared to make a suicidal leap, driven to the edge by an overwhelming loneliness and—

Distant shrieks awoke her. Disoriented, she gathered her robe and rushed to the bailey. The sun was setting below the ramparts. How many hours had she slept? Corba was on her knees, hysterical and fighting to escape Raymond's grasp. The wailing had drawn the Marquessa creeping from her hut.

"They've taken her!" cried Corba. "She wanted to stay alone by the water while we picked berries!"

Esclarmonde searched for Chandelle among the distraught faces converging on her. "Where were the guards?"

Loupe broke through the keening rucks to punish her aunt with a lording stare. "Dismissed from their posts. On your orders."

Corba rushed to Raymond, who stood paralyzed. "Do something!"

"What would you have me—"

"Stop the monks from . . ." Corba stifled a despairing scream.

Loupe finished the aborted plea for Corba. "From bringing her before their tribunal? Is that what you want?"

"I can't live without her!"

Loupe watched with grim satisfaction as the perfects and soldiers turned on Esclarmonde with impugning glares. "You want us to fight to save her?"

"Yes, my God!" begged Corba. "Yes!"

"But is that not contrary to your beliefs?" Loupe raised a taunting brow aimed at Esclarmonde. "To take up arms?"

Corba bent low as if speared in the gut, undone by the reminder of her faith's creed. "I'll break apart if she's taken from me."

Esclarmonde dropped her forehead into her hands in an effort to focus her wrenched thoughts. She could not fathom the terror that Chandelle was now suffering. Would God never stop testing her? There was none dearer to her than this goddaughter, but if she approved a military operation, she would profane the teachings of the Master and the dictates of the Light. Her throbbing temples felt as if her skull was being drilled with a rod. Staggered by the blinding headache, she walked with Corba and Raymond a few steps from the others. "I cannot sanction it . . . but I will not forbid it."

Corba fell to her knees and grasped Esclarmonde's hand in gratitude. Raymond prepared to muster the men for the rescue attempt when Loupe stopped him with a thrust of her sword into the ground.

"Chandelle is not the only one caught in their nets," said Loupe to Corba. "Hundreds more of our people languish in their prisons. And more will die until we chase these monks from our land once and for all. I will do this deed. But only if all members of your faith bless it."

Blanched with consternation, Corba and the Cathars turned to Esclarmonde and Bernard Marti for an indication of what they should do. Marti assessed the willingness of his flock to make the ultimate sacrifice. With eyes lowered in shame, he conceded, "We are no less hypocritical than the Roman monks if we cower behind these walls and allow others to fight and die for our beliefs. Either we must accept responsibility for sending these men to take up arms, or all of us should go forth to join Chandelle."

Esclarmonde's spirit plummeted, sapping the strength from the thews in her legs. She knew that Castres would have found a way to convince them to avoid this snare of the Demiurge. But she could no longer marshal the resolve required to preach his pacifist discipline. In a voice drained of all hope, she allowed, "Each of you must choose as your conscience dictates."

Marti could not look at her directly. "We have tried the Bishop's way and still the Romans break our bones. Mayhaps, for once, we must stand against the Evil One on His own field of battle."

One by one, the Cathars followed Marti's lead and stepped forward to affirm their acceptance of the military raid. Many broke down and wept, certain that they would be returned to this world because they had surrendered to the demands of the flesh. Esclarmonde braced the teary-eyed Marti with a hand on his shoulder to assure him that she bore no ill will for his decision. She then turned and walked slump-shouldered toward the chapel to be alone.

"No!" insisted Loupe. "It is not decided."

Corba crawled toward Loupe in despair. "Is it not enough that the rest of us have forfeited our souls?"

Loupe was implacable. "I said *all* must agree."

At the chapel door, Esclarmonde turned on Loupe with a wrathful glower. Only when Loupe broke off their silent challenge did Esclarmonde resume her entry into the sanctuary.

Inside, she knelt before the altar and prayed for guidance. Yet after an hour of fervent supplication, the Voice had not answered her. In this, her moment of greatest need, she was again abandoned. She had sacrificed Guilhelm, Phillipa, and two children to this rapacious God. Even the Demiurge had held back Abraham's plunge of the dagger into Isaac. She was only a woman of flesh. How could her love for these people be so contrary to the love demanded by the Light? Perhaps Guilhelm had been right in dismissing her faith's abhorrence of violence. He had always insisted that certain acts were so evil that they cried out for resistance and retribution. If he had not killed Jourdaine, she would never have survived to take the Cathar vow and seek the Light's salvatory release from this world. If Trevencal had not hesitated in dispatching de Montfort in the field below Carcassonne, Giraude and thousands of their countrymen might have been spared horrific deaths. If she had driven the knife into Folques's heart that night of the Foix siege, her son would be with her now.

The chapel door hinged open.

Esclarmonde walked into the bailey with deadened eyes. She seized Loupe's impaled sword by its cutting edges to indicate her assent to the raid. Blood trickled down her wrist—until Loupe pulled her aunt's trembling hand away.

Thus force will prevail where gentle persuasion has failed.
- Dominic Guzman

XXXII

Avignonet

May 1242

The labored breath tinged with wine—a sweet Italian vintage, most likely one of the vernages preferred by the northern abbeys for their altars—warmed Chandelle's neck again. Since childhood, her blindness had so heightened the compensating effectiveness of her other senses that some of her fellow perfectas had proclaimed her possessed of the second sight. In truth, she could never be certain when her common faculties gave way to the clairvoyance.

Now, raw fear sharpened her instincts even more.

Her wrists were bound in manacles and her feet stung from blisters raised during the forced march from Montsegur. Fighting fatigue, she stood erect to avoid showing weakness of resolve. Although her captors refused to reveal where she had been taken, she deduced from the cycles of darkness on her lids and the sunburn on the left side of her face that she had been led north for three days. A cacophony of urban sounds and aromas swirled around her. Clanging bread racks were being removed from the kilns, so it was early morning. The yeast, twice-baked for preservation during travel, smelled laced with sawdust, a ploy to deceive unsuspecting pilgrims. The nickering of horses was strenuous and deep, indicating military mounts. Hawkers with strange accents shouted their offers for religious baubles and competed against the percussion of clanking alms cups. The street stalls had been washed with lime and burning candles gave off the fragrance of expensive pork fat. Her eyes watered from the irritation of tannin used to dye wool black. The swishing of heavy robes near her feet was accompanied by the clop of sandals. Despite her fervent prayers that it be otherwise, every indication pointed to an ecclesiastic proceeding.

"Where did you find this one?" That voice was perfumed with cloves used in monastic pompadours to ward off diseased humours.

"Below the heretic mount," said a younger man of small stature, old enough to shave but not deftly; the astringent of sweet gum on his jaw was mixed with dried blood.

She was dragged barefoot through the sucking mud and forced to climb ten splintered steps. A restive crowd below her screamed curses. She heard a jangling of chains; other prisoners were also on the platform, muttering fearful prayers and calling for their families. Below her, musicians halfheartedly played tunes above the din, their keys intentionally off in a veiled act of protest. A slender hand that had never been roughened by a day of hard labor came under her chin and lifted her head.

"Your name?"

A woman shouted, "Give them nothing to write in their death books!"

The hand firmed its threat to force her answer. "Chandelle."

"Who gave you such a pagan appellation?"

She remembered Loupe had warned that the Catholic monks sensed fear like hounds smelled blood. Always offer a question to a question, she had been instructed. "Does not God give us our names before we are born?"

"This one is clever," said the older monk.

"Where am I?" she asked.

"Avignonet."

She was still in Occitania, praise be to God. Esclarmonde had preached in this village situated only a few leagues from Toulouse. There were several Cathar houses here and the populace was known to be sympathetic.

Heavy footsteps circled her. "You wear the black robe."

"Is that forbidden?"

"I will conduct this inquiry, not you."

She bowed her head in contrition. "I was told that the friars wear the black. I thought it was a color pleasing to God."

"What business did you have at Montsegur?"

"Am I to know who questions me?"

"The Inquisitor of the Languedoc."

She shuddered; the refugees at Montsegur had spoken of this new leader of the Dominican persecution as if he were the reincarnation of the devil Folques. The acrid smoke and stench of burnt flesh confirmed that she had not been the first to face such an ordeal here.

"Because you cannot witness God's work, I will describe it for you," said William Arnaud. "Today is the fourth Sunday of the month. The day that our period of grace ends for voluntary confession of heresy. Those moved by God's righteousness have come forward in the hundreds to profess their errors. They wear the yellow cross of lapsed faith."

"What has any of this to do with me?"

"Those sinners who refuse to repent are chained to stakes," said Arnaud. "I urge you to unburden your soul while you have the opportunity."

"I love God."

"Yes, but what Brother Otto and I must determine is whether you *obey* God. A heretic seductress named Esclarmonde de Foix once took refuge on the mount where you were found. Did you know her?"

Why did the name Otto ring familiar? Her faith prohibited the utterance of a lie, so she searched for some answer that might satisfy the Dominicans while giving them no damning evidence. "I have heard of the woman. As have you, it seems."

"Where is she buried?"

She realized that these monks believed Esclarmonde to be dead. Her godmother had not been seen outside Montsegur for years and rumors were rampant throughout the Languedoc that she had passed away soon after Bishop Castres's death. The Cathars had done nothing to dispel the confusion in the hope that the Dominicans would finally give up their efforts to find her. But these black dogs remained hell-bent on digging up her remains to burn them in a public trial. She answered elliptically, "I have never seen her grave."

"Take the Eucharist," ordered Arnaud.

A bitter wafer was forced into her mouth. She tasted blood—she had bitten her tongue in the struggle to refuse the host. The inquisitor's slap stung her nose like ant bites. She flinched with each passing shadow, not knowing when the next blow would land. All she had to do was swallow the crust. It was only unleavened wheat. What harm could come of it? No, it would be a betrayal of her family. There was no transubstantiation. God is not to be forced through the viscera and turned to excrement. The Demiurge was testing her. Even if she accepted this Roman sacrament, the demands would not stop. Next would be the kiss of the crucifix, then the declaration of apostasy. She could never return to Montsegur wearing that despicable yellow cross.

Someone shouted, "Chew their damned morsel and save yourself!"

She spat out the host and clenched her teeth to prevent the abomination from being thrust down her throat. A cheer came from the crowd followed by a collective gasp of warning. Her wrists were hoisted above her head and her tunic was ripped from her shoulders, leaving her back exposed. The air snapped and cracked—her skin burned as if set afire. The lashes came so fast that the lacerations threatened to cut to the bone.

"Who charges this woman?" shouted a man.

The punishment abated as footsteps ascended the steps.

"The Lord Jesus Christ is her accuser!" warned Arnaud.

The protester came another rung up the platform. "Then let Christ Himself appear to testify against her!"

Swarmed by murmurs of agreement, the Dominican guards raised their weapons in preparation to put down the nascent uprising. The platform swayed from the press of the angry mob.

"Today it's that woman up there! Tomorrow it'll be us!"

Arnaud stood behind Chandelle to ward off a hail of rocks. She lost consciousness as the soldiers dragged her down the steps.

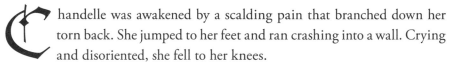

handelle was awakened by a scalding pain that branched down her torn back. She jumped to her feet and ran crashing into a wall. Crying and disoriented, she fell to her knees.

"Sheep's lard. Boiled with bark rind. Smells like rotten eggs, but it will speed the healing."

That was the same man's voice that had come to her defense that morning. She crawled to a corner and gathered the torn tunic around her, listening intently for sounds of his approach. She calmed by telling herself that if the man intended to violate her, he would have done so by now. He touched her back again. She tested him by exposing her shoulder for more balm. As he rubbed the cool liniment across the welts, she tried to conjure an image of him from the tenor of his speech and lightness of his touch. He smelled of livestock and his hands were small and calloused like those of a farmer or field peasant.

"You must know something that monk wants very badly."

She recoiled in suspicion. "Why do you say that?"

After an extended silence, the man said, "He told me I could purchase my freedom if I got you to talk."

She covered herself with the tunic and slid away, reminded that she had violated the priestess discipline of avoiding intimate contact.

"Have you always been blind?"

"Have you always been nosy?" she countered.

He backed off with palms raised in contrition, then remembered that she could not see the gesture. "I'm sorry if I offended you. I am Jean Fressyre. My kingdom consists of twenty mangy sheep and a lazy dog."

"Your dog may be lazy, but at least he kept his mouth shut today."

"You had a chance to save yourself, too."

"You can beat me all you want. I won't say anything."

"You cloggers aren't the only ones hunted by those monks."

"Are you not of the Roman faith?" she asked.

"I've not missed a Lord's Day Mass in ten years."

"Then you're no different than those Dominicans."

He sighed. "Are we all devils to you?"

"Each of us is a child of the Light or the Dark. God has no orphans." She expected a rebuttal, but he was silent. Fearing that she had been too harsh, she asked, "Have you no family?"

"I too will leave no orphans. I suppose you consider that a blessing."

She huffed in exasperation. Would the Roman priests never stop slandering her faith with the falsehood that her people despised children and murdered them at birth? "After a woman has raised her family, she is permitted to take the vow of a perfecta and spend the rest of her life in meditation and prayer. Your nuns are no different. Before death, we are given the Touch of Salvation."

"Have you taken this touch?"

She coughed back a surge of emotion. "I had planned to this year, but . . ."

"But what?"

She hid her face, ashamed that her useless eyes were watering useless tears. "I will die without it."

"What does that mean?"

"I'll be sent back to this world, to seek release from the flesh again. I pray that my brothers and sisters find the Light and avoid that misfortune."

"Then your god is not just," he insisted.

"And your god *is* just? Allowing your pope to hunt us down when all we've done is try to live in the manner of the Apostles?"

Jean contemplated her explanation for nearly a minute. "This redemption that is offered by your religion . . . I've heard said that only another clogger can give it."

"The Touch has been transmitted from disciple to disciple since the time of the Master," she explained. "We try to wait until the last moment to receive it. To sin after taking it dooms one to this world again."

Jean dipped his fingers into the balm and offered to apply another layer, lightly touching her shoulder to avoid startling her. She relented and raised the hair from her bent neck. What did it matter now? She was going to die without the salvation. None of her brothers and sisters would be with her during these last hours to offer her the Consolamentum. She sensed from the slowing of his caresses that he had fallen into deep thought. After several moments of silence, he covered her shoulders with the tunic and retreated into the shadows.

"Thank you for coming to my—"

"Will you give me your sacrament?" he asked.

"You mock my faith?"

"Am I not worthy of it?"

"Yes, of course . . . but aren't you afraid of going to Hell for apostasy?"

Jean gazed through the slit at the smoldering pyre stakes in the square. The air stank from the prior day's burnings that had cost him several cherished neighbors. "Could Hell surpass this misery?"

"You can still save yourself. Call for the parish priest in the morning and ask him to attest to your devotion."

Jean was confused by her reticence to convert him. "I thought you Cathars cajoled others into joining your faith?"

"You must find your own truth."

He saw her shivering and wrapped her with his tattered cloak. "I've watched as your people go willingly to the fires. Why don't you fight back?"

"None of us wish to be murdered," said Chandelle. "But Jesus taught that to turn against what one believes is a fate worse than death." She felt him staring at her and, self-conscious of his inspection, ran her fingers through her hair in a futile effort to render it less unkempt. "There's no need for you to die. You must tell the monks something about me to save yourself."

"No . . . I would take this Touch of Salvation."

"You truly desire this?"

"With all my heart."

For the first time in her life, Chandelle desperately wished for sight. The voice could dissemble but the eyes did not. Could she truly trust him? All members of her faith were required to grant the transmission if requested in earnest. Was he scheming to ferret out the secrets of the ritual for the Dominicans? She had never been clever enough to detect deceit in others, having so rarely been exposed to it. The monks often purchased the loyalty of family members and infiltrated them into the Cathar houses. She remembered the reason that Father Castres had given for his decision to participate in the Pamiers disputation: If but one spark from the Divine Flame can be returned to its source, is it not worth risking the world? With a fortifying breath, she clasped Jean's hands within hers and whispered, "You must promise to stand against the Demiurge and those who trap us in these bodies and keep us from our true home."

"This world is filled with both good and evil," said Jean. "I have seen evidence enough of that."

She listened for the footsteps of the guards. Assured that they were alone, she whispered, "We hold that all living things have souls and should be shown compassion and mercy. We refuse to slaughter animals."

Jean contemplated the strange belief and laughed at the irony of his predicament. "I'll no longer need my sheep. On this night, I declare them free."

She dutifully related the other tenets of her faith, then hesitated before revealing the last commandment, fearful that he would belittle her. "You must also abstain from all worldly desire. No carnal love."

Jean sighed. "I doubt I'll be marrying before the morning."

"Are you certain of this decision?"

He placed her hands on his head. "More certain than anything in my life."

She whispered the ritual prayer over him, "Do you promise to die in Christ, to waver not in the face of fire, to never denounce your faith?"

"I do."

"Do you promise to love all brothers and sisters of the Light and to toil without cease until they are rescued from this world?"

"I promise."

She felt his tears on her hands as she kissed his cheek for the final benediction. "You are a Bon Homme, Monsieur Jean. From this moment hence, walk always in the Light." She tore a ribbon of cloth from the hem of her tunic and tied it around his waist. "It is our tradition that your ministry belt be given now. This will have to do." She sank back into her corner, drained by the Light's use of her body as a channel for the transmission. She thought about her family and those she had left behind at Montsegur. With the passing of so many days, they would have long since accepted her loss to the cycle of reincarnation. She wondered how she would be returned to this world. Would she be blind again? Perhaps she would be forced to suffer another affliction. There must have been some lesson in this life that she had failed to—

"Chandelle, do you accept the baptism of the God of Light?"

She felt Jean's palms press against her forehead—a surge of heat shot across her temples. "What . . . are you doing?"

"I won't let you suffer this world again."

Only then did she discover the true reason he had taken the vow. "You've condemned yourself for me?"

"Our Lord said there is no greater love."

"But—"

"If Jesus is the son of the Good God, then He'll not care if I am Catholic or Cathar."

She sobbed with joy. She had not been abandoned after all. Within hours, she would be with Phillipa and Father Castres. She was so moved by Jean's sacrifice that she could barely utter the credo, "I believe in the God of Light and in His son, the Christ Jesus."

"Do you promise to die"—Jean's voice broke—"to die in Christ, and not waver from the fire?"

"With all my heart."

Jean pressed the Consolamentum kiss to her cheek and placed a small, flat stone into her hand. "A gift. In memory of your special day. I'm not much good at it, but I like to draw. I made a likeness of you while you were asleep."

"But I can't see it!"

"Mayhaps in the world to come."

"I want one of you," she said. "Please. It makes no sense, I know."

Jean etched a self-portrait on the reverse side of the stone. When it was finished, he gave it back to her.

"What do you look like?" she asked.

"That would spoil the surprise for—"

The door clanged open. "On your feet," ordered a menacing voice.

Chandelle tried to arise, but Jean pressed the stone into her fist and hurried from the cell with the soldiers before she could stop him.

*L*oupe and Raymond de Perella muzzled their horses in a thicket of purple beeches above the outskirts of Avignonet. Accompanied by a dozen Occitan knights, they waited in the pre-dawn haze until a lantern flashed three squints from the village's campanile. Loupe counted the sequence again to confirm the prearranged signal. "You are certain that Toulouse has given its sanction?"

"The constable is in Count Raymond's employment," whispered Pierre-Roger, who had been entrusted with the preparations for the avenging raid. He led Loupe and the Occitans down a ridge in stealth, angling from tree to tree. When they reached the entry archway into the village, he held back. "I'll keep the horses at the ready."

Loupe found Pierre-Roger's change of plans suspicious, but she had no time to challenge him. She regretted leaving Bernard behind to protect Montsegur; his uncanny ability to divine an enemy trap would have been invaluable. She and her cohorts stole along the shadows and rendezvoused with the local sheriff, who motioned them into the armory and supplied them with axes. He guided them into the alley adjacent to the abbey and tried the latch. The door was locked. As the Occitans prepared to storm the chapel, the sheriff whispered, "Give the slippery dogs no time to scatter."

Loupe and Raymond made quick work of the planks. They burst into the sanctuary and found William Arnaud behind the altar. Eyes dilated in a start, the inquisitor held a bible at his chest as a shield. Six monks in the side stalls dropped to their knees and began chanting the Salve Regina. Their twitchy voices rose an octave with each verse.

Loupe gripped her ax as she strode down the aisle. "Where is she?"

Arnaud glared his frightened charges to silence. Raymond captured one of the timorous novices by the scruff and dragged him to the altar platform. When the monk refused to disobey his superior, Raymond splattered his brains across the stones. Terrorized by the gruesome martyrdom, the Dominicans doubled the intensity of their prayers and converged in a tight circle. Finding Arnaud still defiant, Raymond hammered another monk to his knees.

Loupe found a scrivener's tome on a table. She tore open its lock and read:

The heretic who revealed herself only by the name Chandelle is sentenced to die at the stake on Our Lord's Day of May 28, 1242.

Loupe tied Arnaud's hands behind his back. She ripped several pages from the ledger and rammed them into the inquisitor's stretched mouth, then lit the protruding wad with a torch. Arnaud snorted and fought to spit the burning fuse as he squirmed across the nave. She ordered, "Take us to her."

Arnaud dripped with flensed skin as he stumbled in muzzled agony toward a side door. The Occitans kicked him down a circular stairwell and rammed open the first cell grille.

Chandelle, shivering and terrified, sat curled up in the corner.

Tears streamed down Raymond's face as he lifted his daughter into his arms. "Come, my love."

Startled, Chandelle raised her bruised face in hope. "Papa?"

"You're going home," said Raymond.

Chandelle struggled against her father's attempt to carry her up the stairwell. "I won't leave without Jean!"

Loupe held the torch under Arnaud's seared face to speed an explanation for Chandelle's plea. The inquisitor reluctantly nodded her toward a far room down the length of the dungeon's gallery. She ran to the door and cleaved it open. Jean's body hung lifeless from a rope. His face was horribly lacerated and his feet bones had been crushed from the instruments of torture. A transcript lay on a table next to a fresh candle and a well of ink. The document's last entry read:

> The apostate Jean Fressyre refused to reveal what he had learned from the heretic captured at Montsegur. He spoke only of a dualist demon and . . .

A trail of splotched ink crossed the floor, evidence that the scribe who wrote the entry had escaped in haste.

From the outer gallery, Chandelle called out, "Have you found him?"

Loupe emerged from the torture cell and signaled for Raymond to say nothing of her discovery. Fearing that the Dominican guards billeted in the village would soon be upon them, Raymond muffled Chandelle's cries and wrestled her up the stairs. The Occitan knights dragged the inquisitor and his monks with them.

Alone in the crypt, Loupe could hear the screams of Arnaud and the monks being dispatched in the nave. She searched the niches in the dripping undercroft and caught a swish of movement in the granary room. She flashed the torch across the top of the bin and watched as a small depression formed in the sea of kernels. She parted the barley and exposed a hollow reed. When she pinched its tip, the grain erupted with the head of a crimson-faced friar. She was about to gut him when her eyes blinked in recognition.

Otto scrambled out of the bin with his hands raised. Gagging for breath, he heaved and wheezed, "I'm only a minor notary."

"Minor enough to preside over an execution."

"I swear I didn't touch the man. I only took down his confession."

Loupe brought the dagger to his arched chin. "The woman you were preparing to burn . . . Do you who she is?"

Otto backed away until trapped by the wall. "Her name was Chandelle. That's all she would say."

She pricked his throat, drawing a grunt. "Your mother's goddaughter!"

Otto's look of trepidation gave way to a glare of spitting disdain. The blue vein throbbed at his temple. "My mother can rot in her grave!"

"You'll have to wait until she gets—" Too late, Loupe saw from Otto's surprised reaction that he had assumed Esclarmonde to be dead. She would now have to kill him to prevent the revelation from reaching his superiors.

"Be done with it!" taunted Otto, exposing his neck.

Loupe drew a thin trail of blood below his ear to test him. "Give me one reason why I shouldn't?"

"We share the same hatred."

"We share nothing."

"I saw it in your eyes when your father spoke her name in Rome. Ours is a bond thicker than blood. Kill me and you will wrong the woman we both despise. Your score with her will then be even." He allowed her a moment to digest the unassailable truth of that prophecy. "And you'll no longer have an injury to hold against her."

Loupe's hand quivered slightly with indecision, confirming that he had hit his mark. This cousin was diabolically possessed of the ability to divine her darkest emotions and twist them to his will. She drove his chin to its limit—and sheathed the dagger.

Released, Otto slid along the wall and escaped into the recesses of the crypt with the darkness shading his long-jawed smile.

In time we shall make them
fully understand our signs.
In the farthest horizons
and within themselves.

- Rumi

XXXIII

*S*eated three tables from the royal dais, Otto shielded his eyes under the dazzling ceiling of Lorris, the ancient chateau that guarded a strategic crossroads ten leagues east of Orleans. On the morning prior, an advance team—led by the French lord chamberlain and comprised of a clattering host of heralds, carders, clerks, scullions, stewards, barbers, ewerers, cooks, carpenters, minstrels, and almoners—had descended on this lugubrious hall and in a miracle of light and color had transformed it into a scaled-down version of the dining chamber in the Palais de la Cité. The sinking rafters were draped with billowing canopies of sapphire velvet and studded with candelabra chandeliers that spun like miniature zodiacs. Savory aromas lingered from the remnants of fricasseed boar. Fresh floor rushes, transported from the nearest baronial barns at Sens, insulated the floor stones and eucalyptus and hibiscus roasted in the warming kettles, infusing the evening's three hundred glutted guests with a soporific balm. All of these preparations had been consummated at an exorbitant expense because the ponderous Capetian court returning from its winter circuit of the duchies had decided that the six-hour journey back to Paris would be too grueling to attempt in one day.

The head table had been cleared and replaced by a cushioned couch where King Louis IX lay sprawled for all to observe. His frail frame and soft beryl eyes belied the fierce reputation he had gained months earlier against Henry III on the field of Taillebourg. Eyes rimmed in a slagish pallor, the young monarch writhed from a thigh wound that had been bandaged in a silk tourniquet.

A blond page ran down the rows of trestles and waved a lance that dripped with a seemingly endless flow of blood. The courtiers gasped and blenched, forced to examine the dolorous weapon up close. Louis fainted into the chaise and moaned as if in his last throes.

Otto closed his eyes and made the sign of the Cross. The shedding of the *sang graal* always reminded him of Christ's breast being pierced on Calvary.

The rear doors opened with an ear-cracking fanfare of trumpets. A wimpled maiden led forth a solemn cortege of white-draped female attendants who carried a large platter laden with silver candlesticks, an ivory dagger, and a vial of burning balsam.

"Make way for Repanse de Joie!" shouted the page.

Bringing up the rear of this fluttering cavalcade was the most imposing woman that Otto had ever laid eyes upon. Announced by a miasma of civet-laced musk, her deltoid face featured a fine layer of powdered lead and her flaxen hair was curled in the fashion worn by ladies half her age. She wore a royal blue mantle of Tripoli camel hair, circumscribed with a wide white belt that was hung low to create the illusion of a lengthened waist.

Among Blanche de Castile's manifold skills was the art of the entrée.

The Queen Mother, twice ruler of France as regent, was exceeded in distaff fame across Christendom only by her deceased grandmother, Eleanor de Aquitane. Having birthed eleven children, Blanche still elicited murmurs of admiration from those required to attend her monthly reenactments of the Holy Grail ritual.

Admiration from all, that is, except Count Raymond VII de Toulouse and King Louis's new bride, Marguerite de Provence. If misery begged company, then these two star-crossed souls had been aptly seated together. Otto's agents had confirmed the gossip: Although Louis had long since reached the age of majority, Blanche continued to hold sway over his affairs. She made no effort, even in public, to hide her disdain for the mousy Marguerite, whose father, the count of that southern domain, had turned traitor against her family. In her prime, Blanche had enjoyed scandalous dalliances with Cardinal Frangipani and the Count de Champagne. But that sordid record did not prevent her from constantly reminding her son that she would rather find him dead than wallowing in the snares of carnal temptation. She had become so militantly pious in her later years that many in the country feared she would drive the impressionable King to the priesthood before he sired an heir.

Poor Marguerite's existence, however, was blessed compared to that dealt Count Raymond. The boy on whom Occitania once placed so much hope had become his feckless father in both degradation of body and callowness of spirit. He sat slumped and bleary-eyed from too much wine, impatiently tapping his fingers on his knee, forced to endure yet another of Blanche's traveling costume performances. His relationship with this meddlesome aunt was composed of equal parts revulsion and masochistic love. She was determined to eradicate the Cathar heresy from his domain by attaching it to the French kingdom. To that end, she had compelled the marriage of her youngest son to Raymond's daughter. Under the terms of that enforced agreement, the Capetians would inherit Toulousia if Raymond failed to produce a male heir.

Raymond had thus been cast upon an all-consuming quest to find a replacement for his deceased wife, one who would earn his aunt's approval while satisfying the Church's law on consanguinity. Dulled by years of accidie and drink, he had only recently discovered that Blanche had schemed to undermine every feminine alliance he nurtured. Sentenced to be scourged again in Notre Dame for failing to round up the heretics with sufficient zeal, he had fled to England to recruit supporters for a rebellion. But his plan to entice the Plantagenet monarchy into an allied invasion was strangled in the crib when French galleys intercepted three of his ships loaded with arms for Marseille. Isolated and paranoid, he was arrested and forced to tramp along with the French court for two weeks, waiting to hear his fate. This evening's drawn-out stage mummery was only more cruel torment for a man who did not know if his head would be attached to his shoulders come dawn.

When the slow Grail procession finally reached the dais, Blanche revived the dying King with a draught of wine from the holy chalice. As always, she played the role of her son's wife in these elaborate productions, a choice that elicited more than a few snickers. Finding Louis at a loss for his lines, she whispered his cue and followed it up with a tight-lipped glare.

"Where is Parsifal, my lady?" asked Louis, dutifully reminded.

"Upon his divine quest," said Blanche.

Louis swept a limp hand to his forehead, swooning from the loss of blood. "This mortal flow cannot be stanched without the Question."

The lance-wielding squire leapt to the dais and posed the penultimate inquiry of the evening, "Whom does the Grail serve?"

The assembly, forced to memorize every word of the play, dutifully replied, "The Grail serves those who serve the Grail."

Louis took an uncertain step to test the cure. "Parsifal has saved me!"

The onlookers burst into wild applause—not from spiritual catharsis, but in relief that their imprisonment to this tiresome ordeal was nearing an end. Lute and viol players broke into melody as Blanche took Louis to her ample embrace. Without warning, she turned on the celebrants with a ferocious mien and screamed, "Out! All of you!"

The startled musicians stopped in mid-chord. Mindful of Blanche's notorious temper, the guests rushed from the hall in a near stampede. Marguerite tried to dredge the courage to remain with her husband, but she too was routed. Otto retreated with the Archbishop de Narbonne, a syphilitic-looking gimp whose skin was so scabrous that he appeared on the verge of molting. The two clerics had nearly reached the portal arch when Blanche called them back.

Blanche took a seat next to her recumbent son. She motioned Count Raymond up and forced him to remain on his knees while the ominous silence stretched out. Finally, she asked, "Have I not been generous with you, nephew?"

The Count hiccuped a nervous laugh as he pawed for her hand. "I am loyal and true, dearest aunt. I was coming freely to do homage when . . ."

She repulsed his reach. "Why do I shower you with undeserved clemency?"

"I have made every effort to maintain my treaties!"

"By murdering monks?"

"I played no part in that affair! I shall swear it on the Holy Book!"

Blanche slapped down his grasp. "No excommunicate touches Holy Writ in my presence!"

"Am I to be condemned without proof? Every hole in Toulousia has been scoured to find the murderers. I firmly believe them to be Gascon ruffians."

Blanche turned toward Otto with calculation. "I am told, Dominican, that you survived the massacre."

That revelation drove the color from Raymond's puffy cheeks. Otto paused to enjoy the baron's discomfiture, holding no doubt that he had given his blessing to the Avignonet murders after receiving assurances that all witnesses to the deed would be eliminated. He allowed Raymond another moment to choke on his astonishment before confirming, "The saints saved me so I might give witness to God's ardent avenger."

"Did you recognize the perpetrators?" asked King Louis.

Otto took an accusing step toward Raymond. "They were outlaws from the heretic den at Montsegur. Commanded by an officer who once served the deceased Count de Foix."

Blanche spat the next words as if having tasted verjuice. "That blighted patch of Hell! Describe for my nephew what you witnessed."

"The rebels broke into the abbey during mass and set upon us with axes," said Otto. "Brother Arnaud's blood still stains the altar. The heretics parade curiosity seekers through the chapel in profane pilgrimages."

Raymond's brows kneaded in suspicion. "If these partisans were so thorough in their butchery, how is it, monk, that you walked away without a scratch?"

Otto bristled at the implication. "God in His infinite mercy saw fit to scatter the curs before they finished me off."

"Indeed, how fortunate." Raymond turned in fawning supplication to Blanche. "What does any of this have to do with me?"

Blanche circled her nephew with a wilting inspection. "Does the name Raymond de Alfaro mean anything to you?"

Louis crunched on an apple, drawing a nervous flinch from the rattled baron. "The man is one of your vassals, is he not, Raymond?"

"And his kinsman," reminded Otto.

Perspiration beaded across Raymond's forehead. "He is, my liege, but—" He took a step back, angling for time.

Otto moved sideways to block the baron's escape. "Alfaro led the murderers to the church."

Raymond was spinning from one accusation to the next, his face a kaleidoscope of choler and fear. "By all that I hold sacred—"

Blanche silenced his whimpering with an upturned hand. "An even stranger story has been brought to my attention. One being spread by those debauched bards who infest your land."

"I don't listen to the fatuous singers," said Raymond.

"Perhaps you should," Blanche advised. "They seem better informed than you about what moves within your borders. There are rumors that the heretics have built a faux Grail castle on Montsegur."

"Preposterous!" Raymond's darting eyes were at war with his denial.

Blanche lifted the gold crown from her head and gazed into its gemstones as if divining the future from their prismatic reflections. "What goes on inside that fortress?"

Raymond feigned indifference, his voice flattening. "I have never made it my business to go there."

Blanche spun the nail of her index finger around the band, generating a grating ring that intensified with each circumnavigation. She asked Otto, "Who commands the defense of the heretic mountain?"

"Raymond de Perella."

"Do you know the name of the lord who the chroniclers say protects the Grail Castle?" she asked.

"I do not, madam," said Otto.

"Perilla," revealed Blanche, her stare opaque.

Otto's mind raced to catch up with the direction Blanche was headed. "A mere coincidence, I am certain."

"What does Montsegur mean in Occitan?"

Otto was nonplussed by the similarities Blanche was finding between the Grail legends and the Cathar refuge. "The Mount of Salvation."

Blanched smiled thinly at Otto's manifest admiration for the workings of her intellect. She walked over to inspect an arras of gold weave that depicted a maiden protecting a dying unicorn within a walled enclosure. "The troubadours claim that the Grail is protected on a mountain called Montsalvache."

Intrigued, Louis tossed aside his apple. "What are you getting at, mother?"

Blanche caressed her son's thick brown hair with loving condescension, resigned to his ignorance in such arcane matters. She resumed her cross-examination of Otto, stealing glances at Raymond to assay his reaction. "The heretics, I am also told, worship a mysterious light on Montsegur. The place is said to be guarded by priestesses who conjure clandestine rituals and spells."

Otto swallowed slowly in an effort to conceal his uneasiness. Had she stumbled on the mystery that Folques tried to reveal on his deathbed? He was eager to divert her from traveling down this path of inquiry, uncertain where it might lead. He had long dreamed of exposing the secrets held by the Cathars and delivering them to the Holy Father in person. He chose his next words with care. "These cloggers spread all manner of falsehoods. I interrogated one of their witches a few days before the raid on Avignonet."

Blanche's gaze flashed hot for a fractured second, but she quickly retreated into a placid comportment. "And what did the woman reveal?"

"She knew nothing of any use." Otto modulated the feigned insouciance in his voice. "I dare say if anything of import was taking place on that mountain, the woman would have given it up under the lash." He prayed that the Queen Mother's inquisitiveness was finally squelched.

Blanche, whose sphinx-like face was rendered even more inscrutable by the thick powder, picked up a viol left by a musician and strummed its strings while pondering what to make of Otto's marked lack of interest in Montsegur. "Was there not a noble lady of some notoriety who once lived in Foix? Worshiped by the heretics as a saint? I seem to recall a chanson extolling her."

Before Otto could gainsay that suggestion, the Archbishop blurted, "You speak of Esclarmonde de Foix. The woman is long dead and sent to Hell, praise be to God. She was hunted for many years by Bishop Folques of Toulouse."

"Ah yes, the Bishop of the Fires. I once heard him warble his inanities in my grandmother's court before he took the vow." Blanche turned back on Otto with an informed smile. "Was he not your spiritual advisor?"

Otto petitioned a goblet from a scullion, temporizing to collect his thoughts. He had insinuated an invitation to this evening's repast with designs to gain introductions in the court. But now he wondered if Blanche had not contrived his attendance all along to draw him out. Her inquiry about Montsegur were troubling enough, but this interest in his upbringing was passing strange. Could she, God forbid, have learned that Esclarmonde was his mother? Folques had sworn to him that he told no one outside the abbey and he himself had arranged the destruction of all documentary evidence concerning his lineage. Desperate to divert this line of inquiry, he scoured his memory for details of the Grail legends. Perhaps the Queen Mother's vanity could be turned to his advantage in gaining his revenge against Esclarmonde. This much he knew: Blanche would countenance no rival, for there could be only one Grail Queen. His plan was fraught with risk; a promising future in the Church hierarchy would be cut short if his connection to the heretic priestess were to be revealed. Nevertheless, he resolved to set it in motion.

"I did overhear one of the murderers at Avignonet speak of this Foix woman as if she still lives," said Otto. "Of course, I gave it no credence. These deranged cloggers converse openly with the spirits of deceased family members as if they are still companions in the flesh. As the Archbishop indicated, the viscountess is certainly dead, or she would have reared her head by now. A couple of the prisoners introduced to the clarity of the interrogation tools did gabble claims about this Esclarmonde having studied the black arts inside that Devil's synagogue." With a calculated smoothness, he casually moved on to another subject, bobbing the cork on the line for Blanche to take the bait. "Speaking of synagogues, I was only this morning advised by my Dominican brothers in Toledo that the chief rabbi there was found hoarding gold worth—"

"What manner of black arts?" Blanche interrupted.

Otto affected a moment's confusion and followed it up with an abashed realization that Blanche wished to continue discussing Esclarmonde. Waving off the supposition he was about to offer, he conceded, "Oh, if I recall correctly, there was some talk of the priestess having covened with Jew necromancers who claimed the ability to ascend to the higher realms." He nearly lost his nerve, withered as he was under her boring gaze. *I should have revealed it sooner. She now suspects me.* He cleared the constriction in his throat. "A fabrication spread to embellish her legend, no doubt."

Blanche mulled these revelations with a locking stare, impossible to read. Finally, she released Otto from her inspection and ordered Count Raymond, "This last heretic haven in your territory must be eradicated at once."

"If de Montfort could not subdue the fastness, how will I manage it?"

Blanche continued speaking as if she had not heard Raymond's protest. "The Seneschal of Carcassonne will command my son's army. Archbishop, you will oversee the adjudications and executions."

The Archbishop's scaly face flamed at the horrid prospect of spending the winter in the Languedoc marches. "Madam, I must minister to my own flock. Lenten season will soon be upon us and—"

"Your flock can wait," she said peremptorily. "There is more pressing work to be accomplished on God's behalf. I expect to receive your report of the mountain's capitulation before the start of summer."

Raymond dithered to his knees to beg release from the infeasible task, but his attempt was rendered stillborn by Blanche's kindled glare of threat. Weighing it the better bargain to leave with a reprieve from treason than to lose his head, he lurched to his feet and, sketching a frazzled bow, backed toward the doors before his aunt's prickly temperament could alter.

"Raymond," she said. "There is still the small matter of your signature?"

"Signature?"

"I've chosen this joyous occasion of your presence to have our understanding drawn up in another treaty. We know how your aging memory tends to falter at the most regrettable moments. The document merely reiterates that because of your shameful role in the murders at Avignonet, your domain will divest to the crown should our prayers for your heir not be granted. My son's attestation has already been inscribed. You need only sign and seal it with your signet, and you are free to resume your search for that special lady who will capture your heart."

Raymond grudgingly accepted the quill from an attendant and stood over the parchment like a condemned man examining the block. Finally, with a barely audible hiss of emasculation, he signed and jammed his ring into the wax so forcefully that his knuckles formed part of the impressed seal, formalizing what he feared would become the death warrant for Toulousia's independence. A magpie screeched somewhere in the night, causing him to question if the ghosts of his ancestors had gathered to haunt him in dissent. Eyes swimming with the pellicle of despair, he bowed slightly and made the shameful walk toward the heralds who were waiting to escort him from the chamber.

Otto feigned his departure with the baron, hopeful that a show of indifference to the Montsegur expedition would seduce Blanche a step further into his snare. As he neared the exit, he heard:

"Dominican . . . I would speak with you on a private matter."

His back still turned, Otto suppressed a victorious smile.

Blanche waved out the flabbergasted Archbishop, who was red with indignation at finding a cleric of lower stature being granted such a privilege. Seeing her son still lounging on the chaise, Blanche asked, "Should you not look upon the welfare of your wife?" When Louis failed to take her hint, she raised her voice in a stentorian demand. "I wish to take spiritual counseling from this monk!"

Bowls of fruit scattered as Louis hurried from the chamber.

Alone with Otto, Blanche traced a finger across the raised stitching of the Flemish Grail tapestry as if attempting to divine the clue to a puzzle. After nearly a minute of this meditative study, she turned to him and ordered, "You will serve as my eyes and ears in this Foix campaign."

Otto shammed surprise while congratulating himself for having inveigled the woman at her own game. He made certain the hook was firmly snagged by pressing his palms together in a plea of inadequacy. "My lady, I am but a lowly notary. There are others more—"

"I have been watching you closely. With the proper intermediary, you will swiftly ascend God's earthly ladder."

Otto bowed adroitly to accept the compliment.

Blanche removed her gloves and extinguished the candles surrounding the Grail goblet, darkening the hall by descending degrees. She fixed her hawkish eyes on him with an unsettling intensity. "In the unlikely event you find this Cathar temptress alive, bring her to me." She enjoyed his fascination with how she tested her threshold for pain by holding her bleached fingers in the penumbras of the flames before guttering them. "When the heretic nest is taken, search it alone. Report to me—and only me—what you discover."

Everyone's death is of the same quality as himself...
- Rumi

XXXIV

Esclarmonde shook the morning cold from her bare feet and cupped her palms to blow warmth into her cheeks. First light had yet to break; frost blanketed the sills and a thin sheet of ice glazed the washing basin. Sixty priestesses sat along the chapel walls with their eyes closed and knees tucked against their stomachs, so gaunt that a litter of scrawny rabbits would have given off more heat. She skipped a pebble across the floor to test their awareness. Several jerked slightly with eyelids fluttering. They were supposed to be meditating, but they had fallen asleep during the day's first session, held before dawn to connect with the power available in that spiritual limbus between night and day.

She arose quietly and retrieved the pot of melted sheep lard that she had hidden under the altar. She sprinkled the fat with crushed sulfur and dried leaves, then placed the pot in the hearth and threw in a burning coal.

Seconds later, the chapel exploded with a crackling flash.

The women erupted shrieking and thrashing. Entrapped in the disorienting twilight between slumber and wakefulness, some fell to their knees in the darkness, others careened into the walls. Corba dragged Chandelle through the tumult and plowed headlong into Bernard Saint-Martin, who had rammed open the door on hearing the tocsins. Corba pummeled him with her fists, convinced that the Dominican henchmen were upon them.

Raymond charged into the dim sanctuary and captured Corba's wrists. "Have you gone mad, woman? I am your husband! What in God's name is going on in here?"

Bernard was on his knees and curled into a ball. He peered over the protection of his elbow, uncertain whether to trust the cessation of hostilities. Raymond fired the tapers to bring more light to the bizarre scene. The women shared confused glances at finding nothing amiss.

Esclarmonde appeared from the shadows. "You men may take your leave."

Raymond and Bernard backed out of the chapel questioning if they had stumbled upon some mysterious feminine rite best left unexamined. "There's a sampling of their pacifist ways," Raymond muttered as he shut the door. "We could have used a battalion of them at Muret. Keep the armory locked."

Corba found the sheep fat sizzling just beyond the hearth grate. "Which one of you pigeon-brains left this grease near the fire?"

"I did," said Esclarmonde with an unsettling serenity. "It was no accident."

The women glared incredulously at Esclarmonde and suspected her of falling victim to another of her demon-plagued trances. The Marquessa leveraged to her scabbed elbows. "Child, have you taken leave of your senses?"

Disappointed in their mistrust, Esclarmonde cowed them with a glower back to their seats. "How will you maintain a steady mind at the appointed hour if you cannot remain calm when confronted with such a trivial distraction?"

"What in God's name are you talking about?" asked Corba.

"It is time."

"Time for what?"

"To prepare for death."

The women shook their heads in mutiny, disgusted by the perverse prank. Corba feared that her old friend was becoming more unhinged from the world with each passing month. "We've had enough of this morbid fascination with the end of our days. It will come soon enough without dwelling on it!"

"It is nearer than you think."

Corba swiped at the air in utter exasperation. "Then let us live in peace with our loved ones until that hour!"

"Chandelle nearly left us without being instructed on the means to return to the Light," said Esclarmonde.

"You think I don't count every hour she's with me?"

Esclarmonde stared down at the threatening hand gripping her arm until Corba removed it. She walked across the chapel to meet each judging face. "All of you are free to leave if you wish. No one holds you here."

Incensed, Corba was on Esclarmonde's heels. "You have no children at your side to protect! Departing this world comes too easy for you!"

Chandelle tried to pull her mother back to sitting. "Let us at least hear what she has to say."

"I've listened to her nonsense all my life! What has it gained me?"

Esclarmonde knew that she had driven these women hard. Many had given up their families to follow her, accepting the stark deprivations of food and sleep and risking capture at the hands of the churchmen, testing their sanity by navigating deeper into the dangerous spiritual realms. But she could no longer put off this final obligation. She removed a tallow candle from the wall sconce and sat on a stool in the center of the circled group while holding the flame in front of her face to protect its precarious life from the drafts. "The Light's approach at death will be more disorienting than the fright you've just undergone. It will seem as if we are suddenly awakened from a deep sleep and find ourselves exiled into a foreign land."

"How do you know this?" asked the Marquessa.

"Father Castres conveyed the mysteries to me before he passed. He made me promise that I would transmit them to you. I should have done so before now, but I could not bring myself to endure it."

The rancor drained from the women's faces. Corba slowly retreated to her position next to Chandelle and dropped her voice to a near whisper, as near an apology as she could muster. "What did he wish us to know?"

Esclarmonde drew a steadying breath to ease the tremors from their confrontation. "The entirety of our lives is but a preparation for this moment of passing. The Bishop assured me that it will be a blessed event provided we cast off our fears and false beliefs imposed by the Lords of Darkness." To offer tangible proof, she came to the unsuspecting Chandelle and rubbed her hand against the blind perfecta's cheek. Chandelle smiled as if having expected the touch.

The Marquessa was amazed by the demonstration. "You didn't even flinch. Why were you not startled?"

"I've learned to expect the unexpected, I suppose," said Chandelle. "It's almost as if my body has given up trying to warn me."

Esclarmonde kissed Chandelle's forehead in reward for her perceptiveness. "When awake, she is accustomed to our presence. But when she falls into the dream state, she forgets, as we all do. Our existence is not unlike spending years in total darkness only to have our eyes assaulted by the midday light at the trice of death. The spiritual Sun that rises at midnight will appear a thousand times brighter than its celestial counterpart."

The Marquessa threw up her grainy hands in dismay. "You can't expect us to tame the phantasms of our sleep!"

"With courage and discipline, it is possible," said Esclarmonde. "We can also relinquish the fear of separating our spirit from the body. This path offers the only true escape from this world."

"If our fears and instincts are so malevolent," asked Corba, "why were we born with them?"

"The Demiurge instilled our nature with the base desires and tendencies to keep us enchained. He wants us to shirk from the Light at the moment of decision and thus be forced to incarnate again."

"How can anyone know what happens after death?" asked Chandelle. "Father Castres was wise, but how could he know?"

Esclarmonde had posed that same question on the night she tried to take her own life. "Each of us has lived and died many times. There is a part of us, our Robe of Light, that remembers our past incarnations."

"I don't remember them," protested Chandelle.

"Do you remember being born?"

"Of course not."

"Do you deny it happened?" Esclarmonde pressed home the crucial point of the lesson. "I have been speaking of the moment of death, but that description is misleading. In truth, there is no one moment of death, just as there is no one moment of birth."

Corba returned in memory to that joyous morning more than forty years ago when Chandelle had entered her world. "We've both experienced the pangs of childbirth. There was no doubt when it happened."

"When was Chandelle born?" asked Esclarmonde. "Was it when the seed quickened? When she emerged from the birth canal? When her head came forth? Her body? Or was it when the Marquessa gave birth to you? Chandelle could not have come to us unless you were born first. Is dying not the same? Do we not begin to die with our first breath and die a little more each night when we fall asleep?"

"At *this* moment," cried Corba, "I know only one thing! My head is pounding like a drum!"

Esclarmonde laughed in relief to find the tension dissipated. She conceded that these teachings were difficult to comprehend and accept. "I tell you these things to explain why we meditate. If we learn to endure longer periods without sensation, we'll not be jolted when the time beyond death arrives. What happens if you place a live chicken in a cauldron of boiling water?"

"The chicken will be scalded," said the Marquessa.

"And if you place it in lukewarm water and slowly heat the pot?"

"The chicken will sit calmly until it dies," said Corba.

"Likewise, we must we raise our spiritual temperature degree by degree to prevent the full manifestation of the Light from scalding us."

"So," said Chandelle to herself, "every meditation is a little death."

"A good passing cannot be attained without years of diligent preparation. The Roman Church insists that our souls were nascent before birth and must face a lone day of judgment to be assigned eternal punishment or reward. But we know otherwise. Our fate hangs in the balance at that instant between flesh and spirit, when the Light beckons us home. If we fail to recognize its fleeting call, all is lost. These fears and desires instilled into our body by the Demiurge are designed to thrust us back into this world again and again."

Corba was not convinced. "What about Purgatory?"

"The Scriptures say nothing about a holding pen for sinners," said Esclarmonde. "Why would the Roman pontiffs invent such a place?"

Chandelle swiveled her delicate head as if to shake forth a connecting thought. "If the priests had not invented Purgatory, they could not sell their indulgences to bind and unbind our sins. But if the Light comes to those of all faiths, why does it matter what we believe?"

"Ah, my clever one, you have bit on the kernel in the nut," said Esclarmonde. "It's not the existence of a place such as Hell that causes our entrapment. No, it's our *belief* in its existence. Our last thought at the transition into spirit will determine if we go home to the Light or reincarnate here."

Anguish scored the crosshatched fissures in the Marquessa's ancient face. "You mean if we live a good life and still hold a fear of Hell in our minds with our last breath, we will be returned to this world?"

"As a man thinketh," reminded Esclarmonde, repeating Christ's own words. "Belief in a nonexistent Hell and Purgatory is the ultimate seduction of the Lords of Darkness. The truth is precisely the opposite of what Rome would have us think."

"Did Phillipa find a good death?" asked Corba.

A heavy silence was broken by coughs of grief. Esclarmonde sidled next to Corba and hugged her. "I believe in all my heart she did. She had a look of peace when . . ." She could not bring herself to speak further of that day in Carcassonne when Phillipa was released to the Light by Guilhelm's arrow.

The Marquessa had suffered too many tragedies to wallow in them again. "You must tell us at once how to make ready." Renewed in their determination, the women nodded and drew nearer to hear the instruction.

Esclarmonde closed her eyes to recall the details of what the Bishop had taught of the final passage from the body. "There are four stations. The first is called the Shedding of the Earth. Its approach will feel as if the channels within our spiritual body are losing their wind."

"I once experienced such a feeling," Chandelle whispered. "At Avignonet. When Jean left me that morning, I could hear the bindings release from his soul." She began weeping softly. "Why was I permitted only a few hours with him?"

Esclarmonde smiled sadly. She had asked Castres that same question about her stillborn daughter. "Was not that night you spent with him more blessed than the thousand others you have passed?"

"Yes."

"Then perhaps his purpose in coming into this world was fulfilled by showing you—showing all of us—the depths of true love."

Chandelle reached into the recesses of her robe and brought forth the flat stone that Jean had given her. "Will you tell me what he looked like?"

Esclarmonde could see that the stone had once held a drawing, but the charcoal had been smudged and partially erased. She hesitated, unsure of how to answer, for she was forbidden by her vows to speak a lie. "I see a beautiful soul who has reached the Light."

Smiling through tears, Chandelle placed the stone back into her robe pocket for safekeeping. "Will I be with him again?"

"Let us do our best to assure it," said Esclarmonde.

"The passage," asked the Marquessa. "Will it be painful?"

Esclarmonde so wished the Bishop were here to explain the arcana. She found it difficult to articulate the mysteries with his subtle clarity. His abiding love for his flock had survived to the end; too feeble to continue his mission in Aragon, he had been brought back to Montsegur to die. In his final hours, he had described each station to her as he passed through them. "He said it felt as if a great mountain were pressing against his chest. The knots that bind the wind in the channels will loosen like snapped moorings of a ship."

Corba clasped hands with her mother, fearful that this reliving of the Bishop's last moments might be too much for her to endure. "Are you certain you wish to hear this?"

"I must," said the Marquessa. "I am nearer joining him than any of you."

Esclarmonde lowered her voice to signal the gravity of what she would next impart. "Then comes the Draining of the Waters. A hazy gauze will spread over our vision, and our veins will release their fluids. When this stage arrives, we will know that our return to the Light is half accomplished. There will be no turning back."

Chandelle cried, "There will be more to endure?"

"Have patience," pleaded Esclarmonde. "Go through each door without rushing. The third station brings the Consummation of the Flame and a coldness ten times the intensity we have ever felt."

"Fire and cold?" exclaimed Corba. "You have lost me again!"

Esclarmonde searched for some means of demonstrating the paradoxical nature of this station. She rushed out to the cistern and returned with a bucket of chilled water. She placed Corba's right hand in the water and her left hand near the fire. "What do you feel?"

A perplexed look came over Corba's face. "I'm not certain."

"Hot and cold are two poles of our limited vision. When our corporeal senses are disintegrated, all opposites will merge into one."

"The last station!" begged the Marquessa, tiring quickly.

Esclarmonde circled the women. "What always accompanies fire?"

"Light!" Chandelle answered.

"A Light whose radiance will be beyond any you can imagine," promised Esclarmonde. "Its approach will be harbingered by a red windstorm. Sparks like dancing fireflies will appear before our eyes, and we will find it difficult to breathe. The air will move so swiftly that we won't be able to catch it. When we reach this maelstrom, we will know the passing is near."

"Blessed Jesus!" said the Marquessa. "How much time will we have?"

"The Scriptures say the sacred radiance will last both the blink of an eye and the eternity of creation."

"The opposites again," Chandelle whispered.

"When the Light comes," said Esclarmonde, "no matter how terrifying it may appear, we must embrace it with all our hearts."

wo weeks later, Esclarmonde sat with her perfectas in their morning meditation. The sun was rising earlier now, warming the chapel with the renewal of spring. The returning larks came fluttering to the window slits to serenade her with their trilling. Even the ceiling beams with their groans of expansion seemed to awaken from the winter freeze. The shimmering rays piercing the embrasures promised the kind of glorious Pyrenean day that she had so relished as a girl, when she would race Corba into the blooming fields to see who could pick the most daffodils.

She reproached herself for letting her mind wander. She always found the meditation most difficult during this time of the year when the mountains exploded with life and the fields blazed with the lavender tongues of toad lilies. Years ago, the courts of love would be held in May, usually on the Nones. The troubadours would arrive in gaudy silks from their hibernation in far-off places such as Mallorca and Sevilla and Rhodes. She wondered how many of them were still alive. The great Vidal had passed away in Aragon; his body was floated down the Ebro and ferried out to sea on a ceremonial barge in the fashion of the old Celtic bards. Cardenal, that flaming comet, disappeared soon after the disaster at Muret, never to be heard from again. Her favorite, Miraval, was so disheartened by the loss of Toulouse that he swore off singing, the only protest he could muster against this cracked world. How different their fates might have been had she not offered up Guilhelm as their challenger in—

Distant alarums echoed in her ear. A foreboding clutched at her breast. She opened her eyes and found the other women unstirred in their meditations, this time giving no heed to the interruption. They kept their breathing calm and even, just as they had been taught. The students, she lamented, had surpassed the teacher.

Raymond, gray-faced and breathless, rushed into the chapel.

She knew before he spoke a word. "Who commands the army?"

"The Seneschal of Carcassonne. He has brought ten thousand men. The Dominicans are with them."

Before the perfectas could make sense of the commotion, Esclarmonde hurried from the chapel and climbed to the ramparts with Raymond's assistance. Her heart was plunged into a frigid bath of despair. The valley churned with black smoke and the western face teemed with perfects scrambling up the pog to escape the pursuing French rutters. There was a searing familiarity to it all. It had been thirty-two years since she had watched a siege army make preparations. The horrid memories of Beziers and Carcassonne came flooding back to her. The gasping moment of terrifying calm was short-lived—the temple exploded in a maelstrom of confusion: women screaming, men shouting orders, birds shooting skyward in a whirlwind of flapping and cawing. Raymond broke open the arsenal and directed his sergeants to pass out the pikes and ballistae. She hurried across the allures and searched the stricken faces converging on the western gate below her. "Where is Loupe?"

"Holding off the French advance in the valley!" shouted Raymond.

Pierre-Roger came running up from the barbican. "If we move quickly, we can still break through to the east passage and reach Queribus."

"And leave these people to the mercy of the French?" said Raymond.

"We can't hold this rock with two hundred men."

Loupe corralled a band of Cathars up the path and led them into the safety of the temple. "I couldn't find them all in time."

"How many were captured?" asked Raymond.

"Fifty, maybe more," said Loupe. "If they break under torture, the French will know every inch of our defenses."

Pierre-Roger took an insistent step toward Raymond. "Do you need more convincing?" Receiving no indication, he pleaded his case to Loupe. "Talk some sense into him. The men will follow you."

The two contingents, one loyal to Raymond and the other to Pierre-Roger, stood on the walls awaiting the decision to stay or retreat. They turned toward Loupe, the linchpin that held the two commanders in yoke.

"How full is the cistern?" asked Loupe.

"Three months' supply at most," said Raymond.

Already parched from the forced climb, Loupe shielded her dry eyes from the sun. There was no well on this rock and the spring rains had been sparse. She had left the management of the cistern to Raymond, who postponed the transportation of additional water from the stream to finish erecting the barbican. Until now, she had not calculated how vulnerable their position truly was. Having seen firsthand the horrors that protracted thirst could inflict, she had vowed never to endure such a Hell again. Firmed in her decision, she tightened the clasps on her leather jerkin and told Pierre-Roger, "Take your men down and hold the gap. We'll follow with as many weapons as we can carry."

Esclarmonde was resigned to Loupe's abandonment of the pog. She turned without a word of protest and walked toward the chapel.

Loupe rushed after her. "You have no time for prayer! The Franks will be on these walls within hours!"

Esclarmonde ignored Loupe and grasped Corba's hands. "You and Chandelle go with the soldiers. Your mother cannot survive a march to Queribus. I will stay with her and care for those who haven't the strength to make the descent."

Riven by indecision, Corba embraced her husband and daughter, refusing to release them. There was nothing more she wished in this life than to abide the rest of her days in peace with them.

Raymond cast his eyes down, withered by Corba's importuning gaze. "The crusaders have destroyed our chateau at Mirepoix," he said, his voice trailing off. "We would live in exile."

"But we would *live*!" cried Corba.

Raymond kissed away her tears. "I cannot leave these people undefended. It is a dying code, I know. I am a relic of a passing age."

Stunned by his refusal to escape, Corba turned in desperation to Chandelle. "Convince your father to come with us."

Chandelle found her mother's distraught face and steadied it in her hands. "Jean sacrificed his life so that I could return to this temple. I can't believe I was brought back here only to leave again."

Corba weakened to her knees. She petitioned a dispensation from her family's duty to remain on the holy mount, but she knew such hope was in vain, for Esclarmonde held no spiritual authority over their souls.

When Raymond signaled his men to prepare the defenses, Pierre-Roger burned Esclarmonde with a galling scowl, incensed that she had managed to disrupt his strategy without uttering a word of contention. "Damn it, Perella! I can't break past the Seneschal's lines without your men!"

"Then our cause will be won or lost here," said Raymond.

Pierre-Roger tried to sway Raymond's troops. "We didn't come up here to be trapped and starved like rats! Follow me and we'll fight another day!"

The soldiers looked to Loupe for guidance, their nervous eyes flicking toward the cordon that the French were tightening in the valley. After a hesitation, Loupe walked across the bailey and joined Pierre-Roger. Some of the men released breaths of relief, but others stirred with misgivings. The prowess of the She-Wolf, the slayer of de Montfort, had become near mythical. She had led them against great odds in every campaign since Toulouse and they had come to trust her judgment. Yet in the past months, a few of the soldiers had developed a grudging admiration for the Cathars and their selfless ways. To abandon them would mean their certain death. A dozen or so remained on the walls, unwilling to accept such ignominy, but most finally broke ranks, averting their eyes in shame while girding their hauberks in preparation to descend the mount. Having won the standoff, Pierre-Roger punished his rival commander with a lording smile of conquest—until Bernard climbed from the allures and stood next to Raymond.

Loupe stared at Bernard with a silent accusation of betrayal.

Bernard took her aside. "What is a country without those who live in it? You never ran from a fight, not even from the Lion."

Loupe was stung by that reminder—no less because it came from the man who professed to love her. She glared with disdain at the Cathars who waited meekly to hear their fate. Only Corba among them had been willing to take up the offer of safe escort. Ignorant bastards! Why should she care a whit about them if they had no concern for their own lives? She could barely endure their presence, sniveling as they did in weakness, renouncing the world while others bled so they could warble their asinine prayers. Esclarmonde had cleverly forced her hand again. Her aunt would become a martyr, lionized for centuries while she herself would be blamed for abandoning these people.

Damn that woman! I'll not give her the satisfaction!

Loupe surveyed the ramparts and tried to imagine how a siege would play out in this cramped mausoleum. Their garrison would have the advantage of the heights and the French would have to fight without trebuchets. If she and Raymond could hold out for two months, the Northerners would become restive in the oppressive Ariege summer, as they always did. She shot a trumping glance at Esclarmonde, then turned to Pierre-Roger, refusing to meet his eyes. "Raymond and I will take our men down the west face. We'll do what we can to draw the French off and cover your retreat."

Pierre-Roger stood gape-jawed, unable to fathom her sudden change of heart. "Have these daft hermits infected you with their lunacy? If we're to have any chance, we must keep our forces combined."

Loupe strapped a crossbow to her back and loaded her side quiver with arrows. "Then you have a decision to make."

Pierre-Roger swung about in disbelief and watched as the rest of Raymond's men came to Loupe's side. He knew he stood little chance of breaking past the French with his small troop alone. He glowered at Esclarmonde, enraged that she had again managed to circumvent his authority. Left no choice, he angrily waved his charges toward the walls to help prepare the defenses. When Esclarmonde's back was turned, he chased her with an obscene gesture.

Armed with loops of hemp rope, Loupe and her contingent of seventy men slithered down the western face and threaded past the rows of barbican stakes that had been posted as the first barrier to the temple. The advent of spring had fleeced the pog with shrubby brush and copses of scrub trees, offering effective cover. Weeks earlier, she had made preparations to counter an assault by ordering slender tracks cut in the foliage on both sides of the switchback with gaps notched in the thicket to allow for the low firing of missiles. Halfway down the pog, she heard the rustling of leaves and breaking twigs. Darkening shadows were accompanied by foreign voices. She whistled for her men to fan out behind the boulders.

The serpentine path was so narrow that the French infantrymen, weighed down by broadswords and scaling ladders, were forced to march two abreast. She bit off a curse of discovery—the Northerners had brought arbalasters with large crossbows that could pierce metal armor. Innocent III had banned the heinous weapons from use against fellow Christians, but infidels and heretics, being deemed less than human, were excluded from the divine protection. The French began shedding their packs, certain that the resistance would be desultory. They kept their eyes trained on the looming fortress while arguing over how much heretic gold they would find.

Loupe held the itching bow fingers of her men at bay. The French vanguard passed so close that their boots were within reach. When the last of the Northerners straggled past, the Occitans threw the rope snares across the path and concealed them with leaves. She stalked the progress of the French, leapfrogging from boulder to boulder, remaining just out of their sight. Nimble as a ferret, she had the bewitching ability to quiet even the jackdaws from cawing on her approach. When the French came within a few paces from the barbican stakes, she took aim with her bow and fired.

The French sergeant straightened and fell.

On the heights, Pierre-Roger and his archers sprang up behind the barbican and let loose with their bows. So many zings filled the air that it sounded as if a nest of hornets had been overturned. Dull thuds of points could be heard impaling flesh. The harried French lurched back and scrambled to form ranks in the dense foliage, but they were unable to discern the direction of the attack. A second volley riddled their exposed legs again. Disoriented and deprived of their officer, they turned, only to be peppered by arrows from their rear. They dropped their weapons and retreated, dragging their wounded.

Loupe scurried down the worming path a few steps ahead of the panicked horde. She whistled the signal for her lurking men to pull taut the hidden ropes. Running blind, the Northerners tripped over the snares and fell tumbling in staves. Those who did not carom from the cliffs were picked off by Pierre-Roger's bowmen on the rocks above. Loupe and her Occitans salvaged the abandoned French weapons, including the precious crossbows.

Below the crag, Otto oversaw the unloading of his new traveling altar, quarried whole from a block of Angers granite and embellished with crockets and grooved columns that were filled with soil from the Holy Land. He ordered it set under a canopy in the center of the encampment where he could say mass framed by a panoramic view of the heretic temple. With the Archbishop of Narbonne not due to arrive until Whitsun Day, he was eager to cross-examine the cloggers and search their lair alone. Earlier that morning, he had sent the levies off on their climb with a rousing sermon from Deuteronomy, reminding them of Yahweh's command to Joshua to wage a war of extermination against the pagan inhabitants of Jericho.

To his dismay, the élan of his carefully crafted homily had been pricked by Hugh D'Arcis, the crusty, pouch-eyed Seneschal of the army. The commander sardonically remarked that the Israelites had been armed with magical horns to bring down Jericho and that the Dominican order, with all of its confiscated largesse, had yet to provide him with such a weapon. This cynical veteran of the western wars against England was embittered by the chafing irony of his new assignment. Defeated in Brittany by the England's Earl of Leicester—Simon de Montfort the younger, son of the deceased crusader—he was being punished with the task of cleaning up the one heretic stronghold that had eluded the father of his vanquisher. So consuming was the Seneschal's hatred of monks that Otto feared he might prove an impediment to the Dominican authority that he had so meticulously installed for this campaign.

While Otto burnished his altar vessels, a tumult of shouts roused him from debating how best to neuter his new agonist. He blinked in astonishment as hundreds of crazed soldiers came running down the pog. Their breeches were bloodied and torn to shreds and their gambesons were quilled with arrows, giving them the appearance of a herd of panicked, upright porcupines.

The Seneschal's serried mouth twitched in white-hot anger as he goaded his roan stallion into the midst of the shambled ranks. He hammered at their heads with the flat of his sword. "Who ordered you back down here? Where is that blind whoreson of a sergeant?"

"Drained dry of his blood!" cried one of the wild-eyed Franks. "The Devil's demons are on that rock!"

"I'll show you the Devil!" shouted the Seneschal, the rucks of his fearsome countenance as rough as emery. "How many?"

"At least five thousand. Maybe ten."

The Seneschal shot a jet of acidic chew into the coward's face, stunning him as if doused by Greek fire. The commander scissored the hapless man to his knees and bludgeoned his bald pate with the haft ball of his blade. "You rattlepated dungworm of a maggot! There aren't that many rebels left in the entire Languedoc!"

Otto came running up with his layered vestments flapping in the breeze like lugsails. Moist from the heat of exertion, he took great pains to keep his chalice level to avoid spilling the consecrated wine. Panting men toppled around him, skirling like castrated dogs and begging to slake their thirst. He held the holy contents of his cup above their outstretched hands, deeming the craven conscripts undeserving of nourishment from Christ's blood. In full hearing of these converging clusters, he seized on the shameful debacle to gain a measure of revenge against the Seneschal for the day's earlier humiliation. "I warned you that mount could not be taken by a direct assault."

Enraged by the imputation of incompetence, the Seneschal lashed at his horse's scarred flanks, causing the animal's hooves to stutter and nearly crush Otto's sandaled feet. "You'll get your damn heretics in due time! Until then, stay out of my way!"

Otto methodically drained the remaining drops from the chalice. He stifled an unholy belch and licked his lips to prevent any of the wine from touching profane ground. "You're off to an auspicious start."

The Seneschal's facial veins were on the verge of snapping when he saw a captured Occitan being dragged down the pog. He ordered the prisoner's neck stretched with a rope from a limb to speed his interrogation. "How many rebels are inside that stronghold?" he demanded.

The prisoner, one of Pierre-Roger's men, refused to speak—until the French officers yanked him airborne with heels kicking and dropped him before he passed out. Reviving with a mouthful of vomit, he looked up to find the Seneschal's blade hovering over him. He stammered, "Two hundred!"

The Seneschal angled his eyes in disbelief toward the pog's crest, unable to comprehend how so small an Occitan force could have repulsed a thousand of his well-armed infantry. The rebels had scouts all over these mountains and were too clever to be trapped up there with such a meagre garrison. The scoundrel was no doubt lying to purchase a few more hours of life. Having detected a familiar cadence in his screechy protests, the Seneschal retrieved a small bag of coins and threw it at the prisoner's feet. "You're a Gascon, no? You people are always selling your allegiances to the highest bidder."

The Gascon prisoner leered at the bribe, momentarily forgetting the painful lacerations that striped the bleeding flesh under his chin.

The Seneschal fingered one of the coins an inch from the Gascon's greedy face and allowed the silver's gaudy flashes to work their seduction. "The King of France will pay you twice what you earn from your rebel liege. And you will have the added advantage of living to spend it."

Unleashed, the Gascon crawled in every direction to retrieve the rest of the scattered treasure—until Otto kicked him in the ribs to reclaim his attention.

"Is there a woman on that rock named Esclarmonde?" demanded Otto.

"There's a whole brood of them go by the name. One's a useless blind nun. Another one fights like a man."

"The one I seek is aged," said Otto.

"Aye, she's up there. They all take orders from her. She sits in her church and performs magic."

Otto smiled at his superb fortune and began silently rehearsing the list of entrapping questions he would soon be inflicting on his perfidious mother.

"How strong are the defenses?" asked the Seneschal.

The prisoner pecked at the grass for the rest of the coins like a rooster in a thrashing stall. "The west side of the scarp can't be taken. Those sabot priestesses mixed the blood of beasts into the mortar to strengthen the walls on that side." He nearly had all the silver in his grasp when the Seneschal dragged him back by the noose, causing him to spill his haul in order to loosen the rope's bite. He rasped coughing and kicking, "There's a shepherd's trail up the other side. Only a small tower and a barbican protect it."

The Seneschal made a dubious study of the eastern approach to the Cathar temple. He kicked the Gascon prisoner off on a yelping roll toward one of the officers. "Take him up with a scouting party after midnight. If the defenses are not as he says, drop him off those cliffs with his Judas bag tied to his neck."

Ye are the Light of the World.
A city that is set on a hill cannot be hidden.
- The Gospel of Matthew

XXXV

Montsegur

December 1243

A sentinel's cry broke the tenuous stillness of Christmas Eve.

As if a log infested with stag beetles had been overturned, the Cathars crawled from their shelters on the terraces below the temple and lifted their pallid faces to a heavenly gift more blessed than manna. Tortured by thirst, they sprawled on all fours and licked the falling snow from the rocks along the narrow crest that had been spoliated of every stripling and sprout of vegetation.

Esclarmonde scooped a wet dollop and savored it on her swollen tongue. Wheezing from the cold in her lungs, she pressed another handful to her burning forehead and shrieked—she had uncovered the bloated corpse of a perfect whose bulging eyes were congealed in their last rivet of terror. She bent to retch, but her stomach held nothing to evacuate. With the ground too frozen to dig graves, she had ordered the corpses stacked against the north wall rather than be rolled down the mount to suffer mutilation. She drew an ice-laced breath to chase the nausea and reminded herself that the remains were only the luring sheaths of the Demiurge. Fearing the onset of catalepsy, she slogged toward the temple, which was shrouded in a blizzard of whiteness. A dark clump near the gate was fast disappearing under the snow, already four fingers deep. She thrashed closer and found Corba unconscious in the sweeping drifts. She shook Corba's shoulders until she opened her eyes. "You must keep moving!"

Corba's head sank against the back of her neck. "Let me sleep."

"Raymond needs you."

Enlivened by that reminder, Corba flailed spread-eagled across the snow in a manic search. "Raymond! Where are you?"

"Calm yourself," pleaded Esclarmonde. "He defends the tower."

A hundred paces below them, the bonfires along the barbican fought for life against a stiffening gale that roared up the crystallized spine. Under the lee of the low wall, Loupe and Raymond crouched with their paltry garrison shivering in their frayed mantles. The temperature had dropped precipitously after dusk, forcing them to hold their bows near the fires to prevent the strings from freezing. They took turns inching their eyes above the stones to check that the French were not launching an attack. No communication had been received from Toulouse since the siege began six months ago, but they still held out hope that Count Raymond was mustering an army to repulse the crusaders. After scaling the eastern approach, the French had thrown up a moveable barricade of bundled stakes, shrinking the battlefield to a sliver of jagged rock no wider than the breadth of the temple. The bottleneck between the barbican and gate was so narrow that only four men could traverse it at one time. The Occitans still held the advantage of the steep slope, but the Northerners brought up more men each night and tightened their ring to cut off escape attempts.

Seething at the French taunts, Loupe pressed her knees against the string of her crossbow in preparation to retaliate, but Raymond signaled for her to lower the weapon. The few arrows they possessed were too valuable to waste on idle vengeance. A stone's throw away, the boisterous invaders enjoyed a Yuletide feast of roasted chicken, almond soup, and a barrel of claret sent as a gift by Blanche from Paris. For amusement, the French heaved their refuse over the palisades and watched with insufferable hoyden as the starving Occitans pounced on the chicken bones to suck the marrow.

At the temple, Corba stirred from her languor and cocked an ear toward a distant chorus in the darkness. "What is that melody?"

"The Franks are singing carols," said Esclarmonde. "The Dominicans have no doubt told them that we don't believe in Christ. They think the Noel hymns will anger us."

"Listen to them!" cried Corba. "They're laughing at us."

The scratchy Gascon accents scattered among the French voices caused

Esclarmonde to think of Jourdaine. His hand had inflicted the same prickly numbness she now suffered in this bitter cold. It would be so easy to lie down and die this night, to retire to her hut and ascend in the Chariot for the last time. She quickly chased such thoughts of abandoning her flock and forced Corba to speed the blood back to her toes by walking and stomping her feet. "The sun will be up soon. The French must not see us like this. We should replenish the cistern before they discover we are out of water."

Drugged by enervation, the Cathar women moved slowly but did their best to follow Esclarmonde's example by scraping the snow with their bowls and carrying their pitiful collections to a vat that hung over a fire. When they had melted as much water as their flagging stamina allowed, Esclarmonde ordered them to return to their huts for rest. She dragged Corba falling and crying into the Marquessa's sparse hovel. The matriarch, colored the hue of chalk, lay on the frozen dirt floor next to the wraithlike Chandelle, their shaking arms entwined. The hearth embers had died, costing the room what little warmth had been trapped. Esclarmonde lowered Corba next to Chandelle and tried to blow life back into the coals.

"I'm sorry," rasped Chandelle. "I couldn't keep the fire tended."

Chandelle's graveled voice was alarmingly altered. Esclarmonde pressed a hand to her sunken chest. The moist swell of mucous in her lungs had risen, a portent of the flux. "There is little wood left to burn anyway." She jangled her bowl to melt the ice and placed a drop on the Marquessa's tongue.

The Marquessa lurched up in a fit of coughing. "What day is it?"

"Almost Christmas," promised Esclarmonde. "On the morrow I will ask Raymond to distribute the last of the lentils."

"Has that snake de Montfort slithered back to Paris?"

Esclarmonde was about to remind her that Simon de Montfort was long dead and buried, but she thought it best to say nothing. Her spectral godmother's failing memory was in truth a small blessing, a place of refuge for her to escape the present horrors. Seeing Chandelle trying to quell her own tremors, Esclarmonde raised the cup to the blind perfecta's lips while steadying her head. "Your humours have worsened. I'll try to find another robe."

"It's nothing," said Chandelle. "Is there word from Father?"

"He still holds the tower. You needn't worry about him."

Despite Chandelle's blindness, Esclarmonde reflexively averted her glance; that was as near a lie as she had uttered since taking the vow. Morale was low. The stores of salted meat and pickled vegetables had long since been consumed, and what little remained of the fava beans, raisins, and honey in the larder was carefully rationed each morning, one handful to the soldiers, half that amount to her Cathars. The strict diet of their faith had proved a mixed blessing; she and her followers were accustomed to small portions, but they had built no reserve of fat to draw on. They had also used up the last of the herbs required to treat the fever that was spreading rapidly. In sieges past, the suffering had been confined to the summers. Unfathomable as it seemed, she now held the blistering heat of Carcassonne preferable to this wretched cold.

"Minerve and Termes lasted less than three months," said Chandelle. "No one gave us a chance to make it until winter. God is watching over us."

Another blast of wind rattled the hut. Raymond entered breathless from running the gauntlet from the barbican. His somber face was sheeted with ice and his hands trembled from the freezing air.

Corba clutched at him. "My love! Stay with me."

Raymond slid to his haunches and pressed his forehead to Corba's cheek. To his dismay, he saw that he was only making her colder. He surrendered to her uxorial ministrations and allowed her to blow warmth to his eyes and straighten his bent fingers, anything that might extend the illusion that she still nurtured a home for him. He attempted a smile that died with a spasm of coughing. "I'll rest a moment. I shouldn't think the French will attempt the wall this night. They're too sated on wine and roasted fowl."

Esclarmonde offered Raymond what remained of the melted snow. He forced it down his seared throat, gulping painfully. After a few minutes of this rare respite, he made known to her with a dart of his eyes that he required a private conference. Each night, he reported to her alone on the progress of the fighting. Before leaving, he gently repulsed Corba's attempt to keep him in her arms and pressed a kiss to her cheek. "I'll return after my rounds, darling."

Esclarmonde was assisted by Raymond's hand to her elbow as they made their inspection circuit. The temple was hauntingly quiet, a ship run aground in a frozen sea of ice. The only signs of life were the steam plumes rising from the breaths of soldiers huddled along the walls. Raymond's gait was slowed and uneven, and he seemed unsteady, as if his sight and balance were out of kilter. He was a stalwart, optimistic man, never one to utter a complaint, but on this night his spirits were so wan that he was barely able to speak.

"Corba is melting away," he whispered.

Esclarmonde gently squeezed his cracked fingers to instill courage. "Come to her as often as you can. Your presence is worth a day's ration."

"I fear there will come a time when she won't recognize me."

"It is in God's hands . . ." Her voice trailed off. She found it increasingly difficult to talk of a divine purpose amid such devastation, particularly in the presence of the soldiers. They suffered even more than her followers, for they were unable to let down their guard and retreat into meditation lest the French ambush them. Watching Corba sink into Raymond's embrace, she had felt a pang of envy for their mutual emotional sustenance. He was neither a man of strong faith nor a skilled warrior like her brother, but he fought for principles of chivalry and love of family, and she had never known a more selfless soul. "Will Loupe be relieved of the watch tonight?"

"You know her. She's as stubborn as your brother was."

Esclarmonde could just make out the round, satisfied faces of the French warming themselves over their fires beyond the barbican. How plump and healthy they appeared, as if they had been engendered from another race of men. "They've made it so near our line."

"Twenty more came up today."

"Will they attempt the walls?"

"They outnumber us ten to one, but it would be a risky gambit even with such advantage. If we repulsed them, they could be hurled off the cliffs."

"What kind of man is this D'Arcis?"

"Cunning but not impetuous. I almost yearn for the erstwhile days. At least with de Montfort we were assured of a quick resolution."

She searched the French lines for some sign of the black-robed friars. "The Dominicans are not on the summit?"

"Safe and warm within their tents in the vale. The Archbishop of Narbonne leads the cabal of inquisitors. Some of the men also overheard the French speak of a firebrand called Brother Otto."

Esclarmonde's heart seized, but she quickly dismissed the possibility. Her Otto was a Cistercian, that much she knew. She had received reports that Folques had sent her son to Rome to serve in the Curia. During the weeks prior, she had not asked Raymond the paramount question on her mind for fear she would be compelled by the dictates of her faith to communicate his answer to the others. On this eve, however, she needed to know the truth. "Raymond, what are our chances?"

He looked toward the scudding darkness above the distant peaks, hoping the clouds might spin out an auspicious augury. "If we can hold on until the March rains, the cistern will be replenished and the birds will fly within range of our bows. God willing and spring arrives early, the berries and roots will sustain us until relief arrives. But if Pierre-Roger . . ." He shook his head in self-chastisement for having broached that subject. He had vowed never to speak ill of his fellow officer, even if the man had become a thorn in his side with his constant complaints and challenges.

"You fear the French may try to purchase his loyalty?"

"He broods, and his men are restless," said Raymond. "I've mixed my knights in with his on the watches just to be safe."

The faint thrum of a chant could be heard coming from the chapel. Esclarmonde pressed a fortifying kiss to Raymond's cheek. "I've promised them a sermon . . . in truth, I don't know what to say."

Raymond drew a gelid breath in preparation to make the dangerous run back to the barbican. "You'll find the right words. You always do."

The bone-thin Cathars and wounded soldiers who had crowded inside the chapel attempted to rise in reverence. Esclarmonde bade them remain on the floor to conserve their strength. She had ordered a roof beam splintered for firewood; snow sifted through the cracks and dusted the floor. She walked among them trying to find an explanation for the torment they now endured because of her faith. She stoked the reluctant fire in the hearth and watched as the chapel began to glow with a lambent radiance. "How precious is this flame. And yet, do you see how its warmth is not diminished when more of us seek its comfort?" She retrieved a candle, the last in her possession, saved for this night. She lit the wick and, cupping the flame to prevent its guttering, passed it down the line for each person to bathe in its blessing. "Why would our Lord have chosen to be born into a world of—"

The creak of the door interrupted her sermon.

Loupe stood at the portal. Accosted by expressions of disbelief, she reconsidered and reached for the latch to leave, but Esclarmonde captured her hand in welcome. Balmed by the warmth, Loupe reluctantly took a seat behind the others, uncertain of how she should act, for this was the first time that she had attended a Cathar service.

Esclarmonde offered Loupe the candle to thaw her face and continued the sermon. "It must have been on just such a night as this that Jesus looked down on this world and made His fateful decision. The Lords of Darkness had ordered all firstborns murdered. Mary and Joseph were forced to leave their home. They sought shelter in a warm inn but were turned away, just as we are turned away this night. Their only refuge was a manger warmed by a solitary candle. Jesus saw that faint flicker and came to us that night. Why? He came to show us the way back to the Light. He came because if a single spark is left stranded, the Eternal Flame will never be complete."

Chandelle edged closer. "Will He come again?"

Before Esclarmonde could answer, Loupe stood in protest. "He didn't come for those at Beziers! Or for those at Minerve and Lavaur! Why would this god of yours save us now?"

"He did not come into this world to save our bodies," said Esclarmonde. "He did not come into this world to save His *own* body."

Loupe's frozen face was strafed with despair. "The Catholics say their bodies will be resurrected on the Day of Judgment, and ours will burn."

"If your arm is severed, are you not still the same person?"

"Of course, but—"

"Then are we not more than our flesh?"

"Why then would Christ take on flesh if it's only a prison?" asked Loupe.

"To demonstrate that what we see and feel and hear is merely a mirage," said Esclarmonde. "Our senses are a trickery perpetrated by the Demiurge. Sheep kept penned all of their lives do not see the opened gate. The Lords of Darkness did not kill Our Lord. They did not kill Him because He was not His body."

Loupe folded her arms in defiance. "I've watched too many die to believe that something blessed occurs at that moment."

"I don't ask you to accept it unless it is first shown to you as truth. When the time comes, you will know it with—"

Distant screams rolled up the eastern spine. The congregants rushed out and found Raymond and his men dragging up three wounded soldiers.

Esclarmonde cried, "Are the defenses breached?"

Raymond was too dazed to form an answer.

Esclarmonde saw Pierre-Roger and his men fighting off an assault at the barbican. Above them loomed a long, slender shadow, cast ghoulishly by the enemy's tapers. She prayed that the cold and hunger were playing games with her mind, but the gut-wrenching image, more at home in some perverse bestiary, would not fade from view. A towering wooden arm—the tallest she had ever seen was being cranked back and bent unnaturally with the groaning twist of a coiled rope. The air seemed to have been sucked from creation; not a breath could be heard. When the diabolical arm was on the verge of breaking, the skein ratchet released and the sling recoiled with such a wrenching bawl that it sounded like a bull being slaughtered. The sky was too overcast for her to see what had been launched. The ominous whistling grew louder and culminated in a skidding crash somewhere in the darkness along the defenses. She had heard that same horrid thud of destruction below the ramparts of Carcassonne and Foix.

Raymond could barely utter the words. "They've brought up a trebuchet."

That report was met by groans of anguished disbelief.

"Those beams are too large to have been carted up on sleds," insisted Loupe.

"They strapped the timbers to their backs," said Raymond. "The Bishop of Narbonne was trained as an engineer. I should have foreseen it."

Esclarmonde tried to gauge the distance between the trebuchet and the temple's north wall. "Can their stones reach us?"

"No, but if they take the barbican . . ." The prediction died on his lips.

Loupe finished it for him. "They'll set the engine at the tower. And then no place on this mount will be out of their range."

During the calamitous days that followed, the Occitan barbican was relentlessly reduced to a heap of stones. Nights were the worst. The darkness prevented the watch guards from predicting the arc of the missiles and the blind whistling spawned more terror than the impacts.

Each morning, Raymond took roll to determine how many of his men had survived the bombardment. The French inched closer by the hour, stalking the temple like wolves frothing to pounce on a stunned prey. Two thousand crusaders now crowded the far angle of the eastern crest and clamored for an assault, no longer fearful of being driven off the cliffs. Barely half the Occitans were hale enough to raise a sword, and those took turns standing guard, a duty that required shouting warnings when the next stone was launched. The severely wounded languished in the bailey with no shelter over their heads. The perfectas, bereft of essential medicinals and bandages, tended to them as best they could.

As dusk fell on the seventh night of the bombardment, Loupe crawled to Raymond's foxhole. "We can't hold this position. They'll be on us by morning if we sit here and do nothing."

"Launch!" screamed Bernard.

The Occitans ducked under their battered shields. The whistling dropped an octave. The stone exploded against the palisades and rained shards.

Bernard peered out from his hole. "If we give up this wall, that chateau will become our ossuary."

"We have to disable their sling," said Loupe.

"That's a dead man's lunacy!" protested Pierre-Roger. "We can't lift our heads without getting brained."

"If you have another plan," challenged Loupe, "let's hear it."

While they argued, Raymond watched as the sun disappeared over the distant peaks and gave way to the slender arc of a quarter moon. If they waited another night, the waxing lunar light would deny them what slim advantage the darkness provided. Reluctantly, he ordered Pierre-Roger, "Divide the men by blind lots. Give those who draw the assignment an extra ration."

An hour after midnight, Loupe returned from the temple with what few loops of extra rope she had managed to scavenge. Having drawn one of the black stones, Bernard was assigned to lead the raid. While testing the temper of his sword, he saw Loupe throw a bundle over her shoulder. "What do you think you're doing?" When she refused to acknowledge his question, he crawled closer to confront her. "You agreed to abide by the fate of the draw."

"I don't believe in fate."

"There's never a dearth of killing here," said Bernard. "Why must you always go looking for it?" She tried to deflect his challenge by occupying herself with fastening and checking the knots. He grasped her shoulders roughly and spun her to face him. "Answer me!"

She was shaken by his raw anger, so uncharacteristic. Turning from his demanding gaze, she revealed in a barely audible voice, "I don't want you to go alone."

The heat in Bernard's face melted into astonishment. He pulled into his embrace. For the first time, she did not resist his advances. He kissed her passionately and whispered, "I don't want to go the rest of my life alone."

She could not meet his eyes. "If I agree to marry you . . . You must promise to come back alive from this raid."

Bernard pulled from his belt pouch the gold wedding band that he had purchased years ago. He took her hand and tried to slide it onto her finger, but the ring was too large. He fashioned a makeshift necklace from a strand of twine and hung it around her neck. This time, it was Loupe, eyes tearing, who took him into her embrace and stole his breath with a kiss.

Disgusted by their maudlin lock of affection, Pierre-Roger snapped a half-hearted signal for the raiders to be off on the mission that he had no faith would succeed. Those chosen to remain behind guttered their torches and began singing ballads to muffle their comrades' exertions. Bernard and Loupe, accompanied by forty men, slithered on their stomachs toward the north cliffs. One-by-one, they fastened the ropes to pinions and descended over the pendent edge. They rappelled in silence along the sheer face toward their target, a precarious drop on the far side of the barbican. One false step meant certain death.

Loupe was the first to breast the French side of the ledge. After several blind attempts, she gained a foothold. She bit on her tongue to sharpen her jangled senses as she inched her eyes over the precipice. She had calculated perfectly—she was several feet behind the crusader line. A few steps from her straining hands, a Gascon guard leaned on a pike. The camp was enveloped by the snoring darkness. She tugged the rope in a signal for the others to swing across the cliff. The trebuchet stood thirty paces away, protected by several armed men. She strangled the guard from behind and brought forward the crossbow strapped to her back. She ignited the tip of her missile with a flint against a rock and fired the flaming arrow into the wooden palisade.

The French wall erupted in flames. The crusaders surrounding the trebuchet rushed to the palisade and flailed at the conflagration with their cloaks. When the French were distracted, Bernard and his Occitans silently climbed the crest and heaved their torches into the engine.

"Attack!" screamed an alerted crusader.

Those crusaders who had been sleeping on the far cusp of the spine roused from their bivouac. Raymond's reserves slowed the reinforcements with a punishing volley. Confused by the attacks from both front and rear, the crusaders beat another retreat to the burning palisade. The crossfire tactic purchased Loupe a few seconds more. Black smoke coughed up from the engine's entrails as arrows cut the ground around her. She begged the flames to grow faster.

A phalanx of crusaders appeared over the brow of the spine.

"Get away!" Bernard turned back and fought off the first wave of attackers. He fell with blood gushing from his thigh artery—an arrow had bored through his femur. A Gascon mercenary ran up to finish his kill. He staggered backwards and looked down at a ragged hole in his chest.

Loupe dropped her spent crossbow. She ran to Bernard and dragged him toward the burning palisades. He screamed in agony, "Leave me!"

The other raiders had retreated to the ropes, believing their assignments accomplished. Hearing Bernard's shouts, several clambered back up to the crest. The French were waiting for them. They cut the ropes and sent the Occitans plunging to their deaths.

Choked by the smoke, Loupe kicked at the flaming palisade stakes and finally caved a hole. She heaved Bernard through the snaking fire and pushed him across the barbican. "Run!"

"My leg's broken!" he cried.

Loupe wrapped his arm around her neck and stumbled with him across the no-man's-land. Raymond led a charge from the barbican to give them cover. Esclarmonde and the Cathars ran from the temple to help carry Bernard to the gate. "Don't die!" screamed Loupe, collapsing. "You promised!"

The next morning, Otto hurried up the path along Montsegur's eastern spine to examine the scene of the previous night's raid. Informed by a courier of the attempt to destroy the engine, he was forced to cut short his first visit to Foix. He had decided to explore that notorious incubator of heresy despite a boyhood vow to Folques never to step foot in the city of his birth. He justified this breach of faith with the need to find witnesses who could arm him with evidence for Esclarmonde's impending interrogation. In truth, he had long burned with a curiosity to see the place of his abandonment.

His fact-finding mission, however, had left him morose and disillusioned. Commandeered by his fellow Dominicans for a regional headquarters, the somnolent burgh had been repopulated with bastide settlers and was nothing like the descriptions he had heard of it during his youth. The few inhabitants old enough to have witnessed his mother's meteoric rise in sin were either senile or refused to admit knowing her. The hall where his stepfather had suffered his great ignominy—yes, the legend of that pivotal confrontation was still passed down in the abbeys—was being used to store livestock fodder. He had found a faint residue of blue paint and gold stars on its concave ceiling. Standing among the hay bales there, he tried to imagine that painted Delilah in those carnal courts fluttering her beguiling lashes to inflame the passions of weak-willed men.

Folques had never spoken to him of that day, but Otto had witnessed the pain in his stepfather's eyes whenever a troubadour song was sung on the street. The room of his birth was now a gossamer-clotted brooding den for spiders and rats. St. Volusien's Church, the site of his baptism, stood a roofless shell overgrown with ivy, its consecration font cracked and fouled by the pigeons that had confiscated it for a splashing bath. In the chateau's bailey, a sinkhole had caved into the limestone, giving one the eerie sense that the looming rock was about to crumble like the salt pillars of Sodom. Heeding the biblical admonition for rejected prophets, he had hurried away shaking the heretical dust from his soles, grateful to have been saved as a babe from the wretched place.

The Seneschal broke a caustic grin as Otto arrived for his first appearance on the heights of the Montsegur pog. "Here's a propitious omen, lads. Circling vultures and tonsured scalps after a battle are certain signs of victory."

Otto ignored the taunt and searched the detritus strewn across the rocks for wounded captives to interrogate, but the crusaders had cut the throats of the few Occitans who survived the fight. "This attempt was madness. They're near the end of their resistance."

"The military genius has spoken!" roared the Seneschal. "Let's give the poor bastards the good news." He signaled for the charred trebuchet to be tested. The stretched arm groaned ominously but survived the recoil. Reassured by its continued effectiveness, the Seneschal turned to his officer. "How many men did the Ocs lose?"

"At least thirty."

"Do they still relieve their barbican watch at night?"

"They don't have the reserves to risk it."

The Seneschal studied the depleted ranks of the Occitans who manned the temple walls. "How many days until you breach it?"

"These people die hard," said the officer. "Another month, at least."

The Seneschal set his teeth in a grimace. The siege was six months behind schedule and had cost him four times the men allotted for the campaign. "That snake in Toulouse could arrive any day to relieve them. Then we'll be the ones trapped like rats. I'm not inclined to sit on this iceberg for the rest of the winter."

Otto was alarmed by the commander's weakening resolve. "The Queen Mother has ordered you to persist until the mount is taken."

The Seneschal cuffed Otto with his shoulder as he walked away. "I answer to the King, not to that witless woman. Support for this diversion is fast waning in the royal court. When I advise the exchequer of the mounting costs, he will convince Louis to overrule—"

"I can take that wall in one night."

Otto and the Seneschal turned to discover the source of that absurd claim. A red-bearded Basque ruffian, accompanied by a small band of mercenaries, had been listening to their argument. These tall, wiry Basques from Navarre—whose name derived from the ancient Celtic word for summit—had only recently joined the royal army. They were a brutish mountain people, half-Spanish and half-goat, born with stubborn temperaments that made them better bandits than subjects to king or pope. For centuries they had been held in low esteem for the dastardly role they had played in attacking the great Roland during his retreat across the Pyrenees with Charlemagne. The French officers laughed at the foolish woodsman and dismissed his burly cohorts as inbred descendents of a depraved race.

The Seneschal did not join in the ridicule. With an incipient smile, he circled the hirsute braggart and examined the fur skins he wore for breeches. "Tell me more."

The Basque gnawed methodically on a green shoot of chamomile, displaying not a whit of concern about protocol in the presence of the commander. "We'll attack them from the rear."

The Seneschal snorted in disbelief at the man's reckless boast. "Your brain has become addled from those opiate weeds you graze on. There is no rear. Their defenses are built to the edge of the cliffs."

The Basque parted his black-stained lips and aimed the gap in his front teeth like the porthole of a war galley. He spat a stream of mossy chaw over the precipice in a deft arc, chasing a crow perched on a ledge several hundred feet below. "Where I come from, this ass pimple would be too flat to live on. Of course, we'll require compensation."

"You're already drawing two francs a day," reminded the Seneschal.

"And we'll be content to sit by and collect them while you bang your bloody heads against that wall."

The Seneschal tried to browbeat a concession from the man with a snarling glare, but the Basque would not be moved off his demand. Finally, the commander gave up with a contemptuous huff and accepted the arrangement, if for no other reason than it might provide a modicum of amusement to chase the boredom of the siege. "A thousand francs if my trebuchet is in range of the heretic hold within the week."

"A thousand *each*," countered the Basque.

"I should string you up for Jewing the crown."

Undaunted, the Basque curled a stubble-rimmed grin. "You have ten thousand conscripts draining your coffers each day you sit up here on your powdered ass. Not to mention the gold you're wasting on this slingshot. Another month and you'll be bankrupt. My offer is a bargain."

The Seneschal begrudged a nod of admiration for the Basque's brass, rare enough among these degenerates and fools that he had been supplied for soldiers. He threw the rope at the man's boots and ordered his sergeant, "See to it he doesn't steal me blind."

The sign of your having this Light
is your vision of the end.

- Rumi

XXXVI

Montsegur

January 1244

Alert to every voice on the pog, Loupe crouched behind the eastern gate and sipped her ration of root broth, keeping it awash in her parched mouth for as long as possible. To thwart the French bowmen from taking accurate aim, she had delayed her return run for the barbican until the sun's tawny filaments were swallowed by the horizon. As darkness finally prevailed, she tightened the bindings on her battered shield and darted across the defile under the cover of rocks thrown by her comrades.

Raymond pulled her into his dugout. "Bernard?"

She cursed her eyes for wasting precious fluids in tears. "The fever hasn't broken." She had endured the privations and freezing better than most, but a sharp burning had begun to eat at her lungs and at times she would lose the feeling in her right arm. "You need rest."

"I can't risk it," said Raymond.

Pierre-Roger called out, "Perella, listen to her!"

The claustrophobic mirk along the spine crawled with shadows. On the night prior, some of the Occitans, disoriented and jittery, had fired on their own. Every vein of ice and shoot of vegetation on their side had been grubbed, but just beyond their reach lay three inches of pristine snow. The French amused themselves by loosing rabbits and shooting them when they scampered close to the defenders. One of the Occitans became so crazed by the torment that he flung himself over the wall. He might have made it back with his catch had he not lingered to slake his thirst. The Northerners used his riddled corpse for target practice.

"Some of the perfects have offered to crouch at our stations to give us a few hours of sleep," whispered Loupe. "If we make the exchange at night, the Franks will think we're only changing the watch."

Raymond blinked in a desperate effort to compose his fragmented mind. The slouching men stared at him with veiled, unfocused eyes. They would soon be of no use if he did not find a way to get them off the line. "I'll take half with me. Keep the sentinels posted at all times. Is that understood?"

Pierre-Roger kicked at him. "I'm not some wet-eared milksop who's never manned a watch! Be gone with you."

After passing the orders down the barbican, Raymond and Loupe led twenty soldiers up the defile, keeping low to prevent the French from spying their departure. Minutes later, Loupe returned from the temple with the volunteers. She supplied the perfects with hauberks and helmets to disguise the substitution. Pierre-Roger tossed over a few swords and shields. The perfects declined the weapons and lowered to their knees clutching their copies of the Gospel of John, which they kept wrapped in reliquaries under their tunics.

Pierre-Roger stuck his nose into the face of a Cathar to test the depth of his meditation. "This one will make a fine guard."

"Leave him be," ordered Loupe.

"Since when did you become so enamored with these cloggers?"

Loupe took aim with her dagger. "My aunt may have been right about you."

Pierre-Roger dared her. "Must be a family weakness. I should've—"

A loud honking cut the darkness behind them. Loupe rubbed her bleared eyes—a plump goose waddled across the rocks. She was about to dismiss it as a hunger vision when Pierre-Roger and his men dropped their blades and gave chase, leaving the Cathars abandoned at the barbican. The spooked bird darted for shelter under the limestone crevices. She could already taste the succulent meat. With no chance to outrun the others, she loaded her bow and took aim, steadying her thrumming hand and—

A sharp jolt slammed her shoulders and drove her into the frozen ground. She rolled to one side to avoid a sword thrust inches from her ribs.

A grinning Basque stood over her.

She blocked his next blow with her boot and kicked the weapon from his grasp. Disarmed, he lunged atop her and dangled her head over the cliff.

I am dying.

The Basque bolted stiff and fell from the scarp with his entrails impaled by a pike. Loupe staggered to her feet and found a dazed perfect staring in horror at his murdering hands. She dragged him to his knees seconds before a volley of barbed arrows whizzed over their heads. Dozens of the Basque mercenaries spawned across the spine like dragon's teeth. More rappelled across the scarp and swarmed over the ledge. The Cathars who had been left behind at the barbican lay dead with their throats cut.

Loupe screamed, "Attack!"

The Occitans rushed back to the barbican, too late. Their weapons had been thrown from the precipice. Outnumbered, they were driven into the chateau.

The French wasted no time in repositioning their trebuchet behind the captured Occitan barbican. By morning, the aerial onslaught had decimated the shamble of Cathar huts on the north face of the pog.

Inside the pockmarked temple, Esclarmonde was surrounded by more than two hundred starving believers and half that many soldiers, many badly injured. Loupe knelt aside Bernard, whose swollen leg had become black with infection. The ill and dying were laid against the south wall with no shelter save for a few crumbling planks. Those soldiers who could stand shared the few swords and bows that had been stored in the reserve armory. The panic caused by the constant pounding was doubled by the wailing of the wounded. Volunteers braved the parapet brattice and tried to predict the landing spot of the launched stones. Below them, the Occitans thronged together in a collective terror. To increase their misery, the French hurled over sacks of dung soaked in urine to douse the cramped confines with a noxious stench.

Esclarmonde crawled among her flock to offer the only consolation at her disposal, the touch of the Light, a ministration that drained her own flagging energy. She knew that unless a miracle was soon granted, all was lost. She asked Raymond, Loupe, and Pierre-Roger to join her inside the crumbling chapel. She stood in impotent silence at the embrasure and watched the funnel of smoke that curled aimlessly from the signal tower of Roquefixade three leagues away, their only means of communication with the outside world.

Pierre-Roger waited to hear a reason for the summons. Receiving none, he said, "If we give up the chateau, the French will allow my soldiers to leave."

"What will happen to my people?" asked Esclarmonde.

Pierre-Roger would not look at her. "I am responsible for my men only."

"There will be no surrender!" insisted Raymond.

"All you give a damn about are those cloggers!"

Raymond grappled him. "Had you had stayed at your post!"

Esclarmonde separated the two men, swirling with vertigo from the effort. "Count Raymond must not be aware of our dire predicament."

Loupe stood apart in the corner, lost in her thoughts. Finally, she said, "Roquefixade may have fallen. The French could be keeping the signal fire stoked to confuse us. We have to get a message out from here."

"No man can get through those lines," said Raymond.

Loupe slid to her haunches, too tired to remain standing. "No man . . . but I will."

That promise was met by astounded silence. Esclarmonde was stunned to find that Raymond did not immediately countermand the foolish plan. "You must order her not to attempt it."

"I won't sit on this rock and wait to die," said Loupe. "I'll try the northwest face. The French line is weakest there."

When neither commander voiced a protest, Esclarmonde reluctantly drew her niece aside. "You are certain of this?"

"It's the only way."

"Take some of Raymond's men with you."

"He can't spare them. I'll stand a better chance if I go alone."

Resigned to Loupe's insistence, Esclarmonde asked Raymond, "Have we any parchment left?"

Raymond thought for a moment, then he removed from his hauberk the letter that Corba had written to him on their wedding night.

"I couldn't use this," said Esclarmonde.

Raymond refused the letter's return. "I would flay the skin from my back if it would keep Corba and Chandelle alive."

Esclarmonde carefully spread open its creased quarters, ragged and torn from having been opened a thousand times. Splotches from tears past had smeared the ink. She saw that Corba had written her favorite of Capellanus's maxims on the margin: *Love can deny nothing to Love.* She wiped the mist from her eyes and turned the letter over to its blank side, then swabbed a sharpened nib with charcoal from the hearth. Her hand shook so fiercely that she had to press her arm against the lintel to brace it as she wrote:

My dearest Count Raymond,

At this hour, your loyal subjects are in the final throes of the King's unlawful siege on Montsegur. Occitania, and all that is cherished in chivalry and freedom of the heart, shall perish if you do not hasten to our aid. My brother, whose soul cries out from the crimes committed on his remains, never failed to heed your call. I pray you not let this stain be laid upon the legacy of your forefathers, who were never known to delay in the defense of all that is noble and good.

Yours in faith, Viscountess de Foix

She picked up a limestone chip that had fallen from the altar and placed it into a draw sack with the folded parchment. She would have the small comfort of knowing that at least one remnant of her temple would escape obliteration. "What do we have left in the larder?"

"A few piles of beans, some almonds and currants," said Raymond.

"Give her what we can spare." Esclarmonde waited for a goodbye, but Loupe remained seated in the corner with her legs crossed and head bowed, preoccupied by a private dilemma. Knowing better than to press her headstrong niece, Esclarmonde prepared to return to the bailey.

Loupe called her back. "I'd ask a favor before I go."

T wo hours before dawn, the Cathars formed a path leading from the chapel's entrance. On Esclarmonde's orders, the last of the kindling had been piled and lit at each corner of the ramparts, offering as much of a *feux de joie* as she could provide. Four knights carried Bernard up on a stretcher and placed him in front of a makeshift altar.

With Chandelle at her arm, Loupe walked from the chapel wearing the emerald satin gown that her grandfather had imported from Cyprus for Cecille's wedding. It was the same dress that Phillipa had worn when she married Roger. Esclarmonde had kept it stored all these years in the hope that Loupe would one day relent in her disdain for marriage. For the first time in her life, Loupe was unsure of herself, feeling awkward in the finery, particularly amid such desolation. She threaded the gauntlet of suffering and knelt next to Bernard. He reached for her hand with a tremulous grasp.

While the betrothed couple publicly professed their love, Chandelle clutched her stone etching and silently vowed to marry Jean in spirit in this same hour.

"South!" screamed the lookout.

This time, the Cathars did not run for protection, refusing to be denied this last remembrance of their lost way of life. The missile fell short and drove stones from the precarious curtain walls. The familiar squeal of rope was heard again—the French engine was being ratcheted and rolled closer.

Esclarmonde steeled her nerves as she read from the Gospel of John:

> *If the world hates you, know that it has hated me before it hated you. If you were of the world, the world would love its own. But because you are not of the world, I choose you out of this world . . .*

The Cathars, who knew the passage by heart, joined in:

> *If they persecuted me, they will persecute you. If they kept my word, they will keep yours also. But all this they will do to you on my account, because they do not know him who sent me . . .*

Several soldiers on the walls knelt and began reciting the verses:

> *They will put you out of the synagogues. Indeed, the hour is coming when whoever kills you will think he is offering service to God. And they will do this, because they have not known the Father, nor me. But I have said these things to you, that when the hour comes you may remember—*

Esclarmonde was stunned to silence: Phillipa's face appeared in the flickering light above Loupe's shoulder. The vision slowly took on more detail, and Bishop Castres came aside her, then Giraude, Aimery, and Roger. They parted to allow an elderly couple to step to the fore of the assembled spirits. A lady clad in black displayed a merel that hung from her necklace. Esclarmonde gasped in sudden discovery—the souls of her mother and father were also present. She moved toward them to speak, but they faded away. Shaken by the encounter, she recovered to the present and found the living staring at her with consternation. Fearful that her legs would fail, she hurried to finish the benediction:

> *This is my command, that you love one another as I have loved you. Greater love has no man than this, that he lay down his life for another.*

"North!" screamed the sentinel.

Esclarmonde touched the heads of Bernard and Loupe to offer the melding of the Light. The hiss of the launched stone became louder. The north corner of the chapel exploded and felled several Cathars, who lay in agony and tried to muffle their moans. She took a deep breath to maintain her mind's balance. *I must finish this before I die.* "Bernard Saint-Martin, do you take Esclarmonde Loupe de Foix as your wife?"

"I do with all my heart," said Bernard.

"Do you, dear Loupe, take this man as your husband?"

"I do."

Esclarmonde gathered their hands together. "Blessed God of Light, we ask that You make this union sacred in Your eyes."

Loupe had not told Bernard of her decision to make the escape attempt, fearful that he would lose all hope and cease fighting for life. Now, unable to delay the revelation further, she kissed him and whispered, "I must go."

A fractured moment passed before Bernard understood what she intended. Tears streamed down his cheeks as he brought her face into his unsteady palms. "I have kept my promise. Now you must promise to return to me."

Raymond's hand came to Loupe's shoulder to remind her that dawn was fast approaching. Stifling coughs of emotion, she pulled from Bernard's embrace and retired with Esclarmonde to the chapel. Inside, she hurriedly removed the wedding gown and returned it.

"No," said Esclarmonde. "It is yours now."

Loupe insisted, "I want to see you give it to my daughter."

That promise for a future caused Esclarmonde to enliven with hope. She struggled to find the words. "I have—"

"There is no need to say more."

Esclarmonde captured Loupe's hands to interrupt her harried preparations. "There is something I should have said to you years ago . . . We have never understood each other. It has been my shortcoming."

Loupe looked away in remorse. "And mine."

"You are so much like . . . I have always been proud of you."

Loupe choked with emotion. "They all expected me to be like you."

"I have tried to turn the other cheek, but I see now that it has brought only more suffering on this family . . . I find myself at a loss of faith."

"My way has met with no more success than yours." Loupe turned aside. "There is something I have kept from you for too long."

"What, child?"

Loupe spoke quickly to blunt the impact. "I saw your son."

Esclarmonde did not trust her ears. "You've seen Otto?"

"In Rome."

"Why did your father not advise me of this?"

"I never told him. I tried to convince Otto to come home, but he wouldn't leave Folques."

Esclarmonde braced with a hand against the wall. "What was he like?"

"He favors the Gascons in features and temperament, but Folques's cunning and treachery have also taken hold in him, I fear." Loupe hesitated before finishing. "Years later, I encountered him again."

Esclarmonde tilted a step closer. "Where?"

"At Avignonet."

Esclarmonde blinked hard, unable to make sense of why her son would have been at the church where the Dominicans were murdered. "With the Inquisitors? But I was told no Cistercians were there."

"He joined the Black Friars. I had the chance to kill him, but I let him live . . . to spite you." When Esclarmonde stumbled from the revelation, Loupe caught her and revealed more. "He's here with the French army."

"What?"

"The day after the raid, I saw him from across the barbican."

"I must go to him!"

Loupe blocked her attempt to rush out. "The Dominicans would do unspeakable . . . " She dared not say what they both knew.

Esclarmonde circled in distress. "I am the reason for this misery!"

Raymond opened the door. "The French guards are changing."

Loupe gathered up the climbing gear and hugged Esclarmonde. "You must promise to hold out . . . I *will* return."

The besieged Occitans cowered for three more weeks, but the signal fire on Roquefixade gave no indication of Loupe's fate. When Esclarmonde could no longer bear the suffering and travail in the crowded bailey, she would ask the soldiers to lift her to the ramparts during lulls in the bombardment. From that vantage, she prayed to catch a glimpse of her son, but all she could see with her failing eyes were the black specks in the valley.

On this fading afternoon, as she stood atop her favorite perch on the western wall, the sun broke through the fast-moving clouds. Filled with a bone-deep despair, she raised her face to soak in the warmth and prayed to the Light, "Tell me . . . what am I to do?"

As usual, no answer came. Resigned to the spiritual abandonment, she was about to descend from the allures when a gray cloud sailed overhead and shadowed her in darkness. The golden rays reappeared on the western slope and illumined the spot near the cliffs where she had contemplated the leap years ago.

Preparation for death takes a lifetime.

Hearing again the words that Castres had spoken on the night of her attempted suicide, she understood what was now required. One last time, she took in the stunning beauty of her homeland. The weather had turned mild, melting most of the snow and revealing napped patches of foliage that hinted at spring. Strangely, this day appeared identical to that morning three months shy of fifty years ago, when she had been initiated into the court of love. Her gaze swept the endless Tarascon forest and the grottes and caves that she had so loved to explore. Beyond them stood the desolate keeps of Aragon where Guilhelm had vowed to seek his exile, never to return. Could he be alive? No, not after thirty years. The Temple would have arrested and executed him. She found solace in the magnificent hues of the Pyrenees: The dark green of the oaks, the robin's-egg blue of the sky, the silver of the rushing river, the dusty tan of the awakening garrigue. She drew a fortifying breath—and turned away from it all.

The Cathars and soldiers watched her like a cast of hawks. Her steps were so purposeful that they were certain she had been gifted with the revelation that would save them from this nightmare. They crowded around her, desperate to hear the message of deliverance.

"This night," she told them, "I will undertake the Endura."

The Cathars froze with a collective gasp of disbelief—then fell to their knees, weeping and shouting protests. The Endura was the most fearsome sacrament of their faith. Castres had taught that under extraordinary circumstances they were permitted to starve themselves to avoid denying their faith. Yet the ritual of suicide had never been invoked. Embracing the sacrament meant that she had failed in her quest to merge with the Light during meditation. If she did not capture the Chariot at the fleeting moment of her passing, she would be returned to this world to suffer and grope in spiritual blindness again.

Corba tried to slap blood into Esclarmonde's cheeks to chase the grip of melancholy. "Someone boil a cup of beech leaves!"

Chandelle groped for Esclarmonde's hands. "Why?"

"The Dominicans will not abandon this siege until they have me. If I go to them alive, I fear what I might reveal under their methods. All we have accomplished would be lost. When the monks have their confirmation that I am dead, they will leave this mount." She ordered Raymond, "Deliver my body to them in exchange for the release of the others."

"Loupe will come," pleaded Chandelle.

Esclarmonde kissed the blind perfecta's streaming cheek and whispered, "Be strong for me. I must do this." She took one last look at her beloved temple, then walked into the chapel to commence her deathwatch.

The flash of lightning is not to light the way,
but a command to the cloud to weep.

- Rumi

XXXVII

Montsegur

February 1244

A commotion at the base of the pog interrupted Otto's morning Lauds. Galled to hear the Sabbath so boisterously violated, he rushed from his consecrated tent to chastise the conscripts and was stopped short by a spectacle passing strange: A tall monk shrouded in a hooded Cistercian robe was lashing twenty barefoot penitents through the lower French encampment. The sinners were burdened with dirt-filled sacks hung from their necks and they dragged large crosses of oak beams tethered with ropes. The crusaders joined in the torment by pummeling the wretches with dung clods and poking their feet with pikes.

"What blasphemous parade is this?" demanded Otto.

"Lapsed Waldensians," said the Cistercian. "My superior, the Abbot of Frontfroide, ordered them to carry the crosses to this mountain of iniquity."

Otto tried to examine the monk's occulted features but could make out only a scraggly gray beard in the shadowed recesses of the white cowl. Penitential processions during winter were unusual, yet the Languedoc abbeys were notorious for their lax enforcement of St. Bernard's regimen and traditions, often allowing facial hair and other pagan vices if the novitiate's familial bequest was generous enough. He had once met Benoit Renault, the patriarch of Frontfroide, an old gasbag who took pride in concocting clever methods for bringing malfeasants to their knees in contrition. This penance smacked of his rigorous method. "Why are they hooded?"

"They must remain cloaked for one year to learn humility."

"And you are?"

"Brother Benedict."

Otto detected a note of condescension in the monk's tone. His own transfer of allegiance to the Dominicans had never been forgiven in the Cistercian abbeys. He was amused to know that this brother considered him a traitor. He commanded the birches and thrashed the feet of the apostates to demonstrate that he alone wielded spiritual authority in Foix. When he finally lost interest in doling out the punishment, he threw the bloodied branches at the monk's sandals and ordered him, "If your Abbot wishes to send his failures to my district for rectification, advise him that I will expect donations for the trouble. Now, return to that Sodom's den you call an abbey and get out of my sight."

The Cistercian looked up at the heights and saw a stone crash into the temple. "Should their atonement be less severe than Our Lord's ascent to Golgotha?"

"Leave off the sermonizing and speak what's on your mind."

"The Abbot's mandate called for the sinners to pray under the shadow of those who deny Christ," said the Cistercian.

The prostrate penitents groaned at the prospect that their agony was not finished. Otto broke a sardonic smile on divining the import of the monk's suggestion. "You have the makings of an inquisitor. Pity you chose the one order that failed miserably in its mission." Never one to impede the mortification of others to the greater glory of Christ, Otto gave his assent to the penitents carrying their crosses up the crag to confess their derelictions below the heretic walls.

"How much longer until the keep is taken?" asked the Cistercian.

"Another week," said Otto, "and that crypt should be filled with rocks."

"The cloggers have not attempted a breakout?"

"One rat managed to scamper past us. He'll be apprehended soon enough."

The brutal climb up the treacherous Pas de Trebuchet was accomplished as the last mauve light of dusk descended. After commanding his weary penitents to their knees, the Cistercian monk strode through the ranks of curious crusaders and produced the abbatial decree for the Seneschal's inspection. "The engine's firing must be halted for an hour."

"By whose order?" asked the Seneschal.

The Cistercian kept his shadowed eyes fixed on the narrow defile beyond the barbican. "By order of God's representative on earth, His Holiness, Innocent IV, who watches over your soul with his faithful servant, the Abbot of Frontfroide."

The Seneschal considered banishing the smart-mouthed Cistercian, but the last thing he needed was the wrath of another monastic order brought down on his head. "Finish it, then get out of my sight."

"I need three cauldrons of boiling water."

"Are you making soup?" chortled the Seneschal.

The Cistercian waited in rigid silence until the guffaws around him dissipated. "The ground must be thawed to dig the holes."

The Seneschal walked among the bent penitents and kicked one in the ribs. "If you're going to all the trouble of staking the crosses, why not crucify them?"

"You mock Our Lord's death?"

The Seneschal lost his smarmy grin, aware that even the King's officers were not immune from being called before the Inquisition tribunals. He grudgingly signaled his men to the task. "If you're foolhardy enough to walk into the range of those hell-spawned whoresons, have at it."

The crusaders threw open a section of their palisade and allowed the Cistercian to whip his penitents over the ruined barbican and up the jagged defile toward the temple. The French deposited three vats of steaming water below the walls, then hurried back to safety. The ragged apostates staggered up to the rocky incline and fell to their bloodied knees under the heavy crosses.

Raymond appeared on the ramparts with a crossbow. "If you value your useless life, monk, you'll remove those Roman abominations from our sight!" Ten Occitan archers joined him atop the wall and took aim.

The Cistercian stole a glance over his shoulder. The crusaders behind the barbican were taunting the Occitans to fire on the sinners. Their bows were stacked and the trebuchet's sling was empty. The Seneschal had retired to his pavilion for his evening repast.

Raymond shouted a second warning, "Are you deaf?"

The Cistercian nodded in a signal to one of his penitents. The sinner untied the beams and fastened them to the cross held by his nearest comrade. Together, the two penitents hoisted their new creation—a cross with three traverse arms. The Cistercian shouted, "Look upon the true cross and be saved!"

Raymond and his men traded confused glances. Why would a Cistercian monk require Catholic penitents to build a Catharist cross?

The Cistercian raised his hand as if offering a benediction.

Without turning his head, Raymond whispered an order to his men. Perplexed, they drew their bows as commanded and fired high into the sky. The arrows landed several feet behind the penitents. The crusaders beyond the barbican roared with laughter and hectored the Occitans for their poor aim. When a second volley filled the air, the Cistercian and his penitents took off on a run for the temple with the crosses on their shoulders. The gate swung open—Raymond and his men dashed out and stole the cauldrons of water.

A scudding silence fell over the French camp. Dining in his open tent, the Seneschal, alerted by the cessation of jeers, nearly choked on a forkful of mince as he sprang from his table. "Bastards! Cut them down!"

The duped crusaders jumped over the barbican and fired their bows at the fleeing penitents. An impaled sinner released his grip on the water cauldron and waved his compatriots on as he fell. Atop the walls, the Occitans loosed another volley to stave off the disorganized French attack.

The Seneschal ran toward the barbican. "Fire the engine, damn you!"

The Occitans dragged the last cauldron through the temple gate seconds before the missile crashed against its planks.

Inside the chateau, the heaving penitents stared with disbelief at the tableau of misery surrounding them. The temple looked like a charnel house. The fever-racked faces of the Occitans were spotted with lesions and their gums were inflamed and crusted white. The Cistercian monk extended his left hand—made of iron—in a dismayed greeting.

Raymond leapt from the walls to embrace his old friend. "Montanhagol! Christ in Heaven, you are a blessed sight! How did you learn of our plight?"

Mobbed by the grateful Occitans, Guilhelm revealed, "The troubadours are spreading the word. We would have been here sooner, but the mountain passes are blocked. We had to find transport by sea from Valencia."

Corba fought her way through the scrum. Too overcome to speak, she pressed a kiss to Guilhelm's cheek. He heard a frail voice call his name and turned to welcome Chandelle into his arms. The blind perfecta was so wasted that he feared she might break in his embrace. He searched for the feisty tomboy who had never been far from Chandelle's side. "Where is the She-Wolf?"

That question cast a sudden pall over the Occitans. Raymond dropped his head in shame and said, "She tried to run the lines."

"How many did you send out?"

"She insisted on going alone."

Guilhelm braced Raymond with a knowing grin. "A Dominican friar with a flapping mouth told me that one from your garrison had eluded their nets."

The Occitans shouted jubilant ejaculations of hope for Loupe's breakthrough. But what next met their eyes transformed the celebration into an astonished silence. Guilhelm's disguised penitents discarded their homespun tunics and revealed themselves to be Aragon knights armed with short swords strapped to their backs. They ripped open the bags that had hung around their necks and poured wheat for the bread kilns. The parched Cathars lined up at the cauldrons and sipped the water with eyes closed to savor its blessed relief.

Guilhelm brought forward one of his compatriots in the deception, a short, white-bearded gentleman with penetrating cobalt eyes. "This is Bertrand de la Baccalaria, the most accomplished engineer in Aragon."

Raymond offered a welcoming handshake. "We are in your debt, seigneur."

The bandy engineer made a quick survey of the temple's broken walls. "Did not Our Lord say that it is better to give than to receive? Bring me your largest stones. It's nigh time the meek inherited some earth."

"The French are massing!" screamed a knight on the walls.

Guilhelm climbed to the ramparts while the engineer and his charges broke down their crosses with a practiced precision. The Cathars watched in amazement as the Aragonese knights mortised the beams to form a triangular frame, then knotted strands of the rope and constructed a sling by piecing together their robes. Within minutes, they had raised a small trebuchet.

The engineer calibrated the trajectory. "Ten degrees left!"

On Guilhelm's signal, the engine heaved its maiden load over the wall. The onrushing crusaders came to a lurching halt, baffled by the appearance of the stone arcing across the horizon. They cast glances over their shoulders toward their loaded engine and again to the sky, convinced that God had wrought some unnatural phenomenon. Before they could make sense of the marvel, the projectile caromed into their ranks. Raymond's men riddled the French survivors with arrows and forced them to retreat in such bewilderment that they left their wounded behind. The Occitans let loose with a hoarse cheer—the first heard on these ramparts since the commencement of the siege.

Guilhelm jumped from the allures and threaded his way through the converging Cathars to find Corba. Drawing a bracing breath for courage, he asked the question that had brought him back to this mount.

The spasms in Esclarmonde's viscera and the tormenting thirst had been replaced by a dull, fragmented awareness. Lying on a stone slab cushioned only by a ragged quilt, she was again reminded of time's torturous passage by the metronomic flapping of the robes draped across the chapel's ceiling to blunt the wind. The hearth sat frozen and sparkling snow dusted the walls. The moon's pallid light cocooned her in a bluish mist. Soaked in cold sweat, she shivered so intensely she could hear her teeth chattering. She tried to look down at her swollen feet in the hope of seeing the purplish mottling said to be the portent of death, but she could not move her head. Having taken no food and only a thimble of water in the five days since commencing the Endura, she was entombed in a body that no longer responded to her commands. Her physical sheath had surrendered its resistance, but her mind had become even more manic, compensating for the recession of her senses. As the icy numbness in her limbs increased, her interior landscape turned frightfully vivid and overpowering, afflicting her with a menagerie of visions, wrenching fears, dissonant thoughts, and once-lost memories, all alloyed in a narrative that seemed always on the verge of profundity and revelation, only to elude her grasp when she struggled to weave them into coherence.

This war between spirit and body brought to her feverish mind a story she had once been told about the Vestal Virgins of Rome. After a disastrous military defeat, the senators immured one of the young female initiates inside the city's ramparts as a sacrifice to the gods. Decades later, when the wall was excavated, the victim's corpse was found with her garments shredded and her fingers eaten off. The poor girl had cannibalized her own flesh.

The memory of that account plunged her into a panic. What if she were not dead when her body was delivered up to the Dominicans? Would she revive in the immolation fires and suffer the death throes anew? Castres had told her of holy men in the East who, after years of practice, gained such mastery of meditation that they could mimic death by suspending their pulse and humours. These magicians of the body would demonstrate their remarkable powers by having themselves buried alive for days at a time. In Occitania, death had become so banal and was met with such indifference by the living that the funeral gangs became slipshod. So numerous were the reports of accidental entombments that many of the dying left instructions for their passage to be confirmed by the insertion of garlic or vinegar into the nose.

Vinegar. The last taste experienced by Jesus before giving up His spirit. Had the Romans offered Him the gall-laced drink to test His survival? She had always wondered about the whispered claims that the Master did not die on the cross. Some believed that He had merely retreated into the little death of meditation, as had Lazarus. She prayed that the claim was true. Why would anyone find hope in such senseless agony on the cross? The popes insisted that God sent His only son to be nailed and flayed to pay off a karmic debt for sins long since lost to our understanding. How could people worship such a cruel divinity?

When, as a young girl, she had listened to the priests describe the horrors of the Way of the Cross, she would think about a tome that she had come across in the library of her Catalan tutor. The work was an Occitan translation of a history written by Josephus Flavius, a Jewish scribe who had gone over to the Romans. What always gave her pause was not the chronicler's confirmation of Jesus's death, but his description of the thousands of Jewish rebels who had also been crucified along the road leading into the Holy City. Those Jews had suffered the same horrid end as Christ for their country, yet their sacrifice had long since been forgotten. Why, she had asked her father, was Christ's crucifixion so elevated in worship when the others were not? He died to save his fellow man, she was told. But so had those Jewish rebels, she insisted, and unlike Christ, they had not been comforted with the divine foreknowledge of their resurrection. She could still remember her father staring down at her in utter perplexity, unable to fathom how a child could—

She heard the door bolt slide open.

A blast of air pricked her skin. She lifted her swollen lids through the filmy gauze and saw the blurred outline of a face. Its doleful features were distantly familiar, but several moments passed before she could place them. Her heartbeat quickened. Yet just as swiftly she sank in black disappointment, having almost fallen for the clever temptation. The Demiurge was again upon her with his deceiving visions.

Allow me to die in peace. Let it come soon, I pray you.

A muffled sob was followed by a cold tear that fell to her cheek with the impact of an avalanche. The apparition took on more detail: Eyes luminous and blue, salted beard, long gray hair speckled white. Her flesh began to awaken as if attacked by spiders. Against her wishes, her body was fighting for life.

"Come back to me," said an echoing voice.

She pressed her sodden eyes closed to chase the Evil One whose cruelty knew no bounds. In these final hours of her life, the Demiurge was conjuring the one image that might tempt a retreat from her duty. She tried to will the pernicious cacodaemon away, but he would not be ignored. Her skin burned from the press of his hand against her forehead. Her fingers were opened and her palm was pressed against the cold surface of rounded metal. She made out the edges of a raised carving—an image slowly took form in her mind: A cross with three traverse beams.

The merel.

"Would Satan know when our eyes first met?" asked the archon. "Would He know how you sent me tumbling down that ladder in Lombrives? Would He know of that sun-drenched day when you stole a kiss on this very mount and promised me another years hence?"

"Guilhelm!"

His warm mouth met her chapped lips and ignited her cheeks with tears that stung like acid. She tried to turn her head to conceal her wasted condition; her hair was matted with grime and her gums bled. "Don't look at me."

"You're the most blessed sight I've ever seen."

Guilhelm's tortured thoughts fled back to that night after Muret, when he had been consumed by rage at her mindless loyalty to this life-hating faith. How many years had he suffered for his impetuous decision to abandon her? Retreating to Aragon, he had absconded from lair to lair across the waste scapes of Christendom, living on bile and venom, nursing his anger against the phantom God of Light that she worshipped. Not a night had passed that he did not angrily defy Christ and His saints, taunting them to retaliate and accusing them of sleeping while the world wept. Until this moment, he thought his reproaches and challenges had gone unmarked. But now he saw that the Almighty's agents of retribution had only been biding their time until the appropriate punishment for his defiance could be arranged. He could barely speak the words. "I am the cause of this."

"You must never think that," she whispered.

He tightened his petitioning grasp on her frail hand. "I once carried you down this mountain. I can do it again."

"You and I are both too old to start over."

"I'll take you to Ireland," he promised. "The people there live to be a hundred. We'll end our days together."

"Would we have horses?"

"Stallions as white as the mountain caps," he said. "Dogs and falcons, too. I shall even find you a unicorn, if you wish."

"And courts of love?" Her voice began to strengthen.

"The Irish bards sing so sweetly, one cannot help but dance."

She smiled weakly. "You never danced. Frivolity you called it."

He raised her limp shoulders and brought her bruised eyes closer to his gaze. He could feel the faint thud of her heart against his. "If you'll stay alive in my arms, I'll never stop dancing."

Listless as a rag doll, she winced from the razored agony caused by even the slightest movement. She began to feel faint from the exertion. He pulled a piece of bread from his knapsack and brought it to her lips. The aroma of barley revived her. She struggled against its seduction by turning away. "I beg of you, Guilhelm. Aid me in this passage."

"You cannot ask me to stand by and watch you die!"

"You and I were not put upon this earth for contentment," she said. "We have been assigned greater tasks."

"We can assign our own fates."

"Each time I have tried to avoid the call, I have stumbled badly." Her vision was tunneling into darkness. She remembered the signs that Castres had said would announce the Light's approach. The end, she knew, was drawing near. "You must bring the others to me."

Guilhelm delayed, desperate to have her to himself in these last moments, but finally he obeyed her request, as he always did. He covered her with his mantle and returned moments later with Corba, Chandelle, and the Marquessa, who was carried in on her pallet.

Esclarmonde's head was propped up so she could see their faces. She could barely make out the tracings of their features. She slid her arm across the slab and wrapped her fingers around the desiccated sinews of the Marquessa's wrist. "Chandelle was right. You will outlive us all." That prophecy had never failed to arouse the matriarch's ire, but for the first time in her life, the Marquessa was too overwrought to form a protest. Esclarmonde reached next for Corba's shaking hand. "Tell me again your favorite maxim."

Corba pleaded, "Esclarmonde, we can still—"

"Must I always start it for you? Love can . . ."

"Love can deny nothing to Love," said Corba, crying.

"You must be strong."

"Loupe will come," pleaded Corba. "Guilhelm has learned that she made it through the French lines. If you will only wait."

Esclarmonde smiled faintly with pride, confirmed in her belief that Loupe could survive for weeks on stubbornness alone. Yet she knew it was too late. Even if Count Raymond and his Toulousian army arrived this hour with the sustenance necessary to reverse death's approach, her internal organs had suffered too severely to mend. She could hear Chandelle's wheeze deepen, evidence that the pneumonia was worse. "Little Candle, you know we'll be together again. Never doubt this."

Chandelle brought Esclarmonde's palm to her own cheek to savor its miraculous touch one last time. "I have never doubted you."

When Esclarmonde's eyes dimmed, Guilhelm hurried Bernard Marti and the other Cathars into the chapel for their final Touch of Love. Those too ill to walk were carried in on stretchers. Raymond, the last to approach, broke down sobbing. "I am lost without your guidance."

"Guilhelm will assist you," she rasped. "Remember, the negotiation must be in writing. The Dominicans will . . ." The blackness was closing faster. A horrible thud shook her soul to its core. The door closed—they were gone. She began to sink into a bottomless whirlpool of despair. Had she given up her spirit so soon? She cried out, "Don't leave me!"

Guilhelm reappeared from the shadows. "Never again."

She refused to surrender his hand. "I must ask one last promise of you."

"I have never been virtuous at keeping them."

Her ears throbbed from a howling wind; the First Station of the Path to the Light was near. "Promise me you'll not let what happened on this mount be forgotten."

He did not answer immediately. "What would you have me—"

"There is an underground chamber. . ." She now fought for every breath. "I never told the others . . . The sun enters on each solstice." She heaved and coughed up blood—the internal moorings were giving way. She reminded herself not to fear the beasts that guarded the entrance to the death realms. She felt Guilhelm's palm pressing against her chest to ease the inhalations. She arched and gasped for air. "Lines intersect."

"How do I find these lines?"

"Connect the crosses on the walls and . . ." The roiling clouds of blackness frightened her. "Guilhelm!"

"I am still here."

"So cold."

He lay beside her and pulled her wasted body into his arms for warmth, attempting to meld her heartbeat with his. Her vows forbade such intimacy, but she had never been so afraid. All her life the God of Light had denied her this man. Would He deny her even this last embrace? She had counseled others to go bravely to their deaths. Hypocrite! The hour was nigh but she could not remain faithful to her own teachings. She then remembered Folques's curse on that fateful night in Foix's chapel:

You will never have him.

Beyond the chapel, the trebuchet's groan and recoil grew louder with each successive launch. That excruciating screech tortured her beyond endurance. She could not bear the thought that this grinding ruination of her temple would be the last sound she would ever hear. She squeezed his hand feebly and begged, "A story."

"I am not a bard."

He had raised that same protest when he had saved her from Folques in the court of love. With great difficulty, she turned her head and looked up at him in fierce desperation. "You are my troubadour!"

Shaken by her desperation, Guilhelm searched his memory for anything that might offer her comfort in these last moments. She was the one who had always been the believer, but now God in His perversity was requiring him to minister to her—the same God who had schemed to keep them apart. What misshapen divinity would sabotage such a love? She had been right all along. The god who ruled this world *was* evil. The same bitterness of old came rushing up his throat. He ran his hand across the coarse weave of her black robe and recalled how she had first appeared to him that first day in Foix: Draped in green silk, flashing with jewels and cinched at the waist to reveal the form that had cost him countless nights. There were few things in his wretched existence of which he was certain, but this was one:

She was never meant to wear black.

He searched the sanctuary and found a small burrell sack that contained what few belongings she owned. Among the rags was the wedding dress that Phillipa and Loupe had worn, the same gown that she had talked of wearing at his side in matrimony. Strips had been ripped from its hem for bandages. He lifted its folds over her shoulders and pulled the silk across her body. He imagined her next to him in this chapel, their hands intertwined in the symbol of infinity. Inexplicably, what next came to his mind was a parable once told to him by a Nasorean hermit in Jerusalem. He eased her head under his arm and whispered, "Do you remember St. Thomas of the Bible?"

"The doubter," she said. "Like you."

That truth drew the semblance of a rueful smile. He coughed back the swell of ragged emotion, reminded that she could still pierce his armor. He held her tighter in the hope of speeding the blood through her veins, then he forced himself to begin the story. "When St. Thomas was a boy, a monk prophesied that he was destined to go to Egypt and find a pearl that could be exchanged for a magical robe." His thoughts turned to the night in Lavaur when he had sacrificed a hand to see her face again. If offered the choice anew, he would gladly give his life for just one night more.

"Guilhelm?" she said, softly calling him back.

He swallowed the lump in his throat. "Thomas gave no more thought to the oracle. For forty years, he toiled in misery, barely staying alive. Then one day, in old age, he had a dream of the monk's promise. Inspired, Thomas resolved to give up all earthly desires and finish the quest to Egypt that he had abandoned so many years before."

A tingling coursed through Guilhelm's arm. Was this the same spiritual heat that had miraculously healed his wounds after the tilting duel in Toulouse? Even in these last moments, her touch still held the ineffable power. Reluctantly, he continued the story, "When Thomas approached the borders of Egypt, he reached into his pocket for his last coin to pay the toll. It was then that he found the lost pearl. The old monk had sewn it into his cloak."

Esclarmonde lifted her drooping lids. "Thomas always possessed what he sought all his life?"

Guilhelm tried to delay the finish, but Esclarmonde's faint press against his hand bade him to go on. "At this moment of discovery, Thomas was transported to Heaven. Jesus met him at the gate with the promised gift, a robe refulgent with a brilliant Light. Thomas asked, 'Lord, what is this robe that blinds me?'"

He paused and waited for her protest to his delay. The brash girl he once knew would have demanded an answer before he could finish. But no such impetuous urging now came. He felt her wrist and found a faint pulse. For the first time since that day his mother had abandoned him at the door of the Temple, he prayed aloud. He prayed that if only one miracle were granted in his life, this woman would be returned to him.

"What did the Master say?" she whispered, eyes closed.

"Our Lord told him, 'Dearest Thomas, this is the Robe you wore before you were born.'"

A dove flapped across the exposed ribbing of the scavenged roof. Startled, Guilhelm looked up to the clear night sky and saw the constellation of Virgo, the celestial abode of the Madonna. One of its stars shot across the black expanse and fell toward the crag, leading his gaze downward again. Esclarmonde was smiling at him with a look of radiant peace. His heart fluttered with hope. Was the star a portent from Heaven? Had the Almighty granted his petition in reward for his service to the Cross? Tears streamed down his cheeks as he kissed her to confirm the blessing.

Her lips were cold.

She had been fixed not on him, but on the Virgin's constellation. Had she witnessed a revelation from another realm? Heaving with grief, he pulled her into his arms and whispered, "Farewell, my pearl. I pray you have found your magical robe."

She had always assured him that, verily, there was a beneficent God who granted the petitions of mortals. But if such a divinity did exist, He had long ago abandoned this desolate mount. The Light of Montsegur—the solitary light in Guilhelm's world—had gone out forever.

If the spiritual universe and the way to it
were shown, no one for a single moment would remain.

- Rumi

XXXVIII

Toulouse

February 1244

hree days of unremitting rain had turned the road north along the overflowing Garonne into a quagmire. Hundreds of starving Occitan refugees were encamped along the approach into the once-proud capital of Toulousia, a battered shell of its past grandeur, its largesse pillaged and spirit crushed by the Dominicans who had installed their inquisition headquarters in the Maison Communale.

Hooded in a tattered cloak, Loupe fought her way through this morass of misery on a crutch to ease the pain in her swollen ankle wrenched during her descent down Montsegur in the darkness. She slogged toward the gendarmes who manned the arched gate of the Narbonnais tower and shouted, "I must speak with the Count!"

Her plea was answered with a halberd's jab. She tried to force a breach, but the guards pummeled her into the rabble of commoners and dispossessed nobles who had come to petition relief from the Dominican reign of terror. Dazed by the blow, she revived to consciousness under the trampling of feet. She staggered upright again and clawed to the fore. "I have a communiqué!"

"A diplomat," scoffed the sergeant of the gate. "From King Louis himself by the look of her fine raiment."

Drenched and wasted, Loupe looked down at her oversized vagabond's rags and only then realized how much she had changed in weight and appearance. "I come from Montsegur!"

The sergeant lost his grin. He glanced with alarm at the claque of black-robed friars who were congregating for their inquests. "Away with you! We have no dealings with your kind!"

Loupe saw that she was standing under the parapet where she had launched the shot that killed Simon de Montfort. The inscription stone set in memory of her deed was weathered and defaced. She could not accept being denied entry into the city that she had once saved. For two weeks, she had clung close to the isolated forests along the Ariege and Garonne rivers, avoiding the French scouting parties while cadging for scraps and surviving on dead carrion and rotted fish heads. Having made it down the pog and across the frozen causses on one good leg, she was determined not to fail at this eleventh hour. She made another attempt on the gate and captured the sergeant's face. "Guiscard Cabresine!"

The sergeant shoved her away. "I'll not have my good name bewitched!"

"We fought together on these walls!"

He spun back to examine her features. "The She-Wolf?"

"Get me in!"

"What has happened to you?" While the Dominicans were preoccupied, the sergeant hurried her inside. "I may lose my head for this."

The mob clamored in protest as the guards slammed the portcullis. Loupe was escorted past the corridor rush lights and up the circular stairway that led into the great hall where de Montfort had once planned his campaigns. There she found a scene starkly different from the one outside. The knights and retainers were in fine mettle, reveling bawdily and stuffing their mouths with exotic viands. A lute-playing minstrel pranced from table to table while several rake-hells hovered over a dice game of Todas Tablas. The music stopped in mid-chord and the men stared at her as if an exhumed corpse had walked into their midst.

At the head table, Count Raymond continued to chomp on a joint of lamb. Belatedly alerted by the cessation of the carousing, he looked up in mid-bite and flung the morsel to the floor in exasperation. "Insufferable mendicants! Can I not take my repast without being plagued by petitions? Who let this one in?"

Loupe moved to pounce on the meat, but she caught herself.

"My lord, this is no beggar," said the sergeant.

Raymond stabbed his knife into a pile of chops and dug out another steaming bite. "If that's no beggar, then I'm no baron."

"You *are* no baron!" shouted Loupe. "At least none worthy of the honor!"

Raymond erupted to his feet, sending trenchers and cutlery flying. "I'll hang that ratsbane tongue from this tower!"

"That staff is already occupied by the Capetian oriflamme," said Loupe. "You'd best dispatch your emissaries to Paris if you plan such bold action. I hear it takes weeks for that Spanish Jezebel to give you permission to wipe your ass."

"Death-courting knave! Your name I'll have before your head!"

Loupe was bent low by a hunger pang. "I am an Occitan who remembers when the Count of Toulouse would defend a faithful vassal!"

Bollixed by the insolent intrusion, Raymond searched his knights for some hint as to her identity. When they shrugged in ignorance, he pinched her threadbare sleeve. "No vassal of mine tramps around like a mangy washwoman."

Loupe slung open the shudders to reveal the gruel lines in the streets below. "I'm well-heeled compared to many who languish in your land."

Raymond reached for his dagger, but Loupe stole it and took aim at his crotch. Slowed by the wine, the baron was staggered by her quickness. The knights moved to his aid until she warned them off with a twist of the blade. "Mayhaps I should hasten Blanche's rights under that feckless treaty you signed."

The Count's eyes dilated in recognition. "Christ's blood."

Loupe produced the scrip she had kept hidden in her belt pouch. Raymond read Esclarmonde's message while glancing nervously at a long-eared Dominican prelate who watched their confrontation from the corner. "Monseigneur, would you excuse us?"

The prelate's brow narrowed with suspicion. "God's ears are all hearing."

"Yes, but we must not try His patience on petty matters of local governance."

The prelate grudgingly departed, but not before burning Loupe's face into his memory. Raymond signaled for his knights to retract their swords. Loupe reciprocated by releasing the baron from the threat of the dagger.

Raymond offered Loupe a slice of meat. Finding her hesitant, he insisted, "Your abstinence will not ease your family's plight."

Loupe chewed the collop of lamb, but she could not keep it down. She was helped to a chair and brought a cup of spiced hippocras. Recovering her strength, she said, "The French have built an engine on the summit."

Raymond walked to the hearth and dispatched Esclarmonde's letter to the flames. "The Dominicans must not discover that your aunt is alive."

"Why haven't you responded to our signals to Roquefixade?"

Raymond shared a guilt-ridden glance with his knights. "My position here is complicated. The cleric is my papal watchdog. He also reports to Blanche."

Loupe was incensed that her family's suffering had been prolonged merely because of this puerile baron's fear of his aunt. She threw the wine goblet at the wall, dousing several of the men. "Drive these meddling monks from your court! The people will rise up and support you as they did against de Montfort."

Burdened by a dilemma, Raymond paced the chamber with his head slung low. "I have petitioned the Holy Father to rescind my excommunication."

"The Church holds your soul hostage?" she asked, incredulous.

"If I send aid to Montsegur, all hope for the restoration of my title and lands will be forfeited. I must think of my future heir."

"Are you that blind? Blanche contrives to deny you of another child!"

"The Queen Mother is my kinswoman and benefactor."

"The woman cares not a whit about your common blood! She seeks only to expand her son's kingdom! There is only one way to restore the rightful governance of your forefathers. You must strike at once!"

Raymond took refuge in his high-backed chair and slumped in a pose of heavy-eyed lassitude. "We will never be rid of the French."

Loupe knelt on one knee before him and grasped his chair arms. "Where is the man I saw stand before all Rome and declare he would never submit?"

Raymond sipped his wine slowly, allowing its soporific effect to wash over his cares. After draining the cup, he stared into the dregs as if attempting to divine an oracle. "I have come to understand my father."

"Have they flogged every drop of Occitan blood from your veins?"

Raymond's sotted gaze was focused inward. "I was forced to watch his body rot in those streets out there. I'll not suffer the same fate."

"My own father's bones lay scattered on fallow ground," said Loupe. "You seek to appease a church that murders the true followers of Christ." She turned to the knights in his court, many of whom had fought with her during the de Montfort wars. "If Montsegur is allowed to fall, all Occitania is doomed."

A blond, gap-toothed squire, no more than fourteen years of age, parted the ranks of the knights and stepped forward. "Is it true what the troubadours say? That the Grail is kept in the chateau on that mount?"

"Be still with your foolishness," ordered Raymond.

The men laughed and ridiculed the lad, but Loupe found a glimmer of hope in his innocent question. "The temple protects a treasure far more precious than a cup. A miraculous Light that appears differently to each seeker."

"Have you seen this Light?" asked the squire.

The knights ceased in their raillery and drew closer, intrigued by Loupe's revelation. She limped to the embrasure and studied the dust motes in the rays that had broken through the rain clouds. "I was too blinded by pride to see it. But my aunt has devoted her life to unlocking its mystery."

"Did she describe this miraculous radiance?" asked the squire.

Loupe now regretted never listening to Esclarmonde's teaching, having always dismissed it as nonsense. She scoured her fatigued mind to remember something in her life that made no sense and yet was beyond doubt. Bernard's face came to her mind's eye. "Is there a maiden who captures your heart?"

The boy blushed. "Yes . . . but I haven't the courage to tell her."

"Why her, above all others?"

He pondered the question. "I don't know."

"Then it is beyond your understanding, this quest for her?"

"Everyone says my love is doomed," he said. "She comes from a higher station and is nothing like me."

Loupe circled the knights on her crutch to chase their smirks. "You make jest of the lad, but you were all once devoted to such a passion before you became inured to the possibilities of lost youth. The holy ones on Montsegur seek this mystical Light with the same fervor that you held for an exalted lady. The perfects cannot explain their faith in the logic of this world, just as this squire cannot explain his star-crossed passion. Yet the troubadours say his love and my aunt's quest for this spiritual radiance share a sacred impulse."

A hush of sad nostalgia and shame fell over the chamber. The squire knelt before Loupe and said, "I will help you save your people." Inspired by his selfless example, several knights stepped forward to join the offer.

Loupe beseeched Raymond to ride at the head of a relief army. "Strike with the fury of your forefathers, my lord! Become the savior of Occitania!"

Surrounded by hopeful gazes, Raymond sought courage in another long draught of wine. He stood unsteadily and studied the sword of his crusader grandfather that was displayed above the hearth. His paunched eyes swam in tears as he looked back into a time when Toulouse was a kingdom as glorious as England and France. He took the blade down from its moorings and strapped it to his belt. Blazoned with the heraldry of the House of Toulouse—a twelve-pointed cross spangled with bobbles—the bejeweled hilt that once crossed the ramparts of Jerusalem and Acre slowly lifted from the scabbard.

Halfway up, the blade halted and slid back into its caitiff repose.

And the Knights of the Grail knelt lowly,
And for help to the Grail they prayed,
And behold the mystic writing,
And the promise it brought of aid.

- Wolfram von Eschenbach

XXXIX

Montsegur

March 1244

Punished by a scudding gale that sliced at exposed skin, the Occitans huddled together inside the temple to hoard what little warmth they could raise over the wounded and dying. Guilhelm had refused to abide Esclarmonde's order to have her body delivered to the Dominicans. Instead, on the previous night—the 2nd of March—he had strapped her shrouded corpse to his back and, in a last-ditch attempt to break past the French lines, led what remained of the garrison down the western face of the crag. He and his men were thrown back with grievous losses, including a severe thigh wound to Raymond de Perella. Unwilling to prolong the suffering, the Cathars asked to be handed over to the Dominicans in exchange for a promise of clemency for the soldiers.

At dawn, Guilhelm and Pierre-Roger walked out with their hands raised. Suspecting a ruse, the French sergeant confronted them from behind the palisade and ordered his bowmen to take close aim. When the two Occitans came beyond the range of the enemy bows, the French officer drove a fist into Guilhelm's gut. "That little sortie last night cost me twenty men."

Guilhelm and Pierre-Roger were heckled and prodded to the Seneschal's pavilion on the far end of the eastern spine. There Otto recognized Guilhelm as the friar who had tricked him with the disguised penitents. "I should have you thrown from these cliffs."

"Harm us under a flag of parlay," Guilhelm warned with level eyes, "and you will spend another summer on this rock."

The Seneschal burned Guilhelm with a minatory glare. "Well? Did you come out for a stroll? Or do you have something of interest to say to me?"

"The fortress will be abandoned and all weapons left inside," said Pierre-Roger. "In return, my men will be allowed to return to their homes. We have no trade with the religion of these cloggers."

"And the heretics?" asked Otto.

Before Pierre-Roger could answer, Guilhelm interjected, "They must be taken before the tribunal in Toulouse to plead their cases."

Pierre-Roger turned on Guilhelm with a questioning look. He had not been told of the Templar's intent to include that condition.

Otto carefully studied Guilhelm. "Does Esclarmonde de Foix still live?"

Guilhelm replied obliquely, "Why do you think these people have been resisting so fiercely?"

"I must have proof," said Otto. "Show her face on the walls."

"I will do you one better." Guilhelm produced a rolled ribbon of cloth that he had found in the chapel. On it Esclarmonde had written a message begging mercy for her flock and telling Otto of her love for him.

Otto began to read her words aloud, "To my dearest son—" He flushed as he pored over the remainder of the message in silence; it was dated and contained intimacies about Folques and Jourdaine that only his mother could have known. He ripped the ribbon to shreds. "Rantings of a deranged witch."

"To her son?" asked the Seneschal. "Why would she—"

"These cloggers address everyone as sons and daughters," dissembled Otto. "A quaint example of their incestuous barbarities."

"Is it from the woman or not?" demanded the Seneschal.

"She's in there," said Otto. "The rebels are yours to do with what you wish. I want that pagan poseur and her heretics."

"There is one more condition," insisted Guilhelm.

"You are in no position to make demands," reminded Otto.

"The surrender must be delayed until the sixteenth," said Guilhelm. "The Cathars will be allowed to remain in the temple with food and water."

"You take us for fools?" scoffed Otto. "You are playing for time until you regain strength to attempt another escape."

"The spring solstice is a holy day for them," said Guilhelm. "They wish to perform a ceremony before offering themselves up."

"I'll not be an accessory to Satan's ritual," said Otto.

Guilhelm searched the monk's clammy features but could find no hint of Esclarmonde in them. How could such a shadow of evil have emerged from her womb? With one lunge, he could throw this viper over the cliff to join his father in Hell—but no, he had committed to seeing her last directive fulfilled. He swallowed his rising anger and calmly asked, "Have you heard of the Endura?"

"Enlighten me," said Otto, haughtily.

"The dualists are permitted to commit suicide to avoid denying their faith," said Guilhelm. "If you reject these terms, the viscountess is prepared to take her own life before you lay a hand on her."

Otto affected indifference with a casual inspection of his fingernails. Would a woman who held to a pacifist creed truly have the mettle to follow through on such a threat? He could not risk that possibility. It was imperative that he interrogate her to extract the secret that Folques had tried to reveal. He would draw her out in confidence as only a prodigal son could. Blanche was the most cunning woman he had ever encountered, but even she had failed to match him in wits. Armed with his mother's capitulation, he would hasten to Rome and personally submit her confession to the Pope before his departure was even reported to Paris. His guerdon from the Church would be a position in the Apostolic Chancery, perhaps even the red cassock of a cardinal. He would be heralded as the monk who had finally crushed the heretics, succeeding where Folques and Almaric had failed. How long he had dreamt of following Dominic's example by forming a new monastic order. His name would be spoken in the same breath with the venerable fathers from Assisi and Clairvaux. He tested the Templar's obstinacy by walking away, but when Guilhelm did not move from the demand, he turned and relented, "The terms are accepted."

Guilhelm captured Pierre-Roger's elbow to speed their return to the temple before the arrangement could be retracted.

"Not so fast," said the Seneschal. "Not that I don't trust you, Templar, but you'll provide us with ten hostages as a surety of your good faith. This woman who seems to be so valuable will be one of them."

Guilhelm feigned indifference, but his pulse was racing in his neck. "You will need to send your men over to carry her out."

"Is she lame?"

"She suffers from a fever that has rendered her legs useless."

The Seneschal and his officers shrank several steps away, fearful that the two Occitan negotiators had also contracted the pestilence.

"Her flock is riddled with it." Guilhelm coughed violently and begged a sip of water, but the French refused their canteens. "The bloody flux eats at the flesh like worms. None of our soldiers will go near her. There is a bishop with them named Marti who remains in good health."

Otto tightened his collar against the infectious vapors. He would arrange for Esclarmonde's interrogation to be held at a safe distance, outside that fouled heap of stone. "The bishop, four heretics and five soldiers, all untainted. If I hear even a wheeze, I'll throw you in a pit with them."

On the 15th of March, the inclement weather gave way to the full warmth of spring. The Cathars, who had not been told the reason for the delay in their capitulation, gathered around Guilhelm inside the temple and waited for the solstice sun to break over the clear horizon. When the golden orb crept above the spine, Guilhelm watched with taut anticipation as a shaft of light pierced the archere slit on the eastern parapet. The beam inched toward the center of the bailey and creased the upturned faces of the perplexed Cathars as it passed. In accord with Esclarmonde's instructions, Guilhelm had ordered a chalk line dusted between the triple crosses that were etched on the northern and southern walls. At last, the solstice ray crossed the chalked demarcation, confirming Esclarmonde's prediction.

Guilhelm impaled his sword on the spot. "Dig here."

The perfects fell to their knees and clawed at the hard scrabble with their bowls. Moved by their desperation, some of the soldiers came down from the ramparts and joined the excavation with pikes. When they had reached an elbow's depth, their tools clanged against a metallic hardness. Guilhelm tapped his sword on a smooth surface that sounded hollow. The men unearthed a hewn stone imbedded with an iron handle. He tied a rope to the ring and signaled for the soldiers to hoist it.

The slab gave way to a tunnel.

Armed with torches, the confounded Occitans entered the descending corridor while the soldiers carried the infirm on blankets and pallets. After a hundred precarious steps, the passageway opened to a dusky grotto. The circular perimeter was surrounded by branching catacombs with low ceilings blackened from the residue of smoke. Esclarmonde had directed them to a subterranean necropolis. The grotte reminded Guilhelm of the ossuaries he had seen in the burial caves around the hills of Jerusalem and in the catacombs of Cappadocia. Hundreds of skulls lay in neat rows with piles of bones below them, all apparently collected not to exalt the bodily remains, but to hide them from the depravations of the Roman monks. Two bundles wrapped in rotted linens lay in niches that had been cut into the soft rock. Etchings marked them as the burial places of Castres and Phillipa. Other luminaries of their faith had also been interred in this hidden hypogeum.

Guilhelm hurried up the stairs to the chapel and returned with Esclarmonde's shrouded corpse. He placed her remains into the empty nook next to Phillipa's resting place. After several minutes of prayer, the Cathars arose from their knees and reluctantly signaled their readiness to leave the crypt. While the others climbed the steps, Guilhelm lingered to say a private farewell and regain his composure. In the far recesses of the grotte, he saw a crude altar smudged dark from smoke and melted wax, remnants of past ceremonies. He came closer and was overcome by a wave of grief. Fighting faintness, he stumbled and braced his hand against the altar to catch his balance.

The lintel moved.

Confounded, he slid the slab a bit more and found a crevice below it. This was not an altar, but a sarcophagus—the same hollowed block of granite that had entombed Esclarmonde during her initiation. He lifted a wooden coffer from the kist's depths and broke open its clasp. Before him lay the Keramion cup and the Mandylion shroud. Had she hidden the relics here all these years? Why had she directed him to find this place only now, when all was lost?

Atop the stairs, the Cathars and soldiers waited for him. Hearing his shout, they hurried back down the passageway and were dropped to their knees by the same mystical effluence that had suffused the chapel in Constantinople. Guilhelm then remembered what the widowed Greek empress had told him: *The sacred relics always find those who are charged with their protection.* After forty years, they had been returned to him. But why now? Inside the sarcophagus lay a sheepskin pouch tied with leather bindings. He carefully unwrapped its dusted covering and found a fragile scroll of great age. Intrigued, the Cathars hovered around him and examined the scroll's strange Levantine writing.

"I've seen this parchment before," said Corba. "It is the gospel that Father Castres carried with him in Lombrives."

Guilhelm had always dismissed Esclarmonde's claim that such a lost gospel existed. Could this be the evidence that had been sought by his Templar Master in the excavations at Jerusalem?

Chandelle ran her hand lightly across the brittle texture of the parchment. "Can you make out its meaning?"

Guilhelm carefully held a torch over the scroll for light. On one section, the marginalia and spaces between the lines contained miniscule notations in Occitan. Castres must have dictated a translation of the Aramaic to Esclarmonde. He brought the script closer to his aging eyes and read her rendition aloud:

> These words, my dear Nasorean brothers and sisters, were spoken to me by James, our beloved Teacher of Righteousness, on the night before his martyrdom in Jerusalem. This testimony I, Barnabas, verily give that you may find comfort and strength in the persecutions you now endure.
>
> And on that night I said unto the Teacher, "There are those who say that your brother Jesus arose from the grave in the flesh."
>
> The Teacher answered, "My brother taught us how to conquer the flesh. Why would he wish to return to its imprisonment?"
>
> "But Peter and his disciples saw him resurrected."
>
> The Teacher said, "What they saw was my brother's Robe of Glory, gained not from death, but from overcoming the flesh in life. Did he not admonish Thomas to avoid touching him in his transfigured state? Did not Peter turn away from the emanations? What flesh has ever shone brighter than the sun? Jesus gave us proof by burning an image of his Robe onto the shroud as a remembrance of the blessed Light that awaits us all."
>
> I asked, "But did not Our Lord return after his crucifixion to trumpet the victory over the body?"
>
> The Teacher answered, "He cared nothing for the flesh. He came to fulfill his promise to reveal the secrets to those who had been prepared."
>
> I protested, "Saul the Tarsian preaches that your brother was a god who died for our sins."
>
> The Teacher lowered his head in sadness. "Did Jesus and I not study at the feet of the same rabbis? Did we not break bread together every day? This Saul is a Pharisee, a Roman citizen who persecuted our people. He never laid eyes upon my brother nor spoke a word to him. Jesus promised that we would all perform the same miracles as did he, and even more. He was no more a god than you or me. And yet he was no less a god than the Father himself, for he knew the precious gnosis that sets us free."
>
> I asked, "Why then do these false claims flourish?"
>
> "The Lords of Darkness chain us with the false creed that claims no salvation is possible outside their synagogues. Their dominion can be exalted only if we falsely believe our bodies will return intact on a Day of Judgment."

Stricken by this revelation, I protested, "But Teacher, many of us have not the strength to seek this return to the Light by our own will."

The Teacher gently corrected my ignorance. "My brother taught that each of us carries a long-forgotten image of the true Light. We must find within us that flame that connects us to the Father directly. If we abdicate this birthright to self-proclaimed priests and rabbis, we will have failed. Did Jesus not promise that each of us shall know the Father in his own fashion and not all in the same way? If He had given to priests the exclusive commission to tell us what doctrines to believe, why would He have admonished us to constantly ask and seek and find? Remember always: It is the awakening of our Robe of Light, not the earthly authority of false prophets, that offers us hope of the precious rebirth."

I said, "But the rebellious ones preach that Jesus rose from the tomb to proffer upon Peter the authority to build his Church and bind believers."

The Teacher said, "That is another falsehood. My brother never spoke of forming a church on earth. His Kingdom was not of this world."

I asked, "Why are the Tarsian and his followers allowed to pass off contrary accounts as sacred mysteries?"

The Teacher's eyes became filled with tears. "There will be as many gospels written as there are stars in the heavens. Those who fail to understand the truth will always seek to destroy it. You must inscribe what I have told you this night and take the remembrance to our brethren at Qumran."

When I took up my quill, my hand trembled, for I was given the duty of preserving the only true account of what the Master had taught.

The Teacher spoke: "To summon the Light, one must spend many lifetimes in preparation. Eat no meat, for the viscera of animals pulls us back into the world. Kill no living thing, for to do so will require recompense. Meditate morning and night to release all binding thoughts. Understand that all corporeal forms are but illusions. Above all else, know this: The Kingdom is not here, or over there, or in the sky; but the Kingdom is within each of us. Beyond this, all is experience and cannot be communicated."

As a great heaviness of the heart came over me, I asked, "Is not our mission already doomed? There are so few of us left to tell the truth."

The Teacher laid his hand upon my shoulder and said, "Do not lose heart, my son. This War between the Light and the Darkness will never end, just as day will never be without night. The Romans and Pharisees will incarnate in future eons with their rich robes and lofty titles altered only in the fashion of the day. And yet, so long as there are sparks still lost, enlightened souls will return to show others the way back home."

Seeing me nearly lose resolve, the Teacher brought his head to mine in prayer. Verily, a brilliant aura of gold surrounded him as he spoke these last words to me: "Take solace, good Barnabas, and know that you have saved many of our brothers and sisters by your selfless incarnation. Know too that the angels and hierarchies watch over you and do constant battle at your side. Together we have fought this war of the spirit many times, and together we shall fight again. Be joyous at the approaching hour of death, for you and I shall soon join hands below the dazzling Throne."

The ensuing silence was broken only by muffled sobs. Chandelle had not realized that she was holding her breath, so entranced was she by these revelations. She carefully rolled the scroll and bound it with the ribands. "These relics must not be allowed to fall into the hands of the Dominicans."

"We can conceal the entrance again," said Raymond.

"They would then be lost forever," said Chandelle. "Rome is trying to destroy us because we were sent into this world to save these teachings. When we are gone, this gospel, shroud, and cup will be the only surviving evidence of our Lord's true mission."

"The monks are growing more suspicious of our delay," warned Raymond.

After all these years, Guilhelm finally understood what the Empress in Constantinople meant by her prophecy: *The relics and the scroll share a common truth.* No one would believe the claims of this gospel unless presented with the physical evidence of Our Lord's radiant manifestation. And no one would perceive the true purpose of the shroud unless instructed in the arcana of the Light by this suppressed gospel. Here was the reason why Jesus appeared to the Apostles on that fateful night: To burn the image of His Light Body into the Mandylion. Only His brother James and the Magdalene comprehended the teachings. They must have taken the scroll and relics from Jerusalem to prevent their destruction. How many thousands had given their lives over the centuries to see these relics preserved? He turned to Raymond, who lay soaked in sweat from the burning fever of his festering wound. "Who are your best climbers?"

"Amiel. Hugues. Paytavi."

"Have them ready to leave with me before dawn," said Guilhelm.

Raymond struggled to his elbows in protest. "The descent is nearly impossible for a skilled mountaineer with two good arms!"

"I made a promise to Esclarmonde," said Guilhelm. "It was the only vow in my life worth the breath. This one I *will* fulfill."

wo hours before dawn, the Cathars gathered their possessions—a few grains of pepper, some family mementos, their worn copies of the Gospel of John—and distributed them to the soldiers. Several of the men tried in vain to convince the Cathars to save themselves by renouncing their beliefs. The perfects gently rejected their pleas and promised that if they reached the Light, they would intercede on behalf of the soldiers' souls. Those who were able to walk filed past Guilhelm and his three volunteer climbers to offer them the Kiss of Love.

Embraced by Corba and Chandelle, Guilhelm fought back tears. "I feel as if I am abandoning you."

"You are keeping our memory alive," insisted Chandelle.

Corba grasped his good hand. "Where will you go?"

"I will try for Usson. Look for black smoke in the west."

During these many years, Corba had delayed taking the Consolamentum. She and the Marquessa had hoped to receive the vow from Esclarmonde, but they had lost courage on the night of her death. Corba was resolved not to let this last opportunity pass. She knelt beside Raymond and kissed him. "My love, you are everything to me. I did not believe that Esclarmonde's Light existed until I saw it with my own eyes. Now I know it is worth dying for."

Raymond tried in vain to rise. "I will take the vow as well."

"No!" cried Corba. "I forbid it!"

"You would condemn me to a life without you?"

"Your faith is life. God asks no more of you. I remained on this mountain at your behest. Now you must grant my request. Promise me you will leave here alive, or I will break!" When Raymond hung his head in surrender, Corba broke from his desperate grasp and took Chandelle by the hand.

Chandelle realized that she had been chosen to administer the vow, which was tantamount to a death sentence. "Do not ask this of me."

"It is your duty," said Corba.

"She will not take it without me!" The Marquessa, sprawled on the ground with the sick and dying, struggled to her scabbed elbows.

Corba cried, "Mother, no!"

The Marquessa crawled toward her daughter and granddaughter with a determination fueled by rage. "I have but one desire left in this cracked world! To confront the god who destroyed my family!"

As the Cathars gathered around the two new initiates, Chandelle placed her hands on the bowed heads of Corba and the Marquessa. "Do you accept the transmission of Light and give oath never to deny your faith, even in the face of fire and death?"

"I do," said Corba.

"And I," said the Marquessa.

"May the Light go with you always to the end of your days."

A weak voice cried out from the rows of wounded soldiers. "They must have an escort!" Bernard tried to stand on his good leg. When he could not manage the effort, four of his comrades assisted him. He turned to express his gratitude and send the soldiers back to their posts, but they remained at his side, intent on joining him in taking the vow.

"You have reason to live," insisted Corba. "Loupe may have survived."

Bernard shook his head. "She would have returned by now."

"You have done enough for us," pleaded Chandelle.

Bernard placed Chandelle's hands to his forehead. "I do this for me."

Resigned to his decision, Chandelle commenced the ritual. "Bernard Saint-Martin, know that you will forfeit your earthly life?"

"I do."

"Accept then the lineage that has been passed from true Christian to Christian since the days of the Master."

When the Consolamentum was finished, Guilhelm climbed to the allures and shook the stiffness from his limbs in preparation for the ordeal that awaited him. He had always possessed an astute eye for assaying the weaknesses of an enemy. During his disguised excursion through the French encampment, he had noticed that the greenest conscripts, Gascon lackwits mostly, were stationed on the south section of the cordon. Most military men were conservative by nature and could be counted on to repeat the oldest of strategic errors, that of refighting the last battle. The actions of the French army during these past weeks had given him no reason to think that the Seneschal would act differently. Loupe had succeeded in threading down the north side, which offered the shortest route to Toulouse. Predictably, the most experienced of the French scouts had been moved there. He would take the south face, which offered the additional advantage of being sheltered from the moon's light.

He made a final check of their precious baggage. Each of his three volunteers would carry one of the relics. The Keramion was hidden inside a water skin, half-filled to conceal its weight. The Mandylion was concealed in the doubled lining of a cloak. The gospel scroll had been meticulously rolled and smoothed around the wooden canister of a quiver, then wrapped in leather. He would be the one most under the greatest suspicion if captured, so he bore on his own person a spurious inventory of bullion and jewels, inscribed on the back of the map brought by the Aragon engineer. Signed by Bernard Marti, the document was contrived with enough detail and cleverness to seduce even the most skeptical of the French into believing it to be the reason for their escape attempt.

He had always prided himself on keeping his emotions under restraint, for a cool head and a cold heart had kept him alive on many a field of battle. But now, gazing down one last time at the Cathars, he was sapped by an overwhelming wave of despair. He had always condemned their ways as folly. Yet they were the only ones who had ever truly loved him. With a huff of bitterness, he turned from their outpouring of farewells and slid down the rope with his three compatriots. The rising night wind suffused the darkness with an unearthly chorus of rustles and whispers. As he hurried in stealth along the cliff's edge rehearsing its clefts and chins from memory, he pondered the strange beliefs that Esclarmonde had espoused: If she were proven right, he would never again see those people, for they would reside in the realm of the Light and he would be incarnated again into this world.

He could still turn back and take the Consolamentum. What did it matter if he spoke a few inconsequential words that he did not believe? He pivoted to return to the temple—and rammed his shin into something hard.

He bit off a muffled curse and looked down to find the culprit. Searing fatigue and the night's shadows blunted his perceptions. Several disoriented moments passed before he discovered that he had stumbled over a small boulder surrounded by blooming flowers. Why did this place look so familiar? He passed his hand across the dolmen's smooth face. His legs buckled in sudden recognition. A hoot howl screeched, chilling him to the bone, and a spate of barking by wild dogs ignited in the vale below. Were the avenging angels assigned to his perpetual torment laughing at him again? He thought it nigh impossible that fifty years could have passed since he had sat with Esclarmonde on this rock. His heart thudded in his chest. He felt a light rain beginning to fall. Raising his good hand to his mouth to stifle a raw cough of regret, he realized that his convulsing face alone was wet.

Damn this blighted mount!

The other climbers stood waiting for him. With surge of anger, he shoved the small boulder over the cliff and resumed his descent without returning to take the rite. He would never again bow in worship to any god, Cathar or Catholic, who stood by and watched the best of this world die so ignobly.

Whosoever is close to me is close to the fire.

- The Gospel of Thomas

XL

Montsegur

March 16, 1244

awn's red tendrils burned off the last wisps of fog as the temple's west gate screeched open on its rusted hinges. Covering their mouths with bandanas, the Seneschal and his French troops led the Dominicans into the ashlar mausoleum and were stopped short by what met their eyes. These hard-bitten veterans of the heretic wars had seen the entrails of many a besieged castle, but nothing so stomach-churning as this farrago of squalor and misery.

"Christ on the Cross," muttered the Seneschal.

Those Cathars who could summon the strength struggled to their pustuled feet. They resembled skulls set on black-swathed stilts as they clustered in an oscillation of misery, shivering uncontrollably from the effects of the flux. Their faces were white as curdled whey and their protruding Adam's apples moiled above the fleshless hollows of their throats. The infirm lay contorted in agony, some curled into balls, others splayed in the muck with lips scabbed and limbs gangrenous from frostbite. A makeshift morgue had been built atop poles at the south end of the bailey and in one corner a fetid privy was draped with shredded robes to provide what little modesty could be had. The sluice rut, clogged with offal and runoff, had turned the ground into a festering mire.

Otto quavered with the nervousness of a novice as he threaded the ranks of the downcast perfectas and searched for features that reflected his own. "Where is Esclarmonde de Foix?"

After a fractured silence, Chandelle stepped forward from the frightened cadre of women. "I am Esclarmonde."

Otto stared at Chandelle without comprehension. Suddenly, dark recognition registered on his face. She was the slippery miniken he had interrogated at Avignonet. He buckled her with a punishing slap. "Deceiving bitch! I know who you are!"

Raymond tried to crawl to his daughter's defense, but the Northern soldiers kicked at his splinted leg to drive him back. "Bastard! Touch her again and—" The butt end of a pike hammered against his jaw.

Blood trickled from Chandelle's sliced lip as she recovered to her feet. She held Otto prisoner in her blind glare. "And we know who *you* are."

"Silence!" demanded Otto. "You will speak only when permitted."

The aged Archbishop of Narbonne cupped a hand to his ear to aid his poor hearing. "What did the woman say?"

"This monk is the son of the woman he seeks to destroy," said Chandelle.

"These heretics will spout any lie to save themselves!" said Otto.

"His veins run with the same blood as ours," said Chandelle. "Take us to the tribunal and we'll prove it."

After another transit around the bailey, Otto realized that he had been deceived about Esclarmonde's presence. He slung Chandelle toward the gate before she could utter more damning charges. "Take them all down!"

The Archbishop stared at Otto for a hazardous moment, but he chose not to act on his suspicion, having no desire to return to Paris and explain his interference with Blanche's orders. With a shrug of indifference, he hurried from the stinking heretic den, eager to return to Narbonne and be done with this noxious business. At the Seneschal's signal, the French soldiers shackled the Cathars to a long chain. The Marquessa was not spared the indignity; unable to raise herself, she was hoisted roughly. Herded to one end of the temple, the Occitan soldiers made a move toward their stacked weapons, but their insurgency was quickly thwarted by the prod of pikes.

When the Occitan knights had been culled from the heretics, Otto advised Raymond, "You and your men will be taken to Carcassonne for questioning."

"Allow my family to accompany me," begged Raymond.

"The cloggers will be given the opportunity to recant." As the Occitan soldiers were led away, Otto found Bernard and twenty of his comrades hold-ing back. He smirked in grim amusement at their misguided chivalry. "As I suspected, some in your ranks have succumbed to Satan's wiles." He ordered a sergeant, "Bind them with the heretics."

The Cathars and lapsed soldiers were shoved through the west gate and required to reveal their names to a deacon who sat at a scrivener's table. Those who tried to speak Occitan were beaten until they answered in French. The Seneschal picked out the healthiest among the captives and forced them to the front of the chained line. The descent would be arduous and his men were in no mood to carry the lame down the pog. The Dominicans chanted *Te Deums* as the Northerners lashed the wretched train to a brutal exodus across the rocks and bramble, dragging those unable to keep up. When the last of the perfects had been banished from the temple, Otto turned to his deacon for the head count.

"Two hundred and five heretics," said the scribe. "Forty-two men at arms."

The Seneschal and his officers lingered at the gate, eager to search the prem-ises for the gold that they were convinced had been hoarded by the Cathars from thefts and familial bequests.

Otto ordered them, "Give me leave here."

"This fastness is the King's property," insisted the Seneschal.

"The King holds it in tenancy for God," Otto said. "I must first exorcise the demonic influences within these walls. On the morrow, you will be allowed to requisition the materiel and possessions." When the Seneschal took a defiant step in anger, Otto brought him to a halt. "You wish me to report to Paris that I was prevented from performing my sacramental obligations?"

The Seneschal was sorely tempted to smite this arrogant monk who had been a thorn in his side for nine long months, but he had even less stomach than the Archbishop for answering to the tempestuous Queen Mother. He burned Otto with a probing glare and tried to divine the true purpose for his insistence to be left alone in the chateau. He had come to know this tonsured viper well enough to be certain that the reason had nothing to do with piety. Finally, he waved off the confrontation and departed with his officers.

Alone inside the temple, Otto slid the gate bolt into place. The sanctuary was eerily still, a confirmation that Satan's dominions were lurking. He tried the chapel door and discovered it locked. He smiled with anticipation, certain that the heretic cache was just beyond the threshold. He found an abandoned ax and hacked at the planks until they caved in.

The small nave of the chapel held only a slab that had served as an altar. The cloggers had swept the room bare of every pebble and speck of dirt except for a small pyramid of ashes in the hearth, still warm. Had they burned their scurrilous writings at the last moment? He rifled through the embers hoping to find a revealing curl of parchment, but the heretics had been thorough in their destruction. He grew more agitated as he searched in vain for hidden niches. Denied his due reward, he rushed back into the bailey and inspected the grounds for evidence of diggings. This scrabbled enclosure of rock and hardpan resembled more an abandoned quarry than a place of devil worship.

Smudged graffiti on the eastern rampart caught his eye. Had the heretics tried to erase these markings? The etching appeared to be an outline of a cross with three beams. He scurried along the inner perimeter and discovered the same symbol on the opposite curtain wall. Their placement appeared haphazard. The crass superstitions of these cloggers were beyond his understanding. Yet he could not shake the gnawing instinct that the markings were of great significance. Where before had he seen such a strange crucifix?

Montanhagol.

He rushed from the temple and ran down the path, ripping his robe skirt on the thick furze in his haste. Panting from the exertion, he reached the base of the pog and found the Cathars crumpled in a pitiful heap, bloodied and torn from their forced descent. The soldiers had brought them into a small clearing near the mouth of the shepherd's path where a stockade of freshly cut poles had been filled with faggots. He walked before the apostate soldiers and examined each face closely. "The impostor friar . . . where is he?"

When the Occitans refused to speak, Otto spun and slapped Corba to the ground. He came next to Chandelle, who swiveled her head, unable to make sense of the groans and shouts of promised retaliation. He knew from her interrogation at Avignonet that she would not be broken by threats to her own life. This time, he would try a different tact. He raised Corba to her feet and cuffed her again, then whispered into Chandelle's ear, "Did they tell you what we did to that swineherd you favored?" He grinned, having gained the paled reaction he sought. "I will offer you one last chance."

Chandelle fought the urge to spit in his face. She steeled her nerves and waited to hear another punishing blow, trying not to succumb.

Otto had learned from Folques the true weakness of these people; they cared nothing for themselves, but could not bear to see their fellow sinners suffer. He demanded again, "Where have the anchoress and the Templar absconded?"

Chandelle heard a sickening thud against her mother's skull. Denied by her faith the right to speak a lie, she struggled to remain mute.

"Damn you, monk!" Raymond tried to claw toward Otto, but the crusaders kicked him to a bloodied submission. "I'll find you in Hell!"

"Tell them nothing!" Corba heaved and coughed, her eyes now swollen slits. She jutted out her battered jaw in defiance. Some of the Cathars rose painfully to their feet, their only means of sharing in Corba's ordeal.

"What did they take with them?" Finding the shivering perfects still clinging to their conspiracy of silence, Otto hammered Corba again and again until she was nearly unconscious. When still none would answer him, he wheeled crimson-faced toward the Seneschal and ordered, "Burn them!"

Raymond fought against the soldiers' restraint. "You promised a tribunal! By the Church's word!"

"They shall have their day of judgment," said Otto, his lips quivering from cold fury. "Before God at the gates of perdition."

The Archbishop was taken aback by Otto's treacherous dismissal of the negotiated conditions for the surrender. "You must afford them the opportunity to recant. Canon law requires it."

"That shall be no impediment!" Otto hoisted a crucifix over the Cathars and tried to force them to look upon the tortured Christ, but they averted their eyes from the despised symbol. "Do you renounce your sins and accept the Holy Roman Church as the true arbiter of faith on earth?"

"They are but words, Corba!" cried Raymond. "Say them!"

Chandelle clutched her mother's hands to infuse her with strength. Corba turned away, unable to look at Raymond for fear of losing resolve.

The perfects recited the Cathar Pater Noster while Otto repeatedly cut the air over them with the sign of the Roman Cross. "By authority vested in me by the Holy Father, I commend your souls to the fires of God's justice!"

When the French soldiers could not decide which of the Cathars to burn first, Otto cut the leather bindings that held the Marquessa's wrist and dragged her toward the stockade. "Give the oldest the honor!"

"Wait!" shouted Chandelle.

Otto hurried to the blind perfecta, certain that she had finally broken. If she recanted, the others would follow. Chandelle extended her strapped hands to be untied. With a sloe-eyed grin of conquest, Otto ordered the soldiers to cut the blind perfecta free.

"My mother and grandmother, as well," said Chandelle.

Bernard Marti and the other Cathars cried softly and hung their heads in defeat, undone by Chandelle's betrayal of the faith to save her family.

"Who else wishes to return to Holy Mother Church?" asked Otto. When none stepped forward, he said, "Perhaps they need some inducement." He signaled for the soldiers to drag the first contingent of the damned into the stockade. "Twelve . . . in honor of the Apostles."

The soldiers chose a dozen victims at random. They shoved the Cathars into the faggots and threw the firebrands over the palisades. Soon a great swirl of sizzling air arose, punctuated by a sharp crackling. The recitations of the Pater Noster grew more frantic. Those Cathars awaiting their turn knelt in grief.

Otto turned to offer Chandelle reassurance. "You have made a wise choice. Now, tell me what I wish to know."

As a second condemned group was dragged to the stockade, Chandelle found her mother's shaking hand. She mouthed a silent word to her father, who was on his knees, sobbing in relief that she and Corba had chosen to live. She captured Otto's face and kissed him forcefully on the lips, then whispered, "I will tell you what you *need* to know. Your mother loved you." Before Otto could comprehend what she meant, Chandelle leaned down and braced the prostrate Marquessa with a hand to her elbow. "Grandma, we must walk a few steps."

Otto broke a wide smile in preening victory. The blind heretic was bringing the others with her to the stern mercy of Holy Mother Church.

The Marquessa squeezed Chandelle's hand to confirm that she was prepared to make the effort. Miraculously, the matriarch, who had not taken a step in years, found the strength to stand. Arm-in-arm, the three women looked up at Esclarmonde's temple and saw the sun's rays strike the pinnacle of the chapel. Blessed with that sign of beckoning, the women turned from Otto and walked toward the burning stockade.

A shadow crossed Raymond's face. "No!"

The three generations of women clutched hands as they staggered closer to the churning conflagration. Corba glanced toward the west and saw a trail of black smoke curled from the mountain fastness of Usson, twenty leagues away. Eyes brimming with hot tears, she whispered, "Guilhelm has made it."

Chandelle whispered a prayer in gratitude that the relics had been saved. As they neared the flames, the heat became so searing that she feared she would lose fortitude. "How much farther?"

Corba bit her bruised lip, drawing a trickle of blood. "A few steps more."

Chandelle could hear the prayers of the dying perfects above the fire wind. In birth, there is no turning back. Only in death can we defy the Lords of Darkness by choosing the moment and manner to leave this world of injustice and suffering. She then remembered Esclarmonde's warning: The opportunity to escape reincarnation will be fleeting. If the passing is met with fear, the doors of salvation will be closed. She whispered hoarsely, "We are going home."

The Marquessa embraced her daughter and granddaughter for the last time. Together, they dived into the stockade.

Engulfed in the vortex of incandescent tongues, Chandelle's breath was sucked from her throat. She reached under her robe and clutched Jean's etching stone. "Watch for the Light!" she cried, barely able to force a sound. "Watch for the Light!" The spitting flames swirled around her. A deafening wind howled in her ears. The first Station was coming. Be brave. Watch for the flash. Her body oozed as if lathered in scalding oil. Is that blood? Do not think of it. Be as resolved as the martyrs before the beasts. My God, why am I so cold?

Come to me, Chandelle.

She instinctively opened her eyes to find the source of that command. The veil of blindness had been torn away. The flames leapt at her like dragons. This is what fire looks like! She turned, and for the first time, saw her mother's face.

Withering in the white heat, Corba sensed the miracle.

Chandelle raised her palm before her own eyes. *How strange, this flesh. It melts like snow.* Her skin dripped around the white-hot etching stone. She brought Jean's drawing closer and saw the outlines of his smiling face. God had granted her this last blessing. Her mother's hand tightened on hers, then released. A storm of embers exploded into sparks and flew toward the one great Sun.

Come to me, Chandelle.

Otto watched in stunned disbelief as the three women turned black in the voracious flames. He muttered to himself, "They walk willingly to their deaths for Satan?"

"For true Christianity," corrected Bernard, who lay on the ground, his red eyes bathed in grief. "A state of grace you will never know." With assistance, he struggled to his feet, wincing from the pain in his swollen leg.

"Where do you think you're going?" demanded Otto.

"To a better place, I pray."

The lapsed Occitan soldiers braced Bernard by wrapping his arms around their shoulders and walked with him into the stockade.

O n the horizon, Loupe reined up with the two hundred Toulousian knights who had joined her relief force. The sky had turned the strange color of molten gold. In the valley, an eddy of slate smoke swirled up. She cantered her chestnut stallion a few paces closer and saw the flames rising above the clearing at the foot of the pog.

Bernard was being carried into the inferno.

She spurred into a gallop. The Toulousian knights, informed that they had arrived too late, turned back north—all but the squire who had come to her defense in Raymond's court. The boy's rouncy pawed the frozen ground in protest, but he finally gained its obeisance and lashed to catch up with Loupe.

Otto walked among the last of the Cathars while perfunctorily hearing their refusals to recant. He glanced toward the far ridge and caught sight of a distant churn of dust. Two riders were charging toward him. He stood frozen, unable to register the improbable sortie, then shouted, "Finish it!"

The alerted crusaders slammed the stockade gate and threaded a pole through its rungs. Inside the burning palisades, Bernard heard the frenetic shouts of the mustering French. He peered through a crack in the stakes and saw the crusaders scrambling for their stacked weapons. His heart leapt—Loupe had survived! He fought to break out but could not force a breach. Denied, he sank to his knees in the churning smoke, coughing and suffocating. He tried to warn Loupe to go back, but his throat was too seared to make a sound above the clamoring of the French rutters who were mounting to meet Loupe's suicidal attack.

"I want her alive!" ordered Otto.

The French archers formed ranks and fired. Loupe's fractious stallion revolted at the enfilade. She heard a crying gasp behind her. The squire was bent back against his cantle, his skivered chest drenched in blood. She leaned into her stallion's mane and circled the engulfed stockade searching for a breach. Bernard's scorched hands slid from the timbers and disappeared. She drew her sword and spurred into the oncoming phalanx. The French were so astonished by her reckless charge that they ceased forming up and waited for her to turn back. Instead, she pierced their line and scythed any who came within reach. She tried to angle toward the stockade, but her horse shied from the roaring flames. She circled the conflagration and screamed, "Bernard!"

The firestorm drowned out Bernard's dying answer. Surrounded, Loupe threw the sword over the palisades in the futile hope that he would hack himself free. The crusaders converged and tried to drag her from the saddle, but she drove them off long enough to lash free and spur west.

*L*oupe was awakened by a distant shout. Her head throbbed like a tabor drum. How long had she been asleep? Recouping her wits, she flinched with a jerk and recoiled into the darkness, reminded of where she had dragged herself. Spent with fatigue, she had abandoned her lamed horse earlier that morning and had climbed for hours up the ragged ridge that led to this cave in the Tarascon wilderness where her father had often taken her on buck hunts as a girl. She prayed that the voice she kept hearing was a figment of the disorienting nightmares. She edged near the yawning gape to make certain. A flicker of torches appeared in the wooded ravine below the ridge.

"Surrender, cousin, and you will be dealt with mercifully."

She muttered a curse. Otto was with the French rutters who had been chasing her. She shouted, "I've seen enough of your mercy!"

Otto's unctuous inflection became more distinct. He was moving toward her. "Tell me what your aunt kept within the confines of Montsegur and I will see to it that you are safely delivered to Toulouse."

She could not see his face to assess the sincerity of the offer. Could information about the Cathar religion truly be all he wanted? She was so tired and hungry from the chase that she could barely force her legs to move. What did it matter now if she revealed the little she knew of these hermits and their superstitions? Bernard and all of her family were dead. Nothing could be done for—

"Loupe! Don't—" That call was throttled in mid-shout.

Startled, she rushed to the entrance for a better vantage. Under the murky light of the torches, Otto held a blade against Bernard's throat. The monk had dragged him from the pyre to use as bait. He forced Bernard a few steps deeper into the cavity to coax her closer.

"Deliver what I want," said Otto, "and he is yours."

On his knees, Bernard tried to warn her away. "Say nothing—"

Otto stifled the warning by pressing the dagger into the seared flesh under Bernard's chin. "You and I are kindred souls. You are not like the others. You once spared my life. Allow me to return the favor."

Loupe tried to marshal her racing thoughts. Montsegur had capitulated. Count Raymond had given up all resistance to the invasion. Her country's cause was lost. Without Bernard, she had no reason to live. She dropped her weapon and came forward to give herself up.

Bernard thrust his windpipe into the knife's edge.

"No!" screamed Loupe.

Bernard fell face first to the ground with his throat gushing blood. Otto stood frozen, avoiding any sudden movement that might spook Loupe. She trembled with despair as she watched the life slowly drain from Bernard. She lifted her vengeful eyes to Otto's expectant face and drew her dagger. She took a threatening step toward him—and retreated into the protection of the cave.

Otto kicked the ground in anger at the lost opportunity. He signaled for his men to give chase.

Minutes later, the soldiers returned empty-handed. "There must be a dozen tunnels in there," reported an officer. "Should we divide up?"

Otto stared at Bernard's lifeless body and curled a scheming half-grin.

*L*oupe groped her way through the oppressive darkness, her calculation of time skewed by the many hours she had endured without light. The damnable roar in her ears was so loud that she could barely hear her own thoughts. She crumpled to her haunches, too exhausted to take another step. She rested against the wall and vowed to take respite for only a few minutes, lest she pass out.

Some time later—how much she could not be certain—the stale air moved around her with a sudden swish. She thought she heard the sounds of rustling, perhaps footsteps. She reached for her dagger, as she had a hundred times in this black subterranean maze. A flint struck a stone near her ear—a small flame was brought to life on the wick of a candle. A dozen gaunt Cathars crawled into its penumbra. She shook her head to chase the hallucination, but the pallid faces remained hovering over her.

An old man in ragged black robes caressed her forehead to confirm his astonishing discovery. "The Templar said you made it past the French . . . but we gave his report little credence."

"What Templar?"

"The one with the iron arm. By God's mercy, he escaped from Montsegur and came to us at Usson with the sacred possessions."

Loupe struggled to her knees. If Guilhelm had reached Montsegur, he would never have left the mount without Esclarmonde. But what did this Cathar hermit mean by sacred possessions? She swayed from the enervation and nearly collapsed, blurred with faintness. "Do you have food?"

The old Cathar cast his scooped eyes down. "We have come here to follow the example of the Mother."

"What do you mean?"

"We are taking the rite of starvation."

"Esclarmonde . . . starved herself?"

The hermit's silence confirmed the incomprehensible act.

Loupe's eyes flooded with tears. She kicked at the wall in impotent anger. Esclarmonde had promised to hold out. Her aunt had taught these people to give up on this world too easily. Otto no doubt believed that he had massacred all of the Cathars of significance in Occitania. If he captured her, the daughter of the Wolf, he could trumpet to Rome that he had eradicated the last heretic noble in Foix. That milksop of the Devil's bastard! She would have revenge on her treacherous cousin yet. She braced the old Cathar man by his frail shoulders and insisted, "You cannot die here. You must keep your faith alive." She shook her head to chase the clodding cobwebs of fatigue. "Follow me."

The Cathars were too weak from fasting to protest. She took the lead and retraced her steps toward the mouth of the cave, reversing in her memory's eye every turn she had taken. After what seemed an hour of crawling, they came upon an expansive grotte with a large stalagmite growing up from its floor. She rubbed her hand across graffiti that had been carved into the stalagmite's triangular formation. She brought the candle closer to the inscription and read:

> On this day of our Lord, the 6th of May 1192,
> Esclarmonde de Foix professed her love for the Templar.

They were in Lombrives.

Esclarmonde had once brought her here as a girl to visit the throne of Pyrene. She remembered from her childhood explorations that the entrance was not far off. She hurried with the Cathars toward the direction of the mouth that she had entered decades ago. Soon the tunnel widened and the floor eased its incline. They were near the end, she was certain of it. She took a few more paces and became disoriented. They should have found daylight by now. She took another step and stumbled over something soft and bloated. The stench of burnt flesh attacked her nostrils. She reached down and felt a viscous wetness.

Bernard's corpse.

She bent to all fours and dry-retched. Why had Otto dragged his body into the cave? She ran her hands across the wall. The stones were creased at intervals. She slid her fingers along the interstices and brought the taste of fresh mortar to her lips. Her mind went blank for a fractured moment. She looked at the Cathars and saw in their blanched faces the reflection of her own fear. She pounded her fists against the stones, but they would not move.

Otto had walled them in.

She sank to her haunches, undone. During the many battles of her life, she had never broken. But now she lay senseless, unable to link coherent thoughts. She watched in detached numbness as the old Cathar calmly prepared his flock for the cruel fate that awaited them. He directed them to lie in a circle with their feet splayed like rays from a sun. Sobbing, she pulled Bernard's corpse to her side, praying against all hope for the miracle of a pulse.

"Do you wish the Consolamentum, my child?" asked the Cathar hermit.

She was stunned by his offer. Her hatred of his faith was well known. Yet this man was willing to share the gift for which he and his people had toiled and suffered their entire lives to gain. A reflection of subdued light crossed her line of sight. She looked down and found a medallion hanging at Bernard's breastbone. She brought it closer and caressed its raised face—a triple cross. It was a merel, just like the one her mother and Esclarmonde had worn.

He took the vow.

Bernard had often confided his growing admiration for Esclarmonde's faith, but she had never thought him serious about conversion. He must have made the decision in the throes of despair. She had let him down. She had let them all down. Her fighting had brought them only more suffering and death. With a cry of anguish, she turned to the old man and, though fearing his answer, asked, "Will I ever see him again?"

"All sparks must return to the Sun," he assured her.

She brushed a finger across Bernard's cold hand. Was his soul confronting the torments of the Catholic Hell or the Cathar Realm of Light? An unbearable sadness plunged her into despair. He had promised never to leave her. But if Esclarmonde's teachings were true, they would never again be together. He had gained release from the cycle of incarnations and she would be returned to this miserable world to pay for her transgressions. In a deadened voice, she heard herself ask, "Must I believe to be saved?"

The old Cathar soothed her with a smile of compassion. "Sheep believe that the shepherd will care for them, even on the day they are led to the slaughterhouse. No beneficent god would condition His salvation on a blind belief in the dogmas of man. The Mother said that the God of Light wishes only that we seek Him with all our hearts."

Loupe brought the expiring taper closer to the old Cathar's leathery face. There was a strange familiarity to his calming voice. She was struck by how much he resembled Bishop Castres. For a fleeting moment, she entertained the possibility, having been told that the mystical holy man had always appeared at the moment of crisis in an initiate's life. But she quickly dismissed the thought as the poisoned product of her fracturing mind. The venerable heresiarch had died several years ago. She removed the dagger from her belt and cast it aside. "I chose the path of violence."

"In the time it takes to draw a breath," the Cathar hermit promised, "the flash of gnosis can redeem a lifetime."

"How does one find this knowing?"

He pressed his palsied hands to her forehead to transmit the blessing of the Light. "It seems you already have."

He was only trying to ease her terrors, she knew. With the blood of a thousand killings on her hands, she could not be so easily saved. Would this world be as depraved when she returned to it? As the darkness enveloped her, she thought she heard a faint voice coming high from a ledge above Pyrene's throne.

You are the Light of the World. You will lead our people to the Kingdom.

She dismissed the echo as only a hunger hallucination. Then, a distant memory from her first visit to this cave came to mind. Esclarmonde had told her that words of truth spoken inside Lombrives never fade. Hundreds of years in the future, she had promised, those who entered this abode of Pyrene with a pure heart would hear the same words resounding up and echoing from the center of the world.

It was only a troubadour's fable. But as Loupe lay waiting for her earthly cares to come to an end, she shouted the name of every brave Occitan who had perished on Montsegur.

The sign of your having this Light
is your vision of the end.
- Rumi

XLI

Zaragoza, Aragon

November 1250

The sheave blocks squealed in warning as the strappado ropes tightened again. Arms bound behind his back, Guilhelm was hoisted into the smoky haze that hung below the slanted timbers of the old Mudejar tower. The diabolical contrivance of pain wrenched his elbows overhead and slowly ripped the tendons from his shoulder blades.

The punishing drop revived him. He awoke in a pool of his own blood with ears throbbing against the wet flagstones. Peppery incense assaulted his nostrils and ignited a spasm of coughing. Through blurred vision he saw what appeared to be a garlanded maiden subduing the jaws of a lion. He blinked the sweat from his swollen eyes, convinced that his mind had finally snapped under the torture. In these last moments before he gave up his spirit, the significant incidents of his life were cascading before him in a menagerie drained of realism yet somehow suffused with symbolic profundity.

The first image faded and was replaced by one of a Roman pontiff holding a staff crowned by the Cathar cross. Next came a burning tower with its defenders leaping to their deaths. And then a woman's hand offered the miraculous Grail with its spiritual waters spouting forth like a nourishing fountain. The visions began floating past him with greater speed: Starving refugees rejected by Mother Church knelt in freezing snow; an armored knight charged into battle at Muret; the Black Harbinger of Death, blessed by the Pope, entered Beziers on a white stallion; a blazing Sun heralded the rebirth of an enlightened soul; a black-robed Cathar hermit stood on a cliff holding aloft the lantern of spiritual gnosis. The litany reached its climax: A wimpled Grail priestess, shrouded in the bluish mist of a silvery moon, sat in a temple bordered by two pillars, one white and one black. In her lap, she held a scroll of incalculable worth.

"Who is this woman?"

That question roused Guilhelm from his anguished reverie. He looked up and saw Otto displaying a hand-painted miniature, one of several in a deck, drawn on scraped rectangles of calfskin and stretched around thin boards. The strange icons resembled the gambling cards he had seen crafted by Mameluke slaves in Egypt. He realized that he had been witnessing not the final roll call of his life, but the gaudy creations of some occult illuminator.

"We found these pagan idolatries in the possession of a bard in Toulouse," said Otto. "They are being copied in stealth and passed from city to city like holy relics. Do you know what purpose they serve?"

Guilhelm turned away, refusing to admit his ignorance.

Otto forced him to examine the card that depicted the seated priestess. "She holds a scroll bearing the letters TORA. Is it a demonic code?"

Guilhelm's stinging eyes widened in sudden discovery. On the night of Jourdaine's death, he and Esclarmonde had scrambled the letters ROMA to form AMOR. He performed the kabbalistic operation again and came up with ROTA. The Latin word for wheel, turning . . .

Revolution.

Whoever had created these cards was trying to preserve the subversive teachings of the Cathars for future generations: The scroll protected by this High Priestess would one day turn the world upside down—but only if it were rediscovered.

Otto demanded Guilhelm's attention with a sharp kick. "Was there a gospel guarded by those witches on Montsegur? Forged by an imposter claiming to be the brother of Our Lord?" Receiving no response, he grasped Guilhelm's sweat-soaked beard. "Were your Templar brethren infected with its lies?"

Guilhelm begged to pass out. "Have done with me!"

"They say you were her troubadour."

"I told you! I knew no such woman!"

"The wretches called out her name from the fires," said Otto. "The dying don't waste their last breaths on the whimsies of minstrels." He turned to a hooded scribe who sat at a tallow-lit table in the corner. "How went the one?"

The scribe read from the confession of an Occitan prisoner who had admitted hearing Guilhelm perform servientes in courts on both sides of the Pyrenees. "'May God save and guard the Guardian Lady of Montsegur, for she is peerless in delicate beauty,'" the scribe droned in a monotone. "'Men would not die, it is my belief, as soon as they do now, if they only knew the joy of such a love.'"

Otto grinned with derision at Guilhelm's love-sick paean. He leaned near the Templar's ear to impart a final indignity, "The conversios say she baptized them in her bed. Yet she never permitted you to taste of her sweetness . . . Is that why you abandoned her after Muret?"

Guilhelm lunged in an attempt to bull the Dominican into the fire, but the ropes wrangled him back to the floor. Groaning, he sank his head between his knees and waited for the rope's retaliation.

Otto grasped Guilhelm's hair and arched his neck. "On the next ascent, stretch the throat," he whispered. "Deliverance will come quicker."

The monk surrenders too soon! Guilhelm cursed under his breath, only then realizing that he had unwittingly given up what the inquisitors had sought all along. If the Cathar gospel did *not* exist, even a Templar trained to endure the horrors of Moslem executioners would fabricate a claim of its survival to avoid such a cruel death. In an effort to throw Otto off the path of the scroll, he had spoken of gold, then of the Shroud and the Cup. But Otto and his conniving friars cared naught about lucre or relics. What they wanted was confirmation of the gospel's existence and—more importantly—its perpetual suppression.

Guilhelm suspected that the Dominicans had finally calculated from the Montsegur rolls that he escaped with the three Occitans on the night before the surrender. His fellow climbers had likely been captured and, refusing to speak, sent to the stake. He himself had survived for six years disguised as an itinerant troubadour, walking from village to village while bearing whispered witness to Esclarmonde's fate. When the Inquisition agents began closing in, he buried the relics and scroll in the barrens of the Languedoc and took refuge in the isolated foothills of Aragon. But the Calatravans, settling an old score, had caught up with him near the monastery of San Juan de la Pena and had handed him over. Now, with his imminent death, Rome would be assured that the only surviving evidence of Our Lord's true mission remained lost forever.

And Esclarmonde's sacrifice will have been in vain.

Perverse and wicked world! As he waited to leave its bloody clutches, he searched his fevered memory and could sift only two verities that had proven constant throughout his miserable life. The first: The Church always appropriated the virtues and spiritual mastery of its buried enemies. He had seen that strategy played out firsthand when the Temple adopted the ways of its fanatical Syrian rivals, the Assassini. Now, Rome was cleverly at work confiscating the very ideals preached by the Cathars that it had massacred. By sanctioning the Assisi monk's new order of mendicants, the Vatican was scraping the palimpsest of history and championing such reforms as fathered *sui generis*. These Franciscans, as they were being called, modeled themselves on the lives of the Bon Hommes by walking barefoot across Christendom and imitating the Apostles in charity, poverty, and respect for the lowest of God's creatures.

The second certitude flowed from the first. Since the days of their wolf-suckling ancestors, the imperious Romans had cultivated a savage blood thirst for turning on their own. Deprived of their popular death games, they had transmogrified the monastic orders into teams of spiritual gladiators, pitting the tonsured dogs against one another in public spectacles just as vicious and tawdry as the ancient Colosseum duels. The rabid Dominicans spread rumors that the Franciscans were rife with the Occitan heresy. The Franciscans countered that the Black Friars had become decadent *bons viveurs* with their false claims that Christ wore shoes and carried a money purse on His belt. The Cistercians, looking down their long noses at both upstart orders, turned Dominic Guzman's famous indictment on its head by condemning their fellow brethren as Pharisees in Christian garb.

"I almost envy you, Templar." Otto yanked Guilhelm's scalp to regain his attention. The monk retrieved the session's testimony and dispatched the parchment to the flames. "Soon you will learn if the woman—"

"Your mother!" reminded Guilhelm.

Otto signaled for the scribe to desist from recording that claim. With a lording smile, he turned back to Guilhelm to finish his taunt. "You are about to learn if the woman was a prophetess or a demoness." After contemplating that mystery longer than faith would permit, the monk nodded for the henchmen to complete their grisly work. He looked down at Guilhelm as if wishing to ask one question more, then thought better of it and departed the chamber.

The strappado raised Guilhelm's limp arms again. He cried out in anticipation of the agony, but this time his mangled body floated miraculously, as if exalted by angels. The Moorish laceria scored into the tiles slowly alchemized into a beatific vision: Before him lay the sun-drenched pog of Montsegur, just as he remembered it when he had first climbed its jagged slopes with the most beautiful maiden in all Occitania.

"You owe me a song," said a dulcet voice above him.

Guilhelm shook the blood from his burning eyes and looked toward the approaching rafters to find the source of that accusation.

"Race me to the top," said the voice, full of playful challenge. "Whilst we climb, you can tell me about your many deeds of valor."

A swirling, golden nimbus descended around Guilhelm's head, nearly blinding him. He protested weakly, "I could never sing!"

"You are my troubadour, and always will be. If I reach the summit before you, I wish a story well sung for my prize."

"I cannot—"

"Look!" teased the voice. "I've gained the crest!"

"Esclarmonde!" he cried. "I failed you again!"

"You have never failed me, Guilhelm."

"The gospel!"

"We have marked the path for others to follow," she promised. "One day, when the world despairs, the way to the Light will be discovered anew . . . Now, my beloved, you must come to me."

"I cannot find you!"

"Have you forgotten?"

"Forgotten?"

"To be in love is to reach for Heaven through your lady."

Reminded of that old troubadour promise, Guilhelm strived with all his waning strength to grasp her outstretched hand. At last he conquered Montsegur's cliffs and dragged his battered body over the precipice. Chaliced in a dazzling white effulgence, Esclarmonde sat waiting for him on their boulder. He crawled to her side and rested his battered head on her lap. In the vale below, rolling waves of bluegrass and goldenrod swept across the Ariege valley like warring armies of shadow and sun. She kissed him sweetly and offered a viol for him to play. He strummed a chord, and paid his final debt:

> *I pray thee, seeker, forget thee not this tale now finally done,*
> *Though priests will wish it never told and knaves will curse it falsely spun.*
> *In once a castled land where sun turned moon and moon turned sun,*
> *Did shine a Light to chase the Dark, my lady, Esclarmonde.*

It is an heretic that makes the fire,
Not she which burns in't.
— Shakespeare, The Winter's Tale

Author's Note

Most Cathar accounts of the Albigensian Crusade have been lost or destroyed. I was therefore required to resurrect the Occitan view of the war utilizing possibilities, extrapolations, and suppositions. As historian Zoe Oldenbourg observed, "If the centuries had preserved the work of some Catharist Vaux de Cernay, telling the deeds and gestes of his spiritual leaders, the miracles God had wrought on their behalf, and describing the grandeur of their work, then no doubt the Crusade would present a radically different appearance to us."

Over the centuries, the three Esclarmondes became merged into one legendary Esclarmonde of Montsegur. The execution rolls of March 16, 1244, confirmed that Esclarmonde de Perella, an invalid perfecta, was burned with her mother, Corba, and her grandmother, the Marquessa de Lanta. The Viscountess Esclarmonde de Foix was not listed among those who surrendered, but she owned the chateau and was believed to have directed its reconstruction. She participated in the celebrated Pamiers disputation against the future St. Dominic and became so celebrated that Pope Innocent III condemned her *ex cathedra* during the Fourth Lateran Council. Angered that a woman would dare contend in matters of theology, the Catholic chroniclers gave her short shrift during the Pamiers debate by depicting an unlikely scene in which she was cowed to silence after being admonished to return to her spinning. She married Jourdaine L'Isle, a staunch Catholic, and gave birth to at least two children, including Otto, who became a champion of the Catholic cause. Her relationship with her brother was acrimonious. Called to account in Rome, Count Roger de Foix publicly denounced Esclarmonde and her Cathar faith. There is no record of her death. Some sources suggest she may have died as early as 1215, but others claim a much later date. The historian Goodrich speculated that she may have undertaken the Endura at Montsegur.

In the preface, I described how the word *Mallorca* appeared to me in the dream that gave birth to this novel. During the writing of this story, I learned that the House of Aragon held land in southern France, including Perpignan, the capital of the short-lived Kingdom of Mallorca, which came to include the county of Foix. The Mallorcan fortress still stands a half-day's drive from Montsegur. The Balearic island of Mallorca, now part of Spain, was a haven for Cathar and Templar refugees. A few decades after the capitulation of Montsegur, a female descendant of the extended Perella family married James, the King of Aragon and Mallorca. After his father's death at Muret, James was entrusted into the care of the Knights Templar in Aragon. His new queen came from Foix—and her name was Esclarmonde.

Folques de Marseilles was an equally fascinating character. As a young troubadour, he enjoyed the patronage of Foix and undoubtedly sang for Esclarmonde. He took the Cistercian vow after being spurned by a lady whose identity has been left anonymous. I posited his romantic interest in Esclarmonde. Their paths crossed many times and his vengeance against her was consistent with his hatred of the woman-worshiping culture that had so injured him. As Bishop of Toulouse, he prosecuted the Occitan massacres with such fury that his name is reviled in southwest France to this day. It was said that he suffered greatly in his last years on hearing his old chansons sung in public. Dante, who has been accused of Gnostic leanings, inexplicably placed Folques in his *Paradisio*.

Less is known about Guilhelm de Montanhagol. He left us servientes extolling Esclarmonde and he was heralded by medieval chroniclers as her troubadour. He became so critical of the Cathar persecution that he was forced to escape to Aragon. I portrayed him as an apostate Knight Templar; there is a record of Templar troubadours, as well as echoes of a covert collaboration between the Cathars and the Temple, which would suffer its own persecution six decades after Montsegur's fall. Both were rumored to have discovered evidence casting doubt on the Roman Church's legitimacy.

Did the Cathars protect the Holy Grail? There are tantalizing similarities between Montsegur and Montsalvache, the Grail Castle of Cretien de Troyes. Some researchers suspect that crusaders brought the Keramion vessel and Mandylion shroud from Constantinople to Montsegur. In France, two camps have drawn battle lines on this issue. Traditional academicians remain suspicious of Cathar involvement with the Grail, Jewish kabbalah, Islamic mysticism, Light meditation, and sacred architecture, contending that the faith had no use for magic or relics. Yet exponents of the more mystical view refuse to rely on evidence extracted by torture and shaped by the Inquisition to confirm a reality that the Church wished to prevail. As was famously said by the French writer Simone Weil, who was sympathetic to the Cathars: "Official history is believing the murderers at their word."

The dubious value of such forced confessions is made even more apparent by the contradictions one encounters when attempting to understand the Cathars. The perfects were said to loathe the world, and yet they embraced, and were embraced by, the world-loving troubadours. The crusade brought utter destruction upon Occitania, but the Catholic nobles of that region persisted in treating their Cathar subjects with great respect and admiration. The perfects avoided sexual encounters and yet they nurtured the ideals of chivalry and considered women their equal in intelligence and spirituality.

Every faith has its cadre of initiates whose esoteric practices are kept hidden from the laity. The Cathar adepts were no exception. They protected the traditions of the first Christians, the Gnostics, and perhaps the Druids. Investigators such as Fernand Niel and Arthur Guirdham have found too many synchronicities to dismiss the Cathars as mere misguided strays. Rather, they contend that the Bon Hommes had inherited the arcana of the soul's individual quest for the salvatory Light from the Egyptians, the Zoroastrians, the Essenes, and the Nasoreans, whose descendants include the persecuted Mandeans of modern Iraq. Oldenbourg confirmed the possibility that esoteric sun worship took place upon Montsegur, and even the most hardened of rationalists concede that a mysterious treasure was taken from Montsegur the night before the surrender. The present ruins, which may have been reconstructed after the surrender in 1244, possess a perplexing design that seemed unsuited for defensive purposes.

The greatest of all the mysteries may be this: Why would the Cathars accept such a horrific martyrdom if they did not possess knowledge of a more authentic version of early Christianity? The question vexed the Cistercians and Dominicans, who deemed fortitude in the face of death to be the exclusive privilege of Christ's true followers.

In the end, we are left with mostly circumstantial evidence: Cave discoveries of skeletons arranged in a circle and accompanied by Cathar etchings; testimonies of the German poet and archaeologist Otto Rahn, who scoured Montsegur and claimed to have found underground Grail chambers; the tantalizing dimensions of Montsegur's ruins that Niel correlated to the seasons of the sun; and claims by local shepherds that Esclarmonde's spirit still inhabits the mountain.

Having stood on these haunting Occitan sites and felt both their power and sadness, I count myself among those who believe that something remarkable happened in these desolate foothills and causses, only to be crushed by a Church that could not bear the impact of the threatened revelations. I also came to suspect that the Cathar gnosis and the suppressed story of that faith's demise were preserved within the Tarot, whose origins become lost in the latter part of the fourteenth century. Halfway into writing the novel, I found confirmation for this intuition in the works of Margaret Starbird, a biblical scholar who has written on Cathar gnosticism and the rejected feminine elements of Christianity.

As the Gnostic gospels warned, Darkness will always seek out the Light. In a tragic irony, the Nazis became obsessed with the Cathars, victims of the first western holocaust. And yet these two groups, one pacifist and the other genocidal, could not have been more different in beliefs and conduct. During the occupation of France, the S.S. became so convinced that the Cathars possessed the Holy Grail that they cordoned off Montsegur and conducted extensive searches.

Today, pilgrims who visit old Occitania can still touch the blackened stones of St. Nazaire in Beziers, explore the refugee caves of Lombrives, feel the wind above Esclarmonde's towers in Foix, gaze upon the reconstructed walls of Carcassonne, climb the Pas de Trebuchet up Montsegur, and stand in mourning on the Field of the Burned. Near these places, on bridges and gravestones and ancient walls, the Cross of Lorraine is seen accompanied by graffiti calling for the return of Occitan independence and the resurrection of the lost troubadour language. These sites remain sacred to those who fight for freedom of spiritual conscience. Their whispering stones were the only voices that Esclarmonde and her Cathars were permitted to leave us.

Children tell stories,
but in their tales are enfolded
many a mystery and moral lesson.
Though they may relate many ridiculous things,
keep looking in those ruined places
for a treasure.
- Rumi

Additional Reading

Most of the primary and secondary sources on the Albigensian Crusade have been written in French, led by Michel Roquebert's multi-volume study, *l'epopee cathare*. The best history in English remains Zoe Oldenbourg's *Massacre at Montsegur*. A 13th-century account, *La Chanson de la Croisade Albigeoise*, has been translated by Janet Shirley in *The Song of the Cathar Wars*. I am indebted to the late Norma Lorre Goodrich for leading me to the tragic story of these Cathar women.

For Cathar beliefs and rituals, Rene Nelli's works in French and Steven Runciman's *The Medieval Manichee* offer the best overviews. For more mystical interpretations, see Arthur Guirdham's *The Great Heresy* and *We Are One Another*. Maurice Magre argues that the Cathars were western equivalents of Buddhists in his *Magicians, Seers, and Mystics*. A moving personal testimony can be found in poet Yves Roquette's paean of loss, *Cathars*.

Fernand Niel, Antoine Gadal, and Deodat Roche have paved the way to the Holy Grail. In English, see Malcolm Godwin's *The Holy Grail* and Ean and Deike Begg's *In Search of the Holy Grail and the Precious Blood*. For Montsegur as a reliquary for the Mandylion shroud, see Noel Currer Briggs's *The Holy Grail and the Shroud of Christ*. Connections with the Tarot are explored by Runciman and Starbird, whose *The Woman with the Alabaster Jar* and *The Tarot Trumps and the Holy Grail* are invaluable. The Nazi quest at Montsegur is recalled in *The Occult and the Third Reich* by Jean-Midral Augebert.

For the role of the troubadours, see De Rougement's *Love in the Western World*, A. J. Denomy's *The Heresy of Courtly Love*, and Linda Paterson's *The World of the Troubadours*. Gershom Scholem sifts the contacts with Jewish kabbalists in his many works, including *The Origins of the Kabbalah*. Robert Eisenman argues for the suppressed role of Christ's brother in *James, the Brother of Jesus*. The best source for the non-canonical scriptures is *The Other Bible*, edited by Willis Barnstone. For their interpretation, see Elaine Pagel's works, particularly *The Gnostic Gospels*.

Sources

any of the songs and verses sung in this novel by Guilhelm Montanhagol and Folques de Marseille were created by this author. Others, in Chapters One and Thirty, for example, are authentic chansons translated by Jack Lindsay in *The Troubadours and Their World of the Twelfth and Thirteenth Centuries* and by Anthony Bonner in *Songs of the Troubadours*. The troubadour poetry in Chapter Twenty-Six is from translations by Lindsay, Bonner, and Ida Farnell in her *Lives of the Troubadours*.

The Tarot images introducing the chapters are from the Royal Fez Moroccan deck by permission from U.S. Games Systems. I am grateful to U.S. Games for its generous agreement for their use. Border enhancements were integrated by Greg Spalenka using art drawn by Edwardian artist Evelyn Paul and licensed from Fontcraft Scriptorium.

Where not apparent, sources for the chapter quotes include: *Jewels of Remembrance,* with the sayings of Rumi translated by Camille and Kabir Helminski; *The Other Bible,* edited by Willis Barnstone; *The Gnostic Gospels* by Elaine Pagels; *The Secret Teachings of Jesus,* translated by Marvin Meyer; Jessie Weston's translation of Eschenbach's Parsifal; Janet Shirley's translation of William Tudela's *The Song of the Cathar Wars,* by permission of Ashgate Publishing; John Matthew, *The Elements of the Grail Tradition*; *The Dead Sea Scrolls,* translated by Michael Wise, Martin Abegg, Jr., and Edward Cook; Zoe Oldenbourg, *Massacre at Montsegur*; and *The Hymn of the Pearl,* translated by William Wright.

The opening quote from Arthur Guirdham's *The Great Heresy* is included with the permission of Random House Group Ltd.

Acknowledgments

Among the many people who helped bring this book to life, a few deserve special mention. My parents, Glen and Betty Craney, never wavered in their support and encouragement. I also thank Natalie Bates and Dorothy Lumley for their editing suggestions; Michelle Millar and Stewart Matthew for their valued friendship and assistance; Margaret Starbird for her generosity in offering comments on the novel; Veraine for her translations of French documents; John Rechy, a marvelous instructor whose encouragement chased my doubts; Harry Essex for his mentoring and friendship, all too short; my brother James Craney for his patient computer instruction; Greg Spalenka, Jeff Burne, and Ivan Lapper for their expert assistance in bringing to life the crucial artistic elements of this story. Also, thanks to the Muessel family, Beth Nissen, David and Ginny Martin, John Jeter, Jonathan Banks, Fred Miller, Laura Miller, Jon Miller, Steve Miller, Elyse LaVine, Kerry Neal, Veronica Schneider, Henrietta Bernstein, Victoria Ransom, Roxana Villa, Darlene Johnson, Claire Carmichael; the members of the Rechy Writers' Workshop; and the waiters at Coogies who kept my glass filled while I slaved away in the corner booth.

Please visit Glen Craney's website at **www.glencraney.com** for the latest news on his books and additional information, including:

- A virtual tour of the historical sites in the novel as they appear today.
- Interviews, media events, newsletter, and book-signing schedules.
- Book-group study guides and supplemental bibliographies.
- Updates on upcoming books and media projects.
- Discussions and correspondence with the author.
- Links to related sites.

Readers are also invited to join Glen in an ongoing discussion about the writer's craft of recreating the past in novels and movies at his weblog, **History Into Fiction** (**www.historyintofiction.com**).

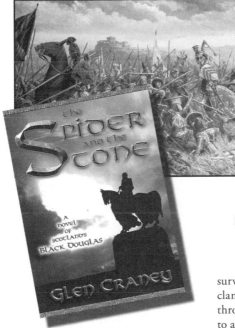

The Siege of Montsegur

1. Chapel
2. Occitan Barbican
3. French Palisade
4. Roc dela Tour
5. Crusader Camp
6. East Gate
7. West Gate
8. Cathar huts
9. Field of the Burned